BRIDES OF TEXAS

BRIDES OF TEXAS

Three Novels in One Volume

KAREN WITEMEYER

BETHANYHOUSE
a division of Baker Publishing Group
Minneapolis, Minnesota

Previously published in three separate volumes:
A Tailor-Made Bride © 2010
Short-Straw Bride © 2012
Stealing the Preacher © 2013

Published by Bethany House Publishers
11400 Hampshire Avenue South
Bloomington, Minnesota 55438
www.bethanyhouse.com

Bethany House Publishers is a division of
Baker Publishing Group, Grand Rapids, Michigan

Printed in the United States of America

ISBN 978-0-7642-1757-9

Library of Congress Control Number: 2015938945

Scripture quotations are from the King James Version of the Bible.

This is a work of fiction. Names, characters, incidents, and dialogues are products of the author's imagination and are not to be construed as real. Any resemblance to actual events or persons, living or dead, is entirely coincidental.

3-in-1 edition cover design by Eric Walljasper
Original cover designs by Dan Thornberg, Design Source Creative Services
Western town image on cover of *A Tailor-Made Bride* courtesy of 1880 Town, Murdo, SD

Author is represented by Books & Such Literary Agency.

15 16 17 18 19 20 21 7 6 5 4 3 2 1

A Tailor-Made Bride

To Wes:

God could not have blessed me
with a more tailor-made husband.
Your love makes life a joy.

Favour is deceitful, and beauty is vain:
but a woman that feareth the Lord, she shall be praised.

PROVERBS 31:30

Prologue

San Antonio, Texas—March 1881

"Red? Have you no shame, Auntie Vic? You can't be buried in a scarlet gown."

"It's *cerise*, Nan."

Hannah Richards bit back a laugh as Victoria Ashmont effectively put her grandnephew's wife in her place with three little words. Trying hard to appear as if she wasn't listening to her client's conversation, Hannah pulled the last pin from between her lips and slid it into the hem of the controversial fabric.

"Must you flout convention to the very end?" Nan's whine heightened to a near screech as she stomped toward the door. A delicate sniff followed by a tiny hiccup foreshadowed the coming of tears. "Sherman and I will be the ones to pay the price. You'll make us a laughingstock among our friends. But then, you've never cared for anyone except yourself, have you?"

Miss Victoria pivoted with impressive speed, the cane she used for balance nearly clobbering Hannah in the head as she spun.

"You may have my nephew wrapped around your little finger, but don't think you can manipulate me with your theatrics." Like an angry goddess from the Greek myths, Victoria Ashmont held her chin at a regal angle and pointed her aged hand toward the woman who dared challenge her. Hannah almost expected a lightning bolt to shoot from her finger to disintegrate Nan where she stood.

"You've been circling like a vulture since the day Dr. Bowman declared my heart to be failing, taking over the running of my household and plotting how to spend Sherman's inheritance. Well, you won't be controlling me, missy. I'll wear what I choose, when I choose, whether or not you approve. And if your friends have nothing better to do at a funeral than snicker about your great-aunt's attire, perhaps you'd do well to find some companions with a little more depth of character."

Nan's affronted gasp echoed through the room like the crack of a mule skinner's whip.

"Don't worry, dear," Miss Victoria called out as her niece yanked open the bedchamber door. "You'll have my money to console you. I'm sure you'll recover from any embarrassment I cause in the blink of an eye."

The door slammed shut, and the resulting bang appeared to knock the starch right out of Miss Victoria. She wobbled, and Hannah lurched to her feet to steady the elderly lady.

"Here, ma'am. Why don't you rest for a minute?" Hannah gripped her client's arm and led her to the fainting couch at the foot of the large four-poster bed that dominated the room. "Would you like me to ring for some tea?"

"Don't be ridiculous, girl. I'm not so infirm that a verbal skirmish leaves me in want of fortification. I just need to catch my breath."

Hannah nodded, not about to argue. She gathered her sewing box instead, collecting her shears, pins, and needle case from where they lay upon the thick tapestry carpet.

She had sewn for Miss Victoria for the last eighteen months, and it disturbed her to see the woman reduced to tremors and pallor so easily. The eccentric spinster never shied from a fight and always kept her razor-sharp tongue at the ready.

Hannah had felt the lash of that tongue herself on several occasions, but she'd developed a thick skin over the years. A woman making her own way in the world had to toughen up quickly or get squashed. Perhaps that was why she respected Victoria Ashmont enough to brave her scathing comments time after time. The woman had been living life on her own terms for years and had done well for herself in the process. True, she'd had money and the power of the Ashmont name to lend her support, but from all public reports—and a few overheard conversations—it was clear Victoria Ashmont's fortune had steadily grown during her tenure as head of the family, not dwindled, which was more than many men could say. Hannah liked to think that, given half a chance, she'd be able to duplicate the woman's success. At least to a modest degree.

"How long have you worked for Mrs. Granbury, Miss Richards?"

Hannah jumped at the barked question and scurried back to Miss Victoria's side, her sewing box tucked under her arm. "Nearly two years, ma'am."

"Hmmph." The woman's cane rapped three staccato beats against the leg of the couch before she continued. "I nagged that woman for years to hire some girls with gumption. I was pleased when she finally took my advice. Your predecessors failed to last more than a month or two with me. Either I didn't approve of their workmanship, or they couldn't stand up to my plain speaking. It's a dratted nuisance having to explain my preferences over and over to new girls every time I need something made up. I've not missed that chore."

"Yes, ma'am." Hannah's forehead scrunched. She couldn't be sure, but she thought Victoria Ashmont might have just paid her a compliment.

"Have you ever thought of opening your own shop?"

Hannah's gaze flew to her client's face. Miss Victoria's slate gray eyes assessed her, probing, drilling into her core, as if she meant to rip the truth from her with or without her consent.

Ducking away from the penetrating stare, Hannah fiddled with the sewing box. "Mrs. Granbury has been good to me, and I've been fortunate enough to set some of my earnings aside. It will be several years yet, but one day I do hope to set up my own establishment."

"Good. Now help me get out of this dress."

Dizzy from the abrupt starts, stops, and turns of the strange conversation, Hannah kept her mouth closed and assisted Miss Victoria. She unfastened the brightly colored silk, careful not to snag the pins on either the delicate material of the gown or on Miss Victoria's stockings. Once the dress had been safely removed, she set it aside and helped the woman don a loose-fitting wrapper.

"I'm anxious to have these details put in order," Miss Victoria said as she took a seat at the ladies' writing desk along the east wall. "I will pay you a bonus if you will stay here and finish the garment for me before you leave. You may use the chair in the corner." She gestured toward a small upholstered rocker that sat angled toward the desk.

Hannah's throat constricted. Her mind scrambled for a polite refusal, yet she found no excuse valid enough to withstand Miss Victoria's scrutiny. Left with no choice, she swallowed her misgivings and forced the appropriate reply past her lips.

"As you wish."

Masking her disappointment, Hannah set her box of supplies on the floor near the chair Miss Victoria had indicated and turned to fetch the dress.

She disliked sewing in front of clients. Though her tiny boardinghouse room was dim and lacked the comforts afforded in Miss Victoria's mansion, the solitude saved her from suffering endless questions and suggestions while she worked.

Hannah drew in a deep breath. *I might as well make the best of it.* No use dwelling on what couldn't be changed. It was just a hem and a few darts to compensate for her client's recent weight loss. She could finish the task in less than an hour.

Miss Victoria proved gracious. She busied herself with papers of some kind at her desk and didn't interfere with Hannah's work. She did keep up a healthy stream of chatter, though.

"You probably think me morbid for finalizing my funeral details in advance." Miss Victoria lifted the lid of a small silver case and extracted a pair of eyeglasses. She wedged them onto her nose and began leafing through a stack of documents in a large oak box.

Hannah turned back to her stitching. "Not morbid, ma'am. Just . . . efficient."

"Hmmph. Truth is, I know I'm dying, and I'd rather go out in a memorable fashion than slip away quietly, never to be thought of again."

"I'm sure your nephew will remember you." Hannah glanced up as she twisted the dress to allow her better access to the next section of hem.

"Sherman? Bah! That boy would forget his own name if given half a chance." Miss Victoria pulled a document out of the box. She set it in front of her, then dragged her inkstand close and unscrewed the cap. "I've got half a mind to donate my estate to charity instead of letting it sift through my nephew's fingers. He and that flighty wife of his will surely do nothing of value with it." A heavy sigh escaped her. "But they are family, after all, and I suppose I'll no longer care about how the money is spent after I'm gone."

Hannah poked her needle up and back through the red silk in rapid succession, focused on making each stitch even and straight. It wasn't her place to offer advice, but it burned on her tongue nonetheless. Any church or charitable organization in the city could do a great amount of good with even a fraction of the Ashmont estate. Miss Victoria could make several small donations without her nephew ever knowing the difference. Hannah pressed her lips together and continued weaving her needle in and out, keeping her unsolicited opinion to herself.

She was relieved when a soft tapping at the door saved her from having to come up with an appropriate response.

A young maid entered and bobbed a curtsy. "The post has arrived, ma'am."

"Thank you, Millie." Miss Victoria accepted the envelope. "You may go."

The sound of paper ripping echoed in the quiet room as Miss Victoria slid her letter opener through the upper edge of the flap.

"Well, I must give the gentleman credit for persistence," the older woman murmured. "This is the third letter he's sent in two months."

Hannah turned the dress again and bent her head a little closer to her task, hoping to escape Miss Victoria's notice. It was not to be. The woman's voice only grew louder and more pointed as she continued.

"He wants to buy one of my railroad properties."

Hannah made the mistake of looking up. Miss Victoria's eyes, magnified by the lenses she wore, demanded a response. Yet how did a working-class seamstress participate in a conversation of a personal nature with one so far above her station? She didn't want to offend by appearing uninterested. However, showing *too* keen an interest might come across as presumptuous. Hannah floundered to find a suitably innocuous response and finally settled on, "Oh?"

It seemed to be enough, and Miss Victoria turned back to her correspondence as she continued her ramblings.

"When the Gulf, Colorado and Santa Fe Railway out of Galveston started up construction again last year, I invested in a handful of properties along the proposed route, in towns that were already established. I've made a tidy profit on most, but for some reason, I find myself reluctant to part with this one."

An expectant pause hung in the air. Keeping her eyes on her work, Hannah voiced the first thought that came to mind.

"Does the gentleman not make a fair offer?"

"No, Mr. Tucker proposes a respectable price." Miss Victoria tapped the handle of the letter opener against the desktop in a rhythmic pattern, then seemed to become aware of what she was doing and set it aside. "Perhaps I am reluctant because I do not know the man personally. He is in good standing with the bank in Coventry and by all accounts is respected in the community, yet in the past I've made my decision to sell after meeting with the buyer in person. Unfortunately, my health precludes that now."

"Coventry?" Hannah seized upon the less personal topic. "I'm not familiar with that town."

"That's because it's about two hundred miles north of here—and it is quite small. The surveyors tell me it's in a pretty little spot along the North Bosque River. I had hoped to visit, but it looks as if I won't be afforded that opportunity."

Hannah tied off her thread and snipped the tail. She reached for her spool and unwound another long section, thankful that the discussion had finally moved in a more neutral direction. She clipped the end of the thread and held the needle up to gauge the position of the eye.

"What do you think, Miss Richards? Should I sell it to him?"

The needle slipped out of her hand.

"You're asking me?"

"Is there another Miss Richards in the room? Of course I'm asking you." She clicked her tongue in disappointment. "Goodness, girl. I've always thought you to be an intelligent sort. Have I been wrong all this time?"

That rankled. Hannah sat a little straighter and lifted her chin. "No, ma'am."

"Good." Miss Victoria slapped her palm against the desk. "Now, tell me what you think."

If the woman was determined to have her speak her mind, Hannah would oblige. This was the last project she'd ever sew for the woman anyway. It couldn't hurt. The only problem was, she'd worked so hard *not* to form an opinion during this exchange, that now that she was asked for one, she had none to give. Trying not to let the silence rush her into saying something that would indeed prove her lacking in intellect, she scrambled to gather her thoughts while she searched for the dropped needle.

"It seems to me," she said, uncovering the needle along with a speck of insight, "you need to decide if you would rather have the property go to a man you know only by reputation or to the nephew you know through experience." Hannah lifted her gaze to meet Miss Victoria's and held firm, not allowing the woman's critical stare to cow her. "Which scenario gives you the greatest likelihood of leaving behind the legacy you desire?"

Victoria Ashmont considered her for several moments, her eyes piercing Hannah and bringing to mind the staring contests the schoolboys used to challenge her to when she was still in braids. The memory triggered her competitive nature, and a stubborn determination to win rose within her.

At last, Miss Victoria nodded and turned away. "Thank you, Miss Richards. I think I have my answer."

Exultation flashed through her for a brief second at her victory, but self-recrimination soon followed. This wasn't a schoolyard game. It was an aging woman's search to create meaning in her death.

"Forgive my boldness, ma'am."

Her client turned back and wagged a bony finger at Hannah. "Boldness is exactly what you need to run your own business, girl. Boldness, skill, and a lot of hard work. When you get that shop of yours, hardships are sure to find their way to your doorstep. Confidence is the only way to combat them—confidence in yourself and in the God who equips you to overcome. Never forget that."

"Yes, ma'am."

Feeling chastised and oddly encouraged at the same time, Hannah threaded her needle and returned to work. The scratching of pen against paper replaced the chatter of Miss Victoria's voice as the woman gave her full attention to the documents spread across her desk. Time passed swiftly, and soon the alterations were complete.

After trying the gown on a second time to assure a proper fit and examining every seam for quality and durability, as was her custom, Victoria Ashmont ushered Hannah down to the front hall.

"My man will see you home, Miss Richards."

"Thank you, ma'am." Hannah collected her bonnet from the butler and tied the ribbons beneath her chin.

"I will settle my account with Mrs. Granbury by the end of the week, but here is the bonus I promised you." She held out a plain white envelope.

Hannah accepted it and placed it carefully in her reticule. She dipped her head and made a quick curtsy. "Thank you. I have enjoyed the privilege of working for you, ma'am, and I pray that your health improves so that I might do so again."

A strange light came into Miss Victoria's eyes, a secretive gleam, as if she could see into the future. "You have better things to do than make outlandish red dresses for old women, Miss Richards. Don't waste your energy worrying over my health. I'll go when it's my time and not a moment before."

Hannah smiled as she stepped out the door, sure that not even the angels could drag Miss Victoria away until she was ready to go. Yet underneath the woman's tough exterior beat a kind heart. Although Hannah didn't fully understand how kind until she arrived home and opened her bonus envelope.

Instead of the two or three greenbacks she had assumed were tucked inside, she found a gift that stole her breath and her balance. She slumped against the boardinghouse wall and slid down its blue-papered length into a trembling heap on the floor. She blinked several times, but the writing on the paper didn't change, only blurred as tears welled and distorted her vision.

She held in her hand the deed to her new dress shop in Coventry, Texas.

1

Coventry, Texas—September 1881

J.T.! J.T.! I got a customer for ya." Tom Packard lumbered down the street with his distinctive uneven gait, waving his arm in the air.

Jericho "J.T." Tucker stepped out of the livery's office with a sigh and waited for his right-hand man to jog past the blacksmith and bootmaker shops. He'd lost count of how many times he'd reminded Tom not to yell out his business for everyone to hear, but social niceties tended to slip the boy's notice when he got excited.

It wasn't his fault, though. At eighteen, Tom had the body of a man, but his mind hadn't developed quite as far. He couldn't read a lick and could barely pen his own name, but he had a gentle way with horses, so J.T. let him hang around the stable and paid him to help out with the chores. In gratitude, the boy did everything in his power to prove himself worthy, including trying to drum up clientele from among the railroad passengers who unloaded at the station a mile south of town. After weeks without so much as a nibble, it seemed the kid had finally managed to hook himself a fish.

J.T. leaned a shoulder against the doorframe and slid a toothpick out of his shirt pocket. He clamped the wooden sliver between his teeth and kept his face void of expression save for a single raised brow as Tom stumbled to a halt in front of him. The kid grasped his knees and gulped air for a moment, then unfolded to his full height, which was nearly as tall as his employer. His cheeks, flushed from his exertions, darkened further when he met J.T.'s eye.

"I done forgot about the yelling again, huh? Sorry." Tom slumped, his chin bending toward his chest.

J.T. gripped the kid's shoulder, straightened him up, and slapped him on the back. "You'll remember next time. Now, what's this about a customer?"

Tom brightened in an instant. "I gots us a good one. She's right purty and has more boxes and gewgaws than I ever did see. I 'spect there's enough to fill up the General."

"The General, huh?" J.T. rubbed his jaw and used the motion to cover his grin.

Tom had names for all the wagons. Fancy Pants was the fringed surrey J.T. kept on hand for family outings or courting couples; the buggy's name was Doc after the man who rented it out most frequently; the buckboard was just plain Buck; and his freight wagon was affectionately dubbed the General. The kid's monikers inspired a heap of good-natured ribbing amongst the men who gathered at the livery to swap stories and escape their womenfolk, but over time the names stuck. Just last week, Alistair Smythe plopped down a silver dollar and demanded he be allowed to take Fancy Pants out for a drive. Hearing the pretentious bank clerk use Tom's nickname for the surrey left the fellas guffawing for days.

J.T. thrust the memory from his mind and crossed his arms over his chest, using his tongue to shift the toothpick to the other side of his mouth. "The buckboard is easier to get to. I reckon it'd do the job just as well."

"I dunno." Tom mimicked J.T.'s posture, crossing his own arms and leaning against the livery wall. "She said her stuff was mighty heavy and she'd pay extra to have it unloaded at her shop."

"Shop?" J.T.'s good humor shriveled. His arms fell to his sides as his gaze slid past Tom to the vacant building across the street. The only unoccupied shop in Coventry stood adjacent to Louisa James's laundry—the shop he'd tried, and failed, to purchase. J.T.'s jaw clenched so tight the toothpick started to splinter. Forcing himself to relax, he straightened away from the doorpost.

"I think she's a dressmaker," Tom said. "There were a bunch of them dummies with no heads or arms with her on the platform. Looked right peculiar, them all standin' around her like they's gonna start a quiltin' bee or something." The kid chuckled at his own joke, but J.T. didn't join in his amusement.

A dressmaker? A woman who made her living by exploiting the vanity of her customers? *That's* who was moving into his shop?

A sick sensation oozed like molasses through his gut as memories clawed over the wall he'd erected to keep them contained.

"So we gonna get the General, J.T.?"

Tom's question jerked him back to the present and allowed him to stuff the unpleasant thoughts back down where they belonged. He loosened his fingers from the fist he didn't remember making and adjusted his hat to sit lower on his forehead, covering his eyes. It wouldn't do for the kid to see the anger that surely lurked there. He'd probably go and make some fool assumption that he'd done something wrong. Or worse, he'd ask questions J.T. didn't want to answer.

He cleared his throat and clasped the kid's shoulder. "If you think we need the freight wagon, then we'll get the freight wagon. Why don't you harness up the grays then come help me wrangle the General?"

"Yes, sir!" Tom bounded off to the corral to gather the horses, his chest so inflated with pride J.T. was amazed he could see where he was going.

Ducking back inside the livery, J.T. closed up his office and strode past the stalls to the oversized double doors that opened his wagon shed up to the street. He grasped the handle of the first and rolled it backward, using his body weight as leverage. As his muscles strained against the heavy wooden door, his mind struggled to control his rising frustration.

He'd finally accepted the fact that the owner of the shop across the street refused to sell to him. J.T. believed in Providence, that the Lord would direct his steps. He didn't like it, but he'd worked his way to peace with the decision. Until a few minutes ago. The idea that God would allow it to go to a dressmaker really stuck in his craw.

It wasn't as if he wanted the shop for selfish reasons. He saw it as a chance to help out a widow and her orphans. Isn't that what the Bible defined as "pure religion"? What could be nobler than that? Louisa James supported three kids with her laundry business and barely eked out an existence. The building she worked in was crumbling around her ears even though the majority of her income went to pay the rent. He'd planned to buy the adjacent shop and rent it to her at half the price she was currently paying in exchange for storing some of his tack in the large back room.

J.T. squinted against the afternoon sunlight that streamed into the dim stable and strode to the opposite side of the entrance, his indignation growing with every step. Ignoring the handle, he slammed his shoulder into the second door and ground his teeth as he dug his boots into the packed dirt floor, forcing the wood to yield to his will.

How could a bunch of fripperies and ruffles do more to serve the community than a new roof for a family in need? Most of the women in and around Coventry sewed their own clothes, and those that didn't bought ready-made duds through the dry-goods store or mail order. Sensible clothes, durable clothes, not fashion-plate items that stroked their vanity or elicited covetous desires in their hearts for things they couldn't afford. A dressmaker had no place in Coventry.

This can't be God's will. The world and its schemers had brought her to town, not God.

Horse hooves thudded and harnesses jangled as Tom led the grays toward the front of the livery.

J.T. blew out a breath and rubbed a hand along his jaw. No matter what had brought her to Coventry, the dressmaker was still a woman, and his father had drummed into him that all women were to be treated with courtesy and respect. So he'd smile and doff his hat and make polite conversation. Shoot, he'd even lug her heavy junk around for her and unload all her folderol. But once she was out of his wagon, he'd have nothing more to do with her.

Hannah sat atop one of her five trunks, waiting for young Tom to return. Most of the other passengers had left the depot already, making their way on foot or in wagons with family members who'd come to meet them. Hannah wasn't about to let her belongings out of her sight, though—or trust them to a porter she didn't know. So she waited.

Thanks to Victoria Ashmont's generosity, she'd been able to use the money she'd saved for a shop to buy fabric and supplies. Not knowing what would be available in the small town of Coventry, she'd brought everything she needed with her. Including her prized possession—a Singer Improved Family Model 15 treadle machine with five-drawer walnut cabinet and extension leaf. The monster weighed nearly as much as the locomotive that brought her here, but it was a thing of beauty, and she intended to make certain it arrived at the shop without incident.

Her toes tapped against the wooden platform. Only a mile of dusty road stood between her and her dream. Yet the final minutes of waiting felt longer than the hours, even years, that preceded them. Could she really run her own business, or would Miss Ashmont's belief in her prove misplaced? A tingle of apprehension tiptoed over Hannah's spine. What if the women of Coventry had no need of a dressmaker? What if they didn't like her designs? What if . . .

Hannah surged to her feet and began to pace. Miss Ashmont had directed her to be bold. Bold and self-confident. Oh, and confident in God. Hannah paused. Her gaze slid to the bushy hills rising around her like ocean swells. *"I will lift up mine eyes unto the hills, from whence cometh my help. My help cometh from the Lord, which made heaven and earth."* The psalm seeped into her soul, bringing a measure of assurance with it. God had led her here. He would provide.

She resumed her pacing, anticipation building as fear receded. On her sixth lap around her mound of luggage, the creak of wagon wheels brought her to a halt.

A conveyance drew near, and Hannah's pulse vaulted into a new pace.

Young Tom wasn't driving. Another man with a worn brown felt hat pulled low over his eyes sat on the bench. It must be that J.T. person Tom had rambled on about. Well, it didn't matter who was driving, as long as he had the strength to maneuver her sewing machine without dropping it.

A figure in the back of the wagon waved a cheerful greeting, and the movement caught Hannah's eye. She waved back, glad to see Tom had returned, as well. Two men working together would have a much easier time of it.

The liveryman pulled the horses to a halt and set the brake. Masculine grace exuded from him as he climbed down and made his way to the platform. His long stride projected confidence, a vivid contrast to Tom's childish gamboling behind him. Judging by the breadth of his shoulders and the way the blue cotton of his shirt stretched across the expanse of his chest and arms, this man would have no trouble moving her sewing cabinet.

Tom dashed ahead of the newcomer and swiped the gray slouch hat from his head. Tufts of his dark blond hair stuck out at odd angles, but his eyes sparkled with warmth. "I got the General, ma'am. We'll get you fixed up in a jiffy." Not wasting a minute, he slapped his hat back on and moved past her.

Hannah's gaze roamed to the man waiting a few steps away. He didn't look much like a general. No military uniform. Instead he sported scuffed boots and denims that were wearing thin at the knees. The tip of a toothpick protruded from his lips, wiggling a little as he gnawed on it. Perhaps General was a nickname of sorts. He hadn't spoken a word, yet there was something about his carriage and posture that gave him an air of authority.

She straightened her shoulders in response and closed the distance between them. Still giddy about starting up her shop, she couldn't resist the urge to tease the stoic man who held himself apart.

"Thank you for assisting me today, General." She smiled up at him as she drew near, finally able to see more than just his jaw. He had lovely amber eyes, although they were a bit cold. "Should I salute or something?"

His right brow arced upward. Then a tiny twitch at the corner of his mouth told her he'd caught on.

"I'm afraid I'm a civilian through and through, ma'am." He tilted his head in the direction of the wagon. "That's the General. Tom likes to name things."

Hannah gave a little laugh. "I see. Well, I'm glad to have you both lending me a hand. I'm Hannah Richards."

The man tweaked the brim of his hat. "J.T. Tucker."

"Pleased to meet you, Mr. Tucker."

He dipped his chin in a small nod. Not a very demonstrative fellow. Nor very talkative.

"Lay those things down, Tom," he called out as he stepped away. "We don't want them to tip over the side if we hit a rut."

"Oh. Wait just a minute, please." There was no telling what foul things had been carted around in that wagon bed before today. It didn't matter so much for her trunks and sewing cabinet, but the linen covering her mannequins would be easily soiled.

"I have an old quilt that I wrapped around them in the railroad freight car. Let me fetch it."

Hannah sensed more than heard Mr. Tucker's sigh as she hurried to collect the quilt from the trunk she had been sitting on. Well, he could sigh all he liked. Her display dummies were going to be covered. She had one chance to make a first impression on the ladies of Coventry, and she vowed it would be a pristine one.

Making a point not to look at the liveryman as she scurried by, Hannah clutched the quilt to her chest and headed for the wagon. She draped it over the side, then climbed the spokes and hopped into the back, just as she had done as a child. Then she laid out the quilt along the back wall and gently piled the six dummies horizontally atop it, alternating the placement of the tripod pedestals to allow them to fit together in a more compact fashion. As she flipped the remaining fabric of the quilt over the pile, a loud thud sounded from behind, and the wagon jostled her. She gasped and teetered to the side. Glancing over her shoulder, she caught sight of Mr. Tucker as he shoved the first of her trunks into the wagon bed, its iron bottom scraping against the wooden floor.

The man could have warned her of his presence instead of scaring the wits out of her like that. But taking him to task would only make her look like a shrew, so she ignored him. When Tom arrived with the second trunk, she was ready. After he set it down, she moved to the end of the wagon.

"Would you help me down, please?"

He grinned up at her. "Sure thing."

Hannah set her hands on his shoulders as he clasped her waist and lifted her down. A tiny voice of regret chided her for not asking the favor of the rugged Mr. Tucker, but she squelched it. Tom was a safer choice. Besides, his affable manner put her at ease—unlike his companion, who from one minute to the next alternated between sparking her interest and her ire.

She bit back her admonishments to take care as the men hefted her sewing machine. Thankfully, they managed to accomplish the task without her guidance. With the large cabinet secured in the wagon bed, it didn't take long for them to load the rest of her belongings. Once they finished, Tom handed her up to the bench seat and scrambled into the back, leaving her alone with Mr. Tucker.

A cool autumn breeze caressed her cheeks and tugged lightly on her bonnet as the wagon rolled forward. She smoothed her skirts, not sure what to say to the reticent man beside her. However, he surprised her by starting the conversation on his own.

"What made you choose Coventry, Miss Richards?"

She twisted on the seat to look at him, but his eyes remained focused on the road.

"I guess you could say it chose me."

"How so?"

"It was really a most extraordinary sequence of events. I do not doubt that the Lord's Providence brought me here."

That got a reaction. His chin swiveled toward her, and beneath his hat, his intense gaze speared her for a handful of seconds before he blinked and turned away.

She swallowed the moisture that had accumulated under her tongue as he stared at her, then continued.

"Two years ago, I was hired by Mrs. Granbury of San Antonio to sew for her most particular clientele. One of these clients was an elderly spinster with a reputation for being impossible to work with. Well, I needed the job too badly to allow her to scare me away and was too stubborn to let her get the best of me, so I stuck it out and eventually the two of us found a way to coexist and even respect each other.

"Before she died, she called me in to make a final gown for her, and we fell to talking about her legacy. She had invested in several railroad properties, and had only one left that had not sold. In an act of generosity that I still find hard to believe, she gave me the deed as a gift, knowing that I had always dreamed of opening my own shop."

"What kept her from selling it before then?" His deep voice rumbled with something more pointed than simple curiosity.

A prickle of unease wiggled down Hannah's neck, but she couldn't quite pinpoint the cause.

"She told me that she preferred to meet the buyers in person, to assess their character before selling off her properties. Unfortunately, her health had begun to decline, and she was unable to travel. There had been a gentleman of good reputation from this area who made an offer several times. A Mr. Tuck . . ."

A hard lump of dread formed in the back of Hannah's throat.

"Oh dear. Don't tell me you're *that* Mr. Tucker?"

2

J.T. slanted a look at the woman beside him. She was dressed as he'd expected, in some kind of fancy traveling suit that had enough extra material gathered along the back side that she probably could have made another whole dress if she'd had an eye for frugality instead of extravagance. Yet he'd be lying if he were to say he hadn't noticed the way the cornflower blue fabric matched her eyes or how the buttoned jacket accentuated her tiny waist. And when she bent over to arrange those dummies in his wagon, he found himself rather thankful for all those flounces and ruffles hiding the shape of what was beneath.

As he watched her bite her lip and try to figure out what to say to him after discovering his connection to her shop, he had to admit that his expectations had only proven true for her clothing. Most beautiful women he'd known over the course of his twenty-seven years possessed an innate skill for manipulation. A seductive smile, pout, or subtle hint woven into the fiber of an ordinary conversation and she would have a man stumbling over himself to please her.

Miss Hannah Richards, on the other hand, didn't seem to subscribe to such artifice. Her yellow hair, trim figure, and pleasant features worked together to form a very handsome woman. Yet when something needed doing, she jumped in and did it herself instead of making sheep's eyes at him or Tom to get one of them to do it for her.

Of course, he had just met her. It was doubtful she'd continue as the exception to the rule over longer acquaintance.

"Forgive me for rambling on like that, Mr. Tucker. I had no idea . . ."

J.T. kept his head straight and his mouth shut, but he watched her out of the corner of his eye.

"All that talk about God's Providence must have been a slap in the face to you. I'm so sorry. It seems unfair that my blessing turned out to be your disappointment." She exhaled a long breath, then bounced in the seat and swung her knees toward him. "I know! I'll give you a discounted rate on any mending or tailoring you need done."

He chomped down on his toothpick. "No thanks. My sister, Cordelia, does all my mending."

"Oh."

Her cheery smile wilted, and he felt as if he'd just crushed a flower. He steeled himself against the regret that threatened to soften him, though. He didn't want any favors from her. Besides, she was only offering in order to make herself feel better.

"Well," she continued, having regained a measure of her previous enthusiasm, "perhaps I could give your sister a discount on a new dress. I've brought a wonderful selection of—"

"No." The last thing he needed was for Delia to get caught up in a bunch of fashion rigmarole. She was too sensible to fall into that trap, but he didn't plan on leaving her exposed to unnecessary temptation.

Miss Richards made no further overtures. In fact, she made no further efforts at conversation of any kind. By the time the first buildings of Coventry came into view, J.T.'s conscience was pressing down on his shoulders like a fifty-pound sack of grain.

"Look, I didn't mean to be rude." He shoved his heel against the wagon's footrest and shifted his hips against the hard wooden bench. "I appreciate you making those offers. But there's no reason for them. You own the shop fair and square. You don't have to mollify me. I can deal with it."

He grabbed the crown of his hat and resituated it on his head so he could see her better as he stole another glance her way. She didn't look at him, but the smile that curved her lips as she stared at her lap made him glad he'd spoken.

"Thank you for your understanding, Mr. Tucker. I hope there will be no hard feelings between us over this matter."

J.T. grunted a response. He couldn't very well tell her that his hard feelings had started before he'd ever met her. That would make him sound narrow-minded. Which he wasn't. Not really. He didn't have any problem with Miss Richards as a person. She seemed likable enough. But her profession was another matter altogether.

He'd seen firsthand what damage such temptation could do to a woman, to a family. Females fawned over Parisian designs until they were no longer content with their lot in life. They looked down on their menfolk for not being able to provide for them in the manner in which they believed they were entitled. And those that did have the funds for such opulence lorded it over those who didn't.

Why, he'd been to some big town church services where the women seemed to be in some kind of fashion competition. Who had the biggest hat? Whose dress was modeled after the latest style? Who wore the most expensive fabric? Wearing one's Sunday best was all fine and dandy, but these ladies acted as if they had dressed to impress their fellow congregants more than the Lord.

Narrow-minded? Not likely. Was it narrow-minded to disapprove of saloons and bawdy houses? They supplied temptations that led people astray. Fancy dress goods did the same thing, only in a more socially acceptable way.

His jaw clenched, and the softened toothpick trapped between his teeth bent in two. J.T. turned to the side and spit out the offending sliver of wood. He wiped his mouth with the back of his gloved hand and rolled his neck in an effort to rid himself of the tension that had built there. Getting all worked up wasn't going to help matters.

Besides, all her talk about God's Providence made him wonder if the Lord really did bring her to Coventry. He supposed if the Almighty could use a woman like Rahab to bring about victory for his people, it wasn't outside the realm of possibilities that he could use a dressmaker for some good purpose, as well. Doubtful, but possible.

Still struggling to believe that she'd finally arrived at her new home, Hannah drank in her first glimpse of Coventry as the wagon rolled by the various storefronts. Two well-dressed men looked up from their conversation in front of a tall limestone building to the right. They nodded a greeting. Hannah smiled back.

"We just finished that hotel a couple months back," Mr. Tucker said as he dipped his chin to the men.

Hope stirred in her. Though Coventry was much smaller than San Antonio, it was growing. A railroad, a new hotel, businessmen coming to town. Businessmen who had wives. Wives who would want fine-tailored dress goods. Yes, there were definitely possibilities here.

Farther down the street, her optimism waned a bit. As Mr. Tucker dutifully pointed out the locations of the telegraph office, bank, and drugstore, Hannah paid little attention, her interest focused on the ladies who strolled down the boardwalk with shopping baskets on their arms. Their dresses were simple, plain. Did they not care for fashion? Or worse, did they not have funds for dress goods? She was pretty sure her designs would draw them in, but if they had no money to spend . . .

Hannah's fingernails jabbed into the skin of her palms. No. She'd not get lost in a pile of *what if*s again. God brought her to Coventry for a reason. It didn't matter if the town was small or if its citizens were ordinary folk. She'd planned for that, adapting patterns ahead of time to reflect more practical styles and selecting fabric suitable to small-town life. Besides, it would be a lovely change to sew for people of her own social standing, women she could befriend and chat with as equals. Maybe even Mr. Tucker's sister.

Hannah glanced at the grim man driving the rig. He didn't seem all that friendly, but that didn't mean his sister would share his reticence. Then again, she'd probably be grumpy, too, if she'd just found out the shop she wanted had been given to someone else.

The horses slowed to a stop, and all at once, her concerns blew away on the wind. They had arrived.

Stomach fluttering, Hannah gazed upon the simple clapboard structure that represented her future. It had a lovely false front and windows facing the street. Ideas blossomed as she considered where she should position the mannequins to best be seen by passersby and which dresses she would use to entice them into her shop. Perhaps the lavender morning dress or the olive polonaise costume she made up last month. Both reflected the latest styles and techniques while not inhibiting everyday duties. No sheaths that wrapped so snugly around the knees that a woman had to take mincing steps. No flowing trains to collect dirt and mud from the unpaved roads and country lanes. Minimal use of silks and velvets or any fabric that wouldn't hold up to normal wear in a western town.

"Do you want a hand down or not?"

Hannah jumped at the growling voice, caught up as she was in the intricate web of her business strategies.

"Oh! Of course." Heat warmed her cheeks. She stood and set a foot atop the raised side of the wagon, then reached out to the irascible Mr. Tucker. Her hands pressed against the corded muscles of his shoulders at the same time his encircled her waist. A frisson of awareness coursed through her as she sunk slowly to the ground, secure in his capable grip. This close, she could smell a bit of horse on him mixed with harness oil. Masculine scents.

"Thank you." She avoided his penetrating gaze and fumbled with the ball clasp on her handbag. "I'll just get the key and unlock the front door."

Hannah extracted a nickel-plated key from the pocket in the lining of her purse and stepped onto the boardwalk. She paused outside the door and pressed a trembling hand to her abdomen. Taking a deep breath, she fit the key into the lock and twisted. A satisfying click sounded, and the door swung open.

Looking past the dirt and grime that had accumulated while the store stood vacant, Hannah crossed the threshold, her artistic mind awhirl with possibilities. A counter jutted out into the room from the left wall about halfway back. It would make a lovely display for her pattern catalogs and fashion magazines. She could put in some shelves along the right wall to showcase her fabrics, stacking complementary bolts together to help her customers visualize the final effects she could achieve for them by blending patterns and colors. The coatrack and wardrobe hangers for her pre-made dresses could be mounted on the left wall, leaving plenty of room for ladies to wander about.

Hannah's boot heels thumped against the bare floor as she made her way behind the counter. She was pleased to discover cubbyholes that could be used to store her till, ledger, and fabric swatches. It appeared there'd be sufficient room for her sewing machine back here, as well, which meant she wouldn't have to hide in the back room. She could save that space for fittings and project storage.

Yes, this little shop would accommodate her quite well.

A shuffle sounded behind her. She turned to see Tom and Mr. Tucker standing inside the doorway, each with a trunk balanced on one shoulder.

"If you're done woolgathering, you might show us where you want this stuff," the liveryman groused.

She supposed he had a right to be testy. With all the excitement of the new shop, she'd completely forgotten about the men. She was thankful she had thought to label the trunks. Colored ribbons tied to the handles indicated which ones contained dress shop items and which held her personal belongings.

"Let's see." She approached the men and fingered the thin strip of grosgrain silk that hung near Mr. Tucker's hand, careful not to touch the man himself. "The ones with blue ribbons can be left down here behind the counter. The ones with pink ribbons need to go upstairs in my personal quarters."

Hannah lifted her chin to meet his gaze and suddenly found it difficult to breathe.

"What color's mine, J.T.? I can't see it."

Mr. Tucker looked away and Hannah drew in a deep breath, willing her stomach to stop its silly fluttering. The man was as prickly as a cactus. Just because he had eyes the color of melting honey didn't mean she had to go all soft over him.

The man gestured with a jerk of his head for Tom to move past them. "Yours is blue. Go put it over yonder and then head back to the wagon and look for any others with blue ribbons. I'll haul this one upstairs." He raised a brow at Hannah. "Whenever Miss Richards decides she's ready."

Riled at his insinuation that she was some kind of lollygagger, Hannah thrust out her chin and marched out the door. "If you'll follow me, Mr. Tucker?"

The nerve of that man. Hannah fumed as she rounded the corner of the building to reach the exterior stairs on the north side. She hoped he was carrying one of the heavier trunks. It'd serve him right if he ended up with a permanent crease in his collar and a crick in his neck. Any person seeing their home or place of business for the first time was bound to need a minute or two to soak it all in. Why, she'd bet a dollar of profits that when he walked into his livery stable for the first time, he gawked like a boy in a gun shop.

Irritation fueling her steps, Hannah slammed her foot onto each stair as she made her way to the top. She clutched the key in her left hand, disregarding the handrail. Pausing before the second to last step, she peeked over her shoulder to gauge Mr. Tucker's progress. He'd had to switch the trunk to the opposite shoulder in order to grip the railing, and was still near the bottom.

"Are you coming?" she taunted in a sugar-sweet voice.

The brim of his hat lifted, allowing her to see his scowl. Satisfaction surged through her as her foot pounded down on the next step.

A crack shouted like thunder in her ear as the board beneath her gave way, and with a surprised squeak, she plummeted feet-first through the yawning hole.

J.T. didn't take time to think. In a single motion, he dropped the trunk and vaulted over the railing. His boots crashed into the earth with a jolt that surged through his bent knees and into his thighs.

Springing out of his crouch, he ran forward, praying that Miss Richards wasn't hurt too badly. But instead of coming upon a pile of crushed blue fluff as he expected, he found himself eye level with a pair of delicate ankles pumping madly through a froth of white petticoats.

Her skirt hung unevenly, hiked up somewhat on the side closest to him. Her black stockings stood out against the white petticoats like coal on snow. The ribbed lines that started above the top of her shoe drew his gaze over the gentle curve of her calf before disappearing into the flurry of white cotton that surrounded them.

J.T. turned away, a cough rising in his throat. The woman was dangling from a second-story staircase, and he was ogling her legs. What kind of a lecher was he? J.T. tugged his hat down and cleared his throat, wishing he could clear his mind as easily.

She must have heard him, for the kicking stilled.

"Mr. Tucker?"

Her voice sounded breathless. Taking firm control of his wayward thoughts, he stepped aside to better assess her predicament. She must have managed to grab hold of the top step as she fell, for her head, shoulders, and arms were blocked from his view.

"I'm here, Miss Richards." He cleared his throat again, despite the fact that his mouth had gone bone dry.

"I seem to have dropped my key."

A quiet chuckle escaped him before he could stuff it back inside. He shook his head, unable to tame the smile that lingered on his lips.

"Yes, ma'am. I believe you have. Looks like you might have dropped one or two other things, as well."

"I'm afraid so."

He chanced another look up, careful to steer his gaze along appropriate paths. Was it his imagination, or was she hanging a bit lower than she had been a minute ago?

"Um . . . Mr. Tucker?" His name came out pinched, and he thought he heard a grunt as she shifted.

"Yes, ma'am?"

"I know it wasn't part of our original agreement . . ." A second noise interrupted. Definitely a grunt. And he swore he could see the edge of her collar peeking out beneath the wooden slats now. She was slipping. His heart rammed against his ribs.

"But might you be willing to catch me? I don't think I can—"

He dove back under her, her quiet gasp ringing in his ears as loud as any scream. Bracing himself against the impact, he scooped her legs into the crook of his left arm before they hit the ground and caught her upper body with his right. He clasped her close to his chest as he fought to stay on his feet. Once his boots were firmly planted, he looked down into her face, concerned to find her eyes squeezed shut.

"Are you all right?"

The lines around her eyelids softened, and her lashes fluttered upward. The twilight blue of her eyes held him captive.

"I . . . I'm fine, I think. Thank you, Mr. Tucker."

She blinked and dipped her chin, breaking the connection. As he lowered her feet to the ground, his chin knocked against her already-askew bonnet. The thing sat lopsided on her head, and one of the flowers from around the crown had abandoned its place to drape drunkenly over her forehead. He reached for it and tried to stick it back where it belonged, but the stubborn stem refused to cooperate. Fed up, he plucked the ornery bloom straight off of its mooring and shoved it at its owner.

"Here."

A hint of a smile played over Miss Richards's lips as she accepted it from him. "Thank you."

She must think him an idiot. And why not? He was one. Trying to fix a stupid flower. What had come over him? Looking around for an escape of any kind, he spied her small purse in the shadow of the building.

"I'll . . . uh . . . look for your key."

She didn't say anything, but he could hear the swish of her skirts as she no doubt set about repairing her appearance. He bent over to collect the purse and searched the area around it for the key.

"Perhaps I should have heeded the wisdom of Proverbs before I allowed my pride to send me stomping up those steps in a huff." Her self-deprecating chuckle drew his attention away from the weed-strewn ground and back toward her. "You know . . . a haughty spirit goeth before a fall."

Her saucy taunts as she'd rushed up the stairs had surely irritated him, but truth be told, he probably shared the blame because of his impatience in the shop. No one had ever accused him of having a silver tongue.

"I don't know about the haughty spirit," he said with a shrug, "but you certainly fell."

Full-blown feminine laughter rang out, and the sound lifted his mood.

"That I did." She started walking his way, a free-spirited smile bedecking her face.

J.T. cleared his throat again and returned to his perusal of the ground beneath the staircase. After a moment, he caught a glimmer of reflected light. The key lay beside the broken pieces of what had once been a secure step. He shoved the purse under his arm and picked up the key, along with one of the defective hunks of wood. The thing was rotted through. He frowned. How many other steps had deteriorated?

Miss Richards slipped up beside him and retrieved the purse and key. "Thank you again, Mr. Tucker. If it weren't for your quick actions, I would likely have suffered a serious injury."

He felt her withdrawal, but he had already started inspecting the other steps and didn't pay her much mind.

"I know you're anxious to return to the livery," she said, "so I'll get the door unlocked in a trice."

She was halfway to the top when her meaning finally sank into his distracted brain.

"Get down from there, woman, before you take another tumble!" His words came out sharper than he'd intended, but fear for her safety had ignited his temper. That and the fact that when he raised his head from his stooped position under the stairs to call out to her, he got another eyeful of stockings and petticoats.

"Don't worry, Mr. Tucker. I'm not stomping this time, and I've a firm grip on the railing. I'll be fine."

Gritting his teeth, J.T. strode out from under the steps and glared up at the stubborn woman whom he had earlier mistaken for intelligent.

"The wood from that broken step is rotten. There might be others ready to give way, as well."

Her eyes narrowed and the skin around her lips drew taut. "Thank you for your concern, but if they held me the first time, there's no reason to believe they won't do so now."

"What if you weakened them the first time?" He crossed his arms and raised a brow in challenge. Just because the steps he had checked so far had turned out to be sound didn't mean the remaining ones wouldn't cause a problem.

The woman deliberately took another step before answering him, her chin angled toward the sky. "You need not treat me like a child, sir. I am perfectly capable of navigating this staircase on my own."

He snorted.

Her nostrils flared. "I promise not to ask you to catch me again, all right? Now stop scowling."

Of course he did no such thing.

Those deep blue eyes of hers shot sparks at him, and he had to work to keep his expression stern. The woman was a firecracker.

"Tell you what," she huffed, "if I fall, you have my permission to gloat as much as you like. How about that?"

Without waiting for his answer, she spun around and marched the remainder of the distance to the top, stretching her stride to span the gulf over the missing stair. He followed her from below as a precaution and didn't relax until she disappeared into the room that would serve as her personal quarters.

Fool woman. She'd rather risk her neck than admit she might not be able to manage something on her own. He jumped up and grabbed hold of one of the higher steps, testing its strength against his dangling weight. It held. The top step, too, remained firmly in place even after all of Miss Richards's clinging and scraping. Apparently, the only unstable lumber was the step she fell through. Didn't matter, though. She still should have waited until he checked it out before trudging up the stairs like Joan of Arc on some kind of crusade.

J.T. pulled another toothpick out of his shirt pocket and wedged it between his molars. His tongue fiddled with it as he stared up through the hole in the staircase. He had to give her credit. Miss Richards knew how to handle herself in a crisis. Not only did she have the presence of mind to latch onto another step to keep from crashing to the ground, but there'd been no screaming, no hysteria, just calm conversation and a polite request to *please catch her*. Any other woman, his sister included, would have shrieked like a hog at butchering time.

Shaking his head, J.T. headed back to where he had left the dressmaker's trunk. The box had tumbled to the bottom of the stairs and now lay upside down. He flipped it over just as Tom came around the corner with the other pink-ribboned trunk hefted on his shoulder.

"I done finished the blue ones, J.T., so I thought I'd bring this 'un to ya. How come you're so slow? I expected you'd be done afore me."

"Miss Richards had a mishap on the stairs."

Tom's eyes widened in glazed panic.

"She's all right," J.T. hurried to assure him. "She's up in her room."

"W-what happened?"

J.T. hauled the trunk off Tom's shoulder and set it down next to his. "One of the steps broke and she fell, but she's fine."

"If she's fine, how come I can't see her anywheres?"

The boy's breathing came in quick shallow gasps, and his head flew from side to side.

J.T. squeezed his arm to get him to focus on him. "You know how womenfolk are, Tom. She's probably up there figuring out what kind of curtains she should hang in the windows and where to put all her knick-knacks. She'll be down in a bit."

The boy glanced up at the open door. "You sure?"

"I'm sure." J.T. stepped behind him and started steering him across the street. "Now, what we menfolk oughta do is fetch a new plank from the lumber pile in back of the livery and fix that step for her so she doesn't have to worry about any more mishaps. You think you can find me a good board while I dig up a hammer and nails?"

Tom's head bobbed up and down. "Yes, sir."

"Good." J.T. thumped him on the back and moved into place beside him. They walked several yards in silence, but when they reached the livery doors, Tom turned back to look at the building across the street.

"You know, J.T., since Miss Richards ain't got no regular menfolk, it'd probably be a good idea for us to look after her. You reckon that's why God brought her to us? So's we could take care of her?"

J.T. chomped down on his toothpick and clenched his jaw. He didn't want to think about the Lord purposefully bringing the dressmaker into his life. He had enough responsibility looking after Cordelia and widows like Louisa James. He didn't want to be bothered with an opinionated, stubborn piece of baggage like Miss Hannah Richards, even if she did fit in his arms like a pistol in a custom-made holster. No, sir. After he fixed her step and finished unloading her paraphernalia, she'd be on her own.

4

Hannah hid out in her living quarters until the muted male voices below faded away. She peeked out the doorway to make sure they were gone, then flopped into the single wooden chair that resided in her room. It tilted to the side and nearly threw her to the floor before she caught her balance with her boot heel. A frustrated scream welled up inside her, held at bay by the barest thread of self-control. Even the furniture plotted to steal her equilibrium.

A scrap of kindling shoved beneath the too-short leg would fix the chair, but what was she to do about Mr. Tucker? One minute he was a gallant knight, rescuing her from a mess of her own making, teasing and charming her, and holding her with arms that made her feel cherished and safe. The next he was an arrogant, overbearing lout who chastised her as if she were a child and ordered her about on her own property. She didn't know if she should kiss his cheek or kick his shin.

Right now, the shin kick was winning.

She sighed and tossed her purse onto the worn oak table beside her, the movement highlighting the ache beneath her arms. More concerned with the state of her clothing than any scrapes or bruises resulting from her fall, Hannah raised each arm in turn and examined the fabric and seams. She found a small tear on the left where the side seam met the sleeve—easily repaired with a few strokes of her needle. The snags on the fabric would be harder to fix, but at least they were in an inconspicuous area. The front of the dress had been spared, and she hadn't lost a single button. Of course, she always double stitched hers, so she'd expected nothing less.

Having assured herself that the damage to her traveling suit had been kept to a minimum, Hannah broadened her inspection to include the room.

A cookstove stood on the left wall flanked by small windows on either side. A primitive-looking bedstead and mattress dominated the back corner. A few hooks protruded from the wall for hanging clothes, but no bureau or washstand could be found. A table and the lopsided chair she sat on completed the tally of furniture. Pretty spare. And it would be more so after she hauled the table and chair downstairs.

Her shop demanded top priority. She needed a work surface for cutting patterns and piecing them together, and a chair was essential for using her treadle sewing machine. Not knowing how long it would take her to build up a steady income, Hannah planned to save whatever money she could.

Once her business was turning a decent profit, she would order furnishings for her apartment. Until then, she'd make do with the trunks she'd brought. She could use them for storage as well as makeshift benches. If she stacked two, they might be tall enough to give her a counter of sorts. An oilcloth cover and her large breadboard would give her a surface for food preparation. That should suffice. She'd have to keep meals simple anyway, with all the time spent in her shop.

Hannah pulled a small tablet out of her purse and began jotting down a list of the items she would need to purchase at the mercantile. Halfway through the word *potatoes* a thought occurred to her. If the store owner boxed up her purchases, she could use the crates for stools and even a washstand. She smiled and nibbled on the end of her pencil. With a little ingenuity, she'd have all the comforts of home in no time. Of course, she'd have to find someone to supply her with fresh milk. She wouldn't last a day without her morning cocoa.

A sudden pounding outside made her jump. Grabbing up her handbag and list, Hannah rushed to the door. Three steps down, Mr. Tucker stood bent over the gaping hole in her stairway, legs straddled, arms swinging as he nailed a new stair into place. As he reached for a second nail, he caught sight of her. He gave her a brief nod and then hammered the nail in with a tap followed by a single sure stroke.

"Tom and I moved your sewing cabinet inside," he said without looking at her. "He's taking the rig back."

Another nail slammed into place. "As soon as I get this step finished, I'll bring up your trunks and leave you in peace."

Still grumpy, Hannah thought, but sweet nonetheless.

"Thank you for fixing the step. I'll gladly pay you for your time."

Mr. Tucker glared up at her as if she had just impugned his honor. "I don't charge for being neighborly, ma'am."

"So I guess I shouldn't offer to compensate you for your heroic rescue of me, either, then." She grinned, hoping to get some kind of reaction out of him, but he never looked up.

"Nope." He accented his refusal with a final swing of the hammer and jumped with both feet onto the new stair.

His craftsmanship held.

"There." He tipped his hat back and finally met her eyes. "That should stand up to any amount of stomping you feel the need to dish out."

His lips stretched, and for a moment she thought he might smile, but his mouth never actually curved. Hannah shifted against the railing, unsure if he had spoken in jest or censure.

"Yes, well, thank you. I never know when the urge to stomp might next come over me." Although she imagined if it did recur, the man before her would somehow be responsible.

He flicked the brim of his hat in salute and turned to go, but she remembered the table and called out to stop him.

"Mr. Tucker? On your way down, would you help me carry this old table to the shop? It's too large for me to manage on my own."

He shrugged and followed her inside. "What's wrong with it? Planning on ordering a roomful of new furniture or something?"

The playfulness she thought she'd detected in his voice earlier had vanished, leaving nothing but frost in its wake. Well, she needed his muscles more than his cheer, so as long as he was willing to help, he could grouch to his heart's content.

"It's a perfectly fine table. The only problem is that I need it downstairs." She set her purse on the seat of the rickety chair and moved around to the far end of the table. Grabbing hold of the edge facing her, she waited for Mr. Tucker to pick up his end. He chose to stare at her instead, with a look that raised her hackles.

Hannah eyed his shins and aimed the point of her toe in his direction. Lucky for him a hefty piece of furniture stood in her way.

"I don't plan to entertain many guests up here," she said, "so I can make do without a table. But I can't very well cut out patterns for my customers on the floor of the shop, now can I?"

He just stared at her, a clouded expression on his face. She was about to shoo him away, determined to move the table without his help, when he stepped up and clasped his side of the tabletop.

"It . . . uh . . . wouldn't be nothing fancy . . ." He stopped and cleared his throat. "But if you want, I could loan you a couple of sawhorses and some spare planks I got piled out back. It'd serve until you could buy a real table."

The heat of her temper mellowed into a warm pool of gratitude. "You would do that for me?"

He nodded, finally meeting her gaze. His mouth held fast to its rigid line, but the hard glitter had left his eyes, giving him an oddly vulnerable appearance despite the steely strength that radiated from the rest of him.

"Thank you, Mr. Tucker." A soft smile curved her lips. "I must warn you, though, that I don't plan to order any furniture until I've successfully established my business, so it could be months before I am able to return the borrowed items."

"Keep 'em as long as you need. I can always make more."

"Really?" The seed of an idea sprouted in her mind.

"Sure. I got a heap of scrap lumber left from when I tore out the dividing wall in the wagon shed last year."

"Enough to spare me four boards that I could use for shelving in my shop? I'd pay you for them, of course."

He leaned over the table toward her. "Now, don't you go insulting me again."

"No, sir," she rushed to assure him, even though there was no heat behind his words. "But I don't want to take advantage of your generosity, either. Are you sure I can't mend a shirt or darn a sock for you in trade? Anything?"

"You can quit your yammerin' and carry this table downstairs so I can get back to minding my own business instead of messing around in yours."

His sudden rudeness set her back on her heels, but as he ducked his head to hide behind the brim of his hat, an internal light dawned. This tough cowboy didn't know how to deal with gratitude. He could repair a step and catch a falling damsel, but try to thank the fellow, and he got all surly. Maybe if she could remember that, he wouldn't rile her so easily.

If he could just remember that she was a dressmaker, maybe his gut wouldn't end up in knots whenever she looked at him like that. It was enough to give a man indigestion.

J.T. bit back a groan and flipped the table onto its side before she could distract him further. Miss Richards grabbed the leg and helped him maneuver the table through the doorway. She anticipated his movements and worked well with him as they eased down the steps, never once complaining about the weight or asking to take a break.

They carried the table through the back door and set it up in the workroom. He then returned to finish with the trunks while she carried her only chair down to the shop, as well. Something about needing it for her sewing machine and using her trunks for benches. Maybe he could check into finding her some real chairs.

After he deposited the last trunk, she locked up her room and followed him down the stairs.

"How much do I owe you?"

J.T. glanced off toward the livery, dodging her gaze. "A dollar for the wagon, and two bits for the unloading."

She handed him a one-dollar note and a silver twenty-five-cent piece. He tucked them into his pants pocket and nodded his thanks.

"Was the dry-goods store down this way?" She bit her lip and pointed toward the south, her blue gaze losing some of the assurance that had blazed there since she'd arrived. "I need to stock up on some supplies before they close this afternoon."

An offer to escort her rose to his lips, but he quickly suppressed it. It was bad enough that he would have to see her tomorrow when he delivered the sawhorses and shelves he'd foolishly promised when the urge to make amends for his hasty judgments temporarily overrode his good sense.

"Yep," he said, choosing the safer option. "It's two doors down. Just on the other side of Mrs. James's laundry."

"Thank you." She smiled in that way of hers, the one that made him feel like he had swallowed his toothpick. He frowned back.

Miss Richards turned away and started down the boardwalk, her skirts swaying in a subtle rhythm. Left. Right. L—

"Oh, Mr. Tucker?" She spun around, and J.T. jerked his focus back to her face. A cough that nearly strangled him lodged in his throat.

"Do you happen to know of someone in town who might be willing to sell me a jar of milk in the morning?"

The Harris family had a small dairy operation on the edge of town, where they sold milk, butter, and cheese to the locals. Will Harris, the eldest boy, usually made deliveries to the folks in town who didn't keep their own cow, but J.T. hesitated to mention him. He was a big, strapping lad with an eye for the ladies. A woman on her own didn't need a man like that coming around to her personal quarters in the early morning hours. Will was an honorable, churchgoing fella, yet the idea of him sniffing around Miss Richards set J.T.'s teeth on edge.

"I'll have my sister bring you some."

She snapped open the clasp on her purse and started swishing those hips toward him again. "Can I pay ahead for a week? I'll give you—"

"You and Delia can settle on a price tomorrow." He waved her off and stepped down into the street. "I've gotta get back to the livery."

"Thank you for all your help, Mr. Tucker," she called out to his back. "You truly have been a godsend."

He waved a hand in acknowledgment but didn't turn around. Clenching his jaw, J.T. pulverized as many dirt clods under his boots as possible while he crossed the road. First he tangled himself up with the dressmaker for another day by promising to make her a table, and now he'd dragged Cordelia into it, too. Exactly what he'd been trying to avoid.

J.T. stormed into his office and shut the door. He pounded the wall with his fist as his rebellious eyes sought Hannah Richards through the window and followed her until she disappeared into the mercantile. With a growl, he spun around and pressed his back into the wall, banging his head against the wood.

A godsend?

J.T. tipped his chin toward the ceiling. "If it's all the same to you, the next time she needs help, send someone else."

5

By the time all trace of pink had faded from the sky the next morning, Hannah had already completed her calisthenic regimen, arranged her trunks and crates about the room, and organized her food supplies and personal belongings. A mountain of work still awaited her downstairs, but that knowledge did nothing to dim the excitement skittering across her nerves. If all went according to plan, she'd have her shop in basic working order by the end of the day and be open for business on the morrow. The very thought sent her into a pirouette. The shortened skirt of her loose-fitting gymnastic costume belled out around her.

Now, if only Miss Tucker would arrive with her milk, the day would be off to a grand start. Fighting off a spurt of impatience, Hannah decided to start in on her devotional time without her breakfast cocoa. Whenever possible, she began the day by sipping chocolate and reading from her Bible, but she couldn't afford to wait on the cocoa with all that had yet to be accomplished.

She had utilized every scrap of yesterday's daylight to knock down cobwebs from the rafters and corners of her living quarters, clean out ashes from the stove, scrub the floor, and curtain off her bedroom area. When the early darkness of the autumn evening had finally forced her to stop, she collapsed onto her lumpy mattress like a dervish that had run out of whirl and slept unmoving until a nearby rooster let out his predawn squawk. Spun back into action by the sound, she'd been swirling about in a frenzy ever since. She was more than ready for a little quiet time.

Hannah pushed the curtain aside, trying to ignore the unattractive fabric as she collected her Bible from the crate next to her bed. When Floyd Hawkins, the dry-goods store owner, heard she was a seamstress, he had dug out a bolt of dusty calico that had apparently been languishing untouched for over a year in his cloth bin and demanded she take it off his hands at the wholesale price. Hannah certainly understood why no one had purchased the appalling fabric. She would swallow a bug before fashioning the orange-dotted cloth into a dress. But knowing she could put it to use, her practical side wouldn't let her pass up the bargain. Tacked up in pleated folds along a ceiling beam, it offered privacy, if not great aesthetic value. Perhaps she could drape an eye-pleasing swag across the top and add a ribbon to the hem to dress it up a bit when things settled down.

Bible in hand, Hannah took a seat on the trunk bench she had positioned beneath the window to the left of the stove. She tugged the red satin ribbon that held her place and opened to Proverbs 16, the passage she had been meditating on for the last month as she made preparations for this day. Morning sunlight illuminated the wisdom on the page. Verse three promised that if she committed her work to the Lord, her thoughts would be established. Yet verse eight cautioned that having little while being righteous was better than great revenues without right. Finally, verse nine, the verse of balance, brought her hopes and fears together in a call to trust.

" 'A man's heart deviseth his way,'" she whispered, "'but the Lord directeth his steps.'"

Hannah read the familiar words one more time before sliding her eyes shut. "Father, you know how badly I long for my thoughts and plans to be established. I have dreamed of this dress shop since my first apprenticeship. You have opened doors for me, doors I could not open on my own, and I thank you.

"At the same time, I confess to wanting success. I want customers to find satisfaction in my designs." Hannah's forehead crinkled as honesty warred with her desire not to appear overly ambitious or greedy before her Lord. "All right, more than satisfaction," she admitted. "I want them to be amazed at my skill. Help me to battle my pride and remember that it is by your grace alone that I have this opportunity.

"As I embark on this endeavor, remind me to cling to righteousness, not to revenue; to look for ways to serve and glorify you, not myself; and to follow where you lead, even if you direct my steps on a path that deviates from the way I have charted. Thank y—"

A quiet knock thumped against the door, cutting off her prayer and accelerating her heartbeat. Hannah shoved her Bible aside and jumped to her feet. She sent a silent amen heavenward and rushed to the door.

She opened the portal to find a softer, rounder, and more feminine version of Mr. Tucker standing on her stoop. The woman's brown hair was pulled into a nondescript knot beneath a plain straw bonnet that seemed more appropriate for a young girl than a grown woman. No frills adorned her brown dress, either. Yet the shy smile on her face erased any semblance of severity, and the aroma of fresh-baked bread that wafted from the basket she held filled Hannah with a sense of comfort and put her instantly at ease.

"You must be Miss Tucker. Please come in. I've been looking forward to meeting you."

The woman's cheeks flushed and her gaze fell to the floor, but her smile widened as she crossed the threshold. "Thank you, Miss Richards. I have the milk you asked J.T. about and brought some of my apple muffins as a welcome gift."

"How thoughtful. They smell delicious. I hope it wasn't too much trouble." Hannah took the offered fruit jar of milk and set it on the arm of the stove while Miss Tucker extracted a napkin-wrapped bundle from the large basket hanging from the bend of her elbow. Hannah spied several loaves of bread and additional muffins before the cloth cover was tucked back into place.

"I supply baked goods to Mr. Hawkins's store, and it was a simple matter to stop here on the way. No trouble."

"A fellow businesswoman." Hannah accepted the muffins and held the offering up to her nose. "And if these taste as good as they smell, you no doubt turn a tidy profit."

Miss Tucker shook her head. "I'm not a *real* businesswoman. Not like you, with your own shop and everything." The blush was back, painting her cheeks a dusty pink.

Hannah examined the woman more closely. She truly possessed some lovely features. Long dark lashes, a dainty nose, full lips. She might be considered a tad plump by some, but Hannah could easily minimize that with the right cut and color of fabric. If she could just get her out of that drab brown and put her into a deep rose or peacock blue. . . .

"I enjoy baking, that's all." Miss Tucker broke into her thoughts, and Hannah refocused on the conversation. "J.T. provides a good living for us, but after all he's done for me, I'm glad to make whatever contribution I can."

"I know what you mean. I still send funds to my mother when I get the chance. She lives with my younger sister and her husband back east and is always worried about being a burden to them. Which, of course, she's not. Emily's the nurturer of the family and loves having Mama around, especially now that a child is on the way."

"Your family's back east?" Miss Tucker eyed her curiously. "How did you come to be in Texas, then?"

Hannah smiled as she moved her Bible to the windowsill and motioned for her guest to be seated on the trunk bench. She gently extricated the oversized basket from Miss Tucker's arm and set it on the floor.

"When I was sixteen, my mother arranged for me to apprentice with an established dressmaker in Boston, not far from our home in Dorchester. After three years, I had worked my way up to first assistant when my employer married the brother of one of her clients. It was quite a scandal, although all of us girls thought it terribly romantic."

"Did she move her business west after the wedding?"

Hannah shook her head as she dumped a bunch of potatoes out of a crate and into an empty dishpan. Turning the crate upside down, she drew the short seat across from Miss Tucker and sat down, folding her crossed ankles off to the side.

"No. Her new husband wouldn't hear of her continuing to work, so she closed her shop. Unfortunately, that left many of us without employment. I could have hired on as an apprentice-level seamstress with one of the other dressmakers in Boston, but the pay would have been a pittance, and my mother and sister depended on the funds I sent them. So when my employer's aunt, also a seamstress, came to town for the wedding and offered me a full-pay position if I was willing to return to San Antonio with her, I decided seeing the great American West was an adventure I couldn't refuse.

"I spent the last two years with Mrs. Granbury, and I must say, I've developed quite a taste for Texas."

"Surely it's hard to be so far away from your family, though."

"Yes." Hannah thought of Christmases missed and how she wouldn't be around for the birth of the niece or nephew who was due in a couple of months. Loneliness permeated, and her posture sagged until she caught herself and stiffened her spine. "But it's not so bad. I've had the opportunity to develop my business out here much more quickly than would have been possible back in Boston. And if I'm blessed enough to make a few good friends in Coventry, my life will be rich."

As she glanced at the quiet girl who was listening so intently, a feeling of kinship rose up in Hannah. Perhaps the Lord was already paving the road for a lasting friendship.

Thinking to offer her guest some refreshment, Hannah rose and stepped over to the stove. She pried open the fruit jar lid and poured the milk into a saucepan. Then she reached to the top shelf and pulled down her five-pound canister of Baker's Breakfast Cocoa, turning it so Miss Tucker could see the trademark Chocolate Lady with her apron and tray. "When Emily and I were girls, Mama took a job at the Baker Chocolate mill to support us after Papa died. She scraped and saved until she managed to buy that first apprenticeship for me. I owe her everything."

"She sounds like a wonderful woman." Miss Tucker smiled, but her eyes held a sad, wistful look.

"Mama's also the one responsible for my chocolate craving." Hannah winked, and steered the discussion in a lighter direction. "Every week, she'd come home with another can of powder, so we drank cocoa religiously every morning. That's the reason I needed the milk. I can't get through the day without my cup of breakfast cocoa. Would you stay and share some with me? It will only take a couple of minutes to warm the milk."

"I wish I could, but Mr. Hawkins likes me to deliver my goods before the store opens." Miss Tucker pushed to her feet and collected her basket. "Perhaps another time."

"We'll definitely find a time." Hannah smiled as she replaced the cocoa canister. "Now, what do I owe you for the milk, Miss Tucker? I would like to pay ahead for the entire week, if that would be acceptable."

"I'll only charge you twenty cents since I skimmed off the cream and kept it for my baking. And please, call me Cordelia."

"Gladly, and I'm Hannah." She handed over the coins and walked Cordelia to the door. "Thank you again for the muffins. Your brother was such a help to me yesterday, and this morning you have made me feel welcome. I am blessed to know you both and would be honored to count you as friends."

"I would like that immensely," Cordelia said, her eyes alight with sincerity. "Oh . . . J.T. asked me to tell you that he wouldn't be able to bring the wood by until later this afternoon. I hope that will be all right."

"Goodness, yes. I'll be up to my armpits in soapsuds and vinegar water all morning, I'm sure. This afternoon will be fine."

As Hannah waved good-bye to Cordelia, her gaze roamed across the street to the livery. An annoying tingle of anticipation wiggled through her stomach at the thought of seeing Mr. Tucker again. Traitorous stomach. The man could seesaw her emotions fast enough to make her dizzy. She didn't need that kind of distraction today. Nevertheless, the insolent tingle remained.

J.T. lumbered toward the dreaded dress shop with the crosspieces of two sawhorses under one arm and six stacked planks under the other. Making two trips would have been easier, but he wanted to get this good deed over and done.

Miss Richards was standing on the boardwalk, rubbing a rag in circles against a pane of glass in her window. When her motions elicited a series of squeaks, she dipped her rag back into the bucket at her feet and moved on to the next pane. J.T. dropped the ends of the boards onto the walkway beside her, making no effort to keep them quiet. Why should he when it was so much fun to watch her jump and squeak at the same pitch as her clean windows?

Splat!

Ah. That's why.

Pungent vinegar fumes scratched his throat and would have made his eyes water if they weren't already wet from the rag that had just slapped across his face. The rag slid down the length of his face in a cold, slimy trail, rolled down his chest, and plopped onto the ground. Blindly, he angled the boards toward the wall and leaned them against the frame of the building, then bent his knees and set the sawhorses down on the opposite side. They clattered and probably tumbled off the boardwalk, but he didn't care. As he straightened, with deliberate slowness, he drew a handkerchief from his trouser pocket and wiped the moisture from his face while the esteemed dressmaker unsuccessfully stifled her giggles. Once he deemed it safe to open his eyes, he glared at her.

"I'm so sorry, Mr. Tucker." She covered her mouth with her hand for a moment, probably trying to stuff the rest of her laughter back inside so as not to spoil the effect of her pretty apology. When her hand fell away, she was biting her lip, but even her teeth could not contain her smile. "You really oughtn't sneak up on a person like that. You startled me and the rag flew right out of my hand." She demonstrated the action as if he hadn't been right there to witness it firsthand.

"Maybe you should pay more heed to your surroundings."

"I'll try to do that. I have a tendency to get absorbed in my thoughts at times, especially when I'm debating strategies." She tipped her head sideways and gave him a thoroughly coquettish glance over her shoulder. "What do *you* think, Mr. Tucker? Would a lavender morning dress be too pale for a window display, or would the demure cut be more likely to attract clientele than a flashy party gown?"

He rolled his eyes, and her laughter showered over him.

"Never mind. I won't draw you into my dilemma. I'm sure you have more manly tasks to pursue."

Unfortunately, he couldn't recall a single one of those tasks as he watched joy flow out of her like a stream of sweet-tasting water.

She stooped to pick up the fallen rag, and he realized she had tied a remarkably similar one over her hair. Some ugly tan thing with orange blotches all over it. One would think such a sight would be enough to make him look away, but even combined with her stained, shapeless work dress, it wasn't enough to deter his gaze.

Hadn't his past taught him anything? Beautiful women were nothing but trouble—shallow, empty husks that would blow away the minute life got a little uncomfortable. J.T. had vowed never to allow feminine beauty to overrule good sense. He wouldn't fall into that trap. If he ever married, it would be to a woman of spiritual depth who selflessly served others. A helpmeet, someone to encourage him and stand by his side as stalwartly in hard times as in easy. Not a pretty piece of fluff who would tangle herself around his neck and drag him down like a millstone.

"One day I'm going to catch you in the grips of a full-blown grin, Mr. Tucker," she said, wagging a finger at him, "and when I do, watch out because I'm going to crow in victory."

"We all need goals in life, Miss Richards." J.T. swung two boards up onto his shoulder and peered down at her. "Mine's to get this stuff delivered before the first snow falls. You think I got a chance at making that happen?"

6

Hannah shook her head and tiptoed up the stairs, determined not to let Mr. Tucker catch her stomping again. He might have crawled under her skin and set her temper to itching, but she didn't have to scratch it.

He set the boards down inside the door and without a word headed back down for the sawhorses. Once he returned, it only took a minute or two to erect the makeshift table. She dipped a cupful of water while he worked and had it ready for him when he finished.

Frowning, as usual, he reluctantly accepted the cup. The competitor within her whooped over the small victory. Mr. J.T. Tucker might tilt her off balance, but from now on, she refused to let him take her feet out from under her. She'd prove her mettle to him, and maybe in the process, she'd finally witness that elusive grin.

"Thanks." He thrust the cup into her hands and turned for the door. "I'll move those shelves inside the shop for you, then be on my way."

Gulping down a quick drink of her own, Hannah tossed the cup into the dishpan on the floor and scurried after him. By the time she locked up and ran down the stairs, he was already inside. She leaned against the door and reached for the handle to follow him, but it fell away from her grasp as he wrenched it open from within. Hannah tumbled through the doorway, her head colliding with Mr. Tucker's chest.

Strong, yet surprisingly gentle hands clasped her arms and steadied her. Heat flooded her face. Hadn't she just resolved not to let this man knock her feet out from under her? The fact that her resolution had been figurative, not literal, gave her no comfort. Twice in as many days she had fallen onto the poor fellow. No wonder he was in such a hurry to escape her.

Not quite able to look him in the eye, she focused on his chin. "I'm sorry to keep throwing myself at you like this, Mr. Tucker. It truly wasn't my intention."

The Adam's apple beneath his jaw rose and fell in a slow movement Hannah found strangely fascinating. Then before she could blink, he cleared his throat and released her so suddenly, she nearly fell into him again.

"I . . . uh . . . need to go." He sidestepped and tried to squeeze past her through the doorway.

Thankfully, Hannah regained her senses and her memory a second before he made it around her. She needed one more thing from him in order to finish the preparations on her shop.

"May I ask one last favor of you, Mr. Tucker?"

He stopped, and she swore she could hear heavy breaths coming from him, as if he were a green-broke stallion fixing to buck his way out of a saddle. "I wouldn't ask except you're the only man I really know in town."

He didn't say a word, just stood there breathing through flared nostrils, making her nervous. Taking a deep breath of her own, she spat out the rest of her request.

"I was hoping I could borrow a couple of tools from you. A level and a screwdriver? I'd return them by the end of the day, or tomorrow morning at the latest. I'd like to get my shelves in place and my display rack mounted before nightfall so I can open the shop tomorrow."

Hannah stared at his profile to gauge his reaction. He stretched his chin out a bit and a muscle ticked in his jaw before he finally spoke.

"Sorry," he said, his voice clipped. "I've got my own business to run. I can't play handyman for you, hanging shelves and things all afternoon. You'll have to ask someone else."

Despite her earlier resolve, Hannah's temper flared. She moved closer to the arrogant, assumption-spewing Mr. Tucker and planted her feet. "Did I *ask* you to play handyman for me? No. I simply asked a neighbor if I might borrow his tools. If you had listened to my words instead of focusing on your own preconceived notions, you might have actually understood that. I am perfectly capable of hanging a few brackets without a man commandeering the task, so you're off the hook. I'm sure Mr. Hawkins will sell me the items I need. I won't bother you again."

She stepped aside to give him his freedom, but he just stood there, so she marched over to her window-washing bucket, slapped the sopping rag against the center pane, and started scrubbing. The entire window had already been cleaned, but she couldn't push past the liveryman statue blocking her doorway to closet herself up in her shop, so she had to settle for ignoring him.

The shop door clicked shut. She refused to turn. His boot heels pounded against the wooden boardwalk, then thudded as they hit the dirt of the road, but she didn't look his way. He'd offered no apology, no parting words.

Grabbing her bucket, she strode into the shop, uncaring that water was sloshing onto her shoes as she went. She held her head high just in case he was watching, but the moment she closed the door, she deflated. Indignation could only fuel her for so long before regret crept in, and her affront had quieted enough to let the voice of conscience through. And the lecture it wrote on her heart shamed her.

She had no right to harangue the man just because he didn't want to help her. After all, she'd done nothing but impose on him since arriving in town. He clearly wasn't the cheerful sort, and while he shouldn't have jumped to such uncomplimentary conclusions about her, he didn't deserve her wrath. He had rescued her from a potentially harmful fall, arranged for his sister to supply her with milk, made her a table without being asked, and even gave her free wood to use as shelving in her shop.

Hannah ran a hand along the edge of one of the boards he had set against the wall just inside the door. Not wanting to get a splinter, she traced it lightly until she realized that the surface was smooth. She took a closer look, handling each plank in turn. All of them had been sanded from stem to stern and cut to a uniform length. Spare wood from a scrap lumber pile wouldn't be this ready for use without someone taking the time to cut and sand each one.

Now she felt even worse.

Why did the man have to be such a contradiction? His actions exuded kindness and consideration, going well beyond the neighborly help she had requested of him. Yet his surly demeanor riled her like a tangled bobbin thread that refused to unknot. Which side of his character was she to believe?

A muted thump sounded on the other side of her door. She probably wouldn't have heard it if she hadn't been standing so close. Hannah pivoted toward the sound and caught sight of a familiar male form passing by her window. Taking a deep breath, she scrambled to find words for a proper apology, then opened the door. She stepped outside to call to him but tripped over something in her path. Lurching forward, she sucked in a pain-filled breath as she caught her balance. By the time she steadied herself, Mr. Tucker was entering the laundry next door.

Toe throbbing and heart equally sore over her missed opportunity to make amends, Hannah turned around and limped the few steps back to the door. Glancing down to see what she had tripped over, she bit her lip, her toe forgotten.

There, in front of her door, lay a level and screwdriver.

She gathered the tools in her arms, her gaze trailing the path Mr. Tucker had taken to the laundry. She might never figure him out, but something told her she had just received an apology, one that spoke with an eloquence that outshone any words he could have offered.

A barrage of steamy heat accosted J.T. as he pushed through the laundry house door. He tugged his hat from his head and closed the door behind him, wishing he could leave it open to create a breeze, but Louisa would scold him good if he let dust blow in to soil her clean wash.

"Pickin' up or droppin' off?" a harried voice called from the back room.

"It's me, Louisa." J.T. frowned as he surveyed the warped floorboards and chinks in the wall. The roof probably leaked, too. If he couldn't move her into a different building, he'd have to find a way to repair this one, which was tricky since the laundress's pride prickled faster than a cactus pear.

"Come on back, J.T."

After consumption took her husband two years ago and left her with three kids to feed, Louisa James had sold her farm and rented this space in town. She'd barely had anything left after paying off the mortgage, but she managed to eke out a living washing trousers and starching shirts for the townsfolk. He admired her grit, yet it was that same toughness that made her reject anything that smelled of charity.

He wound his way past tables stacked with cleaned and pressed items awaiting their owners, empty washtubs, and folded drying racks that could be set up inside when the weather turned rainy. Stepping through the doorway, he found Louisa bent over her ironing table, sadiron in hand, smoothing wrinkles from the sleeve of a man's white cotton shirt. With a practiced motion, she set her iron on the stove, clicked the handle off, and snapped it onto a hotter one while six-year-old Mollie handed the finished shirt to big sister, Tessa, then pulled another garment from the oversized basket on the floor and laid it in place for her mother. Tessa, the middle child at age eight and the most outgoing of the bunch, looked up at him and smiled.

"Hi, Mr. Tucker. Danny's waiting for you out back. He separated out all the small pieces, just like you asked, and saved the big ones for you."

How the child managed to converse and fold at the same time was a marvel, yet the shirt lay in a tidy rectangle by the time she came up for air.

"Thanks, squirt." He winked at her and she giggled.

He tweaked Mollie's nose as he passed her by and nodded a greeting to Louisa. The woman was thin and worn, her hands reddened and creased from her constant labor. Strands of ash brown hair clung to her face, wet with perspiration, yet he'd never heard her complain. Now that harvest was nearly done, she'd be losing her help as the kids headed back to school for the winter term. Many in her position would keep the children home, especially the girls, but Louisa always had them spit-shined and ready before the teacher rang the bell. J.T. figured she didn't want Tessa and Mollie to end up doing other people's laundry for the rest of their lives, and he respected her for that. He just wished she'd accept a little help from folks from time to time.

"I need to speak with you, J.T., before you start in on the wood." Louisa rubbed the underside of her chin with the back of her hand and tipped her head toward the rear door.

"All right." He followed her outside and welcomed the cool breeze that fluttered across the yard as he slipped his hat back on.

"I met the new seamstress this morning," Louisa said. "Ran into her at the water pump at first light."

J.T. nodded as his mind shifted to Miss Richards. He hadn't expected her to be an early riser. The woman was as unpredictable as a Texas cyclone.

"Offered to pay my boy a dollar a week to keep her woodbox full. Said she didn't need much, cookin' for just herself, and she'll gather her own kindlin' during her daily *constitutional*, whatever that is." Louisa crossed her arms over her chest and braced her legs as if preparing for a fight. "I know I ought to've checked with you first, seeing as how you're the one that chops it all, but I accepted her terms, and I don't aim to go back on the agreement."

J.T. reached into his shirt pocket and drew out a toothpick. He took his time moving it to his mouth, and only after it was clamped securely between his molars did he address the widow James, hoping she'd relaxed a bit in the interim.

"I reckon you can do whatever you want with it, Louisa. It's your wood, bought and paid for every time Daniel mucks out a stall at the livery. I pay Tom a wage for the same work."

"The boy's only ten. He works twice as long to do half the work Tom does, and you know it."

"Maybe. But he does the work I ask him to. I don't hold with slavery, ma'am, so if you don't consider my chopping wood for you once a month true payment, I guess I can leave off the wood and start paying the boy in cash money. Which do you prefer?" He switched the toothpick to the opposite side of his mouth and angled a hard look at her.

"You know I ain't got time to chop the wood myself, and the last thing I need is for Danny to try to take over the job and chop his foot off." He watched pride battle with practicality as she gazed at young Daniel dragging large logs over to the chopping stump. J.T. had only asked Daniel to work at the livery so he'd have an excuse to keep her in wood, and Louisa was too smart not to know that. But with all the water she heated for washing and the stove that had to be kept hot all day for the ironing, she ran through her fuel supply faster than she could replenish it.

Practicality won out, but pride put in a fair showing.

"Well, I just wanted to make sure you weren't offended or nothing. I knew we owned the wood all right and proper." She sniffed and, with a twirl of her faded skirts, returned to her work inside the house.

Lord, save me from proud, stubborn women. They seemed to be swarming him lately.

Thankful to be left alone with the only male in the general vicinity, J.T. ducked under a row of clothes still drying on the line and joined Daniel. The kid was a quiet one, which suited J.T. just fine. After tousling the boy's hair and thumping him on the back, he picked up the ax and started swinging. The two worked side by side—J.T. split the logs; Daniel arranged them on the pile. Simple. No ruffled feathers, no pecking accusations, just a couple of men working together without a lot of gab.

Unfortunately, all he managed to think about while he worked were the ruffled feathers and pecking accusations from one hen in particular. Miss Hannah Richards.

J.T. slammed the ax blade into the log below him with a crack that failed to banish the picture of her from his mind.

He swung again, and the log spit unevenly. J.T. scowled.

Now that he'd had time to think on the matter, he realized her protests didn't necessarily mean she hadn't been hinting for him to come help her. She probably just didn't want to admit it. After all, most women didn't know one end of a screwdriver from the other, and she looked pretty beat from her day of cleaning. She'd be too tired to lift those boards high enough to place shelves. He still needed to take care of some business at the bank, but afterward he could stop by her shop to save himself from having to deal with her on the morrow.

An hour and a half later, after he'd split all the logs in the yard, J.T. washed up at the pump, shook hands with the little man who had helped him, and headed for the bank. Louisa might not willingly accept charity, but J.T. had a plan to get around that. She couldn't refuse his help if she was unaware of it, now, could she?

J.T. entered the bank just as the clerk set the *Closed* sign in the window. The fellow nodded a greeting to him before scurrying back to his teller's cage. The proprietress of the local boardinghouse stood at the counter impatiently tapping her foot, apparently displeased by the interruption of her transaction.

"Is Paxton in?" J.T. asked.

The clerk disappeared behind the counter, then opened the gate of his window and met J.T.'s eye around a bent plume in the lady's bonnet. "He's with a customer at the moment, but you can take a seat on the bench outside his office. He should be finished shortly."

"Thanks."

J.T. fingered his hat and nodded to the woman, who glared at him over her shoulder before swinging her accusing eyes back to the unfortunate clerk. After sharing a commiserating look with the two cowhands standing in line, all three males grateful to be on the customer side of the counter, J.T. took his cue and meandered over to the bench.

Too restless to sit, he propped a foot on the seat of the bench and braced one elbow on his thigh. He didn't like sneaking around behind Louisa's back, but the woman didn't leave him much choice. The Good Book taught that a man should give without his left hand knowing what his right was doing. Louisa was just playing the role of the left hand. Still, the secrecy grated on him, made him feel as if he were doing something disreputable.

The quiet swish of a well-oiled door opening drew J.T.'s attention. He dropped his foot to the floor and straightened his stance.

Floyd Hawkins and his son, Warren, emerged from Elliott Paxton's office. The elder Hawkins chatted amiably with the banker while his son separated himself from the conversation.

Warren pushed his overlong hair out of his face and caught sight of J.T. His eyes widened a bit, and his neck stretched as if his collar had suddenly grown too tight.

The kid was always nervous around him. Never used to be. But lately, Warren had been acting different, like he was trying to impress him or something.

Not that his efforts had been paying off. The kid had a chip on his shoulder the size of Gibraltar's Rock. He wasn't a bad egg, just irritating with his sullen looks and woeful attitude. Seemed to think the world owed him something because he was born with a mark on his face. J.T. could sympathize with the embarrassment and frustration that went along with schoolyard teasing, but Warren wasn't a boy any longer. Time to stop the pouting and start acting like a man. Respect wouldn't come any other way.

As if Warren had heard his thoughts, he straightened his shoulders and approached.

"J.T."

J.T. cocked his head. Either his ears needed a good scrubbing or Warren had just lowered the timbre of his voice a couple of levels below normal. J.T. fought the urge to roll his eyes.

"Warren."

The kid tugged on his coat lapels and pushed up on his toes. "Dad and I are considering an expansion of the business. Mr. Paxton is helping us plan the finances."

"That so?" J.T. really had no particular interest in the Hawkins family's business endeavors, but Warren seemed to expect some kind of reply.

"I . . . ah . . . thought your sister might like to join us for dinner one evening to discuss the expansion. Since the change will affect her. . . . I mean, because we sell her baked goods and all."

J.T. arched his brows and shot Warren a look that must have communicated how senseless he thought that comment was, for the kid dropped his gaze and scuffed his toe against the wooden floorboards.

Why would Delia care about them opening another store somewhere? It wasn't like she was going to bake anything for it. Hers was strictly a local operation.

Still, Delia considered Warren a friend, and she wouldn't want J.T. giving the kid a hard time—no matter how much he deserved it. So he cleared his throat and came as close to an apology as he could manage.

"I'm sure Delia would enjoy hearing about your plans one of these days."

Warren's head shot up, and a grin split his face. Seeing his response, J.T.'s conscience flared up. Maybe he should cut the kid a break. He was still young. A little more life experience and he might grow out from under that oversized attitude of his. He'd never really had to fend for himself, what with his father's store always being there for him. And from what J.T. understood, Warren had started taking over more responsibilities—keeping the books, making deliveries, overseeing the inventory. Maybe he should make more of an effort to be tolerant.

"I'll be sure to tell her about it, then," Warren said, swagger restored. "She'd probably enjoy sharing a meal with a man who didn't smell like manure for a change."

Then again, maybe he should just expedite the kid's real-world education and stuff his tongue down his throat.

J.T. stared at him without moving so much as a finger, channeling all his affront into his expression. The snorting laugh blowing out of Warren's nose at his careless jest morphed into a cough and, finally, silence. Even after Warren ducked his head, J.T. did not relent. He wanted to bore his glare into the boy's skull until it stirred up some common sense.

Fortunately for Warren, his father concluded his chat with the banker and came to join them. J.T. lifted his gaze. "Afternoon, Hawkins."

"Tucker." He held out his hand to J.T. and shook it with a solid grip. The man's smile and genuine warmth went a long way to soothe J.T.'s temper. "Sorry for monopolizing Mr. Paxton's time. I didn't realize you were waiting."

"That's all right. I haven't been here long."

Warren edged toward the entrance. "Let's go, Dad. You know how Mother hates to watch the store when she's trying to get supper on the stove."

"You're right." Hawkins offered a little wave as he moved past J.T. "Give Cordelia our best."

"I will."

The two disappeared onto the street, and J.T. barely had time to remind himself why he had come before Elliott Paxton descended upon him.

"Mr. Tucker!" The banker stretched his arms wide in welcome, his nature so ebullient, J.T. would have cringed had it been anyone else. But that was just Paxton's way. After five years, he had gotten used to the banker's fulsome ways. Had the man greeted him with a solemn nod, J.T. would have ordered the clerk to fetch the doctor.

"Come in, young man. Come in." Paxton held the door wide until J.T. entered the office and took a seat. "What can I do for you today, sir?" he asked as he clicked the door closed.

"I want to find out if the owner of the property where Louisa James runs her laundry might be talked into selling."

The banker sat in the chair behind his desk and rapped his finger against its surface. "I could make some inquiries, I suppose. If I remember correctly, the man in question runs a land company over in Waco. Wouldn't be hard to send a few wires to the account manager. I can't say as I'd recommend that building as an investment, though. The place has been in ill repair for years."

"I know." J.T. rubbed his chin. "I'd planned to buy the shop next door, but the owner rejected my offer."

"Ah, yes. It's to be a dress shop, I believe. I spied the new seamstress washing her windows earlier. Lovely woman."

"Yes . . . well . . . I had hoped to be able to offer Mrs. James a more suitable location for her laundry business—one with four decent walls and a roof that doesn't leak. But that opportunity is no longer available. So I figured I could buy the place she's in, lower her rent, and be a proper landlord. You know, fix the roof, keep the pump in working order—that kind of thing."

"I see." Elliott Paxton tapped a finger to his mouth and contemplated him with an intensity that made J.T.'s throat ache.

"That's a commendable plan, son," the banker said. "I'm impressed."

J.T. shifted in his seat and glared at the worn spot on his trouser knee. He hated it when people made too much of things. It wasn't like he was building Louisa a mansion or anything. He just wanted an excuse to help her out from time to time without raising her hackles. That's all. Nothing to be impressed about.

"It's a rare man who would spend his hard-earned money on a worthless piece of property in order to benefit a widow woman unrelated to him. Why, most would scoff at the idea."

Paxton's commendation waxed on and on, extolling his nonexistent virtues until J.T. could bear it no longer.

Jumping out of his chair as if the cushion had suddenly grown teeth, J.T. retreated. He strode to the door in two steps and gripped the knob.

"So, you'll look into it for me?"

Paxton nodded, brows arching in puzzlement. He started to rise. "Of course, but—"

"Thanks." J.T. waved him off and fled the banker's office. But the tightness in his chest didn't loosen until he exited the bank.

He knew Paxton would be discreet. The man had built a reputation on being trustworthy. Still, it would have been easier if Hannah Richards hadn't stolen his building. Then there would have been no need to involve the banker in the first place, no awkward conversation, no sneaking around behind Louisa's back.

A pang of honesty poked at him. Okay, so Miss Richards hadn't exactly *stolen* his building. Nevertheless, the woman was proving inconvenient. Not only did she throw a wrench in his plans for helping Louisa, but thanks to their earlier run-in, he now felt obligated to hang her shelves.

J.T.'s boots clomped over the boardwalk planks as he made his way to the shop situated at the end of the street. He paused outside the door and drew in a deep breath, probing his shirt pocket for a pick. Placing it between his teeth, he clamped down and reminded himself to keep his mouth shut as much as possible. It wouldn't do for him to snap at Miss Richards again. She'd been working hard all day and was probably exhausted. Frustrated, too.

He winced at the image the thought produced. The gal must have had a rough time of it the last couple of hours. If she stuck with it, that is. J.T. stole a glance through the window, curious to see if she had abandoned her project or if she lay buried beneath it. What he found so startled him, he tipped his hat back and looked a second time for verification.

A rack of hooks had been mounted on the north wall, perfectly level and apparently secure, for three dresses hung on display. Eight brackets paired in staggered positions jutted out from the south wall with three shelves already in place. Colorful fabric adorned the shelves, and even his untrained eye could tell they were artfully matched. Several of her dummies, not yet clothed, stood in the corner observing their mistress as she fussed with the way the material draped from the corner of the third shelf.

As his jaw slackened, J.T.'s toothpick dangled unanchored across his bottom lip. Miss Richards's capability had been no idle boast, and her request *hadn't* been a manipulation. But that made no sense. Why would a woman of integrity run a shop that glorified superficial beauty?

8

Hannah awoke to a day full of promise. The sun had not yet crested the horizon, but a soft glow lightened the predawn sky as she dipped water from the stove reservoir to wash her face.

Wednesday—not the usual day to open a new business, but she was too excited to postpone. She'd spent yesterday evening painting pasteboard signs. One carried the words *Open* and *Closed* on opposite sides, and a second one listed her services. *Dressmaking and Fine Tailoring* took top billing in large block letters with *Alterations and Mending* mentioned in smaller script along the bottom. One placard for each window. She would order a larger sign for the front of the building later today. Mr. Hawkins mentioned that the blacksmith also cut and stenciled signs. She could visit with him after she returned Mr. Tucker's tools.

Pushing her thoughts quickly from the annoying livery owner, Hannah returned to her sleeping area and removed her nightgown. Skirts of any kind hindered the extension of her lower limbs during her calisthenic routine, so she preferred to conduct the exercises in her drawers and shift when privacy allowed. Kneeling down, she pulled a small crate full of exercise equipment from under the bed. She selected the two-pound polished maple dumbbells and positioned herself with the heels of her bare feet together and her toes pointed outward.

It took thirty minutes to work through the repetitions. Straight arm lifts to the side, overhead, and forward. Then again with bent arms curling up and punching down, up, or out in keeping with the various positions. She continued with backward leans and leg lunges, all with the dumbbells in hand. Next came the floor sweep, where she stretched to her toes, weights overhead, then bent her knees and crouched, touching the dumbbells to the floor. She repeated each motion twenty times before advancing to the next exercise, and by the time the routine ended, her muscles had been well stretched and carried a satisfying ache.

Hannah sponged the light sheen of perspiration from her body with the wet rag she had used on her face earlier and dressed in her gymnastic costume. She replaced the soiled apron with a fresh one and laced up her low-heeled walking shoes. Since she didn't know the surrounding area well, she planned to walk along the road to keep her bearings. On the way back, she'd venture farther afield to collect sticks and dry twigs for kindling. She looped the strap of a large canvas bag over her head and shoulder and placed the pouch behind her, where it wouldn't interfere with her brisk pace. Then she set out on her first Coventry constitutional.

Not expecting to see anyone out and about in the early morning hours, Hannah nearly tripped when J.T. Tucker appeared along a crossroad that bordered the livery. She swallowed her surprised gasp and kept moving, offering him only a smile and a tiny wave in greeting as she headed north out of town. He returned her gesture with a raised brow that could have stemmed from either shock or disapproval. It was impossible to tell.

Hannah lifted her chin and increased her pace to a near jog, her arms swinging at her sides with gusto. Mr. Tucker didn't intimidate her. He could think what he liked. Vigorous physical exercise was good for a body. Why, it had probably saved her life.

As the distance between her and Coventry lengthened, Hannah's steps slowed to their usual pace, quick but not frenzied. The beauty of the morning calmed her with birdsong and sunshine. A cool breeze ruffled wispy strands of hair from her braid, and she lifted a hand to secure them behind her ear.

Mr. Tucker's response was no different than that of most people. The lady who ran the boardinghouse she'd stayed at back in San Antonio had pointed out often enough that Hannah had to be out of her mind to waste so much energy walking nowhere.

She supposed it did seem a bit strange. Most Westerners labored from sunup to sundown in physically demanding tasks. They had no need for calisthenics and constitutionals. But for a sickly girl growing up in a crowded city, Professor Lewis's system of gymnastic exercise had been a salvation.

Hannah strode up a hill and passed the Coventry schoolhouse. Judging by the cross that jutted up from the belfry, it served as a place of worship, as well. A small footpath veered off to the right behind the building, and Hannah decided to follow it. The grassland turned woodsy the farther she went, and she spied several large pecan trees that promised to provide kindling for her. Not wanting to lose her momentum, though, she trudged on until she came upon a creek and an arched wooden bridge that spanned its width.

Enchanted, Hannah scurried to the center of the bridge and leaned her ribs against the railing. She gazed upriver, drinking in the sunlight sparkling on the slow-moving water, breathing in the smell of moist earth and tree bark, and swaying to the whispering melody of leaves rustling in the wind as sung by the river birch and cottonwood trees that lined the banks.

Lord, how marvelous you are. The beauty of your creation humbles me. If I can imitate even a hint of your artistry with my needle, I will be content. May my craftsmanship reflect your glory and bring you pleasure.

Hannah inhaled long and slow, allowing the loveliness of the moment to infuse her spirit with peace. Never did she feel closer to the Lord than when she was in nature. The busyness of town life distracted and misdirected her, but the Lord sought her out with gifts of beauty. Sometimes she was blessed with an experience like this where she was surrounded by his majesty, unable to do anything but praise him. Other times, he presented her with smaller reminders of his presence and his love. A full moon shining white in a black sky; a wildflower springing up through a crack in the boardwalk; a crimson oak leaf falling from an autumn branch, beautiful in death.

That final thought made her think of Victoria Ashmont and her scandalous red burial gown. A sad smile curled her lips, and she mouthed a prayer for the departed woman's soul. A single act of kindness on her part had changed Hannah's life forever, and Hannah was determined to prove that the old woman's confidence in her had not been misplaced.

Hannah made good time on her way back to town, the weight of the full kindling bag adding to her exertion but not slowing her speed. Coming off the hill by the schoolhouse, she spotted an old man and a mule not far in front of her. The man's stooped shoulders and plodding steps made him the tortoise to her hare, and she overtook them in a matter of minutes. Compassion slowed Hannah's steps as she approached, but then the wind shifted and something altogether different came over her—a suffocating stench that grabbed her by the throat and triggered a powerful urge to retch.

Thankful to have not yet broken her fast, Hannah concentrated on breathing through her mouth instead of her nose and forced a smile of greeting as the man turned.

"Good day to you, sir. It's a lovely morning to be out for a stroll." Her lungs begged to cough, but she wrestled them into submission.

"That it is, young lady. That it is." He smiled in return, or at least she thought he did. It was hard to tell what shape his mouth formed beneath all the whiskers.

His gray, matted beard hung halfway to his belt, an inch or two longer than the stringy hair that draped down his back from under a hat so caked with dust she couldn't determine its original color. The only thing not filthy about him was the tall walking stick clasped in his left hand. She'd never seen one like it. Fashioned from a twisted branch that had been stripped of its bark and varnished to a high gloss, it stood proudly beside its owner, as tall as the man himself. The wood's rich cinnamon color blended with lighter yellow streaks to create a stunning contrast that sent Hannah's creative mind whirling with ideas of how to mimic the effect with fabric.

"What a beautiful staff. Is it made from mesquite?"

"The very same. It shines up right purdy, don't it?" His tone was friendly, but his faded blue eyes groaned with sadness. "I sell 'em down at the depot along with my other carvings."

Hannah examined the mule's load more carefully. What she had initially assumed to be firewood was actually a cluster of handcrafted walking sticks. The animal also packed two large sacks that undoubtedly held the other items he mentioned.

As they neared the edge of town, Hannah discreetly turned her head to the side and gulped in two quick breaths of less potent air.

"If any ladies debarking the trains ask about dressmakers," she said, "send them my way. Today is the grand opening of my new shop here in Coventry. I'm Hannah Richards," she said with a nod.

"Pleased to meet ya, Miz Richards. Ezra Culpepper at your service." He dipped his head and doffed his hat with the walking-stick hand. "You can call me Ezra."

"And you must call me Hannah," she said, charmed despite the unwashed odor wafting from the crusty fellow. Maybe it was his red flannel shirt or the gray hair or the loneliness he radiated, but for some reason, he reminded her of Miss Victoria. The woman would no doubt be horrified by the comparison, but Hannah couldn't escape the feeling of similarity, and her heart softened toward him.

"I'm afraid I don't get the chance to speak to many of them there ladies, Miz Hannah. They tend to give me a wide berth."

She could certainly understand why.

"But I could inform the stationmaster, so's he can pass the word to any females what need new duds."

"I'd be much obliged. Thank you, Ezra."

They passed the livery, where a hay wagon stood out front, a heaping load ready to be delivered, but there was no sign of Mr. Tucker. Unsure if she was disappointed or pleased by that fact, Hannah turned her attention away from the livery and toward her shop.

Pride surged in her breast as she gazed through the clean windows to the well-dressed display dummies. She itched to place the *Open* sign in her window and see who came through the door first. Mr. Hawkins had promised to post a notice in his store to advertise the shop, although she knew she'd be foolish to expect much, having only been in town two days. A seamstress had to build up a reputation before her business could flourish. That required time, satisfied customers, and word of mouth. Nevertheless, little bursts of excitement rebounded through her like popping corn.

"This your place?"

Hannah beamed at the old man beside her. "Yes, sir. What do you think?"

Ezra halted and scratched a spot behind his ear. "Looks nice, I reckon. Don't know much about such things, a course, but if my Alice were still around, I'm sure she'd be knocking on your door." His eyes glistened with moisture as he gazed at the shop window. "Alice was a simple woman, but she always wore a pretty ribbon in her hair. I think she woulda liked having a place like this to visit."

Sensing his grief, Hannah tentatively touched his shoulder. "If you can spare a few minutes, I would love to have you join me for a cup of cocoa." She'd seen Cordelia's milk delivery at the top of the stairs. "I could have it ready in minutes."

"You don't have to do that, Miz Hannah." Ezra dipped his chin, but not before she caught the longing in his eyes. "I know I ain't fitting company for a gal like you."

"Nonsense." Hannah patted his shoulder. A delicate tickle crawled along the back of her hand, sending shivers shooting through her like heat lightning. Keeping her smile bright and praying he didn't notice, she dropped her hand away and shook it vigorously behind her. She wanted to befriend the poor man, but offering hospitality to any vermin he might have been carrying was out of the question. "It would be doing me a favor," she cajoled. "I'm a little nervous about opening the shop today, and having someone to talk to over a cup of cocoa would take my mind off of things. Please?"

"Well . . . if you insist." His eyes brightened a shade as he wagged a dirt-encrusted finger at her, the nail black around the edges. "But I ain't gonna risk your reputation by coming inside. Jackson and I will wait for ya right here." He jabbed his finger toward the boardwalk steps and lowered himself to a seat with a groan.

Ezra Culpepper was a lot more astute than his appearance suggested. Hannah got the distinct impression that he had recognized her gift to him and had responded with one in return.

"Wonderful," she said. "I'll be back in a trice."

She rushed up the stairs, collected the fruit jar of milk Cordelia had placed on her doorstep, and let herself into her room. Using some of the kindling she had brought back with her, she stoked up the fire in the cookstove and pulled out a pair of small pots. She measured two cups of milk into the first and two cups of water into the second. While she waited for them to boil, she rolled up her sleeves and scrubbed her hands with her strongest lye soap—just in case any unwelcome guests had crawled or hopped onto her without her noticing.

The water pot began to bubble, so Hannah grabbed a small bowl and mixed two tablespoons of cocoa powder with two of sugar, added a couple grains of salt, and then stirred in half a cup of boiling water, making a nice paste. She scooped the mixture into the rest of the boiling water for a brief time until she smelled the milk scald. She added the cocoa water to the milk, removed it from the heat, and blended it with an egg beater for two minutes. The aroma of the chocolate made her mouth water, and her stomach let out a hungry gurgle. There was just enough milk left to mix up some biscuits, but she would have to do that later. Ezra was waiting on her.

By the time she returned downstairs, the breakfast cocoa had cooled sufficiently to be drunk without burning their tongues. Hannah handed a cup to Ezra and took a seat beside him on the edge of the boardwalk.

"Ya know, I was thinking while you were gone. . . ." Ezra paused to lift his cup to his nose. He sniffed at it as if unsure what is was. Then he shrugged and gulped down a hearty swig. His eyes lit up and he smacked his lips. "Say, this here's good stuff. Didn't 'spect to like it, seein' as how it ain't coffee, but it's not too bad." He tipped the cup to his mouth again. "Just don't tell the other fellers around town. Wouldn't want them thinking I've gone all soft, drinkin' such a girly concoction."

Hannah set her cup down, placed her right hand over her heart, and raised her left. "I vow not to tell a soul."

Ezra winked at her. "Good. Now what was I saying . . . ? Oh yeah. A bench."

"A bench?" Hannah scrunched her brows.

"Yeah. I was thinking that a man might have cause to wait on his woman a good long time if she were in your shop gawkin' at all those fancy getups. A bench outside might come in real handy."

Warmth seeped through the porcelain cup and into Hannah's hands as she mulled over his words.

"Back at the house I got one that I put together last spring."

"A bench?"

"Yep. Oak. Sturdy legs. It don't wobble none."

Hannah blew a ripple across her cocoa as she weighed his offer. A bench *would* be welcoming to passersby and practical for those needing a place to wait, but she didn't have money for more than necessities right now. Even if the bench were as lovely as the walking sticks. But if she didn't have to part with any ready cash . . .

"Would you consider a trade?"

Ezra nodded and downed the rest of his chocolate in a single gulp.

Hannah examined his tattered ensemble. "I could make you a new shirt, a fine one with fancy stitching. And I'll mend any existing clothes you have." She'd have to boil them first, but she wouldn't mention the laundering for fear of offending him.

"Shucks, Miz Hannah. I don't need all that. I'd give it to you in exchange for sharing a cup of this here cocoa with you every morning." The light that had brightened his eyes suddenly dimmed. "Unless, a course, having a grizzled feller like me outside your shop would be bad for business."

"If we meet early, like we did today, I don't think any harm would come of it." Hannah smiled and reached for his empty cup. "But I am going to make you that shirt. It's the least I can do." Trying not to think too much about what she was doing, Hannah held out her hand to him. "Deal?"

Ezra hesitated. Then he wiped his palm on his trouser leg, which was probably even dirtier than his hand, and clasped hers in a firm shake. The dull eyes that had made her heart ache upon first seeing him sparkled with new life, and she prayed that their morning meetings over chocolate would help keep it there.

"See ya tomorrow, Miz Hannah." Ezra tipped his hat.

"Bring an extra shirt with you when you come," Hannah said. "I can mend any rips there may be or replace buttons, but I can also use it as a pattern for your new shirt. You'll be my first customer."

"I like the sounda that." He picked up his walking stick and used its support to lever himself up. "Gives me braggin' rights, now, don't it?"

Hannah laughed. "I guess it does."

He waved to her, then ambled off down the road toward the railroad station, his mule, Jackson, at his side. Ezra Culpepper was not exactly the type of client she had envisioned for her shop, but somehow she thought Miss Victoria would approve.

An hour later, Hannah emerged from her upstairs room a changed woman. Gone were the loose-fitting exercise clothes and the single braid that had hung down her back. She had set aside her cocoon to stretch her butterfly wings in a smart day dress in deep mauve, button-up heeled shoes, and a tasteful straw bonnet with matching ribbon. Her hair was twisted into an elegant chignon designed to impress but not outshine the women who might visit her shop.

When she reached the bottom of the stairs, she took a deep breath. The idea of opening her shop wracked her nerves, but even more unsettling was the other task she'd have to complete before placing the *Open* sign in her window. She still owed Mr. Tucker an apology for snapping at him yesterday.

Over her arm hung a basket containing his tools along with a peace offering that she hoped would please him. Hannah worried that, with a sister like Cordelia who could bake muffins that melted in a person's mouth, Mr. Tucker would find the biscuits and jam she offered lacking. But they were fluffy and warm, without a single burnt bottom, and the jam she'd bought at the store was sweet. Since he didn't want anything to do with her needlework, food was the best she had to give.

Exhaling a shaky breath, she straightened her shoulders and marched across the street. Better to get the daunting task over with now so she could concentrate on running her dress shop.

She found Mr. Tucker outside the livery, standing in the bed of the hay wagon. Hannah stopped short. The man was slinging giant forkfuls of hay above his head into the loft door as if they weighed no more than feathers. The fabric of his cotton shirt pulled snugly against his muscular shoulders as he scooped the fork forward. . . .

Mr. Tucker certainly has no need of a daily constitutional.

At the same time that thought ran through her head, J.T. Tucker's gaze locked with hers, lighting fire to her cheeks.

9

J.T. caught the rosy blush that colored Miss Richards's cheeks and flexed his muscles. The roses deepened before she turned her head, and something instinctual within him cheered. Just in case she looked his way again, he pitched another two loads of hay, each larger than the last. Remembering the challenge she'd issued of catching him smiling, he schooled his smug grin into an annoyed line, hoping she would think him irritated at the interruption. He wanted to tease her something fierce, but that wouldn't serve his purposes. He was supposed to be putting distance between them, not instigating a flirtation.

That reminder put an edge to his words as he addressed her. "What do you need, Miss Richards? I'm a little busy."

"Yes, I . . . I see that."

Her stammer only bolstered his ego. He guessed it was rather childish of him to enjoy her discomfiture, but for the first time since he met her, he was the one with the advantage, and it felt awfully good.

She tipped her chin up to him, and he swore he could see her spine stiffening. There went his advantage. He stifled a sigh and leaned on the handle of his pitchfork.

"I came to return your tools." She raised her arm, lifting a basket that he supposed contained the level and screwdriver he'd dropped off at her shop yesterday afternoon.

He nodded toward the small door off to his right. "Just put them on the desk in my office."

J.T. tried to dismiss her by turning his back and shoving the fork into the hay, but she didn't take the hint.

"I have something else for you, too, Mr. Tucker. A peace offering."

Of all the harebrained female ideas. The last thing he needed was peace between them. If she started being nice to him . . . well, it would be that much harder to fight his growing attraction.

"I owe you an apology for the way I spoke to you yesterday." Her soft voice sounded much closer. He speared the pitchfork into the dwindling pile of hay and spun around to find her less than a foot away from the wagon.

Her brows arched at his abrupt movement, and he scowled. Why did her eyes have to shine up at him like deep reflections of the mill pond on a spring evening?

"You don't owe me anything, Miss Richards. We both spoke out of turn. Now move along and let me get back to work."

She stiffened and set her jaw. He couldn't help but wonder how hard she was biting her tongue to keep from lambasting him.

"By all means, continue your work, Mr. Tucker. Don't let my olive branch stop you."

J.T. took her advice and grabbed his pitchfork again, half expecting her to find a real branch and start thrashing him with it.

"I came here to apologize, and I aim to do just that. Whether or not you listen is up to you."

Her apology sounded more like a scolding, but he had to respect her for not letting him deter her.

"I had no right to lecture you on being neighborly. You have shown me much kindness since I arrived. Except, of course, for the arrogant, ill-tempered manner with which you seem determined to goad me, for reasons only the Lord above could possibly comprehend." She mumbled that last part, but not so quietly that he couldn't make out the words. "At any rate, I should not have imposed on that kindness, and I am sorry."

He grunted as he pitched a load, cuing her to leave. She took the hint. Out of the corner of his eye, he saw her moving toward his office.

"I brought you some biscuits and jam," she called out to him. "Feel free to give them to Tom or feed them to your horses if you don't want to sully your hands with something I've touched. With as much as you dislike me, they'd probably give you indigestion anyhow."

Were those tears he heard beneath her anger? His conscience roared at him. Keeping distance between them was one thing, but actually hurting her was inexcusable.

He peered through the office window. She emptied her basket, leaving not only his tools, but a generous-sized mound of biscuits wrapped in a bread cloth. Then she swiped a finger under her eye. Twice.

Blast. I did hurt her.

A verse ran through his head, unsummoned: "*. . . neither cast ye your pearls before swine.*" Miss Richards had the pearls, and he was definitely the swine. Not a flattering comparison. He stretched his neck, cracking the first few vertebrae.

All right, Lord. I get the message. I crossed the line and need to put things right.

J.T. dropped the pitchfork. He braced his hand against the side of the wagon and leapt over it to the ground. Miss Richards hadn't emerged from his office yet. She was probably trying to compose herself. A woman as strong-spirited as she wouldn't want to show weakness in front of the enemy. J.T. pounded his leg with his fist as he covered the distance to the open door. He might not want to strike up an intimate friendship with the seamstress, but that didn't mean he wanted her to consider him an enemy.

He burst into the office just as she tried to exit. A tiny gasp escaped her lips as she lurched away from him. She wobbled to the side, her head coming dangerously close to the sharp corner of his tack shelf. He latched on to her elbow to steady her. What was it about them and doorways?

She gently tugged her arm free and ducked her chin. He tried to meet her eyes, but all he could see was the top of her hat.

"I'm sorry. Again," she said, still not looking at him.

He cleared his throat. "I'm . . . ah . . . sorry, too. And not just for nearly running you down. I was rude to you out there." He paused. "Forgive me."

Slowly, the hat tilted back and her lovely face peered up at him. She had freckles across the bridge of her nose, and her lashes were damp. Those blue eyes of hers spoke of her confusion and pain even though her mouth remained silent. But it was the hint of hope shimmering in their moist depths that penetrated his heart. All at once, he could think of nothing save kissing her. His gaze fell to her lips, and he felt himself sway forward.

What am I doing? J.T. jerked back and locked his neck firmly in an upright position.

Clearing his throat, he stepped around her to the desk. "Uh . . . thanks for the biscuits. It was thoughtful of you."

J.T. made a point to unwrap the bundle and take a bite of one of the golden brown halves. The crust flaked, the soft center still warm. The strawberry preserves tempted him to take another bite and relish the sweetness, but the sour feeling in the pit of his stomach told him he was not done with his apology.

"You're a fine cook, ma'am."

She still didn't smile. Two delicate frown lines veed between her brows. "Why do you dislike me so, Mr. Tucker?"

Had he been a cursing man, he would have done so just then. Instead he choked on the bite of biscuit that lodged itself in his throat at her question.

"I don't dislike you, Miss Richards."

She stared up at him, no doubt waiting for an explanation. He stuffed another bite of biscuit into his mouth.

What exactly could he say? That she frightened him and his rudeness was an act of self-preservation? Yeah, that would go over well.

"How's the table working out?" He sat on the corner of his desk, which brought his face level with hers. A mistake. Her gaze bored into him with an intensity that made him squirm. He shoved back up to his feet and strode to the door. She blinked but didn't stand in his way.

"The table's a blessing. Thank you."

He'd forgotten he'd asked the question until he heard her answer. Escape was too close to stop now, though, so he kept moving through the doorway. "Good," he called over his shoulder. "Glad to hear it. I . . . ah . . . need to get back to work. Thanks for bringing the tools back . . . and for the biscuits."

J.T. scrambled up into the wagon as if the ground were suddenly crawling with snakes. He snatched up the pitchfork and starting throwing hay with a vengeance.

"Good day, Mr. Tucker."

He heard her voice but pretended he didn't. After three more pitches up to the loft, he risked a glance behind him. Head high, she was walking down the street toward the blacksmith shop. She looked so prim and professional dressed in her fancy pink dress and bonnet, but when he'd seen her in her plain, loose-fitting work dress, he'd found her no less appealing.

And then she'd waltzed into town with Ezra Culpepper and sat in front of her shop with the man drinking coffee or tea or whatever it was women like her drank in the morning. Which only confused him further. Ezra hadn't bathed since his wife died last spring, probably hadn't changed his clothes, either, just added layers as the temperature cooled. He stunk to high heaven. Even if the woman had no sense of smell, one look at the fellow should have been all it took to turn her away in disgust at his unkempt state. Yet she hadn't turned away. In fact she'd reached out to him.

What seamstress in her right mind would encourage a connection with a dirty, smelly old man? It couldn't possibly be good for business.

Turning back to the task at hand, J.T. gripped the pitchfork and shoved it into the hay. He doubted he'd ever understand Miss Hannah Richards. Trying only made his head hurt.

10

Hannah bit into the bacon sandwich she'd made from her breakfast leftovers, trying not to let discouragement steal her good humor. She'd swept the shop floor, straightened her collection of fashion plates and pattern books at least six times, and repositioned her display dummies twice. Still, no one came. The idleness was about to make her daft.

Didn't word of mouth travel at high speeds in small towns? Surely the women in Coventry knew her shop was open for business. Why didn't they come?

Hannah set aside her half-eaten sandwich. How was she supposed to entice customers? True, it was only the first day, but curiosity if nothing else should have brought potential patrons to her door. Was something wrong with her display? Had she committed some unforgivable social blunder? Was the fact that she was an outsider keeping people away?

Her stomach twisted and a dull throb crept behind her eyes. Hannah moaned and rubbed at her temples. What did she know about running a business? All her professional life, she'd sewn for someone else—someone with an established clientele. She'd had no need to drum up customers. They'd simply been handed to her. Apparently, her assumption that a notice in the general store and an *Open* sign in her window would be enough to bring the women of Coventry flocking to her door had been a tad naïve. So now what should she do?

Not having a good answer to that question, she crammed the rest of her bacon biscuit into her mouth. And of course, that was the precise moment her shop door opened. Mortified, Hannah spun around, cheeks bulging as she tried to swallow the lump of food rapidly expanding in her mouth.

She grabbed her water glass and sipped small drinks until she managed to get the bite down, then turned to greet her customer.

"Good afternoon," she gushed.

Louisa James stood in the center of the shop with a daughter clinging to each hand. After meeting the laundress yesterday morning, Hannah had not expected the hardworking woman to be her first customer, but then again, there was no law against a laundress looking her best when the occasion called for it.

Hannah stepped around the counter to greet the threesome. "What can I do for you ladies?"

"We come by to welcome you to town, official-like—and introduce you to my daughters." Louisa's no-nonsense voice echoed loudly in the quiet room. "You done met my boy, Danny. This here's Tessa," she said, lifting the clasped hand of the taller girl, "and this 'un's Mollie."

"What a pleasure to meet such lovely young ladies. Thank you for stopping by my shop." Hannah kept her smile firmly in place even while her optimism crumbled. Louisa had not come to purchase dress goods.

However, she *had* taken time from her own business to pay a call, Hannah pointedly reminded herself, and such a gift deserved appreciation, not disappointment.

"Welcome to Coventry, Miss Richards!" the taller girl enthused. She dropped her mother's hand and bounced forward to wrap her arms around Hannah's waist.

Surprised yet delighted, Hannah staggered back to catch her balance, a giggle rising up in her throat.

"Tessa!" her mother scolded. "Don't bowl the woman over."

Hannah met Louisa's eye over Tessa's head and smiled. "It's no bother. A hug is exactly what I needed today."

The other woman nodded, understanding glowing in her gaze. "The first couple weeks are the hardest. But business will pick up."

Tessa released her grip on Hannah's waist, and Hannah focused on the young girl. "Thanks for the warm welcome, Miss Tessa. You brightened my day."

"Sure." The youngster smiled with a grin so infectious it was impossible for Hannah to keep hold of her doldrums. Tessa tilted her head toward her sister and whispered in a confidential rasp, "Mollie woulda hugged you, too, but she's kinda shy."

"That's all right." Hannah hunkered down in front of the smaller girl. "I'm glad to know you, Miss Mollie."

Slowly, the quiet child lifted her chin.

"Would you like to see my scrap box?" Hannah asked, an idea blooming. "I have almost every color of the rainbow in there. In fact, if you find a piece of fabric you particularly like, I can make it into a doll for you. Would you like that?"

Mollie had barely begun her nod when Tessa bounded up to interrupt.

"Can I have one, too, Miss Richards? Can I?"

"Of course." Hannah led the girls behind the counter to one of her trunks. She opened the lid and pulled out the top inlaid divider full of ribbons and other notions to reveal the scraps in the bottom. "You can look through these as long as you keep them folded so they don't get wrinkled. Can you do that for me?"

"Yes, ma'am."

Louisa stepped up beside her. "You don't have to do that."

"I know, but it will give me something to do, and hopefully the girls will like them."

"I'm sure they will. Thank you."

Hannah gave Louisa a thoughtful look, the woman's earlier comment about her business picking up returning to mind.

"Did you experience trouble when you first started the laundry?"

Louisa followed Hannah a short distance away from the girls. "Yep. Had a lean couple o' months before I figured out a thing or two. Folks around here are slow to take to change. They like to wait till the shine wears off a bit afore they're ready to try something new. You just gotta convince one or two people to rub off some of your newcomer polish. Then the rest will follow."

"How do I do that?"

The laundress shrugged. "I don't know what'll work for you, but I can tell you what I did. I washed shirts for free."

Hannah's forehead scrunched. "Free? Didn't you lose money that way?"

"Nah. I only washed one free shirt per family. It got people to come in, even if they only brought one thing. I gave those shirts my best effort, and let the quality speak for itself. It took a while to build up a reputation, but now I nearly got more business than I can handle."

Giving things away for free. It seemed so backward, yet Hannah couldn't argue with Louisa's success. But how could she use the same strategy? She couldn't give away free dresses. That would be too costly. She couldn't piecemeal out parts of her service the way Louisa had. A single free seam would do no one any good.

Hannah blew out a breath as she brushed her biscuit crumbs off the worktable and into her hand before dumping them into the wastebasket. She shook out the napkin she had wrapped her lunch in, as well, and idly wove it through her fingers.

"What about making up some of those?" Louisa flicked the dangling corner of the lunch cloth. "You got a bunch of scraps, right?"

Bread cloths. Hannah brightened, her previously infertile mind suddenly sprouting a garden of ideas. "Louisa, that's brilliant! A practical gift the ladies can use, and every time they cover their dinner rolls or wrap up a sandwich, they will think of my shop." Hannah hustled over to where the girls were making their selections and grabbed a sky-blue piece they had discarded. She shook out the folds and held it out before her, tilting it this way and that.

"I could scallop the edges to dress them up a bit and use a wide assortment of colors and fabrics so the women could choose one that fits their tastes." Her gaze found Louisa's. "Do you think it will work?"

"It couldn't hurt." Louisa patted her shoulder and moved past to collect the girls. Mollie had a pink gingham piece in her hand, but Tessa's lap still held three options. "Time to go, Tessa. Hurry and pick one. I got a pile o' pressing waiting back at the laundry."

After a final deliberation, Tessa settled on a saffron yellow calico spotted with tiny green sprigs. She handed her selection to Hannah.

"Thank you for making dolls for us, Miss Richards."

"You are most welcome."

They said their good-byes and Hannah returned to her scrap box. With new energy vibrating through her, she dug through the trunk, pulling out solid-colored broadcloth in earthy hues like tan, rust, and orange. Perfect for the harvest season. Then she found a host of cotton plaids in shades of blue, green, and yellow. Cheerful and fun. Finally she selected half a dozen floral print calicoes for clients who preferred a more feminine design for their baskets.

She spread the pile of fabric across her worktable and cut a folded piece of brown broadcloth into two large, wavy squares. She would sew up one, and if it turned out well, she'd use the second for a pattern. Twenty minutes and one scalloped hem later, she had a fine-looking bread cloth.

Taking up her shears, Hannah began cutting the rest of the fabric into similar patterns. She could keep extra bread cloths on hand in the shop and give them to any new customer who came through her door. That way no one would feel left out. The women from the outlying farms and ranches deserved the same treatment as the ones in town.

Halfway through cut number sixteen, the shop door opened. A customer?

"Good afternoon," she said as she raised her head. "How can I help you?"

Cordelia Tucker crossed into the room. "Oh, Hannah. It's all so lovely."

"Cordelia!" Hannah scurried around the half wall that separated her work area from the rest of the shop. "I'm so glad you came by. Things have been dreadfully quiet."

"I'm sure you'll have more traffic in the coming days. How could you not with such beautiful merchandise?" She fingered a green silk gown that hung on the coatrack, undeniable longing in her eyes.

"Louisa James and her girls are the only ones who've stopped by today. I was growing quite discouraged until she helped me come up with an idea to entice people into the shop." Hannah explained about the bread cloths, relieved when Cordelia showed enthusiasm for the plan.

"And since you are the first one to visit my shop, you get first choice." Hannah steered her friend toward the worktable. "Pick a fabric and I will sew it up while you look around. I have several pattern books you can browse."

Cordelia hesitated. "Oh, but I'm not here to buy anything. I just stopped in to see how you were getting along."

Hannah wrapped her arms around Cordelia's shoulders and gently urged her closer to the table. "You don't have to order anything. Everyone who comes in gets a bread cloth, regardless of whether or not they make a purchase."

The dark blue wool dress Cordelia wore complemented her complexion and figure only slightly better than the dull brown one she'd worn yesterday. Hannah itched to get her into some colors that would bring life to her face.

Cordelia chose green plaid for her gift. She seemed to have a preference for that color. Hannah mentally cataloged the material she had in stock. A sage or hunter shade would be lovely on the young woman.

"You don't have to buy anything," Hannah reiterated. "Just have fun looking. We can talk while I sew."

"J.T. would say it's dangerous to look at things one can't afford." Cordelia made this comment as she tentatively thumbed through the Butterick fall catalog. "It opens the door for temptation."

Hannah gritted her teeth as she sat down at her machine. "I suppose that could be true. But there's no harm in appreciating beauty and letting your imagination run down a brighter path for a little while. It's like playing pretend. Girls have fun dreaming that their mud pies are chocolate cakes, but they have sense enough not to eat them. The joy is in the pretending."

Cordelia looked up from the fashion book and grinned, her eyes twinkling. "I loved playing with mud pies." She glanced over her shoulder as if worried someone would hear what she had to say, then turned back. "I respect my brother a great deal, but J.T. *can* be a bit too straitlaced at times."

"That's stating it mildly," Hannah mumbled.

Cordelia quirked her brow in question. The mannerism must be a family trait. However, it was far less hostile and annoying when Cordelia did it.

"Your brother has been exceptionally helpful to me since I arrived, Cordelia, but he drives me to distraction at the same time with his overbearing attitudes. Is he disagreeable with everyone, or is it just me?"

Hannah pumped her treadle hard and fast, alleviating her frustration while she sewed.

Cordelia giggled, and only then did Hannah realize how her words could have offended. "He can seem a little harsh to those who don't know him well. J.T.'s not exactly what I would call affable, but he has a good heart."

Hannah sighed and her foot slowed. The whir of the machine quieted to a dim hum. "I know he does, and I shouldn't have spoken ill of him. His actions toward me have been nothing but kind. It's his words and demeanor that fire my temper. Perhaps if I could find a way to get the upper hand during one of our verbal skirmishes, I wouldn't feel at such a disadvantage."

With a final turn of the fabric, Hannah finished the hem of Cordelia's bread cloth. She pulled the material free and clipped the loose threads.

"All done." Hannah stood and handed Cordelia her gift. "Here you go. One new bread cloth for the woman who bakes the finest bread in Coventry."

"Thank you." Cordelia smiled and looked over the workmanship. "You did that so quickly. It would have easily taken me an hour to complete this, and it would not have turned out half as nice."

"Swift, quality service. That's my specialty."

A thoughtful look crossed Cordelia's features as she fingered the cloth. Then a downright mischievous sparkle lit her eyes. "You've given me a gift today, Hannah—more than the bread cloth. You reminded me that it is permissible to dream and pretend and think on 'whatsoever things are lovely,' as Scripture says. I want to give you something in return."

She stepped closer and dropped her voice. "J.T. has been extra surly since you came to town. I can only conclude that you are getting under his skin as much as he is getting under yours. And as a female who knows what it's like to live with him when he gets ornery, I would be happy to tip the scales a bit in your favor the next time the two of you spar."

Hannah held her breath.

"Everyone in Coventry knows not to call J.T. by his given name. He absolutely abhors it. From the time he entered school, he refused to answer to anything except J.T. or Tucker, even with Mother and Father. So the next time you feel the need for an advantage, try calling him *Jericho*. I don't know if it will help or simply escalate matters, but it is sure to get his goat one way or the other."

Cordelia's grin was the essence of sisterly devilment. "I only hope I'm there to see his reaction."

"Jericho, hmm?" Hannah felt an answering grin curve her lips. "I suddenly feel a great fondness for that name."

The two women giggled like young girls scheming behind the schoolhouse. Jericho Tucker had no idea what was coming his way.

11

Cordelia introduced Hannah around town on Thursday, and together they handed out close to two dozen of the colorful bread cloths. Word spread, and a steady trickle of visitors came through the shop. Unfortunately, that's all they were—visitors, not customers.

At closing time on Saturday, Hannah flipped her sign so the word *Closed* faced the window, then leaned her shoulder against the door. Not one order. Her mind told her to be patient, that the women who wandered through the shop would return and make purchases in the future. But logic couldn't keep her heart from sinking. Words like *failure* and *mistake* and *disaster* circled through her mind, making faces and taunting her as they spun. Hannah sagged further into the door until she began to slip. She snapped up. In a bid for control, she shook out her skirts and imagined herself brushing off the negativity that clung to her.

"Land sakes, Hannah," she lectured herself, "it's only been four days. Have a little faith."

She marched across the floor and collected the brown-paper-wrapped parcel that waited on the corner of her worktable. Ezra's shirt. He would soon be stopping by to pick it up on his way home from the depot. Hannah fiddled with the string bow that held the package closed, making sure both loops were even and the knot tight. Her first and only customer. Yet he'd paid handsomely. The bench outside her shop gleamed, and more than one visitor had commented on it.

Ezra still insisted on sitting on the edge of the boardwalk while they had their morning cocoa, but she was thankful to have a more comfortable option. The bench was smooth and sturdy and wide enough for three adults. She'd often seen the James children steal a seat there for a minute or two when they were able to get away from the laundry—and whether they were quietly sharing a snack or pestering each other with pokes and pushes, she always enjoyed their antics.

Now the bench sat empty. The weather was pleasant, though, so she decided to make use of it herself while she waited for Ezra. She locked the shop and slid onto the bench, leaning into the crosspieces at her back. Exhaling a long breath, she closed her eyes for a moment and simply breathed. When she opened them again, their focus relaxed. No longer consumed with fabrics and threads, needles and patterns, Hannah let her gaze drift over her surroundings, seeking bits of unexpected beauty. She fancied the search as something of an expedition to uncover God's hidden messages of love. Whenever she found one, she received it as a gift and savored the serenity it brought.

A monarch butterfly fluttered past and landed on the hitching post. Hannah leaned forward for a better view. The orange wings rimmed and veined in black—like stained glass in a church window—winked at her. It lingered only an instant before taking flight once again. Hannah followed its erratic movements until she spotted an interesting knothole in one of the boards near her feet. Golden streaks spiraled inward against a dark brown backdrop, revealing the place a branch once grew. This made her think of trees and how the leaves would soon be changing, covering the area hills in a patchwork of green, gold, and red. Lifting her eyes to examine the outlying hills beyond the town, a particularly fluffy cloud captured her attention. She was in the midst of deciding whether it looked more like an armadillo or a handlebar mustache when a loud bang followed by high-pitched voices jolted her out of her reverie.

"Did not!"

"Did so."

"I'm telling Ma."

"Go ahead. It's your fault we lost it."

Hannah craned her neck in time to see Mollie James stomp back inside the laundry house, apparently intent on carrying out her threat to tattle. Tessa uttered a closed-mouth cry that surely would have been a full scream had her lips parted. Then she spun toward Hannah in a fit of obvious pique and ran blindly for the bench. She pulled up short when she realized the seat was already occupied. Tears pooled in her eyes but didn't fall as she looked at Hannah. Before the child could run away, Hannah patted a spot on the bench beside her.

"I'll share."

Tessa hesitated. Then, with a shrug, she sat down and scooted back until her feet swung freely above the ground. She crossed her arms over her chest and settled into an impressive pout.

Hannah sighed in dramatic fashion and crossed her own arms. "Little sisters can be such a trial. I have one, too, you know."

Tessa's arms loosened a little. "You do?"

"Mm-hmm."

"She ever get you in trouble for something that wasn't your fault?"

"Oh yes, on several occasions." Hannah kept her expression sober even though she wanted to laugh. "I remember the first time Mother let me attend one of her quilting bees. Usually Emily and I had to stay in our room on quilting nights so that we didn't bother the ladies, but this time Mother had deemed my stitching good enough to join the adults. I was so excited and proud. Emily, however, felt left out. She begged Mother to let her help, too, and finally Mother agreed to let her snip threads with a small pair of embroidery scissors.

"The problem, though, was that Mother sewed with a long thread that didn't need to be snipped often. So Emily took it upon herself to snip my threads, too. Only I didn't want her to. I asked politely for her to let me use the scissors, but she insisted it was her job to snip the thread ends. I insisted that I would snip my own threads. Thankfully, the rest of the women's chatter kept them from noticing our argument. Had Emily just given me the scissors, all would have been well, but she refused." Hannah wagged her head at the injustice of sibling interference. "I tried to grab them from her, and we tugged back and forth until I finally won. But that win quickly turned into a defeat."

Tessa wiggled closer to Hannah, her pout replaced by a look of avid curiosity. "What happened?"

"I yanked on the scissors so hard that when they popped free of Emily's hand, I couldn't hang on to them. They sailed through the air and clanked against Myrtle Butler's teacup. She squealed and dropped the cup and saucer, spilling tea all over her dress, and worse, the quilt."

Tessa gasped.

Hannah nodded, a residual shame creeping over her at the memory. "I'd never seen Mother so angry. She yelled at me in front of the Ladies Auxiliary and sent both Emily and me to our room. I wasn't allowed to join the quilting group again for two years, until Emily was old enough to join, as well."

"That's not fair!"

"I didn't think so, either, at the time." Hannah patted Tessa's knee. "But now I understand it better. Emily might have been guilty of instigating the trouble, but my reaction to her is what caused the situation to escalate out of control. If I had simply let her snip the thread, everything would have worked out fine."

Tessa's face scrunched in thought.

"Is that similar to what happened with you and Mollie?" Hannah asked.

"Sort of. Except me losing the button was all Mollie's fault. She bumped into me when I was just sitting there. The button dropped out of my hand and fell through a crack in the floor. Now Mr. Smythe will prob'ly refuse to pay again. He don't pay if anything's wrong with his clothes. And he looks real hard to find something wrong every time. Ma's gonna tan my hide good for this."

Tessa pulled her knees up to her chest and wrapped her arms around them, burying her face in the faded calico material of her skirt. Hannah laid a hand on the girl's rounded back.

"Did the button come off during the washing?"

Tessa nodded against her knees without raising her head. "Uh-huh. I'm the one in charge of sewing them back on. But now I don't have a button, and Mr. Smythe is bound to notice." Her voice hitched, and Hannah feared tears were close to the surface again.

"I've got an idea." Hannah waited for Tessa to lift her face a couple of inches before continuing. "Do you think you can sneak back into the laundry and get Mr. Smythe's shirt?"

"Yeah . . ."

"I've got a whole Mason jar full of buttons in my workroom. I bet we can find something to match."

Tessa straightened, and her legs plopped back to a normal sitting position. Looking at Hannah as if she were a fairy godmother, she blinked away the moisture that had collected in her eyes. "You think so?"

"It's worth a try, wouldn't you say?"

"Yes, ma'am!"

Before Hannah could say another word, Tessa bounded away to retrieve the shirt. She returned in less than a minute. The linen garment had already been washed, starched, and dried but had not yet been pressed. Hannah collected Ezra's package and ushered Tessa into her shop, where she pulled out her jar of buttons. Tessa eyed it with open-mouthed amazement.

"There must be more than a thousand in there," she stated, her gaze glued to the abundant mix of styles, shapes, and sizes.

Laughter bubbled up in Hannah. "Probably closer to two hundred, but I've never actually counted."

She unscrewed the lid and poured nearly half the contents onto the table, spreading them into a thin layer. Black, white, brass, pearl, engraved, plain, two holes, four holes, no holes—the choices were extensive.

"It was a white one," Tessa said. "See?" She laid the shirt on the table and pointed to one of the buttons still in place.

Hannah squinted down at it. "Looks like pearl, or pearl agate. Start searching through the pile, and when you think you've found a match, hold it up to this one to see if it's the same pattern and size. Look for one with a fluted edge that resembles a sun."

"All right."

The two set to work. Several buttons were similar, but something was always off. They were too large, too small, too translucent, or too plain. Hannah started congregating a different set of pearl shirt buttons off to the side as she came across them. If they couldn't find a match to the existing buttons, they could replace all of them with a new set. Most men didn't pay attention to little details like the design of a shirt button, so she doubted Mr. Smythe would notice the difference. But deception was never a good policy, so she would send Tessa back with all the original buttons so her mother could explain to the gentleman what happened and how they had remedied the situation. Hopefully, he would be impressed with their service and not only pay the promised amount, but leave a tip, as well.

"I found it!" Tessa declared.

"You did?"

Relief swept through Hannah. An identical button would make things a great deal easier. She leaned forward to examine it more closely. The button was indeed a match.

"Great job, Tessa! Let me get you a needle and some thread."

Hannah opened the spool drawer on her sewing cabinet and grabbed a reel of white thread. She cut off a strand and handed it to Tessa along with a needle. The girl moistened the end of the thread with her tongue and jabbed it through the tiny eye like an experienced seamstress. Impressed, Hannah grew thoughtful as she watched Tessa knot the end and sew the button into place with precision.

"Most girls your age have trouble threading their own needle, but you seem quite adept. Do you sew more than buttons?"

Tessa tied off the thread and held it out for Hannah to cut.

"Ma keeps saying she'll teach me one of these days, but she's too busy."

"Maybe after my business is better established," Hannah said, thinking aloud, "I can give you a few lessons. If your mother approves, of course."

"Could you teach me to make fancy dresses? Like the ones hanging in your window?"

Hannah smiled as she scraped the leftover buttons back into the jar. The tinkling sound they made as they bounced against the glass mirrored the eager excitement ringing in Tessa's voice.

"We would start with something simpler, like an apron." Tessa pulled a face and Hannah stifled a giggle. "However," she continued, "if you work hard and practice long, by the time you are out of short skirts, you might be ready to make your very own party dress for all those church socials the boys will be asking you to." Hannah winked and Tessa grinned.

The sound of someone calling Tessa's name quickly evaporated their vision of the future.

Tessa jumped. "That's Ma. I gotta go."

She grabbed up the shirt and dashed for the door. Halfway there she stopped and turned around. "Thanks, Miss Richards."

"You're welcome, Tessa."

The girl dashed off, and an unexpected longing rose up within Hannah, catching her by surprise. A longing for a child and a family of her own. Most women her age already had a husband and children, but she had chosen a different path—the path of a seamstress and now a businesswoman. Did that mean she would have to forfeit the chance to share a home and hearth with someone special? She'd never really thought much about it before. After all, she'd known practically all her life that she would be a seamstress, and she'd dedicated herself to making the most of her talent. Now, for the first time, she wondered if it would be enough.

Hannah stepped to her project basket and picked up the cloth doll she'd been working on for Tessa. Mollie's slept peacefully in the basket, complete and ready for adoption. Tessa's lacked a bonnet and a ribbon to cover the bleached-linen head. Hannah cradled the doll to her chest and patted the tiny back. Emily's last letter had been filled with details about the cradle they had purchased and the booties she'd been knitting. Mother had already pieced together two baby quilts in anticipation of the blessed event. Hannah gently lowered the faceless doll back into the basket. Unable to resist the motherly compulsion, she covered the rag creation and her sister with a piece of muslin, tucking them in for the night. Would this be as close as she ever came to motherhood?

Thankfully, Ezra arrived at that moment and distracted her from the dangerous question.

"That young'un nearly ran me down," he said with a chuckle as he stepped up to the door that gaped open after Tessa's hasty departure. He didn't cross the threshold, though. The same invisible barrier that kept him from sitting on the bench with her kept him from entering her shop.

She wanted to believe that it was just his overzealous sense of propriety, but deep down she knew he was self-conscious about his physical state. So why didn't the man simply wash up? He obviously hungered for companionship, yet he pushed everyone away with his lack of basic hygiene. Had the loss of his wife made him reluctant to let anyone else get close? If so, why did he continue coming to her shop every morning to visit and drink cocoa?

No answers were forthcoming, so she smiled and held out the brown paper package as she walked toward him. "I have your shirt ready."

He licked his lips but showed no other sign of eagerness. "I ain't had a new shirt in years, Miz Hannah. I don't rightly know what to do with it."

"Well, I have an idea."

He accepted the package from her, then stepped aside as she exited the shop and closed the door behind her. The strong odor she had come to associate with him assaulted her with its usual pungency, but it seemed she had built up a resistance to it over the last few days, for she managed to breathe without her throat closing up. Definite progress.

Slipping the key into the lock, she secured the building and smiled up at him. "I was hoping you would escort me to church tomorrow. Being new in town, I would feel much more comfortable with someone I know by my side."

His face fell. "Me, Miz Hannah?" He shook his head slowly from side to side, then faster and faster as if to accentuate his denial. "You don't want me to take you."

"Of course I do."

"But I'm . . ."

"I know you know where it is, you rascal," she interrupted, shaking a playful finger at him while inwardly praying that she wasn't making a mistake by pressing him. "We walk by there every morning."

Ezra's shoulders drooped and he hung his head. His fingers dug into the brown paper encasing his new shirt, making it crinkle and pop.

"The truth is, Miz Hannah, I ain't been to church since my Alice died. I don't belong there no more."

She ached for him, this dear old man who had allowed his grief to drive him away from everyone, including God.

"It doesn't matter how long you've been away, Ezra. God is always ready to welcome a child of his back into his house."

He snorted and looked sideways at her. "God might welcome me back, but I doubt the rest o' the town will be glad to have me there, smellin' up the place."

This was the first time she could recall him verbally acknowledging his uncleanness. However, the underlying scorn in his tone made it seem he was repeating a phrase he'd heard others use, not his own opinion. Hannah bristled at the thought of people being unkind to Ezra. So what if he didn't conform to the accepted social norms of personal cleanliness? That didn't give people the right to be cruel.

She tapped her foot and thrust out her jaw. "Well, we can just sit in the back, then. If they don't like it, they're welcome to worship elsewhere."

Ezra met her gaze, his jaw gaping just a hair. Then he blinked the surprise away so that mirth could take over. "You're a regular she-bear when you get riled, ain'tcha?" He shook his head again, but this time the movement had a lightness to it that spoke of suppressed laughter instead of sadness. A corresponding lightness buoyed Hannah's spirit.

"All right," he conceded. "I'll take you to church in the morning, and I'll even wear the shirt you made me. Anything else you wanna wring outta me while you're at it?"

"Just one thing."

He rolled his eyes. "What?"

Hannah took a deep breath before making the final plunge. "Since your shirt is the first made-to-order item I've sewn for anyone in this town, could you do me a small favor?"

Bracing his feet apart on the walk, he nodded once. "Name it."

"Before you take it out of the paper, could you please wash your hands?"

A booming laugh like she'd never heard erupted from Ezra and nearly knocked her over. He hobbled down the stairs and carefully wedged the shirt under one of the ropes that crisscrossed Jackson's back. "You're a hoot, Miz Hannah. Wash my hands. Ha!"

He led Jackson down the road, leaving her with a wave and an unsettled feeling. Was he teasing, or would her first Coventry sale be displayed in church tomorrow as a grubby mess? A dull pain began to throb at the base of her skull.

12

J.T. stood among the horses and wagons in the churchyard as he always did come Sundays. The good Lord hadn't given him the gift of words like the preacher, or music like the fellow who led the hymn singing, or even patience for listening to all the yammering that went on before and after the service. But he had been blessed with a gift for managing horses, so that's what he gave back to God.

He made sure all the wagons and buggies were spaced out enough to prevent tangles and jams when it came time to leave and saw to it that each animal had plenty of grazing space. When he could, he met folks at the church steps and volunteered to take charge of the reins so a husband could enter with his wife. The rich townsmen seemed to expect it as their due and rarely expressed any gratitude, but the farming families and elderly folks always smiled in genuine appreciation, making him feel as if his simple offering was a true ministry.

"Mornin', J.T.," young Daniel James called from several yards away. The boy abandoned his mother and sisters and angled a path toward him.

"Don't you go pesterin' Mr. Tucker, now. You hear me, Danny?" Louisa admonished.

"I won't, Ma." Exasperation dripped from each syllable.

J.T. couldn't blame him. The kid was stuck in a house with nothing but womenfolk all day. He hungered for male attention, and J.T. preferred he got it from him rather than one of the older boys in town who considered rabble-rousing a noble pursuit.

As Danny jogged up the slope toward him, J.T. stroked the dull brown coat of Warren Hawkins's mare. The shopkeeper's son had ridden the old gal up and down this hill since his school days. Cordelia had been a couple of years behind Warren in school, and J.T. remembered her packing bits of carrot or apple in her lunch tin for the pitiful creature. The horse had been old even then.

J.T.'s jaw tightened. The faithful animal deserved to retire. Yet he knew it would never happen. Owning a horse, even a broken-down nag like this one, gave Warren status over the poorer folk who had to walk to church. Cordelia excused his behavior by saying that Warren had never felt accepted by others due to the large birthmark on his face and was only trying to fit in as best he could. But J.T. found it impossible to summon sympathy for a man who treated his animals with callous disregard.

"What's got ya so glum?"

J.T. looked down to find Danny gazing up at him with wide eyes. Clearing his throat, J.T. decided he best start steering his thoughts in a direction more suited for a day of worship.

"I was just thinking." J.T. tapped Danny's forehead and then, with a quick motion, pinned the boy against his body and rubbed the knuckles of his free hand into his hair. Danny moaned and flailed around in halfhearted protest until J.T. finally let go.

The kid scowled up at him in a fairly good imitation of one of his own dark looks, and J.T.'s mood lightened.

"What'd you go and do that for?" Danny whined. "Ma ain't gonna be happy if I show up all mussed."

"Well, we can't have that, can we?" J.T. finger-combed the boy's hair back into place. "There you go, partner. Good as new."

"Thanks," the kid mumbled.

The distant jangle of harness and creaky wheels brought J.T.'s head around. Everyone from town who either owned a buggy or rented one of his was already inside. In fact, the only person he hadn't seen yet was Miss Richards, and he knew she didn't have one. Besides, the woman hoofed out to the river and back every morning, so she surely wouldn't mind the shorter hike to the church. Not that he'd been paying particular attention to her comings and goings. Anyone out and about in the early morning would have noticed. She was hard to miss, after all, with her free-swinging arms and purposeful strides.

"I wonder where Miss Richards is," he mused aloud. He'd expected her to be there by now. The service was fixing to start.

"I reckon that's her coming up in the rig." Danny pointed down the hill. "I saw it sittin' out front o' her shop when we passed it this morning. Some slicked-up old feller was climbin' up the stairs to fetch her."

Jealousy walloped J.T. in the gut and nearly knocked the breath out of him. He strained forward with narrowed eyes, trying to make out the faces of the man and woman in the approaching coal-box buggy. Miss Richards had been in town less than a week, for pity's sake. When'd she find time to snag a beau? The fact that the driver had snowy white hair didn't make him feel any better. Plenty of women married older, more established men. His mother had. Older meant more security and wealth. Pretty women, *fashionable* women, liked that sort of thing. Although he had a hard time picturing the fiercely independent Hannah Richards bending that stubborn streak of hers enough to pander to the whims of a man she didn't respect. Yet if that man offered her the life she wanted without having to work in a shop six days a week . . .

A sharp ache speared through his temples. J.T. forced himself to unclench his molars, but the tension refused to leave. It simply ran down from his head into his neck and shoulders.

"Ma's calling me, J.T. I gotta go."

"What? Oh, yeah. Go ahead, kid. I'll be there in a minute." He chucked Danny under the chin and sent him off. "I just need to get this last buggy settled." Along with his curiosity.

J.T. hung back as the buggy drew near. His tongue would probably get him in trouble again, if he gave it a chance. It always did around the pretty dressmaker. Probably the reason the Lord gave him horse duty.

Miss Richards was wearing a smile brighter than a summer sky and patted the arm of the old man beside her in a familiar way. Too familiar. The spry codger scrambled down to help her alight, then scampered back as she moved up the church steps. The fool was grinning like a giddy young buck. J.T. met him at the edge of the churchyard, legs braced.

As the buggy came closer, it lost some of its luster. The decrepit thing wasn't exactly the stylish gig one usually employed to impress a gal. Oh, the fellow had given it a spit shine, but thick dust remained in the crevices of the folded-down top, and the faded blue stripe on the side combined with the missing spokes in the wheels gave the thing an air of disrepair. It had probably been around since the War Between the States.

"Whoa there, Jackson."

The mule pulling the rig came to a stop, and J.T. grabbed hold of his harness. Something about the beast jiggled a memory, but he was more concerned with taking the man's measure than that of his animal.

"Beautiful day, ain't it?" The old geezer made no effort to tame his irritating grin as he hopped to the ground. "A good day for turning over a new leaf. Yep, Miz Hannah and me is bound to cause something of a stir this morning."

Hannah? Her given name flew off the fellow's lips like it was accustomed to nesting there. And what kind of stir was he talking about? J.T. ground his teeth. If he hurt or embarrassed her in any way . . .

"Best not stay out here too long. You'll miss the fun."

The man winked at him. Winked!

But then something about his voice registered. J.T. pushed his hat back to examine the man more closely. His white hair had been hacked in a ragged line above his shoulders and was held in place by a faded black bowler hat. A tightly trimmed beard clung to his face, matching the well-groomed mustache higher up. The white shirt he wore looked new under a jacket that might have fit him a decade earlier, and his pants had so many crease lines, J.T. imagined him pulling them out of the bottom of a forgotten trunk moments before leaving the house. He smelled like soap and liniment with a touch of mule. 'Course it might just be the mule that smelled like mule. Either way, the fellow had no business courting a woman like Miss Richards. He was old enough to be her grandfather.

That grandfather whacked him on the back and chuckled. "Come on, Tucker. I 'spected Miz Hannah not to recognize me since she didn't know me when Alice was alive, but not you."

All at once the wool fell away from J.T.'s eyes, and shock supplanted the agitation that had blinded him. "Ezra?" he croaked.

"Yep."

How could he have been so stupid? Of course it was Ezra. Just because he hadn't seen the man look this good in a month of Sundays didn't mean he shouldn't have recognized him.

"It's . . . ah . . . good to see you. We've missed you at services."

The man's grin sobered. "Alice always put great store in church-goin' and I know she'd be disappointed in me lettin' it slip, but I just couldn't stomach sitting in there without her by my side. So's when Miz Hannah done made me this purty new shirt and asked me to escort her this morning, I figured it was God's way of telling me it was time to come back."

Ezra stuck out his chest and ran his beefy hands over the fancy stitching that formed a *V* around the buttoned area of his shirt, then leaned forward toward J.T.'s ear.

"You know, that gal fully expected me to show up looking as I have the last several months and was ready to sit beside me anyhow. She's something else, all right. Why, if Alice didn't still hold sway over my heart, I'd seriously think on giving you young fellers a run for your money in courtin' the lady."

J.T. shook his head. He had no intention of competing with the old man or anyone else for the fair Miss Hannah. God would lead him to the right woman one day. He just had to be patient and not get distracted by a complicated piece of muslin who frustrated and confused him at every turn.

Hannah slid onto a bench at the back of the church just as the singing began. She still couldn't get over the change in Ezra. He must have soaked and scrubbed for hours to make such a transformation. If Jackson hadn't been hitched to the buggy in front of her shop, she'd never have believed that the tidy gentleman who came to her door was Ezra Culpepper. His change probably had more to do with entering God's house than with her request to wash his hands, but she didn't care what motivated it. Ezra had made an effort to rejoin the living, and she planned to delight in watching the living accept him back.

Adding her soprano to the congregation as they moved into the second verse of "How Sweet, How Heavenly," Hannah found herself praying that the idea of love and unity the hymn expressed would penetrate the hearts of the people gathered so that they would look past their prejudices and welcome Ezra back into the fold with warmth and joy.

"'When each can feel his brother's sigh, and with him bear a part,'" she sang, her voice growing stronger as the lyrics resonated in her soul. "'When sorrow flows from eye to eye, and joy from heart to heart.'"

A gravelly voice joined hers as Ezra sat on her left, away from the aisle. His fingers gave away his nervousness as they worried the brim of the hat now in his lap. "'When, free from envy, scorn and pride, our wishes all above,'" he intoned slightly off-key. "'Each can his brother's failings hide, and show a brother's love.' "

Boot heels thudded softly against the floor, and suddenly Hannah's wishes were no longer all above. Jericho Tucker strode past her to sit with his sister—across the aisle, two rows up. Memorized words from the hymn continued to flow from Hannah's mouth, but her mind wandered elsewhere—two rows forward, to be precise.

He folded his lean frame into a space that seemed much too small for him. The backless benches that served for pews were better suited for the children who used the building as a schoolroom than for a man of his height. In order to avoid the ample hips of the woman seated in front of him, he had to jut his left leg out into the aisle. Apparently accustomed to such an awkward position, he hung his hat on his bent knee as if it were a fence post and then glanced over his shoulder.

Hannah's heart swelled painfully in her chest. He'd likely intended to look at Ezra, since her seatmate was the one who had drastically altered his appearance, but Jericho's gaze collided with hers instead and lingered. Her singing trailed off midstanza as she tried to interpret his look. He didn't smile. Yet neither did he frown. He just stared at her as if the answer to some incredibly vital question lay in the lines of her face.

If he found any answers there, they must not have pleased him much, for his mouth thinned and he turned away.

Dragging her focus away from the back of his head, she looked down to her lap, at the Bible lying there—reminding her where she was. She lifted her chin and faced forward, determined to return her concentration to the

God they were praising instead of the man across the aisle. She inhaled a deep breath and launched into the final verse of the opening hymn.

"'Love is the golden chain that binds the happy souls above.'"

She tried to imagine those happy souls linked in heaven. She really did. But another image popped into her mind that was frightfully hard to dislodge. The image of a golden chain of love binding her to Jericho Tucker.

Mercy. She couldn't possibly fall in love with Jericho Tucker. The man never smiled. And judging by the number of scowls he sent her way, he probably didn't even like her much. And nearly every time he opened his mouth, he riled her temper. Yet his acts of kindness, despite their disagreements, melted her ire and proved him a man of character.

Those strong shoulders and muscled arms didn't hurt, either.

Ugh. The back and forth was making her head spin.

Hannah straightened and ordered herself to stop analyzing Mr. Tucker. Romance at this juncture would only complicate things. She had a business to run and a reputation to build. She couldn't afford distractions. God would let her know when the time was right to start thinking about a man, and it certainly wouldn't be in the middle of worship.

Jericho Tucker could just keep those consuming glances to himself. She didn't need him complicating things. What she needed was . . . was . . .

"Let us pray." The preacher's voice resonated from the front of the room, and her heart echoed the sentiment.

Yes, Lord. Thank you for the reminder. That is exactly what I need to do.

Hannah bowed her head, but the minute she closed her eyes, all she could see was the man across the aisle.

13

Around noon the following day, Hannah sat at her sewing machine stitching persimmon fabric into a swag. Since she'd finished the dolls for the James girls and had no orders to work on, she'd decided to do something to disguise the unattractive curtains hanging around her sleeping area. She smoothed out the wrinkles from where the material had bunched up in her lap and grimaced slightly at the way the color turned her skin sallow. Did it have to be orange?

Hannah sighed but set her foot back in motion on the treadle. Mrs. Granbury used to remind her girls that an ordinary seamstress could make a beautiful woman look exceptional, but only an exceptional seamstress could make an ordinary woman look beautiful. If the same held true for fabric, this exercise would be a true test of her skills. Thankfully, she wouldn't be wearing the creation, so she didn't need to worry about its effect on her complexion. Hannah finished the seam and tied off her threads. Trying to set her prejudice aside, she moved away from the sewing cabinet and held the cloth up at arm's length, letting it drape over her arms as she eyed it with as much objectivity as possible.

Many people found orange to be warm and cheerful. Of course, most of them didn't look bilious under its influence, but that was neither here nor there. God had painted many things in his creation this color—butterflies, sunsets, and the tiny wildflowers that grew along the path to the river. If the Lord saw beauty in such a color, she could, too. It certainly fit with the time of year, bringing to mind autumn leaves, pumpkins, and the creamy mashed winter squash her mother used to make on cold evenings. The cozy memory made her smile and opened a crack in her heart. Perhaps orange wasn't so bad after all.

Her arms began to tire, so she dropped the swag onto the worktable and folded it into a tidy rectangle. She supposed in the right light it could be considered cheerful. And she needed all the cheer she could get to help her deal with the fact that she had no customers.

Yet.

Hannah pressed her fingers into the sore muscles of her lower back.

No customers, *yet*. That would change in time. It had to. She had spent most of her savings purchasing fabric and supplies. If she didn't start generating some income, she'd be penniless by Christmas.

She had hoped that Ezra's new shirt would pique a bit of interest, but people were more impressed by his physical transformation than the craftsmanship of his garment. Which was only right. Ezra deserved to bask in the welcome of his community after being on the outside for so long. She was happy for him. Truly.

If only she could contract that first custom order. She just needed one woman brave enough to sample her skills. After others saw the flattering effects her fine tailoring had on one of their own, surely they would flock to her door.

Needing to do something other than sit at her empty machine, Hannah grabbed a feather duster and ambled around the shop, swishing the feathers over windowsills, cloth bolts, and anything too slow to get out of her way. As she brushed invisible lint from the shoulders of her display dummies, she caught sight of Cordelia standing across the street, her face etched with yearning as she stared at the olive gown in the window. She fingered the fabric of her plain navy gored skirt and drooped like a flower starved for rain. Then she snapped her wilted posture to attention and marched toward the shop.

Hannah's heart jumped, and she scurried across the room to stash the duster behind the counter. Taking a deep breath, she flattened the pleats of her shirtwaist with a trembling hand and quickly patted her hair before turning to greet her friend and possible first female customer.

Cordelia walked into the shop and closed the door behind her. She scanned the room with a sweeping glance, then turned to Hannah. "I need you to make me beautiful."

The tears that glistened in Cordelia's eyes banished the smile from Hannah's face. Responding to her friend's obvious pain, Hannah rushed forward and wrapped an arm around the other woman's shoulders.

"What happened?"

"He doesn't see me." She hiccuped as a sob tried to break free.

"Who?" Hannah asked. "Who doesn't see you?"

Cordelia buried her face in her hands. The empty basket slung over her arm creaked as her movement squashed it into her side. She might have said a name, but it was too muffled to make out. Hannah extracted a handkerchief from her sleeve and dangled it against the back of Cordelia's hands until she took it.

"Let me close up the shop. Then you can tell me all about it."

When Hannah twisted the key in the lock, the click reverberated in her ear. What if another customer came by? Closing the shop could cost her a sale. Dread churned in her stomach and acid burned the back of her throat. She couldn't afford to lock out a customer. But then one of the verses from Proverbs that she'd been meditating on during her morning devotions floated across her mind.

"Better is a little with righteousness than great revenues without right."

Hannah swallowed the bitter taste in her mouth and flipped over the *Closed* sign without further regret.

By the time Hannah finished with the door, Cordelia had composed herself somewhat. The dear girl was obviously still in a fragile state, however, so Hannah ushered her behind the counter and into her work area. She pulled the chair away from the sewing cabinet and up to the table and gently pushed Cordelia into it.

"Now," she said, dragging her fabric trunk away from the wall and seating herself upon it. "Who is this man with the atrocious eyesight that has you so upset?"

"Only the most wonderful man in all of Coventry."

Hannah could hear the heartbreak in the girl's voice, and her own heart ached in sympathy. "If he's so wonderful, why are you crying?"

"Because he doesn't see me! Not as a woman, anyway. To him I'm just J.T.'s little sister." She wrung the handkerchief between her fists. "I've loved him for ages, and the dim-witted man has no idea."

Hannah smiled. "Dim-witted, huh?"

Cordelia looked up sharply. "Oh, no. I didn't mean that. Not really. He's actually very intelligent. He operates the telegraph and post office down by the bank. You might have met him at church yesterday. Ike Franklin?"

Hannah tried to fish out a visage matching that name from the sea of faces that swam through her memory. Finally one clicked—a thin man in a well-cut gray wool sack suit. Dark mustache. Kind eyes. "Was he the one who led the hymns?"

"Yes." A dreamy look came over Cordelia's face. "Doesn't he have the most luscious voice? It's like chocolate icing, smooth and rich. I could listen to him all day."

"You're making me hungry."

Cordelia giggled. "Sorry."

Hannah reached out and covered Cordelia's hand with one of her own. She didn't want to add to the girl's pain, but she didn't want it prolonged, either. It would be better to face the truth now than to wallow in the misery of unrequited love. Hannah gave Cordelia's hand a gentle squeeze.

"I don't want to dash your hopes, Cordelia, but what if he simply thinks the two of you don't suit and is trying to spare your feelings by pretending not to notice your femininity? It might be better to set your sights on someone else."

"There is no one else! Not for me." She yanked her hand away from Hannah and balled the hankie into her fist. Her knuckles began to whiten, but then she exhaled a long breath and relaxed her grip. "I know you're trying to help, and believe it or not, I've asked myself that same question. But I don't think it's true. The two of us get along famously. We share many of the same interests—books, music, food . . ." She blushed. "He loves my cooking."

What man wouldn't? The woman could bake like an angel.

"About six months ago he hired me to bring him lunch every day, since he's not allowed to leave his post, even for meals. He has to man the wire at all times during his shift." She paused, then her lips curved into a shy smile. "He claims I'm the best cook in the county."

"Well, that proves he's not completely dim-witted, then. He may not be a lost cause after all."

"Oh, Hannah. Do you think so? Do you think I might still have a chance?" Cordelia bounced to the edge of her chair and leaned so far forward that if the table hadn't been supporting her, she would have toppled to the floor. "This isn't just a schoolgirl infatuation. I honestly believe Ike and I would suit. I've come to treasure the friendship that has sprung up between us over the last few months. If the line is quiet when I arrive with his lunch, he sometimes invites me to sit and visit with him while he eats. We talk about books we've read, or he'll tell me funny stories about the scrapes he got into as a boy. He's even taught me how to tap my name in Morse code."

Hannah nodded thoughtfully. Lasting relationships had been built on less.

"If you could fashion me a dress that would somehow make me at least passably pretty, he might finally notice me as a woman and decide to come courting. And if he doesn't . . . Well, at least I would know where I stood and could pack my hopes away quietly."

Hannah could hear the pain and insecurity embedded in Cordelia's words, and they tugged at her heart. There was no question about whether she would help. She'd known she would the minute she flipped the *Closed* sign in the window. The question that plagued her was how. They had only one chance to make a new first impression—an impression so striking that Cordelia's gentleman friend, myopic though he might be, couldn't help but see the beautiful woman in front of him.

The seed of an idea burrowed into her brain and began to take root. This called for more than just a new dress. This called for an Ezra-esque transformation.

Hannah got up and started pacing. "Are there any upcoming community festivities, like a harvest celebration or box social or something of that nature?"

Cordelia's face scrunched up in confusion. "There's the Founders' Day picnic in a little over a month, but what does that have to do with—"

"That's where you will make your debut." Hannah clapped her hands and grinned, but Cordelia failed to catch the excitement.

"It will take you six weeks to make me a new dress? I didn't expect to have to wait that long."

Hannah plopped back down on the trunk and took Cordelia's hands in hers. "I don't need six weeks to sew a dress. I don't need six days. But if you are patient and willing to work hard, I have a plan that will make it impossible for your Mr. Franklin to see you as anything but a desirable woman."

Finally a spark of interest lit her eyes. "Really? You can make me desirable?"

"You've already got all the makings of a beauty. Thick, shiny hair; lovely complexion; dark lashes."

"But I'm fat."

"No you're not. You're just . . ."

Cordelia shook her head. "Don't try to spare my feelings. I see the truth every time I look in the mirror. If I were thin like you, I—"

"You can be." Hannah released her friend's hands to clasp her shoulders. "You can be. I'll teach you my calisthenic routine, and you can join me on my morning walks. Dr. Lewis asserts that if a woman wants to be thinner, she has only to eat less and exercise more."

"Who's Dr. Lewis?"

"Dio Lewis. He's a great proponent of physical education for women and children. He developed a whole new system of gymnastics that can be used by anyone to great result. If you're willing to try, I promise you will see a marked difference. The exercises will improve your health and give you increased energy and strength with the added benefit of trimming your figure. Then, as the day for the picnic draws closer, I can fashion the perfect party dress for you, one in vivid colors and flattering lines that will make it impossible for Mr. Franklin to take his eyes off of you. You'll make as big a splash as Ezra did at church yesterday."

Hannah stood and pulled Cordelia to her feet. "It will mean sacrifice and hard work: changing your morning routine, eating less of those delicious baked goods of yours, and living with some aches and stiffness as your muscles adjust to their new activities. Are you willing to try?"

"Yes! Oh yes. Can we start today?"

Hannah laughed and embraced her friend. "Let's start with the fun stuff. Patterns and fabric. We can start the exercise tomorrow." She flopped her collection of swatches onto the counter and drew Cordelia over to the latest issues of *Harper's Bazar*, *The Delineator,* and *Peterson's Magazine* as well as the Butterick catalog she had brought with her from San Antonio.

An hour later, they were still huddled over the counter oohing and aahing at the fashion plates of elegant ball gowns and sophisticated day costumes neither of them were ever likely to wear, yet both women found great pleasure in admiring the designs.

At last, Cordelia released a sigh of regret and closed the last magazine. "I should probably go. I have to put supper on for J.T., and I've monopolized too much of your time."

"Nonsense," Hannah said. "I can't remember when I've spent a more enjoyable afternoon." She straightened the pile of books and put the fabric swatches back under the counter. "And I look forward to starting our new regimen tomorrow morning. We'll be able to talk more."

"As long as I can still breathe." Cordelia grinned. "J.T.'s told me how fast you walk out to the river."

A little thrill shot through Hannah at the thought that Jericho had noticed. Of course, she had no way to determine whether he found her athleticism appealing or not. Many men seemed to prefer their women soft and fully dependent on the man's greater strength. Would Jericho appreciate a strong woman, or was that just another mark against her?

"I guess I'll have to tell him about my plans to join you on your constitutionals during supper tonight," Cordelia said as she retrieved the basket that lay forgotten on the worktable. "He'll probably take that news better than when he learns I intend to order a new dress. That little discovery will probably send him over the edge."

Hannah frowned. "He would begrudge you a new dress even when you have your own income to cover the cost?" The man could certainly be a grouch at times, but he'd never struck her as harsh.

Cordelia waved off her concern. "No, not if I needed one. But this will be a purely frivolous purchase, the kind he believes leads to vanity. You have to understand . . . J.T. was only sixteen when our pa died, and he'd been running the farm on his own long before that. For years he scraped and saved just to put food on the table. Even now, when he has a successful business and a surplus of money in the bank, he'll only buy himself a new pair of boots when he's worn the soles clear off his old ones. Practicality has been burned into his nature by necessity. He can be incredibly generous to those in need, but he has little tolerance for frivolous spending by those who could be putting their money to better use."

A stone the size of a bread loaf sank into Hannah's stomach. No wonder the man was always so touchy around her. He saw dressmaking as a promotion of vanity and wasteful spending. She'd been foolish to think for even a minute that he might find her attractive.

She understood his point of view. Practicality was certainly a virtue, but so was beauty. The Lord himself wove it into the very fabric of his creation, making it visible to anyone with eyes to see. Why couldn't Jericho perceive the value in that? Just because he was right didn't mean she was wrong. Yes, a love of beautiful things could be taken too far, leading to greed and vanity, but so could practicality. She'd known plenty of embittered misers who sucked the joy out of the lives around them by harping about every little thing that failed to be useful.

Why, if Jericho Tucker were there right now, she'd tell him a thing or two about—

The door rattled. Pounding followed. "Delia? Are you in there?"

A dark shape pressed itself against the window glass trying to peer inside.

Hannah swallowed.

Jericho Tucker *was* there.

14

J.T. stepped back from the window unable to see much past the display. Where *was* that girl? Hawkins had come by the livery twenty minutes ago looking for her. Something about his bread order. The man said he'd already tried the house and she wasn't there. J.T. had promised to pass the message along, thinking it would be an easy task. Cordelia usually went only three places on her own: the mercantile, the telegraph office, or the drugstore, if she got a hankering for a peppermint stick. Since Hawkins was looking for her, that narrowed the options down to two.

Yet she hadn't been either place. Ike said she left his office at half past noon, and it was nearly two o'clock. J.T. had checked their home in case she'd returned, but he couldn't find any evidence that she'd been back since her noon outing. The stove had even grown cold. That's when he started to worry. Delia never let the stove go cold.

He'd been about ready to mount up and start searching along the road when Tom mentioned that he'd seen her go into Miss Richards's shop. But here he stood, and the door was locked, the shop closed. Were the two females together? Were they in trouble? His pulse sped from a trot to a canter.

"Delia!" He pounded the door again. Harder.

Finally, the latch clicked and the door swung open.

"Goodness, J.T. The whole town can hear you yelling," Delia scolded as she grabbed his arm and dragged him inside. "Do hush."

He glowered at her, his relief turning quickly to ire. "Where the devil have you been? I've been looking all over for you."

She gave him one of her looks that questioned his intelligence. "I was here, obviously."

"Doing what?" he snapped.

"Visiting with Hannah and . . ." She glanced away and fiddled with the buttons at her waist. "And ordering a new dress for the Founders' Day picnic next month."

Everything inside him went deathly still. "What?"

"You heard me. I'm ordering a dress. A pretty dress." Cordelia lifted her chin, then dropped it as if drawing an exclamation mark. "I know your feelings on the matter, and I don't mean to hurt you by my actions, but I'm a grown woman and have the right to decide how I spend my money. I've made more than enough with my baking this year to cover the cost."

An invisible vice tightened around his lungs, making it hard to breathe. This couldn't be happening. Not to Delia. She'd been young, but she knew what their mother had become, how her love for fine fashions and the trappings of wealth had surpassed her love for husband and children.

His gaze moved past the women as he sought control. Unfortunately, it landed on the counter, where fashion magazines and pattern books lay strewn. Memories cut free of their bonds and leapt for his throat. He pictured his mother pouring over *Peterson's Magazine* as if it were the only thing in the room, ignoring his questions as he struggled to make sense of his homework. And he could hear the scorn that spewed from her as she upbraided his father for choosing to spend the money he scratched out of the farm on luxury items like flour and coffee instead of the bonnet she craved or the length of lace she would die without.

He fought to break memory's hold, but when he turned back to Delia, for a moment the face he saw was his mother's.

"It's just one dress, J.T." Delia swept by him on the way to the door, but as she passed his side she leaned in to whisper a final argument. "I'm not her."

Before he could manage to respond, she left. He hadn't even given her Hawkins's message.

He couldn't seem to move as thoughts spun round and round his brain. It might only be one dress, but it was a beginning. One dress could lead to another and another and another, until nothing satisfied her any longer.

"What does she want with some fancy getup, anyhow?" he mumbled.

"What any woman wants," a quiet voice said behind him. "To feel pretty."

J.T. pivoted. Miss Richards stood by her counter, probably counting Delia's money in her mind. He jerked a toothpick out of his pocket and jabbed it into his mouth. Clenching it between his teeth, he glared at the dressmaker. He'd known she'd be trouble the first time he clapped eyes on her. Delia never would have gotten this idea in her head if Miss Richards hadn't come to town with all her ribbons and lace and independent ways.

"I'm not going to let you change her." J.T. took a menacing step toward her, his finger pointing at her chest in accusation. His nostrils flared like those of a bull fixing to charge, but instead of shrinking from him, she leapt forward to meet him in battle.

"What are you afraid of, Mr. Tucker? Afraid you'll lose your devoted housekeeper if Cordelia finally catches the eye of the gentleman she favors?"

What gentleman? Cordelia didn't have eyes for any fellow that he knew about. He opened his mouth to say so but never got the chance. The she-cat wasn't done hissing at him yet.

"Is that the real reason you dress her in drab colors and unflattering styles? Because you're too selfish to let her have a life of her own?"

The finger he pointed at her curled into his fist. He squeezed it tight, barely containing the urge to slam it into the nearest wall. "That shows how little you know," he gritted out through clenched teeth. "I would die for my sister."

Clearly too riled to be wary, Miss Richards advanced another step until she was so close to him, he could make out individual sparks glittering in her eyes. "That may be true," she said, biting off each word, "but would you trust her enough to make her own choices?"

The question hit him like an unexpected punch to the gut. For the last decade, he'd appointed himself Delia's protector and provider, making sure she had food to eat, clothes to wear, a place to sleep. He saw to it she finished her schooling even when he'd had to drop out to look for work. She was his responsibility, and he'd shouldered the load without complaint because they were family. All they had was each other. But now that she was out of pigtails, could his protection be smothering her?

J.T.'s frown deepened at the disturbing thought. *Did* he trust Cordelia to make her own decisions?

He shifted the toothpick to the other side of his mouth and narrowed his eyes at his opponent. He had no answer to give, so he opted for silence.

After a tense moment, she banked the fires in her eyes and softened her stance. "I apologize, Mr. Tucker. I may have been a bit overzealous in Cordelia's defense." She took a step back and reached for the counter as if she needed it for support. "I'm not trying to change your sister. She came here in tears this afternoon, begging for my help. That's all I'm trying to do. Help."

"And you think a new dress will solve all her problems." He spat the accusation at her.

"Of course not. Nor does Cordelia. But right now she feels invisible and unattractive. She despairs of ever securing the affections of the man she admires."

"What man?" J.T. shook his head. Why did she keep talking about this nonexistent man? "Cordelia has no beau."

"Not yet." Miss Richards smiled the smile of one holding a secret. "But we hope to change that situation soon."

Cordelia and a man? He'd strangle the guy.

"Did you think she would stay your little sister forever?" Her soft voice held more compassion than censure, but it grated on him nonetheless as he tried to deny what she was telling him. "Cordelia's a grown woman who loves her brother," she said. "But she also longs to step out of his shadow and live her own life. To marry a man who finds her beautiful."

J.T. gazed around him at the fancy dresses hanging on display, symbols of the hollow values he so despised. "Cordelia is already beautiful. She doesn't need your finery. Beauty doesn't come from outward adornment, Scripture says, but from a godly spirit."

"First Peter 3. I know it well. And I agree. However, if you will be honest with yourself, I think you'll realize that on a practical level, men rarely take the time to discover a woman's inner beauty if they are not first attracted to the outer person. How many times have you asked a pock-faced girl to join you on a buggy ride or invited an overly plump one on a picnic?"

J.T. rubbed the edge of his tongue back and forth across the end of his toothpick, the wood abrading his tongue almost as much as her question abraded his conscience. He'd taught himself to look past a handsome woman's face to determine the depth of her character, but he'd never thought much about doing the same for an uncomely gal. And to his shame, he doubted even now he'd be much inclined to try.

Was that what was happening to Delia?

He suddenly wanted to round up all the single men in Coventry and pound some sense into them.

J.T. pulled the toothpick from his mouth and snapped it in two with his thumb, wishing he could do more to expend the frustration roiling around inside him. He shoved the pieces into his vest pocket and glanced up to meet the eyes of the woman who was watching his every move. Upset as he was, he was still drawn to her. Which only heightened his agitation.

"You say you know the Scriptures," he said, "and yet your choice of occupation flies in the face of all they stand for. Clothes are meant to protect the body from the elements and preserve a woman's modesty, not to entice men or put on airs." He flung his arms wide and gestured to the dresses draped so decadently around the room, making no effort to filter the scorn from his voice. "All these items are designed specifically to draw attention to the wearer, to stroke her pride, and to elevate her above others. You may see a room full of harmless fashions, but if you open your eyes, you'll find that, in truth, it is filled with the temptation to indulge in sinful vanity."

Miss Richards pushed away from the counter and planted her hands on her hips, her arms shaking with the force of her affront. "You think *my* eyes are closed? I've never heard such narrow-minded drivel in all my born days."

Her arms fell to her sides, and she marched forward until she stood toe-to-toe with him. J.T. raised an eyebrow but held his ground. If the she-cat wanted to sharpen her claws on him, she was welcome to try. He wasn't backing down. She could hiss and scratch all she wanted. He was on the side of right, and he wasn't budging.

"I'll have you know, there's not a single immodest gown to be found in my collection, nor would I ever consent to sew one. If you would climb down off that high horse of yours for a minute, Mr. Liveryman, you'd see that the only difference between my dresses and the ones you favor from the mercantile is that mine are actually made well, custom-fit to each client.

"There is nothing wrong with bright colors and beautiful lines. If God had wanted the world to be a somber, colorless place, he would have made everything in black and gray. But he didn't. He filled his creation with color and beauty. Why do you think he instructed Moses to call all the skilled artisans to adorn his tabernacle with items of gold, bronze, and silver and with weavings done in blue, purple, and scarlet? Because our Lord appreciates beauty and chose to surround himself with it. I am an artisan, Mr. Tucker, the same as those skilled workmen in the days of Moses. God has given me a talent, and as his Son taught, it would be sinful of me to bury this talent and refuse to utilize it. So I use my gift to bring loveliness into the world."

She waltzed over to the rack that held several gowns and lifted a rosy pink one off its hook. Holding it up to her, she balanced the sleeves upon her arms and caressed the fabric with her fingers. "When a woman puts on one of my dresses and feels better about herself," she said, a faraway look in her eyes, "or smiles in pure enjoyment of the colors and style I've brought together, that's when I know I've created something beautiful, something the Lord could be proud of."

Miss Richards looked at him, and under his unrelenting stare the idealism faded from her eyes. Good. Maybe a dose of reality would wake her up to the truth.

Turning her back to him, she replaced the dress on the rack. "If a pretty dress can bring a woman pleasure, where's the harm in that?"

She really had no idea, did she?

"The harm, Miss Richards, comes when a woman relies on the temporary happiness that a new dress or hat or piece of jewelry can bring her instead of trusting the deeper, abiding joy that can be found in faith and family." J.T. stepped toward her, his slow, deliberate footfalls echoing in the still room.

Hannah Richards stood firm, her chin lifting with every step he took. "You have a poor opinion of women, indeed, sir, if you think we cannot tell the difference between the two."

"My mother couldn't." The words slipped out before he could call them back.

"Excuse me?"

A flood of anger, resentment, and pain rose up in him so quickly he couldn't contain it. "My mother craved the *harmless* pleasure of fashionable dresses, new bonnets, and pretty baubles to such a degree that she abandoned her husband and children in favor of playing mistress to a wealthy railroad surveyor. Delia was only four. Four! Just a baby. And our mother left her with a broken-down man and an eleven-year-old, wet-behind-the-ears kid who didn't know the first thing about taking care of a little girl."

Miss Richards's eyes widened, and the frown lines across her forehead eased, but he didn't want her pity. He wanted her to understand the truth about what her shop represented.

"You might think there's nothing wrong with offering the women of Coventry a taste of fashion and beauty, and for a select few of our citizens, you would probably be right. However, for the majority, what you offer is not beauty but temptation. They will lust after things they cannot afford. They will envy those who can. And they will grow discontent with their current circumstances."

She opened her mouth—to argue with him, no doubt, but he was in no mood to listen any longer. He shook his head and pinned her with a stare that she must have understood, for she clamped her lips tightly together.

"I know that most women would never abandon their families like my mother did, but discontent and selfishness can spread their poison, too, doing just as much damage. The Lord might see value in beauty, but he cares more about a person's heart than the beautiful shell that houses it.

"You asked me to be honest with myself, and now I ask the same of you. Of all the clients you have sewn for in the past, how many do you think derived pleasure simply from the style and color of your design, compared to how many used the beauty of that design to feed their vanity?"

Uncertainty played across her features, and her previously steady gaze wavered. He reached for another toothpick and slipped it into his mouth as he turned away and headed for the door. "Maybe not Delia, but many of the women who walk into your shop will not be strong enough to withstand the temptation you offer. Do you really want to be responsible for putting a stumbling block in their path?"

His fingers closed around the knob, and he glanced back one final time. Stricken eyes in a pale face filled his vision and twisted his gut. J.T. yanked the door open and stomped outside. As the door slammed behind him, he tried to convince himself that hurting her had been necessary, that she would grow from the experience and come to a fuller knowledge of the truth. But as he walked into the livery, her wounded expression haunted him.

Ignoring Tom's chatter, he saddled his best gelding and mounted up without a word. Once beyond the boundaries of town, he urged his horse into a gallop, pushing himself and his animal to the limit. Yet he couldn't outrun the memory of her face or the regret that gnawed on his insides more fiercely than a starving man's hunger.

15

Glad her *Closed* sign was already in place, Hannah tidied up her sewing cabinet and fastened her bonnet strings with numb fingers. She exited the shop, locking it behind her, and climbed the steps to her room, no longer concerned about the loss of potential customers.

Once upstairs, she tore off her bonnet and crumpled onto the makeshift bench by the window. She had left her Bible on the seat that morning after her devotions, and it beckoned to her like a lighthouse signaling a ship lost in the storm. And, oh, how she needed guidance. She picked up the leather-bound book and clasped it to her chest, praying for the Lord to anchor her once again.

"Do you really want to be responsible for putting a stumbling block in their path?" Jericho's parting words crashed against her heart and bruised her spirit.

Was that what she was doing?

She couldn't deny that the majority of the wealthy clients she had sewn for in San Antonio had a selfish bent. Some saw fashion as a way to set themselves apart from the lower rungs of society. Others used it as a means to impress. Most pouted and complained through the fittings, finding fault with everything save themselves.

Yet there were exceptions, too. Women like Victoria Ashmont, who utilized color and style to express her personality while moving in the elite circles necessary to conduct her business. And the awkward young society daughters, fearful of embarrassing their families, whose gasps of genuine delight and relief at the sight of their reflection were anything but vanity.

"Lord, I'm so confused."

For so many years she'd thought she was honoring God by developing the talent he had given her and putting it to use by creating things of beauty. Had she deceived herself? Was she truly a stumbling block?

Searching more for comfort than answers, Hannah bent back the cover of her Bible and flipped to the book of Acts. She needed to reread the stories of her mentors, women of the cloth, like her, who served the Lord faithfully.

She read of Dorcas, a woman well loved by her community because of her ministry to widows, a ministry of sewing coats and other garments. Perhaps God wanted her to be more like this faithful disciple, sewing for the poor and needy instead of those who could pay for her services. Her needlework would truly be a ministry then, not a catalyst for pretentiousness.

But how could she afford to do so? She would run through her savings before winter and then be left unable to provide for anyone, including herself.

Hannah pushed a few more pages aside, the thin paper crinkling in the quiet room. Her finger ran down the length of one column until she came to the passage she sought.

Lydia. What of her example? She was a businesswoman, a merchant, and yet faithful to God's call. She sold purple cloth, the finest, most costly fabric of her time. Her customers had to have been affluent, the social and political elite of Philippi. Yet no one condemned her for selling her finery. In fact, her success in business allowed her to have a home large enough to provide a place for the new Philippian church to meet. And surely funds from her sales made up a substantial portion of the contribution that church later sent to Paul to aid his missionary journeys.

Justification poured over her like a salve on her wounded heart. She'd been right all along. Her dress shop offered a service to the people of Coventry, not temptation and iniquity. Jericho Tucker was simply a bitter man who let the pain of his childhood color his judgment.

So why did that gentle tug on her soul keep nagging her? And why could she not forget the anguish hiding behind the anger in Jericho's face?

Hannah knew the grief of losing a parent, but she couldn't imagine how much worse it must have been for Jericho, having his mother leave of her own accord instead of falling prey to illness, as had been the case with Hannah's father. What else could he conclude but that a closet full of pretty clothes and a handful of trinkets meant more to his mother than her own flesh and blood? No wonder he despised fine clothes.

But was he wrong? She shifted in her seat to press her back more firmly against the wall from whence she had slipped. It would be easy to wrap herself in indignation and toss out his arguments, yet there had been too much truth in them to be discarded.

Balance. She needed balance. Perhaps the Lord wanted her to be both Dorcas and Lydia. Like Lydia, she could run a successful business while at the same time reaching out to the poor and needy as Dorcas did. And now that she was more conscious of the genuine threat of becoming a stumbling block to some, maybe she could make an effort to encourage godly values in her customers. She had no idea how to accomplish that, but she'd pray for wisdom. Of course, she'd need to actually have customers before she could exert any influence. That was in the Lord's hands, too.

Father, I have no desire to be a stumbling block to any of your children. Teach me how to conduct my business in a way that honors you. And if . . .

A physical pang stabbed through her stomach. Hannah squeezed her eyes tight and curled her body down over the still-open Bible in her lap. She didn't want to pray the next words. Her mind resisted where her soul led. However, she knew submission was the only road to faithfulness. With the edge of her Bible digging into her middle, she forced her mind to shape the words that could kill her dream.

If I will do more harm than good by having a shop here, then keep all the customers away and let me fail. But if you can use me—

A thump against her door caused Hannah to jerk upright and suck in a startled breath. It came again, sounding more like a shoe banging upon the wood than a set of knuckles.

"Miss Richards? It's Danny. I brung your wood."

Hannah jumped to her feet and ran a hand over her hair as she hurried to the door. "Hello, Danny. How did you know I was home?"

Arms full of split logs, Danny sauntered in and dropped them into the box by the stove. "Ma saw you come up the stairs while she was bringin' in the wash from the lines. Said to ask if you would come down a minute so's she could ask you something." He dusted off the front of his shirt and then his hands. "If you weren't feelin' poorly or nothin', that is."

"No . . . I-I'm fine. I'd be happy to visit with your mother."

"Great! I'll tell her you're comin'." Danny dodged around her and bounded down the stairs. The echo of his clunky steps worked to pull Hannah out of her haze. She blinked several times, then followed at a more sedate pace.

Mrs. James met her on the back porch, a large basket of sun-bleached petticoats beneath her arm. She passed the basket on to Danny, who nearly disappeared behind the massive mound. "Take these in to Tessa, and add some wood to the stove. Those sadirons need to be plenty hot by the time I get in there."

"Yes'm." Danny wavered under the weight and ungainliness of the basket but made it inside without mishap.

An image of an eleven-year-old Jericho rose in Hannah's mind, unbidden. Only a year older than Danny, would he have been the one to tend to the laundry and cooking after his mother left? She could almost see the determination carved into his young face as he strove to conquer each task. Those determined lines were still evident in his manly profile, likely having been permanently etched into his being.

"Thanks for coming down." Louisa James's voice cut into her thoughts.

Hannah turned toward the hardworking woman and mustered a smile. "Of course."

"I . . . ah . . . never thanked you proper for the dolls you made my girls. They tote them things around everywhere."

Hannah's heart warmed at learning that something she made had brought the girls pleasure. No stumbling block in that. "I'm so glad they are enjoying them. It's been too long since I put my needle to something besides clothing. It was a fun change."

"Well, I also needed to thank you for helping Tessa." Louisa met Hannah's eye. "She told me about the button."

"Oh, yes. She and I had quite a time of it, searching for the perfect match. Did the owner make any complaint?"

"Nope, and that was a first for him." Louisa's mouth tipped up at one corner, bringing a flash of youth back into her haggard features for a moment.

"I was glad to be of help," Hannah assured her. "Tessa is a lovely girl and is a good hand with a needle."

The tiny smile on Louisa's face melted away. She rubbed a spot of perspiration off her temple with the back of her chapped hand and shifted her gaze to the ground.

"That's what I wanted to talk to you about. Tessa told me how you offered to teach her to sew more than buttons." Louisa leaned against a support post and shuffled her foot back and forth several times before she finally glanced back up at Hannah. "I told her you probably said that just to be polite, that you were too busy to be handin' out lessons to little girls. But she keeps pesterin' me about it. Goes on and on about how you meant it and begging me to let her go over there some afternoon."

Hannah heard the question behind Louisa's words and took pity on the proud woman who couldn't quite manage to ask it. "The offer was sincere, Louisa. I would be happy to instruct Tessa when you can spare her."

The other woman's chin began to wobble, but she clamped her jaw shut and stifled the emotional display. "I don't want my girls to end up like me," she said in a hushed voice. "They need a skill so's they can make their own way in this world if their men up and die on them. I done what I had to, and I see no shame in hard work, but they deserve better than raw hands . . . and backs that never stop aching."

Something tingled at the corner of Hannah's eye. She blinked it away as Louisa drew in a shaky breath.

"I can't afford to pay much for the lessons," she said, "but I could do your washin' and Tessa could clean up around your shop. She's good with a broom."

Hannah didn't have the heart to tell her that there was nothing to clean. With no customers to wait on, it took very little effort to keep the place spotless. However, it did give her an idea. One that had less to do with disguising charity and more to do with keeping the doors of her shop open.

"Louisa, there's something I need more than laundering, and I'd be glad to trade sewing lessons for it."

Wary hope flickered in the woman's eyes. "What is it?"

Hannah smiled. "Advertising."

"Advertising?" Louisa huffed out a breath and gestured around her as if Hannah were a simpleton who could not see the obvious. "I'm stuck here from sunup to sundown. I scarcely find time to run to the mercantile when our foodstuffs run low. I can't traipse around town—"

"I don't expect you to," Hannah said. "Cordelia Tucker and I have already gone around town with the bread cloths you suggested, and I've had a few visitors to the shop since then, but I need some way to catch their interest when they have a need. I hadn't thought of it until just this moment, but perhaps I should stop emphasizing my larger services and focus instead on the mending and alterations I can do. Ease people in, like you were talking about."

Louisa's eyes narrowed. "How do you expect me to help with that?"

Hannah grinned, a new enthusiasm building within her. "If you find a tear or worn area in an item that you wash, mention to your customer that the dressmaker next door can mend it for a fair price. Stressed seams or skirt hems that are excessively dirty might mean an alteration would be welcome. I also remake old dresses into more current styles for those ladies who are interested in updating their wardrobe without having to purchase new items."

Hannah stepped close to Louisa and laid her hand on her neighbor's arm. "To be frank," she murmured in a low tone, "I can use all the patrons you can send me. I have yet to make a cash sale."

Louisa patted Hannah's hand and nodded. "I had wondered how you were faring. I'll do what I can to help."

"Thank you." Hannah squeezed Louisa's arm before stepping back, gratitude bringing that moist tingle back to her eye.

It must be true that God knew what his children needed before they asked, for she had barely begun to pray when he interrupted her with an answer. Far from closing down her shop, he had provided her with an opportunity to be both a Dorcas and a Lydia through one simple conversation, and blessed her with a deeper relationship with her neighbor in the process.

Hannah returned home, her stomach calm and her step light. As she reached the landing at the top of the stairs, though, she cast a glance across the road to the livery. A reminder that the path before her still held obstacles.

If the Lord would just work on convincing Jericho Tucker that she wasn't a false prophet sent to lure the fashion-minded women of Coventry down a lacy path to perdition, all would be well.

16

Standing in one of the livery's box stalls, J.T. ran a hand down the right front hock and fetlock of his favorite gray gelding. It'd been two weeks since he'd ridden the animal away from town like an outlaw on the run. Two weeks since he'd spoken to Miss Richards.

Not only had he injured a gal's feelings that day, he'd injured his horse. Eager to gallop, the gray had responded to J.T.'s urgency with energetic strides, but he'd pushed too far. The hard ride over the hilly countryside took its toll. By the following morning, the animal favored his right front leg, and a warm, swollen area emerged above the fetlock. J.T.'s guilt doubled. Unintentionally hurting a woman's feelings was bad enough. At least he could take comfort in the fact that he'd been trying to open her eyes to the truth. But his horse? He'd punished his mount with a heedless, bone-jarring run that left the animal nearly lame. Horses were his livelihood, for pity's sake. He knew better.

His treatment of cold compresses and bandages had restored the gelding's soundness, though. J.T. found no evidence of swelling this morning, only smooth bone and cool skin beneath the gray coat. He turned the gelding out into the corral and lifted his chin to the sky. A cold mist spat in his face. Fitting.

He might've been able to fix things with his horse, but mending things with Miss Richards was a different matter entirely. He wasn't even sure he should. After all, what could he do? He had no intention of taking back anything he'd said; he only regretted that she'd been hurt by it.

Not knowing how to proceed, he'd opted for the easy way around the predicament. He was avoiding her.

At first, he'd harbored hope that their confrontation would discourage her from working with Delia. But it didn't. He'd barely had time to duck behind the chicken coop the next morning when Miss Richards arrived to collect his sister for their walk. Every morning since, he'd made a point to get out of bed thirty minutes early to ensure he was safely inside the livery walls before she emerged from her place across the street.

Not that he didn't still keep tabs on her. He had Delia to consider, after all. And it was amazingly easy to stay abreast of Miss Richards's activities, thanks to Danny. According to the kid, she'd started giving Tessa sewing lessons. At first, J.T. hadn't been too thrilled about the arrangement. The last thing Coventry needed was another fancy seamstress. But then he figured the girl needed to learn how to sew if she planned to take care of a family of her own one day, and as much as he hated to admit it, Miss Richards knew a thing or two about pushing a needle through cloth. If Louisa didn't have the time or energy to train the child, Miss Richards was a logical second choice.

So now, whenever Danny showed up to muck stalls, J.T. engaged him in conversation. He'd learned all kinds of fascinating tidbits. For instance, the mystery beverage that Miss Richards drank every morning with Ezra Culpepper was cocoa. She apparently had a strong hankering for the stuff. Then there was the small matter of her still not having chairs. She did have her new sign, though, and to hear Danny tell the tale, she'd climbed out her upstairs window to hold the thing steady while the blacksmith nailed it to the support boards on her roof. Fool, stubborn woman. Didn't she know prancing around on a roof two stories above the ground was a good way to break her pretty neck? Though he didn't want her to operate her business in this town, he didn't want her dying here, either.

Between his own observations and what he could glean from both Danny and Delia, J.T. was as confused as ever about Hannah Richards. The woman designed gowns for a wealthy clientele while at the same time taking a poor laundress's daughter under her wing. She even found a way to get around Louisa's pride. Two days ago at church, Tessa and Mollie showed up in new dresses cleverly pieced together from smaller scraps of material, like a patchwork quilt. Tessa bragged to everyone who would listen that she had made them herself, which explained why Louisa didn't consider them charity. Tessa's tiny foot might have pumped the pedal, but J.T. had no doubt whose expert hands had guided the fabric through the machine.

J.T. stamped his feet to knock the mud off his boots before trudging through the wagon shed to his office. Judging by her profession, Miss Richards should be a vain, shallow creature, and therefore easy for him to dismiss. Unfortunately, all evidence indicated she was kind, hardworking, and compassionate. He didn't know what to do with that. Especially since she obviously intended to keep her shop open. A woman of true spiritual integrity would never knowingly offer temptation to others. So what did that make her? Sinner or saint?

A shadow bounced across his desk. "Mornin', J.T."

Tom flapped his arm in a greeting much too energetic for this early in the morning. And his lopsided grin only made J.T. grit his teeth.

"I saw Miss Richards and Cordelia playing with some more of those funny toys when I passed your place. You think she'd let me try them things if I asked 'er?"

J.T. ran a hand over his face, weary of the battle raging inside him. "I don't know, Tom. I don't really talk to Miss Richards much these days."

"Why's that? She's nice."

Biting back a groan, J.T. got up and clapped Tom on the shoulder as he wedged past him, needing to escape the kid's black-and-white simplicity. Things were either fun or work. People were either nice or mean. No need to look deeper, to bust a blood vessel trying to guess motives or predict spiritual repercussions.

A quizzical frown stretched Tom's mouth back at one corner as he turned to follow J.T. "I thought we was supposed to be lookin' out for her since she don't have no menfolk. Ain't that kinda hard to do if ya don't talk to her?"

J.T. pulled his hat down over his eyes as he made his way to the livery door, wishing he could shut out the kid's words as easily. "Miss Richards seems to manage just fine without us. She's a capable woman." And beautiful, and fiery, and good-hearted—and a dressmaker. Why did she have to be a dressmaker? J.T. shoved a toothpick between his teeth and bit down until his jaw ached.

"Don't worry about her, kid. I'm keeping an eye on her even if I'm not jawin' with her constantly. She's getting along all right."

But was she? All he really knew was that she showed up for work every day. Work and her morning walks with Delia. And what exactly were those *toys* Tom was talking about? Maybe it was time to stop avoiding the contradictory Miss Richards. After all, the only way to understand something was to study it, and he aimed to figure this woman out.

"The stock is out in the corral," he called to Tom as he strode toward the street. "Start mucking the stalls. I'll be back in a bit." He rounded the corner toward home, determination fueling his steps.

J.T. found the dressmaker with his sister under the large oak tree behind his house. The morning mist had dampened the women's hair flat to their heads, but neither seemed to mind. Their cheeks, rosy from their exertions in the cool air, lent them a healthy glow, and he grudgingly admitted that he hadn't seen Delia look so exuberant since her days of playing tag around the schoolhouse.

"You're doing great, Cordelia. Keep going. Ten more. You can do it."

Something akin to elongated wooden pears hung from Miss Richards's hands. She swung the clubs in a giant *L* shape. The right arm rose straight in the air above her head and the left pitched out to the side at a perpendicular angle. Then the positions reversed. She alternated arms back and forth as she counted off the repetitions. Miss Richards held her arms stiff and strong. Delia's bent a bit at the elbows and didn't quite reach the same height. Her breaths came in heavy puffs as she followed Miss Richards's example, but she didn't quit, and even though she looked ridiculous, J.T. couldn't help but be proud of her tenacity.

"Good. Now lower the clubs to your sides and do the lower pendulums."

Delia moaned. "My arms are burning."

Miss Richards would not be deterred. "That's good. Your muscles are working. We'll do ten of these and then take a break."

"All right."

This time instead of making the *L* above their heads, they formed it in front. The right arm lifted sideways at the shoulder while the left poked straight out in front. Then the alternations began again. They looked like a pair of trainmen flagging down a locomotive.

". . . seven . . . eight . . . nine . . . ten. You did it!" Miss Richards exclaimed. "Go ahead and rest for a minute and then bring the rings over. We'll finish up with those today."

Delia dragged herself up onto the back porch and collapsed into the rocker that sat under the eaves. Her arms draped over the sides, dangling toward the floor. J.T. bit back a grin. The girl was exhausted. Miss Richards, on the other hand, looked as fresh as a yearling colt, antsy and ready to go. While Delia rested, she continued on with a more complicated routine. Lunging with her legs, she twirled the clubs in large, full-bodied circles. The graceful arcs accentuated her flexibility and athleticism, holding J.T.'s gaze captive. Her plain blue dress, dampened by the moist air, clung to her form as she stretched. J.T. tried to swallow, but his mouth had gone dry.

Tearing his attention away from her shape, he focused instead on the silly clubs she was flinging around. He cleared his throat and stepped out of the shade of the house.

"Are you going to start juggling those things next?" Frustrated by his physical reaction to the woman who caused him no end of mental angst, his voice came out with more derision than he'd intended. The little lady jumped and emitted a quiet squeak, much like she had the day she'd fallen through the rotted staircase and into his arms.

That was not a memory he needed at the moment.

He was having a hard enough time clearing his mind of inappropriate thoughts without remembering how good she'd felt bundled up against his chest.

"Goodness, J.T. You scared me half to death sneaking up on us like that," Delia said from her now fully upright position in the rocker. "What are you doing here? You never come home before noon."

"I decided to see for myself what kind of secret activities the two of you engage in every morning." J.T. spared a brief glance for his sister before striding toward the tree and the bristling woman beneath its branches. "Had I known you were entertaining the notion of joining a circus act, Miss Richards, I would have offered to wire P.T. Barnum on your behalf."

"Circus act?" Her lips thinned into a straight line, and she waved the wooden clubs at him.

J.T. halted a few steps away. Perhaps he shouldn't have provoked her while she was still gripping the clubs. They looked less like juggling toys and more like weapons the closer he came.

"I'll have you know, all the implements I use are scientifically researched and proven effective for improving flexibility and strength. Dr. Dio Lewis and Simon Kehoe both published books extolling the benefits of proper and repeated use of the Indian club. In fact, in Mr. Kehoe's volume, he included sketches of several gentlemen who work daily with such clubs. I can tell you their muscular physique would outmatch any man."

The annoying woman made a point to glance at his chest and then roll her eyes away, as if she found him lacking. *Him*. No dandy from New York who passed time swinging some feeble little clubs in a gymnasium somewhere could compete with a man who worked hard for a living. Not on any day of the week. He'd like to see one of those fellows fork hay into a loft for an hour or plow a field of tough Texas soil under the hot sun from dawn till dusk.

And just what was she doing gawking at pictures of men's physiques, anyhow? J.T. shrugged his shoulders and flexed his muscles under his coat.

"You really shouldn't criticize something you know so little about . . . Jericho."

He blinked and narrowed his gaze. No one had dared call him by that name in years. Not since his mother had left. His pa's belt had kept him from back-talking when his mama insisted on using the name despite his protests, and he'd even borne up under his teacher using it. But not one of his peers dared go against his wishes. He'd pummeled the last fellow who'd tried—a twelve-year-old kid who didn't think a nine-year-old could thrash him. The smart aleck hadn't reckoned on how much J.T. hated the name. What boy wanted to be named after a city that crumbled when a bunch of nomads walked around it? Not exactly an image of strength or fortitude.

Besides, *she* liked it. If Mama could abandon him, he could sure as shooting abandon the name she tried to saddle him with.

J.T. silently worked his jaw back and forth. There was only one person who would've dared tell this woman his given name, and she was stifling giggles on the porch behind him. Choosing to ignore his sister for now, J.T. faced the impudent woman whose eyes issued challenges his pride could not ignore.

He prowled forward, jaw clenched so hard his facial muscles ticked. "The name's J.T."

"No," she said, tapping her chin as if pondering some great mystery. "Those are initials. Your *name* is Jericho."

Wiggling his fingers to keep them from curling into fists, J.T. reminded himself that she was a woman. He couldn't deal with her the same way he had the boy in the schoolyard.

"Are you purposely trying to rile me?" His voice rumbled with menace, warning her against such a dangerous path.

An all-too-innocent smile stretched across her face. "Why, yes. Yes, I am. Is it working?"

17

Hannah struggled to keep her expression bland. The incredulous look on Jericho's face nearly made her laugh out loud. He stood stock-still . . . and blinked five times. She counted.

Then his lips twitched. A smile? Surely not. He quickly covered the bottom half of his face with his hand, ostensibly to rub his jaw, but Hannah believed he was hiding something. Perhaps she had finally managed to make a crack in that wall of stoic arrogance he used as a shield. She could hope.

"Care to try them for yourself?" Hannah held out her clubs to him. "Give me thirty minutes, and I bet I can change your opinion of their worth."

"You're on." He rolled up the sleeves of his shirt past his elbows, exposing muscular forearms, and then took the clubs from her. Arms wide, he reached back in a stretch that drew his shirt tight across his chest.

The men pictured in Mr. Kehoe's book suddenly seemed less impressive.

Jericho continued to stretch and Hannah continued to watch until she happened to meet his eye. The look on his face clearly said he'd noticed her noticing. She jerked her attention away and bent to retrieve Cordelia's clubs.

"Usually men use longer and slightly heavier Indian clubs," she said, trying to cover her embarrassment by beginning her instruction, "but you'll have to make do with mine. I'll demonstrate with these."

Hannah showed him the proper way to grip the handles and summarized the different positions. "Now, in order to make this a fair trial, you must put true effort into the exercises. Keep your arms straight, and make your movements fast and strong."

"I'll give you a fair test . . . Hannah."

An absurd thrill shot through her at the sound of her given name on his lips. The mockery in his tone only hurt a little. But she'd brought that on herself. What she had to do now was prove him wrong. And who knew—maybe if he realized he could be wrong about the value of exercise equipment, he might be willing to consider that his view on her profession could benefit from a slight adjustment. Why not wish for the whole pie instead of only a slice?

"All right, Jericho, follow my lead."

He scowled at her use of his name, which only made her want to use it as often as possible. She was done tiptoeing around him. He never smiled anyway, at least not at her, so pandering to his ego would serve no purpose. Perhaps he was one of those misguided creatures who actually preferred vinegar to honey. Well, let someone else try to sweeten him up. She'd take a different tack. Jericho Tucker stood in the way of her finding full acceptance in this community, and she planned to fight her way past him. Starting now.

Hannah swung her clubs into first position, skipping the beginner exercises she'd been using with Cordelia. Jericho needed a more exacting routine. He would expect it to be easy, and it would probably seem so at first, but she planned to double the number of repetitions and increase the level of difficulty without giving him the breaks she allowed Cordelia. It didn't matter that she'd already completed most of her own routine before he arrived. She'd outlast him. Her muscles were used to the movements; his weren't. The determined set of his jaw assured her he'd not quit, but if she could get him to sweat, even a little, that would be victory enough.

After completing all the perpendicular sets, Hannah moved on to arm presses and lunging circles. Jericho stayed right with her. The scoundrel wasn't even breathing hard.

Her arms began to tremble slightly. She locked her elbows into place to hide the tremors and pushed harder, unwilling to let him best her.

"This next move is complicated," Hannah told him, careful to regulate her exhalations so as not to huff at all. "Think you can handle it?"

"I can handle anything you want to throw at me, sweetheart." He cocked a brow at her.

Hannah cocked one right back. He'd not fluster her with his swagger and mock endearments.

"You'll like this one, Jericho," she said. "It's named the Moulinet, or broadsword exercise. Very manly."

"Stop calling me that."

Hannah couldn't hide her grin this time. "What . . . manly?"

His scowl darkened.

"Oh, you mean Jericho." She shook her head. "No, I don't think so. I like it too much. Jericho—a city so sure of itself and its strength that it couldn't acknowledge the possibility that someone else might succeed with methods that appeared foolish and wrong in its eyes. Fits you rather well."

Before he could comment, she began the next movement. It required concentration and a loose wrist to twirl the clubs before tucking in the elbows and circling the arms around in a large arc. Jericho seemed to have a little more difficulty mastering the precision of this one, and Hannah inwardly gloated.

"It's been thirty minutes," Cordelia called out from her vantage point on the back porch. "Why don't you work the rings with him before the two of you quit?"

Hannah winced. She'd been so caught up in proving her point to Jericho, she'd completely forgotten about Cordelia. Her friend didn't seem to mind, though. She leaned forward in her chair, as if she had a front-row seat at an outdoor theatrical.

"Your brother only agreed to thirty minutes," Hannah called back as she brought her spinning clubs to rest. "I wouldn't want to tire him so much that he can't perform his duties at the livery today."

"No chance of that," Jericho grumbled.

Hannah wasn't sure that working the rings with him was a good idea. The apparatus required that two people grip them at the same time, often bringing the exercisers into close proximity. Being near this man tended to have an addling effect on her brain, and she needed all her wits about her to battle him successfully.

"I won't ask you to do the rings," she said, dropping her clubs into the box of equipment at the base of the tree. "You've sacrificed enough time already. I'm sure you'll agree, though, that these instruments are not mere toys."

He came up behind her, reached over her shoulder, and dropped his own clubs in the box. Was that faint musky odor . . . perspiration? Triumph welled in her. Then his arm brushed against hers. Triumph fled, replaced by a wobbly-kneed feeling that rattled her nerves. She stiffened and demanded that her body cease its traitorous behavior, but her pulse ignored her and continued with its giddy little dance.

"I haven't made up my mind yet about your methods," he said, still standing much too close. "I better try these ring things, too. I should make sure they're safe for Delia."

"Of course they're safe," she snapped. "Children use them." She tried to move away, but his piercing eyes kept her feet planted.

"Afraid your contraption will prove ineffective?"

"No." What she feared was that Jericho's nearness would render *her* ineffective. But she'd never been one to back down from a challenge, so she hobbled her high-stepping pulse and looked Jericho square in the eye. "Very well, I'll show you the rings."

He nodded and stepped back, finally allowing her to draw a full breath.

She crouched down by the box and dug out the two cherrywood rings that always found their way to the bottom. Holding one in each hand, she straightened and faced the large man in front of her.

"Those are the rings?" he scoffed. "They can't be more than six inches across. What are you supposed to do with them? Play horseshoes?"

Hannah speared him with a look. "I prefer braining pompous livery owners with them. Should I show you the technique?"

He raised his hands in surrender and mumbled a halfhearted apology. Though his lips didn't twitch this time, the skin around his eyes crinkled. If she could just get the two actions together, she might have the makings of a genuine Jericho Tucker smile. Discarding that thought as too distracting, she focused on the fundamentals of her lesson and thrust her arms out toward him.

"Grab hold of the rings."

The moment he complied, an unwelcome heat surged through her. His broad hands encompassed such a large portion of each ring.

"These were designed to be used by two people of similar height and strength for maximum efficiency." She tilted her chin up to look him in the face. "Since you are taller and stronger than I am, the exercise will not be as beneficial to you, but I think I can present enough of a challenge to give you an idea of how it works."

"We'll see."

Hannah's ire sparked. Hesitation fell away as the spirit of competition took over.

"Match my strength and keep up if you can . . . Jericho."

They began with a series of push-and-pull exercises that mimicked the motion of a piston pumping back and forth. Their left feet stood together in the center while their right legs supported them from behind. At first, he offered her little resistance as she dragged his arm forward and back, but he soon adjusted, and her muscles strained to keep up.

Next, they stood back-to-back and did opposing side lunges with their still-connected arms overhead. Her skirts swished against his legs several times. He gave no indication that he'd noticed, so she affected the same undisturbed mien.

"You should be able to feel a stretch along the outside of your arm," she said. "These routines are excellent for improving flexibility."

Jericho grunted in answer.

They did the same position again, only this time they faced each other. Hannah made certain to lean back as they lunged to avoid coming into contact with Jericho's chest. However, the effects of her extended workout combined with the fact that she was within a hairsbreadth of touching the man whose nearness invited her pulse to polka left her struggling for air.

Which had to be the reason she progressed to the next section of the ring routine without first considering the consequences.

Their right feet together, she and Jericho faced each other and leaned backward as far as possible, using one another's weight as a counterbalance. Then, she explained, on the second count, they would press their arms forcefully outward, bringing their heads and shoulders together. Like a good student, Jericho followed her instructions not to bend his elbows. Unfortunately, she failed to take into account his much longer arms. As he pulled wide, she was helpless to stop her forward momentum and thumped directly into his chest. His well-braced leg kept them from tumbling onto the ground, but nothing could keep them from pressing so closely together that she could feel his heart beating against hers. For an endless moment, he stared down at her, surprise and something much warmer flaring in his eyes. Then common sense prevailed. He released the rings, held her about the waist, and set her on her feet.

"I think I've got the general idea now." Jericho cleared his throat and backed away until he reached the back fence. "I'm heading to the livery, Delia," he called to his sister, never once glancing back at Hannah. "I'll see you at lunch."

Then he left, his long-legged stride eating up the turf at a near run.

Hannah leaned into the tree for support as she watched him go, a sinking feeling settling into the pit of her stomach. She had no idea if she'd proved anything to Jericho with her exercises, but she'd proven something to herself. Something disastrous. She was falling in love with a man who could never return her affections.

18

J.T. took the shortcut home for lunch, through the corral and across the strip of land behind his house. As he passed the big oak, he kneaded his upper arm. He hated to admit it, but flinging around those silly clubs had made him a bit sore.

And the rings? He should have taken Hannah up on her offer to forgo the blasted things. She'd been so close to him, he could smell the mist in her hair, see the sky in her eyes. And when she moved, her skirt brushed against his legs like sandpaper scoring a match.

Until she fell and accidentally ignited the flame. It had taken a wagonload of self-control to set her away from him.

He'd spent the bulk of the morning recounting the reasons she was unsuitable for him and asking God for strength to resist her wiles. Only, deep down, he knew they weren't wiles. Hannah Richards might try to foist her fashionable wares on the people of Coventry, but she'd never foist herself. He'd seen her efforts to maintain a discreet distance between them while they worked through the ring routine, a Herculean task considering they were connected at the fingertips. No, she was just a lovely, misguided woman who tugged at his heart and tempted his body. With God's help, he could resist. He had to. He'd not repeat his father's mistakes.

J.T. thought back to the day his father had taken him aside to tell him the woman they had both loved was gone for good. His face haggard, his eyes dull, he clapped J.T. on the shoulder with one hand while pulling down the wedding photograph from the mantel with his other. Color slowly drained from his knuckles as he tightened his grip on the thin metal frame until his thumb pressed the glass so hard it cracked.

"Don't follow in my footsteps, son."

That was all he said, but it was enough.

J.T. remembered the excuses his father had made when his mother closed herself in her room in one of her huffs, leaving him to finish dinner or soothe a crying baby Delia. He'd said that she was just high-strung, as if that explained anything. Then, more often than not, he had passed the stirring spoon or baby over to J.T. and disappeared behind the closed door to mollify his child bride. It didn't take much imagination to figure out their history.

When his father met his mother, he must have been so taken by her fine looks and youthful exuberance that he willingly closed his eyes to her faults. She'd been fourteen years younger than he, and J.T. supposed his father had been flattered by her attentions, sure that once she matured and settled down, her pretty pouts and artful manipulations would disappear. But they didn't. They intensified. J.T. had seen it firsthand. She birthed him two children and complained all the while about the loss of her figure. She demanded expensive clothes and trinkets until her husband's savings were depleted, threatened to leave him if he tried to tell her no. J.T. couldn't remember her ever sacrificing something for another person strictly out of kindness—not even for him or Delia.

The day they laid his father to rest, J.T. stood at the grave and vowed to take his father's advice to heart. And he had. Until Hannah. Something about that woman weakened his defenses, and he needed to figure out what it was. Soon.

Reaching the house, J.T. paused on the back porch. He shoved thoughts of his parents back into their pigeonholes and threw a mental blanket over Hannah before pushing through the door. The safety of routine restored the last fragments of his control as he stepped into the kitchen and hung his hat on its hook. "What's for lunch, sis?"

"Roasted chicken and parsnips, with apple dumplings for dessert."

Delia opened the warming oven and a blend of savory and sweet aromas filled the kitchen. J.T.'s stomach gurgled in anticipation. He washed up at the kitchen pump and took his place at the table.

Concentrating so hard on keeping everything normal, he was halfway through his meal before he realized his sister was staring at him. Glaring at her over his chicken leg, he swallowed the hunk of meat he'd been chewing.

"What?"

Elbow propped on the table, she braced her chin on her hand. "I think she's right."

"Who?"

"You don't smile. Strange that I hadn't noticed it before." After imparting that keen observation, she turned her attention to her plate and stabbed a roasted parsnip with her fork.

J.T. had no doubt to whom his sister referred. Not wanting to encourage conversation in that direction, he said the first thing that came to mind. "The gray's all healed up."

Of course, thinking of the injured gelding did nothing to stem the flow of thoughts regarding Miss Richards.

"That's good." Delia took a dainty bite of chicken, and only then did J.T. notice that her plate held a much smaller portion than usual.

"You feeling all right?"

She nodded. "I'm fine."

With a shrug, he cut into his dumpling. Baked apple and cinnamon wafted up to him as he slid a healthy portion onto his fork. He lifted the bite to his mouth, already tasting the juicy goodness when he caught Delia grinning at him with a gleam in her eye. The fork clanked down onto his plate.

"Now what?"

"You and Hannah had a lively time this morning. What'd you think of those exercises?"

Swallowing a groan when he would much rather be swallowing his dumpling, J.T. leaned back in his chair. "I think I would've been laughed out of town if anyone had seen me swinging those ridiculous clubs. If you and Miss Richards want to embarrass yourselves with that stuff, be my guest, but don't expect me to touch one of those things ever again."

"But did they work?"

Not yet willing to concede that point, he merely grunted. In response, she reached across the tabletop and snagged his fork. Before he could stop her, she slid the fruity tidbit off the tines and into her mouth.

"Hey!" He made a grab for her arm but missed as she flopped back into her seat.

She smiled in triumph, her lips as wide as they could be while still concealing their prize.

"Imp. Get your own dumpling." He sawed off a second section and crammed it into his mouth before she could steal it.

"I only wanted a bite," she said as she dabbed her lips with her napkin. "I'm taking the others to Mr. Franklin at the telegraph office."

"You didn't make yourself one?" That wasn't like her. Delia loved sweets.

"Not today." She got up to refill his coffee cup, and J.T. considered her more closely. Her brown dress was hanging a bit looser around her middle. She was losing weight.

"You sure you're not sick?"

Delia set the coffeepot back on the stove and began packing a man-sized portion of food into her delivery basket to take to Ike. "I'm fine, J.T. Really. Stop your fussing."

He lifted his coffee to his lips and sipped the hot brew. "Maybe you should cut back on all that walking and calisthenic nonsense. You're getting thin."

"Do you think so?" She looked downright pleased by the idea.

J.T. frowned. "If you're feeling poorly, you should rest, not wear yourself out with crackbrained exercises."

"Actually, feeling poorly is exactly why Hannah got involved with Dr. Lewis's gymnastic system in the first place." Delia collected his empty plate and set it in the dishpan.

He told himself not to ask, but an irresistible curiosity drove him to it anyway. "She was ill?"

"As a child, yes. From what Hannah told me, she nearly drowned the summer she was ten, swimming in a pond near her home. She developed pneumonia, and her lungs weakened to the point that the doctors believed she'd be an invalid the rest of her life."

J.T. drew a toothpick from his pocket to clean his teeth and tried to picture a young Hannah lying in bed with nothing to occupy her beyond a needle and thread. The image didn't fit the woman he knew. It was much easier to envision her as a rambunctious girl bounding over hills and dales in pursuit of rainbows, butterflies, and armloads of wildflowers.

"She's certainly no invalid now."

Delia chuckled as she covered the food basket with a clean napkin. "No, she's certainly not. Apparently her mother ran across a book by Dr. Lewis that emphasized the stimulating effects of sunshine and exercise on curing weak lungs and recommended the use of apparatus such as Indian clubs and lightweight dumbbells. She started Hannah on a simple regimen and built on it little by little until her health was fully restored. Hannah never gave up the habit."

"Gotta go," J.T. mumbled. He pushed away from the table and got up, eager to escape the conversation about Miss Richards. The last thing he needed was another reason to admire the woman. Lots of children faced and overcame adversity. It didn't make her special.

"I'm going to stop by the dress shop on my way home." Delia's giddy grin captured his attention. She gripped the sides of her basket as if trying to keep her hands from clapping together in glee. "We're going to do some preliminary measurements and select fabric."

J.T. scowled at his sister. "I'd hoped you'd abandoned that notion."

She released the basket and blew out a breath. "Land sakes, J.T. It's just one dress. I'm not going to turn into some vainglorious peacock who constantly obsesses about her wardrobe. You raised me better than that. I simply want to wear something nice to the Founders' Day picnic this year. That's all."

He crossed his arms over his chest and broadened his stance. "I'm starting to think that maybe you're spending too much time with Miss Richards. She's a bad influence on you."

Delia gasped. "How can you say that? She's my dearest friend, and she's done nothing wrong—to you or anyone else in this town."

"She operates a shop filled with temptation," J.T. declared, thrusting his finger in the direction of the offensive place. "Her designs aren't simple dresses created to keep a person protected from the elements. No, every last one of them has been specifically crafted to draw attention to the figure of the woman who buys it, stroking the customer's vanity, and giving her reason to snub those less wealthy or attractive than she. And what of those who can't afford the luxury of such clothing? They are left to lust over ruffles and lace, coveting what is out of their reach when they should be content with what they have."

"Which am I?"

J.T. chomped down on his toothpick, tension spearing through his jaw. Delia stood before him with her hands on her hips, daring him to place her in one of those objectionable categories.

"I have the means for the dress, saved from my own earnings," she said, "so that must mean that I'm a status-seeking snob. Is that what you're saying?"

"Of course not. You're different."

"I'm different? Really? Because a moment ago it all sounded very black and white coming from you."

"Delia . . ." She was twisting things around.

"So you're willing to concede that it's possible for a woman, like me, to purchase one of Hannah's creations without plunging into moral decay."

"Yes," he said through clenched teeth, "but she should be more responsible toward those who are weaker. A true Christian wouldn't lay out a stumbling block for others to trip over."

"Jericho Riley Tucker. When did you get so sanctimonious?" Her lips pursed in distaste. "A true Christian, indeed. I guess a true Christian couldn't own a gun shop, then. Too much temptation for those with murderous impulses. Or a bank. Greed leads to all kinds of dissipation, you know. Better not open a restaurant, either. Why, the poor soul who is prone to gluttony would be tempted to order mounds of food each time he entered the establishment."

"Enough! You've made your point." J.T. grabbed his forehead and massaged his temples.

Delia's arms fell to her sides and she sighed. "If Hannah filled her shop with scanty gowns that incited men to lust and promoted an immoral agenda, I would be the first to help you close her down. But she's an honorable woman who makes her living sewing high-quality, modest dresses that glow with the colors and beauty God inspires within her. There is nothing shameful in that.

"You are letting what our mother did cloud your judgment, J.T. She was a selfish woman who craved beautiful things, but that doesn't mean that people who make beautiful things are wrong to do so."

Arguments swirled in J.T.'s mind, setting him adrift. What Delia said made sense, but he feared her logic was another test of his conviction. He *wanted* to believe that Hannah was innocent of any wrong. If she were, there would be no reason to continue fighting his attraction for her. Waves of doubt tossed him to and fro until the verse from First Peter about beauty coming from within and not from outward adornment sprang to the surface like a life preserver. He latched on to it.

"She might not be promoting immodesty, but she is promoting false ideas about beauty that could lead others astray."

"Is that all you can see? Can you not see all the good that she's done in the short time she's been here?" Delia came up to him and touched his arm. He flinched and stepped away from her.

"Do you not see her ministering to Tessa James, teaching the girl to sew and using that opportunity to meet the child's need for new clothes at the same time? Do you not see the happiness her friendship has brought me?" She inched close to him again. J.T. fought the urge to retreat.

"You know I've always struggled to fit in. Between the scandal with Mother and my own shyness, friends have been a rare commodity for me. Yet the first day I brought Hannah a jar of milk, genuine affection sprung up between us."

J.T. frowned. He'd been so busy as a young man trying to keep a roof over his sister's head, he hadn't paid much attention to how she fared with other kids. Had she been lonely all this time?

"And what of Mr. Culpepper?" Delia continued. "How many months did the people of Coventry, you and me included, let that man wander around in the stench of his grief doing nothing about it? Hannah took him under her wing and in less than a week managed not only to get him to bathe but, more importantly, to return to church.

"If anyone can be an influence for good in a shop filled with fancy dresses, Hannah Richards can. She already has."

The life preserver was slipping from his hands, and he didn't know how to reestablish his grip. The truth embedded in his sister's words swirled around him in a current that pulled him in a direction he didn't want to go. Why couldn't he just cling to his simple understanding of what God wanted from his people? It had served him well in the past. But Hannah had muddied the waters with her contradictions. She didn't fit into his clean, simple way of thinking.

J.T. ran a hand through his hair and tugged at the roots. He hissed under his breath at the self-inflicted pain. Then Delia reached out and gently tugged his arm free. Surrounding his large hand with her two smaller ones, she peered up at him.

"You're afraid, J.T. Afraid to believe that someone who values beauty and is so beautiful herself can also be good." She squeezed his fingers, and a small smile lifted the corners of her mouth. "I saw how you looked at Hannah this morning. You're developing feelings for her, aren't you? Despite your rigid rules. Don't let Mother's choices poison yours. Just because *she* broke your heart doesn't mean that Hannah will, too. Beauty in and of itself is not wrong."

Without conscious thought, a verse he'd quoted often while Delia was growing up tumbled from his lips. "'Favour is deceitful, and beauty is vain: but a woman that feareth the Lord, she shall be praised.' Proverbs 31:30."

His sister shook her head, her smile fading. "No one's arguing that a woman should pursue beauty above a relationship with her Lord. Maybe it's time you went back and reread that chapter in Proverbs. Look again at the woman who is praised as a godly example of virtuous femininity. The wife whose value is above rubies. I dare you, J.T. Look for yourself. What type of clothing does *she* wear? How does she earn *her* living? Then maybe we can have this discussion again."

19

J.T. trudged back to the livery, a Bible tucked under his arm. He'd never thought of himself as a coward, but he'd been extremely tempted to toss his conversation with Delia to the wind and ignore her challenge. What if he dug deeper into the Word as she suggested and discovered he needed to adjust his beliefs? Could he do that? They'd been his rock for so long. Guiding him. Shaping him. If they turned out to be shifting sand . . .

Tom waved at him as he approached the office. "Doc came by to rent the buggy. Said Mrs. Walsh was due to have her next young'un any day, and he wanted to pay a call on her. I hitched up the roan. Hope that's all right." He crammed his hands into his pockets and rocked up and back on the balls of his feet.

J.T. slapped him on the arm. "You did fine. I'll add it to his account."

A grin exploded across Tom's face.

The Bible under his arm poked J.T.'s ribs as he moved past the young man and reached for the knob on the office door. A similar jab from within made him hesitate. He glanced over his shoulder.

"Uh, Tom?"

The boy spun around and trotted back to J.T.'s side like an eager puppy. "Yeah?"

"Would you mind sticking around for an extra hour or so? I've got some things to work on, and I'd rather not be disturbed."

"Sure." Tom eyed the black leather protruding from beneath J.T.'s bicep. "If them things need a Bible to figure out, I reckon they must be mighty important. No one'll bother you unless there's an emergency. I'll see to it."

"Thanks." J.T. pulled the book from under his arm and lifted it to the brim of his hat in salute. Then he entered his office and closed the door.

A tangle of harness leather cluttered the top of his desk. With one hand, he scooped it up and tossed it onto a barrel in the corner as he circled the table and lowered himself into his cane-backed chair. He set the Bible on the desktop in front of him, then pushed it over to a corner. The scrape of leather on wood echoed loudly in the small room, but J.T. ignored it. He swiveled away to collect a different book.

He extracted the account ledger from the drawer to his left and flipped to the page that held the current entries. With a nub of pencil, he added a dollar to the doctor's balance and totaled the sum since the man's last payment.

Black leather tugged at his peripheral vision. He scratched an itchy spot on his jaw and turned back to the ledger. Might as well total up all the accounts. It'd make the end-of-month tally much easier. J.T. welcomed the mathematical diversion, his focus only occasionally drifting over to the Bible that sat patiently on the corner. Until the numbers ran out. With no sums to keep his conscience at bay, the black book loomed large, creeping into his line of sight.

He scanned the room for something else to do. The harness still needed work. And he'd been meaning to fix that rickety shelf since last month. The pipe on his potbellied stove was dented. The windowsill needed dusting.

Dusting?

J.T. braced his arms on the desk and pressed his forehead into the heels of his hands. As he exhaled, a self-castigating chuckle vibrated against the wall of his chest. He *was* a coward if he'd rather dust a windowsill than read a passage of Scripture. This was a livery office, for pity's sake, not a fancy parlor. Dust was part of the decor.

With a small groan, he pushed the ledger aside and drew the Bible toward him.

Lord, I don't know what you're aiming to teach me, but I pray for enough wisdom to recognize it when I see it.

Standing the book on its spine, J.T. thumbed the pages back until he found Proverbs. He turned to the last chapter and began to read. Nothing momentous caught his attention in the beginning, except the warning to Lemuel against giving his strength to women. J.T. had been a believer in that philosophy for ages. However, his assurance started dissolving around verse nineteen with the mention of the noble wife's spindle. And at verse twenty-one, it deteriorated completely.

"'She is not afraid of the snow for her household: for all her household are clothed with scarlet. She maketh herself coverings of tapestry; her clothing is silk and purple.'"

Silk and purple? Her household clothed in scarlet? Wouldn't a modest woman wear plain clothes like wool dyed brown or dark blue? Yet God's Word clearly stated that this virtuous woman wore purple silk.

And it got worse the further he read.

"'She maketh fine linen, and selleth it; and delivereth girdles unto the merchant. Strength and honour are her clothing; and she shall rejoice in time to come.'"

Not only did she wear the fancy clothes, she sold them to others. Just like Hannah. And the Bible declared it honorable and worthy of rejoicing.

There was more to the virtuous woman than her occupation and dressing habits, of course. Proverbs painted her as trustworthy, kind, diligent. Strong, productive, and wise. She practiced good stewardship, reached out to those in need, and feared the Lord. All qualities Miss Richards demonstrated, as well.

How could he condemn Hannah for selling fine clothing when the virtuous woman did the same? In the biblical example, her husband and children praised her and called her blessed. For Hannah, all he'd done was tear her down and call her a stumbling block. Not exactly the kind of thing to recommend a fellow as husband material.

J.T. closed the Bible and leaned back in his chair, rubbing his hands over his face. He still believed true beauty came from a woman's spirit, not her physical shape or choice of garment. Yet God seemed to be telling him through this passage in Proverbs that it was possible for a woman to have both. Not only that, but it implied a smart man would claim such a female and count his blessings. J.T. glanced out the window to the shop across the street. *Apparently, I'm an idiot.*

As he stared, his vision blurred with images of what could have been. Thankfully, a dilapidated freight wagon came to his rescue. It rolled to a stop in front of his window and blocked his view. Giving himself a mental shake, J.T. stood and walked to the door. He never missed one of Harley's visits.

The county junkman had befriended J.T. during the dark time after his mother left, a time when his father had been too consumed with grief to worry about where food or other necessities would come from. J.T. had snuck off to town one evening a week and dug through people's garbage, searching for anything that might interest the old man. Cracked mirrors, tuneless music boxes, wheels without spokes—these acquisitions provided shoes for him and Delia, secondhand winter coats, and occasionally a ribbon or some other small pretty to surprise his sister with at Christmas.

Harley never admitted it, but J.T. long suspected that the man set things aside specifically for him and Delia and accepted whatever J.T. could offer in payment, no matter how lopsided the trade. He'd never forget the winter after his father died, when their food stores consisted of little more than a handful of potatoes and one onion. The only thing J.T. had to barter with was a rusted pocket knife that wouldn't close. Harley had exclaimed over that knife, saying that it was a rare specimen, and that once he cleaned it up, he knew of a buyer that would pay a king's ransom for it. He then proceeded to hand over a mound of foodstuff in trade—a sack of flour he claimed had been thrown out because of weevils, a can of lard apparently too dented to sell to anyone else, tinned vegetables that had lost their labels, and a barrel of salt pork that Harley complained took up too much space in his wagon.

Without the junkman's generosity, they would not have survived that winter, and even though J.T. no longer spent his spare time salvaging items for trade, he still made a point to buy a selection of Harley's goods whenever the peddler crossed his path. And deliberately overpaid him each time.

Eager to greet his old friend, J.T. opened the door; but before he could reach the street, Tom ran out of the stable like a guard dog, barking up a storm.

"You gotta come back later, Harley. The boss is working on something real important and can't be disturbed."

J.T. came up behind the youngster and clapped him on the back. "That's all right, Tom. I'm done for now. Why don't you bring out a couple water buckets for the man's horses."

"Yessir. I'll have them out in jiffy."

Tom disappeared into the stable, and J.T. turned back to the stoop-shouldered man climbing down from the seat. He found the ground with a moan, then winked up at J.T.

"Ain't as spry as I used to be."

J.T. grinned and accompanied Harley to the back of the wagon. "I'm not exactly a kid anymore, either."

"Don't feed me that nonsense, Tucker. You're still in your prime." Harley gave him a playful jab with his elbow. "What you need is a pretty young wife to chase after. My Sarah's kept me going for near on forty years."

The grin slid from J.T.'s face as he glanced across the street. His stomach churned, but he covered it up with a forced chuckle. "Well, now, if I could find me a gal like your Sarah, I just might do that, but I reckon she's one of a kind."

"That she is, son. That she is." Harley untied the tarp that kept all his goods from escaping. Each man took a side and rolled the canvas covering back. When they reached the front of the bed, Harley wagged a gnarled finger at him. "Don't get discouraged, boy. The Lord will bring the right woman to you when he sees fit. You just got to keep an eye out for her so's you don't miss your opportunity."

J.T. stared at his boots. "I'll keep that in mind."

But what if a man's eyes didn't open until after he'd already pushed the woman away? Would God, or the lady in question, give him a second chance?

Hoping to distract Harley from his advice-giving, J.T. reached over the side of the wagon and picked up a warped eggbeater. He cranked the handle until it hummed, stirring the air. "What'd you bring today?"

The salesman in Harley overpowered the meddler. A familiar gleam sprang to life in his eyes.

"I've been saving something for you. I think you'll be pleased." He shuffled odds and ends and hefted out a large crate covered in oilcloth. With a flourish, he flipped a corner of the cloth back. "See? What did I tell you?"

Shingles. Enough to repair Louisa's roof before winter hit if he ever got things squared away with the current owner. "You remembered."

Harley drew back, affronted. "Of course I remembered. What kind of a junkman would I be if I didn't acquire what my customers are looking for?" His ready smile reappeared quickly, though, as he leaned over his prize. "They're machine-cut cypress from the sawmill in Bandera. Notice the clean, even lines." He handed one to J.T. to inspect. "Met a fellow who worked down there. He traded 'em for an ear trumpet. Guess all that mill work took a toll on his hearing."

"These will be perfect," J.T. said. "Better than any I could have picked up around here." He tossed his sample shingle back into the crate, replaced the oilcloth, and set the box against the wall of the livery.

As usual, Harley insisted on showing him a handful of other treasures, none of which caught his interest. But when the peddler removed a quilt from a three-legged side table to show him the ornate carvings, J.T. glimpsed a couple of chair backs.

"Are those chairs a matched pair?" he asked.

"Ah, you have a fine eye. They are indeed. Help me lift them out."

They cleared away a mantel clock, a chipped bowl and pitcher set, and several miscellaneous pots and pans from the seats of the chairs before J.T. could lift them out. Careful to position them between the wagon and the livery so no one from, say, across the street could see, he took stock of their condition.

"They're missing a few spindles," Harley said, "but the overall construction is sound. A little sanding, staining, and they'll be good as new."

J.T. sat in each and wiggled the framework. They held his weight fine, and except for being a bit banged up, they were decent chairs. He could shape a couple spindles and refinish them in the evenings. It'd probably only take about a week to get them done.

Once again, the shop across the street drew his gaze and prompted an ache in his chest. He'd have to make up an awful lot of ground if he hoped to win Hannah's heart. In the meantime, he would take care of her practical needs. The woman might not think she needed *him*, but she definitely needed chairs.

20

Cordelia, I'm so proud of you." Hannah marked the tape measure with her thumb and held it up for her friend to see. "You've lost an inch around both your waist and chest. Two inches from your hips. You're making marvelous progress."

A blush rose to Cordelia's cheeks. "J.T. did mention that he thought I looked thinner."

"And he was absolutely correct." At the mention of Jericho, Hannah's mind immediately jumped back to her encounter with him under the tree, but she didn't allow it to linger. Cordelia deserved her full attention.

"Do you really think this will work?" Cordelia asked as she buttoned up her dress. "I just came from the telegraph office, and Ike doesn't seem to notice any difference in me at all."

"Well, the change is subtle. The new dress will be more dramatic." Hannah idly flipped through one of her fashion magazines while Cordelia finished dressing. She'd seen the dresses a hundred times, so her eyes wandered to the bonnets and faces of the models. A pattern began to emerge, and Hannah stood a little straighter. "What do you think about adding a change that's not so subtle, one we can do now?"

Cordelia tilted her head at her reflection in the mirror, then turned sideways to examine her profile. "What kind of change?"

Hannah came up behind her and began pulling pins from her hair. Cordelia raised her brows in silent question.

"It just occurred to me," Hannah said, "that all of those stylish ladies in *Peterson's Magazine* have not only fashionable dresses but fashionable hairstyles, as well." She met Cordelia's widening gaze in the mirror. "If we're giving you a new look, we might as well revamp all of you, including your hair."

She raised a hand to her head. "My hair?"

"Sure." Hannah hugged Cordelia's shoulders as excitement ricocheted through her. "Your hair is one of your best features. It's so thick and wavy. We could cut just a little in the front to give you some bangs. Nearly all the models in the magazine have them. I bet yours will curl up on their own without you even having to crimp them. Then we can exchange your simple bun for a braided chignon. Nothing too fancy, just something different and slightly more elegant. You'll need to wear it lower on your neck so it won't be hidden by your bonnet, but I imagine it won't go unnoticed."

"I . . . I don't know."

Hannah gave Cordelia a squeeze and waited for her to decide. She didn't have to wait long. In the mirror, Cordelia's chin jutted out a bit and her lips tightened in a determined line.

"Let's do it." She turned around and faced Hannah directly. "Now. Before I change my mind."

Hannah grinned and took up her shears, and twenty minutes later Cordelia's new style was complete. Wavy bangs disguised her broad forehead, giving her a more dainty appearance. The looser chignon softened her face and drew attention to the curve of her neck. When Hannah finally let her see her reflection, Cordelia gasped.

"That's me?" She fingered her bangs and twisted her head to get a better view of the rest of her hair. "I can't believe it. I look completely different."

"Do you like it?" Hannah held her breath.

Cordelia's smile beamed the answer. "I love it!"

"We should go for a stroll and see if anyone comments." Hannah handed Cordelia her bonnet and took her own down from the wall hook.

"I don't know," Cordelia hedged. "Maybe I should get used to it first."

"Oh, no you don't. I'm not going to let you crawl back into that shell of yours." Hannah firmly set Cordelia's hat on her head for her and tied the strings. "If you hide from people, men especially, they're not going to see you. You have to carry yourself with confidence. Meet their eyes. Smile." Hannah finished with the hat and grasped Cordelia's hands. "Are you ready?"

"No." Cordelia shot her a wry glance. "But I'll give it a try anyway."

"Good. Let's go."

When they reached the mercantile, a thin young man was out front sweeping the walk. His ash-blond hair hung long over his right cheek, but Hannah made out a large reddish birthmark through the camouflage.

"Hello, Warren," Cordelia said, her head erect, her voice cheery, and her smile warm. Pride surged in Hannah's breast. Her protégée was doing an admirable job.

The man's wary eyes drilled into Hannah with uncomfortable force, but then darted away. When they lit on Cordelia's face, however, they softened.

"Hey." He stopped sweeping and propped his palms on the end of the broomstick. "Dad ordered some new muffin and cake tins yesterday. They should be in next week. I thought you might like first pick."

"Thank you for telling me. I'll be sure to look them over when they arrive." Cordelia, still smiling, moved toward the store entrance, but Warren stopped her with his next comment.

"What'd you do to your hair?"

Hannah could feel Cordelia tense beside her at the man's abrasive tone. Warren was obviously not the most sensitive male of the species. She stepped closer to her friend, tempted to take her hand or pat her arm in a show of support even though she knew Cordelia needed to handle things on her own.

"I decided to try a new style. Hannah cut it for me." Cordelia turned to include Hannah in the conversation and perhaps in the blame should he not like the change. Hannah didn't mind. In fact, she welcomed it. Cordelia would never fish for a compliment, but now Hannah could throw out a line on her behalf.

"Do you like it, Mr. Hawkins? I think it becomes her quite well."

Pink dusted Cordelia's cheeks, and her gaze fell to the ground for a moment before she gathered her courage and looked back up at the shopkeeper's son.

"She looks fine," Warren said, directing his comment to Hannah, "but she looked fine the old way, too. She doesn't need you changing her." Hot accusation burned in his eyes.

Hannah flushed under the scalding look and was grateful when Cordelia linked their arms and led her toward the store entrance.

"Have a nice afternoon, Warren." Cordelia's bright inflection sounded a trifle counterfeit, but Hannah wasn't about to complain. "And thanks again for the information about the baking tins."

"Sure." His scowl melted into a wan smile as he shifted his attention back to Cordelia. "I'll ask Father to let you see them before he sets them on the shelves."

Cordelia waved but didn't speak again until she and Hannah were safely inside the mercantile.

"I'm sorry about Warren," she whispered. "His disposition has always been a little on the sour side."

"That's all right. He seemed more protective than sour. I think he's sweet on you." Hannah winked, feeling more herself now that she was out from under Warren's censure.

"He's only a friend." Cordelia sputtered as if the idea had lodged in her throat like a piece of beef that didn't want to go down.

"It doesn't matter." Hannah batted away her friend's protest with a flick of her wrist. "What he said is true. You *were* just as lovely before we cut your hair as after." Hannah slipped her arm free from Cordelia's, thankful her friend hadn't been disheartened by the events outside. Of course, the young man hadn't aimed any animosity at her. He'd saved that for Hannah.

Cordelia smiled and led Hannah past a pair of gray-haired women debating the merits of leather handbags over the tapestry variety. "You're sweet to say so, but I consider the change an improvement, regardless of what Warren said. I'm glad we did it."

Hannah breathed easier, the knot of uncertainty loosening within her. "Me too."

They browsed through the soaps and feminine toilette items near the rear of the store. The rose and lilac scents of the French milled bars tickled Hannah's nose and soothed her spirit. Cordelia passed them by in favor of a ribbon display.

"Maybe I should change the trim on my bonnet before I visit Ike tomorrow."

"That's a good idea," Hannah said, matching Cordelia's hushed volume. "Make it as easy as possible on the poor man. If he still doesn't notice, maybe you can send him a telegram."

Giggles burst from Cordelia, and she quickly covered her mouth in an effort to stifle the sound.

"Oh, let the little bells free, Miss Tucker. Laughter makes the world a better place."

Cordelia jumped, her eyebrows disappearing into her newly cut bangs. "Mr. Paxton! You startled me."

The middle-aged man swept off his hat and bowed over her hand. "Forgive me, my dear. I thought only to rescue the delightful chimes I overheard clamoring for escape. You really shouldn't imprison such a joyful melody. Music is meant to be shared."

Hannah recognized the banker from her transactions in his establishment. The man was a consummate charmer, yet it seemed he was also a devoted husband who doted on his wife and daughters. The first time she had met with him to set up her account, she'd thought him quite the rogue until she noted the way his eyes caressed the framed photograph of his family that sat on his desk. And since the men of the town treated him with cordiality and respect, she'd concluded that his silver-tongued ways must pose no real threat to the women of Coventry.

As Cordelia blushed and struggled to meet the banker's eye, Hannah glanced between the two, her mind spinning. This could be the perfect opportunity for Cordelia to practice her confidence. Unlike Warren, Mr. Paxton would never say a word to injure a lady's feelings, and though his compliments were smooth, they were never false.

"Miss Tucker is contemplating a new ribbon for her bonnet. Which color would you recommend, sir?" Hannah smiled at the man, hoping he would pick up on her hint.

"Why, Miss Richards," he said. "What an honor to be asked for my opinion, especially by a woman as knowledgeable on the topic of fashion as yourself." His brows lifted ever so slightly, and she gave an almost imperceptible nod in return. "My wife rarely seeks my advice before making a purchase, but I would be happy to offer my meager services if you believe they would be helpful."

"We would be grateful for your assistance."

Cordelia looked as if she wanted to muzzle her with the bonnet in question. Hannah just smiled.

"Let me see . . ." Mr. Paxton leaned back to survey Cordelia. "A brown ribbon would match your dress, but if you are anything like my wife, you'd find that dreadfully dull. Hmm . . . Maybe something bright and cheerful to match that lovely laugh of y—" He stopped midthought and tapped the side of his jaw.

"Mr. Paxton?" Cordelia shot Hannah a nervous glance.

"There's something different about you, but I can't put my finger on it." He stepped to the left and then to the right, studying her. Poor Cordelia looked as if she wanted to make a run for the door.

"I've got it. You changed your hair. Is that it?"

Cordelia patted the tresses that stretched over her temple. "Yes. I thought to try something new."

"Well, the style is most attractive on you, my dear." Finished with his scrutiny, his jovial manner returned. "Most attractive. I think I might recommend a similar fashion to my daughter Eleanor.

"Truly?" A radiant smile broke free across Cordelia's face, and she made no effort to hide it behind her hand.

"Truly. Now, I'm off in search of some tooth powder. Have fun with your ribbons, my dear."

"I will. Thank you." Happy roses blooming in her cheeks, Cordelia wiggled her fingers in a tiny wave as the banker meandered over to the next aisle.

It was amazing how the right words spoken by a man could soothe insecurities. And if things continued progressing as they were, Hannah had no doubt that Cordelia would soon be hearing those words from the *right* man. Unfortunately, the right man for Hannah didn't know the first thing about finding the right words. Although, seeing as how she was so wrong for him, he probably hadn't put much effort into the search.

Oh well. Words weren't everything. Jericho's actions spoke with plenty of eloquence and had the added benefit of being subject to interpretation. If her misguided heart chose to read more into them than he intended and to harbor unwarranted hope, that was her business. She'd face the consequences when she must.

Later.

Over the next week, Hannah and Cordelia stepped up their calisthenic program. Cordelia's improved stamina allowed them to lengthen their morning walks past the schoolhouse to include climbing a second hill instead of stopping at the river. She also graduated to more difficult club and dumbbell routines. Then, since Saturday marked the midpoint of their journey to a slimmer, more confident Cordelia, the girls celebrated by taking in the seams on two of Cordelia's best dresses—a chore they tackled with enthusiasm.

Business at the dress shop had improved, as well. Hannah contracted two alteration projects the previous week, in addition to the steady trickle of mending the town's single men brought to her door. And on Tuesday, miracle of miracles, she sold a ready-made traveling suit to one of the guests staying at the hotel.

Some might have scoffed at the notion that such a sale was a sign from God, but it resonated in her soul nonetheless, fortifying her faith. She had asked the Lord to allow her business to fail if it wasn't in his will, and though she struggled to find significant profits when she tallied her books, she chose to view the sale of one of her original designs as confirmation that she was where the Lord wanted her to be. And as long as the voice within her didn't rise up to contradict her assumption, she would forge ahead.

Or sit and wait, as the case may be.

On the bench outside her shop, Hannah curled her fingers around a cooling cup of cocoa and peered toward the edge of town. She hadn't seen Ezra since church on Sunday. At first, she assumed the rain that had dampened Coventry for the first three days of the week had kept him away, but now she wasn't so sure. The sun had emerged bright and warm yesterday afternoon and returned again today, drying puddles and firming up the roads. She and Cordelia even managed to resume their walking this morning after being confined to Cordelia's parlor half the week doing only calisthenics. There should be no reason Ezra couldn't make it to town, unless something other than the weather was responsible for his absence.

Hannah gulped down her lukewarm cocoa and collected Ezra's unclaimed cup. She climbed the stairs to her room, worry dogging her steps. Was he ill? Had Jackson gone lame? Or worse—could something have happened during one of the storms, leaving Ezra injured with no way to get help? Living alone and as far from town as he did, if an accident befell him, he could go for days or weeks before someone chanced by.

Visions of the dear man being pinned to the ground by a fallen lightning-struck tree or huddled in his sickbed so weak with fever that he couldn't get up to feed himself lent a frantic edge to her movements as she washed and dried the cups along with her dishes from breakfast.

By the time she hung up her apron, she knew what she had to do. She would drive out to Ezra's homestead and see for herself that he was all right. Immediately. Leaving the shop closed for the morning was a small price to pay.

Flinging her black wool cape over the shoulders of her primrose polonaise and fastening the hook and eye under her chin, she dashed for the door. The northern breeze blew cool, and without the exertion of walking, she'd need the hip-length cape to stay warm. She stopped briefly at the laundry to tell Tessa they would have to postpone their lessons until tomorrow, then darted out to the street, only to careen to a halt to avoid a farm wagon lumbering across her path. Too impatient to wait for it to pass, Hannah angled around behind it, skirting the worst of the dust as she crossed the street to the livery.

As she entered the dim stable, Hannah wrinkled her nose at the smell of wet straw and manure. She remembered Jericho's office from the time she'd brought him biscuits, but she was strangely reluctant to knock on his door. He'd kept his distance since their escapade with the exercise rings.

She'd found him looking at her on several occasions, though. At church, on the street—always with the same unreadable expression. And at times she was sure she sensed him staring at her through the dress shop's walls from the confines of his office. It was pure fancy on her part, of course, but it still left her a bit unnerved.

"Hello, in the stable," she called, anxious to put the awkwardness behind her and get on with her business. "Is anyone there?"

"Be right with you." The masculine voice cracked on the first word. Tom.

Relief and disappointment swept through Hannah in equal measure.

The lanky young man emerged from the shadows and grinned when he caught sight of her. "Good to see ya, Miss Richards. You looking for J.T.?"

"Not necessarily. I'm sure you can help me just as well." Hannah hid her grin as Tom's chest expanded. "I need to rent a horse and buggy."

"Where you going?"

"Out to Ezra Culpepper's place. I should have the rig back by early afternoon."

Tom sniffed and ran a hand under his nose. "I could let you take Doc, I guess. Mrs. Walsh done had her baby a few days back, so the real Doc shouldn't need it. It's smaller and easier for a lady to handle. Plus it's got a cover if the rain should start up again."

Hannah nodded to him. "It sounds like just the thing."

"You can sit over there while I fetch it for you." He pointed to a cluster of barrels standing near the wall. "It'll take a couple minutes to getcha all hitched up."

"All right."

Tom left, and Hannah surveyed her seat options. Selecting the cleanest-looking cylinder, she laid her handkerchief over the top and gingerly sat down, trying to ignore the way the raised rim dug into the back of her thighs.

"Miss Richards?"

Hannah jumped back to her feet, her stomach seesawing at the familiar voice—a deep, resonant one, devoid of boyish squeaks.

"What brings you to my side of the street?" Jericho approached not from the office, but from the rear of the stable. His shirt gaped open at the neck and his rolled sleeves revealed powerful forearms that had probably been manipulating a pitchfork moments ago. Smells of horse and hay clung to him in an inherently masculine mix.

Dragging her gaze up to his face, she forced a smile. "I'm renting a buggy. Tom's getting Doc for me."

"What for?"

Hannah frowned and blew out a breath. When Tom had asked, she assumed he was simply making conversation without realizing it was impolite to pry. But now she wondered if he wasn't imitating his employer, a man who should know better. "Do you make a habit of badgering all your customers, Jericho?"

"Nope. Just you." His mouth held its serious line, yet his eyes sparkled with suppressed laughter. She could almost imagine deep chuckles vibrating in his chest.

"Well, since you're paying me such a special courtesy, I suppose I can share my plans with you." She smiled playfully at him, but her frivolity dimmed as the seriousness of her purpose rose to the surface. Twirling the fringe of her cape around her finger, she looked at the ground.

"I'm worried about Ezra." She glanced up and caught him staring at her. His eyes locked with hers and didn't look away.

"He's a grown man."

Hannah finally broke away from his gaze and caught sight of Tom maneuvering the buggy out of the wagon shed. Deciding that was a safer place to direct her attention, she continued watching Tom even though the rest of her senses stayed shamelessly attuned to the man beside her.

"I know he is," she said. "However, he's never missed a morning visit at my shop until this week. I thought perhaps the rain had kept him home, but he didn't come today, either, and the weather is fine."

"There could be a hundred reasons why he didn't make it to town. Maybe he's busy carving up more of those sticks to sell at the depot."

"Maybe. But what if he's hurt or sick?" Needing him to understand, she turned and searched his face. "He lives out there all alone, Jericho. He'd have no way to summon help if something went wrong. I need to go out there. If for no other reason than to reassure myself that he's all right."

He stared at her long and hard. "You're a softhearted woman, Hannah Richards. Hardheaded, but softhearted." He reached out as if to touch her cheek, then dropped his hand to his side. "I'll give Tom a hand. We'll have you ready to go in two shakes."

She stood motionless as he retreated, longing for the contact that had failed to materialize. For a brief moment, the hard lines of his face had relaxed with tenderness, changing his countenance so completely her breath had caught in her throat. What would it be like to feel his hand cup her cheek? To lean into the comfort of his caress? To have him look on her with love?

"It's ready, Miss Richards." Tom waved her forward.

She gathered her wits and joined him by the buggy.

"You know how to handle the reins, right?" The stern Jericho had returned.

"Yes."

"Good. I've double-checked the harness and all the straps. The carriage is sound." He tugged on the leather and kicked at the spokes as if to verify his words. "If you get stuck in mud or have any difficulty with the buggy, just leave it where it stands, unhitch the horse, and ride him back to town. I don't want you stranded out there."

Hannah smiled at the gruffness in his voice. "Now who's worrying unnecessarily?"

She picked up her skirt and placed her foot on the step, but when she reached for the handle on the outside of the seat to pull herself in, Jericho was suddenly there, offering his hand.

She accepted, enjoying the feel of his callused skin against her palm. The contact was far too brief, but it warmed her nonetheless. Reluctantly, Hannah let go and retreated onto the seat, where she extracted a silver dollar from her purse and passed it over to him.

"Can you give me directions to Ezra's place? Except for my constitutionals with your sister, I haven't ventured far from town."

Jericho tipped his hat back and pointed to the north. "Take the main road out of town. Go about a mile past the schoolhouse, then turn right on the road that leads to the river. You'll cross a wagon bridge. Go another two miles or so until you see a post to the left with a hummingbird carved into the wood at the top. His wife loved the things. Follow the ruts that turn off by the post. They'll take you to the house."

Hannah collected the reins, and the horse stomped the ground in anticipation. "Thank you for your help, Jericho."

"Um . . ." Tom sidestepped up to the buggy, shooting leery glances at his employer as he moved. He cupped his hand around his mouth as if to tell her a secret but forgot to lower his voice. "He don't like that name, ma'am. Nobody calls him that."

"I do." Hannah grinned and flapped the reins. The roan set off down the street, leaving a stunned Tom and a scowling Jericho in its wake.

Feeling better than she had all morning, Hannah reveled in the freedom of being out in nature. Thickets of trees covered distant hills, where random specimens boasted the first red leaves of autumn. White clouds rimmed in gray blew gently across the sky, and the same breeze that propelled them pushed the loose tendrils of hair away from her face and cooled her skin. A pair of blue jays flew overhead, scolding each other as they swooped in and out of the mesquite. A lovely morning to be out for a drive.

Jericho's directions proved easy to follow, and Hannah soon found herself at the wagon bridge. Desert hackberry with its dark green oval leaves and bright orange berries combined with prickly graythorn and other shrubs to line the banks of the North Bosque River. The fragrant aromas of juniper and cedar teased her nose and induced a sneeze as she brought the buggy to a halt. The rush of the river seemed unusually loud. She edged forward until she could make out the water below. The usually narrow, slow-flowing stream had swollen with the recent rains. The trestles still cleared it by several feet, though, so she clicked to the horse and rolled from the dirt onto the bridge's planks. The roan's shod hooves thunked against the wooden boards with a hollow cadence that sent a shiver tiptoeing down her neck. Hannah tightened her grip on the reins, but she made it to the opposite side without incident.

Once back on the road, Hannah urged the horse to a trot. The river reminded her of how quickly things could change. She needed to get to Ezra.

When she finally reached his homestead, the sun stood high in the sky. As she stepped down from the buggy, a door on the weathered house creaked open. Ezra hobbled out into the yard, leaning heavily on one of his walking sticks.

"Miz Hannah? What are you doing all the way out here?"

She hurried to his side and steadied him with a hand at his elbow. "I was worried when you didn't make it to town for so many days. I wanted to make sure that everything was all right."

Ezra shook his head and let her lead him back to the house. "You should be in town sewing up some fancy piece of calico instead of checking up on an old-timer like me. I ain't worth your worry."

"Of course you are. Now, let's get you back in the house so I can make you some tea."

Before she could make tea, however, she had to find the kettle. A mound of dishes, pots, and pans littered the kitchen. All of them dirty. The poor man probably hadn't eaten off a clean plate since his wife died. It was a wonder he ate at all in this mess. A half-empty can of beans sat on the table, a spoon standing stiff in its middle. His lunch, no doubt. He hadn't even bothered to warm it up. Hanging up her cape and bonnet, Hannah vowed to make the place habitable before she left.

She located an apron, tied it about her waist, and pushed up her sleeves. Not allowing Ezra to talk her out of her mission, she dragged in the washtub from the back porch, filled it with well water, and started dropping pots and pans into its depths. The plates went into the dishpan along with the cups and flatware, and she left them to soak until she had heated enough water on the stove to clean them properly.

Ezra finally stopped trying to dissuade her and sat at the table whittling while she chattered on about the progress Cordelia was making. She told him about the lovely fern-green wool they had decided on for the main body of the dress, the jet buttons, the fern-and-burgundy-striped skirting, the way the polonaise would gather at the back for a slight bustled effect. She doubted he cared a whit about her babble, but it helped pass the time.

When the dishes and utensils were clean, Ezra insisted on helping her dry. Hannah made him do it sitting down. The way he grimaced and limped around, his pain was obvious. She didn't question him about it, though, until the work had been completed and they both sat at the table with a cup of honey-sweetened tea.

"Did you hurt yourself this week? I can send the doctor out to see you."

Ezra took a sip and shook his head. "Naw. It ain't worth the bother. He can't do nothing for these old joints." He set the cup down and rubbed his leg. "My rheumatism acts up somethin' fierce when it rains. And with the way my knee is aching, I bet we're in fer some more."

"Do you have a soup bone I can use to make stock? I could put together some beef or vegetable soup before I go, to tide you over until you're feeling better."

"No. You done too much already." He slapped his palms onto the tabletop and pushed to his feet. With a hitch in his step, he shuffled over to the window and tilted his head to view the sky. "Looks like that new storm is rolling in. There's a wall of dark clouds to the northwest. No telling how soon it'll reach us. You better head back to town."

Hannah swallowed the last of her tea and stood. "Are you sure there's nothing more I can do for you?"

"I'm sure. Now skedaddle before I have to sic Jackson on you. That mule's as ornery as I am when the weather turns sour."

"All right. I'm going." Hannah held up her hands in surrender as she moved to collect her hat and cape. "I did promise Mr. Tucker I'd have his rig back this afternoon. I wouldn't want him to think me irresponsible."

"From what I've seen, the boy's more likely to think you irresistible," Ezra mumbled with his head aimed at the floor.

A thrill passed through her at his words, but caution quickly rose to quell it. She probably hadn't heard him correctly. However, when Ezra raised his head, his eyes were dancing with roguish light, resurrecting her optimism.

When they stepped outside, the wind immediately whipped over them, tugging Hannah's cape with such ferocity it nearly choked her.

"I think you're right about that storm." She leaned into the wind and moved to inspect her rented horse. The roan lifted its head from the trough where it had been drinking, seemingly unperturbed by the gusty conditions. Jericho had trained him well.

Ezra led the horse around so the buggy faced the road, then handed Hannah up. He took something out of his pocket. Hannah recognized the wood he'd been whittling on in the kitchen. "Here, I made this for you. Alice always liked 'em."

She accepted the offering—a hummingbird, complete with feathered wings and a long, narrow beak. "Thank you, Ezra. It's beautiful." She placed it in her purse. Then, afraid the wind might blow the small bag off the seat, she tucked it deep into the crease of the cushions, leaving only the hummingbird bulge free.

Ezra handed her the reins. "Time to get going, gal. Take care on the way back."

"I will." Hannah set the roan in motion with a flick of her wrist and waved farewell to her friend.

By the time she reached the bridge, fat raindrops were plopping with great frequency against the carriage top. The sky to the north had gone nearly black. She could hear the water rushing, and as she started the buggy onto the bridge, she found the river had risen a good foot since her earlier crossing.

The horse snorted and shook its head, pawing the ground restively.

"I know it looks frightening, but the bridge is solid. We can make it." Hannah spoke to the horse, but she used the words to convince herself, as well.

The storm was still upriver. They had time.

She drove the buggy onto the bridge. Hannah focused on the horse's rump as they traversed the bridge, not trusting her courage to last if her focus wandered to the river.

They were midway across when she heard the roar.

Heart pounding, she looked upstream. A surge of water was thundering toward her, overwhelming the meager banks that fought to contain it.

Flash flood!

"Yah!" Hannah slapped the reins against the roan's back. He lurched forward. They had to get off the bridge.

Ten yards from the end, the water caught them. It crashed over the trestles and threw the horse into the rails. The roan screamed and struggled to find purchase through the torrent that swirled at its knees. The weight of the buggy kept the animal from being swept away, but soon that anchor lost its grip, as well.

The carriage tipped under the pressure of the water's barrage. Hannah released the reins and grabbed the seat handle on the upstream side. She could feel the wheels on that side lifting off the ground. The conveyance shifted and rammed the railing at an angle, splintering the wooden rods that supported the carriage top on the left side. Hannah toppled onto the floor. She clung to the handle above her with both hands as cold water soaked her skirts.

With the underside of the buggy now blocking the main thrust of the floodwater, Hannah crawled up the sloping floor and swung a leg over the side. Tilted and broken, the buggy was useless, but if she could unhitch the horse, perhaps he could get her to safety.

The roan strained against the shafts that twisted toward the river and pinned him to the bridge railing. Hannah debated whether to risk climbing down over the foot of the driver's box in order to get to the horse, but between the flailing hooves and tangled harness lines, it looked too hazardous. So instead, she plunged into the swirling pool beside the upturned buggy. The icy water stole her breath as it reached past her knees, but she slogged forward, fighting the current as she circumvented the wheel. Once at the front, she no longer benefited from the buggy acting as a dam. The water was not as deep, but it rushed faster, nearly knocking her from her feet.

Using the shafts to keep her balance, Hannah edged closer to the horse. She unclipped the driving bit and worked free the straps that anchored the horse to the right shaft. She'd have to find a way to undo the ones on the left next. Wading to the horse's head, she latched on to his bridle and tried to soothe the animal, but his terror was too great. The roan lunged for his freedom, and Hannah lost her footing. She fell to her knees, the violent flow tugging her toward the river. Still holding the bridle leather, she fought the water and managed to stand.

"No more of that. Do you hear me?" She yanked the horse's head down and yelled in his face. "I need you to get me off this bridge. I'll get you free of the carriage, then you'll get me to dry ground. Understand?" The roan jerked his head up and down, probably in a struggle to escape her hold, but she chose to take it as a sign of agreement.

She moved back to the carriage, climbed over both horse shafts, and wedged herself between the second wooden pole and the railing. She undid the first loop but couldn't squeeze her way farther up the shaft. The railing was already digging painfully into her back.

The horse must have sensed the nearness of his freedom, for he strained against the final loop that tethered him to the carriage. His wild movements opened a space for her. She stretched forward and loosened the loop. The roan did the rest. Hannah lunged for the harness saddle so he could pull her free, but she was too slow. The traitor ran for the road, leaving her behind.

"Hey!"

Hannah barely got the shout out before the wooden shaft pounded her back into the railing. The blow knocked her feet out from under her. She flung her arms around the offending pole and tried to pull herself upright as she had done before. Only this time, her legs dangled over the side of the bridge between the rail posts. There was nothing but water to push against. The current tore at her. She slid farther and farther over the side. Her strength waned. Her knees scraped over the side. Then her hips. Finally, the edge of the bridge jabbed its planks into her ribs. Water pounded her face and filled her mouth. She swiveled her head and sputtered, desperate for a breath.

Out of options, she did the only thing she could. She let go of the pole and allowed the river to take her.

22

J.T. peered out the back of the livery, across the corral, and down the road that led out of town. She should have returned by now.

Dark clouds were converging from the north. The light rain that had arrived ahead of them a few minutes ago had sent him out to gather the horses. Now that they were all stabled and dry, he couldn't tear himself away from the open doorway.

Where are you, Hannah?

Surely if something had been seriously wrong with Ezra she would have driven back to town for help right away. So what was keeping her? Maybe she decided to wait out the rain at his place. Or she could have taken a wrong turn.

His gut told him there was more to it.

"Tom!" J.T. spun around and marched through the stable.

The boy stuck his head out of one of the stalls, a currycomb in his hand. "Yeah?"

"Saddle up the gray for me while I get my slicker. I'm going for a ride." Trusting that his order would be obeyed, he strode on without stopping.

"In the rain?" the boy called out after him.

"Yep."

He had just retrieved the oiled raincoat from the nail on his office wall when the pounding of hoofbeats set his heart to racing. He dashed out to the street. The roan ran past him, straight into the livery.

Hannah.

J.T. shoved his sleeves into the arms of his slicker but didn't bother with the buttons as he sprinted toward the gray's stall. "Tom! I need that horse. Now!"

"I got him. I just need to cinch him up."

J.T. ran a calming hand over the roan's heaving sides. "It's all right, boy," he murmured. "You're safe. But where's Hannah, huh? You didn't throw her, did you?" Tension crept back into his voice at the thought of Hannah injured or lost out on the road somewhere. The horse sidestepped, and J.T. backed away.

"Tom," he gritted out through clenched teeth.

"Here, J.T. He's ready."

The second Tom emerged from the stall, J.T. grabbed the reins and swung into the saddle. "Take care of the roan."

Tom eyed the animal, then turned a panicked look on J.T. "B-b-but where's Miss Richards and the buggy?"

"That's what I'm going to find out." Not taking the time to offer any more explanation, J.T. nudged the gray forward and sped out of town.

He held the gelding to a moderate pace so he could scan the brush for signs of Hannah. But as each consecutive section he passed yielded no sign of her, the tension in his gut wound tighter. J.T. rounded the bend that preceded the bridge, a thicket of pecan trees blocking his view of the river. Through the branches, however, he caught a glimpse of a large black object. He reined in his mount and approached with caution.

When his view cleared, his heart dropped to his knees. It was the buggy, all right, but it lay broken and tipped against the railing. Debris cluttered the bridge, and J.T. knew at once that the dripping planks had been drenched by something more sinister than the drizzling rain that fell now.

"Hannah!"

He jumped off his horse, grabbed the lariat from the back of his saddle, and ran onto the bridge. His boots slid on the damp wood, but he didn't slow his pace. Praying that the only reason he didn't see her was because she was huddled inside the carriage, J.T. climbed between the lopsided horse shafts and thrust his head into the buggy's interior.

Nothing.

He punched a fist into the side of the carriage.

Lifting his head, he searched the banks, the water, the brush. No sign of the pretty pink outfit she'd been wearing that morning. Where was she?

Lord, help me find her. Alive. Please, alive.

J.T. scanned the carriage for any clue it could offer. He spotted her purse jammed into the seat cushion and jerked it free. Opening the front of his slicker, he tucked it inside his vest. Something stiff and hard poked him in the chest, but he welcomed the discomfort if it meant having a piece of her close.

He looked back at the empty rigging. The roan would never have been able to free himself without her aid. Therefore, she must have survived the flash flood. At least initially. But he hadn't passed her on the road or seen footprints in the muddy earth. That didn't bode well. Surely she wouldn't have walked back to Ezra's place. Not when the buggy was closer to the town side of the bridge. So where was she?

Cupping his hands around his mouth, he shouted her name loud and long. "Hannnnahhh!"

He waited, straining to hear some kind of response. Anything. But all he heard was the rush of the angry river.

She must have been washed over the side. J.T. ground his teeth. Hannah was strong—stronger than any woman he'd ever known. Physically. Mentally. The buggy had collapsed near the bank. Despite the fast currents, she might have made it to shore. That's where he'd start the search.

He angled his arm through the coil of rope and shoved the lariat up to his shoulder. Leaving the bridge behind, he sunk into the mud lining the west bank. He wove around trees and brush, grabbing limbs and roots to maintain his balance as his boots continually slid out from under him. Twice, he nearly ended up in the river himself.

About a quarter mile from the bridge, he spotted a snippet of color in the distance. There, where the river dipped slightly to the right, a fallen tree stretched out over the edge of the water. Something pink lay in its arms. Pink!

Heedless of the risk, J.T. rushed toward the log. Thornbushes scratched his face and hands. His downhill leg throbbed with the effort of keeping him upright. Mud sucked at his boots and dragged him down, but he charged on.

When he reached the uprooted tree, he lodged himself behind the circular base and unwound his rope. A small cedar stood nearby. J.T. looped the end of the rope around the cedar's trunk and knotted it. He shrugged out of his slicker, folded it up to keep the inside dry, and then tied the free end of the rope around his waist. Taking a deep breath, and petitioning God for an extra measure of strength and agility, he climbed onto the log and began making his way to Hannah.

The log narrowed the farther J.T. went. Not trusting his footing, he lowered himself to his belly and crawled.

He could see her now. Pale hands lying outstretched and limp, alarmingly white against the dark, wet wood. Her face down. Yellow hair strewn every which way, tangled with twigs and soggy leaves. She wasn't moving.

Please be alive. Please.

He inched closer, the river now licking his knees. Nearly there. He could almost touch her. Then the rope snagged, halting his progress. With a growl, he grabbed the cord and yanked. A stub of a broken branch held the rope captive. He yanked again, harder. "Come on!" Finally the branch snapped. J.T. turned back to his goal.

"Hannah?"

She was less than a foot away, but she gave no sign that she heard him.

"Hang in there, darlin'. I'm coming."

The log split into a *V* with Hannah wedged in the middle. J.T. reached for her hand and clasped it. The coldness of her fingers chilled his heart. He folded her hand inside his palm and squeezed. His eyes closed on a wordless prayer, then burst open as determination gripped him. He would compel the river to relinquish its prize. Hannah was not dead. Only unconscious. She could still be revived.

Clinging to that bit of faith, he released her fingers and latched on to her wrist. Once he found a grip on both of her arms, he dug his heels into the side of the tree and pulled. A groan tore from his throat as his muscles strained against the river's hold. Hannah's lower half was still submerged, her skirts weighing her down. He managed to lift her only a short distance before he had to stop and rest.

He needed more power.

Slowly, without releasing his grip on her arms, J.T. scooted his hips forward until he was sitting upright. His balance teetered, but the grip of his legs kept him from falling. Once secure, he unclenched his knees, lifted his bent legs forward, and locked the heels of his boots onto the branches on either side of Hannah.

J.T. kicked at the wood to make sure it would hold, then with a mental count to three, he leaned back and pushed with all his might. His legs straightened little by little as Hannah came to him. He dragged her higher until he could tuck her lolling head onto his shoulder and wrap his arms around her middle. With a final thrust of his legs, she was free.

He wiggled out from under her and drew her backward until he could reach an arm around her knees. Carefully, so as not to throw them both into the river, he lifted and twisted her position until she sat sidesaddle across the log in front of him. He cradled her to his heaving chest and, with a shaky hand, combed the hair out of her face.

"Hannah? Can you hear me? Open your eyes."

He felt along her throat for a pulse. A weak vibration tickled his fingertips. Hot moisture pooled in his eyes. He blinked it away and gathered her close, rocking her back and forth, for his own comfort as much as hers.

"Thank you, Lord."

Turning her body so her back lay flush against his chest, he wrapped an arm around her middle and started shuffling back toward the base of the tree. Once there, he laid her along the length of the log, collected and recoiled his rope, then tried one more time to rouse her. He pillowed her head with his arm and lightly slapped her cheeks.

"Hannah, wake up," he demanded. Too frightened to cajole, he ordered her to comply. "This is no time to be stubborn, woman. Open your eyes."

Her lashes fluttered, and his breath caught in his chest. Then they stilled. He gave her a shake. "Look at me!"

Blue eyes peeked through tiny slits beneath her lids.

"That's it. Come on, Hannah. Look at me."

She blinked and her lashes parted a little more. "J-Jericho?"

He decided in that moment that he loved the sound of his given name. "I'm here, Hannah." He pressed a kiss to her forehead. "You're safe."

"I'm c-c-c-cold." Her eyelids drifted closed again.

J.T. frowned. She needed a hot bath, dry clothes, and a doctor before she came down with some kind of lung fever. Hadn't Cordelia told him she'd had weak lungs as a child? What if she had a relapse?

He wrung as much water from her skirts and petticoats as he could while still preserving her modesty, then retrieved his slicker and wrapped it around her. He doubted it held any residual warmth from his body, but it would block the wind. After buttoning her in, he took her in his arms and started the muddy trek back up to the road.

By the time he made it to his horse, it had stopped raining. J.T. eased his precious burden down to the ground to give him a minute to regain his strength. He knelt behind her so she could lean against him. To keep her head from flopping forward, he cupped her jaw in his hand. His thumb stroked her cheek.

"You're not going to like this next part, darlin', but it can't be helped." J.T. plucked a twig from her hair. "I'm hoping you won't remember it. If you do, I promise to let you upbraid me as much as you like. I won't even frown while you do it. Okay?"

Being as gentle as he could manage, he hoisted her onto his shoulder and pushed to his feet. Then, with a whispered apology, he slung her face-down across the saddle, climbed up behind her, and headed toward town.

23

Delia! Open up!"

J.T. kicked at the front door, his arms full of a still-unconscious Hannah. It was probably for the best that she hadn't awakened during the bumpy ride back to town, but he would've felt a lot better if she had.

As soon as Delia unlatched the door, J.T. pushed his way in.

"What on earth are . . . ?" The question died on her lips, a horrified gasp taking its place. "Hannah?"

J.T. didn't stop to offer explanations. He strode into his bedroom, ignoring the caked mud that clung to both him and his charge, and set Hannah down on his bed. Delia dogged his steps.

"What happened, J.T.? Where'd you find her? Is she alive?"

"Yes," he snapped. "She's alive. I'll tell you what I know later, but right now we need to get her warm and dry." He opened the chest at the foot of his bed and started tossing every blanket he owned onto the floor. "Get one of your flannel nightgowns for her to wear and heat some water for tea in case she wakes and can drink something. I'll fetch the doctor, and while I'm gone, I want you to strip every piece of wet clothing off of her. Everything. Understand?" He waited for Delia to nod. "Good. Dry her with a towel, and tuck her into my bed. If she stays overnight, I can sleep on the cot at the livery."

Delia scrambled from the room to do his bidding, and J.T. stole a few seconds to just look at Hannah. In his bed. Wrapped in a man's bulky coat, her skin smeared with mud, her hair matted and dripping river water on his pillow, she wasn't exactly a picture of feminine enticement. Nevertheless, his heart ached with tenderness.

He hunkered down beside the bed and clasped her hand. "You will not sicken, Hannah Richards. Do you hear me?" His throat clogged as he spoke. Then, before his sister could return, he pressed a kiss into Hannah's palm and returned her arm to her side.

Delia met him in the doorway carrying a steaming basin of water, a nightdress, and two towels slung over her shoulder. The shock that had dulled her eyes when he first arrived had sharpened to a gleaming fortitude. Hannah would be in good hands.

"Take good care of her, sis."

"I will, J.T. Now go get the doctor."

After one last glance at the delicate woman in his bed, he did just that.

Hannah came awake slowly. Flashes of remembered sounds and touches penetrated the fog of her mind. Delia's concern and gentle hand as she combed out Hannah's snarled hair. A man's no-nonsense voice and blunt fingers prodding her ribs. Jericho's arrogant demand to get well and a mysterious softness in her hand. They were no more than vague impressions, yet they lingered with a sense of reality no dream could instill.

The overwhelming weariness that had ruled her lifted. Awareness of her surroundings seeped in little by little. She noticed the quiet first. The angry roar was gone. But so were the voices she remembered. Was she alone? She didn't want to be alone.

Hannah tried to move, but her body wouldn't cooperate. If she could just open her eyes and see where she was . . .

Her lashes parted enough to reveal a flat ceiling, not the sloping roof that sheltered her bed above the dress shop. Panic gripped her, and a whimper vibrated in her throat.

"Hannah?" A masculine voice echoed near her ear. A familiar voice, one that reached beyond the fear and calmed her. "It's all right. You're in my house. Delia cleaned you up, and she's in the kitchen heating some broth. Doc said nothing was broken. You should be fine after a day or two of rest."

She struggled to follow the stream of words. Willing her eyes to focus, she blinked and pried her lashes farther apart. A dark blur materialized above her. Then he touched her. The backs of his knuckles whispered against her cheek, and she turned into his caress. When the features of his face finally converged into a recognizable image, she started to wonder if this wasn't a dream after all.

"Jericho? You're smiling."

"Am I?" He stroked her cheek again. Warm tingles coursed through her, and instinctively, she followed his touch a second time. His smile widened. "I must be happy."

The change in him was quite startling. His amber eyes glowed with an inner light she'd not seen before, and the worry lines that creased his face faded into the background. He looked younger, more vibrant, more . . . everything.

"You're quite handsome when you're happy."

Jericho trailed the back of one finger under her chin. "I'll make note of your preference."

Heat rose to her face as she realized she had spoken the thought aloud. She'd better get a grasp on her faculties before she completely humiliated herself in front of him. Hannah turned her head away in a pointless attempt to hide her embarrassment and heard him scrape a chair closer to the bedside. Only then did she recall the words he had said earlier.

She was in his house.

In a *bed*, in his house.

Her eyes darted about the room. A shaving mug and razor sat next to the ewer and bowl on the bureau. A pair of men's boots lay discarded in a muddy heap by the door. A battered brown hat hung on the bedpost.

She was in *his* bed, in his house.

"I shouldn't be here." Hannah clutched the blankets to her chest and bolted upright. Pain ripped through her head. She moaned and squeezed her eyes shut, releasing the covers to press her fingers against her temples.

"Easy now," Jericho said. "You've got a pretty good knot on the side of your head. If you move slower it won't hurt so much." He wrapped his arm around her shoulders and gently laid her back on the pillow.

The soreness retreated under his tender ministration, and she opened her eyes again. Just in time to see that she was in a nightdress. Before she could do more than gasp, Jericho covered her back up to her chin.

"J.T.?" Footsteps sounded in the hall. "Is Hannah awake? I thought I heard her voice." Cordelia entered the room, carrying a cup full of something that smelled of herbs and beef. "I brought some broth, if you think she can manage a few sips."

Jericho rose from his chair. "Here, take my seat. I'll get some more pillows to prop her up."

Hannah relaxed her grip on the blankets. Having Cordelia in the room restored the propriety of the situation, and the irrational panic that speared through Hannah upon waking in Jericho's bed diminished. There was sure to be a sensible explanation for why she was in their home. She simply couldn't remember what it was at the moment.

Jericho returned with an armload of cushions. He laid them on the foot of the bed and came around to the far side. "I'm going to help you sit up, but we're going to do it slowly this time."

He supported her head and shoulders, lifting her with exaggerated care. Cordelia plumped the pillows and arranged them behind Hannah's back. Jericho eased her down, and she sank gratefully into the cushioned softness.

"Here you go." Cordelia placed the broth cup in her hand. "I let it cool some, so it's not too hot."

Hannah let the warmth seep into her fingers for several seconds before taking a drink. The well-seasoned stock flowed over her tongue and enlivened her sluggish senses. Her nostrils flared to take in more of the aroma and to inhale the heat of the steam.

"Mmmm. It's delicious. Thank you."

She finished most of the broth before her stomach began to churn. Deciding to extend Jericho's advice to eating as well as moving, Hannah didn't push herself to drink the rest. Lowering her arms to her lap, she looked from sister to brother. "What happened to me?"

"You don't remember?" Cordelia reached forward to claim the cup.

Hannah scrunched her forehead. "I'm not sure. Things are jumbled in my mind."

She looked to Jericho for a clue. He'd put distance between them again, leaning against the wall near the doorway, seemingly content to let his sister take over her care. His smile had retreated, too, although warmth still radiated from his eyes. Hannah loved Cordelia dearly, but she missed the unguarded man who had stroked her face and hovered over her with such tenderness moments ago. Would he ever come to her again?

"J.T.," Cordelia said. "Tell her what you know. Maybe it will spark a memory."

One side of his mouth quirked upward. "You went for a swim, and I had to fish you out of the river."

The river.

Images shuffled in her brain, some sharper than others. The storm. The bridge. The flood. An unseen hand pulled mental pictures out of the scrambled deck that was her brain and set them before her in an order that finally made sense. The carriage tipping. The horse running off. The river sweeping her away.

Water everywhere. Over. Under. Currents dragged and flipped her. Which way was up? Her lungs threatened to burst. Flailing her arms, she finally broke through the surface and gulped a breath. She glimpsed the bank. *Swim!* She stroked with all her might but made little progress. Her legs tangled in her skirt. Debris from the flood crashed into her, bruising her body and jarring her off course. *I'll never make it.* Exhaustion sapped her strength. Her muscles rebelled. Unable to do more, she submitted to the river's will. Her shoulders, then neck, then chin sank beneath the surface. As she begged the Lord to take her swiftly, the arms of a fallen tree stretched out to catch her.

"It's coming back to you, isn't it?" Cordelia's soft voice brought Hannah back to the present.

"Yes." The word scratched against her fear-swollen throat.

"J.T. told me you were caught in a flash flood."

Hannah nodded and glanced at Jericho. He watched her with an intent expression yet remained silent in the background. She returned her gaze to Cordelia and drew in a deep breath. She was safe. The river was gone.

"I . . . ah . . . was on the bridge when I realized what was happening." Hannah squirmed beneath the covers. "It was too late to go back. We tried to outrun it, but it crashed into us before we could reach the other side. I managed to get the horse unfastened and tried to hold on to his harness so he could pull me free of the carriage poles, but he was too fast. Then the river knocked the shaft into me. I lost my balance. I tried to hang on, but there was too much water. I couldn't breathe. The next thing I knew, I was hurtling down the river."

"How frightful! It's a wonder you survived." Cordelia clasped her hand. "Surely, God sent his angels to protect you."

Hannah smiled. "Yes, he did. Two as a matter of fact. One that resembled a tree with long arms, and one who looked an awful lot like your brother." Hannah turned her smile on Jericho, who frowned and pushed away from the wall. He'd shuttered his face, withdrawing from her. Why?

"Thank you for pulling me out of the river," she said, trying to scale the wall he was reconstructing. "I'm sure my story would have ended much differently had you not come looking for me."

"I figure you would have found a way to crawl out eventually," Jericho grumbled. "You're too stubborn to let a little thing like a flash flood best you."

Hannah's smile faded at his surly tone. Though he'd played the gallant hero for her, it seemed his attitude hadn't changed much regarding her character. Then she recalled the busted carriage. If someone had borrowed her sewing machine and broken it, even unintentionally, she'd be grumpy, too. Perhaps her accounting of the afternoon's events had reminded him of his financial loss. She'd rather believe that to be the cause of his sudden irritability than a continued disapproval of her as a person, even if it meant shouldering the blame for the buggy's destruction. Besides, it *was* her fault. She never should've driven onto that bridge.

"Jericho, I'm so sorry about the carriage." She spoke before he could escape from the room. "As soon as I'm able, I'll make payments to cover the repairs."

He spun around and glared at her. "Do you think I care about a stupid buggy when you nearly lost your life today? The thing can sit on that bridge and rot as far as I'm concerned." He stormed out of the room, mumbling something to his sister about a cot at the livery.

Hannah just sat and stared, more confused than ever. "I didn't mean to make him angry."

"Don't mind him," Cordelia said. "J.T.'s never been one to accept gratitude from others with much grace. I think your comparing him to an angel got him flustered. As for the rest . . . ?" She stood and fussed with the blankets, smoothing out wrinkles and tugging the edges flat. "You gave him quite a scare today. I don't think he's completely recovered yet. He's just a little testy from all the excitement."

Cordelia helped Hannah lie down, taking out the extra pillows. "Rest now," she said. "You'll feel better in the morning."

Hannah complied, and when she drifted into slumber, she dreamed of Jericho—smiling.

24

Hannah moved back to her own quarters the following afternoon, and by Saturday she was ready to resume her routine. She'd urged Cordelia to exercise without her yesterday, but the girl refused to leave her side. Now that she'd had two full nights of sleep and more rest than she could stand during the day, Hannah planned to eradicate Cordelia's excuse for abandoning her calisthenics. She was still a bit sore and prone to headaches, but Hannah couldn't let her friend down. Founders' Day was only two weeks away. They couldn't stop now.

She stepped into her loose-fitting gymnastic costume and laced up her low-heeled boots. Glancing at her reflection in the small mirror above the crate that held her pitcher and basin, she frowned. Her sleeping braid hung down her back, and frizzy wisps of hair stood out around her head. Most mornings, she flattened the worst of the fluff with a lick to her fingers and a tuck behind her ears before heading out for her constitutional, but today that didn't seem sufficient. What if she ran into Jericho?

Her heart stuttered as she remembered his smile and the husky quality of his voice as he spoke to her when she first awakened. She hadn't seen much of him yesterday, but he had come home for the noon meal and sat with her while Cordelia made her lunch delivery to the telegraph office.

He told her about how he and Tom had gotten the buggy back on its wheels and dragged it to the wagon shed. She told him about Ezra's rheumatism and the whittled hummingbird. Teasing her about the way that bird had stabbed him repeatedly in the chest, Jericho returned her purse. Then he sheepishly admitted to slinging her over his saddle like a bounty hunter's prize and laughed over the justice the hummingbird had doled out on her behalf.

It had been the most delightful hour she'd ever spent in his company. They hadn't argued once.

Hannah undid her braid, dampened the flyaway ends around her face, and brushed the wavy tresses until they shone. Not wanting Cordelia to suspect she had put any extra effort into her appearance, she refashioned her hair into the normal braid that hung just short of her waist. Only this one was tidier.

With a giddy flutter in her stomach at the thought of possibly seeing Jericho, Hannah opened her door . . . and gasped. Two large shadows loomed on her landing. It took her startled brain several seconds to recognize that the shapes resembled furniture more than crouching villains. Sagging against the doorframe in relief, she tried to puzzle out how a pair of oak dining chairs had come to be on her staircase.

"You planning on turning that landing into a sittin' porch?"

Hannah stretched her head over the side rail to see Louisa walking to the water pump between their buildings.

"Seems a bit tight for gettin' in an out o' your door, if you ask me." The laundress winked as she set her bucket under the spout.

"Did you see who left these here? I've no idea where they came from."

Louisa abandoned her bucket and moved closer to the staircase, examining the chairs through an upturned squint. "They look decent. Maybe a friend left 'em. Someone who knows you're a little short on furniture."

Hannah glanced back into her room, blushing a little at the humble trunk benches and makeshift table that adorned her home. She really could use some chairs, but who would know that?

"So you didn't see who it was?" Hannah wedged herself between the chairs and the railing, cupping her hand around the top of the slender rod that formed the outer edge of the seat back closest to her.

"Nope," Louisa answered, retracing her steps to the pump. She offered no further clues as she turned her attention to working the handle.

Hannah sighed. Not knowing the giver's identity was going to drive her batty. She scoured her mind for names of people who could possibly know of her need for chairs. Jericho and Tom had helped her move in. Cordelia, of course. Danny came in whenever he delivered her wood. Neither Jericho nor Cordelia would've said anything to anyone, but Tom or Danny, in their innocence, could have jabbered about it. It was possible that she mentioned something about her accommodations to Ezra during one of their morning chats, but she didn't remember anything specific. With his woodworking skills and soft heart, he would be a logical benefactor, but living so far from town would make it nearly impossible to deliver goods in the middle of the night, especially with his rheumatism.

She searched the empty street below for anyone who might be watching, but as usual, no one was about so early in the morning. At least no one she could see. Unable to solve the riddle, she relegated it to the back of her mind and carried the chairs inside.

They really were quite lovely. A floral pattern was carved into the back of each one and five thin spindles connected that piece to the slat at the back of the cane seat. The legs stood secure against the floor. No wobbles. She placed the chairs at different spots around her plank table until finally deciding to position them kitty-corner, facing the windows.

It looked cozy. Intimate. An image of Jericho sitting there rose to greet her. Him holding her hand or sharing a piece of pie off her plate. That deep voice whispering private messages in her ear. A brush of his lips across hers.

A tardy rooster crowed outside, shattering Hannah's daydream. She jumped and scurried out the door. Cordelia would worry about her if she didn't show up soon.

As she passed the livery, a movement in the office window caught her eye. Jericho was already there. Hannah tamped down her disappointment. It wasn't as if this visit would be her only chance to see him. He'd be at church tomorrow. And maybe she could make him another batch of biscuits or something—a thank-you-for-fishing-me-out-of-the-river gift. A groan vibrated in her throat at the idiotic idea.

Why was it she could give Cordelia advice on securing a man when she didn't have the first idea how to manage the task for herself? Maybe she should just concentrate on being a seamstress and making her shop a success. That had always been her dream.

Yet her dream was shifting. She could feel it. Jericho was weaving his way into its very fabric, and she feared that without him, the whole thing would tear to shreds.

Hannah shook off the dismal thought as she approached the Tucker home. Cordelia rose from her seat in a front porch rocker.

"I wasn't sure if you'd be coming today," she said. "Have you recovered enough?"

"I'm ready to find out." Hannah grinned and motioned Cordelia forward. She hiked past the house without stopping, forcing Cordelia to trot to catch up. "I'll waste away if I spend any more time abed. It feels good to be up and moving again."

"I'm glad you're feeling better," Cordelia said as she came abreast of Hannah.

"Me too."

They strode together in comfortable silence as they made their way toward the schoolhouse. Hannah usually enjoyed the quiet companionship of their walks, but today questions about her mysterious gift kept bobbing to the surface and irritating her like a host of mosquito bites that begged to be scratched.

"Do you happen to know anything about a pair of dining chairs that appeared on my landing this morning?"

Cordelia turned a startled face to her. "Someone put chairs on your landing?"

"Yes." Hannah leaned forward as the road began to steepen. "And what I can't figure out is how this mystery person discovered that I needed them." She looked sideways at her friend. "You didn't tell anyone, did you?"

Cordelia shook her head. "Of course not."

Disappointed not to have learned anything new, Hannah let the conversation lull as they climbed the hill. Then, as they arrived at the top of the hill a moment later, they stopped to catch their breath.

Cordelia bent forward and braced her hands above her knees. She tilted her head and ventured into a new topic. "I had a novel experience at Hawkins's store after I left you yesterday afternoon."

"Oh?"

"A man offered to tote my basket for me," Cordelia said, her eyes glowing with coquettish glee. She straightened and Hannah gestured for them to resume their walk.

"Who was it?" Hannah asked, accelerating the pace now that they were back on flat ground.

"I have no idea." She giggled. "He must have been a rail passenger or some other traveler. But he made such a fuss over me. I've never experienced the like. He followed me around the store, asking question after question," she said between winded exhalations. "He prattled on about the weather, the town, whatever merchandise happened to be near. It was quite endearing. Although I can't imagine why he didn't tire of me immediately. I was so surprised by his attentions, I could barely string two words together."

"A genuine flirtation! How marvelous." Hannah patted Cordelia's shoulder briefly and returned to her arm-pumping rhythm. "Men are noticing you. That's very encouraging."

"Well, it might have been even better, except Warren scared the poor fellow off."

That young man was becoming a thorn in their sides. Cordelia claimed him as a friend, yet he seemed to go out of his way to discourage her from improving herself. First, he made disparaging comments about her hair. Then, aware of her weakness for sweets, he plied her with free penny candy whenever she went in the store, even when she tried to refuse. And each time Hannah encountered him, he glared at her with such animosity, her skin crawled.

Hannah suppressed a shiver. "What did he do?" she asked as she steered them back toward town.

"He swooped in like some kind of avenger and told the man to stop bothering me. Then he glowered at him until he left. It was humiliating." She speared Hannah with a look that clearly communicated her irritation over yesterday's events. "J.T.'s bad enough. I don't need another man playing big brother for me."

Hannah doubted Warren would take kindly to the brother comparison. His actions better fit those of a jealous suitor than a protective sibling. But she kept that observation to herself.

"Did you say anything to him about it?"

"I sure did." Cordelia set off down the hill, her boots slamming into the earth with increasing aggravation. "As soon as the gentleman left, I took Warren to task for his rude behavior."

"I hope he apologized."

"No. Just the opposite." Cordelia marched on like a soldier who couldn't wait to tear into the enemy. "He started lecturing me on decorum! Can you believe it?"

Hannah didn't reply.

"He warned me not to encourage such men's attentions and said he disliked the changes I was making to my appearance and manner. He made some ridiculous accusation about you being a bad influence on me and predicted that if I continued following your advice, I would end up with a man who only cared about my looks, not one who appreciated me as a person. Made me so mad, I left without collecting my bread money."

Hannah's own ire piqued at the man's audacity. How dare he call her a bad influence? She wanted nothing more than Cordelia's happiness.

Yet a niggling truth poked at her beneath the cloak of her affront.

"As much as I hate to admit it," Hannah said, "there is a bit of wisdom in what he said."

Cordelia stopped in the middle of the road. "What?"

Hannah clasped her friend's elbow and urged her forward. "Keep walking." Once Cordelia was matching her stride again, Hannah continued. "There are many men in this world whose affections never run any deeper than physical attraction. I can't tell you how many society wives I've sewed for who were desperate to recapture their youth because their husbands had lost interest in them. A lasting relationship requires an abiding friendship, godly commitment, and an unselfish love that truly makes a couple one."

"But you know I've already given my heart to Ike."

"I know. And I'm sure he's not the sort of man to care only about a pretty face. However, we *are* hoping to turn his head by altering your physical appearance. If we are successful, you must pray for discernment to determine whether or not his interest develops into something that penetrates that surface we created. Because if it doesn't, he is not the man for you."

Cordelia said nothing, and Hannah walked several yards in silence. "Your brother said the same thing to me, and he was right about that part of it," she finally said. "Beauty *is* superficial, and a relationship built on such a shallow foundation cannot last."

Hannah peered at her friend, but Cordelia's eyes remained focused on the ground in front of her. Judging it best to let her think without interruption, Hannah said nothing further. However, in the resulting quiet, her own mind drifted . . . to Jericho.

Where Cordelia longed to have Ike notice her as a woman, Hannah longed for Jericho to appreciate her inner qualities. He was already physically attracted to her. She'd seen that. As well as the fact that he fought his attraction more vigorously than a cattleman fighting a prairie fire. If only he would trust her enough to allow one of those sparks to ignite his heart, she'd prove her faithfulness, remaining loyal to him all her days. She'd love him passionately and be the mother to his children that he'd never had for himself. She'd tease him and fill his days with laughter until that elusive smile became a permanent fixture on his face. If he ever gave her the chance.

Deep in thought, both women trudged on until they reached the house. There, out of habit more than conscious choice, they went inside and quenched their thirst.

Sitting in the kitchen, Cordelia refilled Hannah's glass from a ceramic water pitcher in the center of the table, then turned and met her gaze. "I want to continue with our plan."

Hannah waited.

"I'm in love with him. I can't give up." Cordelia stood and spun away to stare out the window. After a moment, she pivoted, her hands gripping the back of the chair. "I won't settle for superficial. If that's all he can offer me, I'll let him go. But what if there could be more?" She clenched her fist and pounded it against her breast. "What if he does notice me, and that leads to an attraction, and that attraction leads to love? I can't forfeit the chance. I have to try."

Cordelia's passion enlivened the hope that had been flagging in Hannah's heart. Eyes moist, Hannah rose and circled the table. She wrapped an arm around her friend and hugged her close.

"We'll keep pressing on, then." Hannah rested her head against Cordelia's temple and silently vowed to do everything in her power to help the young woman gain her dream. And if the Lord proved merciful, perhaps she'd realize her own in the process.

J.T. raised his gaze to the roof of the meetinghouse and clenched his jaw. He appreciated a good sermon as much as the next fellow, but as a nondrinking man, today's treatise on the evils of drunkenness had grown tedious after five minutes. J.T. changed positions in his seat, twisting slightly toward the center.

He could almost see her out of the corner of his eye. Two rows back, across the aisle. Sitting next to Ezra.

She'd worn that pretty blue dress, the same one she'd had on the day he'd met her at the depot, the one that made her eyes look like moonlit ponds. Crossing his arms over his chest, he ran his hand across the pocket of his shirt. The crinkle of paper as he brushed past afforded him a momentary satisfaction. Hannah had slipped him the note when he'd helped her out of Ezra's buggy prior to services. Her gaze had sought his, and he'd known that whatever was written on the note was important to her and that she trusted him with it. He'd nodded to her, giving wordless assurance that he would take care of it. Whatever it was.

A self-deprecating smirk tugged at his cheek. If she had asked him to chop down a forest to make her a meadow, he probably would have gone home to fetch an ax. But, of course, she hadn't. She demanded no grand gesture of devotion from him. Just a simple act of kindness springing from her compassionate nature—a nature he had once thought shallow and frivolous. What idiocy.

He'd remained outside with the horses, wanting to ensure his privacy before opening the note. Once all the latecomers were safely inside, he ducked behind a wagon and unfolded the half sheet of paper, heart pounding. Her tidy script looped and curled in lovely patterns, fitting for one so enamored with creating beautiful things. Yet as he read, an odd disappointment filled him. The words were friendly but less personal than he had hoped. Which was absurd. Why should he expect the note to contain an impassioned declaration of her feelings when he'd never given her any reason to develop such affection? Nevertheless, he reread the thing a half dozen times, just because she'd written it.

Jericho,

Please don't mention my mishap at the river to Ezra. I fear he will blame himself for my predicament when it was my own lapse in judgment that caused the problem. I'm sure questions about the damaged carriage will arise, and I will gladly accept responsibility for wrecking the vehicle. All I ask is that when you tell the tale, please minimize the danger of the situation so that Ezra doesn't fret.

Thank you,
Hannah

Now, sitting on the hard bench built more for a school-age child than a grown man, J.T. considered her request. It wouldn't be hard to grant. He hadn't said much to Tom about what had happened beyond letting him know that Hannah was all right, so no one besides Delia should be privy to the events surrounding the buggy accident. He didn't figure it was anyone else's business anyway.

The sermon finally ended, and J.T. gladly rose to his feet to sing the closing song. Ike Franklin led them in three verses of "For the Beauty of the Earth." The hymn's lyrics floated through his heart and fell from his lips with newfound freedom. For the first time, he felt comfortable praising God not only for the beauty of the earth and skies, but for the beauty of the people around him, a certain dressmaker in particular. Like any other heavenly gift, beauty could be corrupted. He'd witnessed ample evidence to that effect in his lifetime. However, Hannah had proven that such a fate wasn't inevitable. Her inner character exuded as much loveliness as her physical features—a combination that succeeded in reflecting the glory of her Creator much like a field of bluebonnets or a host of gleaming stars in the night sky.

But what did she see when she looked at him? A grouchy old bear, most likely. J.T. bit down on the edge of his tongue, wishing he had a toothpick to grind. He had no right to hope that Hannah could care for him. Every time he opened his mouth around her, he managed to insult either her or her business.

If she needed him, she might be willing to overlook his bullheadedness, but the woman was as independent and capable as any man. Running her own business. Hanging her own shelves. She even managed to rescue herself from a flash flood. All he'd done was drag her out of the water. Hannah didn't need his money, his strength, or his skills. All he could offer her was his heart. But would that be enough? It hadn't been for his mother. And even though Hannah shared as much in common with his mother as a dove did with a rattlesnake, he couldn't quite banish the doubt that gnawed on his gut.

J.T. added his amen to that of the congregation even though he hadn't heard a word of the prayer the preacher had pontificated. He silently begged God's pardon for his inattention as the hum of conversation escalated around him. Ike Franklin approached and shook his hand.

"Good to see you, J.T."

"Ike."

The fellow darted a glance at Delia and stammered an inane greeting. Delia smiled and stepped closer, which set the man rocking back on his heels.

"I enjoyed the songs you led this morning," Delia said.

"Th-thank you, Miss Tucker." His face reddened, and he stretched his neck as if trying to escape a snug collar. "I . . . uh . . . remembered you mentioning that 'Father of Mercies' was one of your favorites."

Since when did Ike get nervous around Delia? He saw her every day, for pity's sake.

"Indeed it is. The others you selected were uplifting, as well. I especially liked 'Sweet By and By.' The lilting melody put me in mind of a boat of believers sailing for heaven and singing of the joy that awaited them on that beautiful shore."

"I've never thought of it that way, but you're quite right."

J.T. frowned as he shifted his gaze from Ike to Cordelia and back again. Normal people talked about the weather, crops, or their sick aunt Myrtle after services, not poetic song lyrics. What was going on with these two? Poor Ike was probably wishing he'd never opened his mouth. J.T. cleared his throat to gain the man's attention and was about to offer a comment on the recent rains when someone slipped up beside him and touched his arm.

"Excuse me, Mr. Tucker." Hannah smiled up at him, and J.T. promptly forgot about his noble intentions to rescue Ike. "I find myself in need of your assistance. Would you mind stepping outside with me for just a moment?"

"Of course." Ike could fend for himself.

"I hope it's not something too serious, Miss Richards," Ike said.

"Not at all, but thank you for your concern. I'm sure Mr. Tucker will set everything to rights for me in no time."

Feeling like he'd just grown two inches taller, J.T. followed her as she made her way down the aisle. She didn't stop at the steps or even the yard, but strode directly to Ezra's buggy. Did she want him to fix something on the old man's rig? He crammed his hat onto his head and caught up to her, confident he could take care of whatever she needed.

He stripped out of his good Sunday coat and hung it over Ezra's worn leather seat. "What needs fixing?"

Hannah leaned back against the coal-box body of the carriage and drew a line in the dirt with the toe of her shoe. "Oh, I think you've already taken care of it."

J.T. squinted at her. "I don't understand."

She smiled. "I know."

What was she up to? He stared at her until she finally looked away.

A sick suspicion that she'd just manipulated him churned his stomach. A pretty smile, a touch on his arm, and he'd followed her like a pup on a leash. "So you lied to me?" he growled. He was no better than his father after all. "You don't need me." He jerked his coat off the seat and stomped off. *Women!* He should have known better than to let his defenses down.

"Wait, Jericho. I didn't lie." Hannah ran up behind him and latched on to his arm.

He shook off her hold.

"I *did* need you to come outside, Jericho, but that was all. Just come outside."

He spun to glare at her. "What kind of riddle is that?"

The sparkle that lit her eyes a moment ago disappeared. "You were going to interrupt them. They needed more time. Without your interference."

None of this was making any sense. He slapped his fist against his thigh and jerked his shoulders up in question. "Who?" he demanded. "Who needed more time?"

"Cordelia and Ike."

"Delia and . . ." All at once, the scales fell from his eyes, followed by an infusion of sweet relief. She hadn't been manipulating him. Well, maybe a little, but it had only been a harmless ploy to aid his sister, not some feminine machination to twist him to her will. She was simply playing matchmaker.

With his sister.

His ire sparked back to life.

"Delia and Ike? Ike is the man you hinted at all those weeks ago? The man Delia's pining after?"

Hannah glanced around the yard. "Hush. Someone will hear you."

J.T. didn't care about the volume of his voice. His sister was in there flirting with a man. A man whom she visited every day. Alone. With no one to chaperone.

"If he's stepped out of line with her, so help me, I'll—"

Hannah grabbed the ends of his black string necktie to restrain him. He glared down at her in disbelief. She glared right back. "Cool your heels, cowboy. Nothing improper has happened and nothing's going to happen. They're in a church with dozens of other people, for heaven's sake. Stop and think for a minute."

J.T. flared his nostrils and drew in several deep breaths.

"Cordelia's not a girl anymore, Jericho. She's a woman of marriageable age. An intelligent, loving, giving woman who longs to share her life with someone."

He ground his teeth. His mind recognized the truth in her words, but his heart fought against it. Delia was his baby sister, his responsibility, his family.

"Ike Franklin is a decent man, a godly man," Hannah insisted. "He'd make a good husband. Unless you know of some blot on his character that Cordelia is unaware of?"

He'd considered the man a friend for years. Respected him, too. He had no reason to change his opinion just because he'd decided to take an interest in his sister. But Delia married? It seemed too soon. Even if most girls already had husbands and even a kid or two by the time they were nineteen. Not Delia. She'd kept house for him and quietly gone about her duties, never hinting that she was anything but content. And he'd never bothered to ask.

"Jericho?"

He blinked and refocused on the woman in front of him. Exhaling, he unclenched his fists and laid a palm over Hannah's hand, the one still clutching his necktie.

"You're right," he said. Her grip loosened, and he shifted his fingers until she released his tie strings in favor of his hand. It felt awfully good holding her arm against his chest. Delia deserved to feel this way, too. "If I had to pick a husband for her, Ike would be a likely candidate. I guess I just have a hard time picturing Delia under another man's protection."

"She'll always be your family, Jericho. Those bonds won't be severed. But there are some spaces in a woman's heart that a brother's love cannot fill."

He peered into her eyes. A warmth glowed in their depths, daring him to believe that she was speaking as much for herself as for Delia. He covered the length of her arm with his and tugged her close. She came to him, her body only a whisper away. The pink of her lips beckoned to him, promising softness and delight. He wrapped his left arm about her waist. He dipped his chin.

Then the distant drone of voices hit a marked crescendo as the congregation filed out of the building and began swarming toward the wagons.

This was not the time, nor the place.

But as he stepped away from Hannah and released her hand, J.T. vowed to himself that there would be a time and a place. Soon.

26

During the noon hour the next day, J.T. kept one eye on the street as he oiled a pile of spare harness leather in his office. Delia had passed by thirty minutes ago with Ike's lunch in hand and hadn't yet returned. As soon as she did, he planned to have a little talk with the telegraph operator.

Two bridles and a pair of reins later, she finally moseyed by, all smiley and dreamy-eyed. J.T. spat out his toothpick so hard it arced over his desk. His fingers curled into fists, tangling in the breast strap he'd been working on. Breathing deeply, he unclenched his hands and gently set the leather aside.

He trusted Delia. Shoot. He even trusted Ike. But there was something about the two of them together that stuck in his craw. Probably because he wasn't quite ready to admit that his baby sister had grown up. It had been just the two of them for so long—even before Pop died, truth be known—and J.T. had a hard time bending his mind around the idea of turning her care over to another man. Yet she deserved happiness, a family of her own, children.

J.T. pushed to his feet and started for the door. He wouldn't keep her from her dreams, but heaven help him, he'd make sure no one hurt her along the way, either. If Ike didn't have good answers to the questions he was fixin' to get asked, the man could kiss his homemade lunches good-bye.

After telling Tom where he was headed, J.T. marched down the street toward the edge of town, where the telegraph office sat across from the hotel. He chose the dirt instead of the boardwalk to avoid the people milling about. In no mood to chat, he lifted a hand if someone called out a greeting but otherwise kept his mouth shut and his gaze locked on the telegraph office.

"J.T. Tucker! Just the man I'm looking for." Elliott Paxton dashed down the walk on the opposite side of the street.

J.T. tried the wave-and-ignore method, but Paxton had never been one for subtlety. He scurried directly into J.T.'s path and clapped him on the shoulder as if completely unaware of his efforts to avoid him. Then again, the fellow probably *was* unaware. Elliott Paxton had a tendency to see what he wanted to see.

"Hold up a minute, Tucker. I've got some news you'll want to hear."

J.T. kept walking.

"About a certain property . . ." Paxton let his words dangle like a worm on a hook, and J.T. bit back a sigh. No wonder the man always caught the biggest catfish in the county. His bait was irresistible. J.T. slowed.

"You made contact with the owner?"

Paxton gave a quick nod and slid his focus meaningfully around the street. "Come to my office, and I'll tell you about it."

It took J.T. several seconds to drag his eyes away from the telegraph office, but he knew Ike wasn't going anywhere. Not till his shift ended, anyway. Louisa's roof needed those new shingles. The sooner he got things settled with the owner, the better.

"All right. But I've only got a minute."

The banker's eyes twinkled much as J.T. imagined they did when he reeled in a defeated fish. "It won't take long. I promise."

Anxious to get the chore done, J.T. ate up the ground with his long stride and forced the banker to stutter-step to keep pace. Once in the office, he cut to the heart of the matter.

"So, will he sell?"

Paxton shook his head. "No. At least not for the price you offered."

"I can't afford more," J.T. admitted as he dropped into a chair. "Besides, the place ain't even worth what I did offer."

"I know. The fellow claims that he can't get out of his rental agreement with Mrs. James. If he sold to you, he'd have no way to guarantee that you wouldn't turn the woman out."

J.T. slammed his palm against the polished wood of Paxton's desk. "I'd never do that! The whole reason I want to buy the place is to *help* Louisa."

"Yes, I explained that to him, but he refused to relent." Paxton shrugged as he leafed through a stack of papers, setting one aside. "I have no way of knowing if he sincerely cares about Mrs. James's welfare or if he's just using that as an excuse to not sell. Either way, it doesn't bode well for your interests."

"No, it doesn't." J.T. flopped backward into a slouch. Covering the lower half of his face with his hand, he pushed out a long breath.

Slowly, Paxton slid a paper from in front of him over to J.T.'s edge of the desk and rotated it 180 degrees.

J.T. sat forward. "What's this?"

"I still have a few negotiating tricks up my sleeve."

Glancing over the words, J.T. frowned. "This is a contract naming me property manager." He shot a glare across the desk. "I'm no man's lackey, Paxton."

"Of course not, but think about it for a minute. Though the owner's not willing to sell, when I happened to mention the dilapidated state of the structure and how the people of Coventry held him in such low esteem because of his poor oversight, he warmed up to my counterproposal. He agreed to hire a man, on my recommendation, for a small monthly stipend to make repairs and keep the building in good working order. All expenditures will have to be submitted for preapproval, of course, but basically, he would give the manager free reign."

J.T. rubbed his chin, the corner of his mouth tilting up at one corner as he mentally took Paxton's plan a step further. "And if said manager chose to deposit his stipend into Louisa's account . . ."

The banker grinned, and for the first time J.T. recognized the shrewdness in the man's eyes. Paxton continued, "We could honestly tell the widow James that we worked out a deal with the owner to lower her monthly rent in exchange for property maintenance."

"Maintenance I'd be willing to do for her in exchange for . . . say . . . laundry service, since Cordelia is so busy with her baking business these days."

Paxton nodded, and the two men shared a conspirator's chuckle as J.T. signed his name to the contract.

"You brokered me a good deal, Paxton," J.T. said as he thrust out his hand. The banker clasped it firmly.

"Always willing to aid a noble cause."

Leaving in a considerably better mood than when he'd arrived, J.T. bid the banker a good day and crossed the road to the small square building that housed the Western Union office. A bell jangled as he pushed through the door, and Ike emerged from the back room to meet him at the counter.

"Afternoon, J.T. Need to send a wire?"

"Nope. Need to visit with you. About Delia."

The man's face paled and then turned an entertaining shade of red before finally settling on a dull pink. He coughed a bit but then lifted his chin and faced J.T. squarely. "Come around the counter. We can talk in back."

J.T. mentally ticked one mark in Ike's column as he stepped through the doorway that led to a simple room that held only a table with a telegraph machine and a couple of chairs. The room was cozy. Too cozy. He scratched out Ike's mark.

"So what's on your mind, J.T.?" Ike asked, offering him a seat with a gesture of his hand.

"I've noticed that Delia takes longer to deliver your lunches these days than she used to. Makes me wonder what's changed. Especially after the two of you acted different at church yesterday. Friendlier . . . if you get my meaning."

Ike's face darkened a bit, but he held J.T.'s gaze. "I get your meaning. And you're right. Something has changed. At least on my end."

His eyes shifted away, searching out some far-off point in the space that stretched between the room's walls. "Cordelia's easy to talk to. And she laughs at all my stories." He shrugged a bit as a grin tugged at his mouth. "I was comfortable having her around." His grin faded. "Maybe too comfortable."

J.T.'s gut tightened. "What's that supposed to mean?"

"Nothing untoward," Ike sputtered. "It's just that . . . well . . . she started becoming a pleasant fixture in my day. Talking to her, being with her. I guess I started taking it for granted."

J.T. couldn't be too hard on him for that. He'd been guilty of the same attitude.

"Then she started changing little things about her appearance. Her hairstyle, the cut of her dresses. I didn't say anything about it at first. I figured it was just some notion she'd taken up. But then I overheard some old hens gossiping in the mercantile about how Cordelia must have her sights set on some man to make such efforts. Well, it got me to thinking. And feeling. Things I'd never felt before. I didn't want Cordelia cooking lunches for any other man. Only me."

Ike turned to face J.T., and the earnestness glowing in his eyes erased the last of J.T.'s reservations. "It is my hope to somehow win your sister's affection. And if I am fortunate enough to do so, I plan on making her my wife."

The man had gumption, J.T. would give him that. He wasn't afraid to lay his cards on the table and fight for what he wanted. Had to respect that. But other things spoke even more highly of him. The way his expression softened as he spoke about Delia. The way he cared about earning her affection. He would be a good husband to her.

J.T. stood up and held his hand out to Ike. The other man stared at it a moment before grabbing hold.

"If she'll have you, you're welcome in our family."

He could feel the tension drain out of Ike as he released the man's hand and cuffed him on the shoulder. " 'Course, you might have to share those lunches for a while longer. With me."

Ike grinned. "Deal. Until you find a wife of your own, that is."

They shared a laugh, but as J.T. wandered back out to the street, Ike's parting words climbed under his skin and started itching. A wife of his own. Is that where things were heading with Hannah? He cared about her. A lot. But a wife? He scraped his suddenly damp palms against the sides of his denim trousers. His father had loved his mother, and it destroyed him. J.T. had always blamed his mother for that, but what if his father had been at fault, as well? What if issues other than his mother's dissatisfaction had contributed to the demise of his parents' marriage?

As he neared the livery, Hannah's shop drew J.T.'s attention. An ache settled in his chest. If he let himself love her, would she love him in return? Or would he carry out his father's legacy and disappoint her so often that he drove her away?

27

Later that week, Hannah sat at her sewing machine, its low-pitched whir blending with the rhythmic drumming that drifted from next door. Jericho had somehow convinced Louisa to let him install new shingles. He'd spent an hour or two on her roof every afternoon for the last four days.

And every afternoon for the last four days, Hannah had found a small token on her staircase as she made her way to her room after closing the shop. Always on the second to last step—the one that had broken and sent her plunging into his arms that first day.

Hannah's foot slowed its pumping of the treadle, and a bemused tingle danced over her skin as she thought about the collection of pint-sized Mason jars decorating the crate near her bed. Monday's jar had held a polished stone, round and smooth. Its deep reddish hue carried a horizontal line of quartz along the top that made her think of a fine lady with diamonds at her neck. A small note was included in the jar. *For the beauty of the earth*.

Tuesday's note had read *For the beauty of the skies*. The jar contained a perfectly formed feather, the color so blue Hannah doubted any jay would have given it up without a fight.

On Wednesday, he'd deviated from the hymn lyrics to compose a verse with a more romantic bent. *For the beauty of your heart*. A cottonwood leaf in that very shape sat in the glass cage, its stunning yellow color singing the glory of autumn.

And yesterday she'd found a blue hair ribbon with a note that said *To match the beauty of your eyes*. She'd woven the ribbon into her braided chignon this morning in hopes that Jericho would see it.

Her chest rose and fell on a dreamy sigh, the seam in Cordelia's skirt only half finished. Jericho Tucker was courting her, truly courting her. At least she assumed it was him. He never signed his name to the notes. But who else could it be? No one else understood the significance of that particular step. No one else had nearly kissed her in the churchyard. Memories of that almost-kiss had distracted her all week. It had to be Jericho leaving the gifts.

And the notes? Well, they gave her heart the biggest thrill of all. The positive references to beauty in each one led her to believe that he might finally see her as more than a stumbling block and consider beauty more than a plague to be avoided.

The door to the shop opened, startling her out of her thoughts. A guilty blush heated her cheeks as Cordelia came in.

"I'm running a little behind schedule," Hannah said, glancing up, "but I'll have this ready for you to try on in a jiffy." She rocked the foot peddle back into motion and zipped to the end of the side seam.

Cordelia ambled behind the counter, perfectly at home in Hannah's shop, and sat on the corner of the worktable. "I'm in no hurry. In fact, I could use some time to think."

"About what?"

"Warren." Cordelia exhaled with enough force that Hannah felt a stirring on the back of her neck.

Hannah repositioned the fabric, folded in a dart, and continued sewing. "He's giving you a hard time again?"

"Yes." The word leaked out of her, slow and miserable. "He was waiting for me when I came out of the telegraph office. I think he might have overheard me asking Ike to join us for the Founders' Day picnic."

Stopping the treadle, Hannah turned around in her chair. "How did that go, by the way?"

A shy smile temporarily erased the worry on Cordelia's face. "Ike said he was too fond of my cooking to turn down the invitation."

Hannah grinned. "I saw the way he was stammering around you at church last Sunday. I think it's more than your cooking that draws him."

"I'm starting to think so, too." Cordelia ducked her head, her cheeks turning a delighted pink.

"I knew he couldn't stay blind to you forever." Hannah laughed, truly happy for her friend. "I can't wait to see you two together at the picnic next Saturday."

"Seeing the two of us together is what got under Warren's skin."

Hannah clipped off the thread ends and flipped the skirt right side out. "I think Warren's sweet on you, Cordelia."

Her friend let out a groan of frustration. "I didn't want to believe you when you suggested that before, but I can't deny it any longer. He proposed to me. Right there on the boardwalk."

Unable to disguise her shock, Hannah sucked in a too-fast breath and started coughing. Cordelia came over and pounded her on the back. Eyes watering from her choking spell, Hannah looked up at Cordelia's grimacing face. "He proposed?"

"Oh, Hannah. It was the most dreadful experience. He insulted Ike and said that he only looked at me because of the change to my appearance. He said Ike didn't care for the true me—not like he did—and if a man was too ignorant to love me when I was a shy little mouse, he wasn't worth having."

"He actually called you a mouse?" The man had no skill in wooing whatsoever.

Cordelia nodded and started pacing around the table. "I didn't know how to respond, so I asked him why he had never declared himself before."

"What did he say?"

"He claimed he'd been waiting to establish himself in his father's business in order to offer me a secure future. But he's been working there for years and never said a word to me."

"Would you have accepted him if he had?"

Cordelia stopped pacing. "No. At least I don't think so. Oh, I don't know." She crossed her arms over her stomach and hugged her ribs. "I've never had romantic feelings toward Warren, but with no one else knocking at my door, I might have considered it."

"Then I'm glad he never said anything." Hannah laid the skirt aside and went to her friend. "You and Warren would have been a wretched match."

"I know." Her breath quivered as she struggled to contain her emotions. "We were friends in school, though. Two outcasts finding camaraderie with one another—he with his birthmark and me, the shy mouse with the shameful mother everyone gossiped about. We were quite a pair. But having each other eased the loneliness. Whenever he grew too sullen, I would make up silly stories, one more ridiculous than the last, until he smiled. He'd sneak me peppermint sticks and lemon drops from his father's store. There is kindness in him. It's just not as apparent now that he's grown."

Conscience pricked, Hannah closed her lips against the uncharitable comments that had sprung to her tongue. Though sullen and insensitive, Warren deserved a measure of compassion. It couldn't have been easy growing up with such a large mark upon his face. But that wasn't sufficient reason for Cordelia to sacrifice her future by binding herself to a bitter man.

"Did you give him an answer?"

"I tried, but he must have sensed I was working up to a negative response, for he interrupted and said that he would call on me tonight after supper."

Sensing Cordelia's dread over the impending visit, Hannah ushered her into the fitting room. She helped her undress and slipped the new skirt up over her hips. As she made a minor adjustment to the waistline, she met Cordelia's gaze in the mirror.

"You should tell Jericho."

Cordelia looked away. "I know. I just worry that J.T. will toss Warren off the porch or something."

Hannah bit back a laugh as she recalled holding the man back in the churchyard over Ike. "He might at that. But as your brother, he should know of the offer. He can help you decide what to do and be there to back you up should Warren not like your answer."

"You're right. I'll tell him." Cordelia sighed and adopted a woebegone expression that bordered on comic. "I just wish I had a sister to commiserate with after it was all over. Someone like you."

Hannah squirmed a bit as she marked the hem. Had Cordelia guessed her feelings toward Jericho? And if so, what did she think about it? Hannah concentrated on matching up the edges of the skirt's burgundy stripes. "You can commiserate with me anytime you like. You know that."

"Tonight?" Cordelia asked, a touch of genuine pleading blending with the mischief in her tone. "Come to supper. I'd feel so much better with you there. And something tells me J.T. won't mind your company, either."

She *did* know.

Hannah straightened. "Cordelia, I—"

Before she could explain, Cordelia grabbed her in an enthusiastic embrace. "You have no idea how happy having you as a sister will make me. J.T. is a little crusty on the outside, but his heart is true and as big as a mountain. He'd be good to you."

Hannah backed away. "Are my feelings for him so obvious?"

"Only to me. Ever since the day the two of you worked those rings together, I've had a suspicion that something might be brewing, and the way J.T. cared for you after pulling you from the river confirmed it." Cordelia stepped out of the skirt and handed it to Hannah, deliberately holding her gaze. "He may not have fully conceded yet, but I have no doubt that you are infiltrating his defenses."

Hannah's stomach dipped and tickled the way it had when she sledded down Parkman's Hill as a child. Everything within her longed to believe that Cordelia was right. Tentatively, her lips stretched into a smile, and she clasped the hand of the young woman she already loved as a sister. "I'd be honored to join you and your brother for supper tonight."

J.T. answered the knock on his front door, his most intimidating scowl already in place. Delia had warned him of Warren's arrival, and J.T. was none too pleased. He liked and respected the kid's old man, but Warren was immature and so caught up in proving his worth that he rarely looked beyond himself. J.T. had no issue with his marked face or his occupation, certain that a store clerk could adequately provide for a wife. But the kid made that old nag of his drag his sorry hide up the hill to church every Sunday when the animal should have been put out to pasture years ago. If he was selfish in the way he treated his horse, who was to say he'd be any different in the way he treated a wife?

Even if Delia favored such a match, J.T. would have been loath to accept Warren's suit on her behalf. He was thankful his sister's tender heart and girlhood loyalty didn't outweigh her common sense. Ike was a much better choice.

"G-good evening, Mr. Tucker." Warren barely looked him in the eye. Although, to be fair, that was mostly because the kid's long hair dangled in the way. J.T. would've respected him more if he stood up straight, combed his hair back, and took pride in himself. So what if he had a blotch on his face? If he'd stop reminding people that he was ashamed of it by covering it with his hair, folks might actually get used to the thing and forget about it.

J.T. was tempted to educate the fellow, but something told him his advice would not be welcome. Instead, he crossed his arms and stared the young man down. "Warren."

"Is Cordelia at home? I believe she's expecting me." He twitched and flung his hair off his forehead, only to have it fall back in his face.

"She'll be along in a minute," J.T. said. "You planning to visit with her on the porch this evening?"

"Yes, sir."

"Good. I'll keep an eye on you from the kitchen, then."

Warren tugged on his sleeves, looking about as comfortable in his sack suit as a man who had rolled in poison oak the day before.

"Stop terrorizing him, J.T.," Delia said from behind him. "Warren knows how to act the part of a gentleman."

J.T. stepped aside to let his sister pass, his eyes still locked on the man who had come calling. A disturbing flare of insolence crossed Warren's features at Delia's words, as if he were daring J.T. to contradict them. J.T. unfolded his arms and took a step toward him. The insolence vanished. Satisfied, J.T. retreated into the house and closed the door.

He headed for the kitchen and stopped in the doorway. Hannah, a full dishpan between her and the window, was leaning forward, her nose nearly touching the glass.

"I see I'm not the only one interested in what's going on out there."

She jumped, and a plate slid out of her hand, splashing water into her face. "Oh!" She squinted against the unexpected geyser.

J.T. hurried to her side, slid a towel from the bar by the pump, and gently dabbed the droplets from her face. He stroked the cotton cloth over her forehead, cheeks, and chin. Then, just for good measure, he lightly ran it over her lips, as well. Her pink tongue reached out to moisten them again, and heat rose inside him.

"Thank you." Her low voice sent a shiver through him.

He cleared his throat. "You're welcome."

She blinked, and the building fervor in her eyes dispersed, replaced by a teasing twinkle he found almost as alluring. "Now that you've got that towel in hand," she said, "you can dry." Hannah retrieved the sunken plate and handed it to him with a grin.

He raised an eyebrow but accepted the dish. "Just don't tell my sister I know how to do this, or she may put me to work every night."

Hannah extracted her dripping fingers from the water long enough to flick him with a few sprinkles. He frowned, earning him a laugh from the sprite at his side.

"My mama always said dishwater could cure any ailment. It'd be good for you to be close to it more often."

J.T. doubted it could cure what ailed him, but then he wasn't all that sure he wanted to be cured anymore.

They lapsed into a comfortable silence broken only by the clink of crockery and glassware. As he waited for her to pass him another plate, he admired the line of her neck. Slender and pale, with a perfect little hollow near her collar that his lips longed to taste. Veering away from temptation, his gaze roamed up to the braided knot low on her head. A blue thread peeked out at him from between the strands and his heart gave a little leap. She was wearing his ribbon.

A part of him had worried that she'd find his gifts juvenile. Heaven knew he'd felt juvenile leaving them, like a kid in short pants bringing his teacher a fistful of dandelions. After all, what kind of man gave a woman a leaf or a bird feather? Yet after contemplating Ike and Delia's discussion of hymn lyrics, he realized women liked poetry. At least Delia did. His mother would have turned her nose up at a paltry rhyme and objects that cost nothing but patience to acquire. However, he thought Hannah might appreciate them. He'd hoped she would, anyway. A woman who saw beauty in a shiny button and a wooden hummingbird should be able to find it in other small things, too. Right?

He'd stolen the first lines of his poetry from the hymn they'd sung at the close of church last Sunday, only adding a few lines of his own at the end. Each evening, he'd hunted the countryside for the right gift to offer the following day, but he never quite worked up the courage to hand it to her in person. So he'd shoved the things into jars and left them on her step. Not knowing his sister had invited Hannah to dinner, he'd left another gift a mere hour before she showed up at his home. He'd run out of poetic things to say, so he'd simply left the jar, filled with a lopsided bouquet of yellow sunflowers.

Never one to play the coward for long, J.T. steeled himself as Hannah turned to pass him a platter. "So . . . uh . . . did you like the sunflowers?"

Her eyes widened slightly and roses bloomed in her cheeks, but the smile that followed unclenched his gut. "I loved them. And all the other gifts, as well. Thank you."

"You're welcome."

She bent back to her task, rummaging around in the grayish water for something else to wash. "I had hoped they were from you." She spoke in such a quiet tone, he had to strain to hear her. "I would have thanked you earlier, but there was no signature on any of the notes. I didn't want to make a fool of myself if the sender turned out to be someone else."

That's what being a coward got a man—confusion and an uncomfortable spark of jealousy. Forcing a casual air to his voice he was far from feeling, he asked the question that burned in his belly. "You got someone else courting you?"

"No." The fork she'd been scrubbing slid from her hand, returning to the murky depths. "But then, I wasn't sure I had you courting me, either. I seem to recall you expressing a number of objections to my suitability in the past."

"That's because I was close-minded and couldn't see past my own experiences."

Her head spun toward his and the open vulnerability in her eyes branded his heart. For the first time in his life, he wished he were the kind of man who knew how to woo a woman with pretty words. With his luck, though, he'd mangle the attempt and trample her feelings. He'd have to show her instead.

Slowly, he drew her hands from the water and dried them with his towel, aware that she was watching his movements. He ran his palm up her arm and cupped her shoulder. Then, unable to resist, he traced the shape of that delightful hollow at the base of her neck with his fingertip. A tremor passed through her, and the nearly inaudible sound of her breath catching made his pulse throb.

He slipped his hand around the back of her neck. His fingers toyed with the downy hair at her nape while his thumb caressed her cheek and ear. Hannah's lashes fluttered closed, then languidly lifted to reveal eyes darkened to a midnight blue. Her lips parted slightly, and he extracted his hand just enough to trail his thumb across their softness.

"I was wrong," he murmured. "No one could be more suitable."

Digging his fingers into her hair, he dragged her close and lowered his mouth.

The front door banged closed. Hannah jumped and tried to pull out of his embrace, but he wasn't quite ready to let her go. He might never be.

"Jericho." Hannah's frantic whisper restored his common sense, and he allowed the slender fingers that had been clutching his shirt a moment ago to push him away.

Delia stood in the doorway, looking from him to Hannah and back again. He positioned himself in front of Hannah, trying to absorb the majority of the scrutiny, while mentally listing all the reasons he shouldn't strangle his sister.

"Warren leave?" he groused.

"Not happily, but yes, he accepted my refusal and left." She cocked a hip and planted her fist against it. "You know, he could have been out there compromising my virtue for all the attention you paid. Get distracted, J.T.?"

He snatched the towel from the floor and threw it at her. "Finish up the dishes while I walk Miss Richards home." Taking Hannah's hand, he tugged her toward the door, but after a few faltering steps, she stopped.

"Wait," she said. "Cordelia invited me here tonight in order to have someone to talk to after Mr. Hawkins left." Her face was glowing as red as a radish, yet instead of taking the escape he'd offered, she was holding firm to her promise. "Why don't you finish the dishes while Cordelia and I talk? I'll let you know when I'm ready to go."

"Yeah, big brother. Finish the dishes." The imp tossed the towel in his face and then giggled as she absconded with Hannah, the two disappearing behind the door of her bedroom.

Comforting himself with the fact that he could still look forward to escorting Hannah home, J.T. rolled up his sleeves and plunged his hands into the lukewarm water. He never thought he'd be reduced to doing dishes while the two women he loved talked about him behind closed doors.

The tip of a knife jabbed his finger as that thought took hold. The women he loved. He loved Hannah.

J.T. stuck his pricked finger into his mouth to stem the trickle of blood, then dunked it back in the water.

Father had always warned him that love made a man do crazy things. He'd been right. Two able-bodied women were currently under his roof, yet *he* was the one doing the dishes.

28

Did he kiss you?"

Hannah sighed and pressed her shoulder blades into the closed door, wishing she could give an affirmative answer to that question. "We're supposed to be talking about you, remember?"

Cordelia tucked a leg beneath her and sat on the bed. She bounced on the mattress and grinned. "Well, did he?"

Hannah couldn't quite meet Cordelia's eye. "Almost."

Her friend moaned and flopped backward on the bed. "I should have put up with Warren for a few more minutes."

Yes, Hannah's heart cried, but her mind knew better. She moved to the bed and sat on the corner next to her recumbent friend. "Of course not. Now, tell me how things went out there."

Cordelia rolled onto her side to face Hannah. "Some good, some bad. He apologized for waiting so long to tell me of his feelings and then springing them on me without any warning." She fiddled with a button on the front of her dress. "We reminisced a little, which was nice, but then he showed me the ring he'd picked out from his father's store. I panicked."

"Did he propose again?"

"I didn't let him." She finally looked up. "Oh, Hannah, I didn't want to hurt him. I thanked him for being a good friend to me, but he kept shoving that ring in my face as if it would change my mind. I worried that if I didn't escape soon, he would seize my hand and force it onto my finger against my will. I scurried toward the door, said that I was sorry, but I didn't love him the way a wife should love a husband, wished him a good night, and retreated into the house, leaving him out on the porch all by himself." She flopped onto her back and covered her eyes with her arm. "I've never been so rude to anyone in all my life. I feel horrible about it."

"Well, don't." Hannah drew Cordelia's arm away from her face and tugged her up into a sitting position. "Warren was much too forward. He frightened you. You had every right to flee. It would have been foolish not to."

Cordelia laid her head on Hannah's shoulder. "I was so afraid J.T. would storm out and beat Warren to a pulp. When I realized he'd been too hung up on you to even notice what happened, I counted my blessings. I may not want to marry Warren, but I'm not anxious to see him pulverized, either."

A tinge of guilt overshadowed Hannah's joy. What if Cordelia had truly been in trouble? She never would have forgiven herself if she had kept Jericho from intervening.

The thought must have shown on her face, for when Cordelia lifted her head, she gave Hannah a little swat on the arm. "Don't go blaming yourself for anything. If I had needed J.T.'s help, I would have made enough noise to catch his attention. He was distracted, not deaf."

"Just the same, I'm glad you won't have to deal with Warren any longer. He won't continue pursuing you, will he?"

"No. He's not the type to ignore my wishes. He might sulk for a while, and I wouldn't be surprised if he stopped speaking to me, but things will clear up between us eventually. They always do."

"Well, then." Hannah squeezed Cordelia's hand. "Let's put Warren out of our minds for now and focus on Ike, shall we?"

Cordelia grinned and bobbed her head in agreement.

"Founders' Day is only a week away. You and Ike will be together for an entire afternoon. A new dress, a shared picnic, a chance to sneak away from the crowd to talk and possibly even share a kiss."

"If only I could be so lucky."

"We're not going to wait on luck." Hannah arched her brow and gave Cordelia a conspiratorial wink.

"What's dancing around in that mind of yours, Hannah Richards?"

"I might not be able to make Ike kiss you, but I have a plan to ensure he gets a window of opportunity should he wish to try."

Founders' Day arrived, and J.T. found himself in the kitchen again, this time fetching and carrying for his sister.

"Place the two covered dishes in the first crate and the stockpot full of fried chicken in the second while I finish up these deviled eggs." Her skirt billowed out behind her as she dashed about the room, turning in circles fast enough to make him dizzy.

"What's in the covered dishes?" He thought of just lifting the lids and seeing for himself, but when Delia was in a tizzy, one didn't touch her food unless he was ready for a smack from a wooden spoon or some other handy utensil. There were too many knives within her reach for him to tempt fate.

"Carrot salad in one, potato in the other." She didn't spare him a glance as she mashed boiled egg yolks with the back of a silver spoon. "You also need to pack two jars of my pickles. One sweet. One dill."

J.T. lugged the heavy dishes to the waiting crates. "You sure you got enough food, sis?"

Delia stopped mashing her yolks for a second and bit her lip. "Maybe not. With Louisa and her brood joining us, as well . . . I thought I had enough, but . . . Better throw in an extra loaf of bread and some apple butter."

"I was kidding." J.T. chuckled and shook his head at her. "You have enough here to feed the entire town. It's a good thing no one rented the General. We'll need that freight wagon to haul all this stuff to the mill pond. Besides, Hannah and Louisa are contributing, too."

She glared at him. "Just the same, add the apple butter. I already have two bread loaves packed in the basket with the pound cake and cookies. Hannah is bringing a batch of biscuits and preserves, so we probably won't need the extra loaf. Louisa said she'd bring sliced ham sandwiches to go with the chicken."

He dug out the jar of apple butter and carried the crates and bread basket out to the wagon. When he returned, Delia had the egg halves back together and skewered with a mess of his toothpicks. She piled them in a small pail and covered them with a checkered cloth. "Don't take this one out until we're ready to go, and then make sure to keep it out of the sun."

"Aye, Captain." J.T. took the pail from her and saluted.

She shoved him. "Stop it, you rascal. I need to get changed." Delia flounced past him, then stopped short. "Oh! I completely forgot about the tin plates, napkins, forks."

J.T. steered her back toward her room. "I'll gather all that stuff. Go get ready. At this rate, the activities are going to be half over before we get there."

With a reluctant nod, she headed off to change. She couldn't let him handle things completely, though, for every few minutes she shouted through the closed door for him to pack something else. A bread knife, the box of tumblers for the lemonade and cider that would be available, two or three old quilts, and on and on until he started to doubt they'd have any room left in the wagon for passengers.

Once everything was finally loaded, J.T. pulled his suit coat from the back of a kitchen chair and slipped his arms into the sleeves. It seemed backward to him to dress up in his Sunday best for a picnic, but women insisted on wearing their finest to these rare social events, and their men were expected to follow suit. He settled the wool coat on his shoulders, gave it a tug, and strode down the hall to rap on Delia's door. "Come on. You've primped enough. Ike's going to think you stood him up if we don't get a move on."

The hinges creaked as she eased the door open. Delia took a tentative step, then bit her lip and ran a hand down the front of her dress. "I feel like I'm a little girl again, dressing up in Mama's clothes. Do I look ridiculous?"

J.T. couldn't speak. He just stared at the lovely woman his sister had become, wondering how he could have missed seeing it until this moment. The dress's green fabric warmed her complexion and brought her face to life. At the same time, the tailored top and striped skirt flattered her figure, nipping in at her newly trim waist and hinting at the curves that remained beneath. She'd even refashioned her bonnet, adding a green ribbon and delicate sprigs of flowers. Hannah had brought the butterfly out of her cocoon. A little color, a sophisticated design, and several weeks of friendship and encouragement had turned a plain Delia into a rare beauty.

He held his hand out to her and led her into the hall so he could make a circle around her. When he faced her again, he leaned in and kissed her cheek. "You look stunning, Delia. Truly. Not even our mother could compare."

"Do you think Ike will approve?"

Offering Delia his arm, J.T. swallowed his guffaw. "Darlin', I doubt he'll be able to take his eyes off of you long enough to do much else."

Seeing her face light up in pleasure warmed J.T.'s heart. He had kept her a prisoner in those drab dresses for too long. Come Christmas, he'd buy her lengths of cloth in sunshine yellow, bluebonnet blue, and prairie grass green to replace her navy, brown, and gray housedresses. Practical could still be pretty.

And wouldn't Hannah laugh her hat off if she ever heard him say such a thing.

They closed up the house and headed to Louisa's place. The three kids whooped and danced about as J.T. turned the wagon and parked in front of the laundry. Louisa scolded them halfheartedly, unable to keep her smile at bay. Their contagious excitement soon infected them all.

J.T. took her basket laden with still more food and packed it away with the rest of the feast while Louisa fussed over Delia's new dress and shared tips on how best to clean the lightweight wool fabric. The kids scrambled into the bed of the wagon, eager to be on their way. As J.T. rearranged things to maximize space, Tessa jumped to her feet and waved vigorously.

"Miss Hannah! Miss Hannah! Are you ready for the picnic?"

A low laugh sounded behind him. "I most certainly am. And I brought something for all of us to play with after the games are through."

J.T. turned to greet her as the kids clamored for her to show them the surprise that her left hand secreted behind her flowing skirts. He didn't recognize the wine-colored dress she wore, but it did a marvelous job of accentuating her slim figure and setting off her pale hair. The design was simple and almost plain in comparison to Delia's, yet she carried it with such elegance that, to him, she looked like a queen.

Hannah glanced at him as she neared his side and offered a secret smile that immediately set his mind on kisses and long private walks.

"If Mr. Tucker would be so good as to take this pie for me, I'll show you what I brought."

He reached beneath the pie plate in her right hand and grazed her fingers. Making a show of holding the dessert to his nose, he drew whisper-soft circles on the back of her wrist. "Mmmm. Smells like apple." Then he tilted his head to meet her gaze. "I can't wait for a taste."

Fire rose in her cheeks, and she snatched her hand away so fast he nearly dropped the pie. The basket hanging from the crook of her right elbow swung precariously until she steadied it with her hip. She straightened her arm and angled it downward until the handle of the basket slipped into her hand. Then she thrust it at him with a chiding glance that made him laugh.

Throughout it all, she kept her surprise safely out of the children's view with her opposite arm. Stepping away from him, she pulled it out from behind her skirts with a flourish.

"A kite!" Tessa hopped up and down, clapping her hands. The wagon creaked in protest, but no one seemed to care. "And you used the pretty material I like so much. Can I fly it first?"

Danny shot to his feet. "I'm the oldest. I should go first."

"What about me?" Mollie whined.

Hannah grinned at the children. "Everyone will get a turn. I promise." Then her eyes narrowed. "But the next person who asks to go first will wait the longest."

Each little mouth closed, and all three youngsters plopped back down on their bottoms. J.T. was duly impressed.

Reaching around her, he wedged the pie into a protected corner and found a place for the basket, as well. He pivoted back to Hannah and held his palm out. "Your kite, milady?"

She curtsied and handed it to him. "Why, thank you, Sir Tucker. Take care, though. The fabric is wont to snag."

J.T. bowed in return, and the children giggled at their antics. The fabric in question was a rich violet hue that shimmered in the sunlight. He ran his finger across the kite's diamond-shaped body. Its smooth, luxurious texture surprised him.

"Is this silk?" he whispered in her ear.

"Just a small piece." She kept smiling at the children as she spoke to him out of the corner of her mouth. "Tessa has admired that cloth for weeks. This way she can enjoy it."

It had to be one of the most expensive fabrics she carried in her shop, yet she'd made it into a kite to please an eight-year-old girl. "You know it'll probably just get hung up in a tree, right?"

"I certainly hope so." This time she turned her smile on him. "Half the fun of kite flying is rescuing them when they go astray."

Her frolicsome spirit charmed him, heightening his anticipation of spending the day with her.

"All right, everyone," he announced in a loud voice. "Load up. We've got a picnic to go to."

J.T. carefully balanced the kite frame between the bread and sandwich baskets while Louisa seated herself on the tailgate of the wagon, her feet dangling above the road.

"I'll sit back here with my young'uns," she said, waving off J.T.'s offer to ride up front. "That there driver's seat will be crowded enough without me trying to cram in, too."

J.T. tipped his hat to her and made his way to the other ladies waiting patiently for his assistance. He made sure to hand Hannah up first so she could sit next to him. Settling beside her, glad for the tight quarters as his leg pressed against hers, he took up the reins and released the brake. "Everybody ready?"

A chorus of affirmative responses rang out, the women in the front equaling the volume of the kids in the rear. Grinning like a kid himself, J.T. snapped the leather straps and set the vehicle in motion. Something told him this would be a Founders' Day he'd not soon forget.

29

Thanks to the group's high spirits, Hannah didn't think about their need to cross the river at the ill-fated bridge until it was upon them. She tried to hide her unease beneath a pasted-on smile, but Jericho must have felt her tension, for he took her hand and hooked it under his arm before they reached the wooden structure. Grateful to have something solid to hold on to, and equally grateful that he had the good sense to keep both hands on the reins, Hannah gripped his bicep, comforted by the undeniable strength of the muscle beneath her fingers.

The wheels rolled onto the bridge planks, making a series of hollow thumps. The kids chattered, wind strummed through the river birch leaves, and the horses' hooves clip-clopped in a blend of sound that would have brought a sense of peaceful harmony to any other listener. Yet the roar in Hannah's memory drowned out the gentle song. Her hold on Jericho's arm tightened.

She knew she was being foolish. The river had receded. It was no more threatening than a tub of bathwater. Nevertheless, that logic failed to drive out her fear.

Jericho hugged her hand to his side by squeezing his arm against his ribcage, which helped a bit, but when he started humming, she finally began to relax. The low vibrations calmed and soothed her, and the odd thought that he probably used the same technique on his nervous mares made her lips twitch in genuine amusement. The deep melody of "Rock of Ages" moved through her like hot chocolate, warming her spirit and restoring her equilibrium. Jericho sat solid at her side, but there was another who offered an even greater security, and it was that reminder, more than the soothing hum of the music, that finally banished her fear.

As they returned to the road, Hannah slid her hand out from Jericho's arm. He turned and frowned at her, pointedly looking at her hand as if to chastise it for abandoning its post. She smiled at him and mouthed the words *Thank you*. He winked, then refocused his attention on driving.

They turned north and followed the river until they came upon a glen overflowing with wagons, buggies, and more people than Hannah had ever seen in Coventry at one time. Men tossed horseshoes while women tended babies and visited with neighbors. Girls rolled barrel hoops across the open prairie, and boys chased each other around the grounds while trying to snitch food when their mothers weren't looking. Old folks sat in the shade of the limestone grist mill near the edge of the river and oversaw the distribution of lemonade and cider from the large jugs and kegs available on a sawhorse table sheltered by the east wall.

Hannah struggled to take everything in as the wagon bumped off the road and moved toward an oak tree that would offer the horses and picnickers a touch of shade. "Is the entire county here?" she asked as the General waggled over a particularly uneven stretch of terrain. Stuck in the middle with no handle to grab for balance, she alternated pitching into Jericho and Cordelia until Jericho wrapped his arm around her shoulders and anchored her to his side.

"No, only about a third of the county shows up for Coventry's Founders' Day celebration." Jericho glanced down at her, and Hannah blinked. In the cozy pocket beneath his arm, she'd forgotten she'd even asked the question. "Meridian is the county seat, so most go to their events, but we get farmers and ranchers from within a ten-mile radius or so."

The ground flattened out again as they neared the tree, yet Jericho made no move to release his hold on her. Not that Hannah minded. Well, she minded the amused glances Cordelia kept shooting at her, but she discovered that if she leaned her head slightly into Jericho's chest, she no longer saw them.

All too soon, though, Jericho pulled the rig to a halt. "We're here!"

His announcement was met with squeals of delight and clunking footfalls as the James children scampered out of the wagon bed.

"Stay where I can see you," Louisa warned as the youngsters ran to join their friends.

Jericho got out and circled the wagon to help Cordelia alight, then reached for Hannah. His hands lingered at her waist longer than they had on his sister, and a secret little thrill coursed through her. He graced her with one of his rare, glorious smiles that turned her bones to jelly and then left her in her wobbly state in order to unload the mountain of food Cordelia had packed. It took two large breaths and a stern mental lecture on the fortitude of the Richards women before Hannah's bones stiffened enough to allow her to assist the others.

Louisa spread the quilts out and secured them against the wind with rocks and some of the larger food dishes while Jericho took care of the horses. Cordelia shuffled food back and forth, emptying baskets and organizing everything. Not wanting to interfere with her system, Hannah opted to play it safe and unpack the plates and utensils. As she stacked the forks on top of a pile of bleached linen napkins, she caught a glimpse of Jericho walking toward the group of men congregated at a sandy patch of ground that served as the horseshoe pit.

She admired his confident stride and the way the group eagerly welcomed him into their midst. He was a man a woman would take pride in calling husband. And despite the fact that she had no legal claim to him yet, the possessiveness surging through her veins was undeniable.

Like a cowboy working a herd, Jericho wove in and out of the group until he culled out the steer he wanted. Then with a wave, he and the slightly shorter man departed. She couldn't make out the other fellow's features from this distance, but there was no doubt of his identity.

Pushing aside the box of tumblers she had just opened, Hannah turned to warn Cordelia. In an effort to lay everything out to perfection, she was bent at the waist, painstakingly arranging deviled egg halves in the shape of a daisy on a round platter. The eggs were lovely, but Hannah feared Ike would be too undone by the sight of Cordelia's upended back end to notice. Not exactly the first impression they had envisioned for this all-important day.

Hannah rushed to her friend's side and tried to straighten her posture.

"Just a minute." Cordelia resisted Hannah's efforts, all those exercises lending her an inconvenient amount of strength. "I only have two more—"

"He's coming," Hannah hissed in her ear. "You don't want to greet your beloved with your bum in the air, do you?"

Cordelia popped up so fast, Hannah had to dodge sideways to avoid a mouthful of bonnet. Her friend spun around, and when she spotted the two men closing in, she started wringing her hands in front of her.

"Ike's coming." The dullness of her voice worried Hannah.

"Yes, dear." Hannah smiled and reshaped an uneven pleat in the gathered fabric that draped delicately over Cordelia's hips.

"What do I do? What do I say?" The girl's eyes remained fixed on Ike, but all the color drained from her face. Her fainting into the carrot salad seemed a very real threat.

Hannah stepped in front of her friend and deliberately positioned herself to block Cordelia's view of Ike. "This is just like any other day when you bring him lunch. You will smile and chat as you always do. You will act as if nothing is different, for truly nothing of importance is. The only thing you've changed is your clothes."

"Nothing's different," Cordelia chanted under her breath.

Hearing the men's footsteps behind her, Hannah modeled a bright smile, holding it in place until Cordelia matched it with one of her own. Then swinging wide like a book cover revealing the tantalizing first page of a love story, Hannah moved aside.

No one spoke for several heartbeats. Ike stared at Cordelia, his mouth slightly agape and his brows arched higher than the windows of a London cathedral. Cordelia's smile had slipped to a crooked angle, but she had plenty of color in her cheeks now.

A throat cleared behind them. Louisa sidled past. "I'm gonna go fetch my young'uns."

Ike finally snapped out of his stupor and dragged his hat off his head. "Thank you for inviting me to join you, Miss Tucker. I can't imagine a place I'd rather be."

Cordelia ducked her head for only a moment before bringing her chin back up. Seeing that hard-won confidence at work, Hannah's heart cheered.

"I made several of your favorites," Cordelia said, gesturing toward the blankets. "Fried chicken, potato salad . . . oh, and pound cake."

"My mouth is watering already. May I help you lay out the food?"

Cordelia hesitated. "Well, Hannah has—"

"—been waiting for a chance to scout out a suitable place for kite flying." Hannah gave Cordelia a pointed look before turning her attention to Ike. "If you don't mind taking over for me, Mr. Franklin. I plan to take the James children kite flying after we eat, and knowing which direction to go would save time and hopefully keep any squabbling to a minimum."

Ike chuckled. "I would be more than willing to lend Cori . . . er . . . I mean . . . Miss Tucker a hand."

The poor man's face turned a vivid shade of red, but Hannah could not have been more pleased. A man who gave a woman a pet name, even unintentionally, must surely be smitten.

"Thank you. We'll be back shortly." Hannah tugged on Jericho's arm.

He cocked a brow at her. "We? I'm not going anywhere."

Ike swallowed and reached for the edge of his collar.

"Of course you are," Hannah declared with forced brightness. "I need your expertise. I'm completely unfamiliar with this area. Please?" As unobtrusively as she could, she slid her foot atop his and ground her heel into his toe. His frown held steady as he glared at Ike. Not even a wince. *Drat.* His boots were probably too thick. How was she supposed to signal him to stop his overbearing brother routine if she couldn't get his attention? She was debating whether or not to pinch the back of his arm when he surprised her by capitulating.

"Fifteen minutes," he grumbled, and stalked off toward the river.

"Thank you!" Hannah raised her voice, yet Jericho gave no indication that he heard her. She shrugged. "I guess he's eager to start the search."

"Or eager to get back," Ike mumbled.

Hannah bent close to him. "Well, I bought you fifteen minutes. Make good use of it."

His startled eyes shot to hers, and then a grin stole over his features. "An excellent notion, Miss Richards."

"What's an excellent notion?" Cordelia looked as if she wanted to crawl into a hole. Either that or bury her brother in one.

Hannah winked at her. "I'll let Ike explain." Then she dashed after Jericho.

When she caught up to him, he started limping. Dramatically.

"What were you trying to do back there, woman? Cripple me?"

She would have felt more guilt if the hitch in his step hadn't materialized out of thin air. "What were *you* trying to do? Ruin Cordelia's courtship?"

"I was just setting some boundaries." His limp miraculously disappeared.

"Well, you didn't have to scowl so fiercely while you did it."

A mischievous twinkle lit his eyes. "Nope. That was purely for fun."

"Jericho Tucker." She meant to scold him, but the laughter bubbling out of her throat got in the way. "You're terrible."

"Not always." His eyes changed. Their sparkle melted into a heated glow that made her insides flutter. He drew a line down her arm from her shoulder to her wrist and clasped her hand, weaving his fingers between hers. "Hannah, I—"

"J.T.!" A huffing Tom jogged up to them.

Jericho dropped her hand. A chill passed through her as the wind erased the warmth of his grip.

"I signed us up for the three-legged race. The Harris brothers think they can beat us this year, but I told 'em not to get their hopes up." Tom glanced over at Hannah and grinned. "We ain't been beat in three years, not since my legs grew long enough to keep up with his." He thrust his thumb at Jericho, who was doing an admirable job of hiding his disgruntlement over the untimely interruption.

Hannah tried to do the same, but as Jericho turned the conversation to kite flying and the best location for such sport, she bit her lip in frustration.

Five minutes. If Tom had taken just five minutes longer to find them, Jericho would have told her . . . told her . . . well . . . something important—she was sure of it. She had felt the significance of the moment all the way down to her toes. Now all her toes felt were the pebbles that poked against the soles of her shoes as they made their way back to the picnic.

30

The day was too fine for Hannah to let regrets weigh her down for long. Food, however, was a different story. She couldn't remember ever having eaten so much. Hoping to walk off the lethargy that tempted her to lie on the quilt and nap in the sunshine, she let Tessa talk her into a game of graces.

Margaret Paxton, the banker's wife, had brought a crate full of supplies for the game, and several pairs of young ladies loitered near the mill testing their skill. Tessa skipped up to the box and selected a set of dowel rods for each of them.

"What color hoop should we use?" she asked when Hannah caught up to her.

Each of the wooden circles, about the size of a large embroidery hoop, had been decorated with different colored ribbons.

Hannah peered into the box. Three hoops remained: red and white, green and yellow, or brown and orange. "You pick. Just not the orange one." She scrunched up her nose and Tessa giggled. They had long ago agreed that orange was only attractive on round fruit, wildflowers, and butterflies.

Opting for the red and white, Tessa held it away from her and ran to her position a couple yards away, letting the ribbon tails stream out behind her. She hung the hoop over the end of one dowel, then brought the tip of the second into the circle, crossing the two sticks to form an *X*.

"Ready?"

Hannah nodded and stepped out with one leg to broaden her stance. "Ready."

In a quick motion, Tessa flung her arms up and out, uncrossing the dowels. The hoop flew through the air. The object of the game was for

Hannah to catch it on both her rods, but Tessa's throw was short and the wind was tugging the hoop to the left. Too much of a competitor to let the hoop fall to the ground, Hannah grabbed a handful of her skirt and dashed forward. Like a fencer brandishing a foil, she stabbed her dowel through the center of the beribboned hoop and snatched it out of the air.

"Yay!" Tessa cried. "Good catch, Miss Hannah. Nine more and you win!"

She was ahead seven to five when Cordelia and Ike strolled by to watch. Her hand tucked securely into the crook of Ike's arm, Cordelia was beaming. Hannah smiled as the couple passed, so caught up in her friend's happiness that Tessa's next shot arched over her head before she even realized it had been launched.

"Ha! You missed. My turn."

Hannah used her rod to retrieve the hoop from the ground. "All right, you little imp. See if you can catch this one." Hannah sailed it a bit higher than usual, but Tessa got under it and made the snag.

"I did it!" She jumped and gave a little whoop of glee, earning a smile from Mrs. Paxton, who had just refilled her lemonade glass.

"A fine catch, Tessa," the banker's wife said. "But remember, this is a game of elegance and poise, not a rough-and-tumble sport."

Hannah couldn't help wondering if the gentle reproof wasn't as much for her as Tessa. None of the other girls were playing with the same degree of zealousness. Of course, none of the others seemed to be having half as much fun, either. Nevertheless, she supposed she ought to set a more decorous example for her young protégée. Especially with a lady like Margaret Paxton looking on. The woman exuded class and sophistication. All without ever making one feel inferior. It was quite a remarkable talent and surely stemmed from a humble spirit. She would be the ideal client for a dressmaker who longed to promote a balance between inner and outer beauty.

The red hoop sailing toward her head snapped Hannah out of her preoccupation. She leapt backward and raised her sticks at the last minute, deflecting it before it collided with her chin. Unfortunately, she was not deft enough to catch it, only knock it to the ground. Tessa laughed as Hannah retrieved the hoop. The sound was so playful and jolly, though, Hannah couldn't help but smile. She flung the hoop back into the air, and the girl caught it easily.

"Better watch out, Miss Hannah. We're all tied up now."

"So you think you can beat me, do you?" Hannah waved her sticks at Tessa. "Give me your best shot."

In her enthusiasm, Tessa lofted the hoop high and dangerously off course. It veered to the right, directly toward the spot where Cordelia had stopped to chat with Mrs. Paxton. Hannah bolted after it, but she knew she'd never get there in time.

"Look out!" she cried.

Mrs. Paxton turned, and with a skill unexpected in one so genteel, caught the hoop with one hand and flicked her wrist to send it back to Tessa in a perfect arc.

Hannah stuttered to a halt and stared.

"Bravo, my dear!" Elliott Paxton called out from his seat near the cider table. "Just like the old days, eh, Maggie?"

Pink streaks appeared across the lady's cheeks as she waved away her husband's comment, but she turned to Hannah with a welcoming smile.

"Don't look so surprised, Miss Richards," she said. "I haven't always been a staid banker's wife."

Hannah grinned.

"I was just complimenting Miss Tucker on her beautiful new dress," Mrs. Paxton said, expertly shifting the subject away from herself. "The change in her is extraordinary, and she tells me that you are the one responsible for it."

Excitement fluttered in Hannah's stomach. The lady admired her work.

"Cordelia's been a lovely client. She has a wonderful eye for fashion, as you can see in the colors she selected."

"And you have a wonderful skill with a needle to craft such a becoming design."

Cordelia nodded, her eyes bright as they slid from Hannah to Mrs. Paxton. "Oh, yes. Miss Richards tailors everything to perfection. I doubt you could find a better dressmaker in all of Texas."

The banker's wife gave Cordelia's polonaise and skirt another perusal, then assessed the one Hannah wore. "I usually have Elliott drive me to Waco when the girls and I need new gowns, but now that Coventry has a qualified seamstress, I may have to forfeit those shopping trips and invest our funds closer to home."

Fireworks of glee exploded inside Hannah's chest, but she forced her features into a serene expression. "I would be glad to assist you, Mrs. Paxton. Please stop by the shop at any time."

"Thank you. I just might do that."

At that moment, Tessa ran up, grabbed Hannah's hand, and started tugging her toward the center of the glen. "Come on, Miss Hannah. The race is about to start. We've got to cheer on Tom and Mr. Tucker!"

"Tessa, it's not polite to interrupt."

The little girl's face looked properly contrite . . . for all of two seconds. "I'm sorry, but this is important. We don't want to miss it."

No, they didn't. Hannah surveyed the grounds, searching for Jericho in the crowd of men and boys who were lining up at the start. Her heart longed to be at the race; however, responsible business practices dictated she not rush off and risk offending an important potential client.

"Oh my. We can't have you miss the excitement." Mrs. Paxton's hand closed over the end of Hannah's dowel rods, graciously solving her dilemma. "Let me put these away for you."

"Thank you, ma'am," Hannah said.

"Hurry on, now. You don't want to miss the start."

Hannah gave Tessa's arm a little shake. "Let's go." The girl took off, dragging Hannah behind her. Hoping that Tessa's enthusiasm would rate as an adequate excuse for her own hurried pace, Hannah did nothing to slow the girl down. The sooner they got there, the better.

J.T. toed the imaginary starting line, one arm behind Tom's back as the partners gripped each other's shoulders for balance. The Harris brothers stood two pairs down, shooting taunting looks J.T.'s way as the judge inspected the bandanna tied around his and Tom's ankles. Will and Archie would be the only real competition. Most teams consisted of kids or young men with their sweethearts. Fellows typically cajoled their gals into participating just to have an excuse to wrap their arms around them. Such pairings always led to a surplus of silly giggling and quick tumbles.

Although J.T. had to admit that he'd much rather be holding on to Hannah right now than his stablehand. It might be worth a loss. Then again, recalling how hard she'd pushed when she'd challenged him to try those clubs and rings of hers, she might prove to be the toughest competitor of the lot. He wondered if being in a fashionable dress would slow her down at all. He grinned. Probably not.

"What's got you smiling, Tucker?" Will Harris called. "You looking forward to the view of my back as Archie and I breeze across the finish line?"

J.T. snorted. "The only way I'll see your back is if you fall flat on your face at the start. Otherwise, Tom and I will be too far ahead to see much of anything except victory."

Will raised his chin a notch. "Not this year."

The starter stepped into position in front of the racers, and the good-natured ribbing died. A blue bandanna fluttered at the end of his hand.

Having removed his coat for the event, J.T. relished the breeze that fluttered his shirt sleeves. But he would not be distracted. He targeted the finish line. Tom's fingers dug into the muscles at his neck. Together they leaned forward, ready for the signal.

The starter's arm shot straight up, brandishing that blue kerchief like a flag on a pole. "On your mark!" he shouted. "Get set . . . Go!"

His arm dropped and the hobbled racers surged onto the course. Several pairs stumbled as soon as they began, but J.T. paid them no mind. He focused on the ground ahead, alert for any dip or hole that could derail his team as they gradually increased their pace to an uneven hop-jog gait.

Cheers rang out from the sidelines, and for a moment, J.T. wished Hannah hadn't been off playing with Tessa when the racers were called to the field. It was a trivial fair game, not a true athletic contest, but even so, a man liked to have the support of his woman when competing against other males. How else did one get the chance to impress her? Hearing tales of his prowess after the fact never inspired the same degree of awe as firsthand experience.

They reached the halfway point, and J.T. glanced to the side. The Harris brothers were running neck-and-neck with them. The crowd's cheers narrowed to the two front teams. Calls for Tom and J.T. mingled with equal enthusiasm for Will and Archie. But then a different name came through, a name only one person of his acquaintance ever used.

"Go, Jericho!"

His head shot up, and he searched the crowd for Hannah's face. Then his toe struck a rock, nearly sending him and Tom sprawling onto the ground.

"Watch out, J.T. They're gonna pass us."

Tom's strength steadied him as he turned his attention back to the race. A new fire blazed in his belly. There was no way he'd let Will Harris beat him if Hannah was watching.

"Let's take them on the hill."

Tom grunted his agreement.

The last few yards of the course sloped gently upward. It wasn't a hill, really. However, if a team tried to take it too fast, the slight rise could throw them off balance. J.T. had always approached it with caution in the past, but today he planned to attack it like a renegade Apache.

He sped up his metronomic exhalations and their footsteps followed. They pulled a couple steps ahead. Then their balance faltered. They leaned forward, fighting the momentum. They stumbled. The ground rushed up to meet them. With a mighty lunge, they crossed the line and crashed into the earth.

"Tucker and Packard," the announcer shouted. "By a nose."

Hurrahs erupted from the spectators. J.T. rolled onto his back still tethered to Tom. His chest heaved, his knee ached from where he'd landed on it, but he didn't care about the pain. He'd won.

Tom untied the bandanna around their ankles and scrambled to his feet. "We did it, J.T. We did it!"

"Yep" was all J.T. could manage.

Will Harris strode over and extended a hand. "You might've won, Tucker, but at least Archie and I kept our feet. It was worth coming in second just to see you two tripping all over yourselves like that."

J.T. clasped the fellow's wrist and let him help him to his feet. He chuckled ruefully as he dusted the dirt from his trousers. "If you'll promise to put on as good a show next year, I'd consider playing second fiddle myself."

Will grinned. "No promises, Tuck—"

Before the man could finish spitting out his words, a beautiful blonde whirlwind blew past him and launched herself at J.T.

"You won!"

He caught her around the waist and lifted her off her feet, her excitement revitalizing his tired body. She squealed and her smile nearly obliterated the sun as she threw her head back and exulted in the moment, uncaring that others looked on with avid curiosity.

Man, how he loved this woman.

"If I had known this was the prize, I would have fallen on my face to win, too." Will's dry comment brought a blush to Hannah's cheeks, and she straightened her bent legs back toward the ground. J.T. set her down but kept his hand at her waist, staking a claim for all to see.

"Does that mean I get a turn holding her?" Tom asked, and for the first time, J.T. saw him as a man instead of a kid. It was a bit unnerving. Thankfully, Will interrupted.

"I don't think Tucker wants to share, Tom." The men standing around snickered.

"Well, that don't seem fair. I won, too."

"Yes, you did." Hannah stepped away from J.T.'s hold, and he had to grit his teeth to stop himself from grabbing her back. She walked over to Tom and placed a chaste kiss on his cheek. "Congratulations, Tom."

A silly grin spread across his face. "I gotta go tell Ma!" He lumbered off, once again fully the kid his underdeveloped mind dictated that he be.

"So what's the prize for second?" Will asked, looking more at J.T. than Hannah.

J.T. glared at his audacious question, which only made Will grin more. Taking Hannah's hand, J.T. started leading her away. "Sorry, fellas. You'll have to find your own prize. This one's mine."

31

Hannah followed Jericho, eager to escape the men's teasing. Once they separated themselves from the group, the Harris brothers faded from her mind and she became consumed by the way Jericho's warm hand enveloped hers. Strong, capable, protective. And at that moment, connected. To her.

Jericho slowed his pace to a stroll. His callused palm rubbed against her smoother skin, creating a delicious friction that tingled up her arm. He stroked the back of her hand with his thumb and angled his face toward her, curling his lips in the hint of a smile. Hannah's heart thumped heavy and hard. Conscious of the picnic activity around them, she shied away from the heat of his gaze and focused instead on the dips and ruts of the ground. But she had never been more aware of the man at her side.

"I'm sorry I caused such a scene back there," she said, needing to do something to diffuse her growing restlessness. "I didn't intend to throw myself at you, I promise. It just sort of . . . happened."

Jericho tugged her to a halt. "Darlin', you can throw yourself into my arms anytime you like." His tawny eyes shone with humor . . . and something deeper that made her breath quiver. "I promise I'll always catch you." The soft, husky tone of his voice vibrated through her and left her wanting to hide away with him somewhere and explore the meaning behind his words. But she couldn't. She had a kite to fly and children to entertain.

"We should get back," she said, dipping her chin.

Jericho released her hand and cleared his throat. "Tom showed me a good place for kite flying. It's upriver a little ways but easy to get to." He placed his hand at the small of her back and guided her toward the wagon.

Grateful for the ordinary conversation, she tried to subdue her bucking emotions. "That sounds lovely. I'm sure the children will be pleased."

She and Jericho lapsed into silence as they walked across the glen. Hannah glanced his way and caught him staring, the look in his eyes hinting at things unsaid. Her pulse flittered. Would he finish the conversation he had started earlier that day, before Tom had interrupted them?

Hannah held her breath, aching with the need for him to declare his feelings. His warm regard revealed his attraction, and his possessiveness had been evident as he staked his claim in front of the Harris brothers. Yet she longed for the words, for the assurance that she had, indeed, penetrated his heart as he had penetrated hers. Had Jericho grown to care enough for her that he would be willing to set aside his past hurts and tie himself to a dressmaker for the rest of his days? She stole another peek at him, her chest tight with hope. But he looked to the ground without speaking, and her breath leaked out in disappointment.

Grant me patience, Lord. You have promised that things work together for good for those that love you, and whether that good entails a life with Jericho or not, I will trust in your faithfulness. She tried to stop there, but a desire tugged on her soul that wouldn't be denied. She couldn't let the prayer go without at least presenting the request that burned within her. *I love him, Lord. I love him with all my heart. Please grant me a future with this man. Please.*

With a quiet sigh, Hannah released her worry and welcomed the lightness that followed. The sun glowed in the sky, a cool breeze tickled her cheeks, and children's laughter filled the air. It was a beautiful day, a day made for rejoicing. She wouldn't ruin it with unproductive frets.

As Jericho steered her toward their picnic spot, Tessa spotted the children and grabbed the kite from where it had been propped against the tree. She hopped up and down on her toes and waved at them to hurry.

Hannah's feet slowed. "Oh no."

Jericho turned to her. "What?"

"I have no idea how to choose who goes first. They've all been so good. Any suggestions?"

The question hung between them for a split second, as if Jericho couldn't quite believe she was asking him for advice, but in a flash, the glimmer of surprise on his face disappeared beneath his customary confidence. She even detected a swagger in his step as he urged her forward.

"I think I can come up with something that will work."

And he did. A game of short straws, or toothpicks in this case, determined the order. Ike volunteered to help Cordelia pack up the leftover food and supplies, which allowed Louisa to join the kite-flying expedition. Mother and children ran ahead, but Jericho stalled, taking extra time to fold his coat into a lopsided square and lay it on the blanket.

An exasperated Cordelia shot Hannah a pleading look. Hannah deciphered the hint and dragged Jericho away. As they walked, he glanced over his shoulder more than once and grumbled about the folly of leaving his sister alone with Ike when he couldn't keep an eye on them.

Hannah gave him a little swat on the arm. "Leave them be, Jericho. Half the town will be chaperoning them while you're gone. Besides, I think you can trust Ike not to take advantage of your sister," she said. "Just as I trust you."

His lips thinned, but he gave a firm nod. "You're right."

They lengthened their stride to catch up to the James family. As they closed the gap, however, Jericho bent close one more time. "I'm still gonna glare and growl at him, though, to keep him on the straight and narrow until he puts a ring on Delia's finger. Maybe even after."

Hannah smiled. "I wouldn't expect anything less."

The wind proved perfect for kite flying. Each child took a turn holding the string, but young Mollie had trouble keeping the purple diamond aloft. After the third crash, Hannah took charge. Running the length of the clearing with the James children chasing after her, she lofted the kite into the air and sent it soaring. Dangerously out of breath, she handed the spool to Mollie and motioned for Tessa to give her sister a hand while she braced her arm against a tree for support. A wave of dizziness assailed her as her chest heaved.

"You should've asked me to do the running," a low voice grumbled at her side. "You're about to pass out."

"I . . . am . . . not." Somehow she managed to spit out the words between gasps.

Jericho took her arm, but she pulled away, mortified by her condition. She should have been able to run twice that distance without getting winded. Of course, she didn't usually exercise while wearing a corset and twenty pounds of fashionable garb.

"Stubborn woman." Jericho glowered. "Once in a while it'd be nice if you actually admitted that you need my help." He left her standing at the base of that tree with a queasy feeling in her stomach.

She'd hurt him. It'd been there in his eyes. He thought she didn't need him, but nothing could be further from the truth. She needed him so much, she ached with it. But how was he to know that?

Slowly, Hannah's lungs regained a calm rhythm and her mind cleared. She hated appearing weak. All the pitying glances she'd endured after her swimming accident as a child were enough to last a lifetime. When her mother had brought home Dr. Lewis's book and started her on his calisthenic regimen, Hannah had vowed to regain her strength no matter the cost. And she had. Never quitting once, not even when her lungs burned as if she had breathed in a thousand tiny embers or when muscle cramps woke her from a sound sleep, sending teary rivulets down her cheeks as she bit on her pillow to contain her cries. She took pride in her hard-won physical strength. Yet that pride had just pushed the man she loved away.

Jericho was right. She *was* stubborn. Foolish, too.

Determined to rejoin the group and find a way to privately apologize to Jericho, Hannah let go of the tree and stepped forward . . . directly into a prairie dog hole. Her heel caught, her ankle twisted, and she stumbled sideways into the prickly pear cactus plant that she'd been careful to avoid earlier. A pair of pointed spines pierced her skirt and inner layers to stab the tender flesh at the back of her thigh. With a yelp, she jumped forward, only to hear an ominous ripping noise from behind.

Hannah closed her eyes and moaned. Why did it have to be her new dress? Her right ankle throbbed, her thigh stung, and now her skirt was caught on a cactus. The Lord must've decided to help her get rid of that troublesome pride.

"Miss Hannah, come see!" Mollie called from a few yards away. "I'm flying it all by myself."

"You're doing great, sweetheart. I'll be there in just a minute." She waved to the happy gathering, but when Jericho turned to look at her, her hand fell back to her side. "Mr. Tucker? Might I prevail upon you for some assistance?"

He stared at her for what felt like ages without taking a single step in her direction. Then, finally, he trudged across the field, the suspicion lighting his eyes becoming less deniable the closer he came.

Jericho halted a couple feet away and questioned her with a raised eyebrow. Hannah swallowed. Her pride didn't go down easily.

32

J.T. crossed his arms over his chest and waited. *She better not be patronizing me.* Just because he wanted her to admit that she needed help once in a while didn't mean he would stand for her manufacturing some ridiculous predicament in a half-baked attempt to placate him.

A heavy gust of wind billowed across them and Hannah teetered. She shifted her weight to compensate and winced.

He unlaced his arms and took a step forward. "You hurt?"

"Not badly." She tried to smile, but her lips only curved on one side. "My main problem is that I'm stuck to a cactus."

"Stuck to a—" A chortle escaped, obliterating the rest of his sentence. Reining in his laughter, he cupped her shoulders and pulled her forward a bit to judge the extent of the snare. Sure enough, she was stuck. One of the pleats that used to drape so delicately along the back of her skirt now listed gracelessly to the side, gouged by a wicked-looking spine. Several other spines had snagged the wine-colored fabric closer to the ground, as well.

"How'd you manage to get tangled up with a cactus?" J.T. crouched beside her and started extricating her from the prickly plant.

"Well, believe it or not, I was on my way to apologize to you when a prairie-dog hole jumped up and grabbed my shoe heel."

Her turn of phrase made him smile. But the story explained her wince. Probably sprained her ankle. He tugged the last piece of material free. "Shouldn't a seamstress know enough to avoid the sharp end of needles?"

"Oh, we seamstresses jab ourselves all the time, a hazard of the trade."

J.T. looked up at her then, meaning to tell her she'd been successfully detached, but he got lost in her smile and had to answer with one of his own. They stayed that way for a moment until Hannah blinked and twisted her neck as if trying to see the back of her dress.

"How bad does it look?"

It looked pretty good from where he sat. But J.T. figured she was referring to the dress, not the shapely curves beneath. He placed his hands on his knees and pushed to a stand. "There's a fair-sized hole where one of the flounces tore off. But you can't see your bloomers or nothing."

"Jericho!" Hannah's face flamed and J.T. chuckled. Man, but the woman was fun to tease.

He took her arm, thankful when she made no effort to pull away this time. "How's the ankle?"

"Tender but not too bad," she said as she limped along beside him. "I'm sure it will be fine after I rest a bit."

"I should take you home." J.T. wasn't ready for his day with her to end, but she needed to get that ankle propped up.

They approached a stand of mesquite that offered a bit of shade and slowed. Hannah turned to him, but her gaze moved past his shoulder to follow the children who were playing in the clearing behind him. "I wouldn't mind slipping out early to avoid the embarrassment of displaying a torn skirt, but I don't want the others to have to leave because of my mishap."

"Tom can ride back with us," J.T. said as he grasped her waist and hoisted her up onto a bent mesquite trunk that grew at a nearly horizontal angle. She gave a startled little squeal and grabbed his arms for support as he set her on the improvised bench. Her feet dangled a good eighteen inches above the ground, but at least she wouldn't have to stand. "He can drop us in town and drive the General back out here to pick up the rest of the group later."

"All right."

By this time, the kids had noticed Hannah's return and descended upon them with questions about why she was sitting in a tree.

After assuring everyone that Hannah was fine and leaving them strict orders not to let his prisoner escape while he was gone, J.T. hiked back to the picnic area, located Tom, and explained the situation to Delia. It took a while to hitch up the team and maneuver the General over the rough prairie ground, but he managed to fetch Hannah and the James clan back to the picnic without bumping anyone out or breaking an axle. J.T. dropped Louisa and the kids off with Delia and Ike, picked up Tom, and finally steered the rig toward town.

"You think I got time to get back before the square dancin' starts?" Tom called from the back of the wagon as J.T. pulled the General to a halt in front of Hannah's dress shop.

"I reckon so." He set the brake and climbed down, not surprised when

Tom vaulted over the side to meet him and take up the reins. "They had just started setting up the plank floor when we were leaving. The fiddler hadn't even warmed up. You'll have time."

The kid loved a lively tune, and the whole town enjoyed watching his high-kicking antics as he promenaded his ma and any other gals he could get his hands on across the floor. Such vigorous enthusiasm always generated friendly laughter among the spectators, and if Tom got a little mixed up at the caller's instructions from time to time, no one minded. They'd just grin and point him in the right direction. It wouldn't be the same without him there.

J.T. reached up for Hannah and fit his hands to her waist as he lowered her to the street. He held her gaze for a moment. "The ankle holding up?"

She nodded, and he slowly released his grip, making sure she was steady before shifting his attention to Tom.

"Don't be in too big a hurry, son. Hold the team to a moderate pace. You'll get back in plenty of time."

"Yes, sir."

As soon as J.T. stepped away from the wheels, Tom had the General in motion. Shaking his head, J.T. chuckled under his breath. The kid was chomping at the bit more than the horses were.

He turned to share his smile with Hannah, but she wasn't looking at him. Lines marred her forehead as she stared at her shop. Coming alongside her, he linked his arm through hers. "What is it?"

She took a tentative step forward. "I don't know, but something's wrong."

He took a second look, narrowing his eyes to filter out the glare of the sun. He couldn't be sure at this distance, but the door to the shop looked slightly ajar. "Did you lock up before the picnic?"

"Yes."

Hannah pulled away from him and climbed onto the boardwalk. Instinct sent him after her. He clamped a hand on her arm and brought her to a halt.

"Wait. Give me your key."

She obeyed, a question on her face.

"Stay here while I check it out."

Suddenly, she was the one gripping *his* arm. "You don't think someone is in there, do you? I don't want you hurt."

He patted her hand where it lay across his forearm. "I'm sure it's nothing. Probably a flaw in the lock that kept it from latching all the way. I just want to make sure everything's safe before you go in. All right?"

She nodded and let go of his arm.

Senses on alert, J.T. approached the shop door. It was definitely ajar. He flattened his back against the wall, tucked Hannah's key into his trouser pocket, and ran his fingers along the edge of the doorjamb. Splinters where the wood had been damaged jabbed his skin. Someone had pried his way in.

He pressed the toe of his boot against the door and, in a swift move, flung it open. No gunshot or running footsteps broke the quiet, only the squeak of the hinges. Cautiously, J.T. leaned into the doorway. Whoever had intruded was long gone, but he had left an indelible impression behind in his absence. J.T.'s stomach churned, and bile rose in his throat.

Stepping over the threshold, he surveyed the damage. The shelves Hannah had so meticulously hung had been torn down. Bolts of fabric lay unwound and scattered upon the floor. Not only had the miscreant tossed the expensive material on the ground, but he had trod on it, crushing it beneath his heel in several places as evidenced by numerous dusty boot prints and crinkled sections of cloth. Thankfully, the sewing cabinet stood intact, but all of the drawers were missing. J.T. could only assume they'd been dumped somewhere behind the counter.

He balled his hands into fists, longing to mash them into the face of the person or people responsible for this attack.

A tiny tortured cry sounded behind him.

J.T. whirled. Hannah's wounded expression twisted his gut. "Come on," he murmured, forcing her leaden feet back toward the door. "I'll take you home. You don't need to see this right now." Seeing her shiver, he tucked her under his arm and steered her through the doorway. Her neck craned as they went, as if she were unable to pull her gaze away from the destruction. A fierce protectiveness surged within him. He would make this right for her. Somehow, he would fix it.

He grabbed hold of the door and moved to shut it, but Hannah's gasp stopped him. He lifted his head and saw what had distressed her. Tacked to the inside of the door was a note.

You never should have come.

33

A chill snaked through Hannah as she read the ominous words. She would've felt better believing a group of unruly boys were responsible for this violation. Then the deed would have been random, impersonal. But the note destroyed that hope. Someone wanted her gone. Hannah wrapped her arms around her middle.

Jericho snatched the offending paper from the door, crumpled it into a ball, and hurled it into the depths of the shop. He steered Hannah onto the walkway, then slammed the door hard enough to shake the outer wall. Hannah flinched.

He stood with his back to her, the muscles in his shoulders twitching beneath his suspenders. She wanted him to hold her, to comfort her, to convince her she had nothing to fear, but the anger emanating from him made her pause.

"Jericho?"

His chest expanded as he inhaled, and an audible release of air followed. The tension in his neck dissipated. His fisted hands uncurled. When he turned, the solicitous expression on his face eradicated the wall between them.

"I'm so sorry, darlin'. I—"

Hannah dove into his arms and burrowed into his chest. She clung to his waist, anchoring herself to his strength. As his arms enfolded her, the tears she had held at bay fell in earnest.

Why? Why would someone do such a thing? It cut her heart to ribbons. It wasn't so much the damage to her property but the hatred burning behind the act. What had she done to inspire such hostility?

She sank further into Jericho's embrace, her energy flagging as despondency took hold. Her knees wobbled, and Jericho scooped her up. He carried her to Ezra's bench and settled her in his lap.

Neither of them spoke, but his presence, his touch soaked into her soul like a balm on an open wound. Gradually her sobs slowed to occasional hiccups, and he fumbled for a handkerchief. While she dried her eyes and blew her nose, he untied her bonnet strings, set the hat aside, and tucked her head under his chin.

Hannah couldn't say how long they stayed that way, but when she finally raised her head, the sun was swimming on the edge of the horizon. Not quite able to meet Jericho's eyes yet, she stared at his chest. Dark blue splotches marred the sky-blue fabric of his shirt, soggy from her blubbering. She covered the largest spot with her hand. The warmth of his skin seeped through the wet cloth, his heart thumping a steady beat. A beat that seemed to accelerate.

"I'm sorry I wept all over you. I made quite a mess of your shirt." She made to remove her hand, but Jericho covered it with his own and held it in place. Hannah slowly tilted her chin to meet his gaze.

"Are you all right?"

She nodded. "Yes. Thank you. I feel much better." Suddenly shy and uncomfortable, Hannah slid off his lap and stood on the boardwalk. Even her ankle felt sturdier. She plucked her bonnet off the bench but didn't put it back on. "I . . . I should change." She forced a false smile onto her face as Jericho rose to his feet. His eyes narrowed slightly, and she knew she hadn't fooled him. "That's why we're here, right?" she said brightly, as she stepped toward the stairs. "I'll just let you get back to your business while I . . ."

Her hand clutched the rail, but her feet refused to budge. Pulse jumping, mouth dry, Hannah eyed the stairs as if they were the teeth of some feral creature that would chomp into her leg the minute she set foot in its territory. She couldn't do it. What if the same person who ransacked her shop had been in her personal rooms, touching her things, violating her privacy?

Jericho came beside her in an instant. "I'll go up with you."

He took the first step and held out his hand. Taking a deep breath, she fit her palm to his and let him lead her all the way to the top.

The door loomed large, but Jericho faced it down, key in hand. He unlatched it, pushed the portal open, and stepped inside. He returned seconds later, a gentle smile curving his lips.

"Everything's still neat and tidy."

Thank you, Lord. Hannah swayed in relief and gripped the railing to her left as she steadied her shaking legs. After a moment, she stepped inside, her eyes scanning the room from wall to wall, searching for anything out of place. Jericho remained behind, giving her the privacy to explore on her own. Moving through the chamber, she fingered the cloth that covered her table, toyed with the spindles of the new chairs, traced the nickel-plated design on the stove, and ruffled the pleats on her ugly orange curtain.

Normal. Everything was blessedly, wonderfully normal.

"Put together a bag of clothes and whatever else you might need. You're staying with Delia tonight." His voice rumbled through her with a comforting authority.

Jericho's arrogant manner had irked her in the past, but hearing the tender concern behind his soft-spoken command made all the difference. He wasn't trying to dictate to her. He was trying to protect her. And she was only too eager to surrender. After all, she truly had no desire to stay in her room tonight. Alone. Vulnerable. Just a thin door standing between her and the person who wanted her gone. Suppressing a shiver, Hannah nodded and ducked behind the curtain to collect her things.

Later that evening after a light supper, J.T. sat at the kitchen table across from Delia and Hannah, drawing circles around the rim of his coffee cup.

"I can't believe it," Delia said once Hannah finished her tale. "We've never had vandals in Coventry. Do you think they were after your money?"

"I made a deposit yesterday, so there wasn't much in the till." Hannah glanced up at him and swallowed. He could sense her lingering unease, and it tore at his heart. More than anything, he wanted to take that from her, absorb it into himself if need be. He held her gaze, as if that limited connection could siphon off some her distress. And perhaps it had, for she sat a little straighter when she turned back to Delia. "I don't think the vandal was after money. I think he wanted to scare me. He left a note saying I should never have come here."

Delia gasped and set aside her tea to squeeze Hannah's hand. "How awful for you." She shook her head. "To think someone we know could do such a horrible thing. . . . Well, it . . . it defies belief." A thoughtful look crossed her face. "Do you have any idea who the culprit could have been?"

J.T. halted his cup halfway to his mouth at his sister's question. He'd been wanting to ask Hannah the very same thing ever since they got back to the house, but he'd not had the chance.

Hannah hesitated, her focus dancing from Delia to him and back again. "I can only think of one person who has ever treated me with any degree of hostility."

His cup clunked against the tabletop. "Who?"

"I . . . I have no proof it was him, of course."

J.T. pressed to his feet and leaned over the table. "Who?"

Hannah glanced back to Delia, then looked down at her cup. "Warren."

Delia made a little choking sound. "Warren Hawkins? Surely not. I've known him since we were kids."

J.T. gritted his teeth and pushed away from the table. He whirled toward the wall and gripped the edge of the cabinet that held Delia's baking supplies. Digging his fingers into the wood until his knuckles whitened, he struggled to master the rage that speared through him.

Warren. First he'd tried to force Delia into a match she didn't want, and now he'd taken out his anger on Hannah. The scoundrel needed someone to pound some sense into him. J.T.'s biceps twitched at the thought of fulfilling that duty.

"I'm sorry, Cordelia, but I can think of no one else." Hannah's quiet regret inflamed his need for justice. She was the last person who needed to apologize for anything.

When Delia finally responded, her voice broke, as if tears were near the surface. "It's because of me, isn't it?"

"No. Of course not," Hannah asserted, but when J.T. turned around, Delia was nodding.

"Yes. Yes it is. He blamed you for the changes he saw in me. He probably thought that if you hadn't come to Coventry, Ike would've never paid me any mind. When I refused his proposal, he struck out at you." Her lip trembled as tears rolled down her cheeks. "Oh, Hannah. Can you ever forgive me?"

Now they both were apologizing! A growl built in his throat, though he pressed his mouth into a thin line to keep it from escaping.

Hannah grabbed both of Delia's hands. "You've done nothing wrong, Cordelia, and I won't have you thinking you did. We don't know for sure that Warren is the one who broke into my shop. But even if he was, you're not responsible. He made the choice to act shamefully, not you."

J.T.'s jaw ached from clamping it so tight. He hoped the Lord would keep Warren out of his path tonight, because he wasn't sure he would stop himself from pummeling the man. But Hannah was right. They needed proof.

"I don't recall seeing Warren at the picnic today. Did you see him, Delia?" He kept his tone as neutral as he could manage but apparently wasn't too successful, for Hannah's head spun toward him.

Delia sniffed a couple times, then met his eyes. "I don't think so. But he might have been avoiding me since I was with Ike. A conversation between us would have been awkward."

J.T. strode to the door and took his hat down from the peg. He fingered the brim for a moment and then set it on his head. "I'm going out for a while, but I'll be back."

Out of the corner of his eye, he saw Hannah rise and move toward him. "Jericho? What are you—?"

He didn't wait to hear the rest of the question. Without looking back, he stepped into the night and closed the door behind him.

34

J.T. pounded on the back door of the mercantile. "Open up, Hawkins. I need a word with you." He waited a couple seconds and started pounding again.

"Yeah, yeah. I'm coming. Keep your boots on." The store owner cracked the door and peered out. "This better be an emergency. I don't do business after hours."

"This isn't business."

"Tucker?" Hawkins pulled the door wide. "What in the blue blazes are you doing hammerin' a hole in my door?"

The man had a napkin tucked into his shirt collar, and crumbs speckled his mustache. However, J.T. could summon little regret for disrupting his meal.

"Your boy home?"

"Nope. Took the train down to Temple this afternoon."

The Gulf, Colorado and Santa Fe didn't depart until around three o'clock, which left plenty of time for Warren to sabotage Hannah's shop before leaving town. A convenient arrangement.

"Thinking 'bout opening a second store there now that they're building up the place," Hawkins rambled. "Used to just be a bunch of railroad men thereabouts, but since they sold off town lots back in June, it's really growing. I tried to convince Warren to go several months back, but he weren't interested till recently."

Probably because of his spontaneous plan to marry Delia.

"When do you expect him home?"

The abrupt question put a halt to the storekeeper's chatter. He eyed J.T. with suspicion.

"A couple days. Why? You got a problem with him?"

J.T.'s lips tightened into a grim line. "Yes, sir. I do."

Hawkins yanked the napkin out from under his chin and tossed it aside. "Now, see here, Tucker. Warren told me about his plans to hitch up with your sister, and if you're thinking to try and scare him off with your high-handed ways, you can forget it." He advanced on J.T., poking him in the chest.

J.T. held his ground—and his temper. Barely.

"I thought you were above judging a person by his appearance," the storekeeper spat, "but you can't see past his birthmark, can you? You have no right to come to my house, interrupt my supper, and accuse my son of not being good enough for your sister. Get out of here."

The man's face had gone quite red, and veins popped out of his neck. He backed into the house and would've slammed the door in J.T.'s face had J.T. not shoved his foot into the opening.

Jaw clenched, J.T. grabbed the edge of the door and muscled it open until he could see Hawkins's eye. "I don't give a fig about Warren's face. It's his actions and attitude that I take exception to. Did he tell you that he sprung a proposal on Delia without a single act of courting? Did he mention that Delia turned him down? And did you happen to notice that instead of accepting her answer with gentlemanly grace, he blamed Miss Richards for his troubles, a woman innocent in this whole affair?"

Some of the color faded from the man's cheeks. "Cordelia turned him down? Warren said she wanted some time to consider his offer. I figured he was hoping to win her acceptance with the financial promise of the new store."

J.T. released the door and stepped back. "Look. I don't have any great love for your son, but Delia has considered him a friend since their school days. Out of respect for her, I wouldn't have come about Warren's actions, but the safety of someone I care about may be at stake." He paused a moment, an idea taking root. "Can I show you something? It won't take long."

Hawkins seemed to measure him with his eyes and finally gave a jerky nod. "Let me fetch my coat."

When he returned, J.T. led him to Hannah's shop. He still had her key, having forgotten to return it during the process of getting her settled.

"Why did you bring me here?" Hawkins asked as J.T. fit the key into the lock.

"You'll see." The door swung in, and J.T. entered, his boot heels click-clacking against the floorboards in a hollow rhythm that echoed eerily in the abandoned room. Hawkins followed. Sunset had come and gone, but the twilight of early evening sufficiently revealed the destruction amid the shadows.

J.T. wove through the maze of fabrics and notions, careful not to do any further damage as he made his way to the far wall, intent on collecting the paper ball resting in the corner.

"Was Miss Richards harmed?" Hawkins choked out the question.

J.T. didn't turn. "No. She discovered this mess when I escorted her home from the picnic this afternoon." And it had devastated her. J.T. could still feel the heat of her tears as she'd wept against his chest.

He gently lifted a length of blue cloth from the floor and draped it over the counter to clear a path and noticed Hannah's collection of fashion magazines and pattern books scattered over the counter's surface and the floor behind. Pages had been ripped from the bindings and showered like giant confetti. A cover from *Peterson's* lay beside the blue fabric. The fashionable woman on the cover seemed to glare at him in accusation.

How many times as a child had he wanted to do the same thing? To tear up his mother's magazines, to set them on fire, or sink them in the river? He'd blamed the world of fashion for stealing away his mother in the same way Warren had blamed Hannah for Cordelia's lack of interest. The reality hit him like a blow. It sickened him to think he shared anything in common with that worm. But it couldn't be denied. His hatred of fashion was just as irrational as Warren's hatred of Hannah. Deep down, he knew this. The truth had been growing in him over the last several weeks. Hadn't Christ taught that money itself was not evil, but the choice of men to love it, crave it, and make it their god was the sin that destroyed their souls? So it was with fancy clothes.

Pretty fabric and stylish designs held no innate power to corrupt. It was the sinful desires of the heart that turned one to vanity, condescension, or covetousness. If one could learn to manage his money without greed consuming him, surely a woman could do the same with clothing. Hannah lived out such balance every day, and now that he thought of it, so did many other women of the community.

His mother had been weak, and she'd made destructive choices. Yet with a child's loyalty, he'd been unable to place the responsibility on her shoulders. So he'd blamed the clothes, the man who'd taken her away, and even his father for not fulfilling her needs. He'd thought his growing love for Hannah had erased his prejudice, but with a flash of insight, he realized he'd never be completely free until he let go of the final weight dragging on him.

J.T.'s hand shook as he reached for the magazine cover and smoothed out the bent corner.

Mama, you were wrong and you hurt me. But . . . I forgive you.

His eyes slid closed as a gentle lightness enveloped his soul. For a moment he even forgot where he was and what he was doing. That is, until Hawkins shuffled up behind him.

"My heart goes out to the poor gal," he said. "She's a good customer. Always goes out of her way to be kind and include the mercantile in her business. I'm sorry this happened to her, but I don't see what this has to do with me or my son."

J.T. snapped back to the present. The hunger for justice still growled to be fed, but the anger that had previously accompanied it had cooled considerably. He sidestepped an overturned display dummy and reached for the wad of paper he sought.

"Miss Richards was reluctant to voice her thoughts when we asked her if she had any idea who could have done this. She had no proof of a specific person's involvement, but she did mention one name—a man who had treated her with disdain in recent days." Taking care not to tear the crumpled paper, J.T. opened the ball and pressed it against his thigh to iron out the creases.

Hawkins blew out an impatient breath. "Come on, Tucker. This was probably just a bunch of kids getting into mischief while everyone was away at the picnic. Boys do stuff like this all the time. It's not some personal vendetta."

"That's where you're wrong." J.T. handed him the note. "Do you recognize the handwriting?"

The storekeeper stared at it, and his hand trembled just enough to rustle the paper. "It's . . . uh . . . hard to tell, what with all the wrinkles on the page and the dim lighting." But there was a nervous edge to his voice that confirmed J.T.'s suspicions.

"I think we can safely conclude this wasn't a prank, don't you think?"

Hawkins pushed the paper back at J.T. as if it pained him to touch it. "The note does seem to . . . uh . . . indicate a more personal agenda. But the woman wasn't hurt. No lasting damage done." He looked frantically around the room as if in search of something to validate his desperate words. "The sewing cabinet is intact, the windows unbroken. A true criminal would not have spared those. And really, this is nothing more serious than a large mess. It can be cleaned up, most of the material salvaged. It could have been much worse."

J.T.'s temper sparked anew. "You didn't see her face when she walked through the door. You didn't hold her while she sobbed or feel her tremors as her heart broke. You didn't taste her fear when she faced the staircase, terrified that a similar violation had occurred in her personal quarters. Who's to say the man who did this will stop at one attack? How is she ever to feel safe?"

Hawkins backed away, sputtering excuses.

J.T. trailed him and held the note up in front of his face. "Hannah named Warren as the man who has been acting embittered toward her, blaming her for Delia's rejection of his suit." He set his mouth close to the other man's ear. "Is this your son's writing?"

"I . . . I can't be sure."

J.T. folded the paper into a small rectangle and stuffed it into the man's coat pocket. "Take it home. Examine it in better light. Compare it to an inventory list or something that Warren has written. Take care of this matter with your son, Hawkins. Because if you don't, I will."

35

Hannah stood in Cordelia's kitchen after church the next day, drying the dishes while her mind wandered to the shop. Although shivers coursed through her at the prospect, she needed to spend the afternoon sorting through the debris to see what she could salvage. As tempting as it was to take refuge among friends and let Jericho watch over her, she couldn't allow fear to dictate her actions. Or lack of action, as the case may be.

"Thank you for letting me stay here last night," Hannah said as she reached for the platter Cordelia held out to her.

Cordelia laid a damp hand on her arm, and the warm moisture soaked through Hannah's sleeve. "You can stay here as long as you like."

Hannah shrugged. "Jericho said that Warren would be out of town until Tuesday, so there's no reason to impose on you any longer."

"You're not an imposition. How could you be? You're practically family."

A little thrill shot through Hannah at Cordelia's words, but she couldn't let them sway her. She needed to move forward.

Founders' Day had been a rousing success in showcasing Cordelia's new style and Hannah's design skills. In fact, several women had spoken to her about dressmaking projects that morning after services. Retreat now would destroy the momentum she had gained yesterday. And worse, it would mean giving Warren or whomever was responsible for vandalizing her shop exactly what he wanted.

Hannah inhaled a fortifying breath and rubbed the dishtowel along the decorated edge of the oval dish. She stared at the tiny blue flowers instead of the sympathetic eyes of her friend, afraid that the warm acceptance in their depths would erode her determination. "I appreciate all you and Jericho have done for me. Truly. But I can't hide here. The longer I stay away, the harder it will be to return." Hannah set the platter on the table and reached for the dripping pan.

Cordelia released the pan, her mouth flattening into a tight line as she shoved a greasy pot into the dishwater. Her elbows wagged as she scoured it with enough vigor to rub a hole through the bottom. "I wish this whole mess with Warren had never started. You've done nothing to deserve such vile treatment."

Guilt lingered behind her friend's frustration, and Hannah rushed to dispel it. "Don't worry about me," she said with a grin and a playful bump to Cordelia's flapping elbow. "I'll be too busy catering to all my new customers to think about anything else. Besides, maybe the vandalism will draw extra attention to the shop, and God will turn something Warren meant for harm into a blessing. All I need is an afternoon to tidy things up a bit, and I'll be back in business. Better than before. You'll see."

An answering smile eased across Cordelia's lips. She lifted the scrubbed pot out of the water and started to extend it to Hannah, but stopped and slipped it back into the dishpan. "Why don't you take J.T. his lunch since he rushed off in such a hurry today? Then, as soon as I finish cleaning the roasting pan and set my bread dough to rise for Monday's loaves, I'll come lend a hand."

"Perfect." Hannah draped the dishtowel over Cordelia's shoulder and untied the borrowed apron from around her waist. Having help would greatly lighten the work, but more than that, it would give her company. Despite her brave talk, she really didn't want to be alone in the shop. Not if she didn't have to be. She trusted the Lord to answer her prayers for courage, but in the meantime, a friend to share the load would be a blessing indeed.

Hannah collected the basket Cordelia had set aside for her brother and headed for the livery. She'd thought Jericho had been acting strange when he rushed off after seeing them home, but Cordelia had assured her that he often had to tend to his animals and rigs after services since several townspeople rented them for the drive to church.

Still, a little niggle of disquiet picked at her. He'd been so hard to read last night, coming in from his undisclosed outing with no more to say than that he'd talked to Mr. Hawkins and Warren would be out of town until Tuesday. Then he'd urged her to get some sleep, which had been nearly impossible, what with his pacing in the kitchen like a soldier on patrol. By the time his boots finally fell silent, Hannah had been ready to tie him up herself.

He'd been solicitous that morning, though, watching for Ezra at her request and notifying the older man that she would attend services with the Tuckers. Jericho's solid presence beside her held her fears at bay and allowed her to focus more clearly on worship. But then he'd ushered them back to the house only to leave them the minute their feet hit the porch. The abruptness of it all had left her feeling shuffled and dumped and more than a little confused.

Did Jericho regret becoming involved with her? Hannah's stride faltered at the thought. Perhaps all the trouble with the shop reinforced his previous view that her profession was a stumbling block—not only to women, but now to him. After all, he was being dragged into something that undoubtedly put him at odds with men he considered friends and business associates.

What could she do to make it up to him? Close the shop? A swift, stabbing pain speared her side and brought her to a halt at the edge of the livery stable. Could she do that? Sacrifice her dream in order to share a life with the man she loved?

Hannah swallowed hard. She visualized herself in a flourishing dress shop, a full-grown Tessa working by her side. Happy clients. A sizable bank account. Yet she'd go upstairs to an empty room every night. No strong arms to embrace her and soothe away her hurts, no tender kisses to make her heart sing, no one to tease and to be teased by in return. Without Jericho, success would be hollow. Could she give it up? Yes . . . if she knew he loved her in return, she could. But did he?

A moan vibrated in her throat. Why did everything have to be so complicated?

A verse floated through her mind about not taking thought for tomorrow since today carried sufficient trouble unto itself. Her lips twisted into a wry grin. The Lord could not have sent her a more apt reminder. Hannah straightened her spine. She'd deal with today's problems and leave tomorrow in God's hands. That's where it belonged anyway.

Stepping into the dim interior of the stable, Hannah paused as her eyes adjusted to the lack of sunlight. The pungent smells of manure and old hay wrinkled her nose, but she made no effort to block the odor with her handkerchief. She needed to get used to it if she hoped to be a livery owner's wife.

A movement near one of the middle stalls caught her eye. "Jericho?" She started forward.

"Nope. Just me." Tom turned, a grin stretching wide over his teeth. "Oh, and Mr. Culpepper."

"Ezra?"

The older man emerged from inside the stall.

"What are you doing here?"

"That you, Miz Hannah?" He shuffled closer and heaved a sigh. "Old Jackson threw a shoe. With the smithy closed on Sundays, I convinced young Tom to let me stable him here until tomorrow. I'll rent a horse to take me and the buggy home, then return it when I come to the depot in the morning. Don't want Jackson going lame trudging up to my place without a shoe."

"Of course not."

"I am glad I ran into you, though." Ezra winked at her as he moved past, heading for his buggy. "I brung you something."

Hannah followed him, her curiosity piqued. "You did?" A tiny thrill of excitement coursed through her at the prospect until a more logical explanation came to mind. "Do you have more mending that needs to be done?"

Ezra's laugh boomed through the stable, eliciting an answering bray from old Jackson. "Now, why would I bring you mending on the Lord's Day, Miz Hannah?" He shook his head as he reached to retrieve a small paper-wrapped parcel from the seat cushion. "Nah. I brung you a gift." He presented it to her with a gleam in his eye.

"I meant to give it to you when I picked you up for services this mornin', but you'd already made plans to trade in my company for that Tucker fellow."

The parcel sat heavy in her hand, but she ignored it, worried that she had truly hurt the man's feelings. "Oh, Ezra. It wasn't like that at all. I just—"

His chuckle cut short her apology. "No. No. I'm just giving you a hard time. A gal as purty as you deserves to be courted by a young buck. Besides, I seen the way he looks at you. Reminds me of when I was courtin' my Alice."

Warmth crept into Hannah's cheeks, and not knowing what to say, she dipped her head to examine the gift her friend had given her. The brown paper crinkled as she unfolded it. She lifted one side, and a small silver cylinder rolled into her hand. The needle case was delicately tooled with a leaf pattern that flowed up the side and over the pull-off lid.

"This is beautiful." Her hushed voice echoed a reverent tone as she drank in the loveliness of the silver case. "But it's too much. I can't accept it." She tried to hand it back, but Ezra took her hand and folded her fingers back over her palm, trapping the gift inside.

"Alice would want you to have it."

Tears welled in Hannah's eyes. He was giving her something of Alice's?

A wistful look passed over Ezra's face. "I decided to finally go through her things. The day after you paid me a call, as a matter of fact. I figure on giving most of her clothes to the poor box at church . . . since I ain't never gonna wear 'em." He winked at Hannah and she smiled, thanking God for how far this grieving man had come. "And I'll prob'ly send a box of stuff back to her sister in St. Louis. But when I saw this here case, I knew you were the one who had to have it.

"Alice would have liked you, Miz Hannah. And she would've appreciated what you done for me. Maybe having something of hers will help you feel like you know her even though you two never met."

Hannah bent forward and touched a kiss to Ezra's cheek, right above his whiskers. "I feel as if I already know her—through you." She stepped back and held the needle case to her heart. "Thank you, Ezra. I will treasure this."

Tom brought out a horse and started hitching it to the buggy. As he adjusted the collar, he shot a questioning glance at Hannah. "You lookin' for J.T.?"

"Yes," she said, stepping back to give him room to work. "I brought him some lunch. Is he here?"

"Nope. Ain't seen him since church."

"That's odd. He said he had business to take care of." Something twinged in her stomach. Had he manufactured an excuse to get away from her? Surely not. Jericho was an honorable man. But why . . . ?

For heaven's sake. All this negative thinking was getting her nowhere. She'd just received a lovely gift from a dear friend. She had no cause to feel morose. Careful not to drop the precious needle case, Hannah slipped it into her skirt pocket and patted it against her side. Such a thoughtful gift, equally as thoughtful as . . . her chairs.

"Ezra?"

The man had moved away from her to help Tom buckle all the necessary straps. Upon hearing his name, though, he turned.

Hannah smiled to cover her discomfiture over the question she was about to ask. "Did you by chance leave another gift for me on my landing? I only ask because I found a pair of oak dining chairs there with no note or other clue as to who they were from. With all your woodworking, I thought maybe they were from you."

Ezra scratched his beard. "No. Can't say they were. They just showed up?"

"Yes. I'd like to thank whomever is responsible. If I can determine who that person is."

Tom worked his way down the horse's back, checking the harness. "Mighta been J.T."

Hannah's heart gave a little leap. "You think Jericho left me the chairs?"

Tom shrugged. "Don't know fer sure. He bought a couple from the junkman a couple weeks back, though, and I saw him working on 'em in the corner over there a few times." He pointed to a recess hidden by buggies and buckboards. "They aren't there now."

"I knew that boy was smitten," Ezra murmured just loud enough for Hannah to hear.

She stared at the empty corner, a grin breaking free across her face. Cordelia had warned her that Jericho didn't handle gratitude well. That's probably why he hadn't said anything. But he best prepare himself. The next time she saw him, she was going to bombard him with thanks. In fact, she thought as she glanced down at the lunch basket still slung over her arm, maybe she could finagle a meeting in the next hour or so.

"I need to be going, gentlemen." She eased her way toward the livery door. "Tom, if you happen to see Mr. Tucker, tell him I have his lunch. He can stop by the dress shop whenever he wishes to claim it."

Tom yelled an "okay" to her back as she bustled across the street. She smiled, both at Tom's limitless exuberance and at the warmth that radiated through her at the thought of Jericho's painstaking attentions on her behalf.

As she neared her shop, though, her step faltered. Beyond the display window, a dark figure was roaming about inside. Had they been wrong to assume Warren's guilt?

Whoever he was, the person inside had no right to be in her shop. Indignation swept over her like a prairie fire. Hannah jutted out her chin and stalked forward. The vandal had escaped detection last time, but not today. Nothing was going to stop her from uncovering his identity.

Caution kept her boldness in check as she concealed her body behind the wall that stretched between the two shop windows. It wouldn't do to have the villain catch sight of her and flee before she figured out who he was. Balancing one hand on the back of Ezra's bench, she pressed the other to the glass. She squinted against the reflective glare and leaned in until her forehead rested against the curve of her fingers. The shadowy figure finally took shape. Her heart pounded in anticipated victory. Then he turned, and Hannah gasped.

36

Tears burned the back of Hannah's eyes. Jericho stood in the middle of her shop, flower-sprigged fabric tangled around his torso. Having pivoted too quickly, he teetered while trying to avoid stepping on a coil of lace that lay directly under his raised boot. He managed to regain his footing, but almost took a tumble in the process. A muted laugh puffed out of her at the same time a tear fell from her lashes. Her rugged liveryman was draped in pink calico.

Jericho Tucker, a self-proclaimed despiser of fashion, flounces, and frills, was chin deep in feminine trappings. All for her.

Hannah sank onto the bench, her legs suddenly too weak to support her weight. Jericho's actions had always spoken more eloquently than his words, and at this moment, the message could not be clearer. He loved her.

J.T. lopped off the soiled section of fabric with a pair of Hannah's shears and finally freed himself from the ridiculous pink cocoon that nearly felled him. He folded the cloth over his arm, its raggedly cut end leaving pink strings stuck to his sleeve. He brushed at them, but they held firm. Rolling his eyes, he let them be and continued working. Once he had the material folded into a shape that loosely resembled a square, he slapped it on top of the four others already piled on the counter.

As he reached for the bit of lace near his boot, he glanced over the room. He'd wanted to have most of the mess cleaned up before she arrived, but not knowing where things belonged or even what half of them were had slowed him down. He was tempted to fetch a pitchfork and muck the place out like one of his stalls, but he supposed Hannah wouldn't appreciate that type of efficiency.

The creak of door hinges brought his head up.

"You're a hard man to find." Hannah strode into the shop, letting the door close behind her. She raised an arm toward him and revealed a basket. "I brought you some lunch."

"Thanks." J.T. straightened and tossed the bit of lace in his hand onto the counter. An unexpected awkwardness closed off his throat. She probably expected some kind of explanation for his furtive behavior, but his tongue felt about three feet thick. He doubted anything intelligible would make it out of his mouth even if he tried.

It wasn't like he hadn't expected her to show up at some point, but something about the way she was looking at him made his breath shallow and his pulse accelerated. Beyond affection, beyond desire, a new light glowed in the depths of her eyes, one that seemed to penetrate the core of his soul and lay bare his secrets.

Setting the basket on the counter, she sauntered toward him, the intensity of her gaze unrelenting. He cleared his throat and took a step back, but Hannah didn't let him retreat. Like a mesmerist, she held him enthralled. He couldn't have moved if he wanted to. Which he didn't. She reached up and stroked his jaw, freeing the small muscle beneath her fingers to twitch. Then she braced her hands on his shoulders and rose up on her tiptoes. The lashes framing those fathomless blue eyes fluttered closed, and her lips brushed against his. The feathery caress lingered only an instant, but his insides trembled. Closing his own eyes, he savored the velvety touch.

"I love you, Jericho Tucker."

For a moment he forgot how to breathe.

What miracle had led him to this woman?

He opened his eyes to find hers shining up at him with a love so real even his carefully cultivated cynicism could not deny its existence. At first, he was so humbled by the sight, he could do nothing more than drink it in. Then joy and possessiveness like he'd never known exploded in his chest. Pulling her to him, J.T. claimed her mouth. His hands slid up her back, pressing her close. She leaned into him and raised up on her toes as she returned his kiss. The taste of her lips tantalized him, stirring a craving that begged a lifetime to explore.

After a moment, Hannah slid back down to her flat feet. J.T. followed, caressing her cheek with the pad of his thumb, his forehead bent to hers. She inhaled a shaky breath and then stepped back. Reluctantly, he let her go. She bit her lip and turned toward the counter, pressing her palms into the wood. A long tress of golden hair had fallen from the knot he had thoroughly mussed. Hunkering down, he retrieved two hairpins from the floor, then stood and moved behind her.

"Here," he mumbled, setting the pins on the counter next to her left hand. "Sorry. Your . . . uh . . . hair . . ." He was stammering like an idiot. Yet she smiled at him anyway, a tinge of pink dusting her face.

"Thank you." She gathered the pins and edged around the counter, heading for the dressing room. He watched her until she disappeared behind the wall. Then he leaned against the counter and blew out a harsh breath.

He should have said something. Told her what was in his heart or at least spouted some romantic nonsense that women put such stock in. But no, he'd just stood there, mute as a fence post as she'd spoken the words he'd ached an eternity to hear.

"It looks like the fitting room escaped unscathed." Hannah emerged from the back, her hair once again pinned up properly, although she dropped her bonnet on the worktable as she walked by. She smiled, but her gaze shied away from his as she drew closer. "The mirror's intact and the skirt panels I'd been piecing together on the tailoring dummy are undisturbed."

"That's good." He couldn't seem to look anywhere but her mouth. Her lips were moist, as if she'd just licked them, and all he could think about was tasting them again. Just one kiss. One . . .

J.T. snatched a toothpick out of his shirt pocket and shoved it between his teeth. There. He couldn't kiss her now without impaling her. Surely that would help him hold on to his common sense. All they needed was for someone to walk into the shop and catch them in an embrace like that last one. Not likely with everything closed on Sunday, but he couldn't afford to take that chance. Hannah's reputation would be shredded. J.T. chomped down hard and prayed for restraint.

They set to work, Hannah organizing all the smaller items that had been dumped out of her sewing cabinet, and J.T. continuing his self-assigned task of separating the blemished fabric from the salvageable. Cordelia arrived a short time later, and within a couple of hours, the three of them had the place back in order.

After a cold supper of chopped ham sandwiches at the Tucker house, J.T. and Cordelia tried to convince Hannah to stay at their house another night, but she insisted on returning to her own place. So J.T. escorted her home, carrying her bag as they strolled down the quiet street.

When they passed the livery, Hannah peeked up at him, an impish sparkle in her eye. "Thank you for the chairs."

His brow furrowed. "What chairs?"

She giggled. "The ones you left on my landing."

J.T. halted in the middle of the street. "How did you—"

"Don't worry." She spun around in front of him and he could see laughter in her face. "I won't tell anyone that you're really a sweet, caring man underneath all those frowns."

"Good. A man has his reputation to consider," he grouched, forcing his features into a scowl when what they wanted to do was grin. "That'd be almost as bad as you trying to hang curtains in my livery."

Her eyes danced. "What a lovely idea! Why, that pink calico you wrapped yourself in earlier today would be just the thing."

J.T. growled and lunged for her. With a sound that was half giggle, half squeal, Hannah darted out of his reach. But not for long. He chased her down and captured her waist in the crook of his arm. She pivoted to face him, her joy stealing his breath with its beauty. Unable to help himself, he dropped a quick kiss on her forehead before recalling they were in the middle of the street. Quirking a half grin, he tugged her forward. "Come on. Let's get you home."

When they reached the staircase, she didn't hesitate to make the climb. He took that as a good sign that her fear had receded. When they reached the small landing at the top, she pushed her key into the lock and turned to face him.

"Thank you, Jericho. For being there when I needed you yesterday, for helping with the shop, for everything."

Uncomfortable with her gratitude, he ducked his head so the brim of his hat shielded his face from her, using the excuse of setting her bag down to justify bypassing her earnest expression. He mumbled something that he hoped would pass for a reply, while all the time his heart was pumping faster and faster under his ribs.

He'd intended to tell her how he felt when they got here. To the top of the steps. It was the perfect time. They were alone. The fading light softened the surroundings. He'd even spent the better part of the afternoon rehashing the words he could say. Not that he'd come up with anything good enough, but that didn't matter. She deserved the words. Even if he mangled them in the process.

So sure he could say them this time, he looked into her face. And froze.

She waited.

Nothing came.

A sick sensation swirled in his gut. He wanted to tell her, he just . . . couldn't.

If he spoke of his feelings, there would be no going back. What was left of his defenses would be stripped bare, leaving him completely vulnerable.

Like his father.

J.T. stared at her, willing her to read the apology in his eyes. Her smile never dimmed, but her shoulders dipped slightly—and that tiny show of disappointment knifed through him.

What is wrong with me? He'd fight a rabid cougar with his bare hands to protect this woman but he couldn't spit out a handful of love words. It was pathetic.

Angry at himself, he turned away and coughed to loosen his throat. "I'll be sleeping at the livery until we get things settled with Warren. I don't expect trouble, but I wanted you to know I'd be close at hand should you need anything."

"Thank you."

Out of the corner of his eye, he saw her stoop to collect her bag. Then the sound of the door unlatching clicked loud in his ears.

Panic clawed at him. *Say something!*

He spun around and grabbed her arm. "Hannah, I . . ."

She came to him easily, too easily. Instead of forcing the words he needed to say past his lips, he pulled her into his embrace, tucking her head into the hollow between his shoulder and his chest. A perfect fit.

J.T. tightened his hold, trying to communicate through his arms what his mouth was unable to say. But then Hannah patted his chest near where her head lay, and her quiet voice drizzled over him like honey.

"It's all right, Jericho. I can hear your heart."

And he got the strangest feeling that she could.

37

Over the next few days, business poured into Hannah's shop, and she gladly welcomed the distraction. Whether the client wanted a simple alteration, an old dress remade into a more current style, or a completely new, custom-designed ensemble, Hannah gave each woman her utmost attention and courtesy. She planned to prove to the women of Coventry that she could be trusted with their fashion needs and exceed their expectations by completing the promised items ahead of schedule and with impeccable quality.

Needless to say, when she finally dragged herself up the stairs each evening, she barely managed to keep her eyes open long enough to eat a cold biscuit and wash her face before collapsing into bed. A soft lantern glow from the livery's office across the street filtered through her window to warm her room and her heart as she eased into slumber. True to his word, Jericho was watching over her.

When she awoke on Thursday morning, her eyelids felt like sandpaper as they scraped open. She'd stayed in the shop until after midnight trying to piece together the perfect bodice for the eldest of Mrs. Paxton's daughters. This was to be the girl's first dress with long skirts, a gift for her sixteenth birthday.

By angling the pattern pieces in a judicious manner, Hannah recovered enough undamaged material from the length of trampled pink calico to cut several usable panels. However, necessity demanded smaller than normal seam allowances in order to avoid the soiled sections. This made assembly more difficult. She'd had to rip out one seam five times before everything finally lay just right.

Unwilling to quit until she'd accomplished her task last night, Hannah was now paying the price for her obsession. Not even a splash of cold water could enliven her wan complexion or remove the lavender circles from under her eyes. Maybe a brisk walk would add some color to her cheeks. She didn't want to meet her customers, or worse, Jericho, looking as if she belonged in a box at the undertaker's.

Lacing up her low-heeled boots, she thanked the Lord for the blessing of many clients, reminding herself that the added work *was* a blessing, and asked for sufficient energy to meet the demands of the day. Then after a few calisthenic exercises to animate her muscles, she headed outside.

And found Jericho sitting on her steps.

He stood, took one look at her face, and scowled so darkly she would have flinched had she the energy to spare.

"You look terrible."

Hannah sighed. "Just what every girl dreams of hearing from her beau."

Unfortunately the sarcasm bounced right off him without leaving so much as a dent. He took her arm and helped her down the rest of the stairs as if she were an invalid, frowning all the while. "You didn't put out your light until the wee hours last night. You're working too hard."

"I'm fine, Jericho." At the bottom step, Hannah tugged her arm free. "I know my limits. You don't have to worry about me."

"But I do anyway," he muttered, letting her go.

Touched by his concern yet irritated at the same time by his overbearing manner, Hannah edged away from him. It didn't matter that he was right. She was too tired to guard her words, and if he started lecturing her, she'd probably say something she'd regret. That surely wouldn't aid her in getting him to admit his feelings. No, best to retreat before swords were drawn.

Hannah gave her best imitation of a perky smile, despite the fact that the corners of her mouth seemed to weigh fifty pounds each, and threw some spring into her step as she strode toward the outskirts of town. After a few steps, she turned to wave farewell. "My morning walk will put everything to rights. You'll see."

And it did, for a while. But by midafternoon, she found herself repeatedly snapping her neck up after nodding off at her sewing machine. The first three times, she shook her head and set back to work. The fourth time, she got up and paced the length of her shop. Twice. The fifth time, however, she stopped caring and laid her head in the crook of her arm, willing to let sleep claim the victory.

Thankfully, she wasn't so far gone that she failed to hear the door as it swung open on its unoiled hinges. Bolting upright in her seat, she swiped at her eyes to remove any sleep residue lurking there and fluffed the peacock blue fabric pooled in her lap, hoping she looked industrious instead of like someone who'd just been caught napping.

"I'll be right with you," she called.

"It's just me." Cordelia's familiar voice filled the room.

Hannah sagged in relief.

"I came to invite you to supper." Her friend sauntered behind the counter and leaned against it as Hannah set the blue fabric aside and rose to meet her.

A quiet dinner with friends sounded heavenly, but she really needed to finish this alteration so she could get back to work on the Paxton dress. And with all her little dozes, the chance of finishing by suppertime was rather remote.

"I would love to come, but I've got so much to do here. Perhaps one day next week when things slow down again?"

"J.T. said you'd be stubborn about this."

Hannah bristled. "Did your brother put you up to this? For pity's sake, Cordelia, I'm a grown woman. I don't need someone to tell me when to eat, when to sleep, when to—"

An ill-timed yawn interrupted her diatribe. Hannah hid her gaping mouth behind her hand and glowered at Cordelia as if it were somehow her fault.

Cordelia just smiled. "J.T. did volunteer to forcibly remove you from the shop if you refused to come, but I assured him such tactics wouldn't be necessary. After all, you're a sensible woman who can recognize the signs of having pushed yourself too far. Say . . . falling asleep in the middle of a sewing project?"

The smug look on Cordelia's face was really quite annoying. Hannah crossed her arms over her chest, not yet willing to concede the point.

"The truth is, when J.T. suggested you come for supper, I leapt at the chance. Not just because I enjoy your company, but because I could use your help." Cordelia's smugness disappeared behind a pleading expression, one that was much more difficult for Hannah to dismiss.

Hannah's arms flopped to her sides. "What kind of help?"

"Ike's coming to dinner, too. And I'm afraid J.T. will hound him with questions about his intentions and so forth. The poor man will probably never want to have dinner with me again."

"Nonsense," Hannah declared. "If it means spending time with you, a little verbal sparring won't keep him away."

"But if you were there to distract J.T., our time together could be so much more pleasant. Please?"

Hannah rolled her eyes to the ceiling and sighed. "Oh, all right. I'll come."

Cordelia beamed. "Thank you!" She practically skipped to the door. "Oh, by the way, we're having beef roast with potatoes, carrots, and onions; cornbread; cabbage salad; baked tomatoes; and fresh apple pie. Ike's favorites."

Hannah had always supposed Ike was a man of good taste, and this confirmed it. Her mouth was already watering. She hadn't taken the time to cook a decent meal for herself all week. She'd fried up a little bacon yesterday and nibbled on some boiled eggs at noon, but beyond that, her diet had been sadly lacking. Maybe she did need a break.

When closing time arrived, she set aside the alteration project with two feet of the hem left to sew. Her fingers itched to complete the task before leaving for the day, but thoughts of Cordelia's roast set her stomach to growling, and the sound drowned out the siren call of the unfinished project.

Wanting to make a better impression on Jericho at supper than she had that morning, Hannah closed the shop and rushed upstairs to tidy her appearance. She couldn't do much to disguise the shadowy circles under her eyes, but she could change into the blue dress he liked and twist her hair into a more fashionable chignon than the plain knot at the base of her skull now. After brushing and braiding, pinning and primping, Hannah surveyed the results in the small mirror above her washstand. Not perfect, but hopefully good enough to erase Jericho's scowl and keep the lectures at bay. As a final touch, she pinched her cheeks several times and then headed downstairs.

A cool breeze carrying the smell of rain drifted over her and drew her face toward the overcast sky. She closed her eyes and inhaled deeply. Her spirit absorbed the quiet, replenishing the peace that had been worn threadbare by busyness. In an effort to please her clients, she'd become consumed by work and forgotten the need to be still in the Lord's presence.

Forgive me.

Perhaps Jericho's arrival on her step had a divine purpose as well as a human one. A reminder to keep things in balance. If there was a time to be born and a time to die, a time to kill and a time to heal, surely there must be a time to work and a time to rest. Or better yet, eat.

With a grin, Hannah opened her eyes and set out across the road. An impromptu tune rose inside her, dancing a cheerful jig across the roof of her mouth and buzzing against her lips. Her fingertips tickled the wood siding of the livery as she passed, and her mind drifted to Jericho. Was there something she could do to make it easier for him to declare himself? She saw his love in his eyes and in his actions, yet some unseen barrier blocked the words.

Maybe it would help if she stopped calling him by the name he despised. She'd started calling him Jericho to irritate him, but now she considered it more of an endearment, a name only *she* called him. But what if he still hated it? Kindness would dictate she stop using it and defer to his preference—J.T. She doubted such a small gesture would free his tongue in and of itself, but it couldn't hurt. And tonight at dinner would be the perfect time to try it out. And again when he walked her home. Would he be so pleased that he'd kiss her again outside her door? She bit her lip to keep the tingling sensation in her chest from erupting in an embarrassing giggle. Not that anyone was around to hear. This end of town was quite deserted at suppertime.

She rounded the corner and the Tucker home came into sight. From a distance, she could make out Cordelia and Ike on the porch, laughing and talking. Her hand in his.

Hannah stopped before they could see her and scurried behind an oak tree several feet off the road. Cordelia would no doubt welcome her arrival with a smile, but Hannah suspected her friend would prefer a few more minutes alone with her suitor. She planned to give her just that.

A rustling in the brush to her right drew her attention from the happy couple. Before she had fully turned, though, a man lunged at her. Hannah shrieked, but the man clamped a bony hand over her mouth and slammed her into the tree. The back of her head crashed against the unforgiving trunk. Pain ricocheted through her skull. Stunned from the blow, she offered little resistance as he pressed his forearm against her collarbone and trapped her legs with his weight. As pain receded, panic surged. She grabbed at the arm that imprisoned her and frantically twisted her head from side to side, wanting freedom, wanting away, wanting to deny that this was happening. Her nails dug into the man's wiry forearm. He hissed but did not lessen his hold.

"Be still or I'll cut you. Understand?"

Hannah stilled. She knew that voice.

The pressure at her neck lessened as her attacker lifted his arm to brandish a pocket-sized knife close to her left cheek. The fading light glimmered off the short silver blade. A frisson of fear slithered down her back. Yet it had more to do with the man than the weapon. Flaring her nostrils to take in as much air as possible above iron fingers that smelled of ink and onions, Hannah shifted her focus from the knife to the hardened face behind it. Small eyes brimmed with accusation. Overlong hair. Blotched skin growing redder and more pronounced as she stared.

Warren.

38

As J.T. had prepared to leave the livery, one of the horses he'd been stabling for a traveler at the hotel began showing mild signs of colic. After lunging in the paddock for twenty minutes, the animal seemed some improved, and J.T. led him inside to a stall. He offered the sorrel a small handful of grain to see if he would eat, and when the gelding nuzzled it from his palm, J.T.'s spirits lifted. A truly colicky horse would have turned his nose up at the feed.

Stroking the sorrel's side, he backed out of the stall and handed the empty lead line to Tom. "Keep an eye on him till I get back. Don't give him anything to eat. He can have a little water but nothing else. Got it?"

"Yes, sir. No feed. Got it."

"And if he gets restless or tries to roll, come get me at the house, right away."

Tom nodded. "I'll watch him real close. I promise."

J.T. clapped the young man on the shoulder. "I know you will. You're a good liveryman, Tom."

The grin that split the boy's face was a mile wide and brighter than a full moon on a clear night. J.T. thumped him on the arm and left, confident the kid would keep a faithful vigil.

On his way out, he passed through his office to lock up. J.T. glanced at the clock on his desk as he shoved his ledger into the top drawer and frowned. He should've been home ten minutes ago. Cordelia would skin him alive if his tardiness caused Ike's meal to be less than perfect. Although the delay did afford him the opportunity to check on Hannah, kidnap her if necessary. If the woman couldn't see the wisdom in taking time to rest, he had no qualms about forcing a bit on her.

J.T. raised two fingers to his temple in a parting salute to Tom and jogged across the street to Hannah's shop. He peered through the window, checking to see if she was inside. When he didn't find her, he nodded to himself in satisfaction.

Good. The woman possessed some sense after all.

How could she have been so senseless? Hannah swallowed a moan. She'd been aware of Warren's return to town earlier in the week, but with her nose to the grindstone at the dress shop, she hadn't spared him more than a passing thought. Now she'd practically thrown herself into his path with her silly matchmaking efforts. There was no telling how long he'd been spying on Cordelia, stewing about her burgeoning relationship with Ike. His fuse was already lit, and she'd walked right into the explosion.

Defiance burned in his eyes as he bent his head close to hers. "Father's sending me away, you know." He spoke conversationally, as if they were passing time in the aisles of the mercantile. "Says it's time for me to stand on my own two feet and run a store of my own, but I think there's more to it than that." He pressed the flat edge of the knife against her cheek.

Hannah whimpered and shut her eyes, afraid to move as he trailed the cool metal downward. The pointed tip caught slightly on her skin as it reached the edge of her jaw. She squeezed her eyes tighter.

God, help me!

Warren laughed at her, a quiet little huff, but it was enough to goad her pride. Then, as if the Lord himself were speaking to her, a verse rang in her head. *"God hath not given us the spirit of fear; but of power."* It was time to tap into that power. She'd quivered enough for this little weasel. No more.

Hannah opened her eyes and glared at Warren. The snide grin on his face slipped for a moment, but he recovered quickly. He held the blade before her eyes as if inviting her to examine its sharpness, but when her eyes stayed fixed on him instead of the knife, his lips curled into a snarl.

"Cordelia should have been mine," he spat. "Ever since we were kids together, I knew we would marry. Then you swept into town with your fancy ways and started changing her. Changing everything."

Hannah shook her head, the bark of the tree scraping against her scalp. She mumbled a denial against his hand, but he ignored her.

Warren glanced at a spot beyond the tree—probably the Tuckers' porch—and his eyes softened. Sadness dulled the rage.

"She liked me," he said, an undeniable wistfulness in his voice. "*Me.* People always see the mark on my face, never me. But Cordelia was different. She looked me in the eyes when we talked. She brought me gifts and baked cookies on my birthday. She would've made me the perfect wife."

But you would've made her a terrible husband.

Warren pierced her with a glare as if he'd heard her thoughts. "You stole my future from me," he accused, his face mere inches from hers. "You dressed her up in showy clothes, made her do those ridiculous exercises until she no longer even resembled herself, and started throwing her at every available man in town."

If Hannah could've found a way to open her mouth, she would've bit him for that. How dare he describe Cordelia like some kind of hussy? And her like a madam in a bordello? Hannah scratched at his eyes. The fiend!

Warren jerked his head back and swore.

"Maybe you need to see what it's like to have people stare, to whisper behind their hands when you walk by." He brought the knife back up to her face, this time the sharpened edge pressed against her skin. She froze. Her eyes slid to the corners of her lids as she tried to monitor the threat. Would he really cut her? Hannah's heart throbbed, swollen with fear. She'd pushed him too far.

Her chest heaved, yet she struggled to draw sufficient air into her lungs with her mouth still covered and her nose suddenly too small for the job. Her vision began to blur. Through a sheen of tears, she refocused on Warren, pleading silently.

His wicked smile taunted her. "Just one slice is all it would take. Just a little pressure . . ."

The blade pricked her cheek near the corner of her left eye. Hannah winced. A drop of something warm trickled past her ear.

Warren's eyes rounded in horror. His grip loosened. "I . . . I'm sorry." He yanked the knife away from her face and stepped back, releasing her. "I only meant to scare you. I never intended to actually—"

A growl from behind him cut off his words as Jericho wrenched Warren away from her and flung him to the ground. The knife tumbled into the grass and leaves at Hannah's feet. She braced herself against the tree trunk, sucking in fresh, sweet-smelling air as tremors quivered through her limbs.

"You all right, Hannah?" Jericho called without taking his eyes off Warren.

"Yes." Her first attempt came out in a wisp of breath. She cleared her throat and said it again, stronger. "Yes. I'm fine." When she trusted her legs to support her, she bent to retrieve the knife in case Warren thought to use it on Jericho. With shaky hands, she folded it shut and slipped it into the pocket of her skirt.

"You need someone to take your frustrations out on, Hawkins? Try me." Jericho's low voice rumbled the challenge. Back on his feet, Warren crouched, apparently preparing to take Jericho up on his offer.

The two men paced in a circle, shooting each other wary glances as they moved deeper into the cover of the surrounding mesquite brush. Hannah guessed neither of them wanted to draw Cordelia's attention or Ike's interference. The house was a good fifty yards away, but if the couple happened to look up, the old oak would only block so much of their view. The denser brush would afford a more private place for the men to pummel each other.

Hannah followed, determined to keep an eye on Jericho as well as conceal her position from her friend. Cordelia had a tendency to blame herself for Warren's attacks. She didn't need guilt plaguing her tonight of all nights.

Despite his smaller size, Warren was the first to make a move. He launched himself at Jericho with surprising speed. Hannah bit back a cry as Jericho stood his ground and let the man come. Warren landed a blow to Jericho's midsection an instant before Jericho wrapped a muscled arm around his neck and tossed him aside.

Warren shook it off and charged again. This time Jericho sidestepped the assault and kicked out a leg to trip his opponent. Warren stumbled to a knee but jumped back to his feet. He spun around and made another pass. And met Jericho's fist with his belly. He doubled over with a moan.

"Are you done?" Jericho asked.

Although he was obviously no match for Jericho's strength and skill, Warren shook his head no.

Hannah cringed as the man slowly straightened and turned to face Jericho. Did he actually think he could win? Or was he welcoming the pain as some kind of punishment?

As much as she longed for justice after Warren's foul treatment of her, his repeated humiliation was becoming a torture to watch.

Warren staggered forward again, swinging his arms widely. Jericho struck a clean blow to the man's chin, felling him like a hewn tree. He lay still for a moment, then rolled to his stomach and pushed up to his hands and knees. Jericho gripped him under his arms and put him to his feet. Drooping and bent, he swayed sideways, but still managed to advance once again.

Jericho sighed.

Hannah couldn't take it anymore. Warren hadn't really meant to hurt her. The look of horror on his face when he realized what he'd done had proven that. It was an accident. One brought on by his idiotic refusal to accept that he couldn't have what he wanted, but an accident nonetheless.

"Catch him and hold him, Jericho. He's had enough."

Jericho did as she asked, swiveling the fellow around to trap his arms behind his back. He held him fast, and by the way Warren sagged, Hannah got the impression Jericho was holding him up more than pinning him down.

Hannah walked up to Warren, no longer compelled to demand justice but to offer mercy. "Go home, Warren," she said. "Start your new store. Leave all this bitterness behind and give yourself a fresh start. It's over."

Warren tugged his arms free and, with effort, managed to straighten to his full height. He made no further apology, yet something shone in his eyes she didn't remember seeing before. The seeds of a newfound maturity? She prayed it was so.

Jericho dusted the man's back, sending a shower of dirt and leaves to the ground. Then he moved to Hannah's side. "When do you leave, Warren?"

Warren stretched out his neck and looked Jericho in the eye. "Monday."

"I expect you to keep your distance. If I catch you anywhere near Miss Richards or my sister between now and then," Jericho growled in a voice laced with steel, "I'll wire the county sheriff and have you brought up on charges. Understand?"

"Yes."

"Good." Jericho jerked his chin in the direction of the road. "Now, get out of here."

As Warren trudged back to the road, Hannah nestled into Jericho's side. He wrapped his arm around her and hugged her tight as he watched Warren disappear around the corner. She buried her face in his shirt and breathed deeply, the scent and nearness of him soothing away the last of her agitation.

He pulled back slightly and placed a tender kiss on her forehead. Then he touched his lips to the cut below her eye. He pulled a handkerchief from his trouser pocket and held it to her face. "It doesn't seem too deep. I think it's already clotted. We can wash it up at the house."

"Do you think Cordelia will notice?"

"Probably, but that can't be helped."

Hannah sighed. "Well, let's get going, then. Cordelia's waiting on us." Hannah stepped out of his embrace and tugged on his arm when he didn't move fast enough for her. "Come on, Jer . . . I mean, J.T. I'm starving."

39

What did you just call me?" J.T. raised a brow and refused to budge. The words had come out more like an accusation than the simple question he'd intended. But then, that was probably due to the fact that his insides were still churning.

I could have lost her.

The image of that knife slicing into her cheek would haunt him for weeks. Years, maybe. It had taken all the self-control he possessed not to thrash Warren to a bloody pulp for putting his hands on her and accosting her with that blade. The man could have put out her eye or slipped and nicked a vein in her neck. The very idea made his blood run cold.

Hannah looked at the ground and kicked at a fallen acorn, the simple motion a reminder that she was safe. The danger had passed.

"I thought you preferred being called by your initials," she said.

"By everyone else, sure. But not you."

Her head snapped up. "Not me? Why?"

J.T. closed the small distance between them and cupped her jaw in his hand. He brushed his thumb over her lips, delighting in the breathy sigh that whispered past his knuckle. "There's something about the sound of my given name coming from you that makes me proud to own it."

A mist settled over the deep blue of her eyes, and the knot in his chest began to unravel. He slid his hand from her neck to her shoulder and gently massaged the muscles beneath his fingers. "Do you remember telling me that the name Jericho suited me?" He pulled a wry face. "I think you were trying to jab my pride at the time with a rather uncomplimentary comparison, but you were right. It does suit me. Or at least it has since the day I met you."

For once, Hannah seemed to be the one incapable of speech. She just stared at him, a cautious hope shimmering in her eyes. J.T. trailed his hand from her shoulder to her wrist and twined his fingers with hers. He'd not disappoint her. Not this time.

Glancing down at their joined hands, he cleared his throat. "I wanted to protect myself from making the same mistakes my father made. He let a beautiful woman into his heart only to have her tear it to shreds. I couldn't fall into the same trap. So I built a wall—a wall like the one that surrounded the city of Jericho in the Bible."

Her breath caught.

J.T. squeezed her hand and lifted his eyes to meet her love-filled gaze. "You were beautiful, fashionable, and independent—everything I considered a threat. Yet you laid siege to my heart anyway. You walked circles around me, Hannah, and somewhere along the way, that wall of mine crumbled, and you captured my heart."

He brought her hand to his mouth and pressed his lips to her knuckles. Her chest rose and fell between them, her breathing uneven. Slowly, he slipped his fingers free of hers, drawing out the touch as he watched her eyes darken. He cradled the sides of her face, the softness of her skin heaven in his hands.

"I love you, Hannah."

He touched his lips to hers in a delicate kiss, sealing his love chastely upon her. But as he drew back, the feisty, independent woman in his arms clasped his face with both hands and pulled his mouth back down to hers. Willingly surrendering his freedom, J.T. yielded to his captor, claiming victory himself as the taste of her filled him. He wrapped his arms around her and deepened the kiss. His mind, his heart were consumed with her as he gave all of himself, holding nothing back. She answered in equal measure, and a moan rose in Jericho's throat. He pressed her close, marveling at the way her soft curves conformed to the angles of his arms, the way her lips fit so perfectly against his, the way her love erased all his past hurts. She'd been tailor-made for him.

Slowly, he pulled away and watched as her light brown lashes fluttered open. Her mouth curved in a satisfied smile that warmed his blood.

"So you really don't mind if I call you Jericho?"

"Nope." He held up a cautionary hand. "On two conditions."

Hannah blinked up at him.

"First, you have to marry me. I can't let just anyone go around calling me Jericho, after all. Only family gets that privilege. Second—"

"Wait a minute." Hannah pressed her fingers against his lips to silence him. "Was that a proposal? Did Jericho Tucker, the man who disdains fashion and all its trappings, just ask a dressmaker to marry him?"

J.T. gazed into her beloved twilight eyes and shook his head. "No. Jericho Tucker, the man who thanks God every day for bringing beauty back into his life, is asking a dressmaker to marry him." He inhaled a shuddering breath and captured her hands between his own. "Will you, Hannah? Will you marry this grouchy old liveryman who loves you more than life itself?"

A radiant smile burst across her face as she nodded again and again. "Yes, Jericho. Oh, yes!"

Triumph and joy shot through him. With an exultant shout, he lifted her from the ground, her feet kicking back behind her. She laughed, and the sound sprinkled over him like a gentle summer rain, refreshing his soul. She was his. Really and truly his.

J.T. lowered Hannah until her toes touched the earth, and for a moment they just grinned at each other like a pair of empty-headed fools. A pair of very happy empty-headed fools.

"What's the second condition?" Hannah asked, finally breaking the silence.

J.T. squinted in confusion. "What?"

"I agreed to marry you. What else do I have to do in order to call you Jericho?"

Ah, yes. He'd nearly forgotten. Wrestling his smile into a more subdued, serious line, he placed his hand over his heart. "You must vow never to name any of our sons after Canaanite cities. I may have developed a new appreciation for *Jericho* in recent months, but no boy should be saddled with a name like Gezer or Eglon." His body convulsed in an exaggerated shudder.

Hannah's lip protruded in a delicious little mock pout. "Oh. But I had my heart set on naming our firstborn Megiddo."

A chuckle vibrated in J.T.'s chest as he steered Hannah back toward the road and the house he would soon share with her. Life with this vibrant woman was sure to be filled with rich colors, frequent laughter, and bountiful love. What could be more beautiful?

SHORT-STRAW BRIDE

To Gloria and Beth
my eagle-eyed critique partners and beloved friends.

You strengthen my stories, encourage my heart,
and corral my characters when they get out of hand.
Thanks for walking this road with me.

Bear ye one another's burdens,
and so fulfill the law of Christ.

Galatians 6:2

Prologue

Anderson County, Texas—1870

Ten-year-old Meredith Hayes balled her hands into fists as she faced her tormentor. "Hiram Ellis! Give me back my lunch bucket this instant!"

"Oh, I'm sorry, Meri. Did you want this?" His voice dripped sarcasm as he dangled the small pail in front of her.

She lunged for it, but her hands met only air as the older boy snatched it away and tossed it over her head to his snickering brother. Meredith ricocheted between the two, never quite fast enough to get more than a finger on the tin.

Why was she always the one to get picked on? Meredith stomped her foot in frustration. She thought she'd gotten enough of a lead today after school, but Hiram must have been watching for her. He'd had it out for her ever since her family moved to the area last spring. Probably because the land they bought used to belong to his best friend's family.

"Meri, Meri, quite contrary," Hiram sang in a ridiculously high-pitched voice, skipping in a circle around her and swinging the lunch bucket back and forth. A group of girls came around the bend and stopped to giggle behind their hands. Meredith asked for help, but they just stood there smirking and whispering behind their schoolbooks. Even Anna Leigh, her desk mate and the one girl Meredith thought a friend. Angry tears pooled in her eyes, but Meredith blinked them away. She'd not let Hiram win.

"You're a bully, Hiram Ellis."

"Yeah?" Hiram stopped skipping and glared at Meredith. "Well, you're a carpetbagger's daughter."

"My papa's not a carpetbagger. He's a teacher, just like your sister."

Hiram's face scrunched up like a pumpkin that had started to rot. "My sister teaches white kids. Not good-for-nothin' darkies."

Meredith raised her chin and repeated the words she'd heard her father say countless times. "They're freedmen. And they have just as much right to learn as you do."

"If those *freedmen* were still slaves, like they oughta be, Joey Gordon's pa wouldn'ta been killed by Yankees, and Joey would still be here." Hiram glowered and strode toward her, his boots pounding into the earth. Meredith instinctively retreated a step before she remembered she wasn't afraid of him.

"You want this stupid tin back?" Hiram growled out the question as he halted a couple of feet in front of her. "Go fetch!"

He sprinted to the edge of the road and hurled the pail through a thick stand of pine trees. Meredith watched it fly, wondering why God thought it fair to give a mean-tempered boy such a strong throwing arm.

The bucket clipped a tree limb and disappeared over a small rise. A hollow clang echoed through the pines followed by a series of quieter thunks as it tumbled down the back side of the hill.

Meredith winced. Mama was going to skin her alive for bringing her pail home dented and busted. The only thing worse would be not bringing it home at all.

Meredith glared at Hiram and trudged forward.

"Meri, no!" Anna Leigh ran up and clutched Meredith's arm. "You can't. That's Archer land."

Archer land? Meredith looked around to get her bearings and swallowed hard as recognition dawned. Anna Leigh was right.

"No one steps on Archer land. Not if they value their life." Anna Leigh shook her head, eyeing the trees as if their branches might reach down and snatch her off the ground. "Just let it go, Meri." She backed away, tugging on Meredith's arm. But when Meredith made no move to follow, Anna Leigh released her with a heavy sigh.

It couldn't be as bad as all that. Could it? Meredith gazed through the pines, to the small hill that hid her lunch bucket. Her heart thumped against her ribs. It wasn't very far. If she ran, she could get her tin and be back before the Archers even knew she'd been there. Then again, everyone in Anderson County knew the Archer boys were trigger happy and plumb loco, to boot. What if one of them was hiding out there somewhere, just waiting for her?

"I hear they got bloodthirsty hounds that can sniff you out the minute your foot steps off the road." Hiram spoke in a low, husky voice. "Dogs that'd sooner gnaw your leg off than look at you."

Meredith told herself to pay him no mind. He was only trying to scare her. But she couldn't quite banish the image of a big black dog barreling down on her, teeth bared.

"You know Seth Winston . . . and his hand?"

Meredith didn't turn around, but she nodded. The man ran a store near her father's school. He only had three fingers on his right hand.

"Travis Archer shot them two fingers clean off when Winston tried to pay a call after old man Archer died. Woulda done worse if Winston hadn't hightailed it outta there as fast as he did. And don't think you'd be safe just 'cause you're a girl. They peppered Miss Elvira's buggy with buckshot when she came to collect the young ones to take them to the homes she'd found for them. Nearly put her eye out."

"At least . . ." Meredith's throat seemed to close. She forced a little cough and tried again. "At least they weren't hurt too bad."

"Only because they escaped." Hiram came up beside her and spoke directly into her ear. "Five other men weren't so lucky. They came out here at different times, each with hopes of buying the Archer spread. None of them were ever seen again." Hiram paused, and Meredith couldn't fight off the shivers his words provoked. "Their bodies are probably buried somewhere out there."

Something rustled just beyond the pines. Meredith jumped.

Hiram laughed.

She should go home. Just leave the pail and go home. Mama would understand . . . but she'd be disappointed.

"I dare you," Hiram said, finally drawing Meredith's attention. "I dare you to go after that tin."

"Don't do it, Meri," Anna Leigh begged.

"Oh, she won't. She's too scared." Hiram's cocky grin resurrected Meredith's pride.

Crossing her thin arms over her chest, she glared up at him. "I'll get it. Just see if I don't."

The girls behind her gasped, and even Hiram looked a bit uneasy, which only served to bolster Meredith's determination. She marched to the tree line, turned back for one last triumphant glance at the stunned Ellis boys, and dashed off in the direction the pail had disappeared. Her shoes crunched on fallen pine needles and twigs as she ran, her breath echoing loudly in her ears as she huffed up the hill.

She stopped at the top and clutched her aching side as she scanned the ground for her lunch bucket. Something shiny glinted in the sunlight down and to the left. Meredith smiled and hurried forward. *This isn't so tough.*

Her fingers closed around the handle of the battered tin, but when she turned to head back, the hill blocked her view of the road. Suddenly feeling very isolated, she bit her lip as forest noises echoed around her. A twig snap to her left. A rustle to her right. Then from somewhere in the distance behind her, a dog barked.

The Archer hounds!

Meredith fled, scrambling up the hill. But the sandy soil was too loose. Her feet kept slipping. She clawed at the ground with her fingers, to no avail.

Another bark sounded. Closer this time.

Meredith gave up on the hill and just started running away from the barking. The slope gradually lessened, and she spotted a flat section up ahead where the pines turned back toward the road. Aiming for the opening, she veered between the trees.

As she looked up to gauge how close she was to the road, her right foot hit something metallic. A loud crack rent the air a second before a pair of steel jaws snapped closed on her leg.

"Good girl, Sadie." Travis Archer folded his wiry adolescent frame as he hunkered down and stroked the half-grown pointer. "We might turn you into a huntin' dog yet."

She still barked too much when she got excited, frightening off the game, but she'd successfully pointed a rabbit and held when he called *whoa*, so even though the hare scurried away before he could get in position to shoot, Travis was proud of the pup's progress.

"Let's try again, girl. Maybe we'll find some quail for you to flush. Jim's getting tired of fixin' squirrel mea—"

An agonized scream cut Travis off and raised the hair on his arms. He hadn't heard a cry like that since his mother died birthin' Neill.

Sadie barked and took off like a shot. Travis called for her to stop, but the pup ignored his command and ran west—toward the road. Snatching up his rifle, he gave chase. If a new threat had wandered onto Archer land, he'd do everything in his power to protect his brothers.

The barking intensified, and it sounded as if Sadie had stopped. Travis slowed his pace and brought his rifle into position against his shoulder. It wouldn't be the first time some greedy land grabber tried to draw him out, thinking four boys were easy pickings. He might not be full grown, but he was man enough to defend what was his. No one was going to drive him and his brothers out. No one.

Travis wove through the narrow pines, catching a glimpse of Sadie's black coat. He recognized the spot. It was one of several places he'd hidden coyote traps. He'd posted warning signs, but some idiots were too cocky for their own good. Hardening himself against any pity he might feel for the interloper, Travis fingered the trigger on his rifle and stepped around the last tree that stood between him and his target.

"Hands where I can see 'em, mister, or I'll put a bullet in . . ." The threat died on his lips.

A girl?

Horror swept over him, loosening his grip on the rifle. The barrel dipped toward the ground.

"D-don't shoot. P-p-please." The girl turned liquid blue eyes on him. "I didn't m-m-mean any harm." Her tearstained face stabbed him with guilt as she bravely tried to swallow her sobs.

"I ain't gonna shoot you." Travis relaxed his stance and set the weapon aside. "See?" He held his palms out and took a cautious step toward the girl sitting sideways beneath the tree. "I thought you were someone else. I ain't gonna hurt you." Although judging by the blood staining the edge of her ruffled pantalets, he already had.

"W-what about your d-dog?" She eyed Sadie as if the pup were some kind of hellhound.

"Sadie, heel." The pointer quit barking and padded over to Travis's side. He motioned for her to stay, then gingerly approached the frightened girl. "I'm gonna get that trap off your leg. All right?"

She sucked in her bottom lip, her eyes widening as he approached, but she nodded, and something inside Travis uncoiled. He'd no idea what he would've done if she'd gone all hysterical on him. Thankfully, this gal seemed to have a decent head on her shoulders. Travis smiled at her and turned his attention to the trap.

His stomach roiled. The thing was clamped above the ankle of her right leg. She whimpered a bit when he reached for the spring mechanisms on either side of the trap, no doubt anticipating more pain. The metal chain clanked as she moved.

"Try to keep still," he instructed. "Even when the trap opens, don't pull yourself free. Wait for me to help you. Your leg might be broken, and we don't want to do anything to make it worse. Understand?"

Another brave little nod.

Travis grabbed the release springs and was about to compress them when the girl spoke.

"Can I . . . hold on to you?"

Closing his eyes for a second, Travis swallowed, then gave a nod of his own. "Sure, kid."

Her hands circled his neck as he bent over her, and she leaned her head against his shoulder.

He cleared his throat. "Ready?"

The side of her face rubbed against his upper arm. "Mm-hmm."

Travis pressed the spring levers with a firm, steady pressure until the trap's jaw released. Once it clicked back into its open position, he gently removed her foot from the trap.

"I need to check your leg to see how bad it is." Her arms still around his neck, Travis rotated her until her back brushed the tree trunk. "Rest here."

He eased away from her hold and lifted the edge of her pantalets a few inches up her shin. The skin had been broken, and there was a deep indentation where the steel had clamped her leg, but she'd had the good sense to keep still, so the bleeding was minimal. There seemed to be swelling and discoloration around the indentation, though, and that worried Travis.

"Can you move your foot?"

The girl flexed her foot and immediately hissed in pain. "It hurts." Her voice broke on a muted sob.

"Just be still, then." Travis gritted his teeth. Probably a fracture. "I'm gonna look for some sticks to splint your leg with, and then I'll get you home. All right? Don't worry."

On his deathbed, his father had made him swear never to leave Archer land, to protect it and his younger brothers at all cost. And Travis had done exactly that for the last two years. But today, he was going to have to break his promise. He had to make things right with this little girl. Had to get her home.

Travis stood and scoured the ground for splint-worthy sticks while silently vowing that, before he went home, he'd spring every stinking trap on his property. No way was he going to run the risk of something like this happening again. He'd thought that any troublemakers who found themselves snagged would be able to free themselves with a minimum of fuss and leave with a sore leg to remind them not to return. The traps were too small to do significant damage to a man's leg, especially through the thick boots most of them wore. But a child? A *girl*? Travis never even considered such a scenario.

By the time he made his way back to the tree, the girl had composed herself. "What's your name?" he asked, thinking to distract her as he fit the splint to her leg.

"Meredith."

He pulled a handkerchief from his pocket and tied it firmly around the sticks just below her knee. "I'm Travis."

"*You're* Travis?" She said it with such disbelief that he stopped what he was doing to stare at her. She blushed and stammered. "I just . . . uh . . . thought you'd be meaner or bigger or . . . or something."

Travis shook his head and chuckled softly. "That's exactly what I want people to think. Me and my brothers are safer that way."

He looked around for something else to use to tie the bottom of the splint. Finding nothing, he took out his pocket knife and used the point to tear a hole in the seam at his left shoulder. Then he yanked until the sleeve pulled free and slid it down over his hand. He knelt back down and fastened it into place around her ankle.

"You know what you could do for me, Meredith?"

"What?"

He made sure the knot was tight, then smiled up at his patient. "When you get back and your friends start asking you questions, make me sound as big and mean as possible. The fact that I helped you get home can be our secret. Okay?"

Her eyes glowed with something besides pain, and she actually smiled. The weight dragging on his conscience lightened.

"Grab onto my neck again—I'm going to pick you up." Travis shifted to her side and maneuvered an arm under her knees.

"Wait! I need my tin."

He pulled back. "Your what?"

"My lunch tin. Hiram threw it into the trees. That's why I came onto your land in the first place. I can't go back without it." She twisted and tried to reach behind her.

"Hold still," Travis barked, not wanting her to hurt herself. "I'll fetch it." He grabbed the beat-up pail and handed it to her. Meredith cradled it to her middle, and Travis decided that if he ever met this Hiram person, he'd find another pail and give the numskull a wallop or two upside the head.

Travis slid his arms around Meredith and lifted her from the ground. The little warrior never cried out, just tightened her grip on his neck as he pushed to his feet. He examined the ground for the smoothest path to the road, even when it meant going out of his way. It was crazy, really—this urge to protect her. He'd spent the two years since his father died building barriers to keep the outside world out. But when this slip of a girl looked at him with trust blazing in her bright blue eyes, all he could think about was protecting the one piece of the outside world that had found a way in.

When he made it to the border of his property, Travis halted and inhaled a deep breath as his gaze tilted up toward heaven.

Sorry, Pa. I gotta do it.

Then, with a prayer for his brothers' safety resounding in his mind, he leaned forward and stepped off Archer land.

Palestine, Texas—1882

"I don't think I can do it, Cass." Meredith peered up at her cousin through the reflection in the vanity mirror.

Cassandra pulled the hairpin from her mouth and secured another section of Meredith's braided chignon. "Do what?"

"Marry a man who wants me only for the land I can bring him."

"How do you know that's all he wants?" Cassandra leaned down until her face was level with Meredith's and winked at her in the mirror. "If you ask me, the man seems rather smitten, paying calls on you every Saturday night for the last month."

Calls where he spent more time discussing the lumber industry with her uncle than conversing with her. Wouldn't a man who was smitten spend his time talking to the woman he hoped to marry rather than her guardian?

Meredith sighed and turned to face her younger cousin. "I know I should be thrilled. Uncle Everett has told me again and again that Roy Mitchell is an excellent catch, and your mama nearly swooned when she found out he'd proposed. But something doesn't feel right."

"Maybe that's because saying yes would mean letting go of a girlhood dream."

Meredith squirmed under her cousin's knowing look. Cassandra was the only person Meredith had ever told about her infatuation with Travis Archer. An infatuation based on a single encounter. It was silly, really. What girl would dream about a young man whose hunting trap had nearly taken off her leg? Yet something about Travis Archer had left a permanent impression upon her heart.

Cassandra understood that.

During holidays and family visits, the two cousins used to huddle together beneath the covers of Cassandra's bed and spin romantic tales of the heroes who would valiantly rescue them from rockslides and stampeding cattle and even a polar bear or two when they were feeling particularly inventive. Meredith's hero always wore Travis Archer's face. Even now, she couldn't stop herself from imagining what he must look like twelve years later. He'd been handsome as a youth. What would he look like as a man?

Standing abruptly and moving to the open wardrobe where she could riffle through her dresses instead of looking at her cousin, Meredith mentally crammed Travis back into the past, where he belonged.

"Goodness, Cass. I'm far too sensible to hold on to a bunch of silly daydreams. I put those thoughts from my mind years ago."

Cassandra reached around her and took down the rose-colored dress Meredith only wore for special occasions. "You might have put Travis from your mind, but I think he still claims a piece of your heart."

Meredith reluctantly accepted the polonaise and matching skirt and laid them on the bed. But instead of removing her wrapper to dress, she hugged her arms around her waist and flopped onto the mattress. "You're right."

And where did that leave her? She hadn't seen the man once since that day. It was doubtful he even remembered her. If he did, the memory was probably a vague recollection of some scrawny kid who'd gotten caught trespassing. Not exactly a vision to inspire romantic feelings. Besides, none of the Archers ever stepped foot off their land. Waiting for Travis would be about as fruitful as waiting for a snowstorm in July.

"Give Mr. Mitchell a chance, Meri. Maybe he's the kind of man who doesn't know how to express his feelings." Cassandra sat beside her on the bed and patted her knee. "It'll be just the two of you today at lunch. Papa won't be around to distract him with business talk. Get to know him. You might be surprised by what he can offer you."

Meredith glanced sideways at her cousin, a grin tugging at the corner of her mouth. "You know . . . I'm supposed to be the wise one here, not you."

"I may be three years younger," Cassandra said with a wink, "but that doesn't mean I don't know a thing or two about men."

"I can't argue with that. You've probably collected more courting experience in the past two years than I've had in the last five." Meredith smiled and nudged her cousin with her shoulder. "Look at the way Freddie Garrett follows you around."

"Freddie Garrett's barely fifteen, you goose. He doesn't count." Cassandra grabbed a pillow and swatted Meredith on the chin. Meredith, of course, had to retaliate. The two dodged and giggled until their sides ached so much they had to stop.

"I think you're going to have to fix my hair," Meredith said as she blew a loose strand off her forehead. The ornery thing fell right back across the bridge of her nose, which set the two girls to laughing again.

Cassandra gained her feet first. "Come on," she said between chuckles. "Let's get you dressed, and I'll see what I can do about your hair."

Twenty minutes later, dressed in her best polonaise with her hair artfully rearranged, Meredith stood by the window looking out over the street. Her cousin had kissed her cheek and wished her well a few minutes ago and left her to gather her thoughts before her suitor arrived. The only problem was, her thoughts were so scattered, Meredith was sure she'd never pull them together in time.

Roy Mitchell had many admirable traits. He was ambitious and prosperous, and would certainly support a wife in fine style. His dark hair and eyes were handsome to look upon, and his manners were impeccable. Yet he stirred no strong feelings in her. And as far as she could tell, she stirred none in him.

What am I to do, Lord? Do I marry Roy and hope that affection comes, or do you have someone else in mind for me? Please make your will clear to me.

A brisk knock sounded on the door, but before Meredith could answer, her aunt swept into the room, her brows lifted in a scrutinizing arch. "I'm glad to see you had the good sense to dress for the occasion."

Meredith bit her tongue. After living with the disapproving woman for several years, she'd learned to speak as little as possible during their private . . . discussions.

"Come here, child, and turn around so I can see you."

Trying to ignore the *child* remark, Meredith did as instructed while her aunt clicked her tongue and sighed like a martyr who had been given a heavy cross to bear.

"Can you do nothing more to disguise that awful limp? We can't have Mr. Mitchell second-guessing his offer before the engagement is official. I've already done all I can to ensure you every advantage. Cassandra has strict instructions not to enter the parlor while he's here. Don't want the man drawing unfavorable comparisons, do we?"

Aunt Noreen narrowed her gaze, as if she could sense Meredith's inner doubt. "You'd best not do anything to sabotage this proposal," she said, shaking her finger under Meredith's nose. "Everett and I have too much riding on this for you to dillydally around. The man expects an answer today. And that answer had better be yes."

When Meredith had asked God for guidance, she'd never expected him to shove it down her throat with a dose of her aunt's less-than-flattering opinions. Was this really the answer she sought? Was God speaking through

Aunt Noreen, or was Aunt Noreen just spouting her own agenda? Meredith didn't mind rebelling against her aunt, but rebelling against God was another matter entirely.

Needing to get away from the waving finger in order to think straight, Meredith stepped over to the wardrobe to collect her shawl, exaggerating her limp as she went. When Aunt Noreen moaned, Meredith smiled. She knew it was petty of her, but she refused to let the woman browbeat her without striking back at least a little.

In reality, the hitch in her gait was barely noticeable except on those days when she overexerted herself. Years ago, the doctor had explained that the bone damage she'd sustained from the steel trap had hindered the completion of normal growth in her right leg, eventually causing it to be slightly shorter than her left. With custom-made shoes that added half an inch of height to the right heel, she got along without much trouble. Unfortunately, Aunt Noreen tended to see mountains where the rest of the world saw only molehills, especially when it came to Meredith's shortcomings.

Wrapping her ivory shawl around her shoulders, Meredith stared at the silky fringe instead of her aunt as she cautiously ventured into the conversation. "Papa always encouraged me to choose a husband with utmost care since the bond would last for life. I aim to follow his advice. Roy Mitchell has many fine qualities, but I need more time to get to know him before I can make this decision with confidence." She glanced up and found scowl lines furrowing Aunt Noreen's brow. "Today's luncheon will certainly help me achieve those ends," Meredith hurried to add.

"More time?" The woman sounded as if the words were choking her.

Aunt Noreen eyed the open doorway and prowled three steps closer to Meredith. "Did I ask for more time when your father requested lodgings for you in my home so that you could attend the Palestine Female Institute five years ago?" she hissed. "No. And two years after that, when your father's dealings with those . . . those *Negros* finally resulted in the end I predicted, did not Everett and I give you a permanent home?"

Meredith swallowed hard, trying to fight the memories of the fever that had taken first her papa and then her mother. They hadn't allowed her to come home, too afraid she'd catch the sickness. She'd tried to go to them anyway, but when her father refused to unbar the door and gazed at her through the front window, palm pressed to the glass, sunken eyes silently pleading with her to leave, she'd had no choice. She returned to her aunt and uncle's house and wept in Cassie's arms.

"My food has fed you," Aunt Noreen muttered, bringing Meredith back to the present. "Your uncle's income has provided a roof over your head. You've been given more than enough *time*."

Noreen sniffed and crossed her arms, looking uncomfortable as her focus jumped to the doorway before returning to Meredith. "You might not be aware, but your uncle's business has experienced some setbacks in the last few years. We need the stability that a connection with Roy Mitchell would provide. He's promised to partner with Everett once his land deal goes through. All his lumber will be cut exclusively by the Hayes mill. But the deal hinges on your marriage. No marriage, no partnership."

Because Roy Mitchell needed her land—the land her father had left in her uncle's care, intending that he restore it to Meredith when she married or turned twenty-five.

"Would you jeopardize Cassandra's future simply because you're unsure of your feelings?"

Meredith blinked. If she refused Roy Mitchell's proposal, *would* she be hurting Cassandra?

Footsteps echoed in the hall outside the room for a moment before Cassandra's smiling face appeared in the doorway.

"Papa sent me to fetch you, Meri. Your suitor's here."

Aunt Noreen gave her a pointed look and nudged her toward the door. "Go on, now. Let's not keep Mr. Mitchell waiting."

As Meredith stepped into the hall, Cassie's eager smile, so full of innocence and romantic dreams, lit up her face. Guilt pricked at Meredith like a row of sewing pins protruding through her corset seam.

Cassandra deserved the best, and if marrying Roy would provide her cousin that opportunity, perhaps Meredith should make the sacrifice.

Yet when she entered the parlor and Roy walked toward her, she couldn't quite stem the quivers of panic that convulsed in her stomach.

Lord, I asked for guidance, and so far everything seems to point me toward marrying Roy. But if you have another plan, any *other plan, I'd gladly consider it.*

Roy extended his arm to her, and Meredith fought for a polite smile as she slid her hand into its expected place.

2

By the time Meredith finished her slice of chocolate cake, she'd given up on finding common ground with Roy Mitchell. After the soup, she'd asked him what he enjoyed doing in his free time, and he'd answered that he was fond of traveling. This perked her up initially, until his description of a recent trip to Houston turned into a quarter hour of rambling about the area's booming lumber industry.

Then, when the waiter arrived with their entrées, blessedly interrupting the *Ode to the Big Thicket's Virgin Pine*, Meredith slipped in a question about what he liked to read. Roy smiled and confidently assured her that he much preferred to experience things firsthand rather than read someone else's view on the subject.

"For example," he said as he leaned across the table in obvious enthusiasm, "I've made careful study of the lands here on the edge of the Piney Woods. Acres of forest stand virtually untouched, just waiting for the right man with the right vision to capitalize on the opportunity. Reading books only teaches a person about the past. I'm a man who looks to the future."

He went on to describe how his forward thinking led him to line up a handful of investors to supply capital for the manpower and equipment he'd need to expand his small logging operation. All he lacked were a few parcels of land that would allow him direct access to the railroad. And those he would soon have in his possession.

Desperate by the dessert course, Meredith broke all the etiquette rules her mother had taught her and asked about religion, questioning Roy about the role he expected God to play in his expansion plans. The man chuckled and offered some sort of platitude about God helping those who helped themselves before he tucked into his apple pie.

The meal could not have left her more disheartened. She supposed Roy was simply attempting to convince her of his ability to provide for a wife, but what he'd succeeded in doing instead was paint a dreary picture of the two of them sitting on a porch, staring at a field of tree stumps with no fodder for conversation because all the virgin pines were gone.

"Are you ready to go, my dear?"

Meredith blinked. "Oh . . . yes." She dabbed her lips with her napkin and smiled up at Roy as he hurried around the table to assist her with her chair. "Thank you for a lovely meal. I don't often get to eat in such elegant surroundings."

"That will change once we're married. As my wife, you'll dine in the finest establishments in the state. Houston, San Antonio, even the capital."

"Mmmm." Meredith couldn't seem to vocalize anything more committal as Roy helped her on with her shawl and escorted her from the hotel dining room.

The two strolled down the boardwalk in front of the International Hotel in silence, and for the first time since leaving her uncle's house, Meredith relaxed. Maybe being with Roy wasn't so bad after all. His firm grip steadied her uneven gait, and the people they passed didn't look through her as they usually did. Men tipped their hats and women gazed at her with new respect. Being on Roy Mitchell's arm apparently made her a person worth noticing.

But did it make her the person she wanted to be?

A hat in the milliner's window caught Meredith's eye, and she slowed. Ever the gentleman, Roy steered her closer to the shop, but she found it nearly impossible to concentrate on the bonnet, for she could feel him scrutinizing her face.

"Have you given much thought to my proposal, Miss Hayes?"

Meredith's stomach lurched. *Not yet*. She wasn't ready.

He released her arm and placed his palm in the small of her back. "I confess, I have thought of little else," he murmured.

The warmth of his hand penetrated her clothing, but the intimate touch left her chilled.

Lord, I need a sign here. A hint. Anything.

"Mr. Mitchell?"

Roy's hand fell away from her back as he turned to face the burly man approaching him from the street. "Now's not a good time, Barkley."

"I'm sorry to interrupt, sir, but it's important."

Roy held his hand out to Meredith, and she took it, letting him drag her to his side. "Nothing could be more important than what I'm doing right now."

What he was doing right now was pressing her for an answer she was unprepared to give. Mr. Barkley's interruption could not have pleased her more.

"I don't mind, Roy," she said. "Truly."

Roy patted her hand. "Nonsense. I'm sure whatever Barkley has to say can wait until after I see you home."

"But he says it's important," she insisted, praying he'd do the unchivalrous thing for once. "I'd hate to be the cause of a delay that ended up hurting your business ventures."

Roy hesitated. He glanced back to where Mr. Barkley stood shifting his weight from foot to foot. "Can it wait an hour?"

"You . . . ah . . . you said you wanted to be informed the minute Wheeler returned with an answer, boss." The man finally looked Roy directly in the eye, and a silent message seemed to pass between them. "He's back."

Meredith held her breath as Roy battled with himself over which course to choose. Then he squeezed her hand, and she knew she'd been granted a reprieve.

"I'm sorry, my dear, but this really is an urgent matter. I promise not to be long."

"Take as much time as you need." Meredith slipped her hand from his loose hold and wandered back toward the shop window. "I wanted to examine the new bonnets more closely anyway."

Roy favored her with an appreciative grin and gestured for Mr. Barkley to meet him at the end of the boardwalk. The two met at the edge of the milliner's shop and ducked into the alley that stretched alongside.

Meredith had just set her mind to figuring out a way to postpone responding to Roy's proposal when the man's voice echoed back to her from around the corner.

"He's back from the Archer spread already? That doesn't bode well."

The Archer spread? As in *Travis* Archer? Meredith strained to hear more, but Roy's voice faded as he walked deeper into the alley.

Meredith ambled down to the far end of the display window, careful to keep her eyes on the hats while diverting all her focus to her ears. A wagon rolled past, harness jangling and horse hooves clomping, making her want to scream in frustration as the men's words got lost in the din. Giving up on the hats, Meredith moved to the building's corner and pressed her shoulder against the brick, getting as close as she dared without being seen. Thankfully, the noisy wagon turned down an adjacent street, and she could finally catch pieces of the conversation again.

". . . can't be convinced to sell?"

"Wheeler offered him twice what the property's worth . . . man threatened to shoot . . . ain't selling, boss."

". . . connects the northern properties to the railroad. . . . my investors will pull out. I have to . . . one way or another."

"I thought . . . Hayes spread, too."

"That's in the bag. You . . . that crippled gal was hanging on to me. I'll have my . . . deed before the month is out. No, Archer . . . only serious obstacle."

Meredith sucked in an outraged breath. *Crippled gal?* Of all the nerve. If he thought he was going to get his greedy hands on her father's legacy that easily, he couldn't be more wrong. Why, she had half a mind to—

". . . issue my threat?"

Threat? What threat? Meredith shoved aside her indignation and fixed her attention back on the men in the alley.

"Yep. Wheeler warned . . . didn't sell there'd be consequences."

"Good. Burn . . . . tonight. Target the barn. Then . . . offer half the previous price to take . . . off their hands."

Meredith gasped. Roy had just ordered an act of arson with the same nonchalance as he'd ordered their beefsteak at the hotel.

God had given her a sign, all right, and it clearly read *Stay Out!*

But what about Travis? Fires could be deadly. She had to do something to help him.

One set of footsteps echoed in retreat while a second grew louder. Meredith lunged awkwardly back to the window, her pulse throbbing.

"Have you decided which you like best?" Roy came up beside her, once again the solicitous gentleman. Revulsion crept over her, but Meredith forced herself not to shy away.

She wanted to spit on him or slap him or shove him off the boardwalk and into the mud where he belonged, but she couldn't do any of those things without tipping him off that she had overheard his plans. So she smiled instead, vowing to beat him at his own game.

"I'm leaning toward the blue one with the flowers. What do you think of it?"

"I think it would look lovely on you. But then, you have a way of making everything lovely." He smiled and lifted a finger to stroke her cheek.

Meredith's stomach roiled.

"Oh dear." She quickly covered her mouth with one hand and her stomach with the other, thanking God for the excuse to cut their time together short. "I think something from lunch may not be agreeing with me." That something being Roy Mitchell.

An impatient frown darkened Roy's face before he quickly replaced it with a look of concern. "Would you like to sit and rest for a moment? There's a bench outside the drugstore across the street."

"No. I think I should lie down." She hunched herself over and added a quiet moan for good measure. "Can you take me home, please?"

"Are you sure?"

Meredith nodded vigorously, keeping her hand over her mouth.

"Very well."

Roy took her arm and helped her navigate the three blocks back to her uncle's house. When they reached the front gate, however, he used his grip to slow her to a halt.

"I'm so sorry to have ruined our afternoon," she blurted, not wanting to give him the chance to ask her anything. Besides, the longer she thought about what he planned for Travis, the more ill she truly became. She looked up at the brick house, longing for the escape it promised.

"Meredith, darling," Roy said, turning her to face him, "please, just tell me that I can move ahead with our wedding plans."

The idea was so nauseating, Meredith didn't have to prevaricate. Her stomach began to heave all on its own. Roy must have seen the truth in her face as she bent forward, for his eyes widened and he quickly stepped back. Meredith covered her mouth and ran for the house.

"I'll come by later this evening," Roy called after her, but Meredith didn't slow until she was safely inside.

The kitchen stood empty, so Meredith made her way to the sink pump, hoping that a glass of cool water would help settle her stomach. She needed to calm her body so her mind could focus on how to help Travis. If Roy's henchmen planned to strike tonight, that left her precious little time to strategize. The Archer ranch was a good two and a half hours' ride to the north. A well-conditioned horse could possibly shave thirty minutes off that time, but that still left her less than an hour to implement a course of action.

"Mercy me, Miss Meri. You look like someone done wrung you out and hung you up to dry. You all right?" Eliza, the cook Meredith's aunt employed, strode into the room cradling a selection of carrots, onions, and potatoes in her upturned apron.

Meredith managed a wan smile. "I'm not feeling well, I'm afraid. Is Uncle Everett back from Neches yet? I need to speak with him."

Not for the first time, Meredith longed for her own father's counsel instead of her uncle's. She missed the days of occasionally riding beside him in the buggy out to the freedmen's school he continued to run even after the Freedmen's Bureau shut down—missed the talks they had, the dreams they shared.

Papa would've known what to do about Roy and Travis. But Papa was gone.

Eliza dropped the vegetables into a wash pan with a cascade of thumps, then shook her apron out over the dry sink. "Master Hayes told me not to expect him till suppertime."

Meredith's shoulders sagged. Suppertime would be too late.

"Miss Meri, you better go up to bed and rest some. You're looking right peak-ed."

"I don't need—" Meredith stopped herself as she recalled Roy's promise to return. "Well, maybe I will." She'd not want to face her aunt, either. "In fact, with my stomach as unsettled as it is, I'll probably forgo dinner tonight. Would you mind asking Aunt Noreen not to wake me?"

"Of course, child. You go rest."

Why was it when Aunt Noreen called her a child she felt degraded, but when Eliza did it, she felt nurtured? Meredith set her half-empty glass on the table, the churning in her abdomen finally beginning to subside.

"And in case ya get hungry later," Eliza said, pointing to the cookstove, "I'll leave some of my stew broth on the warmer. You just sneak on down here and help yourself. Ya hear?"

Meredith smiled and, on impulse, hugged the older woman. Eliza flapped her hands and shooed her away, embarrassed by the display of affection. "Go on with ya, now."

Meredith climbed the stairs and closed herself in her room. At least Aunt Noreen would not be home to pester her. She and Cassandra always paid their social calls on Tuesday afternoons. Usually Meredith accompanied them, but Roy's luncheon invitation had taken precedence over the weekly torture of censorious glances and nose sniffing that Aunt Noreen and her friends enjoyed while expounding their ponderous opinions. Unfortunately, that meant Meredith wouldn't be able to confide in Cassandra, either. That left only one person she could think of who might be willing and able to help her.

Changing out of her fancy polonaise, Meredith pulled a more practical dress out of her wardrobe and buttoned herself up into her favorite dark green calico. Just in case anyone should look in on her, she lumped an extra quilt under her covers to make it appear she was sleeping, then tiptoed down the stairs and slipped quietly out the back door.

Meredith chose an indirect route to Courthouse Square, studiously avoiding any avenues where her aunt might be visiting. She hurried down Market Street until she reached the jail, then circled around to the north and entered the sheriff's office.

The man lounging behind the desk bolted upright, dropping his booted feet from the corner of the desktop to the floor. He braced his palms on the arms of his chair to boost himself up until his eyes met hers. Then he promptly slouched right back into his negligent pose.

"Well, if it ain't Meri Hayes. Come to ask me to the church social?"

Hiram Ellis. Of all the rotten luck. The fellow was just as obnoxious grown as he'd been as a kid.

"I'm looking for Sheriff Randall." Meredith ignored Hiram's cocky smirk and glanced around the office as if he were beneath her notice. "Do you know where I might find him?"

"Still as contrary as ever, I see." Hiram slowly rose to his feet, puffing out his chest as if to emphasize the deputy's star pinned to his coat. "The sheriff's transportin' a prisoner over to Rusk County to stand trial, so it looks like you're stuck with me, darlin'."

Could this day get any worse? Hiram Ellis was the last person she'd trust with her troubles. But then, they weren't *her* troubles. Travis Archer and his brothers were the ones in danger. A spark and an unruly gust of wind could easily set their home ablaze, killing them in their beds.

Meredith gritted her teeth. If Hiram was her only choice, so be it.

"I overheard a threatening conversation today." Reluctant to reveal Roy's part in the scheme due to his connection with her uncle's business, she kept the account as anonymous as possible. "Two men were discussing Travis Archer's land and how he refused to sell. One man ordered the other to set the Archers' barn on fire in an effort to convince him to reconsider."

Hiram leaned a hip against the edge of the desk. "So what do you want me to do about it? It ain't no crime to run off at the mouth. You probably didn't hear them right anyhow. How close were you to these two fellers?"

"Around the corner," Meredith admitted, "but I heard them clearly enough. And I can assure you, this was no idle talk. It was menacing and authoritative. You have to ride out to the Archers' place and keep this terrible thing from happening. At the very least, warn Mr. Archer that trouble is headed his way."

Hiram shook his head. "I ain't riding all the way out there on the say-so of some woman who can't be sure of what she heard. You always were the kind to get all worked up about one thing or another for no good reason. Besides, I gotta stay here and protect the good citizens of Palestine while the sheriff's gone. We can talk to Archer when Randall gets back."

"By then it will be too late!"

Hiram just shrugged. "I'll make a note in the log book that you came by to make a report. That's the best I can do."

Of all the lazy, arrogant, self-aggrandizing men she'd ever had the misfortune to meet, Hiram Ellis sat at the top of the list.

As Meredith marched out of the sheriff's office, one thing became exceedingly clear. If there was to be any hope of getting a warning to Travis Archer in time, she was going to have to deliver it herself.

3

A half hour later, Meredith penned a note to her cousin.

> *Cass,*
>
> *I need your help. Roy Mitchell is not the gentleman he pretends to be. With my own ears, I heard him order the burning of Travis Archer's barn because the man refused to sell his land. Thankfully, Roy doesn't know I overheard him. However, he's planning to call tonight, and I need you to tell him I am feeling poorly and have retired early, since I'll be on my way to warn Travis.*
>
> *Tomorrow you can tell Uncle Everett that I decided to visit the old homestead, for that is what I plan to do right after stopping by the Archer place. I will stay out there a few days, cleaning and preparing the house for winter, and return to town by the end of the week.*
>
> *I'm sorry to put you in an awkward spot, but Roy's men are headed to the Archer place tonight, so there's no time to delay. I know you'll understand.*

She signed her name at the bottom, knowing Cassandra would cover for her. There was no one she trusted more. Yet when she returned, nothing would be the same. Rejecting Roy's proposal meant sabotaging the Hayes family business. Her aunt would resent her more than she already did, and Uncle Everett's disappointment would be hard to bear. Perhaps it was a good thing she was spending a few days at the old house. She might very well be taking up residence there again soon.

With a sigh, Meredith folded the ivory paper and walked down the hall to her cousin's room. She tucked the note into the basket that held Cassandra's hair ribbons, a place where her cousin would be sure to find it but one that would make the note inconspicuous to others. Then she retrieved the small leather valise she'd packed with a spare dress, sleeping gown, and necessary toiletries and slipped out the back to where she'd tied her horse.

The man on duty at the livery where she boarded Ginger had been kind enough to saddle the animal for her, and Meredith had already tucked a few days' provisions into the saddlebags, so all she had left to do now was mount up and go. Yet as she gazed back at the redbrick building that had been her home since losing her parents, an odd reluctance filled her. It was almost as if she were saying good-bye.

But then the image of a young man with sun-kissed brown hair and compassionate eyes lured her back to her mission. She would find a way to warn Travis Archer and deal with the repercussions later. She owed him that much.

The sun had started to streak the sky orange by the time Meredith reached the turnoff to Travis's property. Losing light and warmth in the shadows of the trees, she shivered beneath her cloak as she urged Ginger from the main road onto the little-used path that wound through the Archer pines.

Several yards in, a wooden gate rose from the brush to bar her way. Two hand-painted signs nailed to the top slat of the gate glared up at her. The one on the left read *Trespassers will be shot on sight*. And the second wasn't much friendlier. *To conduct business, fire two shots and wait*.

The Archers certainly weren't long on hospitality, but what really concerned her was the padlock that held the gate secure. With barbed wire stretching out on either side as far as she could see, it would be impossible to get Ginger through. And with no gun, she had no way to summon any of the Archers to her position.

For the first time since she'd left Palestine, urgency gave way to uncertainty. She'd known Travis and his brothers were reclusive, but by the look of things, they were downright hostile when it came to outsiders. They obviously wanted no news or visits from the outside world.

But they had no idea of the menace waiting to strike.

Meredith inhaled a deliberate breath and dismounted. She'd come this far. She might as well see it through. With trembling hands, she secured Ginger's reins around the gate post and stroked the mare's neck.

"I'll be back soon. I'm just going to deliver a message. It won't take long. You'll be fine."

Ginger reached her head down to nibble at some grass, apparently unperturbed at the prospect of being left alone. But as Meredith hiked up her skirt and wedged her left foot onto the bottom slat of the gate, the confidence she'd projected into that little speech evaporated.

She scaled the gate quickly and paused at the top to swing her leg over. Closing her eyes for a moment, she straddled the gate and whispered a quick prayer.

"Please don't let them shoot me."

Then before she could talk herself out of it, she scrambled down the far side and started walking.

The last time she'd trespassed on Archer land, she'd ended up with a broken leg and a nasty scar. Last time she'd had an excuse, and there'd been no fences. This time she didn't have the innocence of childhood to protect her. Was Travis still the kindhearted man she remembered, the one who hid his tender side behind a harsh reputation and a wall of secrecy, or had he hardened into the unyielding, coldhearted man people thought him to be?

Meredith shoved that last thought aside. She refused to believe it. She'd seen his heart that day. Travis might put up a ruthless front, but gentleness was too ingrained in his character to disappear over time.

But just to be safe, she walked with her arms angled away from her sides, palms facing forward, to present herself in as unthreatening a manner as possible. No point in putting her theory to the test if she didn't have to.

The smell of woodsmoke tickled her nose, and Meredith's heart skittered. The house must be close. An odd-sounding birdcall echoed somewhere in the distance off to her left. Her head swiveled in that direction. Then another bird answered from up ahead of her to the right. A chill passed over her. In all her years in Anderson County, she'd never heard a bird that sounded quite like those surrounding her. Then again, she'd been in town for quite some time. Perhaps she'd forgotten.

The trees began to thin, and Meredith spotted a clearing ahead. She picked up her pace, anxious to have her errand over and done. But before she took more than a dozen steps, four men emerged from the woods and surrounded her, each pointing a rifle directly at her chest.

What in blue blazes was a woman doing waltzing onto Archer land at the brink of dark?

From his vantage point behind her, Travis couldn't see much of her face, so he had no way of judging her intelligence. But anyone crazy enough to come onto Archer land without an invitation was sure to be unpredictable, and he wasn't taking any chances.

The woman kept her hands a healthy distance from her sides, and he could see her fingers quivering. Yet despite her obvious nervousness, she stared at each of his brothers in turn and even twisted around to examine Neill and finally . . .

Travis raised his head from sighting down the rifle as shock radiated through him. Those eyes. Such a vivid blue. It was as if he'd seen them before. But that was impossible. Females didn't exactly pay them calls on a regular basis.

Clearing his throat, he readjusted his rifle. "We don't cotton to trespassers around here, lady. You best skedaddle back the way you came."

"I will. But not until I say my piece." She pivoted to face him fully, her lashes lowering for just a moment before she aimed her gaze directly at him again.

Even knowing what was coming didn't stop the jolt from ricocheting through his chest when those piercing eyes latched onto him.

"I came to warn you, Travis."

Travis? She knew who he was? Most folks meeting the Archers all at once had no way of knowing him from Crockett or Jim. Yet she said his name with the confidence of recognition.

He squinted at her. "Look, lady. I don't know what kind of game you're playing, but I want no part of it."

"This is no game. Please, Travis. Just listen."

"You know this gal, Trav?"

Out of the corner of his eye, he saw his youngest brother start to lower his rifle. "Hush up, Neill, and hold your line." The kid obeyed without question, firming up his grip.

"The man who wants to buy your land is sending men out here tonight to persuade you to change your mind. They plan to set fire to the place while you sleep and force you to accept the next offer in order to recoup your losses."

Her announcement closed around Travis's heart like a vise that slowly began to tighten. Why wouldn't people just let them alone? Whether it was the do-gooders fourteen years ago who thought they knew best and attempted to take his brothers off to some orphanage, or the string of men who came after, trying to take advantage of a green kid with prime land, he was sick to death of people interfering in his affairs.

There was plenty of other land to be had, after all—although none of the available acreage had a house and outbuildings already built or a creek that didn't run dry in the summer. The more honorable vultures had sought to buy him out at a price far below market value, assuming he was too inexperienced to know the difference. The less honorable ones tried to take the land by force.

He still shuddered every time he thought of that bullet in Jim's shoulder—the one Crockett dug out, holed up in the cellar, while Travis drove the rest of the attackers from their land. Jim had been a pup at fifteen. Crockett, seventeen. And nine-year-old Neill had been the only one left to stand guard. They'd almost lost Jim to the fever afterward, but in the end, God had spared his life.

And now, according to this woman, another round was about to begin.

Travis glanced at each of his brothers. Being well trained, none had dropped his guard, but he could sense their wariness, hear the questions hanging unspoken in the air.

"Please, Travis. You have to believe me," the woman pled. "You and your brothers are in danger."

"Look, lady," Travis ground out between clenched teeth, "I don't know what you're up to, but I do know that if someone was planning to attack us, they sure as shootin' wouldn't go around announcing that fact to the general public. That tells me that if what you're saying is true, you're a part of it somehow, and I can't trust you."

Pain flashed in the woman's eyes, but she quickly blinked it away before jutting out her chin. "The man my aunt and uncle want me to marry is the one who wants to buy your land. While in his company earlier today, I chanced to overhear a private conversation between him and one of his subordinates. I was horrified by what I heard and knew I had to warn you. After your kindness to me, I couldn't stand by and do nothing."

Travis drew back. "What *kindness*? I've never even seen you before." Yet the familiarity that continued to stir at the edge of his consciousness made him question the accuracy of that statement.

"But you have." The crazy woman actually took a step closer to him, completely ignoring the rifle he was still pointing at her chest. "I was a trespasser then, too, only a much younger one."

She reached for something in her skirts, and he cocked his weapon. "Don't move, lady. I don't want to hurt you."

"I know."

Instead of shrinking away from him, her eyes held his, filled to the brim with . . . trust? That made no sense. Maybe the woman *was* crazy.

"You told me it was all an act on the day you helped me. Do you remember? After you freed me from that trap and splinted my leg, you made me promise not to tell anyone about how you were helping me. Said it would be safer for your brothers if everyone continued to believe you a mean-hearted, trigger-happy fiend. I kept that promise. And now I'm back to return the kindness you extended to me twelve years ago."

She reached for her skirts again, and heaven help him, all he did was lower his rifle barrel so he could watch her better. He remembered that girl and those abominable traps. How brave she'd been. How trusting. But this couldn't be her, could it? Surely time hadn't passed so quickly. She'd been just a child. This woman couldn't be the same person.

Travis fought his reaction to her and regained his stance. "This is some kind of trick—some way for you to worm into my good graces so your fiancé can step in and steal my land."

Her eyes narrowed. "This is no trick, and that man will never be my fiancé." She tugged on her skirts again. "I can prove who I am, Travis, if you'll just give me the chance." She lowered her gaze to somewhere near the ground. "Look at my leg."

He might be a recluse, but even he knew what she asked wasn't proper. But apparently Neill was too young to have any qualms.

"Ah, that little scar ain't nothin'. Jim's is better."

A quiet growl rumbled out of Jim, but Crockett actually laughed. Travis turned a glare on the man to his left. Crockett swallowed his mirth.

Fed up with this girl's shenanigans, Travis finally glanced down at her ankle, at the small amount of skin exposed above the top of her shoe and below her hem. Sure enough, a thin scar marred the pale flesh there.

In a flash, he was seventeen again, tending her wound, and carrying the little girl in his arms all the way to her home. He'd thought of her often—wondering what became of her. Travis examined her face again. Her hair was a little darker now, but a few golden streaks remained, evidence of the tow-headed girl he'd met so long ago. Her vivid blue eyes cut through him just as they had back then, when they'd been full of tears. The curves she sported now were definitely new, but the determination and bravery he remembered clung to her bearing like a grass burr to a pant leg.

That scrawny little kid had grown into a right handsome woman.

Travis lowered his weapon. "Good to see you again, Meredith."

4

He *did* remember. Even her name. Meredith couldn't hold back the grin that begged for release.

"So, brother . . . how come you never told us about your little friend, here?" The teasing drawl from the man at Travis's left drew Meredith's attention. He deliberately looked from her to Travis and back again. Then he winked. She couldn't believe it. Biting her lip to keep her embarrassment in check as well as to keep from smiling too wide, she dropped her gaze to the ground.

"Shut up, Crockett," Travis grumbled as he stalked forward to take her arm. "It was a long time ago." His grip was gentle but exerted enough force to propel her toward the clearing. "She wandered off the road and stepped into one of those traps we used to have set up. I freed her, splinted up her leg, and took her home. End of story."

As they rounded the last stand of trees, the house came into view off to the right. The snug cabin with its trail of smoke curling up from the stone chimney beckoned Meredith with an earnest welcome completely at odds with the rifle-wielding foursome who had met her on the path.

"Wait a minute." Crockett jogged around them and planted himself in front of her.

Travis tried to maneuver around his brother, but the quick change of direction gave Meredith no time to compensate for her weaker leg. She stumbled a bit, her limp becoming more pronounced. Travis frowned down at her leg as he drew her to a halt.

"Did you say you took her home? You actually left our land?"

"Her leg was broken. What did you expect me to do?" Travis demanded. "Leave her for the coyotes?"

"Of course not. It's just . . ." Crockett stood there staring at him, the incredulous look on his face almost comical. "I never thought you'd cross that line."

"It was one time. Don't make more of it than it is."

Good advice for her, too, Meredith realized as Travis shouldered past Crockett and continued escorting her across the clearing. The fact that Travis had kept their meeting a secret from his brothers didn't mean something private and personal existed between them. Most likely, all it meant was that he didn't want to give them an excuse to follow his example and venture too far from home. Allowing the warmth expanding all too rapidly inside her to cloud her judgment would indeed be foolish.

Too bad his hand felt so good on her arm and his solid presence at her side confirmed all those heroic imaginings she'd indulged in as a young girl. It made sensibility far less attractive.

A horse whinnied somewhere behind the house, though, and reason returned as she recalled Ginger tied up at the gate. Coupling that with Travis's comment about the coyotes, Meredith knew her errand had taken too long already.

Before he could haul her up to the covered porch that stretched the length of the log house, Meredith tugged her elbow free and stepped a couple of paces away from the steps. "Thank you for offering the hospitality of your home, but I really should be on my way. I left my horse tied at your gate, and she tends to get restless if left alone too long."

Travis's gaze bore into her. Gone was the compassion she'd experienced as a child. And the gratitude she'd expected to see was nowhere in evidence, either. The only thing glimmering in those greenish-brown eyes of his was steely determination.

"I'm not bringing you to the house to offer you hospitality, Meredith." Travis closed the distance between them with one long stride. "I'm bringing you here so that you can tell us everything you know about this former fiancé of yours and his plans for our ranch."

"But . . ." Meredith looked from brother to brother. Even the teasing Crockett looked implacable. "I've already told you all I know," she insisted.

The Archers surrounded her once again and started herding her like a stray cow. Before she knew it, she was up the porch steps and through the front door.

This was not how things were supposed to go. The heroic Travis of her dreams would never dictate to her in such a way.

"It's nearly dark. I really have to go. It's not proper for me to be here." Her protests fell on deaf ears as they drove her toward the kitchen. Warmth from the stove permeated the air along with the smell of some kind of roasted meat.

Travis pulled out a chair from the kitchen table and glared at her until she sat down. He set his gun against the wall and leaned close to her face, one hand on the table, one on the back of her chair. "I'm sorry, Meredith, but I can't take any chances. Protecting my brothers and my land always comes first with me. Always." His words rang with righteous conviction, leaving little room for argument. "You'll stay here and answer my questions until I'm satisfied that I've gotten all I can from you."

Meredith's temper flared, although she didn't know if she was more upset about being coerced to stay or about her hero acting in such an unchivalrous manner. "So it's to be an inquisition."

"A friendly one. I promise." He smiled, and for a moment, the hardness in his face relaxed and a touch of kindness leaked through. But all too quickly, he shut it off. "I wouldn't worry about propriety if I were you. I'm guessing no one knows you're here, so your reputation is in no danger."

"My cousin knows." The argument was weak, even to her own ears, and probably accomplished as much good in changing his mind as sticking her tongue out at him would have, but she couldn't stand to leave his smug assumption unchallenged.

"Your cousin, huh? Well, I doubt a family member would risk tarnishing your good name."

Heavy footsteps clomped around behind her as the other brothers made their way to the table. She didn't feel threatened by them, but having four men tower over her in a confined space didn't exactly boost her confidence, either. Travis must have noticed her unease, for he lowered himself into a nearby chair and gently touched her shoulder.

"You have nothing to fear from us, Meredith. You have my word." Her gaze locked with his, and something passed between them. A remembered bond from that childhood encounter? She wasn't sure, but she was certain she could trust him.

She sat a little straighter and lifted her chin. "What about my horse?"

Travis smiled and turned to the youngest Archer. "Fetch the lady's horse, Neill."

The boy was standing by the stove and had a spoonful of beans halfway to his mouth. Undeterred, he jabbed the spoon between his lips and talked around the mouthful as he dropped the spoon back into the pot. Meredith cringed.

"I don't want to miss all the discussin', Trav. The horse'll keep."

"If you hurry, you might make it back before we eat all the vittles."

"Eat the . . . ? You wouldn't dare!" Neill scowled, then shot an anxious look toward the stove. Meredith ducked her head to hide her smile. Amazing how much sway food could hold over a young man's decisions.

Travis shrugged. "We have a guest, which means less to go around. Might be slim pickin's if you dally."

Neill growled low in his throat, like a cornered animal, and after aiming a final glare at Travis, he snatched up his gun from where it stood propped against the wall and stomped out of the room.

Travis shook his head and smiled at the kid's back, his affection obvious despite his firmness in dealing with him. But as he turned his attention to Meredith, his smile faded, leaving nothing but stoic resolve lingering in his gaze.

As if by silent cue, Crockett and the other brother who had yet to speak lowered themselves into chairs across from where she and Travis sat and stared her down. Meredith instinctively shrank away from them and edged closer to Travis.

"What do they plan to target?" Travis hardened himself against the surge of protectiveness that rose in his chest as Meredith leaned toward him, her cloak brushing his arm. He hated being so brusque, but it was imperative that he learn everything possible about his attackers. And quickly. The woman might be privy to valuable insight or a clue to his enemy's scheme without even being aware of its significance. Such knowledge could prove vital when it came to defending his home. This was no time to go soft.

"Meredith?"

She looked past him to the doorway, and for a moment, he thought she might bolt, but then the level-headedness he remembered from twelve years ago reasserted itself. She folded her hands together atop the table in a serene prayerlike pose and kept her attention riveted on them while she spoke.

"The barn."

It made sense. They'd already put up most of their winter stores. The hayloft and corncrib were full, and with the nights getting so cold lately, a lot of their stock was sheltered there. Losing the barn would cripple them during the winter. Not that it would convince him to sell. Nothing could do that.

"How many men are coming?" Crockett probed.

"I don't know."

Travis tried coming at the question from the back door. "How many men does this fiancé of yours have working for him?"

Meredith's head swiveled around, her blue eyes shooting sparks. "He is *not* my fiancé—never was. And I'd appreciate it if you'd quit referring to him as such."

Travis held up his hands in apology. "All right."

She inhaled slowly and refocused on her hands. "The man's name is Roy Mitchell, and I have no idea how many men work for him. He owns a logging company, so I imagine there are a good number in his employ."

And they'd be physical men, too. Comfortable in the woods. Not a bunch of city-bred dandies. Travis tapped his thumb against the pine tabletop as his mind spun.

Crockett cleared his throat. "We'll have to move the stock out."

Travis nodded his agreement. "But we can't just leave them all in the paddock. If Mitchell's men get close enough to see that the stock are safe, they might suspect we're on to them and burn the house instead."

"We could tether the draft horses down by the creek."

"Good idea, Jim. Being near the water will help calm them if fire does break out." Travis tipped his head up to stare at a rafter in the ceiling, the ordinary view helping him concentrate. "Each of us can keep a saddled mount near our position when we set up a perimeter. That will help spare the tack, the horses, and give us a way to chase the vermin off."

"What about the mule?" Crockett asked. "You know how cranky Samson gets at night. If we try to take him down to the creek bed, he'll bray his fool head off and give away his position."

Travis nodded. Old Samson was as cantankerous as they came. If he wasn't in his stall come dark, he'd pull a tantrum worse than Neill used to at bath time. "I guess we better leave him in the paddock. Maybe if we keep Jochebed tied out there, too, it'll keep him calm." The milk cow occupied the stall next to Samson, so having her close might soothe him. Then again, it might just endanger their milk supply. But he didn't see as he had much choice. "Two animals outside the barn shouldn't draw much suspicion."

"And the fodder?" Crockett asked. "I was thinking we could store the contents of the corncrib in the shed." He turned to Jim. "If that's all right with you."

The shed was Jim's domain, a workshop for the furniture he made from the walnut, pine, and oak that grew on their land. He was as protective of that space as a squirrel was with a cache of nuts. But he nodded acquiescence, as Travis knew he would. Family needs came first.

"I'll clear out a space."

"Good." With each solution they generated, Travis regained a piece of the control he'd lost when he'd learned of the pending attack. His confidence growing, he posed the last issue. "What about the hay? Any ideas of where to store it?"

The smokehouse was too small, as were any of the other outbuildings. And if they stacked it in the open, it would prove an easy target for a lit torch. Travis looked to Crockett and then to Jim, but his brother's faces were as blank as his mind. Silence stretched around the table. The control restored to him was once again slipping from his grasp.

"The hay wagons that deliver to the liveries in town are always heaped to the sky. Why don't you load as much as you can into your wagon and drive it down to the creek bed or into the woods somewhere? You can cover it with a tarp for added protection."

Three pairs of Archer eyes turned to stare at the female in their midst—a female they had all but forgotten was there. At least Travis had. But looking at her now, he couldn't quite fathom how that could've happened.

"It's a good idea," Crockett said.

Travis was about to agree when pounding hooves echoed from the yard. In an instant, he was on his feet, rifle in hand. He felt his brothers behind him as he dashed down the hall.

5

Travis sighted down the barrel of his Winchester. A rider on an unfamiliar white-and-chestnut paint thundered toward the porch. Travis released a nervous breath and steadied his aim. The dimness of twilight made it difficult to distinguish features, so he went for the high-percentage shot and drew a bead on the man's chest. But as he moved his finger to the trigger, a sense of recognition registered. The rider had a very familiar posture. Travis jerked the Winchester away from his shoulder, his heart thumping with the dread of what could have happened.

Neill pulled up short of the porch and leapt from the horse's back before the paint had fully stopped. "I ain't too late for supper, am I?"

Travis stormed down the steps and shoved his kid brother hard enough to land his butt in the dirt. "What were you thinking, riding in here without giving the signal? I could have shot you!"

The shocked look on Neill's face gave way to one of abashment. "Sorry, Trav. I thought you'd know it was me, since you sent me to fetch Miss Meredith's horse."

"Did you forget we were expecting other visitors tonight? Unwelcome visitors?" Travis extended his hand to his brother and yanked him to his feet. "With the poor light and you on a strange mount, for a minute there, I thought you were one of them. You gotta think with more than your belly, Neill."

"I'll do better next time. I swear."

Travis gripped the boy's shoulder and offered reassurance with a squeeze. "I know you will. You're an Archer."

"Jim," Travis called up to the man waiting on the porch with Crockett, "dish up the vittles. We can't afford for this boy to be distracted. We got too much work to get done."

Neill's ready smile reappeared, and the tension in Travis's gut relaxed. A little.

As Jim led the way back into the house, Travis hung back and scanned the darkening woods, wondering from which direction trouble would strike.

Lord, I'd be obliged if you'd get us through this night in one piece.

Watching the Archer brothers eat was like watching a twister blow through the room. Meredith sat with her elbows tucked close to her side, afraid to do more than occasionally raise her fork to her mouth for fear of being rammed by a reaching arm or thumped by a tossed biscuit. The venison steak was overdone, the beans gluey, and the biscuits were dry as unbuttered toast, yet the Archers attacked their food like a pack of dogs fighting over a fresh kill. No one spoke. They just ate.

Well, not all of them. The one called Jim slowed down enough to glare at her over his dish and grunt as he chomped down on what must have been a particularly tough piece of venison, giving her the distinct impression that he held her responsible for the condition of the food. Which was probably true. Her arrival *had* delayed their supper. And with the threat of Roy's men so imminent, she supposed haste was more important than decorum. Still, it was a bit unnerving to be surrounded by such ravenous appetites. Therefore, when Travis pushed away from the table and started giving orders not five minutes after the meal had begun, Meredith found herself as much relieved as amazed.

"Jim, you're in charge of the corncrib. Crockett, bring the wagon around and get started on the hay. We won't be able to get it all, but we should be able to save a decent portion. I'll give you a hand as soon as I fill Neill in on what to do with the stock."

A chorus of chair legs scraping against floorboards echoed in response as each of the Archer brothers stuffed final bites into their mouths and rose to follow Travis. Not one of them spared her so much as a glance, all of their faces set in grim lines.

Feeling left out, Meredith jumped to her feet. "What can I do?"

Travis pivoted, quickly scanning her from head to toe, hesitating ever so briefly on her weak leg. "Stay in the house. As soon as this is over, I'll see you home." And with that, his long strides carried him away from her and out into the night.

Meredith chased him down and grabbed his arm from behind. "I can help, Travis."

The dark brown vest Travis wore flapped open as he spun to face her.

"This isn't your fight. Just stay in the house and keep your head down. You don't know your way around out here, and it'll only slow me down to answer your questions."

Even though he didn't say it, she could easily imagine what he was thinking. That telling glance in the kitchen had said it all. He believed her to be weak. A liability.

Meredith made no further protest as Travis left her to jog over to the barn, but as she made her way back to the house, she vowed to prove to him that she was more than just a girl with a limp. She was smart and strong and capable, and any man who thought different needed his opinion adjusted.

She charged through the front door and down the hall to the kitchen. A table full of dirty dishes and a stove covered in food splatter called out a defiant challenge. Meredith narrowed her gaze and stripped out of her cloak. Rolling up her sleeves, she moved to the table and started stacking dirty plates and utensils. It might not be the most glamorous of jobs, but she'd have their kitchen shinier than a new copper kettle by the time those thick-headed Archers returned.

Besides, her mind did some of its best work while her hands were in dishwater. And she had some serious thinking to do. The men were focused on saving the contents of the barn, but they'd really taken no time to strategize ways to protect the barn itself. That would be up to her.

Once the dishes were done and the stove scoured, Meredith set about enacting phase one of her newly hatched plan. First, she pulled out every stockpot, bucket, and washtub she could find. Then she searched the cupboards for medical supplies. She prayed Travis and his brothers would escape injury, but she'd make sure things were ready just in case. Next, she dug through the bedrooms, gathering old blankets. There was more than one way to fight fire, and she aimed to have as many weapons at her disposal as possible.

Meredith piled the blankets in the largest washtub and threaded her arm through the handles of three buckets. Then, with the *cling-clang* of the tin pails bouncing against her hip, she hefted the washtub and headed for the back door she'd discovered in a small room off the kitchen. She scanned the yard, squinting against the dark shadows, until she found a shape that fit what she was looking for. Squaring her shoulders, she made her way to the edge of the paddock.

The men had been busy. The mule and milk cow were already in the corral along with four fully outfitted saddle horses, and she saw the back of the wagon from around the corner of the barn. Male voices called to one another from within the structure, and Meredith guessed they were finishing up the hay. She'd need to hurry if she wanted to be back in the house by the time the men came in to get their coats before they headed out.

Meredith grasped the pump handle and worked it until water gushed from the spout into the horse trough beside the paddock fence. She filled the trough to the brim so it would be easy to refill the buckets quickly should the need arise. Then she filled the washtub and each of the pails. She stacked the blankets beneath the trough to protect them from the wind and returned to the house for the stockpots. When she finished, an entire line of vessels stood ready to extinguish and douse. Meredith nodded in satisfaction and headed back to the kitchen.

From the window, she could barely make out the dark outlines of the trough and bucket line she'd put together, but knowing it was there filled her with a sense of accomplishment. It was odd, really, the protectiveness that welled in her whenever she thought of the barn burning. She'd been on Archer land less than two hours, but a strange sense of belonging flowed through her when she looked out over the yard.

"I know your men are coming, Roy," she whispered to the darkness, "but I'm going to fight you with everything I've got."

The sound of the front door opening and the heavy thumping of booted feet turned Meredith's attention away from the window. Wrapping a dish towel around her hand, she grabbed the coffeepot she'd put on earlier and started pouring the steaming brew into cups.

As the coffee worked its way up the sides of the fourth cup, Meredith became aware of a complete lack of sound coming from the men. She tipped back the pot and cautiously glanced up. All four Archers stood bunched in the doorway staring at her as if they'd never seen a woman pour coffee before.

"I thought you'd like something to warm your insides before you set out. The night will be cold, and there's no telling how long you'll be out there." She smiled as she fought to control the nervous tickle in her stomach.

Finally Travis stepped forward and accepted a cup from her. "Thanks." His gaze met hers, and a warmth that had nothing to do with coffee penetrated her.

Meredith ducked her head and grabbed another cup, handing coffee to Crockett, Jim, and then Neill. Each man murmured his thanks and dipped his head in deference, but none of them inspired the same quivery feelings as their brother.

Careful, Meredith. You're going home after this. Don't be leaving your heart behind with a reclusive cowboy whose life has no room for you.

"I brought Sadie to keep you company while we're out." Travis gave a low whistle and a big black dog pushed her way past the Archer legs blocking the doorway. Her nails clicked against the wood floor, and her stiff gait stirred Meredith's sympathy. At a motion from Travis, the animal padded over to Meredith and sat down.

"This is Sadie? The ferocious pup I thought was going to chew me to a pulp?" Meredith grinned at the slightly arthritic dog and bent to pat her head. Sadie's tail swished across the floor in friendly response. "Now that I'm bigger and you're older, you're not nearly as frightening."

"Frightening? Sadie?" Neill scoffed. "She's just a retired bird dog. Who'd be afraid of *her*?"

"Neill." Travis spoke the name like a warning.

Meredith laughed softly. "That's all right." She hunkered down and rubbed the dog more thoroughly along her neck and sides. "Anyone can tell that Sadie is a loyal, sweet-spirited animal. But to a ten-year-old girl with an overactive imagination, who had stories of the vicious man-eating Archer hounds ringing in her ears, Sadie's enthusiasm was easily misinterpreted."

"Man-eating Archer hounds? What kind of nonsense—"

"Never mind about that, Neill." Travis cut off his question. "We have other issues to deal with. Grab your coat and mount up."

Neill complied, followed by Jim and Crockett, leaving Meredith alone in the kitchen with Travis. He shuffled his feet for a moment, then thunked his coffee cup down on the table. "Sadie might be old," he said, his gaze not quite meeting hers, "but she's a good watchdog. She'll bark if she hears anything, so keep her close at hand."

"I will." Giving Sadie a final pat, Meredith straightened.

Travis gripped the back of the chair nearest Meredith, his hands massaging the wood as if he wasn't sure what else to do with them. An odd gesture for a man who wore authority like a well-broken-in hat. The hint of vulnerability in his movements now made Meredith's pulse skip.

"Stay in the house," he said. "You'll be safe." His eyes finally met hers. "If anything should happen to me, the boys have orders to see to your protection, so you don't have to worry about anything."

She lowered her lashes and peered back up at Travis. "Be careful."

He cleared his throat and looked away. "I will," he mumbled, then collected his coat from its hook and shoved his arms through the sleeves. "Oh, and, Meredith . . ."

"Yes?"

"Thanks."

As Travis strode out of the room, Meredith smiled. Whatever the night held, the trip to the Archer ranch was definitely worth it.

Each of the brothers set out on horseback to their assigned positions, needing the cover of the woods to conceal their presence. They had considered hiding out in the barn, but that would have given them only two vantage points instead of four. If Mitchell's men came in from the east or west, they'd be nearly impossible to spot. Out among the trees, he and his brothers stood a better chance at stopping the attackers before they drew close enough to the barn to toss a torch.

Besides, he wanted to keep an eye on the house, as well. And Meredith. He still couldn't believe she had come out to warn him. A pretty woman like that should have better things to do with her time than brave the den of a bunch of mangy men who'd lost touch with civilization years ago.

But she'd come. Because she felt beholden to him. Travis shook his head as he dismounted and pulled his rifle free of its scabbard. He'd noticed the woman favored her right leg, an injury he was no doubt responsible for, but instead of laying blame, she went out of her way to help him. Not your average female.

Not that he had much experience with females. He'd quit school after the eighth grade to run the ranch with his father, and a few years later he was raising his siblings on his own. Outside of a couple church socials he'd attended when he was fourteen, he had no experience with the fairer sex. That didn't mean he was too ignorant to recognize the effect of one, though.

Travis rubbed the stubble on his chin and frowned, wondering for the first time what kind of impression he'd made on her. She probably thought him half wild, pointing guns at innocent women and snapping out orders like a general. Yet when he and the boys had dragged in after clearing out the barn and found Meredith in a spotless kitchen, pouring hot coffee with a welcoming smile, his gut had tightened with longing. And he wasn't the only one suffering such a reaction. Crockett and Jim had felt it, too. He could tell by the strange tension radiating from them. Even Neill's youth had not kept him immune.

As Travis stared out into the darkness, watching for any movement that didn't belong, questions churned in his mind, distracting him. Would his reaction have been the same for any woman standing in his kitchen looking homey and inviting, or was it something specific about Meredith that kindled his appreciation and protective instincts?

Travis crossed his arms and leaned his shoulder against the trunk of a nearby tree. It was a shame she'd be leaving so soon. He would have enjoyed trying to figure that one out.

6

Meredith's chin jerked up from its resting place on her chest, and she blinked several times, trying to get her bearings. She stared into the darkness from her seat on the porch rocker but failed to see anything amiss. Rearranging the thick folds of her quilt cocoon, she burrowed into the coverlet and leaned the side of her head against the back of the rocking chair, allowing her eyes to slide closed once again.

A low growl resonated near her feet, culminating in a sharp bark.

Meredith's eyes flew open, and she bolted upright. "Did you hear something, Sadie?" she whispered. Meredith freed her arms from the quilt and reached for the old shotgun she'd found in the den.

Sadie lurched to her feet, her posture stiff, her ears pricked. Meredith rose, as well. Clutching the shotgun across her middle with trembling hands, she squinted into the night, trying desperately to make out the form of someone moving about where he didn't belong. But the barn was nothing more than a dark, hazy form against a landscape of black and gray.

Then a shadow separated itself from the others. And divided into two . . . no . . . three smaller silhouettes. Meredith's heart dropped to her stomach. Her pulse thrumming erratically, she inched her way to the porch railing. Had Travis and the others returned to check on things, or had Roy's men somehow reached the barn undetected?

While she debated with herself over what to do, a breeze ruffled the loose strands of hair around her face—a breeze that carried a familiar, cloying scent.

Kerosene!

Meredith darted off the covered porch and lifted the shotgun to her shoulder. Pointing the double barrels into the air, she braced herself for the recoil and pulled the trigger. The blast shattered the silence, its alarm echoing in the stillness.

That should bring the Archers down around their ears!

Meredith lowered the weapon, satisfaction filling her as the man-sized shadows around the barn began to scramble. Then an answering gunshot cracked. Meredith yelped as a bullet kicked up dust a foot in front of her. She darted back into the darkness of the covered porch and hunkered down behind the rocker she'd been dozing in moments earlier. Sadie followed, protectively flanking her right side.

"Good girl." Meredith grabbed the dog's neck and pulled her down behind the chair, too.

No longer concerned with stealth, Roy's men scurried around the barn with new urgency until one of them finally struck a match.

That tiny spark ignited a bonfire of dread in Meredith's chest. For it didn't stay tiny for long. It ignited a torch. Then a second. And a third.

Sadie barked despite Meredith's efforts to shush her. The mule in the paddock brayed and kicked against the fence with sharp thuds that carried all the way to the house. Meredith closed her eyes and prayed until the sound of hoofbeats descending upon the barn interrupted her pleas.

Travis!

A pair of horsemen emerged from the woods near the front of the barn, rifles drawn. Gunfire erupted and male shouts punctuated the air. Was one of the riders Travis? And where were the other brothers? Were they on the far side of the barn, hidden from view? How many of Roy's men were over there? Meredith peered between the spindles of the chairback, her grip on Sadie tightening until the dog finally squirmed away. If only she could see what was happening!

Soon the other two brothers rode in, and the torches were discarded in the fray as guns and horses became more important. For a few minutes, Meredith believed the barn would be spared, but when Roy's men gained their mounts and scattered into the woods, and Travis and his brothers gave chase, the smell of smoke wafted back toward the house. A stronger odor than could be explained by a few smoldering torches lying in the dirt.

Meredith came out from behind the chair and cautiously made her way down the porch steps. With one barrel of her shotgun still loaded, she shouldered the weapon and stole across the yard. She scanned from the barn to the corral to the trees, checking for any man-sized movement. Just as she determined that all was clear, Sadie rushed past her, ducked under the lowest rail of the corral fence, and set to barking at the barn entrance.

Tightening her grip on the gun, Meredith bit her lip and followed. "Anyone there?" she called.

The only answer came from the mule, Samson, which was still kicking up a fuss. The milk cow was nervous, too, sidestepping and moaning an occasional complaint. As Meredith strained to hear any evidence of a human threat, her ears picked out another sound altogether—a muffled crackling from within the barn.

Hurrying forward, Meredith straddled the bottom fence rail and squeezed her body through the opening between the slats, then ran to Sadie's side. A blast of heat hit her face when she crossed in front of the doorway.

Greedy flames were climbing the interior walls.

The thugs had lit the *inside* of the barn! Anger surged through Meredith's veins as she hiked up her skirts and sprinted to her bucket line. Travis and his brothers had no way of knowing that their barn was afire when they set off after Roy's men, so they'd be in no hurry to return. Capturing the men responsible would take precedence. Which left Meredith alone to fight the blaze.

In case Travis wasn't too far afield to hear a warning shot and grasp its meaning, Meredith fired the final shell from her shotgun and dropped the weapon on the far side of the trough. She grabbed two of the full pails she'd prepared earlier and walked as fast as she could without sloshing too much water over the edges.

"Of all the times to have an uneven gait," Meredith grumbled. The moment the words left her mouth, her right foot hit a divot in the earth and water splashed onto her shoe. With a grimace, she redirected her path but didn't slow her pace.

Once in the barn, she maneuvered to the east wall, where the fire seemed to be the strongest. She tossed the bucket contents onto the burning wood, rejoicing at the hiss of dying flames. But in an instant, new ones rose to take their place.

Meredith ran back to the trough. "Lord, help me make a difference. Please. It's not right for good men to suffer on a wicked man's whim."

Back and forth she ran. Dumping water over and over until the trough was nearly dry. Her arms felt like rubber, and her back screamed at her to stop. Her lungs burned from the smoke and heat, but she refused to quit.

Wiping a soot-covered arm across her brow, she turned away from the barn to inhale a deep breath of clean air. Then, ignoring the weariness that threatened to claim her, Meredith dropped a blanket into the trough and soaked up the last of the water. She'd beat out what flames she could, then refill the buckets at the pump. Surely the Archers would return soon.

Circling well out of the reach of Samson's hooves, Meredith trudged back into the barn and turned her attention to the west wall. She slapped at the flames with the wet blanket, but they seemed to tease her, dancing upward, out of her reach.

Then, as if a furnace door had suddenly swung wide, light flashed above Meredith's head and heat swooped down on her in a massive wave.

Lord, have mercy.

Fire had exploded across the hayloft.

Mitchell's men had escaped. Every last one of them. Travis glared at the cut wire that left a gaping hole in his boundary fence and ground his palm into the saddle horn. If it hadn't been so dark, things might have been different. But Archers knew better than to endanger a horse by racing over rough terrain at night.

Would there be another attempt? Without Meredith to warn them next time, Travis held little hope they'd be as successful in thwarting Roy Mitchell's efforts.

"Look at the bright side—they didn't get the barn, and none of us were injured in the fray." Crockett's quiet statement seeped into Travis. He shifted his focus from the damaged fence to the three hale-and-hearty brothers congregated around him.

"You're right." Travis cleared his throat, buying time to squirrel away his own disappointment and muster a half-hearted smile for the boys. "Things could certainly be worse. With the way those bullets were flying, it's a miracle no blood was drawn."

"I still don't know how those skunks got past us in the first place," Neill groused. "I didn't fall asleep, Travis. I swear it!"

"I know you didn't, little brother. Don't sweat it. What's done is done." Travis nudged his chestnut gelding forward until he sat even with Neill. "There was too much ground for four men to monitor, and too little light to see more than a stone's throw in any direction. I knew going in that our best chance was to have them stumble onto one of us as they were coming in, since they expected us to be at the house, sleeping in our beds. But it wasn't meant to be."

"Speaking of sleeping in our beds . . ." Crockett tugged on the reins until his horse faced homeward. "I'm more than ready to do just that. Let's head back."

Travis nodded, his own energy giving way to weariness now that the danger had passed. "Lead the way."

They wound through the trees, sticking to the well-worn paths that would cause the horses the least amount of trouble. No one spoke, too exhausted and dispirited to do more than keep themselves upright in their saddles. But as they climbed the rise that led to home, Neill broke the silence.

"It's a good thing you got off that warning shot when you did, Trav, or we wouldn'ta had a chance of stoppin' 'em."

"Wasn't me." Travis reined his horse around a large rock, keeping his gaze trained on the ground in front of him. "I saw a muzzle flash near the house. My guess is that Meredith fired the shot."

"Meredith?" Disbelief tinged Neill's voice. "Didn't you tell her to stay in the house? What was she doin' out there, and where did she get a gun? You don't think she was helpin' 'em, do ya?"

"Of course she wasn't helping them," Travis snapped. "If she were, there'd be no point in making all that racket to bring us charging out of the woods like the cavalry, would there?" Travis bit back the rest of the words that sprang to his tongue, shocked at his vehement reaction. Neill didn't know Meredith. Shoot. None of them did, really. Including him. Questioning her loyalty was reasonable—more reasonable than blindly defending her character based on two encounters that totaled less than a day's worth of time in her company.

Travis grimaced. Was he really so susceptible to a pair of bright blue eyes and a pretty smile? He'd better get a grip on his reactions before he ended up doing something stupid.

"She probably found one of Pa's hunting guns," Crockett said. "The case in the den isn't lock—"

"Quiet!" Jim's sharp voice brought Travis's head up. "I smell smoke."

Smoke? Travis sniffed the air, and alarm gouged through him. He smelled it, too.

Had a spark from one of the fallen torches managed to catch? He'd not seen any evidence of fire when he signaled the boys to give chase. Had he left their home unprotected?

Had he left Meredith unprotected?

"Yah!" Digging his heels into his horse's flanks, Travis charged toward home.

7

As the trees thinned, the smell of smoke grew stronger and an eerie orange glow winked at him from between the pines. Travis tightened his grip on the reins and leaned low over the saddle, urging his mount to a pace that bordered on hazardous. So close to home, though, the ground was familiar, and Bexar responded without hesitation.

The barn came into view, and Travis gritted his teeth. The thing was glowing from within like a jack-o'-lantern, an occasional flicker of flame licking through the hayloft door to tickle the outer walls.

How could he have been so stupid? He hadn't even thought to check the interior of the barn before he went tearing off after Mitchell's men. He'd simply assumed he'd interrupted them in time. His thirst for justice had outweighed his common sense.

Travis reined his horse around to the side of the barn closest to the trough pump and pulled up short. A host of empty pails, tubs, and even cooking pots lay scattered beside the trough, firelight gleaming across their tin surfaces.

Surely she wouldn't have . . .

Travis leapt from the saddle and scaled the corral fence. "Meredith!"

Sadie shot out of the barn and circled his legs, almost tripping him. She barked and dashed back toward the barn. Travis sprinted after her.

Thick, dark smoke hovered near the rafters, and the stench of burning wood and hay enveloped him. He squinted through the haze, searching the ground for any sign of Meredith. When he spotted a feminine figure battling the blaze along the west wall, relief hit him with such force his knees nearly buckled. Then anger stiffened his joints and propelled him toward the woman whose dark green dress had faded to a sooty gray.

"What do you think you're doing?" Travis snatched the damp blanket from Meredith's grip as she swung it behind her shoulder. The rag pulled free without any resistance. Her obvious exhaustion only heightened his ire. "I told you to wait at the house."

Meredith pivoted toward him and blinked as if she couldn't quite understand what she was seeing. "Travis?" A spark of clarity flashed in her eyes before she launched herself at him, wrapping her arms around his waist. "Thank God you've come."

The contact was so unexpected, it nearly threw him off-balance. Travis didn't quite know what to do. He'd been shouting and scowling a second ago, and now he had a grateful female pressed up against him. How had that happened?

"I tried so hard, Travis. I really did." She tipped her face up to look at him. The soot smeared across her cheeks and forehead made the blue of her eyes even brighter. "I had the east wall put out and started on the west when the flames reached the loft. Do you think you can save it?"

"Don't know. The boys and I will try, though." He separated himself from her and took her hand. "We need to get you out of here first."

She stumbled along behind him as he steered her out to the corral. Crockett was already working the pump to fill the trough while Jim and Neill righted the buckets.

"The heart of the fire is in the loft," he called out to his brothers. "Do what you can, but don't put yourself at risk. If the roof catches, get out. We'll move to containment. Make sure the house doesn't catch."

Travis didn't release his grip on Meredith until he had her at the fence on the far side. "Go up to the house."

"I can help."

"No, Meredith! I don't want you anywhere near that fire." The very thought made him shiver despite the heat pouring out of the barn.

"I managed not to burn myself to a crisp for the thirty minutes it took you to get here." She crossed her arms and glared at him, her spunk reviving. "I think I can find a way to preserve that tradition a little longer."

"The answer's no." He turned his back on her and strode away, praying she'd obey. If she were one of his brothers, there'd have been no question. He was the head of the family, and his word was law. But she wasn't an Archer. And he had no idea how he'd handle her if a direct order didn't work.

She leapt past him and moved into his path, forcing him to halt. "Let me work the pump."

"You're too tired to lift the handle." Travis cut her off with a wave of his hand when she opened her mouth to protest. "I don't have time to argue. My barn's burning." He sidestepped her and resumed his long-legged pace. This time she let him go.

Travis and his brothers fought the blaze as best they could. With ladders inside and out, they doused the loft simultaneously from the barn's center as well as through the loft window, but it wasn't long before the fire reached the roof.

When Neill arrived with another pail of water, Travis waved him off. "Go help Jim and Crock outside." He shimmied down the ladder, his voice hoarse from the smoke, his face scalded like a cow's hide after branding. "I'll get the animals a safe distance away, then meet you there."

Neill nodded and jumped to obey, but the determination in his eyes dimmed. Even at seventeen, the boy could recognize defeat when he saw it. And Travis figured that was exactly what the kid saw when he looked into his big brother's face.

It killed him to lose twice in one night. The arsonists' escape had been hard enough to swallow, but believing the barn had been spared had made it tolerable. Now everything was sticking in his craw.

He pulled the ladder down, kicked dirt over the few flames that had taken root on the top rungs, and carried it outside. As he tossed it over the corral fence, cool air bathed his stinging face. He wanted nothing more than to close his eyes and relish the coolness, but all he could afford to do was cough some smoke out of his lungs and turn back to the task at hand.

Which apparently included scolding a certain hardheaded woman for not heeding his instructions. Meredith glared at him from where she stood pumping water into the trough, not a hint of apology in her demeanor. Travis stormed past her and worked the knot on Jochebed's lead line. "I thought I told you to go up to the house."

The pump arm creaked as she gave it a series of vigorous yanks, then fell silent as water gushed into the trough. "As I recall," she said, rubbing her palms into her skirt, "you never forbade me from working the pump. You simply expressed your doubts as to my ability to do so."

Travis's grip on the cow's rope tightened. "Don't play word games with me, Meredith. You knew what I meant."

"Did I?" She reached for a stew pot and dipped it into the trough. "Seems to me that a man who claims protecting his brothers and his land always comes first wouldn't be so quick to refuse able-bodied help just because that body happens to be female." She set the full pot on the ground and crossed her arms over her chest.

Travis's eyes followed the movement, noting the curves it accentuated. Yep. Definitely female. He wouldn't be arguing that point.

Crockett rounded the barn at a jog, an empty washtub banging against his leg. Meredith unclasped her arms and immediately returned to the pump.

Travis made no move to stop her, deciding it wasn't worth wasting more time or breath debating. Having her there *did* speed the process, and even though he still didn't like her being so close to the fire, she was probably in no immediate danger.

At least Jochebed obeyed him without question. More than eager to get away from the burning barn, the milk cow lumbered along beside him to the back side of the corral, where Travis removed the fence rails from their notches and set her free.

Next he went after Samson, but the old mule was too busy throwing a fit to recognize what was good for him.

"Enough of that," Travis reprimanded as he grabbed hold of the mule's halter and forced the animal's head down. Samson tried to jerk away, but Travis held firm, asserting his dominance until the animal calmed. "That's it. Settle down, now." Travis patted Samson's neck and slowly unfastened the hitching strap. At the same moment, a thunderous *pop!* exploded from within the barn.

Samson's eyes went wild, and with the sudden strength of his namesake, he wrenched free and tore across the corral. Travis gave chase in an effort to steer him toward the fence opening, but the old mule was either too blind to see the downed railings or too terror-stricken to comprehend their meaning. Instead, the fool beast raced straight into the barn.

Stunned, Travis stared at the entrance. What would possess him to run *into* the fire? Sure the cantankerous thing would run right back out, Travis braced his legs apart and prepared to make a grab for him. Only he never came. The old mule was probably standing in his stall—third one on the right, under the loft—too stubborn to leave.

"Stupid critter," Travis muttered under his breath. He had half a mind to leave him in there. Of course, he never could stomach the thought of any living creature suffering. Not when it was in his power to do something about it.

Digging his handkerchief out of his coat pocket, Travis marched up to the entrance. Heat flared against his skin. Steeling himself, he turned his head and sucked in two deep breaths, then tied the red bandanna over his nose and mouth.

"No, Travis!" Meredith's voice barely penetrated the roar of the fire. "Don't!"

But he didn't have a choice. The longer he waited, the more dangerous it would be. Ignoring her calls, he ran into the barn.

Travis lifted his arm to shield his face from the heat and his head from any debris that might fall as he made his way to Samson's stall.

Not daring to get near the mule's hooves, he entered the adjacent box and scaled the half wall near Samson's head. "Easy, boy." The mule shied, but Travis snatched the halter and yanked the animal's head around while pushing on his shoulder. "Back," he ordered. "Back."

Samson pinned his ears down and bit at Travis's arm. With a quick move of his elbow, Travis dodged the teeth and smacked the mule's neck with the flat of his hand. "Quit!"

The mule blinked and retreated a step, but Travis dragged the mule's head around until Samson faced the doorway leading to the corral. The fire raged directly overhead in the loft. Sweat and smoke stung his eyes and blurred his vision. Burning air scalded his throat, making it hard to breathe. If he didn't get the animal out soon, he'd be forced to leave him behind.

Travis tugged the mule forward and Samson actually complied. He'd only taken a handful of steps, however, when the loft floorboards gave way. Fiery debris plummeted. Planks of wood struck across his shoulders, and lit hay showered upon his back. Spooked but unharmed by the downfall, Samson brayed and pulled against Travis's hold, trying to retreat farther into the barn.

"No you don't. We aren't going through that again." Travis shook off what he could from his back and swatted Samson's neck a second time. The mule tossed his head, but obeyed. However, Travis had a new problem to contend with—a focused heat was radiating through the back of his coat, and he feared some of the flames from the debris had taken hold.

"Get up *now*, mule." Travis walked backward, tugging on Samson's halter with one hand while trying to undo his buttons with the other. He had to get that coat off.

The heat on his back grew painful, and panic made him clumsy. He arched away from the fabric clawing at him and was about to release Samson and tear the coat off with both hands when a gush of blessedly cool water hit him from behind.

"Thanks." Travis swiveled to see which brother had just saved his hide, only to find Meredith standing there, an empty stockpot in her hands. His gratitude evaporated.

"Get out of here!" he shouted.

The woman was as bad as Samson.

He tried to order her out again, but a chest-heavy cough blocked the words as it pummeled his ribs. It bent him forward, and Meredith took advantage of his weakened state. She dropped the pot and pulled something from under her arm as she rushed toward him. Clicking her tongue, she latched onto the opposite side of Samson's halter and tapped his hindquarters with the end of a long stick.

The mule hopped and kicked, but the movement carried him closer to the door, so Travis bit back his protest. They'd nearly made it outside when the roof collapsed. Twenty feet behind them, timber beams splintered the weakened loft floor and slammed into the ground of the barn with a deafening crash. Meredith screamed. Samson bucked and contorted. Meredith lost her hold on the halter and stumbled sideways. Travis strained to lead the animal away from her, but Samson finally grasped the danger the barn represented and kicked wildly for his freedom.

Travis released his grip on the halter. "Go!"

The panicked mule kicked out a final time and ran out to the corral.

Travis spun toward where he'd last seen Meredith, and a new terror twisted his gut. She lay crumpled on the hard ground.

"No." The whispered denial fell from his lips as he ran to her. He dropped to the ground and yanked his gloves from his hands. "Meredith?"

She gave no answer. Not even a moan. He reached beneath her head to support it as he hoisted her into his arms, his only thought to get her away from the fire. But something sticky wet his fingers.

Blood.

8

Travis gathered Meredith close to his chest and ran out of the barn. He didn't stop until he reached the pump. Neill was at the trough filling a pail. He straightened when he saw Travis approach.

"What happened?" His eyes roamed over Meredith's limp form, and beneath the soot, his face paled.

"Fetch Crockett." When Neill just stood and stared, Travis's voice sharpened. "Now!"

Neill flinched and dashed off, leaving his pail behind.

Cradling Meredith's head in the crook of his arm, Travis slowly knelt and lowered her to a dry patch of ground. He combed her hair from her face, and a feather-light stirring of air brushed against his palm. She was breathing.

"Thank you, God," Travis murmured.

He shrugged out of his coat, folded it inside out, and gently cushioned her head with it. Careful of her wound, he angled her face so that the right side of her skull would take most of the weight, leaving the left side exposed for Crockett to examine.

She lay so still, it hurt to look at her.

This never should have happened. He should have let her leave as soon as she'd issued her warning. What had he been thinking, dragging her into this mess?

Desperate to do something—anything—to help her, Travis yanked the bandanna from around his neck and dipped it into the trough. Then, kneeling in the dirt beside her, he rinsed away the worst of the soot smears from her face, all the while praying for her eyes to open.

He was so focused on Meredith, he didn't realize his brothers had surrounded him until Crockett hunkered down and touched his shoulder.

Emotion clogged Travis's throat. He cleared it away with a rough cough. "I think the mule kicked her." He tilted her head to expose more of the bloodied area to Crockett's view. His brother was no doctor, but he was the closest they had. Ever since the day Jim had been shot, Crock had taken it upon himself to memorize the two medical books in his father's study, *Gunn's New Domestic Physician* and *A Dictionary of Practical Medicine*. Travis just prayed there'd been something in those books that could help Meredith.

Crockett pulled off his gloves and probed the wound. Meredith moaned and thrashed her arms, but her eyes didn't open. Travis took her hand in his, wishing he could do more.

"She can feel the pain," Crockett observed. "That's a good sign. But I'm going to need to get her into the house, where the light is better, before I can tell you more."

Crockett made as if to pick her up, but Travis nudged him aside. "I'll carry her." His brother shot him an odd look. Travis ignored it. Meredith was injured because of him. She was his responsibility.

After pushing to his feet, he shifted Meredith's weight in his arms and turned to Jim and Neill. "The roof's gone, so let the barn burn itself out. Keep an eye on it, though, and don't let any sparks spread to the house or shed. Neill, when it's under control, fetch the draft horses and Miss Meredith's paint from the creek bed, and tie them up by the old lean-to behind the shed. Jim, take care of the barn. Oh, and one of you better keep watch in case Mitchell's men decide to return. I'll come spell you when I can."

"Take care of the girl," Jim said. "We'll handle things out here."

Travis nodded and strode toward the house.

Crockett had every lamp in the den blazing with light by the time Travis arrived. "Set her on the sofa," he said. "I need to wash out that wound and see if any bone has chipped or if the skull is dented from the blow."

Travis laid Meredith across the cushioned seat, arranging her head at the end nearest the lamp table where Crockett had piled several squares of toweling.

As Crockett moved in with basin and sponge, Travis backed away and paced the room's perimeter.

Why was it that every time Meredith's path crossed his, she ended up hurt? First her leg in one of his traps, and now her head kicked by his mule. Both were accidents, of course, yet Travis couldn't shake a growing sense of guilt. If he had made different decisions, neither would have happened.

He dipped his chin and rubbed the aching area above his eyes. *Help her recover, Lord. Please. Don't make her pay the price for my mistakes.*

Travis circled past the woodstove, his mother's rocking chair, and his father's bookshelf, and then found himself once again at the foot of the sofa. He studied Meredith's face. Her dark lashes lay delicately against her pale cheeks, fluttering slightly. Tiny frown lines puckered her forehead between her brows as Crockett probed her wound, and quiet whimpers vibrated in her throat. An insane urge to shove his brother away and spare her the pain of his invasion had Travis balling his hands into fists, but he restrained himself from interfering.

After several more minutes of cleaning and probing, Crockett finally set aside the washbasin and pushed to his feet. Travis met his eye, silently seeking answers.

"The bleeding has slowed, and she continues to react to the pain—both of which are good signs. The cuts are fairly minor and won't require stitching. I've treated them with salve. It's the impact to her head, not the abrasions, that I'm most worried about, but best I can tell, there are no skull fractures."

Travis acknowledged his brother's words with a slight dip of his chin, and then reached out to grip the back of the sofa, bracing himself for the rest of the news.

"The fact that she hasn't awakened could be a problem. There is no way to know the extent of the damage inside her skull. The only thing I can recommend is to make her as comfortable as possible. Let her rest and heal at her own pace."

At first, Travis said nothing, just silently absorbed the verdict. So much of his life revolved around controlling his environment. Control meant security. That's why Archers never left their land and why few people were ever granted permission to cross their property line. Control minimized risk. But all his efforts to minimize risk tonight had failed. Mitchell's men escaped, the barn burned, and Meredith—a woman whose only "crime" was trying to perform a good deed—lay unconscious on his mother's sofa, and there was nothing he could do to remedy the situation.

Travis pressed his fingers into the wood trim of the sofa back and straightened. "My room's closest," he said. "We'll put her in there. I can bunk with Neill."

"Someone should probably sit up with her until she regains consciousness." Crockett raised a brow and searched him with a look that seemed to ask more than one question. "I'd be happy to—"

"No. I'll do it." Travis bent and lifted Meredith from the sofa. "She came here because of me. It's only right that I be the one to tend her."

Crockett nodded, a slight smile curving his lips. Travis glared at him, uncomfortable with his brother's shrewd expression. Crockett's grin widened at his reaction, but he wisely said no more and, instead, strode down the hall to open the bedroom door and pull back the covers on the bed. Travis carried Meredith through the doorway and lowered her to the mattress.

"We should probably . . . um . . . try to make her more comfortable." Crockett glanced at Travis from the opposite side of the bed, his face reddening.

Travis took secret pleasure at his brother's discomfort until the meaning of his words settled into Travis's brain. His mouth suddenly dry, he looked from Crockett to Meredith and back to Crockett again.

"We can't—" He cleared his throat. His shirt collar seemed to be shrinking. There was no way he was going to undress her. Especially not with Crockett looking on.

"I'm not suggesting we do anything improper." Crockett blew out a heavy breath. "Well, not *too* improper. Aw . . . blast it, Travis. I'm trying to be practical here. Her breathing is shallow, and if we loosen her stays, that might help. That and taking off her shoes so she can rest better. That's all I'm saying."

Shoes. He could handle shoes. Travis swallowed hard and moved to the end of the bed, where her feet hung off the side of the mattress. It was true that she didn't look very comfortable, her legs skewed at an odd angle. If he was lying there, he'd sure want his boots off. So why did he feel like the worst kind of cad when he touched her ankle?

"Throw the blanket over her legs," Travis ground out between clenched teeth. She'd shown them all the scar above her ankle when she first arrived, but that had been her choice. Neither he nor Crockett needed to see anything besides shoe leather now. Once the covers were in place, Travis waved Crockett over to his side of the bed. "Come help me with the other shoe." The faster they completed the task, the better.

They undid the laces and gently tugged off the shoes.

"Just like when Neill was a kid, right?" Crockett said.

"Right," Travis agreed. Only it didn't feel anything like putting Neill to bed when feminine wool stockings rubbed against his hands as he poked her toes under the covers. Nor was he able to picture Neill's sleepy little boy form when it came time to take care of the second order of business.

Travis looked to Crockett. His brother shrugged.

"It has to be done, Trav. She needs to be able to breathe freely. If you don't feel right about it, I'll do it."

He sure as shooting didn't feel right about it. But he felt even less right about letting anyone else do it.

Travis sat on the edge of the bed and reached for the buttons at Meredith's midsection. But before he touched one, he stopped. His eyes moved to her face. "Meredith," he said in a firm, loud voice. "Meredith, can you hear me?"

Her head shifted slightly on the pillow, but she gave no sign of waking.

"Meredith, I'm going to loosen your . . . ah . . . clothing to help you breathe. I swear that's all I'm doing. All right?"

She made a slight moaning sound, then quieted. He'd have to take that for permission. Setting his jaw and focusing strictly on the task that needed to be accomplished, he made quick work of the buttons on her bodice. Unfortunately, instead of the laces he expected to encounter, he uncovered another layer. Some white frilly thing offered up a second set of buttons. Travis bit back a groan but tackled the obstacle with businesslike precision. Finally, he found the stiff, boned corset he sought, but there were still no visible laces.

Why couldn't a woman just throw a shirt over her head like a man? This was ridiculous. At least there were metal fasteners of some sort running down the front.

"I swear, if there's another row of buttons under this, I'm gonna get my knife and cut her out," he grumbled under his breath. No wonder her breathing was shallow. She was wrapped up tighter than a roped calf at branding time.

However, the moment he unclasped the last fastener and the corset fell open to reveal another layer of white fabric, Meredith let out a sound that could only be described as a sigh. Her breathing deepened, and Travis's frustration melted away. He quickly drew the covers up to her chin.

"She'll rest easier now," Crockett said from behind him, "and that will give her the best chance to recover."

Travis nodded. Her recovery was more important than any awkwardness or embarrassment his actions might have caused. He just hoped she saw it the same way when she awoke.

9

Meredith rolled to her side and grimaced when pain throbbed behind her ear. She squeezed her eyes more tightly shut and gingerly rolled back the way she'd come, only to have something stiff jab her in the soft spot below her ribs. Had she fallen asleep reading again? She felt around for the book that must have worked its way under the covers, eager to remove the impediment and go back to sleep. However, when she extracted the poking object from beneath her, it felt nothing like a book and everything like a . . . corset? What was her corset doing in her bed? She always stored it carefully in her bureau drawer at night.

Cassandra had secretly given her the pink satin undergarment for her birthday last year, letting Aunt Noreen believe her gift had been nothing more extravagant than the package of stationery she'd presented at the family dinner that evening. But later she had taken Meredith's hand, dragged her upstairs to her room, and closed the door. Eyes twinkling with suppressed secrets, she had pulled a brown paper package from her wardrobe and presented it with giddy delight. The pink satin corset trimmed in white lace and covered with embroidered roses had been the most beautiful thing Meredith had ever seen. She treasured the garment and would never discard it haphazardly. So why was it in bed with her?

Meredith's mind flitted from dreamlike memories of her cousin to the puzzle of her present circumstance. Yet the more she tried to make sense of things, the more her head ached. Then another ache made itself known—the ache to use the chamber pot. Meredith swallowed a moan, hating to forfeit sleep. Maybe if she hurried, she could bury herself back into the covers before Aunt Noreen banged on the door.

Pressing her palms into the mattress, she started to lever herself up, but when she lifted her head from the pillow, stabbing shards ricocheted through her skull. She mewled and reached for her head.

"Easy now." A deep voice resonated near her ear. Strong hands supported her shoulders and propped a second pillow beneath her. "Are you awake, Meredith?" A warm fingertip drew a line across her forehead and gently smoothed back a piece of hair. "Please, God, let her wake," the voice murmured.

Meredith struggled to open her eyes, to make sense of the voice. It was familiar, masculine. Nothing like Uncle Everett, though.

Her lashes slowly separated. A face hovered over hers. She blinked, trying to bring it into focus. Craggy features, a strong jaw that seemed to tighten as she watched, and eyes . . . eyes that looked like home.

"Travis?" Her voice came out scratchy and cracked. "What are you doing in my room?"

Those eyes—not quite green, not quite brown—crinkled at the corners. "I'm not in your room, darlin'. You're in mine."

What? Maybe she was still dreaming. That would explain why Travis was here and why nothing was making a lick of sense. But the throbbing behind her ear seemed awfully real.

"My head hurts."

"You were kicked by a mule."

A mule? Meredith frowned. Uncle Everett didn't own a mule. Had she been injured at the livery fetching Ginger? And why was Travis grinning at her? Shouldn't he be more concerned?

"It's not very heroic of you to smile at my misfortune." *Really.* This was her dream after all. Her hero should be more solicitous. Of course, usually in her dreams, Travis rescued her before any injury occurred. The man was getting lax. She'd started to tell him so when he laid the back of his hand on her forehead as if feeling for fever. The gentle touch instantly dissolved her pique.

He removed his hand and met her gaze. "I'm smiling because I'm happy to see you awake. We've been worried about you."

"Awake?" Meredith scrunched her brows together until the throbbing around her skull forced her to relax. "Travis, you're not making any sense. I can't be awake. You only come to me when I'm dreaming. Although you're usually younger and . . . well . . . cleaner, and not so in need of a shave.

"But don't get me wrong," she hurried to assure him. It wouldn't do to insult her hero. "You're just as handsome as always. I don't even mind that you didn't save me this time. The important thing is that you're here."

She smiled at him, but his grin faded and frown lines appeared above his eyes.

"Don't you remember riding out here to warn me about Mitchell? The fire, Meredith. Remember the fire? You were fighting the blaze on your own until me and the boys returned."

Something important tugged on the hem of her memory, something she should know. Something Travis expected her to remember. Meredith grew uneasy under the intensity of his stare. He was disappointed in her. She could see it. Disappointed that she couldn't remember. She *had* to remember. Travis might leave her if she didn't. She didn't want him to leave.

Despite the pounding in her head, she searched deeper into the foggy recesses of her mind. Images flashed just out of reach. Flames. A line of pots. A gray blanket in her hand. The pieces jumbled in a confusing blur. Then she saw a building. Big. Open. Fire climbing its walls.

"A barn!" she cried triumphantly. "Your barn was on fire, and I was helping put it out. Right?" She found his hand and grabbed hold. "That's right, isn't it? See, you don't have to leave me, Travis. I can remember. I won't let you down. I promise."

Travis's face started to swim in front of her and her lashes grew too heavy to keep parted. Her fingers started to loosen their grip on his hand, too, and fear clutched her chest. He was leaving her!

"Don't go, Travis. Please." Her mouth stumbled on the words as darkness descended over her again. "Don't leave me."

Then a firm, warm hand closed over the top of hers and held on with the strength she could no longer muster for herself. "I'm not going anywhere, Meredith. Go ahead and rest. I'll be here when you wake."

Peace settled over her then, and as she slipped back into the darkness, her spirit smiled.

Travis held Meredith's hand for several minutes and watched her sleep. Perhaps it was his imagination, but she seemed to be resting more peacefully now than she had before, as if knowing he was there actually brought her comfort. Then again, it probably wasn't *his* presence specifically that eased her. She hardly knew him, after all. Most likely she simply didn't want to be alone, and he was handy. Crockett or even Neill would have filled the bill equally well.

But, despite the logic of that observation, Travis couldn't quite shake the feeling that it didn't ring true. The things Meredith said during their brief, and thoroughly bizarre, conversation had sounded personal. So personal, they'd rattled him. And stirred an odd warmth in him, too.

Did she really dream about him?

Travis lowered himself back into the chair he'd placed at the side of the bed and slowly released Meredith's hand. He fingered his eyes, trying to massage the exhaustion out of them, then rubbed his palms down his face. Whiskers scratched his skin, eliciting a rueful chuckle.

She was right. He did need a shave.

A floorboard creaked in the hall, and Travis glanced up to find Crockett—barefooted, pants hastily donned, shirt untucked—standing in the doorway. "I thought I heard voices."

"You did." Travis pushed to his feet and waved him into the room. "Meredith woke a couple minutes ago. She was disoriented and confused, and most of what she said didn't add up." He turned his attention from his brother to the woman sleeping in his bed. "Thought she was at home in her own room and didn't recall the fire until I mentioned it. Even then, she seemed to have to dig real deep to muster any recollections."

Travis worked his jaw back and forth, trying to churn up enough courage to ask the question he was afraid to have answered. "You don't think her mind's been damaged, do you?"

"Not permanently, no." Crockett leaned over the bed and felt Meredith's head for fever, just as Travis had done earlier, and pivoted to face him. "Confusion and memory loss are to be expected. Her brain took a hard knock. I wouldn't worry unless she fails to improve after a day or two."

"So she'll be staying with us for a while?"

"Yep." A defensive edge crept into Crockett's voice, as if he expected Travis to argue. "I don't want her out of bed until we're sure she's fully recovered. If we send her on her way too soon, she could succumb to a dizzy spell and fall off her horse or get disoriented and wander from the path only to get lost in the woods. I know you don't like having strangers here, Travis, but I'm going to have to insist."

"Meredith proved herself an ally last night," Travis conceded. "She can stay as long as is necessary."

He cleared his throat, afraid Crockett would sense how easy it was for him to break his own rules where Meredith was concerned. "But as soon as she's healthy, she has to go. I don't want a bunch of townsfolk poking around out here because one of their own is missing. It wouldn't do her any good, either, to be found alone on a ranch with four men." The last thing he wanted to do was cause Meredith more grief. He'd done enough of that already.

"Agreed." Crockett clapped him on the back. "Why don't you grab a few winks before the sun comes up. I'll sit with her for a while."

Travis shook his head. "No. I promised to be here when she woke, and I aim to keep my word." He scratched at his stubbly chin and caught a glimpse of himself in the mirror above his chest of drawers. *Haggard* was about as kind a description as could be applied to what he saw. *Filthy saddle bum* painted a truer picture. "I might take a few minutes to clean up a bit, though. I could stand a wash and some fresh clothes."

"Yes, you could." Crockett twisted his face into a look of mock disgust, then broke into a smile. "Go on." He pushed Travis toward the drawers that held clean trousers and shirts. "She probably won't wake for a couple hours. You got plenty of time to make yourself pretty."

Travis whipped off his sweat-stained shirt and hurled it directly at Crockett's head. The joker ducked, and the sound of his quiet laughter followed Travis down the hall.

The next time Meredith woke, the sun was well on its way across the sky. Travis had been dozing in the chair when her quiet moan stirred him. He shifted closer to the bed. Would she be more clearheaded this time?

"Don't move too fast," he warned as she rolled to her side and propped an elbow beneath her. "It'll make your head ache worse." He stilled her with a hand to her shoulder.

"Travis?" She blinked and struggled to fully open her eyes.

"I'm here, Meredith."

She smiled at him then, and the gesture did something funny to his insides. Not wanting to examine the phenomenon too closely, he cleared his throat and reached for the glass of water he'd brought in with him after cleaning up.

"Are you thirsty?"

Her eyes instantly lost their peaceful glow. She bit her bottom lip and gave her head a tiny shake. "You have to leave," she said in a wobbly voice.

"Leave? Why?" First she'd begged him to stay, and now she wanted him to go. Travis blew out a breath and ran his hand through his hair. The woman's confusion must be addling his own mind.

Her face flushed crimson, and her gaze dropped to somewhere below his chin. "I have to attend to . . . to personal business." Her voice dipped so low at the end, he had to strain to hear her. Once he deciphered the words, however, an uncomfortable heat crept up his neck.

"Oh."

What in blue blazes was he supposed to do now? She could barely move about in the bed with the pain from her wound. How was she supposed to manage standing and walking about the room? What if she grew dizzy and fell?

Travis clenched his teeth. He'd get her up, but by Jove, she was going to have to find a way to accomplish the rest on her own. Heaven help her.

Without further discussion, Travis dragged the chamber pot from beneath the bed and set it beside the footboard so that Meredith could hang onto the carved bedpost for balance. He scanned the room for anything else that might be of help, and his eyes lit on the small bag Neill had retrieved from Meredith's horse last night. Without asking permission, Travis strode over to the bag and rummaged through it. Finding a white cotton nightgown, he draped it across the end of the bed, then dropped the bag on the floor nearby. That way she could reach it should she feel the need.

By the time he turned back to Meredith, the woman had already pushed herself up to a sitting position and had her legs dangling over the side of the mattress. Deep lines furrowed her brow, and her left hand gingerly cupped the side of her head, but her chin was set and her back straight.

The woman had grit. If he hadn't learned that truth last night, watching her power through her pain this morning would've proved it.

Travis rushed to her side and wrapped an arm around her middle. Something pink and lacy winked at him from within the sheets. Recognizing the corset, he loosened his hold on Meredith in order to grab the frilly thing and flip it down to the far corner of the bed. Maybe if she found it with her other belongings, he'd get lucky and her confused mind would assume she'd taken it off herself.

Cinching his arm back around her ribs, Travis took her weight on himself and slowly raised her to her feet. "Easy now," he said. "I'll help you get to the end of the bed."

She leaned into his side as they moved slowly toward their goal, her left arm circling his waist. When they reached the bedpost, Meredith released him to grasp the oak column, and Travis found himself missing the contact. He maintained his grip another moment until certain she was secure. Finally, he slackened his hold and slipped his arm free.

"I'll be right outside the door." He ducked his head and shoved his thumbs beneath his suspender straps. "Call out if you need anything."

He couldn't quite bring himself to look at her with her dress half undone, but he heard her quiet "Thank you" as he strode to the doorway.

Once the door had been pulled closed behind him, he pressed his back into the wall and exhaled a long, slow breath.

Fifteen minutes later, Meredith called him back into the room. She'd managed to change and crawl back under the covers. Sitting with the blankets held up to her chin, she bit her lip and hid her eyes from him behind lowered lashes.

"I didn't want to bother you," she said softly, "but I couldn't reach all my hairpins. It hurt too much to twist my head back and forth."

Travis crossed the room and, lowering himself beside her, reached for the first pin he could see. She hissed a little when a tangled strand pulled painfully against her injured scalp. Travis scowled. His rancher's fingers were too thick for this. But who else was gonna do it? Setting his jaw, he reached for another pin. This time she didn't make a sound as he extracted the thin black wire. His confidence building, Travis searched for more. By the time he found the last one and added it to the pile next to his hip, Meredith's eyes had closed and her back slumped against his chest.

Travis eased her down to where her pillow waited. Scooping the discarded pins into his palm, he pushed to his feet only to have the bed groan at the loss of his weight. Meredith's lashes fluttered open.

"Travis?" she whispered, her voice groggy.

"Yes?"

"You're the best hero I ever dreamed up."

And in that moment, Travis wanted to be more to her than a dreamland hero left over from her childhood. He wanted to be her hero in truth.

But his wants never came first. His brothers, the land—those were what he swore to protect. And with Meredith's connection to Mitchell, he couldn't afford to indulge in selfish whims. No, when Meredith recovered, he'd see she got back where she belonged—far away from him.

10

Meredith drifted in and out of sleep most of the day. Each time she woke, she'd ask the same questions: Where was she? What happened? And each time, Travis gave her the same answers. Despite her continued memory trouble, however, her disorientation improved. No more talk of dreams or heroes, for which he was exceedingly grateful. If Crockett had overheard one of those statements, he'd never let Travis live it down. Besides, the less he thought about those early conversations, the better. He had no business trying to be someone's hero. He had enough to worry about.

Like the fact that someone was trying to drive him off his land. And because of that, he had no barn, only half the hay stores he'd need for winter, and an injured woman whose presence kept him in the house when he should be out helping his brothers build a temporary shelter for the stock. Travis paced over to the window and raised an arm to cushion his head as he leaned against the wall.

"I'm sorry about your barn, Travis." Meredith's soft voice settled over him like a comfortable, well-worn shirt. He turned and found she had bolstered herself on the extra pillows without his aid and was regarding him with remarkably clear eyes.

How had she so accurately deciphered his thoughts? He pasted on a smile, not wanting to burden her with his worries, and stepped away from the window. "It's nothing for you to be sorry about. The boys and I can build another."

"But it will cause you hardship. Perhaps if I had gotten here sooner . . ."

Travis's mouth hardened into a stern line. "None of the blame belongs on your shoulders, Meredith. Mitchell's the one responsible. Without your warning, things could've been a lot worse."

Travis dropped onto the bedside chair ready to scold some more, but it suddenly hit him that she hadn't asked him her usual questions. "Do you remember what happened?"

She started to shake her head but stopped with a wince. "Not really. I remember coming out here and helping fight the fire, but I have no memory of you and the others returning or anything else from last night."

"Do you recall me explaining how you got injured?"

"Samson, right?"

He nodded, and she smiled like a pupil trying to impress her teacher. "You told me when I awakened a while ago."

"And four times before that." A true grin split his face. She was getting better. "I'm glad it finally sank in."

Her brows knit in bewilderment. "Four times? How long have I been . . ." She glanced down at the bed, as if only then recognizing the significance of where she was, and slid down on the pillows until the blankets came up to her chin.

So much for bypassing the awkwardness.

"It's nearly suppertime. I'll have Jim bring you some broth if you think you can manage eating."

"Suppertime?" she squeaked. "I was here all night and all day?"

"And you probably won't be leaving anytime soon." Judging by her horrified look, the prospect didn't exactly thrill her. Well, being chained to a sickroom when he had work to do wasn't his first choice, either. If he could deal with it, she sure as shootin' could, too.

"Look, Meredith. We have no choice in the matter. That lump on the side of your head ain't there for decoration. You're seriously hurt. Crockett knows what he's talking about when it comes to things like this, and he insists that you not leave until you've recovered to the point that there's no chance of you blacking out on the way home or growing so dizzy you fall off your horse. Until now, you couldn't even remember where you were. No way was I going to dump you outside my gate just because propriety said you shouldn't be here. Propriety wasn't kicked by a mule."

Travis sucked in a breath and reined in his temper. It was only natural for her to be alarmed. She was in her nightclothes in a strange man's bed. Any sane woman would protest. It only proved how delirious she'd truly been when she'd rambled on about him being handsome and the hero of her dreams. He should be thankful for the evidence that she was in her right mind again.

So why wouldn't that pang in his chest at the thought of her leaving go away?

"I understand." Meredith looked at him with those big eyes of hers and made an effort to clear the trepidation from her face. But when she bit her bottom lip, he knew she still harbored worries.

"I see our patient's awake again." Crockett leaned a shoulder against the doorjamb. His trousers and shirt were streaked with soot, but his face and hands glowed from a recent scrubbing. "How are you feeling, Meredith?"

"Stronger, thank you." Her lashes remained lowered, and her grip on the blankets tightened.

Travis moved to the foot of the bed to shield her from his brother's view. "She remembers things, too," he said. "Not everything, but enough that I don't have to repeat explanations."

"Well, that's good news." Crockett angled his head past Travis and projected his voice across the room. "Another couple days of rest, and you should be up and about."

Meredith's quiet moan was all the catalyst Travis needed. He strode to the doorway and, taking Crockett by the shoulders, manually pointed him toward the kitchen.

Crockett resisted, concern creeping into his voice. "Is she in pain?"

"Only if she moves." Travis strong-armed his brother into the hall. "Why don't you get her some of that soup Jim's heating up? She hasn't eaten since yesterday."

Crockett pulled out of Travis's hold and turned on him. "What's wrong with you?" he hissed. "You're acting as if you think I'm going to hurt her or something."

"It's not that. It's just . . ." Travis let out a heavy breath. "She's not too pleased about having to prolong her stay, and your reminders aren't easing her worries none."

Crockett jutted his chin. "Well, she's going to have to get used to the idea, because I'm not letting her leave until I'm sure—"

"I already made that plain to her," Travis interrupted. "And she's coming around. She just needs some time to settle things in her mind." He glanced back toward the open doorway. "Meredith's tough. She'll weather whatever storm comes."

"She's got spunk. That's for sure."

Hearing the admiration in his brother's voice, Travis turned to scowl at him. "Just get the soup."

Crockett's gaze returned to the doorway to Meredith's room, giving Travis the distinct impression that the man remembered all too well what she looked like tucked up in bed.

He gave his brother a shove. "Get going."

"All right. All right." Crockett caught his balance and finally moved toward the kitchen. "I'll brew some willow bark tea, too. It'll help with her pain."

"Fine."

Travis marched back to his room and made a beeline for his chest of drawers. He grabbed the first shirt his hand touched and yanked it out of the drawer. His bootheels clomped against the wood floor, then muffled as he hit the rag rug at the side of the bed.

Meredith watched him, her brows slightly quirked.

"Arms up," he said as if she were a child and not a very beautiful, very grown woman. "Crock is gonna bring some tea and soup in a bit, and you won't be able to eat if you've got a death grip on those blankets." He scrunched the shirttails in his hands and stretched the unbuttoned neck hole wide. "Put this on. It'll cover you up and still allow you to eat."

She hesitated for a moment, then released the blankets and stuck her arm through the sleeve, her disgruntled expression making him smile.

With Meredith's condition no longer critical, Travis joined his brothers outside the following morning. He and Crockett split her care between them, and at her insistence, only checked in on her when a break in their work allowed it. Her head still pained her, though the willow bark seemed to take the sharpness away, but it was the dizziness that kept her in bed. He'd provided her with a book to read, Ballantyne's *The Wild Man of the West*, and while he doubted a less feminine book had ever been written, she'd assured him it helped pass the time.

Late that morning, Travis headed to the pump. It was his turn to look in on Meredith. He pulled off his work gloves, tucked them into his coat pocket, and ran his hands under the icy water streaming from the spout. Then he dampened his handkerchief and wiped the sweat from his brow. As he moved the cool cloth around to the back of his neck, two shots fired in close succession echoed from the direction of the road.

Company.

In a blink, he unfastened the protective loop on his holster, his fingers testing the freedom of his Colt. After Mitchell's attack, he and the boys had taken to wearing their gun belts even when close to the house.

"Neill, take position by the shed!" Travis yelled as he ran to the corral. He ducked through the fence and grabbed his saddle from where it lay slung over the top rails. He caught a glimpse of Jim running around the corner of the shed and called out for him to guard the road.

Crockett appeared at the corral with a horse blanket, and Travis whistled for his gelding. As the two worked in tandem to get the animal ready to ride, Travis ordered Crockett to see to Meredith's protection.

"She warned us Mitchell's man would return to make another offer after the fire. Things might get ugly when I spit in his face." Travis mounted, and Crockett moved to open the railings.

"I'll watch over her, Trav. Just keep your head out there."

He nodded to his brother and nudged Bexar into a run, his eyes only briefly touching on his bedroom window as he charged past the house.

11

Meredith shivered as a draft from the open window passed over her skin, yet her trembling had more to do with her concern over Travis than the cold. Crockett had assured her that his presence in her room was simply a precaution, but the rifle he held and the way he constantly scanned the trees outside as if searching for invaders did little to put her at ease.

What would Roy do when Travis still refused to sell? For he *would* refuse. She was certain of it. Would there be another fire? Would the house be targeted next? Or would Roy finally give up?

Please, Lord, let him give up.

But in her heart she knew he wouldn't. Roy's ambition ran nearly as deep as Travis's loyalty. Something drastic would have to occur before either man gave an inch.

Something drastic . . . Meredith's breath grew shallow.

"You don't think he's walking into a trap, do you?"

Crockett spared her the smallest of glances before turning back to his vigil. "Travis is smart. He'll assess the situation before revealing himself, and even then, he'll keep his gun trained on whoever's there. He can handle himself."

If Crockett was so confident of Travis's abilities, why was he clutching his rifle like a soldier about to be called to the front line?

"What if Roy sent more than one man? What if they lured him with their shots, then cut the fencing wire and caught him unaware? Someone should check on him. He's been gone too long."

"He's fine. Now hush." The gentle reprimand had the intended effect, but her fears must have been communicated at least a little, for when Crockett returned his attention to the window, he fidgeted with his rifle grip and shifted his stance three times before settling.

Meredith held her tongue, but her worries festered. She watched Crockett watch the yard. Every time his focus snapped to a new location, her breath caught.

Just when she thought she'd surely go mad from the waiting, a distinctive low birdcall drifted through the window—one she vaguely recalled hearing the afternoon she arrived. Crockett relaxed immediately and pivoted to wink at her. "I told you he was fine."

Thank you, Lord!

Meredith sagged against her pillows, relief bringing the sought-after comfort that had eluded her earlier. She grinned at Crockett, but before she could ask any questions, he slammed the window shut and strode out of the room, rifle in hand.

What did that mean? Was danger still afoot? Perhaps he was simply eager to greet his brother and hear the details of his encounter. *Hmmm . . .* She wanted to hear those details, too, and she doubted the Archers would make a point to share them with her. They were forever telling her not to worry. A rather bothersome trait, that.

Why did men think they had to protect women from reality? She didn't mind being protected from wild animals or murderous villains, but from the truth? Meredith made a face as she threw back the bedcovers. The more she knew about a situation, the less likely she was to worry, not the other way around. If she was to stay with the Archers another day or two, she needed to know what was going on.

Holding a steadying hand to her head, she swiveled her legs to the edge of the bed and dangled them over the side. She blinked as the floor seemed to tilt forward and back and waited for the dizziness to pass. Grasping the top of the headboard, Meredith stood slowly, her bare toes digging into the rag rug to aid her balance. She still wore Travis's shirt over her nightdress, and it bunched uncomfortably at her waist. With her free hand, she tugged it down over her hips and untwisted the skirt of her sleeping gown before attempting to move.

A door slammed somewhere in the distance, and male voices poured into the house. Agitated male voices.

More curious and determined than ever, Meredith leaned her leg against the mattress and shuffled along the side of the bed, chilled air nipping at her ankles. If she could just make it as far as the doorway, she could listen in on whatever the Archers said when they congregated around the kitchen table.

Having reached the bedpost, she inhaled a deep breath, straightened her shoulders, and took her first unaided step. Her foot met the hardness of the wood floor and wobbled, but she found if she stared at the ground a few inches in front of her toes, the room didn't spin quite as much. She concentrated so hard on remaining upright, however, that she failed to hear the approaching footsteps until two pairs of boots appeared at the top edge of her vision.

An audible gasp sucked the air from the room. Meredith stilled.

"Heaven help us. You've ruined her."

Meredith jerked her head upright. "Uncle Everett?"

Pain shot through her skull at the too-fast motion. She staggered sideways, unable to maintain her equilibrium as the floor seemed to undulate beneath her. Then all at once she found herself braced against the firm wall of a man's chest. *Travis.* He caught her arms above the elbows and steadied her as she sagged into his safe harbor.

"You shouldn't be out of bed," he scolded in a soft voice, then promptly picked her up and delivered her back to the pillows.

"Good grief, man! Have you no shame?" Her uncle's voice followed her across the room. "You carry on with my niece in front of my very eyes?"

Horrified by her uncle's outburst, Meredith turned her face away from Travis as he set her down. Tension radiated through him as he released her, and when she found the nerve to look at him again, a muscle twitched at the edge of his jaw.

"She's injured, Hayes. Or don't you care about that?" Travis ground out. "I thought I explained her condition quite thoroughly on the way here."

Uncle Everett stomped into the room, pulling his arms from his coat. Once he had the garment off, he stormed down the opposite side of the bed and forced it around Meredith's shoulders, drawing it closed under her chin.

"You failed to mention that her condition included a nightdress and a place in your bed!"

Travis leaned across the bed and grabbed Uncle Everett's wrist. "You insult her again with talk like that, and I'll throw you off my land with a buckshot escort."

The sound of a rifle cocking drew all eyes to the doorway. "Buckshot's too tame, Trav. I say we each carve out a piece of his hide with a .44." Crockett stood just inside the room, brandishing his Winchester. Jim and Neill flanked him on either side, hands hovering above their holsters.

Meredith diverted her gaze to the ceiling, wishing she could dissolve into the covers. Could her humiliation be any more complete?

Travis tossed her uncle's wrist away from him and straightened his stance to face the man squarely, arms crossed over his chest. Uncle Everett straightened, too, though not until he'd done up three of the buttons on the coat he'd forced upon her. The two glared at each other for what seemed like an age before Uncle Everett finally looked at her and let out a hefty sigh.

"Meri. You've thrown everything away, girl. How could you be so foolhardy?" The disappointment in his eyes cut her to the quick.

"I had to warn them, Uncle Everett. You were away, the sheriff was gone, and the deputy just laughed off my concerns as if I didn't know what I was talking about. I had no choice but to come."

"You should've stayed at home and let the Archers take care of themselves. That's what they're best at." He aimed a pointed glance at Travis before taking a seat on the edge of the bed. "Ah, Meri. There'll be a high price to pay for this bit of foolishness." He patted her hand. "When I think of everything your aunt and I did to secure your match with Mitchell only to have you throw it all away on a crazy whim . . . Why, it breaks my heart. What would your papa say?"

"Papa would be proud that I followed my conscience." Meredith sat forward, indignation fueling her speech. "I want no part of Roy Mitchell, Uncle. He's the one behind the fire that destroyed the Archers' barn. I heard him give the order myself."

"Nonsense, girl. You misunderstood. Roy explained everything to me last evening."

Travis lurched forward. "You told him she was *here*?"

"Of course. As her betrothed, he had a right to know. The poor fellow feels dreadful about everything. He kept castigating himself for not noticing your upset and clearing up the confusion immediately. He is very concerned about you, my dear."

"He's concerned about my land, not me," Meredith grumbled under her breath. Uncle Everett didn't seem to hear, but Travis raised a brow at her before turning his attention back to her uncle.

"What exactly did you tell Mitchell about Meredith?"

"At first, nothing. After all, I had no idea where she was." He patted her hand once again, as if she were a child to be placated, then stood to address Travis, dismissing her from the conversation. "I arrived home for supper Tuesday night only to find my wife inconsolable. Cassie had told her Meredith was ill, but when Roy arrived to pay his respects, she went to fetch her anyhow. Noreen is very set on this match taking place. When she found our Meri missing . . . well . . . she flew into a tizzy."

More likely a rage, Meredith thought as she pictured Aunt Noreen storming about the house.

"She questioned our daughter, Cassandra, until the girl admitted that Meri had gone to the old homestead. Noreen insisted that I fetch her back at first light. However, when I arrived at the place yesterday morning, I could find no evidence that she had been there. By the time I arrived home again, Noreen had scoured the house and found the note Meri left for Cassandra. Mitchell arrived soon after, and when Noreen showed him the note, he put the pieces together and explained the situation."

"Whatever he said was a lie," Meredith interjected. "The charred remains of the Archers' barn prove it."

"No, dear. They prove the villainy of one of his competitors." Uncle Everett pulled off his hat and set it on the corner of Travis's bureau with a nonchalance that made Meredith want to scream. "Roy explained how one of his men interrupted your time together, and how you must have overheard bits and pieces of his conversation and jumped to an inaccurate conclusion. He doesn't fault you, of course. He's too much of a gentleman. There was quite a bit of traffic on the road that day, I understand, and the noise surely interfered with your ability to decipher what was being said."

"I know what I heard." How could her uncle dismiss her intelligence and judgment so easily? Did he think she would risk her reputation and personal well-being if she wasn't sure?

"I fear you only know what you *thought* you heard." Though he smiled, condescension laced his tone. "Roy's man had come with news of a rumor regarding a large outfit from Houston. They planned to force him out of the bidding for local lumber by burning out those property owners who stood between him and the railroad. When the devastated owners were forced to sell, the Houston outfit would offer higher prices, thereby securing the necessary land. Roy would be out of the running. Needless to say, he was sickened by such underhanded tactics and intended to inform the sheriff as soon as the man returned.

"He even assured me he'd still marry you after your misadventure, but now that I see the extent of your ruin, I can't expect him to hold to that promise. A man in his position cannot afford to have such a scandal attached to his good name."

"You're wrong." Moisture gathered in her eyes at her uncle's betrayal. He was her father's brother. Why did he believe Roy Mitchell's sly explanations over those of his own niece? She would expect such a turn from Aunt Noreen, but Uncle Everett had always been kind to her in his own negligent way. It didn't help that every time she looked at him, she saw features that reminded her of her father. "You want to believe Roy because he's promised to triple your business at the mill, but he's behind this attack. I'm certain of it."

She glanced from her uncle's shaking head to Travis's unreadable expression. Did *he* believe her? Somehow the thought that he might doubt her cut deeper than Uncle Everett's lack of faith.

"You wound me, Meri," her uncle said, putting his hand to his chest. "I would never put my own profit ahead of your well-being. In fact, I aim to do all that is within my power to rectify this mess you've gotten yourself into."

"There's nothing to rectify. I'll be well in a day or two and can return to town then." Not that she relished the idea of being back under Aunt Noreen's roof, but at least she could commiserate with her cousin.

"I'm afraid it's not that simple. When your aunt realized that this is where you must have spent the last two nights, she implored me not to bring you back into our home. Noreen is convinced that doing so would throw a shadow of scandal over Cassandra, hurting her prospects for a suitable marriage. I had hoped to calm her concerns with the truth of your circumstances, but if I tell her in what condition I found you . . . well . . . you know your aunt. I'd never hear the end of it." He gave her that haggard look, the one he wore whenever Aunt Noreen got a bee in her bonnet.

Meredith bit the inside of her cheek in a bid for control as her uncle's meaning sank into her brain. She was to be the sacrifice laid upon the altar to appease Aunt Noreen's wrath. Instead of standing up for his niece, Uncle Everett would do what he always did—take the path of least resistance.

"Word of your little . . . escapade . . . is bound to get out," he said, as if that excused his behavior. "These things always do. Noreen threatened to take Cassie away from me and move in with her sister if I don't bend to her wishes. I can't allow that to happen."

Meredith jutted out her chin. She had imagined such a scenario, although deep down she'd never truly believed it would come to pass. "I'll live at the homestead, then. The house is in fine condition—"

"No," Uncle Everett cut in. "I'd never be able to rest knowing you were out here alone. Your father entrusted me with your care, and I must see this through." He clasped his hands behind his back and rocked from heel to toe. "The way I see it, there's only one way to salvage this situation."

He looked pointedly at her, then scanned the rest of the room's occupants with a steely determination she'd never witnessed in him before. "You're going to have to marry one of the Archers."

12

What?" Crockett, Jim, and Neill chorused the word as if it were one of the hymns they sang in the parlor on Sundays. But Travis said nothing. He wouldn't give Everett Hayes the satisfaction of knowing the pronouncement had rattled him.

Meredith, apparently, had no such compunction. "For heaven's sake, Uncle. You can't just foist me on them like an abandoned puppy. The Archers have been nothing but kind to me. They don't deserve such ill treatment from you."

Travis ground his teeth. Nothing but kind? They'd welcomed her at gunpoint and refused to let her leave after she warned them of the coming danger. Meredith was the kind one, not them. Shoot, his mule kicked her in the head.

And hearing her talk of herself in such unflattering terms, as if marriage to her would be a punishment to whomever found himself tied to the other end of the knot, riled him even more. He itched to hit something, preferably good ol' Uncle Everett, since the man made no effort to correct her assumptions.

"It can't be helped, Meri. It's the only honorable option. And if the Archers are honorable men—" the man stared meaningfully at Travis—"they'll take responsibility for you."

Travis felt more than saw his brothers step deeper into the room.

"Now you're *really* making me sound like an unwanted puppy," Meredith grumbled. Then she drew her legs up under her, and taking hold of the headboard for support, she turned her back on her uncle.

"Pay him no heed, Travis," she pled in a soft voice. His gaze moved to meet her bright blue eyes. "I have a perfectly good house on the land my father left me, and an allowance that will see to my needs. You don't have to give in to his bullying."

The thought of her living alone had his gut clenching. Wild animals, wilder men . . . He didn't want to think about what could happen. And what of Mitchell? He'd heard Meredith's comment about the man only being interested in her land. If she didn't marry him, to what lengths would he go to ensure she sold it to him? Would he burn her out, too? No, Meredith living alone was out of the question. It was the one thing he and Hayes agreed on.

Meredith's lower lip trembled slightly as he contemplated what course to take. She was a brave, fierce little thing, but vulnerable, too.

He gently chucked her under the chin. "Don't fret, pup. We'll figure something out."

Her nose wrinkled at the puppy reference, and he nearly laughed aloud at the resemblance. As he shared a smile with her, a strange urge burgeoned inside him—the urge to stroke her hair and tuck her into his chest as he would one of Sadie's pups. But he was certain the instant he touched her, puppies would be the furthest thing from his mind.

"Well, Archer?"

Travis hardened his expression as he returned his focus to Everett Hayes. The man was all bluster. He had no power in these negotiations, and he knew it—not when surrounded by four armed men. His only choice was to appeal to their sense of honor. Hayes wanted protection for his niece, Travis would give him credit for that, but he was too lily-livered to take care of it himself, letting his shrew of a wife kick Meredith out of his house. Meredith deserved better.

"I'll have a decision for you tomorrow. Come back then." Travis signaled to Crockett. His brother handed his rifle off to Jim and strode forward.

Hayes retreated toward the wall. "Tomorrow's not good enough, Archer! I demand—"

"You're in no position to demand anything," Travis snapped, his patience depleted. "My brother will show you to your horse."

"This way, Mr. Hayes." Crockett spoke through clenched teeth as he gripped the man's shoulder and firmly steered him toward the door.

Meredith's uncle grabbed for his hat as he dragged his feet and twisted his neck to glare at Travis. "What of my niece?"

"She's not well enough to travel. She stays with us."

The man frowned but offered no argument as Crockett shoved him out into the hall. "Mark my words, Archer." Hayes latched onto the doorframe, momentarily halting his exit. "I'll be back in the morning. And I'm bringing a preacher."

Travis said nothing, just stared the man down until he finally released his hold on the wall and submitted to Crockett's not-so-gentle guidance.

"Travis?" Meredith's quiet voice drew his head around and had him fortifying his resolve. She might not like the way he'd treated her uncle, but courtesy could only be stretched so far. He refused to be polite to a man who would insult his own niece and try to fob her off on a virtual stranger. She should be grateful that he—

"My uncle will need his coat." Meredith undid the buttons and shrugged out of the heavy overcoat. Then she handed it up to him with a smile that offered no censure.

When he took the coat from her, she adjusted the too-long sleeves of his brown plaid shirt, the one he'd lent her the night before, and hugged her arms to her middle. She gave him a brief nod, and all he could think was that she had just removed herself from her uncle's protection and entrusted herself to his.

He stared at her a moment, then nodded in return.

"Neill." Travis pivoted away from Meredith. "See that Hayes gets his coat." He tossed the garment, and his kid brother snagged it out of the air. "Jim, follow our guest to the road. We wouldn't want him to have a mishap on the way home."

Jim nodded, his expression assuring Travis there'd be no more surprises that day.

When the two men left, Travis turned back to Meredith a final time. Her eyelids were drooping, and her shoulders seemed to sag against the pillows. The strain of her uncle's visit had obviously depleted her strength.

"Get some sleep, Meri," he said, moving closer to the bed.

Meri. He liked the nickname. It reminded him of the young girl he'd encountered in the woods a dozen years ago, a girl with a brave spirit and trusting eyes, a girl who had grown into a woman of conviction and courage with a quiet beauty that awakened things in him he didn't quite understand.

Lifting the covers, he helped her lie down. "The boys and I will see to things."

She smiled sleepily. "I know."

He tucked the blankets around her, then crept out of the room and met Crockett on the porch. The two stood silently for several minutes as they watched Everett Hayes ride away, Neill at his side, Jim somewhere in the trees. Crockett never turned to face him, but Travis could hear his question before the words hit the air.

"You know one of us is gonna have to marry her, right?"

Travis inhaled a deep breath, prolonging the final moment before his world changed irrevocably. Then with a sigh, he let it go. "Yep."

All through dinner, Everett Hayes's demand hung over the Archer table like a boulder perched on an eroding precipice. No one spoke of it, as if fearful that doing so would bring a rockslide down on their heads, but everyone knew it was there.

Travis scraped the last of the rabbit stew from his bowl, mentally rehearsing how to relay his decision to his brothers.

As the oldest, it was his duty to do what was best for the family. It always had been. Therefore, he was the logical choice to marry Meredith. After all, it was because of him that she'd come to their land in the first place. None of his brothers should have to sacrifice his freedom for an unexpected bride just because—

"I'll do it." Crockett's proclamation slammed into Travis's carefully formulated rationale and shattered it like a stone hitting window glass.

Travis gulped down his mouthful of stew, his empty bowl thunking onto the table as he pierced his brother with a hard glare. "What do you mean, you'll do it?"

"I'll marry up with her." Crockett shrugged and glanced around the table, his palms turned upward before him. "What? She's decent enough to look at and handles herself well in a crisis. A man could do worse."

A man could do worse? *That* was his reasoning? Travis could just imagine the kind of husband Crock would make with that attitude. What was he thinking? There was no way—

"I'll wrestle you for her." Jim propped his elbow on the table, his open hand extended in challenge.

"Hold on!" Travis pushed out of his chair and braced his arms on the edge of the table next to Crockett, his heated blood pumping hard through his veins. "No one is going to wrestle over Meredith as if she were the last piece of Christmas pie. Show some sense. Besides, I've already decided that I'm the one to marry her. It's my fault she's here. She's my responsibility."

Instead of looking abashed, Jim quirked a cocky grin at him. "'Fraid you'd lose to me, big brother?"

"I'd whip you any day of the week, *Bowie*, and you know it." Travis threw the despised name in Jim's face, ready to wrestle more than his arm if need be.

Jim kicked his chair out of the way and lurched to his feet, his face a thundercloud. The two squared off, hands fisted, eyes narrowed, the table the only thing separating them. Travis stepped around the barrier. Jim mirrored him, no longer his brother but a rival—a man who matched him in height, breadth, and most likely strength. Everything but experience.

And desire.

Yesterday he had come to grips with the idea of Meredith returning home to her uncle and perhaps marrying a druggist or banker someday, a man he didn't know and would never see. But there was no way he could stand to have her living in his house, belonging to one of his brothers. If an Archer was going to lay claim to her, by George, it was going to be him!

"You're not really gonna whup him, are you, Trav?" Neill's wide eyes came into focus at the edge of Travis's vision, and like a well-aimed snowball, the truth of what he was about to do slapped him in the face and left him cold.

Immediately, Travis relaxed his stance and opened his hands. "No, I . . ." Had he really been contemplating thrashing his own brother? His fingers trembled slightly as he lifted his hand to rub his jaw. "Sorry, Jim. With everything that's happened lately, I suppose I'm a bit on edge."

Jim raised a skeptical brow, but Travis held his gaze without further apology. Finally, Jim nodded and bent to retrieve his chair. The tension in the room dissipated. Travis exhaled a long breath and returned to his seat.

"So how do you propose we decide which of the three of us gets her?" Crockett asked, dashing Travis's hopes that the others would simply accept his wishes.

"Three?" Neill piped up. "Don't be leavin' me outta the mix."

As if Crockett and Jim weren't bad enough.

Travis stared at his youngest brother, his left temple suddenly throbbing. "You're barely old enough to shave, Neill. You wouldn't know what to do with a wife."

"I'm as much a man as the rest of you." Neill sat forward with a confidence that demanded respect. "I do the same work, wear the same clothes. I ain't gonna be cheated outta my chance to have a gal of my own just 'cause I'm the youngest. Shoot. She might not even want an old geezer like you, Trav."

A chuckle erupted from Crockett, and Travis shook his head, feeling older by the minute.

"The kid's got a point," Crockett said when his laughter subsided. "We don't exactly come into contact with marriageable females on a regular basis out here. Who's to say how long it'll take the Lord to drop another one in our lap."

Travis leaned his forearms on the table, unable to argue the truth of that statement. "Any suggestions?"

Crockett rubbed his neck. Jim crossed his arms. Neill eyed the ceiling.

Travis glanced around the room for inspiration, as if the perfect idea might be hiding behind the coffeepot or under the stove. He needed some way to assuage his brothers while still ensuring Neill didn't end up as the groom. As the head of the family, he could simply claim first rights, but that could cause a rift. And the last thing they needed with Mitchell breathing down their necks was a lack of unity. No, there had to be a better way.

His gaze traveled over the cabinet that held his mother's dishes and drifted past the doorway to the bathing room. Something tickled his peripheral vision, and he looked back to the wall. A broom stood in the corner. Travis sat up straighter, a germ of an idea taking root. It would require some trickery, but he should be able to pull it off.

"Boys," he said, slapping his palms on the tabletop. "We're going to draw straws."

13

A loud crash awakened Meredith. Blinking, she eased herself to a sitting position and listened, trying to piece together what was happening.

The Archers were arguing about something in the kitchen. Something that had them quite upset. Meredith frowned and tossed back the covers. It probably had to do with her uncle's embarrassing demands. The whole episode came back to her with humiliating clarity. The only good thing about the entire encounter was that Uncle Everett had declared her no longer good enough for Roy Mitchell.

Never had she been so thankful to be found wanting. She just wished it hadn't hurt so much to hear him say so.

As Meredith stretched her toes toward the floor and reached for the headboard, the discussion in the kitchen escalated. She heard her name and something about Christmas pie. She had no earthly idea what Christmas pie had to do with anything, but one thing was clear—the argument involved her.

Meredith frowned and hauled herself to her feet. This was not the Archers' problem to solve. It was hers. She never should have let Travis believe differently. She'd just been so weary when her uncle left, that handing over her burden for a time had been too comforting a prospect to resist.

Well, her energy had been restored, and it was time to reclaim ownership of the situation. Meredith stepped away from the bed, determination subduing her dizziness as she tottered across the room. Her heart might have fluttered at the thought of Travis becoming her husband, but what woman wanted her man forced to the altar? No. She'd have to find another way to deal with this mess.

As she reached the doorway, another thought brought her up short. If she didn't marry an Archer, would Uncle Everett make her marry Roy? Meredith inhaled a shaky breath and leaned her back against the wall.

If Roy coveted her land half as much as she thought he did, he'd waste no time convincing Uncle Everett that her sullied reputation meant nothing to him. He'd probably even offer to marry in all haste to minimize the scandal, further endearing himself to her aunt and uncle and blinding them to his true nature—a wolf hiding beneath a fancy wool overcoat.

Aunt Noreen would insist the marriage take place, and if Meredith proved incapable of swaying Uncle Everett from that course—a most likely prospect—she'd have no recourse but to flee. Away from Roy Mitchell's schemes. Away from her aunt's controlling ways. A lump lodged itself in her throat. Away from Travis.

A dull ache spread across her chest. All her life she'd dreamed of marrying Travis Archer. But he wasn't a dream. Not anymore. He was flesh and blood and just down the hall. Could she really give him up when he was finally within reach?

Travis hunkered down next to the broom and broke off a handful of straw from an already frayed edge. After selecting the pieces most similar in length—and tucking one of them inside the cuff of his sleeve—he strode back to the table.

"Everyone's agreed that this will settle the matter, correct?" Travis eyed his brothers and waited for each of them to nod. "Good." He tossed four pieces of straw onto the table. "Crockett, shorten one of the straws."

Crockett snapped about an inch off the end of one of the straws and tossed the leftover piece onto the floor. Then before anyone else could volunteer for the duty, Travis snatched the straws up and turned his back.

He arranged the straws in his fist, making sure each end stood at a height equal to the others. But instead of including the short straw, he withdrew the fourth long straw from his shirt sleeve and added it to the mix. A pang of guilt shot through him. He'd always demanded honesty from his brothers and never gave them anything less than that himself. Until now.

Not wanting to examine his motives too closely, Travis shoved the short straw into his sleeve and told himself what he was doing was for the good of the family. Then, with a deep breath, he spun around to face his brothers.

"All right. Who's first?"

Neill reached out a hand. "Here goes nothing." He closed his eyes and grabbed. When he spied the long straw, a crooked smile twitched across his face an instant before a more solemn expression crowded it out. "Well, it ain't gonna be me, fellas."

Travis's guilt eased at the boy's obvious relief. He swiveled toward Jim next, and when he, too, pulled out a long straw, there was no indication of strong feelings one way or the other. He simply waggled his brows at Crockett and Travis, then propped a foot on the seat of his chair and leaned an elbow on his knee.

"Guess it's you or me, Crock." Travis extended the final two straws to his eldest brother, tightening his grip to ensure the fourth straw didn't escape when the third one was tugged free.

Crockett eyed both options and frowned a bit in concentration. Travis had to focus to keep his hand steady. Was Crock trying to pick the short one or the long one? Did he actually have feelings for Meredith? His offer to marry the gal earlier had seemed practical, not personal. But what if there was more to it than that?

Travis clenched his jaw, his thoughts growing defiant. What if there *was* more to it? Crock didn't share a history with Meredith, and he sure as shootin' wasn't the guy Meri had said she'd dreamed about.

"Loosen your grip, Trav," Crockett said, breaking into his thoughts. "I can't pull my straw out."

Heat climbed up Travis's neck. "Sorry."

Crockett shook his head and grinned as he pulled the third straw free, but his smile faded as he examined his piece. "It's a long one."

"Guess that means Travis gets her," Neill proclaimed.

Crockett grasped Travis's wrist. "Let's see the straw first."

Panic shot through Travis. How was he going to make the switch? He needed a distraction—something unexpected, something . . .

"You're drawing *straws*?" Meredith stepped into the kitchen, her night-gown swirling about her ankles, her hair mussed, her eyes shooting blue fire.

Every male eye in the room locked onto the honey-haired virago. Travis had no idea how many seconds ticked by before he realized that Crockett's hand had fallen away. He quickly dropped the long straw, scraped his boot over it, and sent it skittering back toward the wall as he shook the short one down into his cupped palm.

When he looked back up, her anger pierced him. However, it was the hurt hiding behind the sparks in her eyes that made his heart ache. "Meredith, I—"

"Four grown men put their heads together," she said, cutting him off as she reached to the wall for support, "and *this* is the solution you come up with? *Drawing straws?*"

"Jim wanted to arm wrestle—*oomph*." Neill's explanation died as Jim's elbow connected with the kid's stomach.

Meredith speared the two of them with a quick glare, then dropped her hand to her side and stalked toward Travis. Crockett sidled out of range.

"So this is how you see to things, is it? How diplomatic of you to leave my future in the hands of chance. I'm surprised you didn't throw an extra straw in the mix for Roy Mitchell. Might as well give him a shot, too. But then he'd have my land, which would increase his determination to get his hands on yours in order to complete his enterprise, and you couldn't allow that. After all, the land always comes first with you. Isn't that right, Travis? The land and your brothers."

Somehow Travis managed not to flinch under the barrage of sarcasm. He held her gaze until she finally dropped her eyes from his face to someplace lower. Her hand closed over his. A shiver of pleasure mixed with dread snaked up his arm. She drew his fist up between them and gently extracted the short straw from his grasp.

"The land and your brothers," she repeated softly. "Of course you drew the short straw. How else could you spare your brothers from the burden of being shackled to me?"

"It's not like that, Meri." Travis reached for her hand, but she pulled it away the instant his fingers grazed her knuckles.

"I expected better from you, Travis." Her words hacked into him like an ax in a tree trunk, and he swayed a bit from the impact. The trust he'd grown accustomed to seeing in her eyes had dimmed to disappointment.

"I expected better from all of you." She stepped back, creating an invisible chasm between her and the men who had let her down. "Did it never occur to you that I might actually want some say in my future? Or did you assume I would meekly accept whatever the four of you decided and thank you for lifting the heavy burden of thinking for myself off my weak female shoulders?"

Silence smothered the room.

Travis swallowed the excuses he'd been feeding himself—the fact that she'd been asleep, that she was under his protection, that she'd seemed to welcome his assistance when he'd promised to see to things for her.

He knew what it felt like to have fate decide your future. If he had stayed home and watched over his brothers like his father had told him to that day fourteen years ago, he never would have been caught in a thunderstorm. And if his father hadn't gone searching for him, he never would have been thrown from his horse when the lightning stuck. And if his father hadn't been thrown, he never would have incurred the wounds that led to his death.

Travis fidgeted as old guilt erupted to mingle with new.

Joseph Archer had extracted an oath from his son that day. An oath borne of desperation and a desire to protect the sons he was leaving behind. An oath that placed a heavy burden on the thin shoulders of a fifteen-year-old boy. But that boy took it on without complaint. Travis's dreams and plans no longer mattered. He had to atone for the damage his disobedience had caused. Guarding Archer land and the Archer family became his sole duty—his road to redemption.

Meredith's situation, however, had no root in disobedience. It was kindness alone that set her on this path. Unlike him, she didn't deserve to have her future wrested from her hands.

"You're right, Meredith." Travis shifted his weight and forced himself to meet her gaze. "We should have waited and discussed the matter with you."

"Yes. You should have."

"Would you like to discuss things now?" He held out his palms and took a cautious step forward.

"I'm not a spooked horse that needs to be placated." Her dry tone halted him in his tracks. He lowered his hands, a reluctant grin curving his lips.

He *had* been approaching her that way, hadn't he? Funny that he'd failed to recognize it until she called him on it. The gal was perceptive. And intelligent. Perhaps it was time to take the kid gloves off and treat her as he would one of his brothers.

Travis leaned his hip against the corner of the table. "All right, Meredith. No placating. No sugarcoating. Here's where we stand."

She crossed her arms and braced her legs apart like a warrior willing to talk peace while still prepared to battle should talk prove ineffectual. With an arched brow, she nodded for him to continue.

Travis ticked off his arguments on his fingers. "Your reputation is tattered. You have no home except for a house on a piece of land that Mitchell will do anything to get his hands on. You can marry Mitchell and live the rest of your life with a man you despise, or you can refuse his suit and see what vile scheme he concocts to steal your land from you. He could burn you out like he tried to do with us, or he could compromise you in order to force you to the altar. No matter how capable or careful you are, a woman alone has little chance against a man like him."

Meredith kept her head high and her face schooled, but the fabric around her knees wavered. Travis grabbed two chairs. Whether it was trepidation or her injury that was causing her to tremble, he didn't know. But he wasn't about to let her fall to the ground. He set one chair beside her and turned the other around and straddled it. Then he continued his assessment as if it didn't matter to him if she sat or not.

"Your only other option is to marry one of us." He paused. "Me." Travis suddenly felt the need to clear his throat. "This alternative would repair your reputation, give you a place to live, and provide the protection of four able-bodied men. Unless you have something else to suggest . . . ?"

"Actually, there is something else." Her quiet statement startled him.

"There is?" He glanced over at Crockett. His brother shrugged.

Meredith slowly lowered herself into the straight-back chair, the fight draining from her. "I could leave Anderson County. I could go farther west to where the railroad is opening new towns, or head to a larger city where no one knows me." Her chin jutted upward. "I could find work. Make a clean start."

Leave Anderson County? Travis frowned. He hadn't considered that option. Didn't really want to, either. It was reckless. Dangerous. And for some odd reason . . . disappointing. Besides, he'd already settled his mind on this marrying business. No sense muddying the waters.

"You're a good man, Travis. An honorable man." Meredith plucked at her sleeve. "You drew the short straw, and you're willing to stand before a preacher because you feel responsible for me. But you're not. I made the decision to come here, and I'll deal with the consequences. You deserve to have a wife of your own choosing, not one forced on you through circumstances outside your control."

"It's not like that, Meredith. It's . . ." Travis sighed and rubbed his jaw. Why did she say nothing about what *she* deserved? He didn't know much about the workings of the female mind, but he knew one thing—she deserved a choice.

"I'm not going to force you, Meredith. If you believe leaving is the best option, I'll not stop you. But if you think you might be able to make a home for yourself here, with a bunch of unrefined men, we'd like you to stay. *I'd* like you to stay."

Stretching his hand across the space that separated them, he caressed her cheek with his knuckles, then let his arm fall away. "You're a fine woman, Meredith Hayes. You're strong and brave and kind. And should you decide to take a chance on me, I'd be honored to make you my bride."

14

Meredith gripped the edge of the chair seat with her left hand as a new light-headedness assaulted her. Travis Archer had just proposed. Really proposed. Sure, he'd made no mention of love, but he had only been in her company for three days—four if she counted the day she stepped in that trap twelve years ago. The man needed time to catch up. After all, she'd been in love with him since she was ten. She had a bit of a head start.

But did he really want her? What if his pretty words were just flattery? Travis didn't strike her as the manipulative type, yet if she agreed to marry him, she'd be risking her entire future on an idealized impression. What if she was wrong?

"Meredith?"

She blinked and refocused on the man in front of her. The man who could be her husband if she gave the word. The man she wanted more than any other. The man who could hurt her more than any other.

She bit her lip and glanced at the other Archers spaced about the room. All eyes lingered on her. Waiting. Leaving the decision in her hands.

How was she supposed to know what to do? If she married Travis and he never returned her feelings, she'd be miserable for the rest of her life. But if she ran away when there *was* a chance for her and Travis to find love together, she'd be running away from her greatest hope.

"Meri? Are you all right?" Travis's rugged features softened in concern. He lifted his hand as if to touch her cheek again, and Meredith bolted out of her chair. Out of his reach. Her head throbbed at the sudden movement, and the floor seemed to roll beneath her feet, but she couldn't let him touch her again. His tenderness would cloud her judgment.

Recalling how Travis had extricated himself from her uncle earlier in the day, Meredith took a shaky step backward and employed the same tactic. "I'll give you my decision in the morning."

Travis's eyes met hers for a long penetrating moment. Then he nodded. "Fair enough."

He didn't offer to see her to her room, and though a small part of her was disappointed, a larger part was grateful. He seemed to sense her need to exert what little control she had over her situation and respected her choice to do so.

She limped back to her bedroom, the air taking on more of a chill the farther she moved from the kitchen. Logic said it was the loss of the cookstove's heat, but Meredith feared it had more to do with walking away from Travis.

A solitary tear rolled down her cheek as she closed the door. She leaned her back against it and sucked in a quivery breath. Why was this happening to her? How had things become so complicated? All she'd wanted to do was help Travis, yet instead, she'd trapped him—trapped him in his own honor, an honor more ironclad than the steel trap that had closed around her leg all those years ago.

She should grant him his freedom. Just as he had freed her from the steel jaws of that trap, she should free him from his self-imposed responsibility.

Stiffening her spine and her resolve, Meredith marched across the room to the bed. But when her hand closed around the bedpost and she sank down to the mattress, both her spine and her resolve weakened. She opened her right fist and stared at the short straw in her palm. Out of all the brothers, Travis had ended up with the short straw. Was it a sign that she should stay? God's will?

Meredith pressed her forehead against the curved wood of the bedpost and groaned. Why did the choice have to be so hard? Why couldn't God make his will simpler to discern?

"Seek the Lord, and his strength."

Meredith lifted her head. Those words. They were from one of the Psalms her father had helped her memorize as a child.

"Seek the Lord, and his strength."

They ran through her mind again, eclipsing all other thought, resonating with her soul. The answer to her immediate dilemma remained as murky as before, yet a new clarity emerged. She'd been seeking answers within herself, not from the Lord.

No wonder none of this makes sense, God. Only you can see what the future holds. Therefore, only you can guide me in the direction that is best. Please make the way clear. Help me make the right decision.

Meredith tightened her grip on the bedpost and hoisted herself back to her feet. Travis had mentioned something about a Bible he kept in his bureau when he brought her that book of western tales yesterday—in case she preferred it to the male adventure novel. She hadn't thought much of it since, but suddenly her spirit hungered for the wisdom it contained.

She found it in the second drawer she opened, next to a mahogany keepsake box. The black leather cover was well worn, with cracks running parallel to the spine and part of the gold lettering rubbed away from the bottom of the *H* in *Holy*. It fit comfortably in her hand, as if it belonged there, and for the first time since she'd awakened, a hint of peace fluttered about her heart. It didn't fully alight, but its nearness brought her a much-needed assurance that she was on the right path.

Clutching the Bible to her chest, Meredith petitioned the Lord again for guidance and understanding, then crawled onto the bed, propped the pillows against the headboard, and settled in for a long night of prayer and searching. Whenever a verse tugged at her memory, she'd look through the Scriptures until she found it. She'd read it and reread it, trying not to form conclusions but simply absorb what God's Word was saying. On several occasions, she dozed off in the midst of a prayer, yet when she stirred, her fingers still marked the passages the Lord had led her to. As the first hint of dawn lightened the room, she read back over the verses she had marked.

"Be kindly affectioned one to another with brotherly love; in honour preferring one another . . . Distributing to the necessity of saints; given to hospitality."

She flipped from Romans to Hebrews.

"And let us consider one another to provoke unto love and to good works: not forsaking the assembling of ourselves together, as the manner of some is; but exhorting one another. . . ."

Meredith turned a couple of pages to the next passage. "*Let brotherly love continue. Be not forgetful to entertain strangers: for thereby some have entertained angels unawares."*

And finally, the verses from First Peter that filled her with purpose. "*Likewise, ye wives, be in subjection to your own husbands; that, if any obey not the word, they also may without the word be won by the conversation of the wives."*

Over the course of the night, a growing sense of certainty had blossomed within her as she meditated on the verses the Lord had led her to. A thread of similarity ran through them all—a theme of service, of love, of hospitality. She had thought her decision hinged on what was best for her, but as the approaching sunrise tinted the sky with pink, she finally understood that, in truth, it hinged on what best fit in with God's plan. A God who was faithful, a God who desired his children to serve one another in love and to spur one another on to good works, a God who could use a wife to gently sway a husband to a life of greater faith.

Even when sleep claimed her during the night, she'd dreamed in images and ideas. The Archers imprisoned on their own land. The sign at the gate threatening away all visitors. Loneliness. Isolation. *"Love thy neighbour."*

She'd found no promises of any love more than brotherly love. She'd found no assurance of happiness beyond the joy inherently found in hope. But what she had found was purpose and a belief that God could work through her to bring about good for Travis. And the rightness of it resonated in her soul.

Meredith turned the pages back to Romans, to where she had placed Travis's short straw as a marker. Once again she read the precious promise written in the eighth chapter. *"And we know that all things work together for good to them that love God, to them who are the called according to his purpose."*

She inhaled deeply through her nose, and her eyes slid closed. "I don't know if Travis will ever love me, but I pray you will help me to trust in your promise, Lord. Help me to believe that you will work things out for our good so that I will not fall prey to bitterness or discontent. I'm leaping, Lord. Please don't let me fall."

Exhausted from the long night, yet oddly invigorated at the same time, Meredith climbed out of bed and padded over to the window to watch the sunrise brighten the trees. The dull ache in her head reminded her of her injury, but the floor respectfully stayed put instead of rising and falling as it had yesterday. She smiled and silently thanked God for small blessings. It wouldn't do for the bride to stagger around like a drunkard on her wedding day.

Travis stared at his jawline in the small square of mirror that hung in the bathing room and drew the straight razor down his cheek. He winced as the blade nicked the edge of his ear. Adjusting his grip, he rinsed the shaving soap from the razor and reached up for another stroke. His fingers trembled. Travis frowned. A lack of sleep combined with a prolonged sense of uncertainty had stolen his usual steadiness.

How was a man supposed to prepare for his wedding day when he didn't even know if the bride was going to show up? Not that he blamed Meredith for her indecision. A person needed time to settle something this big in her mind. It was just that he was accustomed to being the one who did the settling. He gathered input from his brothers, chewed over the ramifications, rendered a verdict, and put it into action. Simple. Direct. Practical.

Meredith, on the other hand, left him stuck in the chewing phase while she mulled through her problem without his assistance. He'd been tempted more than once to knock on her door and ask if she'd reached any conclusions, but good sense had prevailed and he'd left her alone. Now that the sun had crested the horizon and it was officially morning, however, the desire to know his fate had him back on edge.

The razor snagged a spot on his chin, and Travis scowled as a drop of blood beaded on his jaw. *Great*. With the way things were going, he'd end up with enough scratches on his face to have Meredith thinking one of the displaced barn cats had mistaken him for a mouse. Not exactly the impression one wanted to make on a woman who had yet to make up her mind concerning his worthiness as a mate. He'd dug himself into a deep enough hole last night without inviting more unfavorable scrutiny this morning.

"Coffee's on," Jim growled in a sleep-roughened voice as he plodded through the bathing room, the wire egg basket dangling from his meaty fingers.

Travis had never really noticed how incongruous a picture the big man made carrying the thin basket, since Jim had been in charge of all food chores and cooking duties since the time he was ten. But as Travis held his razor away from his neck and watched his brother exit, he couldn't help imagining what it would be like to have Meredith squeeze past him with the basket, her skirt brushing his pant leg, maybe a smile curving her lips as their eyes met in the shaving mirror.

The sting of the blade biting into his neck brought him back to reality. "Thunderation!" He hadn't been this clumsy with a shave since he was Neill's age.

"Nervous, Trav?" Crockett stood in the doorway, one shoulder propped against the jamb. The fellow looked far too well rested and chipper for Travis's taste, and the teasing gleam in his brother's eye rubbed over him like sandpaper.

"Worried she'll turn you down, or afraid she won't?"

Travis glared at him in the mirror and swiped the razor under his chin for the final stroke. Ignoring the quiet chuckle behind him, Travis set the blade aside and rinsed the soap residue from his face before toweling dry. If he was lucky, Crockett would be gone by the time he finished.

He lowered the towel from his face and stole a glance toward the door. *Drat*. Luck never had favored him much.

"You know, I could stand in for you if you're not up to the task."

The words lit a fuse in Travis. He twisted to face his brother fully and jabbed his finger into Crockett's chest. "Leave it alone."

Tossing down the towel, he shoved his way through the blocked doorway and stormed over to the stove to check the coffee. As he reached into the cupboard to retrieve a mug, however, his conscience nudged him. Taking the cup in hand, he slowly reined in his temper. After a long moment, he reached for a second mug.

Travis poured two cups of coffee and motioned for Crockett to join him at the table. "Sorry I snapped at you."

Crockett shrugged and slid into a chair. "I knew the spot would be sore when I prodded it."

Travis shot a glare at him. "Then why'd you bring it up? For pete's sake, Crock, we're in enough of a mess without you stirring up more trouble. The matter's been decided. If Meredith chooses to marry, she'll marry me. That's the end of it."

Instead of firing back, Crockett stared at him over his coffee cup as he sipped the steaming brew. The silent survey lasted so long, Travis grew uncomfortable and finally dropped his gaze, suddenly finding it imperative that he unroll his shirtsleeves and fasten the button at each cuff.

The sound of Crockett's mug coming to rest on the tabletop brought Travis's head back up. The sparkle he was accustomed to seeing in his brother's eye glowed once again.

"I needed to be sure Meredith was marrying the right Archer."

Travis raised a brow. "And?"

Crockett smirked and lifted his cup to his lips. "Let's just say my concerns have been addressed."

15

Meredith twisted from side to side, examining her appearance in the mirror above Travis's bureau. Some bride she made, dressed in faded calico. In her dreams, she'd always worn blue brocaded satin with lace at the neckline and cuffs. She'd imagined her hair done up in an elaborate style. Perhaps a pearl comb or a spray of tiny flowers tucked into her tresses, depending on the time of year.

But with over half of her hairpins missing following her run-in with Samson, the best she'd managed was a braided chignon low on her nape. Her bangs had lost most of their curl and frizzed a bit at her forehead. She wound a strand around her finger, counted to fifty, and released it, but the rebellious ringlet failed to hold its curl. Huffing out a breath that sent all her bangs fluttering, Meredith smoothed a hand over her tremulous stomach and lifted her chin.

So what if this wasn't to be the wedding of her dreams. She was marrying the *man* of her dreams. That would be enough. Besides, a wedding was only an event. It was the life together following it that truly mattered. *Grow up, Meri. It's time to start putting sensibility ahead of sentimentality.*

Her shoulders sagged a bit as she examined the worn navy housedress hanging from her frame in all its wrinkled glory. *Was it too sentimental to wish for a prettier dress to wear?* She sighed. At least it didn't smell like smoke. The green dress she'd worn the night of the fire stank of the stuff, and she worried she might not be able to get all the soot stains out. One thing was for sure—when she took over the cleaning duties around here, laundry was going to top her list.

A knock sounded on the door. The butterflies she'd willed into submission earlier burst forth in a flurry of batting wings.

"Meri?" Travis's voice. "Your breakfast is ready."

"Thank you. I'll . . . I'll be right there." She spun away from the mirror and gripped the bedpost a final time, more to steady her nerves than her feet. Closing her eyes, she mentally recited her version of the promise of Romans 8:28. "*All things* will *work together for good. All things* will *work together for good.*"

Then, with a lift of her chin, she opened her eyes and strode to the door. She grasped the handle and pulled, only to find Travis waiting for her. He straightened from where he'd rested his back against the opposite wall, his widening eyes traversing from her face, down the length of her, and back up to her eyes. When his gaze connected with hers, the flare of male appreciation he failed to tame sent warm tingles skittering over her skin before he hid it behind a look of apology.

Meredith felt a blush warm her cheeks, but oddly enough, she felt no need for his apology. If anything, the look he'd given offered hope that, in time, there might be more than a relationship of duty between them.

"You're looking . . . better this morning," he said, breaking the silence at last. "How's your head?"

Meredith suddenly found it hard to hold his gaze. Her attention slid to the floor as she fidgeted with the edge of her sleeve. What was wrong with her? She'd been staring at the man just fine while he gawked at her, but now that he offered polite conversation, she turned into a mess of jumbled nerves. Really. It was too ridiculous.

She coughed softly and forced her chin up. "The dizziness is gone, so long as I don't move too quickly, and except for a dull ache behind my ear, my head is much improved." Darting a glance into his brownish-green eyes, she added, "Thank you for asking."

He smiled, then looked at the wall behind her. "I'm glad to hear it."

Now he was the one fidgeting. Meredith nearly giggled as the sole of his boot scraped back and forth over the floorboards. And what were those red marks along his jaw? The poor man looked like he'd been in a tussle with an angry chicken. She thought of one of her mother's laying hens that always used to peck at Meredith's hand. She'd been terrified of that bird until the day Mama finally tired of its antics and served it up for supper. Meri had never taken more delight in stabbing a knife into a chicken thigh than she had that night. Perhaps she ought to add roasted chicken to the Archers' menu this week.

"Did you . . . ah . . . arrive at any conclusions during the night?" Travis asked, lifting a hand to cover the red spot on his neck.

The chickens roosting in Meredith's mind vanished.

"I did." She fortified herself to look at him and waited until his eyes touched hers to continue. "If your offer still stands, Travis . . . I accept."

She sensed him sigh, even though no sound or movement evidenced such an event. And while she wouldn't necessarily describe his demeanor as overjoyed, the way his mouth curved up at one corner combined with the slight crinkling around his eyes communicated a positive reaction to her response that stretched beyond mere politeness.

"Good." He nodded once and gestured for her to continue on to the kitchen. "Jim held back some eggs for you in the skillet, and if Neill didn't get to it first, you might be able to scrounge up a scrap of ham, too. I'm gonna round up some clean clothes while you eat." Travis pointed to her room and headed that direction.

Well, technically it was *his* room. Although after spending so much time there the last few days, it felt like hers. Meredith crossed into the kitchen and picked up the empty plate that sat waiting for her on the table. When her hand closed over the spoon handle to ladle up what was left of the scrambled eggs, however, a new thought froze her where she stood.

Would it be *their* room tonight?

Meredith blinked and reminded herself to breathe as she scraped the last of the eggs and a tiny square of ham onto her plate. Somehow coffee ended up in her cup and her rear ended up in a chair, despite the fact that she had no recollection of accomplishing those tasks herself. As she bent her head to pray, thankfulness for her breakfast didn't even cross her mind.

Lord, I'm not sure I'm ready to be a wife. It seems a lot more daunting now that it's staring me in the face. I thought I was prepared, that my affection for Travis would make things easier, but all those lovely daydreams seem so juvenile in light of what is truly to come. Please don't let me embarrass myself. Give me the courage to be the wife he needs.

As she chewed the lukewarm, overdone eggs, Meredith vowed to be like the biblical woman Rebekah. If she could enter Isaac's tent on the first day they met and become his wife, surely Meredith could manage the same feat after knowing Travis three times as long.

Although . . . Rebekah had ended up with twins.

The square of ham she'd just swallowed lodged itself sideways in her throat. Meredith grabbed her coffee cup and gulped down a swig of the strong, bitter brew in an effort to keep from choking.

Good heavens. Contemplating the realities of life with a husband was frightening enough. Motherhood could wait a bit.

At least she didn't have to worry about facing Travis's brothers yet. Meredith eyed the mound of dishes waiting for her in the washtub with a wry quirk of her lips. It seemed they'd already abandoned the house to her care. Either that or it was their custom to save the dish washing till the end of the day.

Maybe they drew straws for that duty, too.

Travis yanked on the too-short sleeves of his father's old suit coat and scrunched his shoulders for fear of tearing out the back seam. His dad had always been such a large figure in his mind, Travis never imagined that his coat wouldn't fit. The thing was as old as the hills and musty as month-old bread, but it was the only decent suit coat in the house. Travis and his brothers certainly had no need for fancy duds, living the way they did. Or they hadn't until today.

So much for dressing for the occasion. Travis shrugged out of the coat and returned it to the bottom drawer of his bureau, where it would probably sit unused for another couple of decades. At least he had a clean shirt to wear. Of course, it was the scratchy white cotton one that always made his neck itch, but it was probably more appropriate wedding attire than the dark brown flannel he usually wore. And he could dress it up with his dad's black string tie—the one part of the suit guaranteed to fit.

Travis took out his mother's keepsake box and ran his hand over the rose pattern carved into the top of the mahogany lid. After seventeen years without her, his memories had faded. He remembered her smile, the way her arms felt around him when she hugged him in the morning before sending him off to school, the way she fussed at him for tracking mud into the house. But he couldn't recall the particular sound of her voice, or the precise color of her eyes. He thought they might have been green, but perhaps they'd been more brown, like his.

What would she think of his marriage? Would she approve? He didn't doubt that she'd like Meredith. Mama had always been a fighter, even at the end when the childbed fever finally claimed her life. Meredith possessed the same quality, in spades.

Travis opened the mahogany box and fingered the hodgepodge within. His father's watch, a packet of old letters, the three-legged dog he'd whittled for her one Christmas. Then his hand closed over the slender band he'd sought. Plain and not as shiny as he would have liked, yet the ring warmed his palm as if the love his parents shared still radiated from within its circle.

He didn't have a proper suit of clothes or a white clapboard church to offer, but his bride would have a ring—a ring representing all he hoped their relationship would one day become.

Before closing the box, he snatched the black ribbon that wove in and out of the treasures and strung it through the center of the ring. After knotting the ends of the tie securely around the gold band, he shoved both objects deep into his trouser pocket. With his father's tie and his mother's ring on hand, he'd be ready whenever Mr. Hayes showed up with the parson. In the meantime, he had work to do.

Travis slid his brown wool vest over the scratchy cotton shirt, wincing as the stiff material pressed against his back. He did up the buttons and grabbed his hat, catching a glimpse of himself in the mirror as he turned for the door.

Meredith wasn't getting much of a prize in their arrangement. Travis frowned at his razor-nicked face and saddle-bum clothes and thought about how pretty she'd looked stepping out of his room with her hair done up and her eyes glowing shyly at him. Seeing her only in a shapeless sleeping gown the last couple of days, he'd nearly forgotten what nice curves she had. The faded dress she wore with its snug bodice and trim waist brought all those memories rushing back.

Meredith Hayes was a fine specimen of a woman. And sometime later today, she was going to be his.

A rogue with a devilish grin stared back at him from the mirror. Travis winked at his reflection, settled his hat into place, and fought the urge to whistle as he headed outside to tend to his chores.

Roughly two hours later, before the sun hung fully overhead, the expected sound of gunfire ricocheted through the pines. Travis looked up from the pile of scorched tack he'd been sorting through, his gut suddenly knotting. *This is it.*

The banging over by the shed where the boys were reinforcing the lean-to halted. Neill and Jim emerged from the west side, hammers moving from right hand to left as they reached for their gun belts. Even knowing who their guest would be, they were ready for any trouble that might be riding shotgun. Travis straightened, pride infusing his stance. His brothers were competent men—Archers through and through. Whatever came through that gate, they'd handle together.

And it was a good thing, for when Crockett finally rode into view leading their guests, Travis noted that the wagon Everett Hayes drove carried a passenger who bore little resemblance to a preacher. Jim's indrawn breath echoed loudly in Travis's ear, and one glance at the dazed look on his brother's usually stoic face confirmed that trouble had indeed ridden shotgun—and their normal defense tactics would be useless.

16

The minute Everett Hayes reined in his team and set the wagon brake, the young gal at his side shot to her feet and grabbed a handful of pink skirt as if she meant to leap to the ground then and there. Travis had never seen Jim move so fast. Usually the deliberate one of the bunch, Jim's movements blurred as he holstered his weapon and dropped his hammer to the dirt, all while hustling toward the wagon before the pretty little blonde could alight on her own.

"Why, thank you," she said as she rested her hands on Jim's shoulders and allowed him to lift her to the ground. She beamed a smile at him that must have blinded the poor fellow, for all Jim could do was blink at her after he set her down. "Are you Travis?"

Jim's head wagged slowly in the negative, his eyes never leaving her face.

Travis's eyes rolled in a sardonic arc at his brother's absorption while he strode forward. Apparently an introduction was beyond Jim's abilities at the moment. He lifted a finger to his hat brim when he reached Jim's side and nodded to the petite lady with the china-doll face. "I'm Travis, ma'am. Travis Archer."

She examined his face and glanced over the rest of him, yet her inspection held such innocence, he couldn't exactly call her bold. Curious was probably a more apt description.

"A pleasure to meet you, sir. I'm Cassandra Hayes, Meredith's cousin." She turned one of those glaringly bright smiles loose on him, but his vision remained unaffected.

Oh, she was pretty all right, and there was something about the joy inherent in those smiles that made a man want to hang around and see how many he could draw out of her, but nothing significant stirred in Travis when she turned the full force of her sky-blue eyes on him. They were pale compared to the vibrancy of Meri's and didn't evidence the same depth of living.

"You *are* going to marry my cousin, aren't you?"

The young lady was certainly direct. Travis grinned and scratched a spot on his jaw with the back of his thumb.

"Cassie, dear," Everett Hayes murmured as he moved around the horses to position himself between his daughter and the Archer brothers. "We wouldn't have brought the preacher with us if there wasn't going to be a wedding."

Travis glanced past the pair in front of him to see Crockett talking quite animatedly to an older man climbing down from the back of a mule.

"Yes, Papa, but you only said she was marrying an Archer. You didn't specify which one."

When Jim continued staring at Cassandra, Everett Hayes scowled a warning at him, then took his daughter's arm and tugged her close to his side before smiling at her in a way that was so indulgent it bordered on condescending.

"It doesn't matter which one, darling. All that matters is that she marry."

Cassandra pulled her hand free and stared up at her father, tiny lines creasing her porcelain brow. "How can you say that, Papa? Of course it matters. Meredith has to marry Travis."

Everett's smile flattened. "Why?"

Travis tilted his head, eager to hear the answer himself. But before Cassandra could say anything, another voice rang out from the porch.

"Cassie?"

The distance did little to disguise the wonder on Meredith's face—wonder that quickly transformed into happiness so radiant that Travis wished he'd been the one responsible for it. Then she let out a little squeal and charged down the steps as if she hadn't just spent two days in bed after being kicked in the head by a mule.

Her cousin broke away from Everett and ran to meet Meredith, surprisingly unconcerned about the hem of her pretty pink dress dragging in the dirt. The two women embraced, and at once, Travis recognized the bond between them. Meredith loved her cousin the way he loved his brothers.

"How did you ever convince Aunt Noreen to let you come?" Meredith asked as she gently untangled herself from the embrace.

"I didn't ask." Cassandra waved away Meredith's arched look. "She never would have agreed, so there was no point."

"But she'll be livid about you exposing yourself to the scandal of the situation."

"I'm here with my father and a man of the cloth—surely that will protect me from any imagined taint. I couldn't miss your wedding. Not after all we've shared. I would have rented a horse and ridden here unescorted if I'd had to."

Meredith laughed softly. "You? On a horse? That would've been something to see."

Cassandra pulled a face and shuddered. "A horrendous sight, I'm sure. But I would have done it had Papa not relented and allowed me to join him in the wagon."

Travis's impression of the little princess bumped up a couple of notches. Perhaps there was a woman of character behind all the flirtatious smiles, after all. But the quick glance she darted toward Jim before linking her arm through Meredith's left no doubt that her being here still spelled trouble.

"The first thing we have to do," she said, as she steered Meredith toward the house, "is find you a different dress. You can't get married in that old thing."

"But I don't have—"

"Yes you do. I packed your trunks." Cassandra paused long enough to toss a softly pleading look Jim's way. "If one of these strong Archer men would be kind enough to bring them inside for us?"

In answer, Jim strode to the back of the wagon. Travis followed. It was only fitting that he help cart his future wife's belongings. Crockett could deal with Everett Hayes and the preacher.

The women left the front door ajar behind them, and when he and Jim entered the house, the aroma of cinnamon and baking swirled around them. Jim twisted toward the kitchen and raised an eyebrow but didn't pause on his way down the hall. Travis, on the other hand, took a moment to breathe in the delicious scent. He hadn't smelled anything like it since his mother passed on.

Cassandra was showing Jim where to set the first trunk when Travis arrived at the bedroom, so he took the opportunity to sidle up next to Meredith. "What're you baking?"

"Cinnamon rolls. They just came out of the oven." She dipped her chin as if embarrassed, although about what he couldn't figure. "I hope you don't mind. I know it probably seems silly considering the unusual circumstances surrounding the wedding, but I thought it would be nice to have some way to mark the occasion. You didn't have much sugar left, so I decided against a cake. I found a tin of cinnamon buried behind the coffee and thought sweet rolls might be an acceptable substitute."

He grinned. "I can't wait to taste them."

She smiled back, and a little frisson of pleasure coursed through him. Reluctantly, he stepped away and pulled the trunk off his shoulder to place it against the wall next to the one Jim had brought in. Travis turned back to Meredith, but before he could continue their conversation, Cassandra maneuvered between them and expertly shooed him out of his own room.

"Thank you, gentlemen. Why don't you show my father around while I help Meredith change?"

She closed the door before Travis could answer, which was probably for the best, since she was bound to dislike his response. There was no way he'd be showing Everett Hayes anything on his land except maybe the charred shell of his barn. The man was in business with Mitchell, and despite the ties he had to Meredith, he was the enemy.

"I have a surprise for you." Cassandra released the door handle and spun to face Meredith, her eyes glowing with secret glee. "Come see."

Meredith's tummy fluttered in anticipation as she followed in Cassandra's wake. Her cousin unbuckled the straps of the first trunk and threw open the lid with a flourish. "It's polished muslin instead of satin brocade, but it's blue and there's plenty of lace. What do you think?"

She twirled around, an Egyptian blue-and-ivory-striped gown pressed to her torso.

Tears welled in Meredith's eyes. "You're letting me borrow your courting dress?" Aunt Noreen had commissioned that dress from a local seamstress, and to the best of Meredith's recollection, Cassie had only worn it once.

"No, I'm giving it to you. Consider it a wedding gift. I let out the hem last night, so it shouldn't be too short." She slid an arm under the skirt and held it out for Meredith's inspection. "My stitches aren't quite as fine as the dressmaker's, but no one will be looking at your feet."

"Oh, Cass. It's b-beautiful." She barely got the words out before a sob lodged in her throat and cut off her ability to communicate.

Cassandra laid the dress on the bed and rushed to Meredith's side. "Now, don't start crying," her cousin admonished in a teasing voice. "You don't want your eyes to be all red and puffy when you exchange your vows with Travis." She reached into the pocket of her skirt and retrieved a handkerchief, then paused with her hand only half extended. "You *are* marrying Travis, aren't you?"

Meredith nodded vigorously as she wiped her cheeks with the back of her hand.

Cassandra let out a hearty sigh and handed her the lacy handkerchief. "Good. For a minute there, you had me worried."

Meredith dabbed her eyes and blew her nose before setting the soiled handkerchief aside and lifting her chin. Cassie was right. Travis wouldn't want to see her all red-eyed and weepy. He'd told her he admired her courage and fortitude. He wouldn't want a maudlin bride. She drew in a deep breath and squared her shoulders.

Cassandra nodded her approval and gave her a gentle push toward the bed, where the dress lay. "Now, let's get you changed."

Meredith smiled at her cousin as she reached for the buttons at her neck. "So, dear fairy godmother, did you bring me glass slippers, too?"

Cassandra laughed. "Didn't you hear? Glass slippers went out of fashion last century. All the fairy godmothers are providing kid leather nowadays." She knelt down by the trunk again and rummaged around until she finally pulled out Meredith's Sunday button-up heels. "See?"

The two giggled just like they had as girls huddled together on Cassie's bed, reading Perrault's tale of *Cinderella*. Meredith's worries floated away on the laughter. She felt lighter than she had in days.

Stepping out of her simple work dress, Meredith reached for the blue-striped skirt of Cassie's courting costume. "You really are my fairy godmother, you know," she said in all seriousness, fitting the skirt over her hips. "I was trying so hard to be practical about this impromptu wedding, telling myself that little things like a dress and a cake and a bouquet of flowers didn't really matter, but deep down I ached over not having them. Then you roll onto the ranch with everything I need to make this day special. Including yourself."

Cassandra helped her with the fastening at the back of the skirt, and once it was in place, Meredith twirled around and wrapped her arms around her cousin. "Getting married without Mama and Papa is hard enough, but I was certain that Aunt Noreen would keep you away, as well. Having you here is like a miracle, Cass. A lovely miracle that gives me hope for my future."

The two hugged each other tightly for a moment, then separated. Cassandra reached for the solid blue polonaise with the striped trim that fit over the skirt and held it out so Meredith could slip her arms into the sleeves. As it settled into place with its elegant draping in the back, Meredith snuck a peek at herself in the bureau mirror. "I've never worn anything so fine, Cass. I feel like a princess."

"Well, you should." Her smiling eyes met Meredith's in the glass. "Your prince is certainly handsome. No wonder your infatuation lasted all these years. The Archer men are a comely bunch—those rugged physiques and the mysterious air surrounding them. Did you ever learn why they are so adamant about keeping to themselves?"

After twelve years, the Archers were grown men and no longer faced the dangers that threatened them when they were children, but even so, Meredith couldn't bring herself to share what little she knew. It seemed disloyal to Travis somehow, and if he was to be her husband, he deserved her loyalty. Perhaps if he grew to trust her, he would grow to love her as well.

Meredith turned away from the mirror and gathered up her shoes along with the button hook Cassie had dug out of the trunk. "I've been laid up in bed, Cass, recovering from an injury. We haven't exactly had time to delve into the Archer family secrets."

"I suppose not. More's the pity." She sat on the bed behind Meredith and began undoing her cousin's braids. "I guess I forgot about your injury in all the wedding excitement. You seem to be much recovered."

"The dizziness has passed, for the most part, but my head still aches a bit. Oh, and the area behind my left ear is rather tender," she warned as Cassandra tugged a hairpin free near the spot where Samson's hoof had collided with her skull.

Cassie's hands immediately gentled. "I'll be careful."

Once the braids were undone, she ran the brush through Meredith's hair and Meredith closed her eyes as the bristles massaged her scalp, sending delightful tingles along her neck.

"It's too bad we don't have time to roll your hair in rag curls," Cassie said. "You look so pretty in ringlets. But the wave from your braids will give us just the right volume for a lovely French twist. And I have ribbons to dress it up even more. Travis won't be able to take his eyes off of you when we get done."

Meredith allowed herself a smile as she submitted to her cousin's artful ministrations. She knew she was no great beauty, and the prettiest hair in the world couldn't hide her limp or make up for the fact that she was a bride of duty instead of love. But if Travis could look at her this morning with appreciation flaring in his eyes when all she'd worn was a faded housedress, perhaps seeing her in full bridal finery would dissolve any lingering regret he harbored from drawing that short straw.

She'd vowed to the Lord last night to do her best to be the wife Travis needed, but in her heart of hearts, she desperately wished to be the wife he wanted.

17

Travis paced along the front of the house. An hour. Meredith and her cousin had been closed up in his room for an hour. How long did it take a woman to change her dress, for pity's sake? He was going to be out a full day's work at this rate.

Crockett was doing his best to keep the visitors entertained. Well, the parson, at least. The two of them were sitting on the porch discussing sermon topics and spiritual flock tending as if they had known each other for years.

Jim and Neill had returned to work on the lean-to, promising to come as soon as the women were ready. That left Travis with Everett Hayes, a man he respected little and trusted even less. They'd run out of things to say to each other after the first five minutes. So now, Everett Hayes sat on the porch eyeing the Archer pines as if he were measuring them for his mill while Travis paced the yard in front of the house, tension coiling tighter in his gut with each pass.

By the time the front door finally opened, he'd wound himself so tight, he nearly sprang out of his boots.

Cassandra stood in the doorway, one of those dazzling smiles on her face. "Thank you for your patience, gentlemen. We're ready for you to take your places in the parlor."

As she slipped back into the house, Travis mumbled, "It's about time."

Everett Hayes had the gall to wink at him. "Better get used to it, Archer. Things are never the same after you install a woman in your house."

"That is true," the parson said as he pushed up out of his chair, his expression slightly censorious as he glanced at Everett. "But if the Lord is installed, as well, the changes can bring blessing to a man." He shifted his attention and peered at Travis. "Marriage is a sacred union, son, and not something to dread. As Ecclesiastes says, 'Two are better than one, because they have a good reward for their labor. . . . A threefold cord is not quickly broken.' Keep God woven into your relationship and this union will make you stronger. But if you treat it as a burden, it will become one."

Travis stared into the kind eyes of the preacher and nodded. This was not the time to fret over work going undone or to stew about Everett Hayes and his connection to Mitchell. This was the time to focus on family, old and new. For that is what Meredith would be after today—family. And as such, she deserved his consideration and his patience. The work would keep.

"You all go in," he said. "I'll fetch Jim and Neill."

Travis made his way toward the lean-to, and when his brothers came into view, he called out a greeting and waved them in.

Neill jogged over to meet him. "It's time, Trav?"

"Yep."

"It's sure gonna be strange having a girl livin' here." Neill leaned against the wall of the shed, his knees and elbows poking out at odd angles. "I reckon I'll hafta start pullin' on my trousers before I go use the outhouse at night, huh?"

Travis fought to keep a straight face. The boy looked seriously aggrieved by the inconvenience. "Yep, I reckon so. But at least you won't have to worry about the washing anymore."

Neill's face brightened considerably at that. "Jim told me that she'd be taking over the cookin' but he didn't mention nothing 'bout the washin'." He bounced away from the shed and gave a little hop toward the house. "C'mon, Trav. Get a move on. We gotta get you hitched!"

Travis chuckled. "Go clean up at the pump, scamp. I'll be there in a minute." Neill trotted off, and Travis turned to Jim. "You think the kid's glad to get off laundry detail?"

"He might change his tune when all his duds start smellin' like flowers," Jim groused.

"Why would they start smelling like flowers?"

Jim shrugged. "Just stands to reason that if a woman starts handlin' a man's clothes they'd start smellin' like her. And women smell like flowers."

"Meredith doesn't smell like flowers." Travis frowned. He remembered the rose scent the schoolmarm used to douse herself in. He'd never misbehaved in class for fear he'd suffocate if he had to stand in the corner next to her desk. Meredith smelled nothing like that. She smelled . . . well . . . like Meredith. Like cinnamon and sunshine.

"Cassie does."

Travis hadn't noticed anything particular about the way Meredith's cousin smelled, but he wasn't about to argue. Instead, he clapped his brother on the shoulder and quirked a grin at him. "We'll all have some adjustments to make—Meredith included. And no matter what our clothes end up smelling like, the woman's family, now. Remember that."

Jim's mouth curved slightly upward. Then he nodded and clasped Travis's arm, sealing the silent pact. Archers stood together, no matter what. Not even frilly-smelling laundry could tear them apart.

Jim released his grip and moved past. Travis pivoted to follow, but something caught his eye near the fence surrounding the garden plot behind the house. Near the gate stood a small brushy shrub, its branches intertwined with the wooden pickets. Most of the tiny white blooms that had dotted it earlier that fall had faded, but one section still blossomed. Travis altered his course.

Meredith might not smell like flowers, but that didn't mean she wouldn't like some. His mother had always kissed his cheek whenever he picked wild flowers for her. She'd fussed over them and put them in a jar with some water and told him what a thoughtful boy he was for bringing her such a pretty present. It seemed like a paltry offering now that he was older, but maybe he'd get lucky and it would make Meredith smile.

Hunkering down beside the fence, he took his pocketknife and hacked off the thick stems holding the largest clusters of flowers. The reddish centers of the calico asters stood out against the spiny white petals as he ordered and reordered the stems, trying to decide which arrangement looked the best. Not having a clue how to make such a judgment, he finally just shoved them together and pulled a white cotton handkerchief from his pocket. After the awkward job of rolling the fabric diagonally against his thigh with one hand, he wrapped it around the stems like a bandage around a wounded arm and knotted it off.

Travis shoved his hand deep into his trouser pocket to make sure his mother's ring was still there. He'd removed it from the string tie after bringing in the trunks and fashioned the black ribbon into a floppy bow under his shirt collar in anticipation of his imminent marriage. Only the ceremony hadn't been as imminent as he'd thought, so the thing had strangled him for the last hour. But his bride was finally ready to put him out of his misery and get the deed done.

Hating to be the last one arriving at his own wedding, Travis jogged up to the back porch and entered the house through the bathing room. He paused long enough to check the straightness of his tie in the shaving mirror, then inhaled a deep breath and strode through the kitchen and down the hall to the parlor.

The parson stood at the front of the room near the woodstove, an open Bible in his hand and a welcoming smile on his lips. His brothers stood in a line in front of the sofa, while Everett and Cassandra Hayes held places near the bookcase.

The one person he didn't see was Meredith.

Then a soft rustling from the corner behind him drew his attention. "It's not too late to change your mind, you know." Meredith's husky whisper met his ears before he'd fully turned.

A gallant denial sprang to his lips, but the moment he saw her, his ability to speak vanished. She was a vision. Her honey-colored hair was rolled against her head in thick, soft twists accented by loops of blue ribbon with long tails that draped along the side of her neck. Travis's fingers itched to follow the trail of those ribbons, to brush the tender skin at her nape.

Her lashes were lowered, and he wondered at her shyness until he recalled that he hadn't answered her comment. "Meri, look at me," he murmured in a quiet tone that no one would overhear.

Those thick, dark lashes lifted slowly, and the blue of her eyes, made even more vibrant by the blue of her dress, pierced his heart. Her teeth nibbled her bottom lip as she forced her gaze to hold his.

"I'll not be changing my mind."

Her shoulders relaxed and a tentative smile tugged at the corners of her mouth. His own mouth curved in response. Then he remembered the awkward bouquet he'd brought. Feeling a little sheepish, he raised his arm and held it out to her.

"It's not much, but I thought you might like them."

Her breath caught and for a moment she did nothing but stare at the rustic offering. Unable to see her eyes, Travis's doubts grew. "I know they're just a bunch of weeds, so don't feel like you have to carry them. It was probably a stupid idea anyway." As his mumbled excuses tapered off, Meredith's head snapped up.

"Don't you dare call them weeds, Travis Archer. They're glorious!" Her eyes glistened with moisture he didn't understand. "No bride could have a finer bouquet. Thank you."

The softness of her palm caressed his knuckles as her hand circled the stems, and the contact had an odd tightening effect on his chest. He offered her his arm and led her to the parson.

To be honest, Travis didn't remember much of what the preacher said during the brief ceremony. He supposed he answered at the appropriate times and vaguely recalled Meredith doing the same, but when the parson announced that he could kiss the bride, his senses came on high alert.

How did one kiss a bride he'd never expected to have, one he'd known less than a week? Thinking to buss her chastely on the cheek, he leaned forward. But he couldn't seem to pull his attention from the fullness of her lips or the way they parted slightly as she drew in a breath, and somehow his mouth found her lips instead. The kiss was brief, gentle, but exquisitely sweet. If not for the hoot Neill let out, he would have returned for another.

A pretty blush colored Meredith's face as she turned away to accept her cousin's congratulations, and Travis had to fight the urge to swagger when he approached his brothers.

"I guess this means you won't be bunking with me no more, huh, Trav?" Neill snickered as he elbowed him.

More than ready to give up the cot in his brother's room, Travis scowled without any heat and shoved his kid brother's shoulder.

Crockett clasped Travis's hand and reached around to slap him on the back. When he stepped back, however, the knowing grin he wore communicated his thoughts all too clearly. "I'm sure he'll miss your snore terribly, Neill, but I imagine Meredith will distract him from the loss."

Travis felt his neck grow warm. "Leave it alone, Crock," he warned as he turned to accept Jim's hand.

In truth, he'd been so caught up with worries about Mitchell, the barn, and whether or not a wedding would even take place, he'd given very little thought to what would happen after the exchange of vows.

His gaze found Meredith across the room, the ribbing comments of his brothers fading from his awareness as he lingered over her profile. The curve of her cheek. The way the ribbons caressed her neck, inviting him to do the same. The slenderness of her waist. The curve of her—

Meredith glanced up at that moment, and Travis jerked his attention back to his brothers.

All right, so he *had* thought about it. Just not in any . . . uh . . . practical sense.

Instinctively, he knew that Meredith would not refuse him his marital rights. She would consider it her duty as his wife. Yet most husbands had first been suitors, courting their prospective brides with sweet words and gifts of affection. Except for the handful of weeds he'd presented her that morning, he'd given her nothing but a scarred leg and a dented head.

"What's got you frowning, brother?" Crockett jostled him with a shoulder to the arm. "You want me to hurry this party along so you can have some time alone with your bride?" His eyebrows wiggled suggestively, but Travis ignored the bawdy gesture.

He nudged Crockett aside and lowered his voice so the others wouldn't hear. Jim had already wandered into Hayes territory anyway, trying to get closer to a certain gal in pink, and Neill was smart enough to take the hint and turn his attention to the parson.

"Do you think I should give her some time to adjust before I move into her room?" Travis stretched his neck from side to side in an effort to rid himself of the kinks that suddenly arose.

"Shoot, Trav. It's *your* room, not hers."

"I'm serious, Crockett. It would be the considerate thing to do, don't you think? This situation has been thrust on both of us without any warning."

The teasing light in Crockett's eyes dimmed, and his mouth stiffened. "Are you saying you're not attracted to her in that way?" His voice was tight. "You should have never gone through with this if you—"

"Of course that's not what I'm saying," Travis hissed. "Just look at her. A man would have to be blind not to be attracted."

Crockett's face relaxed.

"I just thought, maybe I should, you know, court her a bit first." Travis kicked at the edge of the rug with the toe of his boot. He'd rather she be a willing partner than simply a dutiful one.

"When do you plan to court her, exactly? While we rebuild the barn? Or maybe out among the cattle while we search out new places for them to forage, since half our fodder went up in smoke? Thanks to Mitchell, we have more work on our hands and less time to accomplish it with winter already knocking on the door." Crockett looked to the ceiling and blew out a breath before turning back to his brother. "I don't know what the right answer is, Travis. I've even less experience than you when it comes to women. Talk to Meredith. Decide together what is best for the two of you. And pray for the Lord's guidance."

"Travis?" Meredith's soft voice gave him a start.

He spun around. Had she overheard any of their conversation? He prayed not and schooled his features as best he could to keep his chagrin hidden.

"I thought our guests might like to eat those sweet rolls now." She spoke with hesitation, and her eyes had difficulty holding his, but her smile reached inside him and undid the knots in his gut.

Travis offered her his arm and called out to the rest of the room. "My wife informs me that it's time to eat. And I, for one, am eager to sample my bride's cooking."

"It takes a brave man to marry a woman without proof of her ability to keep him from starvation, Archer," the parson said on a chuckle as he bustled forward.

"Says the man in the greatest hurry to get to the kitchen."

Meredith giggled at his jest, and Travis smiled. He slipped his hand over hers where it rested on his forearm and enjoyed the feel of his mother's ring beneath her glove.

"I said *you* were brave, lad. Not me. I've tasted Miss Meredith's baked goods and know precisely what quality of treat waits for me in the other room. And I plan to snatch the largest roll." He broke into a bouncy jog as if afraid someone would beat him to the prize. The room erupted in laughter.

Emboldened by the man's high spirits, Travis leaned down and whispered in Meredith's ear. "If they taste half as sweet as the one who baked them, they'll be delicious indeed."

"Travis," she chastened in low voice, her lovely cheeks matching her cousin's dress.

He grinned unrepentantly and urged her forward.

He was going to enjoy this courting business.

18

Meredith winced as she straightened from the wash basket and lifted one of Travis's shirts to the line. Laundry day had always made her lower back throb with all the bending and heavy lifting required, but as she surveyed the neat rows of male clothing, sheets, and table linens flapping in the chilled air, a proud smile curved her lips.

These were her family's things. Her *husband's* things. Amazing how that simple fact took the drudgery out of the chore.

Smiling to herself, she tossed the shirt over the line for a moment, then pushed her palms into the small of her back and turned her face up toward the sun as she stretched. The sound of a door shutting brought her head around.

Jim clomped down the back steps, his stocky build making his stride heavier than Travis's loose-limbed gait. His hair was a shade lighter than her husband's, but his eyes were similar, only they didn't have the intriguing touch of green she saw in Travis's.

Meredith raised a hand in greeting as he walked down the clothesline. The taciturn man favored her with a lift of his chin but not much else. He was a bit of a curmudgeon, but she didn't let it bother her since he acted the same way around his brothers. The only one he didn't act that way with was Cassie. But Cassie had that effect on men. She could charm a rock into floating on water with one of her smiles.

"I've got some stew simmering for supper," Meredith called out as he passed. He stopped and turned, but instead of answering her, he grabbed one of the trouser legs from the line and held it to his nose.

Was he . . . *sniffing* it?

He released it with a grunt, one that sounded rather like the ones her father used to make when he'd find the answer he sought in one of his research books. Then he glanced up and briefly met her gaze.

"Stew needs salt." And with no further commentary, he strode on to his shed.

Meredith didn't know whether to be offended at his opinion of her cooking or pleased that he'd actually spoken to her.

Turning back to her task, she pulled a clothespin from her apron pocket and fastened one shoulder of Travis's plaid flannel shirt, the one he had loaned her, to the line. As she worked to pin the other side, a ray of sunlight glinted off the gold band on her left hand. Meredith paused to admire it.

A married woman. Her. Meredith Hayes.

No, she corrected, *Meredith Archer.*

Her smile widened as she reached into the basket at her feet and retrieved her nightdress. A sigh escaped her as she shook out the wet, wadded cotton—the virginal white fabric a reminder that she was not yet a wife in all respects, only a bride. She forcefully flicked her wrists, snapping the gown into its full length.

She'd spent her wedding night alone.

Oh, it was out of consideration for her feelings. Travis had explained all that. And in her mind she understood his kindness and even appreciated the time he was giving her to truly get to know him before their relationship became more intimate. But in her heart? Well, deep down his consideration felt a lot like rejection.

Had he not felt the pulse-stopping current she had when their lips met during the ceremony? She guessed not, since he seemed in no hurry to repeat the experience. Travis hadn't kissed her once since the wedding three days ago.

She'd waited twelve years for that kiss, and now that she'd had a taste, three days without one felt like an eternity. Maybe Travis was the one who needed time. Meredith tilted her head as she pondered that idea. Perhaps he'd suggested they wait to consummate their marriage because *he* needed time to adjust. It wouldn't be surprising, really. Her uncle had practically forced the man to the altar. Meredith let out a sigh. She supposed she'd have to be patient.

At least Travis didn't seem adverse to her touch. His hand had a tendency to brush hers when they passed food around the supper table. And when they'd shared the sofa yesterday during the worship service the Archer brothers conducted in their parlor on Sundays, Travis had held the hymnal and sat close enough to her that she could feel the length of his leg whenever she leaned to the side to get a clearer view of the page.

The Lord probably didn't appreciate her feigning nearsightedness in order to repeatedly lean into her husband when she should've been concentrating on the meaning behind the hymn she was singing. It was no doubt her shameful behavior that prompted his divine hand to intervene in the song selection. When Neill accidentally announced the wrong song number, he decided to lead the unplanned hymn anyway. After three verses of "Nearer, My God, to Thee," Meredith's vision miraculously improved.

She reached for another garment, the green calico she'd had to scrub three times on the washboard, thanks to all the soot stains. When she straightened, the tune from that convicting hymn found its way to her lips. As she hummed the lilting melody, she recommitted her priorities. God first. Husband second. Yet when the words of the refrain ran through her mind, they brought with them recollections of a verse from James. *"Draw nigh to God, and he will draw nigh to you."* Meredith couldn't help wondering if such a strategy would work on husbands, as well.

Two shots fired in close succession rent the air. Meredith startled and dropped the clothespin she'd just extracted from her pocket. Then she remembered the sound was her husband's version of a doorbell and ordered her pulse to settle.

"One of these days I'm going to convince Travis to get rid of that awful sign," Meredith muttered as her hand closed around another wooden pin.

Just yesterday, Crockett had preached a fine lesson on the parable of the Good Samaritan. He'd kept looking at her with those twinkling eyes of his, leaving her to wonder if he saw her in the role of the Samaritan, performing a good deed in warning Travis of Mitchell's attack, or if he'd cast her in the role of the poor traveler who'd ended up half dead upon the road. Either way, Jesus clearly told the story to teach his followers to love their neighbors through acts of kindness and charity. How exactly did Travis think he and his brothers would fulfill this calling if they closed themselves off from anyone who might be considered a neighbor?

That sign had to go.

"Meredith?" Travis called out to her as his long strides ate up the distance between the shed and the trees that supported her wash line. "I need you to go into the house."

"I only have a few things left to hang. It'll just take a min—"

"Now, Meredith. Do as I say." The hardness in his voice surprised her, and the firm set of his jaw made it clear he expected her to jump to his bidding.

She *had* vowed to obey her husband, but she'd made no promise to jump like a scared rabbit every time he took to ordering her around.

Meredith lifted her chin. "Why must I go into the house, Travis?"

"Because," he gritted out, "there might be a threat, and I want to ensure that you're safe."

"What kind of threat?"

Travis yanked off his hat and swatted his thigh with it. "Confound it,

Meri. Will you just do as I ask?" He slapped the abused hat back on his head, then took her by the arm and pushed her toward the back steps. "I don't know what kind of threat, but I don't take chances. For all we know, Mitchell could have sent more men to convince me to sell."

"Or my uncle could have stopped by for a visit." Meredith didn't resist his forced guidance. His grip wasn't rough, just insistent. But she meant to make it clear that she didn't appreciate his high-handed tactics.

When they got to the back porch, he released her. "I know you haven't been here long, Meredith, but you're an Archer now, and you've got to learn how Archers do things. We always expect the worst. It keeps us alive. And when someone gives an order, you don't question it, you follow it. Explanations take time away from setting up our defense, and that leaves us vulnerable. Trust me to do what's right for you, Meri. It's for your own protection."

She frowned at him, letting him know she wasn't too pleased with his methods, but dutifully nodded her agreement. "All right."

Travis clapped her upper arm in a movement probably meant to convey his satisfaction over her compliance, but the hard lines of his face never softened. She would have preferred a smile. She'd have to make do with the brotherly thud on the arm, though, for he was already striding away from her, heading to the corral, where his mount waited.

"One of these days you're going to have to learn that the whole world isn't out to get you," she said softly to his retreating back, unsure if he heard her or not, even more unsure if she wanted him to hear. "You're keeping out more friends than foes with that gate, Travis." This last observation she whispered to herself.

She'd follow Travis's instructions and trust him to protect her, but she'd also follow the directives the Lord had placed on her heart. The Archers might be experts when it came to defense, but they were sadly lacking in their execution of hospitality.

Meredith marched through the bathing room and into the kitchen. After stoking up the fire in the stove, she took out a mixing bowl and scooped out three large portions of flour from the bin. She sprinkled a pinch of salt into the bowl, then cut in enough lard and cold water to make a dough. Taking the rolling pin from the drawer, she quickly rolled out the crust, not caring what shape resulted from her hasty efforts. Instead of reaching for a pie pan, she selected a large baking sheet from the cupboard and greased it. She cut the dough into strips, laid them in the pan, and dusted them with the leftover cinnamon-sugar mixture she had reserved after making the sweet rolls. While the crisps baked, she tidied the kitchen, then bustled back to her room to tidy herself.

If their guest proved not to be foe, as she suspected, the brave soul would be showered with neighborly hospitality. It was time the Archers were known for something other than seclusion.

Travis charged through the trees on Bexar's back, left hand on the reins, right hand on the butt of his pistol. Catching a shadowy glimpse of a wagon, he slowed the chestnut's pace and steered him off the path to take cover in a thicket of young pines. Crockett must have heard his approach, for the call of a white-winged dove floated on the breeze. White-winged doves rarely nested this far from the Rio Grande Valley, so when Joseph Archer taught his three older boys to imitate the call, they immediately turned it into a game of secret communication. Later, when they were on their own, it became an essential tool of stealth, allowing them to communicate to one another without being seen.

Taking his hand from his pistol, he patted Bexar's neck and waited for the second call that would signal all was well. When it came, the tightness in his chest lessened, and he drew in a deep breath. Strangers on his land made him tense at the best of times, but now that he had a wife to protect, fear for her safety intensified the usual concern that poured through him every time shots echoed from the road. At least he knew it wasn't one of Mitchell's agents. Crockett never would've admitted a wagon through the gate if he didn't know the driver.

Travis cupped his fingers around his mouth and returned Crockett's call. When the wagon drew abreast of his position, he urged Bexar forward with a touch of his heels and added his escort.

"Travis, my boy!" the bewhiskered driver boomed. "Good to see ya. I wondered where you were hidin'."

"I'd hate to grow predictable on you after all these years, Winston." Travis grinned at his father's old friend, the only man with a free pass onto Archer land.

"Shoot, that'd take all the fun out of it. Coming to see you boys is about the only excitement I get nowadays." He reached under his coat and scratched a spot on his chest with the three fingers left to him on his right hand. "Jim got my cabinets ready?"

"Yep. Finished the fourth one a couple weeks back."

Early on, the Archer boys had traded livestock for supplies—a cow or a hog, whichever they could best spare, in exchange for three months worth of flour, cornmeal, lard, coffee, sugar, and other necessities, like garden seeds, tools, and medicines. But when Jim started dabbling in woodworking and turned out to have a true talent for carpentry, Seth Winston quickly renegotiated their standing arrangement. They could keep their animals if Jim would fashion pieces Winston could sell to the local farmers' and ranchers' wives in his shop. Winston's general store and post office, along with a saloon and a church that doubled as the local schoolhouse, were the only buildings in the nearby tiny settlement known as Beaver Valley, but having the store situated on the market road between Palestine and Athens provided a place for the locals to congregate and therefore a steady trickle of customers. Customers who apparently appreciated rustic oak and pine furnishings.

"Can't wait to see 'em. Pansy Elmore's been badgerin' me somethin' fierce about that open cupboard I promised her. You know how antsy them women can get." Winston slanted a glance at Travis and let out a cackle. "No, I reckon you don't, do you?"

"Oh, he's learning," Crockett offered in a wry voice.

Winston twisted to eye the younger Archer. "Whadda'ya mean, he's learning? You four are livin' in bachelor heaven. You ain't even seen a female in fourteen years. Lucky dogs. Womenfolk're more trouble than they're worth, if you ask me. Always naggin' a man to death. I tell ya, there's been many a time I thought about holin' up out here with you boys just to get some peace."

"Your sister still pestering you to move down to Palestine and retire?" Travis asked, eager to veer the conversation in a different direction.

"As if I'd want to be surrounded by her clan. Nellie's brood is all girls. And not a one of 'em has up and married yet. I'd be stuck in a house with five females. Five! Can ya imagine the torture? All that yappin' and carrying on. It'd drive me batty." His violent shudder made Travis smile. Seth Winston was a grouchy old cuss, but beneath all that bluster beat a loyal heart. If a person ever managed to find a way to his good side, he'd have a friend for life.

When Joseph Archer helped him rebuild his store after a twister tore off the roof, he'd landed himself on Winston's good side. And fortunately for Travis, Joseph's sons inherited the man's favor when their father passed.

"Yessiree. You boys are the smart ones. Protect what you got out here, Travis." Winston pointed at him with the trio of fingers on his right hand. "Don't let no woman come in and start changing things. She'll suck the freedom right outta ya."

They arrived at the front of the house right as he made that statement. Jim and Neill set aside their rifles and stepped down from the porch to help unload the wagon.

Crockett grinned and winked at Travis over the old man's head. "I think your warning came a couple days too late, Seth."

Travis shot him a quelling look, but Crockett just chuckled and dismounted, wisely staying on the opposite side of the wagon, out of his big brother's reach.

Winston squinted up at Travis, consternation furrowing his brow. "Tell me he's jokin', Travis. Tell me you didn't—"

The sound of the front door squeaking open stole the rest of his sentence. Meredith backed through the doorway, her arms occupied with a tray. When she turned, a cheery smile lit her face even as her eyes darted nervously between all the men assembled in the yard.

"Consarn it, Travis! What is *she* doin' here? Ya gone and ruined everything, haven't ya?"

Staying atop his horse so he could hold Meredith's widening gaze from the far side of the wagon, Travis tried to communicate his apology with his eyes. Her smile only slipped a little before her determination propped it back into place.

Man, he was proud of her.

"Seth Winston," Travis intoned, a touch of steel lacing his voice. "My wife, Meredith."

"Wife?" The man nearly shouted his outrage. "Good gravy, boy. It's worse than I feared."

19

Of all the sour-minded, pig-headed . . . Meredith breathed through her nose, careful to keep her smile in place. Of all the people God could send her to practice her hospitality on, did it have to be Seth Winston? The man had scared her to death as a child when her mother took her shopping in his store, always glaring at her like an ogre from one of her fairy-tale books. She hadn't seen the man since she started school in Palestine, and truth be told, she'd gone out of her way to avoid him even before that, so it didn't surprise her that no recognition flashed in his eyes. And that was fine with her. She'd take every advantage she could get in this battle. For a battle it would be—one she had no intention of losing.

It was time to slay the ogre. And though she longed for a sword, her weapons would have to be cleverness and kindness instead.

Meredith marched forward, head held high. Until she noticed their visitor's gaze drop to her feet. It wasn't the first time her limp had garnered a rude stare, but it was the first time her imperfection reflected on someone other than herself. Not trusting herself to glance at Travis to gauge his reaction, she focused on the ground as she navigated the steps.

What was that verse from Romans? *Oh yes. "If thine enemy hunger, feed him; if he thirst, give him drink: for in so doing thou shalt heap coals of fire on his head."* She peered at her tray of cinnamon crisps, and smiled over the fiery coals waiting to be consumed.

Mr. Winston clambered down from the wagon bench and eyed her approach as if she were a bobcat looking for someone to sharpen her claws on.

"I know you," he said pointing a hand at her that lacked a couple of fingers. "You're Teddy Hayes's girl. The one with the bum leg."

"And I know you, Mr. Winston," she answered before Travis could say anything. "You're that cranky old store owner. The one with the bum hand." Unlike their guest's vinegarish tone, Meredith infused her barb with a thick dollop of honey.

The man blinked at her, his mouth slightly agape, as if he couldn't quite believe her audacity.

"You used to tell the most gruesome war stories when I came to your store with my mother," Meredith continued, her smile still in place as she swept past Crockett, Jim, and Neill without a sideways glance. "Even though they gave me nightmares, I couldn't stop myself from listening. You have quite a gift for storytelling."

She held the tray out to him when she reached the place where he stood. "Cinnamon crisp? They're fresh from the oven."

He didn't move, just stared at her as if she were an oddity he couldn't decipher.

Meredith continued holding the tray as if she had nothing better to do than ply the recalcitrant man with sweets. "You know, when I was a girl, Hiram Ellis nearly convinced me that Travis shot off those two missing fingers of yours when you trespassed on his land. I'm glad I didn't believe that nonsense. You've obviously been on friendly terms with my husband for quite some time." She emphasized the word *husband*, hoping to rile the grumpy cuss. Two could play at his game. "Why don't you come up to the house? You can entertain me with more of your stories while Travis and the other, younger, men unload the supplies."

Mr. Winston turned an accusing glare at Travis. "She fer real?"

Travis nodded, and a grin stretched across his face. He even winked at her before he dismounted. "She's real, all right."

"She know it's rude to insult comp'ny?" The old codger shot a challenging look her way before turning back to Travis, obviously thinking he'd bested her by excluding her from the conversation.

Little did he know that Meredith Hayes Archer never backed down from a challenge, spoken or not. "Oh, she'd never insult a guest, Mr. Winston," Meredith answered on her own behalf as Travis came around the front of the wagon. She moved to stand by his side. "Like any good hostess, she's sensitive to the preferences of her callers and is careful to address them in the same manner in which they do her. Anything less might make them feel ill at ease, and that would never do."

Someone tried unsuccessfully to stifle his guffaw. Probably Crockett. But Meredith dared not take her eyes off of Mr. Winston to verify her theory.

The man grunted, then snatched three of the sugared pie-crust strips from her tray and proceeded to bite the ends off all of them at once. Crumbs fell into his beard, but his mouth stayed closed while he chewed. It was more than she had hoped for from the ill-mannered fellow. And really, at this point he could have spat on her shoe and she wouldn't have cared. She had bested him!

Her smile grew as she watched him stuff her snacks into his mouth. She knew a delaying tactic when she saw one. He couldn't come up with anything else to say. The man couldn't even hold her gaze.

Then all at once, his jaw stilled, his eyes feasting on something behind her. He swallowed. Slowly. "So, Travis," he said, his voice deceptively pleasant. "You marry this harpy before or after she burned down yer barn?" He tossed the rest of the crisps into his mouth and chomped down, victory written all over his face.

"After." Travis couldn't resist; he was having too much fun watching their sparring.

Meredith's sharply indrawn breath roused his conscience, though.

"I did *not* burn down your barn, and you know it!" She shoved the tray into his stomach so hard he almost failed to steady the thing before all her little treats fell into the dirt. That would've been a crime. Jim had an able hand for making stew, but he never could bake worth a hoot. Meredith's desserts were precious commodities.

When Travis had all the goodies safely balanced, he glanced up and caught the vivid blue fire of his wife's eyes. "And I am *not* a harpy!"

With that dramatic pronouncement, she strode back toward the house, giving Crockett a censoring shove when he laughed. He managed to contain his mirth until the front door slammed closed behind her. Then it burst forth even louder than before. Neill joined in, and even Jim cracked a smile.

The woman had held her own against Winston like a seasoned verbal warrior. So why had one teasing word from Travis ignited her temper?

Winston clapped Travis on the back, unsettling the cinnamon things again. "That's one ornery spitfire ya got there, Travis." He grabbed another handful of pastries and ambled to the back of the wagon to lower the tailgate. "She just might make a halfway decent Archer yet."

If she ever let him near her again.

Travis blew out a heavy breath and headed for the house, passing the tray off to Neill as he went. This business of wooing one's wife was complicated. The pitfalls were so well hidden, a man didn't even know they were there until he'd fallen into one.

"Good luck, Trav." Crockett's voice wobbled on the end of a chuckle. Travis shot him a glare and pounded up the porch steps.

She wasn't in the kitchen. The bedroom, either. He checked the parlor and even peeked into the boys' rooms on his way down the hall. Nothing.

"Meredith?" He held his volume to a minimum, not wanting the others to know he'd lost his wife. He lifted his hat, scratched at a spot on his crown, and fit it back into place. She'd only been a minute or two ahead of him. She had to be somewhere in the house.

The only place he hadn't checked was the bathing room. Travis crossed the kitchen in six long strides and pushed through the unlatched door. "Meri?"

The room was empty, but cool air whistled through the back door, where it hung ajar. When he nudged it open, he spotted her stomping between the clotheslines as if she were squashing a wolf spider with every footfall.

Travis shook his head at the picture she made—arms swinging like a soldier, bonnet flapping against her back, pieces of hair coming loose and dancing about in the breeze. He took off after her and caught up just as she snapped the wrinkles out of a damp petticoat.

She had to realize he was there. He stood less than a foot away, for pete's sake, yet she refused to look at him. Her lips pressed together in a tight line as she jabbed a clothespin over the cotton garment.

Travis crossed his arms, his own temper rising a notch. "You gonna tell me what I did wrong, or am I'm gonna have to guess?"

"You betrayed me!" She spun to face him, and for the first time he noticed the tears behind the fire in her eyes. But the accusation she flung at him burned away any soft feelings that might have been evoked.

"Whoa, now." Travis uncrossed his arms and held up a hand of warning. "Archers don't betray their own."

"I must not be one of your own, then."

Travis stepped closer and glowered down at the woman daring to impugn his honor. "You agreed before God to take my name. Have you forgotten?"

"No, but it seems you have." She glowered right back at him. "I complied when you ordered me into the house. I even put together refreshments on the rare chance that someone might actually be welcomed onto sacred Archer land. Then when you did bring a guest to the house, he turns out to be the grumpiest woman-hater north of the Rio Grande. But did I shy away? No, sir. I faced Seth Winston head on. And I was making progress, too. Until you"—she poked him in the chest—"chopped the legs right out from under me."

He knocked her finger away. "One word, Meredith. One lousy word. You're getting all worked up over nothing."

"Nothing?" Her voice rose. "With that one word, you sided with the enemy. You as much as conceded that I had something to do with that fire and agreed that I'm some kind of ill-tempered harpy!"

He raised an eyebrow and stared at her until she realized the irony of the shouted statement.

At that moment the starch went out of her. She glanced away and kicked at the edge of the laundry basket with her shoe. "You didn't defend me."

His anger evaporated at the tremor in her voice.

Travis cupped his fingers under her chin and turned her face back up to his. "You didn't give me the chance." He stroked the edge of her jaw with his thumb. "Meri, you are my wife, a part of my family. I will never betray you." Her eyes stared up at him like a doe's in an early morning mist. Travis dropped his hand away from her chin and shoved his fingers into his trouser pocket, worried he'd pull her close and kiss her if he didn't. "The truth is, I was so blasted proud of the way you were handling Winston that I couldn't resist a little teasing. I fully intended to clarify that you had nothing to do with the fire, but you stormed off before I got the chance."

"I ruined everything, didn't I?" She sounded so forlorn. "I let him goad me into losing my temper. I shamed you."

"You did no such thing." Travis frowned down at her. "Did you not just hear me tell you how proud I was of you?" Compliments seemed to slip off his wife as if they were covered in grease. Nothing stuck.

"But that was before I started acting like a harpy."

"For pete's sake, woman, you are *not* a harpy!"

Her startled eyes darted to his. Then without warning, a giggle erupted. Travis felt his own lips twitch, and soon they were both laughing.

"Hey, Trav," Neill called from the back porch. "Winston wants to know if you want to add anything to your usual order since we got us a female on the place now."

Travis winked at his new wife, her cheeks rosy from their shared merriment. "Tell him we'll be up there to discuss it with him directly."

Meredith moaned and turned to reach for the last item in her wash basket. "Do I really have to face him again, Travis? The man will be insufferable after besting me as he did."

Travis grinned and grabbed up the empty basket. "You can handle him. I've got faith in you."

He held his hand out to her after she finished pinning a second petticoat to the line. She glanced uncertainly at his offering, then slipped her palm into his. On impulse, he tugged her arm, causing her to stumble into him.

"We're Archers, Meri," he murmured as he tucked her briefly against his chest. "We can face anything if we do it together."

After five days of marriage, the shine was starting to wear off. Meredith grimaced as she stirred a bowl of cornbread batter. She'd cleaned the house from top to bottom, kept the men fed and their clothes mended—done everything a wife was supposed to do. Well . . . almost everything. And therein lay her trouble. Except for the quick hug he'd given her when encouraging her to face Mr. Winston, Travis had offered her virtually no affection, leaving her feeling more like a housekeeper than a wife.

She'd told herself he was being gallant when he suggested they take some time to get to know one another before sharing the intimacy of the marriage bed, but now she wondered if that had just been an excuse to avoid her. After all, he hadn't wed her out of love but rather a sense of responsibility.

"Quit being pitiful, Meri." She forced herself to stop pulverizing the cornmeal and poured the batter into a square baking pan. Love needed time to grow. It was unfair to expect her husband to blossom overnight into the idealized romantic hero she'd spent her adolescence mooning over. Besides, she was a woman now, not a girl, and she needed a man to stand at her side, not an imaginary hero.

But she still wanted that man to care for her.

With a sigh that was still far too pitiful sounding for her peace of mind, Meredith opened the oven door and slid the pan into the heart of the stove. It was then that she noticed the quiet. Travis and Jim were supposed to be tearing out damaged boards from the sections of the barn that were still standing, while Crockett and Neill checked the cattle out on the range and scouted new pastureland. There should have been voices, the crash of wood planks hitting the scrap heap, something. But even when she held very still, all she could make out was a faint chatter from the chicken coop.

Heart thumping in her breast, Meredith crept over to the bathing room and grabbed the broom. It seemed a particularly opportune time to sweep the front porch. If trouble was afoot, she'd surely see it coming from there. Wouldn't hurt to have the shotgun at hand, either. Meredith took a detour through the den to collect the gun and tuck a handful of shells into her apron pocket. She stood the weapon against the wall of the entryway, then opened the door to find Sadie blocking her path.

"Shoo, girl." Meredith nudged the dog's side with her knee. Sadie held fast, her ears pricked, her attention focused somewhere down the path.

Meredith angled herself over the dog's back, jutting her shoulders through the doorway in order to glance around the yard. No sign of the men. She pressed harder against Sadie's side. "Come on, now. Let . . . me . . . through." Meredith's greater weight finally prevailed as she displaced the dog far enough to squeeze past. But before she could take more than a step or two, Sadie scrambled around to block her progress once again.

"What has gotten into you?" Meredith stroked the dog's fur, hoping a friendly rub would restore the animal's usual good humor. Sadie refused to relax, however. Her back remained stiff and straight, her legs braced like a soldier on guard duty.

All at once the pieces clicked into place. "Travis ordered you to stand guard, didn't he?"

Sadie twisted her neck and looked at her mistress with eyes that seemed to reprimand her for being so slow in comprehending the obvious, then turned her attention back to the path.

Meredith straightened and peered in the same direction. The trees obscured her view, and the uncertainty of what was happening behind their cover set her pulse to thrumming. Whatever had lured Travis away had been urgent enough to preclude him from stopping by the house to warn her.

Had Roy Mitchell's men returned? What of Crockett and Neill? Had something befallen one of them?

Her hands tightened around the broom handle. *Please, Lord, keep my family safe.*

A flash of color tickled her vision, dodging in and out of the pines. Meredith dashed around Sadie to the far end of the porch and leaned over the railing to get a better view. The dog barked once in protest, then bounded to her side.

Meredith squinted, the railing digging into her stomach. She spied a man. No. Two men. One tall and large, the other slender. Both dark-skinned. The path took them behind another tree, and Meredith bit the inside of her cheek in frustration. The tall one wore an odd-looking feather in the band of his tan planter hat. Even from a distance, she could make out the black plume against the lighter-colored headpiece.

She'd seen a hat like that before. As the memory slowly awakened within her, the hard voice of her husband cut through the late morning quiet.

"Take one more step, and I'll shoot you where you stand."

Like a pair of ghosts, Travis and Jim materialized out of the trees, their rifles pointed directly at the man who had built her father's school.

"No!" Meredith cried. "Wait!" She shooed Sadie with her broom and managed to evade the animal long enough to gain the steps. Dropping the broom, she hiked up her skirts and ran toward her husband.

He didn't look too happy to see her. The glare he aimed her way was downright furious, as a matter of fact. But Meredith refused to be cowed. He could yell at her later. Right now she intended to broaden the stubborn man's horizons.

"Meredith, get back to the house." Travis called out the demand, then shifted his stance to match her angle of approach, putting himself between her and the visitors.

A stitch in her side kept her from answering at first, but she knew he'd figure out her refusal once she reached the gathering. She stopped a few feet behind him and struggled to catch her breath as she surreptitiously rubbed her right leg. The punishment of running on the shorter limb had set it to aching.

Travis would have to be deaf not to be aware of her presence, even with his back turned. Yet he paid her no heed, just continued on with his threats.

"You're trespassing on my land." Travis aimed the barrel of his rifle at the larger man's chest. "The sign at the gate warned you of the consequences. Now turn around and leave before I put a bullet in you."

The big man held his arms out from his sides in a gesture of conciliation, but he made no move to leave. "I didn't read no sign."

"That doesn't change the fact that you're trespassing."

The younger fellow, just a boy, really—he looked about the same age as Neill—backed a step away from Jim, his eyes wary. "Let's go, Pa. Mr. Winston was wrong. They don't want our help."

"That's cuz they don't know what we're offerin' yet." The man's face gave nothing away, but Meredith could feel the challenge hanging in the air.

"The only offer I'm interested in is the one where you offer to leave my land." Travis waved his gun in the direction of the road.

Meredith lifted a hand to Travis's shoulder. Her touch was light, yet he flinched as if she'd burned him. "Travis. Please. I know this m—"

"Strangers aren't welcome here," her husband ground out, cutting off her explanation. But the others heard.

Moses Jackson peered past Travis, and when his eyes landed on her, his composure fell away. "Miss Meri? That you?"

She smiled and stepped out from behind her husband. An answering smile began to crease Moses's face when Travis shoved her back behind him. In an instant, the black man's good humor vanished and the hands that had hung harmless at his sides balled into fists—giant fists that looked like they could fell a tree.

"You here against your will, Miss Meri?"

Jim and Travis both tensed, and Meredith's stomach plummeted to her toes. *Merciful heavens*. If Moses started swinging those fists, Travis was bound to be the first target. And if one of the guns went off? Well, it didn't bear thinking about.

Just as she had with Sadie earlier, Meredith dodged around her husband's protective stance and dashed directly into the line of fire.

Travis immediately raised his rifle barrel into the air, but the look he shot her felt just like a bullet tearing through the flesh near her heart. She prayed he'd forgive her once she'd explained. There was nothing to do now, though, but brazen her way through.

"Travis Archer, may I present Mr. Moses Jackson? Mr. Jackson built the freedmen's schoolhouse a mile west of Beaver Valley, where my father taught for several years." Meredith watched Travis's face for signs of softening, but his jaw remained as clenched as ever as he stared down the large black man. She turned to Moses only to find his face equally implacable. "Moses, Travis is my husband. I am here quite willingly."

Finally, Moses surrendered the staring battle to glance at Meredith. He relaxed his fists, and a hint of a smile played about the corners of his mouth. "Your man ain't the friendly sort, is he, Miss Meri."

She laughed, her nerves getting the better of her. "Not at first. But he can be a trusted ally once you get to know him." Meredith peeked back at her husband. He still looked none too pleased, but his eyes were no longer shooting bullets at her. It was a start.

Travis tipped his rifle barrel onto his shoulder, pointing it harmlessly away from the visitors, but his right hand continued gripping the stock in a way that would allow instant readiness should the occasion call for it.

"Why'd you come, Jackson?"

"Lookin' for work. Heard ya had a barn what needed rebuilding."

"I've got three brothers." Travis jerked his chin in Jim's direction. "That one's even a carpenter. We'll manage the task."

Moses crossed his arms over his chest. "Before the next rain comes?" The question hovered for a moment, everyone knowing the answer. "My boy's good with a hammer, and I've built just about everything there is what has walls and a roof. With us working for you, you can cut yer building time in half."

Travis's jaw worked back and forth.

"We need a place to store what's left of the hay," Jim stated with flat practicality as he shifted his rifle, pointing it toward the ground.

Travis made no outward show that he'd heard his brother, but Meredith sensed the battle inside him. The hay would mold if rain came before they got a roof on the barn, and in Texas, the weather was harder to predict than a hummingbird's flight path. It could hold off for a month or a storm could roll in tomorrow. But having strangers on Archer land went against everything Travis had clung to since his father died.

"I can't pay in cash money."

Meredith held her breath. He was bending.

"I'd work for provisions, foodstuffs to see me and mine through the winter."

Travis frowned. "I can't spare much. We've already laid in provisions for the winter and won't receive more until spring. We hadn't planned on needing extra for barter."

Meredith considered offering to go to town should they run low on supplies, but figured she'd pushed her husband far enough for one day. Perhaps discretion would be the better part of valor in this instance. Her gaze seesawed back to Moses, praying he'd not refuse. Travis needed his help whether he admitted it or not. And not just with the barn. He needed a connection with the outside world, with someone other than that dreadful Seth Winston, someone who could help him see that reaching out to others was as important as protecting one's own.

Moses uncrossed his arms. "I'll accept whatever you think fair."

Silence stretched over the pair as they continued to size each other up. Finally, Travis thrust out his hand. Moses grasped it with his own, and the two shook. Giddy pleasure gurgled through Meredith, but she contained it behind a soft smile.

"One of us will meet you at the gate each morning to escort you in," Travis instructed. "You and the boy can take your midday meals with us while you're working and collect your payment at the end of the week."

"Yessir, Mr. Archer." Moses dipped his head in compliance.

"Call me Travis. If we're going to be working together, there's no need for such formality. That there's Jim," he indicated with a thrust of his chin. "Crockett and Neill are out on the range. You'll meet them in a bit when they come in to eat."

Moses shook hands with Jim and introduced his son, Josiah. Meredith stepped back and watched the whole thing unfold, pride in her husband seeping through every pore. She'd worried, just for a moment, that the color of Moses's skin might have played a part in Travis's reluctance to accept his help. But clearly that was not the case. Not with him offering the use of his Christian name. No, Travis would have treated any stranger with the same discourtesy.

A giggle tickled her throat. Oh, that's right—he had. She'd nearly forgotten about her own inhospitable Archer welcome. That day felt like a lifetime ago now.

"Jim, why don't you take Moses and Josiah up to the shed and show them the sketches you've been working on," Travis said. "Meredith and I will meet you at the house in a couple minutes."

Jim nodded and led the Jacksons toward the shed. Meredith waved to Moses when he tipped his hat to her, then turned a beaming smile on her husband.

"Oh, Travis," she gushed. "You won't regret this. Moses is a good man and a talented builder. I know the two of you will get along famously. Papa always held him in high esteem even though he and his older boy never came to the reading classes. Too busy sharecropping. That's probably why he didn't heed your sign. I don't think he can read. But his wife and younger son attended and were fine pupils. Why—"

"Meredith," Travis snapped and grabbed hold of her arm.

The well of frothy babble inside her dried up in an instant. She met his gaze, and her heart started a painful throb in her chest. She'd experienced his irritation and even an occasional flash of true frustration, but never had Travis directed a look of raw anger at her.

Suddenly she very much wished she had let Sadie keep her penned in the house.

Travis glared down at the woman who'd nearly given him a heart seizure. Her blue eyes had gone wide. *Good*. Maybe he'd scare some sense into her.

"Don't you *ever* step in front of my weapon like that." He ground the order out between clenched teeth. "Do you understand me?"

Meredith gave a quick little nod, her chin quivering. Travis hardened himself against the urge to set aside the lecture and gather her into his arms. This was no time to be soft. Just thinking about what could have happened made his blood run cold.

"A bump against the barrel, an involuntary jerk of my hand . . . anything could have set the gun off, and then where would you be?" He let go of her arm and stalked off a pace before whirling around, his finger jabbing toward the earth, where he visualized her bloody, prostrate form. "On the ground, that's where. Dead."

A shiver passed through him, and he raised a hand to his face to try to rub away the torturous image.

"I trust you, Travis." Meredith took an uneven step toward him. "I know you would never harm me."

"Not intentionally, but accidents happen. You need to exert better judgment, Meri. Stop rushing in to help all the time."

"Stop rushing in . . . ?" She stiffened her posture.

A tickle of unease gathered in Travis's gut.

"It wasn't *my* faulty judgment that placed me in front of your rifle, Travis Archer. It was yours." Her index finger collided with his chest.

Travis frowned. If she thought she was going to turn this around on him, she could think again. *She* was the one who needed to learn how things were done on his land. *She* was the one who needed to quit putting herself in harm's way, conducting those good deeds of hers that always seemed to go awry. *She* was the one—

"I tried to explain who Moses was when I first came across your little welcoming party," she said, intruding on the satisfaction of his inner tirade, "but you were so set on driving him away that you rebuffed my efforts. Had you simply listened, there would have been no need for me to get your attention through drastic measures. Perhaps I did put myself in harm's way, but only because you drove me there."

"I'm sure you could have found other, *safer*, ways to secure my attention." Travis crossed his arms. Let her try to refute that argument.

Meredith crossed her own arms. "Maybe, but none of those options would have put me between you and Moses. And that was precisely where I needed to be. Or did you fail to notice the way his hands curled into fists when he thought I might be in trouble?" She paused, as if daring him to comment. "He would have flattened you if I hadn't intervened."

"I would've held my own," Travis grumbled.

"Would you have shot him?"

Travis rubbed the back of his neck and stared at the tops of his boots. Meredith knew he'd never shoot an unarmed man, he could hear it in her voice. So why was she pressing him?

She took a step toward him and braced her hands on her hips. "One of these days someone is going to call your bluff, Travis, and you'll either have to take whatever they dish out or pull that trigger and live with the consequences. I didn't want today to be that day.

"Moses outweighs you by at least forty pounds." Meredith eyed him dubiously. Travis straightened to his full height and glared at her. "You might've been willing to take him on, but I wasn't willing to let you try, not when I had the ability to clear up the misunderstanding with a simple explanation. So I did what I had to do. I'm an Archer, remember? We protect our own."

He wanted to throttle her. He truly did. Throwing his words back in his face as if the crazy woman actually thought he needed her protection. It was his job to protect her, not the other way around. Yet hearing her declare herself an Archer filled him with such satisfaction, he chose not to correct her misguided notions.

For now.

"Just promise me that you won't put yourself in harm's way again."

She lifted her chin. "I promise not to intentionally put myself in harm's way . . . *unless* I deem it necessary to protect the well-being of another."

Did she have to make everything so complicated? Travis bit back a sigh. At least she agreed to comply with his dictate for the most part. That'd have to be good enough. He'd just ignore the obstinate set of her mouth.

Only he couldn't.

He stared at her lips. Watching them soften as her defiance faded. Imagining the feel of them against his own. Would she welcome a real kiss from him? Not another chaste meeting of lips like at their wedding, but a deep, intimate joining?

Travis jerked his gaze to the sky and flared his nostrils as he strove to subdue the stampede of desire thundering through him. He'd always found his wife attractive, but he'd not been prepared for this sudden ambush of cravings—to kiss her, touch her . . .

Could she read his thoughts? Was he frightening her? 'Cause he was sure as shootin' scaring himself.

"I don't mean to make you angry, Travis," Meredith said, her expression more stubborn than fearful, thank the Lord. "But I can't promise to do something that may violate my conscience."

Angry? What was she talking about? "I'm not mad at you, Meri."

Her brow furrowed. "You're not? I could have sworn you were counting to ten or something, trying to keep your temper in check."

Travis nearly laughed aloud. His sweet, innocent wife had no idea what he'd been trying to keep in check. And he wanted to keep it that way. At least until he learned how to control it a little better.

"I promise I'm not m—"

Meredith's gasp cut him off.

"Oh my stars!" Her panicked eyes darted past him to the house and had him reaching for his rifle to confront the threat. "My cornbread!" She grabbed a fistful of skirt and sprinted down the path and across the yard.

Travis let out a breath and watched her go, propping the unneeded rifle on his shoulder. She sure was a pretty thing. Feisty, too. And even though he hated that she'd put herself in danger, he had to admit that her courage and tender heart were the things he admired most about her.

Perhaps it was time he got serious about courting his wife.

Travis secretly schemed during supper, determined to wait for the right moment. When Meredith cleared away the dessert plates and the empty pie tin that earlier had been filled with sweet, flaky apple goodness, he excused himself to go check on the stock.

If the woman was trying to sweeten him up, she was doing a right fine job of it. He couldn't remember ever tasting anything as delectable as that apple pie. It only made him more anxious to get his wife alone. When he carried his coffee cup to where she stood washing the dishes, he caught the faint aroma of cinnamon and apples clinging to her even after the pie had been fully consumed. He couldn't wait to see if the taste lingered on her lips, as well.

After checking that the horses had adequate feed and water for the night, he headed back to the house with Sadie trailing at his heels. The sun had already dipped beneath the horizon, and light quickly faded from the sky. The moon promised to be bright, though—the perfect backdrop for a courting stroll.

He bent to pat Sadie's head, but the sound of the front door opening urged him back to an upright position. Jim crossed the porch, an unlit lantern in hand.

"Heading to your workshop?" Travis strode forward to meet him at the base of the steps.

"Yep." Jim halted when he reached the ground and hesitated, as if waiting to see if any other conversation would be necessary.

"Whatcha making this time?"

Jim tipped the brim of his hat back and shrugged. "One of them chests womenfolk like to store blankets and such in."

"Oak or pine?" Travis asked, not concerned so much with the answer as in keeping the conversation going.

"Oak."

A question burned on the front of Travis's tongue, but he couldn't quite seem to spit it out. It was only when Jim started to move past him that the words tumbled forth.

"Do you think I did the right thing in hiring Moses and Josiah?" Travis peered into his brother's face, hoping for a sign of approval yet worried that Jim might confirm the uneasy niggling in the back of his mind that accused him of giving Meredith too much influence over his decision.

As always, Jim took his time answering. "The man knows building," he finally said. "And his idea about using stonework for the first three or four feet of the walls is sound. We'll be able to get more use out of the lumber we've salvaged from the original barn, plus the stone at ground level will be less likely to catch fire should a torch ever be tossed down beside it."

"You think he's trustworthy?"

"Dunno. But he and the boy are hard workers. They sanded the scorch marks from about half the boards in the scrap heap after lunch and tested them for weak spots while you and Crockett checked the grass up by Horseshoe Rock. Said he'd bring along his own tools tomorrow, too, so he wouldn't have to borrow mine. Seems a decent enough fella."

"Good." One of the knots in Travis's belly loosened.

"I think Neill got a kick outta having someone his own age around. Once those two started yakkin', they hardly ever stopped."

Which could mean anything from swapping names and a pleasantry or two to jabbering like a pair of magpies. It was impossible to tell with Jim making the observation. To him, a sentence with more than two words qualified as verbose. He'd probably said more in the last two minutes than he had all day.

"Well, I'll look forward to seeing them in action tomorrow."

Jim nodded and headed off to the shed. Sadie padded after him, leaving Travis alone with the other knot in his gut—the tangle of anticipation and nerves.

Surely Meredith was done tidying the kitchen by now, and hopefully Crockett would be off in the den working on Sunday's lesson or taking Neill on in a game of checkers. The last thing Travis wanted when he asked Meredith to walk with him was an audience.

As it turned out, no audience waited for him in the kitchen, but then, neither did Meredith. Travis moseyed down the hall in search of his wife, trying to look as nonchalant as possible despite the porcupine rolling around in his stomach. He ducked past the den before Crockett could see him, figuring he'd look there last. No sense opening himself to a round of teasing if it wasn't necessary.

Her bedroom door stood open, but when he peeked inside, he found no trace of her. When he turned, however, he was treated to the sight of his wife's backside wiggling toward him as she struggled to pull Neill's door closed while clasping a wad of clothing in one hand and her sewing box in the other.

Travis reached around her to assist, enjoying the contact as his arm brushed against hers. She jumped into a straighter position, and the movement pressed her back snuggly against his chest. He liked that even more.

"I didn't mean to startle you." Which was true, but he sure didn't mind taking advantage of the results. He breathed in the scent of her as he rubbed the side of his jaw against her hair.

Meredith lingered a moment, then stepped away. Travis bit back his disappointment.

"I was gathering the mending," she said, her shy gaze not quite reaching his. "I didn't realize you were behind me."

"No harm done." Travis smiled at her, hoping the grin would pass for charming. Sadie was the only female he'd ever tried to coax into sharing his company before, and something told him gals of the two-legged variety might be a little trickier to convince. "Would you . . . um . . . like to take a walk with me? There's a pretty spot down along the creek that I've been meaning to show you."

"It sounds lovely." Her lips curved encouragingly, then fell. "Oh, but I told Neill I'd repair the cuffs on his favorite work shirt. One snag and the raggedy things are bound to tear clean off."

Hoping the regret he heard lacing her voice was genuine and not just wishful thinking on his part, Travis gently collected the sewing box and pile of shirts from her and tucked them under his arm. "It'll keep," he said.

He led the way to the kitchen, set the mending items on the table, and then took her cloak from the hook on the wall and held it out for her to step into. "Shall we?"

She hesitated, looking at the mending before reaching out to him again. But when she bit her lip and nodded, a spark of eagerness danced in her eyes that set his pulse to thrumming. Meredith reached behind her back to untie her apron, then slid her arms into the sleeves of her cloak and allowed him to fit it over her shoulders. His hands smoothed down the edge of her arms as she did up the top few buttons, and he fought the urge to draw her into a more intimate embrace.

Finally, she turned to face him, her smile sending that porcupine tumbling around inside him again. Bowing slightly, he offered his arm, and once her fingers settled near his elbow, he led her to the door.

22

As they left the yard to stroll along the path his parents used to take when they wanted to escape prying eyes, Travis felt more like a married man than he had since the day he took his vows. Moonlight lit their way, its soft glow adding a touch of enchantment to the pines and walnut trees that surrounded them. He took care to modulate his stride to accommodate her shorter one. The hitch in her gait didn't slow her down, but he found himself taking extra care to guide her around pebbles and uneven ground that he usually didn't give a second thought.

Travis tried to think of something romantic to say, something charming or witty to entertain his lady, but his tongue remained glued to the back of his teeth. The scenery would have to be poetry enough.

"Do you hear the music, Travis?" Meredith glanced his way, her eyes luminous. "The rippling water, the humming crickets, the leaves rustling in the breeze. It's like a lullaby I vaguely remember from childhood coming back to soothe me after a long day."

Travis grinned. It seemed his wife had enough poetry in her soul for both of them.

"My father and I used to sit on the porch when I was young and listen to the night sing to us. He said it was the best cure for a weary spirit. And he was right. I would curl up in his lap and listen to the sounds of the night while the steady beat of his heart matched the rhythm of the rocking chair. No matter what had happened that day, my worries fell away while we rocked."

Her voice had turned so wistful, Travis could easily picture her as the young girl she'd been when first they met, snuggled up in her father's arms, her head lolling against the man's chest as sleep claimed her.

"The last three years must've been hard on you without him."

Meredith stumbled to a halt and turned startled eyes on him. "How could you know that? That he passed three years ago?"

"That's when Christmas stopped." Travis smiled softly at his wife's scrunched expression. "Well, I guess Christmas didn't exactly stop, but that was the first year there was no gift at the gate."

"I don't understand." Something more than confusion sparked in her eyes, though. Something deeper. A longing to regain a piece of what had been lost.

He prayed what little he knew would ease that ache.

"The first gift arrived the Christmas after I carried you home. A couple old primers, an arithmetic book, and *The Old Farmer's Almanac*. Christmas Eve night he fired off two shots by the gate and left the books for me to find. The only reason I knew it was him was because he had inscribed the front of the almanac with a note thanking me for taking care of his daughter."

Meredith's eyes grew dewy, but her lips turned up at the corners. "Do you still have it?"

Travis nodded, his smile matching hers. "I do. I can show it to you tomorrow."

"I'd like that."

Wrapping his fingers around hers where they still rested in the crook of his arm, Travis gently urged her back into their stroll.

"He surprised me with more books the next year. He always included some kind of schoolbook and the newest almanac, but then he started passing along back issues of the *Palestine Advocate*. On Christmas morning, Crockett and I would take turns reading the stories aloud to the others." A chuckle rose up in Travis's throat as he recalled how young Neill and Jim had been back then. It seemed like ages ago. "It became a tradition. We would all sit outside on the porch on Christmas Eve and listen for the gunshots. I would retrieve the parcel and the boys would swarm me before I could get off my horse.

"Sometimes there would be a novel, once there was a book on animal husbandry, and Crockett's favorite was the year we got a collection of Charles Spurgeon's sermons. There were twenty-seven sermons in that little book if I recall, just enough for Crockett to preach each of them twice to us over the course of a year. I think he did that for three or four years before he finally started writing his own."

"I never knew he did that," Meredith murmured. "I knew he put parcels together for the families of his students. I even helped wrap them in brown paper and tie the strings. But I never knew that one of those parcels ended up on your doorstep."

"Three years ago, even though most of us were grown men, we still sat on the porch waiting for those shots just like we did when we were kids. Only that year, the shots never came." Travis tried to tamp down a rising lump in his throat.

"We grieved that Christmas, Meri. Not because we missed the joy of the gifts, but because we knew something had happened to the giver. I think all along it was the idea that someone remembered us and cared enough about our education and upbringing to give the books rather than the books themselves that made such an impact on us. Your father was a kind man, and I am proud to be married to his daughter."

Meredith brushed the pad of her thumb beneath her eyes, but the smile she turned on him was glorious.

"Thank you," she said, her eyes glistening—the longing replaced by gratitude and something else that made his heart turn a flip.

The path widened as they approached the pool at the base of a small waterfall. The creek only tumbled a few feet over the rocky ground, but it was enough to create a decent fishing hole. And near the edge sat a large boulder where his father used to sit with his mother.

Travis had never forgotten the time he'd cut through the trees with his pole and jar of worms only to find his father lifting his mother onto the boulder before nestling in beside her. Travis had hid among the pines and watched his mother lean her head on Father's shoulder. Joseph Archer had taken her hand and held it to his lips, then turned to his wife and whispered words that had made her smile and lift her face to accept his kiss.

Not accustomed to seeing more than a quick peck or two between his parents, Travis grew uncomfortable when that kiss stretched longer and longer. He'd quietly retreated and returned to the house, ignoring Crockett's teasing about his inability to catch a fish. He never told Crockett about what he'd seen. It felt too private. But from that moment on, the rock at the fishing hole had been dubbed the Kissing Rock in his mind. He'd never climbed on it since, promising himself that the next time he sat there, he'd have a girl of his own to kiss.

"What a beautiful place," Meredith exclaimed as he drew them to a stop by the rock.

"I'd hoped you'd like it." Travis watched her face as she took in the surroundings with wonder and delight. "I thought we could sit and talk for a bit, if you wanted."

"I'd like that." The mistiness had disappeared from her eyes, yet they continued to sparkle in the moonlight.

"This rock makes a good seat." Hearing the huskiness in his voice, he quickly cleared his throat. "I'll . . . uh . . . just help you up."

He fit his hands around her waist, his gaze mingling with hers. Then, not trusting himself to linger too long, he lifted her onto the rock and scampered up the side where smaller stones offered footholds. He settled close to her side, brushing his legs against hers and bracing his right arm behind her back. He stole glances at her while pretending to be as lost as she in the beauty of their environment. Her mouth drew his attention again and again, and he found himself desperately wishing he knew what his father had whispered to his mother to make her offer him her lips.

So consumed was he with thoughts of kissing, that when Meri opened her mouth to speak instead, it took a moment for her words to register.

"I studied to be a teacher." She turned her head and looked at him. "Did I ever mention that?"

As he tried to refocus his brain on conversation, she stretched her arms behind her to support her back and inadvertently rubbed her forearm against his bicep. His muscle twitched at her touch, and Travis had to work to keep his mind on their conversation. "No. I . . . uh . . . don't think you did."

A faraway look came over her, and her gaze shifted to hover somewhere above the creek. "After the Freedmen's Bureau shut down in '70, Father continued teaching at the freedmen's school. The students and their parents were so hungry for the education that had been denied them, they made great sacrifices to continue paying him a salary.

"When I got older, he occasionally took me with him, let me read to the little ones and help them with their alphabet. Before long I was as enamored with teaching as he was, and for the first time in my life, I felt . . . useful and appreciated."

She crossed her legs at the ankle and swung them out and back, her heels thumping quietly against the rock in an easy rhythm. "I attended the Palestine Female Institute and planned to sit for the teacher's exam, but then my parents came down with that fever." Her feet stilled for a moment. Then she sat straighter and swung them back into motion. "I had hoped to continue Papa's work at the freedmen's school, but Aunt Noreen wouldn't hear of it. She declared it unseemly to involve myself with such people and insisted it was too dangerous for a young woman to travel such a distance alone."

Travis hated to agree with anything the old bat had to say, but just the thought of Meredith traipsing about unprotected made his stomach churn.

"Seeing Moses again today awakened those old dreams." Meri aimed her blue eyes on him, hope glimmering in their depths. "I want to teach at the school again, Travis. Just one day a week. Saturday—when the largest number of students are able to attend. I would only need to be away from the ranch for a few hours. I could leave right after the noon meal and be back before supper. I promise I won't fall behind in my chores. You probably won't even know that I'm gone."

Her sentences flew at him in such rapid succession, they made him dizzy. And the churning in his gut intensified.

"Please say you'll let me go."

"No." Travis's throat closed over the word, as if an unseen hand were choking him. Her crestfallen expression pierced his heart, but he wouldn't be swayed. He tightened his jaw and looked up to the moon.

Leave the ranch? Alone? There was no way he'd let her do that. Anything could happen to her. Anything.

Her legs halted their swinging, and she twisted to look him full in the face. "Why?"

A buzzing expanded through his brain like a swarm of bees growing more and more agitated. "Archers don't leave," he ground out.

Meredith laid her hand over his. "Why?"

A muscle in his thigh jumped. Why was she questioning him? Why couldn't she just let things be? His leg twitched again and his arm began to shake. Her palm stroked the back of his hand as if to calm him. She'd noticed. She thought him weak. Afraid. But she didn't understand.

Travis jerked his hand out from beneath hers. He needed to leave. To escape. To run.

"Why do Archers never leave the ranch, Travis?" she persisted.

"A promise." The creek disappeared before him, replaced by a vision of his father reaching out to him from his sick bed, clasping his hand and making him swear. "I promised to keep them safe. Together. 'Don't leave the land, son,' he said. 'If you do, they'll take it from you. They'll split you up. Stand together. On the ranch, you're strong.'"

Travis blinked away the image of his father and turned to Meredith, his voice little more than a whisper. "On the ranch we're strong."

Meri lifted her hand and caressed his face. His eyes slid closed.

"You're strong anywhere, Travis. You all are."

Her hand felt cool against his cheek, and for just a moment he allowed himself to rest in her confidence. Slowly, he opened his eyes and found hers gazing back at him filled with trust and admiration—sentiments he wasn't sure he deserved.

"Your father was right to urge you to stay together and seclude yourself from others who would try to take advantage of your youth, but you're not boys anymore. Not even Neill. You're men. Strong Archer men. This ranch has been a haven for you for years, but if you're not careful, it will become a prison."

"It's not a prison." He pulled away from her touch and jumped down from the rock. "It's a home." He fisted his hands as if he could fight off her words.

The slide of fabric against stone whispered behind him, punctuated by a tiny grunt as her feet hit the ground. "A home where no one is free to leave? A home where all who come calling are treated like criminals? How long do you think the others will be content to live here in your shadow? Did you not see how hungry Crockett was to talk to the minister on the day of our wedding? He stayed at the man's side, throwing question after question at him about shepherding congregations and seminary and sermons.

"He has a gift for preaching, Travis. I can tell that after only one Sunday service in your home. God placed that desire on his heart and equipped him for the task, yet because of his loyalty to you, he has done nothing to pursue his calling."

Travis spun to face his wife, his accuser. "Maybe God called him to minister to his family. Or is that not grand enough for you? Perhaps you think a man can only serve God if he impacts hundreds or thousands, that three souls are not significant."

"Even one is significant."

Why was she looking at him like that? As if she were no longer talking about Crockett but about him. This wasn't about him. Everything he did was for his family. To protect them. To support them. And now this . . . this outsider who had known them for all of . . . what, less than a week? . . . had the gall to insinuate that he was trapping his brothers in some kind of prison, binding them with family loyalty, and stealing their freedom. She understood nothing!

Travis pounded up to the creek bank, barely containing the fury that burned in his gut. "You want to leave?" He spun around and marched back up to her. "Fine. Take your horse and leave. You're not really an Archer anyway."

She staggered back, her right hand pressed against her middle as if staunching a wound.

All at once he realized what he'd said. Remorse nearly cut his legs out from under him. Travis rushed forward and clasped her free hand between both of his. "Meri, forgive me. I didn't mean it. I swear I didn't." He drew her hand to his mouth and laid kiss after kiss upon her knuckles, unable to look at her face.

Meredith tugged her hand free of his grasp and turned her back.

"I don't want to leave you, Travis. I just want to help others." Her quiet words flayed him. "But helping others isn't the Archer way, is it?" She pivoted, her delicate chin jutting forth like that of a soldier. "Archers hide in their trees, too scared of what *could* happen to risk reaching out to someone in need."

"I reached out to you."

"But only because you felt responsible." Her chin dipped a bit, some of the fight going out of her.

Was she right? Had he only married her because he felt obligated? If so, why did the thought of her taking him up on his insistence that she leave chill his blood?

Travis closed the space between him and his wife with a single step. "You think I'm scared, Meri? Well, I am. Scared to let you go. Scared that something will happen to you." *Like what happened to my father.* He lifted one hand to her face and stroked her cheek with his thumb. "I can control things to some extent on the ranch, but away from it? I won't be able to protect you."

"Oh, Travis." She shook her head at him, her mouth twitching into an ironic smile. "You do realize, don't you, that the two most serious injuries I've endured in my life have happened while on your property? Not by any fault of yours, of course, but one could argue that I'm actually safer off the ranch than on."

A groan vibrated in his throat, turning into a reluctant chuckle. The woman had a point.

"No matter how many precautions we take, none of us are truly in control. Only God can claim that kind of authority. All we can do is use the good sense he provides and trust him to guide us." Meredith stroked his arm from shoulder to wrist, then lightly clasped his hand. "If you want to protect me, Travis, prayer is just as powerful a weapon as that gun you carry."

Travis blinked, stunned by the simplicity of that statement. Did he believe it? When was the last time he'd prayed, really prayed, for the Lord's protection over his family? He'd been depending on himself for so long, he'd forgotten how to trust another with that duty. Even God.

Reaching for a faith that was more than just Sunday-deep, he inhaled a shaky breath and cleared his throat. "This teaching thing. It's important to you?"

She nodded. "Yes. But not more important than our marriage. If you don't want me to go, I'll respect your wishes."

He didn't want her to go. Not at all. Yet he couldn't keep her a prisoner, either. How would she ever come to love him if he stole her freedom?

"You're not to tarry. You hear me? Straight there and straight home. And you'll take a rifle. Prayer is all well and good, and I imagine I'll be sending a constant litany heavenward while you're gone, but I doubt a little earthly defense will offend our Maker."

She bounced up and down on her toes, her smile bright enough to rival the moon. "Thank you, Travis. Thank you, thank you, thank you!" Before he knew what she was about, she grabbed his shoulders and planted a kiss on his cheek.

His blood heated in an instant. He snaked his arm around her waist and drew her firmly against his body. "If you're gonna thank me, Meri, do it proper."

Travis bent his head and captured the startled little sound that escaped her parted lips. His emotions were too raw, too close to the surface to contain, so he kissed her with everything inside him. Desire, fear, yearning, and a touch of desperation fueled his passion. He melded his mouth to hers, trailing his hand upward along her back until his fingers buried themselves in the hair at her nape.

He told himself to stop, afraid he'd frighten her, but just as he steeled himself to pull away, she moaned deep in her throat and wrapped her arms around his neck. Travis's pulse leapt, her response too sweet to ignore. He slanted his lips over hers again, deepening the kiss until he felt her tremble. Only then did he gentle his assault, loosening his hold as he softened his lips. He moved his hands to cradle her face and leaned his forehead against hers. Eyes closed, lips inches apart, their ragged breathing mingled in the air between them.

"You belong to me, Meri," he whispered hoarsely. "You *are* an Archer, but more importantly, you're my wife."

She said nothing, but he felt the slight bob of her head as she tried to nod. Something deep inside him relaxed.

He'd not driven her away after all. Thank God. He wanted to kiss her again, and more. Much more. But he'd already taken enough backward steps tonight. He'd not rush things. Meredith deserved a proper courtship, and she was going to get one, even if it killed him.

And kill him it might, if it meant sitting back and watching her ride off to teach at that school of hers. But he couldn't imprison her at the ranch and expect to earn her loyalty. Nor her love. Such commodities had to be given freely. As did trust—something he'd have to learn to give more freely himself.

Keep her safe, Lord, he prayed as he pulled Meredith into his embrace and tucked her head under his chin. *Keep my wife safe.*

He didn't know how or when she had become so important to him, but as he stood there holding her, he was certain of one thing. He never wanted to lose her.

23

Swear to me you'll be careful."

Meredith smiled at her husband's stern expression. Travis demanded the same thing every time she left. Of course, this was only her third Saturday to travel to the school, so perhaps he was still adjusting. Nevertheless, her heart gave a little leap every time she heard the protective growl that proved he cared.

"I swear it."

He took the flour sack that held Neill's old primers and tied it to Ginger's saddle, then checked the cinch for the third time. Meredith chuckled and laid a gentle hand on his shoulder.

"It's secure, Travis. You saddled her yourself, remember?"

He looked up, his eyes scanning her face as if trying to commit every feature to memory. She ducked her head as her cheeks began to warm.

Travis cleared his throat and kicked at the dirt. "You got the gate key?"

"Yes." Meredith lifted her hand to her chest in confirmation. The key hung from a chain around her neck. Its outline was barely discernible to her touch through the layers of her dress and cloak, but she could feel the metal press against her skin.

Knowing what question he'd ask next, she answered before he finished drawing a full breath. "Yes, the rifle is loaded. And yes, I'll come straight home after the last lesson."

"You better." His lips twitched as he struggled to maintain his serious mien. Then before she could react, he grabbed the folds of her cloak and pulled her to him. His lips came down on hers, possessive, demanding, and so intense her knees shook.

"Come home to me, Meri," he whispered, his voice husky and deep.

"Always." The single word was all she could manage just then, but she infused it with all the love in her heart.

He'd still made no move to come to her room, not even after that soul-stirring kiss they'd shared down by the creek. He and the rest of the clan had been so busy with rebuilding the barn and driving the cattle to wherever they could find undepleted pasture, that she rarely even spoke to her husband except at meals. But on Saturdays he made a point to see her off. On Saturdays he kissed her. On Saturdays he gave her hope that their marriage could be based on something deeper than hastily spoken vows.

She adored Saturdays.

Travis laced his fingers together and bent to give her a leg up. Meredith reached for the saddle horn, placed her left boot in the stirrup, and put her right into her husband's keeping. He helped her into the saddle and patted Ginger's neck as Meredith gathered the reins.

"I'll be watching for you." His hat shielded his face from her view as he ran his fingers along the chestnut-and-white pattern of Ginger's shoulder. His hand reached the cinch, and she thought the daft man was going to check it a fourth time, but he skimmed over the strap and settled instead upon her ankle. The solid presence of his hand filtered through the leather of her boot top as he assured himself that her foot sat securely in the stirrup. It seemed an intimate, husbandly gesture, and Meredith's heart swelled. Then his thumb stroked upward and brushed against her stocking. Her breath caught.

He finally lifted his face to hers, and the heated look in his eyes left no doubt in her mind that the touch had been deliberate. "Hurry home." The words lingered as his gaze melded to hers. Then he stepped back and swatted Ginger lightly on the hindquarters to set her into motion.

The paint's bouncing trot demanded Meredith's attention. She turned forward in the saddle and took charge of the animal. Moses called down a farewell from where he and Jim were nailing shingles onto the barn roof, and Meredith raised a hand to wave at them as she rode past. Jim saluted her with a lift of his hammer—a gesture so typical of her stoic brother-in-law that it normally would have brought a smile to her face. But Meredith was too consumed with thoughts of Travis to pay Jim much heed.

Could it be her husband felt something more than protectiveness toward her? More than obligation? She'd let herself believe so when he kissed her, but even then the fantasy didn't completely dispel the hint of desperation she sensed in him. It was as if he needed to stake his claim on her before he could let her go.

What would it be like to have him kiss her simply out of desire? Out of love? Suddenly Saturdays seemed inadequate. She wanted to be kissed on a Tuesday. No special occasion. No threat to her well-being. Just a warm sharing of affection between a husband and wife. To see that heated look in his eyes again, as if she truly meant more to him than duty.

And what of your vow to be content in your marriage?

The thought brought a swift end to her self-pity.

Forgive me, Lord. I'm turning my mind in the wrong direction, aren't I? I became so consumed by what I didn't have that I forgot all about what I do have.

Just like those times when Aunt Noreen's caustic personality wore her down and bitterness started to leak into her soul. She had to take charge of her thoughts and steer them in a more positive direction. It was time to count her blessings.

One—she was married to the man of her dreams. Two—Travis had allowed her to continue her father's legacy by teaching at the freedmen's school. Three—she belonged to a family of godly men who would protect her with their lives. Meredith turned her gaze toward heaven and smiled, the burden on her heart already beginning to lift. She truly was blessed. Just thinking about how far her relationship with Travis had progressed over the last few weeks stirred songs of thanksgiving in her soul. She could only imagine what strides they could make in the next few weeks.

Help me to be patient. To accept your timing.

Her grin widened as the gate came into view. Perhaps one day soon, she would unlock Travis's heart as easily as she was able to unlock the gate to his land. All she had to do was find the right key. Or become so trusted by him that he unlocked it himself. Wouldn't that be something?

Buoyed by hope, Meredith slid from the saddle and drew the chain around her neck upward until the gate key freed itself from her clothing. Humming a cheery tune, she made short work of the gate, leading Ginger through and carefully relocking it before climbing atop a nearby stone to remount.

Travis might feel safe behind all his fences and gates, but she aimed to show him that freedom was sweeter. Especially when founded on love.

Urging Ginger into a canter, Meredith leaned forward in the saddle and let the exhilarating rush of the wind tug at her hairpins and sting her cheeks with its frosty bite. If she arrived disheveled and chapped, so be it. Her students understood the significance of freedom. They'd not condemn her for indulging in a spirited ride.

But fifteen minutes later, when she reined Ginger to a walk in front of the schoolhouse, a host of concerned children swarmed from the schoolyard to surround her.

"What done happened to your hair, Miss Meri?"

"Didja fall off your horse?"

"Why was you ridin' so fast?"

"Was som'un chasin' you?"

"I'm fine, children," she assured them, laughter bubbling up to accompany her words. "I simply chose to give Ginger her head today." She patted the paint's neck.

When the children continued to press closer, Ginger halted. The horse didn't seem too perturbed by the crowding, just cautious.

"Get back, now, and give Miss Meri some air." Myra Jackson moved through the throng, shooing children back toward the schoolhouse. "How's she gonna teach us anything if'n she can't get off her horse?"

The children moaned but obeyed, filing off toward the schoolhouse to find their desks.

"Joshua, you stay and tend to Ginger. Rub her down real good, you hear?"

"Yes'm." Myra's younger boy stood at the horse's head, waiting patiently for Meredith to dismount.

Once her feet were planted on the ground, Meredith tossed him the reins. "Thank you, Joshua." She untied her supply bag and stepped aside.

As the boy led her horse away, Meredith sidled up next to Myra. "You know, I think he's going to catch up to Josiah soon. He's nearly the same height."

"Don't I know it?" Myra's mouth turned up in a proud motherly smile. "And him three years younger. The boy's got his father's hands, too. Big as fryin' pans they are."

Meredith grinned, remembering how Moses had curled those big hands of his into fists. Getting hit with one of those would probably feel a lot like getting walloped with a skillet. "Joshua seems to have inherited your love of books, though. Has he finished *The Last of the Mohicans*?"

Myra nodded. "Mm-hmm. Two days ago. He tol' me you promised to bring a new one this week."

"That I did." She opened her bag and pulled out her copy of *The Adventures of Tom Sawyer*. "I don't think you've read this one yet, Myra. It was only published a few years ago, so it wasn't among the books my father used to loan you."

"Joshua might have to fight me for it, then." The older woman winked at Meredith and tucked the book under her arm.

Meredith laughed and followed her friend into the classroom. Myra Jackson kept the small building as tidy as herself, which was saying a lot since the woman's apron was always starched and pressed, her black hair always combed into a perfect knot, and her dress always so pristine that dust wouldn't dare approach its folds. Meredith reached a hand to her own hair and sighed. Freedom had more than taken its toll. No wonder the children had stared.

Taking a minute to repair the wind's damage, Meredith remained at the back of the class while Myra called the group to order and asked them to take out their primers. The worn books were the same ones her father had started the school with over a decade ago. They'd been well cared for, though. Unfortunately, there were never enough to go around, which was why she'd asked Travis if she could borrow Neill's old schoolbooks.

Taking the slender volumes from her bag, she distributed them to the adults who sat on benches at the back of the room. The surprised faces and reverent strokes of the covers warmed her heart. These parents hungered for learning even more than their children did, yet they insisted the younger generation have first access to the few books and other materials available. Such noble souls. She wished she could do more for them.

As Myra asked one of the female students to stand and read a passage aloud, Meredith moved to the front of the room and quietly began writing a series of arithmetic problems on the blackboard.

Despite a lack of formal training, Myra had done her best to continue where Meredith's father had left off, teaching the local children the basics of reading, writing, and arithmetic. And when Meredith mentioned to Moses her idea of teaching at the school, she'd made it clear she had no intention of supplanting Myra in any way. She only wanted to make herself available to assist.

Myra, however, responded as if Meredith's offer were a gift from above. The first Saturday they met, she pulled Meredith into a fierce hug and praised the Lord right there in the schoolyard. She'd been praying, she'd said, for the Lord to provide a teacher for her advanced students, someone capable of preparing them for future studies or for professions that would utilize their minds instead of breaking their backs. She dreamed of her students one day becoming teachers themselves, or shopkeepers, or even doctors. Education opened doors, and Myra was bound and determined to fling wide as many portals as possible.

So, for the three hours Meredith spent at Myra's school every Saturday, she taught advanced mathematics, grammar, and history to the half-dozen students who already excelled in the more elementary lessons. Joshua was particularly bright, and Meredith had high hopes of him continuing his studies at Wiley College up in Marshall. Her father would've been thrilled to have one of his former students attend the new school, and she couldn't deny that she, too, would be proud to have played some minor role in the boy's success.

But first she needed to help him master algebra.

Turning to face her group of students, Meredith caught Joshua's eye as he slid into his seat after seeing to her horse. She smiled and motioned him forward. "Joshua, would you please come to the board and work the first equation?"

"Yes, Miss Meri," he said, matching her quiet tone so as not to disturb the rest of the class.

And so it began. Each of the older children took turns working problems, and when not at the blackboard, they practiced on their slates. If one student made an error, another could volunteer to make the correction. Once the algebra problems had been completed, Meredith administered the oral quiz she had prepared over the Boston Tea Party. The students had only one history text between them, but they had worked out a system that allowed each person to take possession of it on a different day, and she was pleased by how much they had retained.

The students had just started reciting their grammar lesson when the light from the doorway abruptly dimmed. Meredith glanced up to see a large man standing in the entrance.

"Moses?" The concern in Myra's voice sharpened Meredith's attention.

Why had he come? Had Josiah been hurt? Or . . . Travis? Meredith took an involuntary step closer to the aisle, her heart thumping painfully in her chest.

"I need a word with Miss Meri." He pointed the hat he held in his hand toward her, his gaze finally leaving his wife to settle on Meredith.

"Finish your recitations, children," she murmured as she took her cloak down from the nail on the side wall. "And study lessons seven and eight for next week."

Her students nodded but did nothing to break the unnatural hush that had fallen over the schoolroom. The quiet only amplified Meredith's unease, and every time a floorboard squeaked as she made her way to the door, the echo frayed her nerves further. By the time she reached Moses and followed him outside, her hands were shaking.

Moses tried to lead her a discreet distance away, but she grabbed hold of his arm, needing answers more than privacy. "Has something happened to my husband?"

"No, ma'am." He turned to face her, his earnest expression spearing relief through her. "Everybody be fine."

She exhaled a heavy breath. "Thank heavens."

"But there sure 'nough be trouble of some kind, 'cause Mr. Travis, he done tol' me to fetch you right quick."

Meredith slipped her arms into the sleeves of her cloak and worked the fasteners. There was no question—she would return at once. Travis needed her. "Do you have any idea what the trouble is?"

"No, Miss Meri. But it might have somethin' to do with their visitor."

A visitor? Meredith jerked her attention from her buttons to the grim line of Moses's mouth.

"I noticed a strange horse in the corral when I come in from the barn. It weren't wearing the Archer brand."

Meredith's pulse picked up speed again. Had one of Roy's men come to make more threats? For the first time, she realized how Travis must feel when things began spiraling out of his control. The horrible helplessness that swamped her at the thought of her family being in trouble while she was too far away to help made her ill.

"I need my horse." She rushed past Moses only to see Josiah leading Ginger toward her.

Moses came up behind her and lifted her into the saddle. Meredith thanked him and kicked Ginger into a gallop. This time the wind in her hair brought no feeling of freedom, only a growing urgency as she raced home.

24

When Meredith rode into the yard, she scanned the barn and outbuildings for any hint of what the trouble could be, but nothing seemed out of place. None of the men were in evidence, either, which sent a frisson of alarm skittering down her back. Meredith reined Ginger to a halt in front of the house and jumped to the ground, ignoring the twinge of pain that shot up her weak leg. She tossed the lead line around the porch railing and pounded up the steps.

"Travis?" His name echoed through the house as she threw the door wide.

The sound of muffled voices drifted to her through the parlor wall. Meredith hurried the short distance to the entrance and nearly collided with her husband as his form filled the doorway. He looked blessedly hearty, if a bit haggard. She laid her palms upon his chest, needing the solid feel of him to reassure her that he was indeed unharmed.

"You're all right?" The breathless whisper escaped before her mind could stop it. The man probably thought her a nitwit. Of course he was all right. He was standing right in front of her, for goodness' sake.

Yet something that flashed in his eyes dissolved her chagrin. He claimed her hands in his larger ones and gave them a gentle squeeze before a wail from somewhere behind him broke the spell.

"What on earth . . . ?" Meredith tilted her head to see around her husband's shoulder. A familiar set of blond curls peeked at her over the back of the settee. "Cassie?"

Her cousin pushed away from a beleaguered-looking Jim, whose wet shirtfront attested to the length of time he'd offered himself as a human handkerchief, and twisted to peer at Meredith.

"Oh, Meri. Thank the Lord you're home." Her reddened eyes and blotchy complexion spurred Meredith to her side. Cassie had been known to shed a strategic tear or two when trying to get her way, but Meredith had never seen her so distraught.

Squeezing onto the settee between her cousin and the sofa arm, Meredith grasped Cassandra's hands. "What happened?"

Cassie's face crumpled. "Papa's done something awful, Meri. Truly awf-f-fullll." The last word ended on another wail as Cassie threw herself into Meredith's arms.

Wrapping her cousin in a tight embrace, Meredith glanced around the room at her brothers-in-law, questioning them with her eyes.

They all wore the same bewildered expression, offering no help whatsoever.

"We haven't been able to get much out of her," Travis said softly, his hands gripping the wooden trim on the back of the settee near her shoulder. "She insisted on waiting for you."

"Well, I'm here now." Meredith spoke more to Cassie than Travis. She patted her cousin's back a final time, then gently clasped her arms and sat her up straight. "Whatever Uncle Everett has done, we will deal with it." Meredith reached a hand to Cassie's hair and began rearranging the disheveled curls. "Now, let's get you presentable so you'll feel better. You really are quite a wreck." She smiled fondly at her cousin to take the sting from her words. Yet the delicate prick to Cassandra's vanity sparked the exact reaction Meredith intended.

Her cousin immediately set about putting her appearance to rights, wiping the tear tracks from her cheeks, smoothing her skirts, and straightening her posture. The quick self-conscious glance she directed toward Jim as he rose from the settee didn't go unnoticed, either. Cassie wouldn't be falling apart again—not in front of the men, anyway.

"I never thought Papa would steal from his own flesh and blood." Cassie gave a little sniff. "It's not like him at all, you know. But when Mama insisted it was the only way to save the business, he gave in." Cassandra placed her hand atop Meredith's, her earnest face pleading for understanding. "You must forgive him, Meri. His financial troubles are much more dire than I imagined. I'm sure he felt this was the only way."

"Cass, you're making my head spin." Meredith's forehead crinkled as she tried to make sense of the convoluted story. "What, exactly, has he done?"

"Before I tell you, promise me that you won't hold it against me. I want no part of this scheme. I said as much to Papa, but Mama slapped my face for talking back and said I'd do what was right for the family, that I'd been pampered long enough, and it was time for me to do my duty."

"Aunt Noreen actually struck you?" The shock of it pushed Meredith back against the arm of the sofa. Her aunt had always doted on Cassandra.

Meredith couldn't even remember the woman speaking to her daughter in a harsh tone.

"Yes." Cassie's chin wobbled, but she fought to keep the tears at bay. "That's when I knew that I couldn't cajole Papa out of the idea. There was too much at stake. My only chance to escape was to beg you to take me in."

"You are always welcome in my home, Cass. You know that. But you really must cease all this beating around the bush and tell me what is going on."

Her cousin lowered her lashes as if too ashamed to meet Meredith's gaze. "Instead of signing over Uncle Teddy's land to you upon your marriage, as he and Uncle Teddy arranged, Papa plans to use it as a dowry. For me."

"He's stealing my land?" Meredith could barely get the words out, so deflated was she by the revelation. "The home I grew up in?"

A warm hand settled on her shoulder and stroked the skin at her neck. *Travis.* His quiet support kept her from shattering. But she couldn't look at him. What would he think? That land was the only thing of value she'd brought to their marriage. She'd hoped to pass it down to their children one day, just as his father had passed down the Archer ranch to him and his brothers. Her dowry had just been stolen from him to be given to another.

To Cassie.

Meredith stiffened. The only reason Uncle Everett would use the land as a dowry for Cassandra would be to entice a prosperous suitor into making an offer. A man who would value the land.

Meredith's stomach lurched. She prayed her intuition was wrong. "Who do they expect you to marry?"

Cassie finally looked up, her eyes twin pools of sorrow. "Roy Mitchell."

Tension speared through Meredith's shoulders beneath Travis's fingers. He tried to massage some of it away, but his own muscles had bunched so tight, he doubted it was very effective.

How could Everett Hayes be such a weak-livered dunce? What little respect Travis held for the man due to his relationship with Meri evaporated. Even if Hayes was fool enough to believe Mitchell innocent of the attack on Travis's barn, he should have enough qualms to prevent him from handing over the daughter he claimed to love simply to boost his deteriorating business.

He glanced at each of his brothers, all of them wearing the same stony-eyed expression, and made his intention clear by moving to stand directly between the backs of the two women sitting on the settee. Travis slid his hands along the wooden trim of the sofa until his spread arms encompassed them both. Meredith loved Cassandra like a sister. That made her family. Archers protected family.

Crockett, Neill, and Jim all met his stare and gave their nod of assent. Jim held Travis's gaze the longest and took a deliberate step closer to their visitor as he clenched his jaw in determination. His meaning was clear. Jim had just staked a claim. And made himself responsible for Cassandra's welfare.

"You can't go along with it, Cass." Meredith shoved up out of her seat and started pacing, her uneven gait agitated and unsteady as she crossed the rug. Travis moved farther into the room, wishing he could spare her this latest betrayal.

Cassandra shifted to the edge of the settee. "I know. That's why I came here. You were obviously right about Mr. Mitchell. He must have only been after your land if the bride accompanying it makes so little difference to him. I can't marry someone who cares nothing for me."

"It's worse than that." Meredith spun to face her cousin. "He's dangerous. Or did you forget about him sending men to set fire to the Archers' barn?"

The younger woman tilted her chin at a quizzical angle as she slowly rose to her feet. "Papa assured me that was a misunderstanding. That it was one of Roy's competitors who set the fire."

"I heard him give the order, Cassie. There was no misunderstanding." Meredith crossed her arms over her chest. Instead of lending her a look of determination, however, the movement gave her an air of vulnerability, as if she strove to protect herself from another family member's disbelief.

"Papa wouldn't lie to me. I'm sure of it."

Travis strode to Meredith's side, the instinct to protect her driving him forward. His jaw tensed as he glowered at the young woman before him. "Your papa *wants* to believe in Mitchell's innocence because he needs the man's partnership." His words came out clipped and impatient even to his own ears. Little Cassie would just have to deal with it, though. He couldn't stomach another Hayes gainsaying Meri in order to make excuses for the man who destroyed his property and plotted to steal his land. "Money clouded his judgment, and he accepted the word of a stranger over family."

"Isn't there the slightest chance you misheard, Meri?" Doubt clouded the girl's features as she scrambled to keep her doting father from sliding farther off his pedestal.

"No," Meredith answered, her voice rich with compassion. "I'm sure of what I heard. But even if there *was* a chance, would you be willing to risk your future happiness on such short odds?"

Cassandra bit her lower lip and shook her head. Meredith rushed to her side and wrapped her arms around her.

"What am I going to do?"

Meredith smiled that brave smile of hers that always made Travis's chest puff with pride. "We'll think of something. For now, though, you're going to come to the kitchen and help me make supper."

"You know I can't cook."

Meredith tucked her cousin under her arm like a mother hen with a chick and led her toward the door. "Well, it's about time you learned, don't you think?"

Meredith twisted her neck to meet Travis's gaze before she swept out of the room. He felt her thanks without her having to say a word, and the fact that he could read her looks as well as those of his brothers made him pause. She was becoming part of him.

Once the women's voices receded, Travis turned back to face his brothers. They all gravitated toward the center of the room.

"What's the plan, Trav?" Neill asked.

"She ain't marrying Mitchell." Jim glared at Travis, daring him to argue.

Travis clapped him on the shoulder. "Cassandra will stay here under our protection until we decide what needs to be done. In the meantime, it might be a good idea—"

A pair of shots echoed in the distance, cutting Travis off. He instinctively looked to the window. Cassandra's father had made good time.

"Have you noticed that we've had more visitors in the last few weeks than we had all of last year? Maybe we should consider opening a hotel." Crockett's sarcasm earned him a punch in the arm from Jim.

Travis bit back a reply. He couldn't deny that things had started spiraling further and further out of control ever since Meredith showed up on their ranch, but even with all the trouble, he didn't regret her appearance. How could he? She was family.

A tiny seed of a thought surfaced in his mind, that perhaps she was even more than family, but he didn't have time to examine it too closely. He had an irate father to deal with and a brother to restrain from shooting said father. That was about all he could handle at the moment.

"Jim, you're with me. Neill, take position near the barn. Crockett—" he paused long enough to smirk at his oldest sibling—"you can man the Archer Hotel."

Crockett's chuckle followed him as he and the others filed out the front door.

25

Travis and Jim approached the gate from among the trees instead of using the path, taking the opportunity to observe their quarry before making their presence known. Everett Hayes paced back and forth beside the gate, muttering under his breath. The rifle gripped in his right hand gave Travis pause.

Perhaps his customary show of force wasn't the best course of action this time. The man had already worked himself into a lather, and with Jim's temper being riled, as well, things could get ugly fast. Meredith's warning about someone calling his bluff one day floated through his mind.

With a silent motion, Travis lifted his rifle from its ready position across his lap and angled the barrel into the scabbard attached to his saddle. He shoved it home.

"What are you doing?" Jim hissed.

"Put your gun away."

"Not a chance." He tightened his grip on the weapon and braced the stock against his thigh.

Travis frowned at him. "Do you really think that putting a bullet in Cassandra's father is going to endear you to her?"

Jim shifted slightly in his saddle.

"If Everett Hayes is foolish enough to believe Mitchell's lies, he's foolish enough to start something with that gun of his that we'd have to finish. And if one of us puts a bullet in him, we'll have to take him up to the house and let Crockett patch him up. Not the best scenario for keeping him away from Cassie, is it."

Jim said nothing, just eyed Everett Hayes through the trees, his jaw clenched. After a long minute, he expelled a full breath through his nostrils like a provoked bull, then flipped his rifle around and crammed it into his scabbard.

Thanking the Lord for his brother's cooperation and adding in a quick plea for Hayes to see reason as easily, Travis nudged Bexar out into the open and raised a hand in greeting to his wife's uncle.

Hayes started at the sight of Travis and Jim emerging from among the pines and snapped his rifle to his shoulder. "About time you got here." He glowered at Travis over the barrel of the gun with eyes that looked a little too wild for reasonable conversation. "I want my daughter back. Now!"

"Cassandra's safe," Travis said. He figured if *his* daughter ran away, fear for her well-being might make him a bit crazed, too. The least he could do was put that fear to rest for the man.

"Safe with *you*? Ha! The last female of my household that came to visit you unescorted ended up half dead with a soiled reputation. I'm not about to let Cassie share the same fate."

Travis leaned forward in his saddle, his brief flash of sympathy hardening to stone as he glared down at the older man from his position atop Bexar. "Put the gun away, Hayes, and we'll talk. Keep waving it at me, and you can forget about gaining my help with your daughter."

The man held his position, but Travis could see indecision playing across his face as he glanced from one brother to the other. Finally, he lowered his rifle and stepped closer to the gate.

"All right, Archer. Now let me in so I can fetch my daughter."

Travis stood in the stirrups and swung his leg over Bexar's back. Jim dismounted, as well, and the two strode forward. When they reached the gate, Travis hung both arms over the top of the highest crossbar and braced a foot on the lowest, trying to appear as friendly and nonthreatening as possible. Jim, on the other hand, stood as straight as a soldier and kept his gun belt within easy reach. Neither made a move to unlock the wooden barrier that obstructed the man's entrance.

"Cassandra will be staying with us for a while," Travis informed Hayes, the sternness of his voice belying his casual stance. "My wife is thrilled to have her company, of course, and will gladly serve as her chaperone."

"Impossible!" Everett Hayes blustered. "Cassie is coming home with me, at once."

Jim took a single menacing stride forward. "She's staying."

Travis brushed a bit of dust from his sleeve. "I'm sure she'll calm down in a day or two and see reason again." He shook his head and expelled a sympathetic chuckle. "The poor girl actually believes you plan to marry her off to Meredith's former beau. Can you imagine? I did everything I could to convince her that you couldn't possibly be thinking of forcing her into a union with that barn-burning, land-grabbing fiend, but she seems quite convinced. Even went so far as to gain my promise that I wouldn't let you take her away. So, unfortunately, I cannot let you in."

"Curse your lying hide, Archer!" Hayes seized the top rail of the gate and rattled it on its hinges. The rails shook with such violence that Travis had to step away to keep from having his chin pummeled. "You said you'd help me."

Travis held up a conciliatory hand. "Simmer down. I said I'd help you, and I will. I cannot break my word to Cassandra, of course, but I'd gladly deliver a note to her if you wish to clear up the misunderstanding. Surely after she learns she was mistaken, she'll be eager to return to her family."

"You're meddling in affairs that do not concern you." Hayes jabbed his finger at Travis over the gate. "If you won't bring Cassie to me, I'll take her myself." He leapt forward, intent on scaling the barricade, his rifle still clutched in one hand.

In a flash, Jim had his revolver clear of its holster, and the sound of the gun being cocked echoed loudly in the air between them. Hayes halted his climb.

"I wouldn't recommend trying to take her by force," Travis said. "We do have a policy about trespassers, after all, and I'm sure it would distress my wife if I let Jim put a bullet in you. Oh, and should you consider sneaking in after dark, I think it only fair to warn you that my hound is a fierce guard dog. She doesn't take kindly to strangers skulking about and is likely to take a piece out of your leg. I'd hate for you to become injured after I promised to help you and all."

Hayes swore under his breath and dropped down from the gate. Jim lowered his revolver. Travis grinned.

"Why don't you go back to town and get some rest? Give Meri and Cassandra a few days to visit, and when your daughter is ready to come home, I'll see to it that she is delivered to you safely. You have my word."

"I don't want your word. I want my daughter." Nevertheless, Hayes stomped off toward his horse. The animal danced sideways, unnerved by the hostility emanating from his master.

Hayes jerked the reins with a rough hand and hauled himself into the saddle. He steered his mount in a tight circle as he fought for control, then turned his attention back to Travis. "If Cassandra is not home in three days time, expect an armed posse at your doorstep. And I'll shoot any man or beast who tries to keep me from her." His narrowed eyes shifted to Jim and lingered for a heartbeat or two before he brought his horse's head around and dug his heels into the animal's sides.

Neither Archer spoke until the hoofbeats from Hayes's horse faded into the distance.

When the sound could no longer be heard, Travis pivoted away from the gate and faced his brother. "You think he'll follow through on that threat?"

"Yep." Jim holstered his gun and strode to his horse.

Travis's mouth settled into a grim line as he followed. "Me too."

Meredith and Cassie managed to have a simple supper of skillet-fried ham, mashed potatoes, and green beans ready when the men came home.

"Why don't you take the biscuits to the table while I whip up a batch of redeye gravy." Meredith nudged her cousin over to the counter, where the biscuits sat in a pair of towel-covered pie tins. Ever since Travis and Jim returned, Cassie hadn't been able to concentrate on any task for more than a minute or two. And no wonder. The men had been terribly tight-lipped over what had happened at the gate.

All Meredith had ferreted out was that their visitor had indeed been Uncle Everett and that they had managed to convince him to allow Cassandra to stay for a few days. She hoped that once everyone sat around the table, Travis and Jim would give a more detailed accounting.

Meredith poured about half a cup of coffee into her skillet with the ham drippings and deglazed the pan, scraping every bit of ham from the bottom and sides that she could. As the gravy simmered, she glanced over her shoulder to check on Cassie's progress. The girl had gotten all the biscuits into the serving bowl, but the bowl hadn't quite made it to the table. Meredith hid her grin by turning to stir the gravy.

Cassie hovered at Jim's side near the doorway, the biscuit bowl in the crook of her arm. It was hard to tell if Cassie was attracted to the stoic man or if he just made her feel safe, but one thing had become abundantly clear—she preferred Jim's company to any of the others. Which Meredith found surprising. She would have guessed that Crockett's charm and gentle teasing would hold more appeal for the usually effervescent Cassie. But it was Jim who drew her.

While Meredith added salt and pepper to the redeye gravy, she spied Jim taking the biscuits from Cassie. He thumped the bowl onto the table and immediately put a hand at her waist to guide her to a chair—one that sat directly next to his.

Her cousin wasn't the only one smitten.

Meredith's gaze wandered over to where her husband stood near the head of the table. Was Travis smitten? Did he long to be close to her like Jim longed to be near Cassie? She inwardly pleaded with him to look at her, to assure her of his affection. But he didn't. He just kept jawing with Neill and Crockett about the barn roof. Oblivious.

Biting the inside of her cheek, Meredith turned her attention back to the gravy. Her elbow flapped as she stirred the drippings with a tad too much zeal. Foolish fancies. What did she expect? That he would read her mind and suddenly cross the room to take her in his arms? He was a man, not some kind of clairvoyant wizard. Unrealistic expectations would do neither of them any favors.

Yet . . .

Her hand stilled, and the gravy ceased its frantic whirl.

Travis had looked at her earlier today. *Really* looked at her. After he'd kissed her and held her tight against his chest, he'd helped her mount and caressed the base of her calf. A touch that still made her shiver when she thought of it. And the heat in his eyes as he'd gazed up at her? That heat had warmed her blood and stolen her breath. Oh, he'd looked smitten then.

Perhaps if they could find an opportunity to be alone . . .

Meredith removed the skillet from the stove and twisted toward the counter to pour the gravy into a small bowl. The ocean blue of Cassie's dress loomed up from the corner of her vision like a wave sent to dash Meredith's hopes. She couldn't exactly instigate a rendezvous with her husband when her cousin was sharing their room, could she? Now wasn't the proper time for that kind of thing, anyway. Cassie was in trouble. Her needs took precedence.

"Neill, grab the beans, would you?" Meredith called to the youngest Archer as she set the gravy near Travis's end of the table.

Travis stopped talking at her approach and finally turned. His eyes met hers, and though she sensed his distraction and concern over what had happened with her uncle, she also sensed a connection, as if her presence actually comforted him. It wasn't a heated look of attraction like the one earlier in the day, but it warmed her just the same—deep in her heart, where her most protected dreams dwelt.

Crockett moved past her to take charge of the potatoes, reminding Meredith of her duties. She scurried back to the stove and removed the ham platter from the warming oven. Travis stepped forward to carry it to the table. Meredith wiped her hands on her apron and double-checked the counters to make sure she hadn't missed anything. Then, praying the men would assume the stove was responsible for her flushed cheeks, she joined her family at the table.

The instant the blessing ended, the men tucked into their food with their usual gusto. Cassie, on the other hand, spent more time pushing her ham around her plate with her fork than actually eating.

Hoping to lighten the mood and perhaps spark her cousin's interest, Meredith leaned forward to see around Cassie and addressed her brother-in-law at the end of the table. "So . . . Jim. I've been meaning to ask you a question."

His jaw halted midchew. He glanced around the table as if looking for another man named Jim to respond. Not finding one, he swallowed what was in his mouth and scrubbed the back of his hand across his chin. "What?"

Cassie's head came up, and Meredith secretly cheered. Straightening in her seat, she set aside her napkin and peered down the table. "Well, I've managed to figure out that all you Archer men have names connected to the Alamo. Travis"—she turned to smile at her husband at the head of the table to her right—"of course refers to Lieutenant Colonel William Travis, who took over command of the regular soldiers at the Alamo in relief of Colonel James Neill"—she pointed to the youngest Archer, across from Cassandra—"who had to leave San Antonio de Bexar to tend to a sick family member. Crockett most certainly is named for Davy Crockett, the famous Tennessean who arrived at the Alamo only two short weeks before Santa Anna. So, logically, I would have to assume that you were named for James Bowie, the commander of the volunteers. What I don't understand is why you are the only Archer who doesn't go by your hero's surname."

A dull red color seeped up Jim's face, and Meredith immediately regretted asking the question. She'd only wanted to distract Cassie from her troubles, not embarrass the poor man.

"Never mind. I didn't mean to pry. I—"

"You're not prying." Jim interrupted her babbling. "You might as well know the truth."

Perhaps it was the sideways glance he darted in Cassandra's direction, but Meredith got the feeling he wasn't really aiming that last comment at her.

"Ma was real big on remembering the Alamo. And you're right. She didn't name me James. My given name is Bowie." He ducked his head and stabbed a bean with the tines of his fork, though he made no move to lift the vegetable to his mouth.

"And none of us can figure out why he doesn't like it," Crockett said, his eyes full of teasing. "It's not like it sounds like a hog call or anything. Boo-ie! No, wait. Soo-ie!"

Neill laughed out loud, nearly spewing mashed potatoes all over the table. Travis grinned and shook his head, a little huff of laughter puffing out his nose. Meredith couldn't resist a little smile of her own.

"I think Bowie is a wonderful name. It's strong. Heroic." Cassie's passionate defense brought Jim's head back up. His eyes focused on her with an intensity that left Meredith feeling as if she was intruding on a private moment.

"However, I can certainly understand your preference for a nickname." Her cousin blushed a bit under Jim's regard. "I myself prefer being called Cassie. It's so much friendlier and less pretentious than Cassandra, don't you think?"

Jim never took his eyes from Cassie's face. "I think they both fit you right fine. One is elegant and graceful, the other fun and lively."

Cassie's cheeks flushed a deeper red. "What a lovely compliment. Thank you."

After that, Crockett turned the conversation in a less intimate direction with stories of how the Archer brothers used to reenact scenes from the Alamo battle as boys. Jim had even whittled an imitation Bowie knife to use during their skirmishes, which sparked his interest in woodworking.

While Meredith cleared the dishes and refilled coffee cups, Cassie begged to see the knife Jim had carved so long ago. He offered to show it to her along with his carpentry workshop, and Cassie didn't hesitate. With an eager smile, she took his arm and allowed him to lead her from the room.

A look passed between Jim and Travis over the top of Cassie's head, and at once Meredith knew that Jim had just taken it upon himself to explain the situation with Uncle Everett to her cousin. Meredith glanced at Travis and deliberately reclaimed her seat at the table. The dishes could wait. Explanations could not.

26

Travis wrapped his hands around his coffee cup and stared into the dark depths. He could feel Meri as she lowered herself into the chair next to him, his senses attuned to her movements. He didn't have to turn, he *knew* she was there—knew she was looking at him, waiting for a recounting of what happened with her uncle. Waiting for a solution he hadn't yet devised.

Her gaze bore into him almost as fiercely as it had earlier when she'd been setting out the food. He still couldn't recall a word of what Crockett had said about the barn shingles. He'd just nodded and tried to look contemplative when all the while he'd wanted nothing more than to cross the room and wrap his arms around his wife.

My wife.

Heaven help him. He was past ready to make Meri his wife in truth. To hold her throughout the night and wake with her in his arms every morning. He'd plotted all afternoon how best to approach the topic with her that evening. After she'd kissed him with such fervor and even allowed—no, welcomed—the boldness of his touch on her leg, he'd been able to think of little else.

Now, thanks to Everett Hayes and his idiotic scheme, he'd have nothing but thoughts to keep him warm as he scrunched himself onto the too-short cot in Neill's bedroom again tonight. Travis closed his fingers around the crockery mug before him, wishing it were Hayes's throat.

"So, Trav—" Crockett made a grand show of finishing his coffee and plopping the empty cup against the tabletop—"what did Hayes have to say?"

Travis forced his fingers to relax their stranglehold on the mug and leaned back in his seat as he expelled a heavy breath. "We convinced him to let Cassandra stay for a visit." He hesitated, trying to come up with some way to soften the rest of the facts for Meri's sake.

"Spit out the rest of it, Travis." Meredith nodded to him, but he could see the strain around her eyes where tiny lines creased her skin. Apparently she didn't care about soft. She just wanted the truth.

Knowing the truth would be painful, he worded a short, silent prayer, and then summed up the situation as succinctly as possible. "If Cassandra's not home in three days, Hayes will round up a posse and take her by force."

Meredith tried to muffle her moan, but Travis heard it. And the sound cut right through his heart. Not caring about what his brothers might think, he reached around the side of the table and grabbed one of the spindles on the back of Meri's chair. He dragged her to his side, the chair legs scraping against the floor in a loud racket, took her hand in his, and cradled her entire forearm against his stomach. She laid her head atop his shoulder and leaned into him.

Crockett tapped the edge of his thumb against his thigh. "Is he set on marrying her off to Mitchell?"

"Seems to be. He didn't come right out and say so, but every time I hinted at such a union being a mistake, he sputtered something about me minding my own business and not meddling in his affairs."

"Travis, she can't marry that man." Meredith raised her head and stiffened her spine.

"I know, darlin'." Travis hugged her arm closer. "We'll figure something out."

She looked past him for a moment, catching her lower lip between her teeth. When her eyes met his once again, determination glowed in their vibrant blue depths. "I'll go talk to him. Give him permission to sell the land to Mitchell straight out. No dowry, no need for a wedding. All Roy wants is the land, anyway."

Crockett shook his head. "I don't think it would do any good."

"Why not?" she demanded, jerking forward in her seat. "Roy gets the land, and Uncle Everett would have him in his debt. Both of them get what they want."

Travis stroked the exposed skin on the back of her arm from the wrist joint all the way to her elbow, where her rolled sleeve sat bunched against her bicep. "Your uncle wants a stronger tie to Mitchell, one that will ensure his business for years to come. A marriage contract would bind him more fully than a bill of sale."

"The homestead was supposed to be my inheritance. Maybe if I got a lawyer . . ." Her words died when Crockett shook his head.

"If the deed is in your uncle's name, I imagine he can do whatever he wants with it, even if it goes against your father's last wishes. Now if the land was specifically deeded to you . . ." He left the sentence hanging, a thread of hope holding it aloft.

She shook her head and snapped the tenuous thread. "No. Papa trusted my uncle to look out for my interests since I was not of age. Nothing is in my name."

Meredith slumped, and Travis tugged her back into his side.

"I just can't believe that Uncle Everett would do this. Papa trusted him. His own brother. He was supposed to oversee the property on my behalf, not sell it out from under me or give it to his daughter. And Cassie . . . Oh, Travis." She turned anguished eyes on him. "He's not just stealing my land, he's selling his daughter. How could he do that? He loves Cassie. I know he does. This doesn't make any sense."

Travis kissed her forehead and murmured into her hair. "Desperation can warp a man's mind. Keep him from seeing things clearly. Your uncle must be in a financial crisis."

"I don't care what kind of crisis he's in." Meredith drew back, a sob catching in her throat. "What he's doing is wrong!"

"I know it is, love." He gathered her close again, aching to fix what Everett Hayes's betrayal had broken. "We'll find a way to protect Cassie. I swear it."

"Already found one." Jim's deep voice rumbled in from the bathing room an instant before he and Cassandra stepped through the doorway into the kitchen.

Travis frowned. How had he not heard the back door open?

Cassie bounded forward, arms outstretched to Meredith. The smile Travis had noted during her first visit had made a miraculous reappearance. Reluctantly, Travis relinquished his hold on Meri, freeing her to clasp her cousin's hands.

"You'll never guess our plan," Cassie gushed as she slid into the chair next to Meredith. "It's perfect. And it was all Jim's idea. He's so clever." She smiled at her accomplice over her shoulder as he, too, reclaimed a seat at the table.

"What didja come up with?" Neill elbowed Jim, speaking up for the first time since dinner.

"It's the most brilliant plan." Cassie's enthusiasm bubbled over before Jim could shape his mouth into a response. Not that the fellow seemed to mind. Having someone do his talking for him was probably a dream come true.

Cassie released Meredith's hands in order to include everyone at the table in her gaze. "First, we're going to give Papa his three days. I'll stay here at the ranch, making my objection to his scheme clear. And perhaps with the six of us praying, the Lord will see fit to nudge him into a more rational stance."

Travis took a swallow of his coffee, hoping to hide his skepticism. Everett Hayes would need more than a nudge from the Lord to help him see the error of his ways. A wallop upside the head with one of the charred pine planks from the barn might be better.

"Then on Tuesday," Cassie continued, "I'll return home and tell Papa and Mama straight out that I will not be coerced into marriage. No matter how they plead, I will not be dissuaded." She lifted her chin in such a way that Travis had to smile. She looked so much like Meri. Brave and determined. Perhaps the princess had gumption, after all.

Crockett hunched forward over the table and scraped his coffee cup across the wooden surface as he drew it closer to his chest. "I don't mean to dash your hopes, but I highly doubt that a little time and stubbornness on your part are going to accomplish much. If your father is truly set on this marriage, all he would have to do is find someone to officiate who could be convinced to ignore your protests. And unfortunately, Mitchell's got enough money to bribe a man into forgetting his scruples."

"That's where your brother's cleverness comes into play." Cassandra's smile didn't dim for a second.

Travis raised a questioning brow at Jim, but the man made no effort to enlighten him, his face as stoic as ever.

"If Papa insists on the wedding despite my protests, then we move to stage three."

"What's stage three?" Meredith asked when Cassandra decided to pause for dramatic effect.

Cassandra rose from her chair, her eyes glowing. "Only the most brilliantly simple idea ever." She clapped her hands together beneath her chin and slid over to where Jim sat, his gaze centered somewhere between the table and his lap.

Travis's jaw began to twitch. He couldn't quite figure out where this was headed, but his gut told him he wasn't going to like it.

"Papa can't force me to marry Roy if I'm already married to someone else."

"Jim?" The single word clawed its way out of Travis's throat as he tried to convince himself he'd misunderstood Cassie's meaning.

His brother finally lifted his head, defiance glittering in his eyes. "I offered to be her groom should she find herself in need of one."

Travis shot up so fast his chair tipped backward onto the floor. "You did *what*?"

Jim slowly pushed to his feet and crossed his arms over his chest. "Why so surprised, Trav? I'm just following in your footsteps."

"Jim?" Cassandra's smile wobbled, and uncertainty clouded her features.

"Everything's fine, Cassie." Jim patted her shoulder, but his eyes never left his older brother. "Travis just doesn't handle surprises well. He'll get over it."

"Outside," Travis ground out between clenched teeth. "Now."

He rounded the table and strode down the hall, his arms throbbing with the need to hit something. When he reached the front door, he wrenched it open, not caring that it thudded against the wall with enough force to loosen the hinges.

What could Jim be thinking? He'd known Cassandra Hayes for all of about two minutes. How could he possibly make a decision that would affect the rest of his life on a . . . a whim? Travis paced the length of the porch, the heels of his boots pounding against the pine boards. He was on his second pass when Jim finally got around to joining him.

"You can save your breath," Jim said as he pulled the front door closed, "I ain't changin' my mind."

Travis stalked up to him, his hands fisted at his sides. "Think about what you're doing, Jim. You don't really even know the woman."

"I know enough."

"What do you know, exactly? That's she's pretty? Quit thinking with your eyes and try using your brain. The girl's been pampered her whole life. She can barely sit a horse, she can't cook, probably can't sew or garden, either. What happens when those pretty smiles of hers turn into pouts because she hates being a rancher's wife? Will you follow her to town?"

"Maybe."

Fear coiled in Travis's heart at Jim's dark expression. Would he actually choose town life with Cassie over the ranch?

Jim drew himself up to his full height and set his jaw. "Meredith's got a bum leg and a penchant for meddling, yet you seem willing enough to overlook her faults. It's no different with Cassie. I can teach her what she needs to know. And if there comes a time when she wants to return to town, I can handle that, too. I'm sure Palestine could use a new carpentry shop."

An invisible vise clamped over Travis's chest. His lungs refused to draw in a full breath. His heart throbbed as if his rib cage were shrinking.

Meredith's words came back to him, flaying his defenses like a skinning knife cutting away a hide. "*How long do you think the others will be content to live here in your shadow?*"

Would they really leave? All of them?

"Marriage is forever, Jim." Travis leaned a bent arm against the doorframe, needing its support. "You can't just jump into it on a chivalrous impulse."

"Like you did?"

"That's different," Travis sputtered. "I knew that I lo—" *That I loved her*. The shock of that thought sent him reeling. He pushed away from the wall and staggered over to the railing. His palms dug into the wood as he locked his elbows and braced himself against the truth swirling around him.

He loved her. He had all along. That's why he'd not protested when Everett Hayes demanded a wedding. That's why he'd rigged the straws. It wasn't to spare Meri's reputation or an act of brotherly duty. Nothing so altruistic. He'd wanted her for himself. Needed her.

Somehow, on a gut level, he'd known she was the one meant for him, and he'd made up his mind to do everything in his power to keep her.

Jim's quiet footfalls sounded behind him. "Look, Trav. It's a last resort. Neither of us plans to rush into anything. I might have a strong hankerin' for the woman, but if I marry her, I want her comfortable enough around me that I don't have to bunk with one of my brothers while she adjusts."

"Hey!" Travis spun to face his brother, fists clenched. But the half grin on Jim's face stole his ire. He thumped his fist against his brother's arm anyway, though he put no real force behind the blow. "Yeah, well, I'll listen to your advice when you actually have some experience as a husband. Until then, keep your thoughts to yourself."

Jim thumped him with his own fist, and Travis grinned as he staggered slightly to the side. Suddenly their problems didn't seem quite so dire.

"So would you really do it, if it came down to it?" Travis asked.

Jim raised a brow. "What? Marry Cassie?"

"No. Willingly tie yourself to a pair of in-laws like Everett and Noreen Hayes?"

Jim growled and lunged for Travis, but Travis sidestepped his brother and darted up to the porch, a chuckle vibrating deep in his throat.

Maybe he wouldn't have to worry about Jim moving into town after all.

27

Eager to get Cassie alone, Meredith shuffled her cousin off to the bedroom the minute the dishes were done. The men accepted her excuse of being tired easily enough. Heaven knew all the emotional upheaval they'd endured in the last few hours would exhaust the most robust of women. Yet in truth, sleep was the furthest thing from her mind.

"Will Travis need to come in to get a change of clothes?" Cassie asked as she laid her small satchel on the bed. "I can wait to undress until after he gathers his things."

"He has clothes set aside already. Don't worry about him." Heat suffused Meredith's cheeks at the awkwardness that lay in that conversational direction. She quickly focused things back on her cousin. "You just make yourself comfortable. It will be like old times, the two of us snuggled under the covers, telling stories. And believe me, I expect to hear all about how you and Jim concocted this plan. Are you really prepared to marry him?"

Cassie paused in the midst of her unpacking, the hairbrush she'd pulled from the satchel quivering slightly in her hand. "I am."

"Even though you hardly know him?" Meredith came up behind her cousin and started unpinning her hair.

"When you had to choose between Roy Mitchell and Travis, you chose an Archer. I'm doing the same. You don't regret marrying Travis, do you?"

Meredith took the brush from Cassie and gently tugged it through the blond waves. "I don't regret it. Not for a moment. But I've harbored feelings for him all these years. It will be different for you. Jim's a good man, but he's a stranger to you. How do you know you'd suit?"

"He kissed me," Cassie whispered.

Meredith stopped brushing, the shock of Cassie's admission slamming into her with the force of Samson's hoof. She dropped the brush onto the bed and took hold of Cassie's shoulders. Slowly she turned her cousin around to face her. "He kissed you?"

Silent, stoic Jim?

"Mm-hmm." Cassie nodded, her rosy face glowing. "And it wasn't a little peck on the cheek, like the ones my past suitors pressed on me. It was strong and deep and . . . wonderful."

The sigh that escaped her held all the drama of a young girl's first love. Meredith couldn't help but smile. After all, she felt much the same about Travis, only her yearning had passed the early stages of attraction weeks ago. Her love for Travis had intensified to the point where she couldn't imagine her life without him.

Meredith blinked. When had her schoolgirl crush turned into this soul-deep need? She'd called her young infatuation *love*, but when she looked into her heart now, nothing there resembled those girlish feelings. Everything was so much richer and deeper—as if what had come before was simply an artist's preliminary sketch, void of detail and color, and over the last few weeks, that same artist had brushed the canvas of her heart with masterful strokes, creating a vibrant work that left her breathless.

"Do you think it's shameful for me to hope that Papa *won't* change his mind about Roy?" Cassie asked in a hushed voice, bringing Meredith's mind back to the matter at hand. "So that Jim will have an excuse to marry me? Not that I wouldn't prefer a proper courtship and time for us to get to know each other, but part of me worries that without the urgency, he'd stay out here on the ranch and forget about me altogether. The Archers don't have much use for towns, you know."

Meredith stroked Cassie's arm and gripped her hand in reassurance. "The Archers are honorable to the core, Cass. If Jim kissed you the way I think he did, the last thing you need to worry about is him forgetting you." Meredith gently steered her cousin around until her back faced her, then took up the brush again and resumed detangling her long tresses. "Besides, the Archers aren't as reclusive as they appear. They've just been secluding themselves for so long it's become a habit. I don't imagine Jim would let a little thing like a town keep him from calling on you. He's too smitten."

Cassie's head swiveled to the side. "Do you really think so?"

"Yes." Meredith grinned and nudged Cassie's chin back to the forward position. "The question is, are you smitten with *him*? Would you still want to marry him if the situation with Roy and your father didn't exist?"

Meredith expected a quick, affirmative response. Cassie wasn't known for having an overly contemplative nature, after all. But silence stretched between them. Meredith had set the brush aside and plaited a braid halfway down Cassie's neck before her cousin finally answered.

"I feel safe, cherished when I'm with him. He held me while I cried today and never once asked me to hush. In his workshop, he vowed to protect me from Roy and even my father if it came to that. And when he looks at me . . ." She pivoted to face Meredith, her eyes soft and dewy.

Meredith tied off the braid with a piece of ribbon, and the two girls sat on the end of the bed.

"When he looks at me, Meri, he makes me feel like the most beautiful woman in the world, as if he could gaze at me for a lifetime and never grow tired of my face. As if he sees not just who I am, but who I can become. And when I look at him, not only do I see a handsome suitor who makes my heart flutter, I see a solid, dependable man who can be counted on no matter how difficult the road may become. A man who wants more than a pretty ornament to dangle on his arm. A man who wants a partner."

Cassie dipped her head and traced the line of a fabric fold in her skirt. "It seems too soon to label what I'm feeling love, but whatever it is, it is more intense than anything I've felt for any other beau." She bit her lip, then finally raised her chin. "There is something strong between us, Meri. Something that promises to last. Would I marry him if we weren't in this crazy predicament? Yes. I believe I would."

Moisture gathered at the corners of Meredith's eyes. "Then that's all that matters." She clasped Cassie to her breast and hugged her tight.

Guide her in this, Lord. Work this out for your good and hers.

Once the two separated, Meredith rose to her feet and began removing her own hairpins as she strolled toward the bureau. "You know what this means, of course," she said, meeting Cassie's gaze in the mirror.

"What?" Cassie stood and unfastened the buttons of her dress.

"We're finally going to be sisters."

Cassie gave a little squeal, and Meredith barely had time to turn before she was assaulted by her cousin's spirited embrace.

The trials facing them seemed to fall away as the two cousins giggled and prattled like a pair of adolescent schoolgirls while they readied themselves for bed. Once they'd scrubbed their faces, changed into their nightclothes, and crawled under the covers, however, reality started to creep back in. At least for Meredith.

Curled up on her side, she stared into the darkened room, her thoughts centered on Travis. Somehow she'd imagined he'd be the first one to share this bed with her. Not Cassie. Scrunching her pillow to her face to muffle her sigh, Meredith closed her eyes and waited for sleep to rescue her from her discontent. But it didn't come.

Frustrated, she flopped onto her back, careful not to flail her arms. When Cassie wiggled closer to her edge of the bed, as if trying to give Meredith more room, the urge to confide in her cousin grew too strong to ignore.

"Are you awake, Cass?" Meredith whispered, promising herself that if her cousin didn't answer she'd just bite her tongue and roll back over.

"Yes."

A staggering relief flowed through her at the quiet answer—followed by a rush of nerves.

"Umm . . . Can I ask you a question?"

"Mm-hmm," came the sleepy reply.

Cassie made no move to roll toward her, and Meredith relaxed a bit. Staring at the dark ceiling somehow made it easier to voice her secret fears.

"When we were talking earlier, you said that if you had your preference, you'd rather have a normal courtship with Jim so the two of you could get to know each other better. But if you were to marry him tomorrow, would you still want that courtship? I mean, before the two of you . . . you know . . ." Meredith closed her eyes as mortification poured over her in a heated wave.

"I'm not sure," Cassie said, sounding decidedly more alert. "I enjoyed his kiss, so I'm pretty sure I would enjoy other aspects of . . . well, of married life, but I imagine it would be easier if we didn't feel so much like strangers." She fell quiet for a moment or two, then cleared her throat. When she spoke, her whisper was so low Meredith had to strain to catch the words. "What was it like with you and Travis?"

Meredith bit back a moan. "I can't tell you, Cass."

"I'm sorry. I shouldn't have asked. It's just that I don't know what to expect, and Mama surely isn't going to tell me anything. I'm not certain I'd trust her opinions on the matter, anyway." Her words tripped over themselves trying to cover up her obvious hurt. "I just thought that since you and Travis were in much the same situation when you married that you might be able to give me some advice, but it's much too personal, of course. I shouldn't have—"

"Stop, Cassie." Meredith rolled toward her cousin and laid her hand on her arm. "It's not that I don't want to answer your question. I wish with all my heart I could."

"What . . . ?" Cassie squirmed sideways until she faced Meredith. "What do you mean?"

Meredith nibbled her lip as she summoned her courage. "Travis sleeps on a cot in Neill's room."

"Oh, Meri." It was too dark to see, but it sounded very much as if there were tears in Cassie's eyes. "I know how much you care for him. How awful. Why, I have half a mind to storm into that room and kick his sorry hide off that cot and onto the floor. The dog. How could he treat you so cruelly?"

A chuckle escaped Meredith's lips as Cassie swung from sleepy little girl to sympathetic confidante to vengeful angel all in the course of a single minute.

"What are you laughing at?"

"You." Meredith smiled into the darkness. "Travis hasn't rejected me." Although it was harder to believe that when she lay alone in the big bed with nothing but a spare pillow to hold. "He is trying to be chivalrous. To court me first."

"So he's kissed you?"

"Yes." Meredith pressed her palm against her stomach as she recalled the heart-stopping kiss they'd shared by the creek.

"More than once?"

Warmth spread through her midsection as she thought about the kiss he'd given her that very afternoon. "Yes."

Cassie shifted to a sitting position an instant before her pillow collided with Meredith's face. "I hear that dreamy, besotted sigh in your voice, Meredith Archer."

Meredith grabbed the pillow and retaliated, smiling in triumph when it plowed into the side of Cassie's head. "No more than the way you sounded when you talked about Jim."

"But I haven't been mooning over Jim for half my life the way you have Travis. You're tired of the chivalry, aren't you?"

"Yes." She couldn't believe she'd just admitted it aloud. Although, truth be told, it was possible Cassie hadn't even heard her, so tiny was her whisper.

But Cassie *had* heard, for she sought out Meredith's hand and gave it a squeeze. "On Tuesday, when Jim takes me back to Palestine, I think you should find Travis and tell him that you're ready to be a wife to him."

"Just tell him straight out?" Meredith pulled her hand from Cassie's grasp and clutched at the neck of her nightdress as if trying to protect her modesty. "I couldn't do that. I'd die of embarrassment. It's highly improper for a lady to speak of such things. Why, there's no telling what Travis would think of me."

"Seems to me he'd be glad to know you'd welcome him in the marriage bed." Cassie's dry answer made Meredith cringe.

It sounded so simple. But what if she made her feelings clear and Travis still didn't come? She couldn't bear that. The rejection would be real then, and no clever argument could dismiss it.

The sheets rustled as Cassie settled back down on the mattress. "Do you have any married friends you trust enough to ask for advice? Seeing as how I have no actual experience in this area, it might be wise to seek another opinion."

Myra immediately came to mind. "There is one lady," Meredith admitted, her mind already spinning with ideas about how to convince her husband to let her leave the ranch on a Tuesday. "She's the wife of one of the men Travis hired to help rebuild the barn. They've been married for probably twenty-five years, and she and Moses seem devoted to one another even after all that time. I could ask her."

"Good," Cassie said, a yawn distorting the word. "That's what you should do."

As Cassie's breathing deepened, Meredith's mind continued to turn circles. Her heart told her it was time to take action. But *which* action was the right one?

28

Tuesday dawned gloomy and gray. Meredith shivered beneath her cloak as she stepped away from the house and received the full brunt of the northern wind against her side. Crockett led a pair of saddled mounts out of the barn while Jim bundled Cassie into one of his old coats. The thing nearly swallowed her, but the added warmth would be a blessing on the long ride to town.

When Jim turned to fasten a pair of saddlebags behind the cantle of his mount, Cassie buried her nose in the collar, and Meredith imagined her inhaling his scent.

Meredith came alongside Travis and slid her hand down the length of his sleeve to let him know she was there without interrupting him while he instructed Neill on where to check for strays. When her fingers reached the back of his hand, she thought to taper away, but he twisted his wrist and captured her palm against his. Then he laced his fingers through hers and tugged her into his side in a motion so natural, it felt like a well-rehearsed dance instead of a spontaneous improvisation.

Meredith leaned her head against the side of Travis's shoulder and looked toward the ground, not wanting to witness Neill's reaction to his brother's show of possessiveness.

Possessiveness. The thought struck Meredith hard, and a delightful little shiver worked its way up from her stomach to her heart. Travis *was* acting possessive, wasn't he? But did his behavior stem from a growing affection for her or was it simply an expression of his protective nature?

What she wouldn't give to have something more substantial than intuition to guide her. She was afraid to trust hers. Roy might have stepped out with her a time or two, but she'd never had a true beau. How could she possibly comprehend the workings of a man's mind? And now her only confidante was leaving. She had to see Myra today. She couldn't wait for Saturday. The uncertainty was driving her mad.

"You're awfully quiet," Travis said close to her ear. "Are you worried about Cassie?"

Meredith drew her head back, surprised to see Neill had already mounted and was heading out to check on the stock. She hadn't even noticed him leave. Giving herself a mental shake, she turned her attention to her husband.

"Jim knows to set a slow pace, right? Cassie's not too comfortable atop a horse."

"He'll watch out for her." Travis rubbed the pad of his thumb over the top of her hand, but she sensed a strange tension coiling beneath the surface.

Meredith searched her husband's face as he turned to watch his brother make final preparations for the journey. A muscle ticked in his jaw, and all at once insight dawned. "You're worried about Jim."

Travis tightened his grip on her hand. He said nothing for a long moment, then dipped his head and spoke in a low voice. "None of us has left since Pa died."

"Except for you," Meredith gently reminded him.

He finally met her gaze. A small smile curved his lips. "Only because of a pretty little trespasser."

Warmth spread through Meredith's chest. She reached across her body, clasped his arm, and hugged it close to her side. She'd been so consumed with her own worries, she'd never even considered what this day would mean for her husband.

"I'm proud of you, Travis."

His eyes widened a bit at her words.

"I am," she confirmed. "Letting Jim go can't be easy for you, yet you never once tried to talk him out of it." A gust of icy wind blew across her face, whipping tendrils of hair into her eyes.

He dragged his finger along the edge of her cheek, collecting stray hairs and tucking them behind her ear. "You're the one who gave me the courage, Meri." He grew silent again, and Meredith simply leaned into his side, enjoying his closeness. Yet instead of relaxing as she expected him to, Travis stiffened. Meredith lifted her head.

"Pa died because I left the ranch." The stark statement hung in the air between them like the fog of their breath. "I was supposed to be at home watching out for my brothers, but I left. Snuck out to meet a group of boys down at the swimming hole. I don't even remember why now. All I know is a fierce storm blew in, and Pa came looking for me. A clap of thunder spooked his horse and he fell. He died later that night."

Meredith clung to Travis, blinking away the sudden moisture that blurred her vision. She wanted to weep for the young boy who had watched his father die, for the boy who carried such a heavy burden of guilt so unnecessarily.

Give me words to ease his burden, Father.

"He died because he fell from a horse, Travis. Not because you left the ranch."

Her husband tried to release her hand, but she refused to let go. "He wouldn't have fallen from that horse if I hadn't disobeyed him."

"It was an accident, Travis. A tragic accident. One you are no more responsible for than I am for the sickness that struck my parents."

"It's not the same."

"No?" She kept hold of Travis's hand but shifted her body to stand partly in front of him. "Why not? I disobeyed my parents many times. Maybe their death was my punishment, too."

"That's ridiculous." He shoved his hat back and rubbed the lines of his forehead.

"Yes. It is." Meredith stretched up on her tiptoes and laid a slow, tender kiss on her husband's tanned cheek. "God forgave you long ago, Travis. Your father, too, I imagine. It's time to forgive yourself."

As she settled back onto the flat of her feet, Travis's eyes met hers. The intensity shimmering in his eyes was so intense, Meredith couldn't move. Couldn't breathe. He slipped his arm from her grasp and wrapped it around her waist, his hold so strong she wanted nothing more than to melt into him. Travis angled his head. His gaze shifted to her lips.

Meredith lifted her face to him, the love inside her swelling.

Then Crockett strolled up with Travis's horse, and cleared his throat. "You send Neill up to the north pasture?" he asked, completely unsuccessful in his feigned innocence. The rogue knew exactly what he was interrupting and wasn't the least bit repentant.

Travis cleared his throat and released her. He adjusted the way his hat sat on his head, angling it more sharply over his eyes. "I plan to join him out there in a bit," he said, gravel in his voice. "I didn't figure you and Moses would need me on the barn. With the roof done, all you'll need to do is bring in the hay and add those two extra stalls we talked about."

"I figured as much." Crockett handed Bexar's reins over to Travis and climbed aboard his bay. "I'll ride with Jim to the gate and wait for Moses there. He and Josiah should be along shortly."

The mention of Jim brought Meredith's attention back to her cousin. They'd already said their good-byes in the house, but Meredith couldn't resist one final word of farewell. As Jim gave Cassie a leg up into the saddle, Meredith quietly approached.

Seeing her, Jim nodded once and backed away, allowing them a private moment.

"I'm going to miss you." Meredith reached her hand up, and Cassie grasped it, her gloved fingers tightening around Meredith's bare ones.

Tears glistened in Cassie's eyes and her chin wobbled slightly, but she pulled her mouth taut and managed to keep her emotions under control. So proud of her, Meredith raised her other hand and cocooned Cassie's between both of hers. It was one thing to plot and plan when safely removed from a threat. It was another matter entirely to ride out to meet that threat. Yet her little Cassie was doing exactly that.

"Whatever comes, God will see us through." Meredith punctuated her words with a squeeze to Cassie's hand. "Trust him, Cass. Lean on his strength."

"I will." Her voice quivered, but when she pulled free of Meredith's grip, she sat erect on the rented livery nag and even found a tiny smile.

As Jim led her down the path, Travis came up behind Meredith. The welcome weight of his arm settled atop her shoulder. He didn't say anything, just hugged her to his chest and let her rest her head against him. As she watched Cassie enter the trees, Meredith sank into Travis's strength, comforted by his solid presence.

"Thank you for staying with me this morning," she murmured once Cassandra had completely passed from sight. "It would have been much harder to say good-bye alone."

He tightened his hold on her, and she felt the gentle pressure of his lips against her scalp as he pressed a kiss into her hair. Meredith's eyes slid closed.

"Travis?"

"Yeah?"

She turned to face him, his arms loosening to accommodate her movement. Immediately she missed his warmth. "Would you mind if I rode out to Beaver Valley to visit with Myra for a short while this afternoon? I won't be gone long. I promise. I just . . . Well, I feel the need of a woman's company. I think it would help me adjust to Cassie's leaving and give me a chance to talk to her about something besides teaching."

Something like husbands.

Travis stared hard at the sky. "I don't like the look of this weather. It could turn nasty if the temperature keeps dropping."

"Or it could be sunny by noon. One never knows in Texas."

He resituated his hat and blew out a quiet breath. "Visiting with Mrs. Jackson is that important to you?"

No, having a marriage filled with intimacy and love was that important to her. But since talking with Myra was her best chance to achieve that . . . "Yes. I really think it will help."

"All right." He grumbled as if he would have much rather given a different answer. "But only if it's not raining. Rain can turn to sleet in an instant on a day like this, and the ice would make the roads treacherous. Promise me?"

Meredith nodded, unable to hold her grin at bay.

Never had she flown through her morning chores so quickly. So far the weather was holding, but the clouds were turning an ominous shade of gray. If she didn't leave soon, she might not be able to leave at all. After adding an extra flannel petticoat beneath her skirt, Meredith dug out her woolen mittens and matching scarf. She wrapped the scarf around her head to protect her cheeks and ears from the bitter wind blowing out of the north and fastened her cloak over her shoulders. The ride wouldn't be long, but she'd be facing the wind much of the way. Coming home would be easier.

Having told Crockett her plans when she'd taken sandwiches out to the barn a few minutes ago, she wasn't surprised to see Ginger saddled and ready at the end of the porch. With anticipation dancing in her chest, Meredith descended the steps and hurriedly untied the lead line from the porch pillar.

"Need a leg up?" Crockett emerged from around the corner as if he'd been waiting for her.

His sudden appearance startled her, but Meredith managed to greet her brother-in-law with a smile. "Thank you." She fit her boot into his laced fingers and soon found herself on Ginger's back. "I'll return in time to fix supper."

"If I were you, I'd return long before then." Crockett hesitated before handing her the reins. "There's a storm coming. It'll do you no good to be caught in it."

"I'll be careful," she assured him.

And she was. She held Ginger to an easy canter on the road and didn't even take the shortcut across Beaver Creek. She stopped by Seth Winston's store, but only long enough to give the crotchety old man a dozen of the oatmeal cookies she and Cassie had baked yesterday. He might have won their first skirmish, but she was determined to win the war.

"Ya tryin' to poison me, woman?" Winston grouched as he untied the knot on the napkin-wrapped treat.

"Nope, just sweeten you up some."

"Doggone women, always thinking they gotta change a man. Infernal creatures. A fellow'd be better off with a mule than a wife."

Meredith let the insults slide off her back, knowing she didn't have time to rise to his bait, and wished the storekeeper a good day.

Braced for the cold, she turned the knob and stepped outside, giving the door enough of a tug to allow it to close behind her. But the thud she expected never came. She turned to reach for the knob a second time only to find Seth Winston filling the doorway. The ornery old buzzard had followed her.

She offered a brief smile, then spun away and scurried down to the street to unhitch Ginger.

"Always thought them Archer boys was too smart to let a female hog-tie 'em." Winston called after her.

"Guess that proves my gender's superiority over the male of the species," Meredith called back, unable to hold her tongue any longer.

"How's that?"

Meredith didn't respond until she was safely in the saddle. "Not only are we smarter, but we tie better knots."

With that, she reined Ginger around and touched her heels to the mare's flanks. She could have sworn she heard a bark of laughter from behind her, but that was impossible. It must have been the wind.

Since Myra only taught at the freedmen's school during the morning hours on weekdays, Meredith rode past the schoolyard to the small pine cabin that sat a quarter-mile behind it.

"Miss Meri? That you?" Joshua called out from beside the woodshed where he'd been splitting logs. "Everything all right with Pa?"

"Yes. He and Josiah were helping Crockett fork hay into the loft when I left. I just wanted to visit with your mother. Is she at home?"

"Yes'm." He leaned his hatchet against the chopping stump and rubbed his palms along his trouser legs. "Go on up to the house. I'll see to your horse."

Meredith smiled at the young man as she dismounted. "Thank you."

By the time she reached the cabin, however, her smile had twisted into a nervous grimace. Second thoughts leapt through her mind, causing havoc with her stomach. Marriage was a deeply private affair. Perhaps discussing her relationship concerns with Myra wasn't such a good idea.

But how else was she to figure out what to do?

A verse from Titus surfaced through the panic. A verse about older women teaching younger women how to love their husbands. Surely the answers she sought fell into that category.

Meredith inhaled a long, steadying breath, then raised her hand to knock. When Myra answered, Meredith blurted out the thought uppermost in her mind.

"I need you to help me end my husband's courtship."

29

"The cold musta done froze your brain, Miss Meri, 'cause you ain't making a lick of sense." Myra took Meredith by the arm and drew her into the house. "I got water on in the kitchen. I'll make some tea. Maybe once you thaw out, I'll be able to understand what in the world you're sayin'. I could've sworn I heard you say you wanted to stop your husband from payin' court to you."

"Yes, but that's not exactly—"

"Uh, uh, uh." Myra held up a hand and shook her head. "Not until we get that tea."

She bustled Meredith into the toasty kitchen, collected her cloak, and directed her into a chair, then reached into the cupboard and took down a tea canister.

Grinning at her friend, and a little at herself, Meredith dutifully kept her mouth closed as she unwound her scarf and slid her hands free of her mittens. The strains of a familiar hymn wove through the air, so quiet at first that Meredith couldn't tell if she actually heard them or if they resonated only in her mind. But when Myra turned to set a teacup on the table in front of her, the melody rose like the sun cresting the horizon.

"Father of Mercies." A stillness came over Meredith. Little by little, her frantic desperation dissolved as her mind filled in the lyrics extolling God's abundant blessings. She became so caught up in the prayerful attitude of the song, that when Myra stopped humming in order to pour tea into their cups, she had to blink several times to return her focus to her surroundings.

"Take a sip, Miss Meri. Then tell me what you come here to say."

Meredith did as instructed, then set her pink-flowered teacup back on its saucer and faced her friend. "I find myself in need of advice—from someone accustomed to dealing with a husband."

"I see." Myra paused as she lifted her cup to her lips. "Travis causing you trouble?"

"Not really, it's just that . . ." Meredith sighed. "We married under unusual circumstances, and Travis thought I deserved a proper courtship. So for the last few weeks he's been courting me."

"Honey, if you got yourself a man who's willing to pay court to you even after the vows are spoke, you got yourself a treasure, not a problem."

"You don't understand. He's courting me like a suitor, not like a . . . a husband." Meredith dropped her gaze to the tabletop. She toyed with the corner of her napkin as she revealed the rest of it. "He sleeps on a cot in Neill's room. Not with me."

"And you're ready for that arrangement to change?"

Meredith bit her lip and nodded.

Myra set her cup on her saucer and scooted them both out of the way. "Miss Meri, if your man is attracted to you at all, I can promise you he's been thinkin' of little else than changing that arrangement. He's prob'ly just waiting for some kind of signal from you to let him know he'd be welcome."

"That's the problem. I feel like I've been signaling more than a flagman on the rails, but Travis fails to notice. I respond to his kisses, I come up with excuses to be near him, I never pull away from his touch. How many signals does a husband need?"

A mild laugh rumbled in Myra's chest. "Oh, Miss Meri. You gotta remember them Archer boys grew up with only themselves for comp'ny. They ain't been around womenfolk to learn how to interpret them quiet signals of yours. You're gonna have to take a more direct approach, I reckon."

Meredith's hand shook as she reached for her teacup, setting it to rattling against the matching saucer. She managed to get the cup to her mouth without dribbling anything on Myra's tablecloth, but the brew did little to fortify her.

"How direct?" Meredith glanced around the kitchen to ensure they were still alone. She'd be absolutely mortified if Joshua were to overhear their conversation. The rhythmic *thwack* of a hatchet splitting wood outside, however, gave her the courage to continue, albeit in a whisper. "I don't want Travis to think I'm some sort of . . . loose woman."

Myra smiled, but this smile was different. Far from the friendly, open grins Meredith was accustomed to receiving, this one spoke of secrets—seductive secrets. "A lady can be direct and still be a proper lady, Miss Meri."

Meredith leaned forward. "How?"

"Have you ever been the one to start a kiss?"

Heat climbed up Meredith's neck. "Not really. I did kiss him on the cheek earlier today, but Travis has always been the one take the lead with . . . well, real kisses."

"Then the next time the two of you are alone, surprise him. And not with some little buss like his ma woulda given him. Take his face in your hands and kiss him the way your heart tells you. Slow. Sweet. Full of all the love you been storin' up."

Could she do something that bold? Meredith ran her fingertip around the rim of her cup. Even if she could find the nerve, would she be able to find him alone? There always seemed to be another Archer around once the evening chores were finished.

"Even when you're not alone, you can make it feel that way," Myra continued as if she had read Meredith's mind. "Meet his gaze from across the room. Let down your guard and show him the truth of your feelings in your eyes. Men fear rejection, too, you know. Give him every reason to believe you'll say yes, and he'll find a way to ask you the question."

"But what if I can't get him alone or he can't read my eyes? Is there anything else I can do?"

"Honey, if the man is that dense, you can drag that cot he been sleepin' on into your room, nab his clothes, and lay in wait for him. When he comes lookin' for his things, lock the door and settle the matter once and for all."

"Myra!" Meredith gasped in shock, then promptly started laughing at the picture that came to mind of a bewildered Travis searching high and low for his bed.

"You ain't got nothing to worry about, Miss Meri." Myra reached across the table and patted her hand. "From what Moses says, your man's got a good head on his shoulders. He'll figure it out. And if it takes him longer than you like, you can always let him *accidentally* see you with your hair down, or tangle your apron strings in such a knot that you need his help to undo them. Find excuses to touch him, even if it's just passin' the potatoes, and look him in the eye while you do it. Trust me, that cot will find its way back into storage faster than you can fold the sheets."

Myra winked at her, and the insecurities that she'd been dragging around for days finally lifted. She could do it. She could woo her husband.

Meredith sat a little straighter in her chair and finished off her tea, ideas churning in her mind. Myra stood to refill her cup, her secretive smile no longer quite so mysterious. With confidence blossoming, Meredith felt a similar smile stretch across her face.

Knowing she needed to get back to the ranch, Meredith downed her tea as quickly as politeness allowed. Myra didn't seem to mind. She just peered at her over the rim of her still half-filled cup, her eyes gleaming with a light that made Meredith's cheek warm.

"I'm sorry to rush out on you, Myra. I promised Travis not to stay long." Meredith stood and collected her mittens and scarf. "The weather, you know."

"Mmm-hmm," Myra murmured, that secretive gleam of hers only growing brighter.

Meredith ducked her head to hide an embarrassed smile. It was the middle of the day, for heaven's sake. She probably wouldn't even see Travis for another couple of hours. It wasn't as if she were rushing home to put their plans into action.

All right, maybe that accounted for *some* of her urgency. But the coming storm was cause for concern, too.

Just as she reached for her cloak, Joshua stomped through the back door, letting in a gust of wind that pricked her skin like tiny ice needles.

"Lord have mercy!" Myra inhaled sharply. "When did it turn so cold?"

Joshua closed the door behind him, but Meredith still shivered. She hurriedly donned her cloak and crossed her arms over her middle, trying to reclaim the heat she'd lost.

"It's been droppin' for the last hour, Ma," Joshua said as he moved closer to the stove. "And now it's rainin'. Ain't much more than a drizzle, but the water's freezing on its way down. I suspect we'll get snow overnight."

Myra jumped to her feet. "I had no idea." She tossed an apologetic look Meredith's way. "You *do* gotta get home. Joshua, saddle her horse for her."

"Already done it. Ginger's ready to go when you are, Miss Meri."

"Thank you, Joshua." Meredith stuffed her hands into her mittens and wrapped her scarf high around her neck. "I best be on my way. I don't want my husband to worry."

And heaven knew, Travis would worry. He'd specifically warned her about the freezing rain. If she didn't get home soon, he might not let her leave the ranch for the rest of the winter.

Myra helped fasten the buttons on Meredith's cloak, since mittens didn't allow for much dexterity. Meredith thanked her and pulled her friend into a brief embrace.

"I'd be lost without you, Myra."

"You and Mr. Travis will find your way through this," the older woman whispered fiercely in Meredith's ear. "I have no doubt."

Meredith followed Joshua outside, heartened by the woman's words and eager to get home to put some of Myra's strategies into practice.

Icy drizzle stung her cheeks, and the wind seemed to know the location of every crack and crevice in her clothing, chilling her instantly. Ginger stamped her hooves and twisted her head away from the wind.

"I know, girl," Meredith soothed, stroking the paint's neck. "Let's get you home to that new barn."

"Pa always takes the cutoff by Beaver Creek," Joshua said after helping her mount. "It could save you some time gettin' back."

Meredith nodded as she took up the reins and turned Ginger's head toward home. "Thanks."

Moses and Josiah usually traveled on foot, not on horseback, but Meredith trusted Ginger to handle the terrain. It wasn't truly raining, after all, just drizzling. The ground didn't even feel muddy when they left the road.

By the time she reached the edge of the creek, however, the drizzle had worsened into a light shower of sleet. Her soggy mittens only intensified the cold as the wind blew through the knit, leaving her fingers numb.

Meredith reined Ginger in and tugged her mittens off with her teeth. She tucked them into the pocket of her cloak, then lifted her hands to her mouth and tried to warm them with her breath.

"All right, Ginger," she said as she guided the horse to the lowest spot on the creek bank. "Home's not much farther. Let's get across."

The paint tossed her head but obediently trudged forward. The creek wasn't more than a foot deep, but the banks were getting slick as the rain increased. Halfway down, Ginger's back hoof lost purchase and sent her staggering to the right. Meredith grabbed the horse's neck, barely managing to stay in the saddle.

"Easy, girl." Heart thudding in her chest, Meredith righted herself and ground her teeth together as she urged Ginger into the water.

They splashed across without much problem, so Meredith relaxed her grip on the saddle horn. Then, as Ginger surged up the opposite bank, her hooves slid on the mud. Her hind legs buckled, and she fell hard onto her haunches. Meredith flew backward. She screeched and grabbed desperately for the pommel, but her numb fingers were too slow to connect. The reins tore from her hand, and she toppled end over end—right into Beaver Creek.

Meredith gasped. Frigid water slapped her face. Cold rushed up her arms and legs, her cloak offering little protection as she lay half submerged in the creek. She scrambled to her feet and quickly waded to the bank, but already she could feel the added weight in her skirts.

Wiping water from her face with the back of her hand, she searched for Ginger. The horse had made it up the small embankment, but the way she kept lifting her rear left foot sent a frisson of dread through Meredith.

After wringing what water she could from her petticoats, Meredith hiked up her skirts and planted her boot on a thick tree root protruding from the muddy bank. She grasped a handful of tall grass from atop the rise and crawled out of the creek bed.

"So maybe we should have taken the longer way around, huh, girl?" Meredith scraped her mud-caked boots on the yellowed grass and carefully approached Ginger. "We're definitely both going to need a bath after this."

She collected the dangling reins and wrapped them around the pommel, then ran a calming hand down the paint's neck and shoulder. Slowly, she stroked her way back toward the mare's hind legs.

"Let me take a look, girl. Easy." Meredith ran her palm down Ginger's left leg, over the hock and down along the fetlock. Ginger tossed her head and snorted as if in discomfort, but otherwise submitted to the examination. Nothing seemed to be broken, thank the Lord, but something was definitely paining her. Hopefully, it was just a bruise. But it could be a sprain or even a fracture. One thing was for certain, Meredith wasn't about to risk causing her horse further injury by forcing her to carry her added weight. They'd have to walk the rest of the way.

Meredith unwound Ginger's reins and limped up to the animal's head. "It's only a couple of miles, girl. We'll be home in no time."

Unfortunately, that promise proved to be a bit optimistic. As the temperatures continued to drop, Meredith's pace slowed. With every step, shards of pain tore through the arch of her right foot and up into her calf and thigh.

"We . . . make quite a . . . pair, don't we, Ginger?" Meredith ground out as she bent to retrieve a dead branch to use as a cane. It didn't offer much relief, but a little help was better than none. "Two girls with bum legs limping home."

After another dozen or so excruciating steps, her weak foot came down on a stone hidden beneath a scattering of leaves and pine needles. Meredith cried out and crumpled to the cold, wet ground, her ankle twisting beneath her. As her knees hit, she released Ginger's reins.

Meredith drew in a few deep breaths and willed her mind to disregard the agony in her leg. She could rest when she got home—home to Travis.

Travis. Meredith concentrated on her husband, on her plans to encourage his attentions, to become his wife in truth. Gripping the oak branch with both hands, she levered herself to her feet again, a groan vibrating in her throat.

They were close, maybe only a quarter mile away. *I can do this*.

Ducking her head against the sleet that continued to pelt down on her head, she planted the walking stick firmly against the ground and lifted her right leg. The moment her foot came down and took her weight, however, the weakened limb gave way.

"No!" Angry tears filled her eyes as her hip collided with the earth. Why did her body have to be so feeble?

Ginger sidestepped her mistress and swung her head back around, her big brown eyes seeming to convey the truth Meredith was loath to accept.

Time to part company.

Meredith pushed up onto her good knee, blew out a heavy breath, and nodded. "All right, then. Go fetch the men, Ginger." She swatted the paint's rump with her walking stick. "Hyah!"

The horse trotted off, still favoring her back leg.

Using her arms, Meredith dragged herself over to a nearby pine and leaned her back against the trunk. Only then did she remember the key on the chain around her neck. The Archer gate would block Ginger's path.

She closed her eyes for a moment, her mind turning heavenward. *Help Travis find me, Lord. And don't let him worry too much. Or blame himself.*

The more she thought about Travis and the conversation they'd had that morning, the more Meredith's heart ached for her husband. *Don't let this accident reinforce his fears. Bring him beyond that, to the assurance that can only be found in depending wholly on you.*

Exhaustion pressed upon her and kept her eyelids closed. She'd just rest for a few minutes, regain her strength. Then she'd crawl home if she had to. Travis needed her.

30

Travis and Neill rode in from the range, rain and sleet sliding off their hat brims and oilskin ponchos. When the house came into view, Travis nudged Bexar into an easy lope. What he wouldn't give for a hot cup of Meri's coffee right about now. If he was lucky, she might even have some of those oatmeal cookies left over. Well, if Crockett, Moses, and Josiah hadn't already finished them off.

Those three had had it easy that afternoon, working under the cover of the barn roof. Nevertheless, Meredith had most likely packed up half the kitchen for Moses in payment, including the cookies. Travis couldn't begrudge the man the treat. He and Josiah had worked as hard as any Archer over the last couple of weeks. They deserved a healthy payment.

He'd come to respect Moses's abilities, his work ethic . . . shoot, the man himself. He and Josiah were going to be missed now that the barn was finished.

Crockett must have heard their approaching horses, for he pulled wide the barn doors and allowed Travis and Neill to ride directly inside.

Josiah stepped out of a newly fashioned stall and moved forward to take charge of Bexar. Travis tossed him the reins as he dismounted, scanning the shadowy interior for Moses. He finally spotted him up in the hayloft, examining the ceiling.

"Any leaks?" Travis called out.

Moses grinned down at him, his white teeth glowing against his dark face. "No, sir." He patted the barn wall to his left. "She's holdin' together real fine."

"I suspected she would." Travis strode to the ladder and met Moses on his descent. "You've done well, my friend." He offered his hand.

Moses shook it. "Mr. Jim's the master carpenter. I just supplied some extra labor and a bit of experience."

"More than a bit." Travis winked at the big man, then pulled his soggy hat from his head and tried to reshape the brim. "We wouldn't have had the barn up in time for this storm without your help."

Crockett joined them at the base of the loft. "Yep. It's going to seem strange not having you and Josiah around every day."

"I can still meet up with Josiah on Saturdays to go fishin', can't I, Trav?" Neill's raised voice drew Travis's attention to where the boys stood rubbing down the horses. The two had become fast friends, and Travis had no intention of forcing a separation.

"Absolutely. The Jacksons are welcome here anytime."

Neill nodded with all the cockiness of a young man coming into his own, but he couldn't quite stifle the grin that lit up his face. It was nearly as bright as the one he sported the Christmas they gave him his first rifle. Meredith had been right about the boy needing a companion his own age.

Meredith. The urge to see her spurred him forward.

"Why don't we walk over to the house and get you some hot coffee before you head out?" Travis clapped Moses on the arm. "I'm sure Meri's got a pot warming on the stove."

"Uh, Trav?" Crockett edged closer, his eyes uneasy. "She's not back yet."

Travis stiffened. "Not back? You mean you let her go out in this mess?" Fear-spawned rage flared with such unexpected force, he had his brother by the collar before he even realized he'd moved. "I trusted you, Crock. If anything happens to her, I swear I'll—"

"Whoa!" Crockett brought his arms up in a sharp motion and broke Travis's hold. "She left two hours ago, before the storm hit. You're the one who gave her permission to leave as long as it wasn't raining. Don't go laying this on me."

Travis backed away, drawing a trembling hand over his face. Crockett was right. This was his fault. He never should have let her sway him from his better judgment. He should have—

"Josiah and me will check the path by the creek," Moses said, striding toward the barn entrance, buttoning his coat as he went. "Myra mighta sent her back that way when she saw the ice. It's shorter."

"Neill, go with Moses," Travis ordered, his mind racing ahead. "If you meet up with her, send up a couple shots. Crock and I will check the road."

Neill left with the Jacksons on foot while Travis and Crockett saddled fresh mounts.

"Sorry." Travis glanced over at his brother as he tightened the cinch. He didn't have time for a lengthy apology, but Crockett didn't seem to need one. He nodded his acceptance as he fit a bit into his horse's mouth.

"We'll find her, Trav."

Travis planted his foot in the stirrup and hoisted himself into the saddle. "We better."

Not waiting for his brother to finish, he set off at a canter and overtook Neill and the others before they reached the gate. The wind whistled in his ears, the wind and something that sounded vaguely like a horse's neigh.

Meri.

When he rounded the last stand of trees, Travis spotted Ginger's distinctive chestnut-and-white patches.

"Thank God," he breathed. But his relief lasted only a moment.

If Meri was at the gate, why couldn't he see her? It was possible she had just arrived and dismounted, but his gut told him otherwise. Travis slowed his gelding and leapt from his back before the animal came to a complete halt.

"Meri!" He called her name as he dug in his trouser pocket for the key he always kept there. "Meri!"

Travis shoved the key into the padlock. When it clicked open, he yanked the steel clasp free of the chain and tossed it into the dirt. Grabbing the middle rail of the gate, he pried it open with one hand, just far enough to squeeze himself through. He held out a calming hand to Ginger, noting the way she shied from putting weight on her left hind leg.

What happened? Had Meri been thrown? Was she even now lying hurt somewhere? Travis scanned the ground as far as he could see, cursing the trees he loved for obscuring his vision.

Turning his attention back to the horse, he captured the bridle and patted the paint's neck. Her coat was soaked. Ice crystals had accumulated in the dip of her saddle and in the dark strands of her mane. The ground had been churned into a muddy mess from her hooves.

God have mercy. Travis staggered back a step. How long had she been out here? How long had *Meri* been out there waiting for help while his locked gate kept Ginger from alerting anyone of trouble?

Stupid! Travis fisted his hand around the pommel and leaned his forehead against the seat. Meri had warned him about the gate, told him he didn't need it anymore. But did he listen? No. He knew what was best. He knew how to protect those he loved. Idiot!

He raised his head to the sky, not caring about the sleet that stung his face. "Help me find her, Lord. I need you. Please."

A firm hand on his shoulder brought his head around. Crockett's determined expression reignited Travis's spirit.

"Send the paint back toward the barn, then follow me with the horses." Once again in control of his emotions, Travis handed Ginger's reins over to Crockett. "Moses," he called to the man crouched down a few feet from him, examining hoofprints in the mud. "Help me track her."

"Don't worry, Mr. Travis," Moses said as he pushed to his feet. "As long as the rain don't start pourin', we oughta be able to follow her tracks good enough."

The men advanced on foot, Crockett and Neill keeping the horses behind the rest to ensure the tracks were not obscured. Travis's focus remained glued to the ground, jumping from one hoofprint to the next as he half-jogged down the path.

"Here!" Josiah shouted from several yards ahead. "Mr. Travis. Over here. I found where the horse entered the road."

Travis lifted his head. "You sure?" The tracks were getting harder to spot as the rain wore them down. He couldn't afford to waste time following a false lead.

"That's about where me and the boy cut through to go home," Moses said in a low voice, assurance lending power to his words. "If she done took the shorter route, she woulda been headed here from that direction."

Careful not to tread on any of the existing tracks, Travis raced up to Josiah's position. The markings were harder to spot among the pine needles and leaves, but when he examined them, he had to agree that they were most likely from Meri's horse.

"Good work, Josiah." Travis braced his palms against his thighs and pushed up from his crouch. He peered into the darkness of the forest, his gut clenching. He should be feeling relief that they were getting close, but all he felt was an increasing sense of urgency.

He cupped his hands around his mouth and yelled his wife's name into the shadows. "Meri!"

No one moved as they listened for an answer. Nothing came.

"Neill, stay here with the horses." Travis motioned impatiently to his youngest brother. "Mark our place in case we have to retrace our steps. Moses?" He turned and pleaded with the man he'd come to trust. "Show me the way."

With a sharp nod, Moses took off through the trees. Travis followed on his heels, scanning the surrounding trees. He called out Meri's name every dozen steps or so, his heart pleading with his ears to capture a response over the rustling of their footfalls against the leafy ground.

When it came, he nearly stumbled.

"Hush!" he ordered. The men halted abruptly, their labored breathing the only sound beyond the wind and sleet.

"Meri!" He closed his eyes and willed the response to come again. *Please, Lord. Help me hear.*

A small sound carried above the wind. Soft yet distinct.

Thank you!

Travis sprinted past Moses and veered slightly to the right, something deeper than instinct guiding him. A tiny movement at the base of one of the pines caught his attention.

"Meredith." Immediately he changed course. He'd nearly passed her by, the dark brown of her cloak blending in with her surroundings. Thank God for white petticoats. If that ruffle hadn't winked at him from near her boot tops, he might never have seen her.

Travis dropped to his knees at her side. "Meri? I'm here, darlin'. Are you hurt?" He ran his hands lightly over her arms and down her legs, assessing for breaks. Alarm surged through him when he realized how wet her skirts were. Ice particles had collected on her clothing just as they had on her horse's mane, making the fabric stiff. Her limbs must be frozen through. She didn't even react when he touched her, as if she were too numb to feel his hands.

"I'm sorry, Travis." Her voice whispered over him, stilling his movement. He turned his face from examining her leg and watched the hood of her cape lift as she raised her chin. She was conscious. Yet her face was so pale, he feared that state wouldn't last for long. "The storm came up too fast . . . Ginger fell . . ." Meredith's eyes glazed. "I didn't want you to worry . . ."

Her chin slumped forward then, as if it required too much energy to hold up.

Travis levered his left arm beneath her legs and his right between her back and the tree trunk, pulling her tight into his chest. Close to his heart. He pushed to his feet and called to his brother.

"Crockett. The horses. I need to get her home."

Crockett dashed through the trees, hollering Neill's name. Travis followed with his precious burden, thinking to save every second he could by shortening the distance between him and the horses. Moses and Josiah shadowed him, their worried faces offering him little comfort.

Thankfully, Neill and Crockett galloped through the trees a moment later. Crockett dismounted and held his arms out to Travis. "Let me take her while you mount. Then I'll hand her up to you."

Travis didn't want to let her go, even for a moment, but he knew his brother was right. He gently transitioned her into Crock's arms, then mounted his gelding. Wishing he had the better-trained Bexar with him, he did his best to still the gelding with the pressure of his knees while he reached out for his wife.

"All right. I'm ready."

As he bent to collect Meri, his horse sidestepped, agitated by the weather and all the odd happenings. Instantly, Moses appeared at the beast's head. He took the bridle with a firm hand and ordered the animal to be still.

Travis solidified his hold on Meri and drew her up onto his lap. She burrowed her hands under his oilskin in search of warmth as she secured herself to his waist. Even through his flannel shirt, her fingers felt like ice.

"Get that gal home, Mr. Travis," Moses said as he released the bridle.

"Thank you, my friend. For everything." Travis hugged his wife's half-frozen form to his chest and made for the ranch as fast as the storm and the extra weight on the horse's back would allow.

31

Meredith felt herself falling. With a tiny cry, she struggled against the lethargy that bound her and scrambled to reclaim her hold on the warm rock that was sliding away from her.

"Shh, Meri. It's all right," the rock said. "We're home. Let go for just a minute, sweetheart, so I can get down. Then I'll carry you inside."

But she didn't want to let go. Without her rock, she'd fall. She'd be alone in the cold again. "No," she murmured, tightening her grip.

Something soft and very unrockish touched her brow. It left a small circle of heat against her skin, like a promise. "Trust me, Meri." More warmth fanned across her cheek, warmth and familiarity. Strange how much her rock sounded like Travis.

Strong hands gripped her wrists and gently pried her away. Meredith whimpered but didn't fight. She trusted her husband's voice—whether he be rock or man.

As the rock shifted out from under her cheek, the hands returned, propping up her shoulders as she slumped forward. She tried to hold herself erect, but apparently her spine had turned to mush, for her body slumped to the side, following the hands as they edged farther down.

"I've got you, love."

The falling finally stopped as she came to rest against her warm rock once again. But when the rock began moving, her head jostled in a way that kept her from slipping back into the comfort of oblivion. Annoyed, she strained to open her eyes, just enough to glare a complaint. But the stubbled jaw that blurred in and out of focus a few inches from her face looked nothing like the rock she'd expected. Oh, it was set at a hard angle and clenched tight in concentration, but it was definitely flesh.

"Travis?" she croaked.

His chin dipped, and the brown eyes she loved so dearly caressed her face.

"I'm glad you're my rock." She knew it wasn't quite the right thing to say, but so much fog swirled in her mind, it was the best she could manage.

Travis's jaw softened a touch, and one corner of his mouth lifted. "I'm glad, too."

A sharp gust of wind slashed across her face, bringing her mind into momentary focus. Cold. She ached with it. Everywhere. It ran so deep she feared she'd never be able to cast it out. She burrowed closer to Travis, but even he seemed to lack heat. The place she had laid her cheek against his oilskin during their ride had chilled.

"I'm c-c-cold." Shivers began coursing through her with such violence she worried she might shake herself free of Travis's arms. But he held fast.

"You'll be warm soon, Meri. I swear it."

As he climbed the porch steps, another horse pounded into the yard, two riders on its back. For once, Travis didn't bellow any orders to his brothers, he just continued on to the house. Meredith would have smiled if her teeth hadn't been chattering so shamefully. Her husband was learning to surrender control—trusting his brothers more fully, and perhaps God, as well. Dare she hope that one day he might even trust *her* enough to bestow his heart?

When he carried her across the threshold of her room, she could think of little else. Her eyes slid closed, and she imagined herself in the blue-and-white-striped dress she'd worn at her wedding, her husband's arms around her, his eyes full of love and laughter as he escorted her into their room. *Their* room. The room where they would belong solely to each other, where love would be shared and children conceived. A room where she could truly be a wife.

"Meri? Can you stand?"

Why did he need her to stand? Wouldn't it be easier just to lay her on the bed? Her dress would look so pretty fanned out around her. She could open her arms, and he could bend down and kiss her . . .

"I need you to try to stand, sweetheart. If I lay you down, you'll get the bed all wet."

Wet? Meredith scrunched up her nose. What an odd thing for a husband to say. It wasn't at all romantic.

"Come on, Meri. I need you to help me get your clothes off."

Meredith sniffed. That wasn't very romantic, either—all gruff and businesslike. Where were the sweet words a husband used to woo his bride? And why wasn't he kissing her? Everything would be so much better if he'd just kiss her. Then he could do whatever he wanted with her clothes.

She leaned forward to show him what she wanted, but for some reason, her lips missed their target and landed somewhere on his neck. At least it felt like his neck. Not that she'd ever kissed him there, of course. But it felt much like she expected a neck to feel. She thought to adjust her aim and try again. However, she couldn't quite summon the energy. Oh well, necks were nice, too.

"Meredith!" Travis's bark combined with a brief, jarring shake tore away the curtain of her delirium, leaving her exposed to the harsh light of reality.

She hung like a rag doll from Travis's arms, her feet dragging the floor, her face plastered against his neck. No wedding dress. Only mud-smeared calico and a soggy wool cloak.

"I need your help." This time she heard the fear in his voice. "Please."

The hovering darkness promised escape, but she resisted its pull. Travis needed her.

Meredith reached her hands up to her husband's shoulders and drew her feet more firmly beneath her. Bracing her weight on her good leg, she gazed into his eyes as she forced herself to stand. His eyes held hers, infusing her with strength.

Keeping one hand at her waist to aid her balance, Travis used the other to undo the cloak's fastenings. Once he had it undone, he helped her slip each arm through the sleeves and tossed the sopping garment into a heap near the wall. He had just reached for the buttons that ran the length of her bodice when a masculine voice intruded.

"How is she, Travis?"

Meredith twisted her head away from Crockett, feeling exposed and vulnerable.

"She's frozen, half delirious, and weak as a newborn kitten, but I think if we can get her warm, she'll be all right."

"I've got water heating for some tea and a pair of bricks heating in the hearth. I brought some toweling, too." Crockett raised his arms to indicate the small bundle, then walked into the room and set it on the bed. "Need any help?'

Meredith gasped. She thought the man wanted to be a preacher. How could he make such an improper suggestion?

"Yeah. Come hold her up for a minute while I get out of this slicker."

"Travis, no," she moaned.

His eyes widened slightly, then crinkled at the corners. "Don't worry," he whispered close to her ear. "I'll send him away before we undo any more buttons."

What on earth had possessed him to say such a thing? Travis stripped off his hat, slicker, and coat, tossing them to the floor. The woman was soaked to the skin, her teeth chattering faster than the rattle on a snake's tail. The last thing she needed was a flirtatious husband. Yet it *had* brought a touch of color back to her cheeks.

Travis took a minute to rummage through the bureau drawers and find one of Meri's nightdresses before he relieved Crockett. His brother stepped aside, then winked at Travis, careful to keep the gesture hidden from Meredith.

"A little different from last time, huh?"

Images of the two of them bumbling over Meredith's corset after her encounter with Samson scurried through Travis's mind. "Very," he ground out.

Thank the Lord Meredith was conscious enough to cooperate this time, for there was no way he'd let Crockett assist in her undressing. That duty belonged to her husband. And only her husband.

Crockett slapped him on the back and strode to the door. "I'll knock when the tea and bricks are ready," he said, all teasing gone from his voice as he grabbed the knob to pull the door shut. "Feel better, Meredith."

"Th-th-th-hank y-y-you," she stammered in reply.

Travis gently tugged her head toward him until it lay against his chest, and then he ran his hands briskly up and down her arms, trying to ward off her convulsive shivers. His own legs were cold inside his rain-soaked trousers, but his comfort could wait. Meri's couldn't.

Together, they managed to get her dress, petticoats, and corset off. But when Travis started to toss the pink, lacy undergarment on top of the pile of wet clothes, Meredith shrieked and grabbed his arm with more strength than he would have given her credit for.

"Drape it over the b-b-back of the ch-chair."

He figured it was safer not to argue with her, so he did as she instructed and hurried back to her side, grabbing the toweling off the bed as he went. He wrapped her in the dry cloth as if it were a shawl and urged her to lean on him as he rubbed her back and arms. So focused was he on getting her warm that it wasn't until he was kneeling before her, running a second towel up and down her calves, that he realized how well her damp chemise and drawers clung to her curves.

Travis immediately turned his attention to her feet.

After a moment of carefully regulated breathing and a stern internal lecture, Travis stood and faced his bride. "Do you think you can handle the nightdress on your own?"

She gave a jerky little nod, and he exhaled in relief. Her shivers had calmed somewhat, but she still looked unsteady on her feet.

"I'm going to turn around to give you some privacy, but I'll be right here if you need me. All right?"

Another nod.

Travis turned his back and immediately started naming the books of the Bible in his head. Then the twelve apostles, thirteen if one counted Matthias, which he did because he needed all the distraction he could get to keep himself from imagining what was transpiring behind him. He added Paul in for good measure, too, and then started on the twelve tribes. Although, really, there were thirteen there, too. What with Joseph's descendants split into two tribes and named after his sons, Ephraim and Manasseh. But then again, the Levites didn't inherit any land, so—

A muffled cry banished the Israelites from his brain. Travis spun around to find Meredith bent sideways clasping her calf through the white cotton of her nightdress. He was at her side in an instant.

"What is it?"

"Cramps," she whimpered. "In my w-weak leg."

He picked her up and carried her to the bed.

"I sh-shouldn't have put any weight on it. I know b-b-better."

Travis pulled the covers back and laid her on the sheets. "What can I do?"

She squeezed her eyes shut and rolled toward him, curling up into a ball. "It'll p-pass eventually."

That wasn't good enough. Travis tucked the blankets up to her chin, knelt on the rug that ran alongside the bed, and reached for her leg—the leg his trap had weakened all those years ago, the leg that had brought this incredible woman into his life.

Meredith groaned and tried to ease the limb away from him, but he wouldn't allow her to retreat. Using a light touch at first, he worked his way up her calf to just above her knee, then back down to the arch of her foot and even her toes. Gradually he increased the pressure of his massage, working the knots out of her muscles until she finally began to uncurl from her protective posture.

When Crockett's knock came, Meri's eyelids had relaxed, and though she continued to shiver slightly, her breathing had evened enough that Travis suspected she might have drifted off to sleep. Slowly, he drew his hand down her calf, over her ankle, and across her foot, enjoying the feel of her skin one last time just for the pure pleasure of it before rising to answer the door.

"How is she?" Crockett asked, lowering his voice to a whisper when he noticed her lying in bed.

"Better, but she's still shivering. I'm worried she might have caught a chill."

"Yeah, well, I'm worried *you're* going to catch a chill unless you get some dry clothes on yourself. Go change while I try to get some of this tea into her. Neill's gathering the bricks now. We'll have her warm in no time."

Travis glanced back at Meri, reluctant to leave. But Crockett was right. He'd be no good to her if he was ill.

"I left a mug of hot coffee for you on Neill's dresser."

"Thanks." Travis strode down the hall, determined to change in record time.

His wet trousers made the going slower than he would have liked, clinging to him like woolen leeches. He eventually succeeded in peeling them off, along with his drawers and socks. The dry clothes went on much easier, and within minutes, Travis had gulped down his coffee and was helping Neill arrange the cloth-wrapped hot bricks under the sheets at the bottom of Meredith's bed.

Crockett got about a cupful of tea into Meri before she waved him away. Her haggard expression elicited Travis's protective nature, and he immediately shooed his brothers out of the room. Meredith inched her way back down in the bed, no doubt drawn to the heat of the bricks, but once there, she still curled herself into a ball, as if the added warmth failed to penetrate her.

"Are you still cold?"

"Mm-hmm," she mumbled against the pillow.

Travis could think of only one other way to help her get warm. He walked around to the opposite side of the bed and lifted the covers. His heart throbbed against his ribs. After more than a month, he was finally going to share a bed with his wife.

The mattress took his weight, and Travis tentatively shifted closer to Meri. As if someone had shot off a starting gun, she rolled over and burrowed into him with such haste that he barely moved his knees in time to avoid a collision. Her legs tangled with his while her arms folded up between them. Frigid toes rubbed against his calf where his trouser leg had bunched up, shocking him with the sheer cold that continued to cling to her despite the blankets and heated bricks. He sandwiched his legs around her feet, hoping to speed their thaw. Her hands eventually wiggled their way beneath his untucked shirt, and when her icy fingers found his bare chest, she let out a tiny sigh that made his heart flip.

One thing was for sure. Crockett needn't worry about him catching a chill tonight. With Meredith touching him like she was, he'd be lucky not to go up in flames.

32

Travis woke before the sun, pangs in his stomach prodding him to rise and make restitution for skipping supper the night before. But he resisted. Contentment lay over him like an extra blanket, so foreign yet utterly captivating that he didn't want to move for fear it would dissipate. Then it shifted, blowing a warm puff of air against his neck. Travis's mind sharpened in an instant.

Meri.

Travis opened his eyes and turned his head, ever so slowly, so as not to disturb the woman whose face lay in the crook of his shoulder. She was so beautiful. Her long lashes resting peacefully against the creamy skin of her cheeks, her hair cascading behind her, finally freed from the confines of its pins. As he watched her sleep, he couldn't resist the urge to stroke the deep blond tresses, their softness quickly becoming an addiction to his fingers.

He wanted nothing more than to gently kiss her awake and finally claim her in the way God intended. But as he leaned forward to touch his lips to her sleepy eyelids, he noted the faint smudges of exhaustion still evident beneath her eyes and pulled away. She needed rest.

Turning his gaze to the ceiling, Travis exhaled. He might as well get up. Sleep was well beyond his grasp now, and Meredith would rest better without him tossing and turning beside her. But, oh, how he hated to leave. One thing was for certain, though, if she would have him, he'd be spending all future nights in this bed with her. Their courting had gone on long enough. It was time to begin their marriage.

Careful to disturb her as little as possible, Travis cupped the back of Meredith's head as he slid his arm out from under her cheek and eased away. Her mouth puckered into an adorable little pout as she grumbled her displeasure in her sleep before resettling. Tenderness welled inside him as he smiled down on her. What a precious gift he'd been given.

A gift he'd nearly lost yesterday.

His smile faded as he padded on bare feet over to the window and looked out over the predawn landscape.

How am I supposed to protect my family, Lord?

Twice now the measures he'd taken had come back to haunt him, and both times Meredith had been the one to pay the price. She could have lost her leg the first time, and yesterday she could have frozen to death waiting for him to find her.

All my life I've striven to protect those you've entrusted to my care. Yet no matter how hard I try, my efforts are never enough. What do you want from me?

As the first hint of light softened the sky, a verse from Proverbs illuminated his heart. *"Trust in the Lord with all thine heart; and lean not unto thine own understanding. In all thy ways acknowledge him, and he shall direct thy paths."*

Conviction speared through him, and Travis had to place a hand against the wall to steady himself. He'd been shouldering the burden of guarding his family since his father charged him with the duty fourteen years ago. And all that time he'd trusted only himself to take care of them. Rarely had he sought the Lord's guidance. His father had always said that God gave man a mind and expected him to use it, but perhaps he had taken that admonition too far.

Travis glanced back at Meredith. *Show me how best to take care of her. How to be a good husband, provider, and protector.*

Hungering for direction, he crossed the room on silent feet and eased open the dresser drawer where he kept his Bible. Then he crept out to the kitchen, lit a lamp, and settled into a chair at the table. His brothers would be up soon, but right now the morning was quiet—a good time to listen for the Lord.

Not sure where to start, Travis thumbed the pages open to Proverbs. For much of his life, he'd clung to the wisdom of a particular verse in chapter 27. He ran his finger down the page until he found verse 12: "*A prudent man foreseeth the evil, and hideth himself.*" That's what he had been doing the past fourteen years, trying to predict what evil might threaten his family and taking steps to hide away from it. But the disquiet in his soul made him wonder if perhaps the season for that tactic had passed. He and his brothers were no longer vulnerable boys who needed to hide. They were grown men who could fight for what was right.

His gaze drifted over the page, not truly focusing, until the word *brother* caught his attention, just two verses up from where he'd been reading.

"Thine own friend, and thy father's friend, forsake not; neither go into thy brother's house in the day of thy calamity: for better is a neighbour that is near than a brother far off."

Don't forsake friends. Depend on neighbors. Your brothers might not always be at hand when trouble comes. Travis rubbed his brow, bracing his elbow against the table. Friends? Until Meredith had talked him into letting Moses help rebuild the barn, he hadn't had any. Seth Winston might count as a friend of his father, but the old man only came around four times a year.

And neighbors? He recalled a few schoolmates who'd had farms in the area, but he had no idea if their families were still around or not. Hadn't Christ said that except for loving God, the most important command was to love one's neighbor? Kind of hard to do that if he didn't even know who his neighbors were.

Another verse floated into memory, one about not only looking out for one's own interests, but also to the interests of others. Travis began flipping pages toward the New Testament, but before he found the verse, something stuffed between the pages in Romans caused him to halt.

A straw. A broken, short straw.

She'd kept it.

He wasn't quite sure why that fact make his heart jump around in his chest, but it did. His hand even trembled slightly as he moved to take it out of the book's crease. The brittle piece felt thin and delicate in his rough fingers. He stroked its length with his thumb and thought of the wife it had brought him.

Meredith deserved better than a reclusive life. Whenever she talked about teaching on Saturdays, her whole face lit up. Myra and the children brought her such joy and gave her life a sense of purpose beyond daily chores. And she'd been right about his brothers, too. No matter how badly he wanted to keep them tied to the ranch, he knew the Lord had planted ambitions in them that could one day take them away. Jim had his carpentry and his newfound attachment to Cassie. Crockett had his preaching. And Neill? Well, the kid had an entire world of possibilities to explore.

"Travis?"

He swiveled toward the sleepy voice. Meredith stood in the doorway, her nightdress floating about her legs as she squinted into the lamplight.

"Is everything all right?" Her fingers clenched nervously at the shawl she'd wrapped around her shoulders.

Travis got to his feet. "What are you doing out of bed? You should be resting." He closed the distance between them, thinking to lead her back to the bedroom.

"I missed you." The hushed admission froze him in his tracks and drove all other thought out of his head.

She missed him? Beside her? In bed?

His gaze flew to her face to gauge if perhaps he'd misunderstood, even while his heart raced with the hope that he had not. She dipped her chin away from him, a delightful shade of pink coloring her cheeks.

"I . . . I was cold." She still couldn't meet his eyes, and he prayed it was because his heat wasn't the only thing she missed.

Travis moved his hands up her arms to her shoulders, his fingers digging through her hair. "You know," he said, probing her gently. "Now that winter's here, you're apt to be cold often. I'd be willing to help you stay warm on a more regular basis. If that was something you wanted."

She angled her face away from him and nibbled on her bottom lip.

"Meri?" He forced himself to breathe slowly as he waited for her to turn and look at him. When her lashes finally lifted, the longing he read in her blue eyes matched the desire pulsing in his chest. "Is that what you want?"

"Yes."

Tightening his grip on her nape, he drew her to him and slanted his lips possessively over hers. He stroked her jaw with the side of his thumbs and urged her to deepen the kiss. A tiny moan escaped her, and she melted against him. He was about to sweep her into his arms and take her back to his room where they could make good on the promise passing between them, but the creak of one of the hall doors brought him back to his senses.

Reminding himself they had years to be together, Travis gentled his kiss and then pulled away. The fact that Meredith didn't seem to want to stop nearly derailed his good intentions, but he managed to disentangle himself from her hold on him, pleased by her reluctance to let him go.

"The others are starting to rise, Meri," he murmured low in her ear. "Why don't you go back to bed? The boys and I can fend for ourselves this morning."

"I don't mind seeing to things, Travis. I can—"

"Shh." He placed a finger on her lips. "With all you went through yesterday, you need to rest. Besides, I have a special project I thought you might like to help me with later this morning. You won't be able to help if you're too worn out."

Her eyes lit. "What sort of project?"

"I thought we could dismantle the front gate. Oh, and those warning signs, too. Something tells me we don't really need them anymore."

A beatific smile blossomed across her face as she clasped his hand and drew it to her middle. "Oh, Travis. Do you mean it?"

His chest expanded as he returned her smile. A man could get used to his woman looking at him like that.

"Yes, darlin'. I mean it. I think it's time for the Archers to rejoin the world."

Meredith stretched up on her tiptoes and touched a kiss to his cheek. "You *are* my world."

Her husky comment made his gut clench, but before he could do more than blink, she released his hand and trailed away from him. Which was probably a good thing seeing as how Crockett was standing right outside the doorway trying to look inconspicuous.

Meredith bundled her shawl more tightly around her shoulders before ducking her head and scurrying past his brother. Travis knew he probably looked like a lovesick pup just standing there watching her go, but he didn't care. Crockett even came into the room and stared into the newly emptied hall alongside him, obviously trying to taunt him out of his stupor.

"So when are you finally going to tell her that you're insanely in love with her?" Crockett asked, only a hint of teasing in his voice.

Travis rubbed a hand over his whiskery jaw, reaching his fingers up to the place she had kissed. "Tonight. Definitely tonight."

33

Meredith whistled and danced her way around the kitchen, drying the lunch dishes and wiping down the stove, her happiness too large to contain. Had there ever been a finer day? Yesterday's storm had passed, and the blue sky left in its wake portended a bright future.

Wouldn't Myra be surprised to learn that all their plotting had proved unnecessary? A tiny giggle bubbled out of Meredith as she returned a stack of clean plates to the cabinet shelf. She hadn't needed to use even one of Myra's suggestions in order to get Travis to stay with her last night. Of course, she'd slept through nearly the entire experience, but there were enough lingering memories of his scent close to her face, his chest beneath her hand, and his touch at her waist to reassure her that it hadn't been a dream.

And this morning? Meredith sighed. Her hands stilled as she stared at the doorway where Travis had kissed her. She recalled the way he'd looked at her afterward, the possessive heat in his eyes, the way his lips quirked slightly as if eager to return to hers, the touch of his fingers through the sleeve of her gown. At that moment, all her self-doubts had vanished. She'd actually felt beautiful. Desired. Not at all like a woman who'd been foisted upon a reluctant bridegroom.

Could it be that Travis no longer saw her as simply a responsibility but as something more? Had duty deepened to . . .

Meredith couldn't quite bring herself to name the emotion, not even in her thoughts. The disappointment would be too keen if his affection didn't prove to be as deep as such a name would imply. His fondness for her had already grown so much. Getting greedy now would only risk halting their progress. Better to let the words come naturally. In their own time.

As she tried to convince herself that she was patient enough to wait however long it might take, pounding hoofbeats approached from the direction of the road, seizing her attention.

After working close to the house that morning, Travis had left after lunch to help Crockett and Neill assess the damage the storm had done to the herd. With cattle scattered all over the northern pasture, she didn't expect him back until suppertime. Meredith reached for the loaded shotgun she'd propped against the wall near the back door, having sworn to her husband that she wouldn't leave the house unarmed, and moved to the front room, where she could get a better look at the rider.

Catching a glimpse of her brother-in-law's scowling face as he leapt from his horse's back, rifle in hand, sent relief spiraling through her—quickly followed by new alarm as she tried to guess what unseen foe had him so on guard.

Jim climbed the porch and positioned himself with his back to the door, his rifle aimed across the yard.

"Travis!"

Meredith jumped at the sheer volume of his yell. Heavens! The man was louder than a grizzly. Ordering her heart palpitations to cease, she moved to the door, intending to inform the bear of his brother's location, but the instant the hinge squeaked, Jim crouched and spun, bringing the barrel of his rifle in line with her chest.

Meredith's heart stopped altogether then. Her shotgun clunked to the ground as her breath hitched in her throat.

"Confound it, woman. I could have shot you!" Jim yanked his rifle out of her direction, but he scowled at her as if the mishap were somehow her fault. Then he noted the shotgun at her feet, and his irritated expression immediately turned wary. He placed himself in front of her and began scanning the yard again.

"Where are Travis and the others? Did Mitchell's men attack?"

"Everything's fine, Jim. Truly." Meredith stepped from behind him. "They're all out checking the herd. Why would you think Roy's men had returned? Unless . . ." She grabbed his arm. "Did you see someone on the road?"

His brow furrowed. "No. But the gate was down. Travis never leaves that gate open. I figured something must've happened."

Meredith's breath released in a soft whoosh. "Something did happen," she said, a grin stretching across her face. "Your brother decided to rejoin the world. Travis and I took the gate down this morning."

Jim's jaw hung slightly slack as he stared at her. "Travis took the gate down? *Travis?*"

She nodded, pride for her husband nearly unbalancing her as she rose up onto the balls of her feet. "He took the warning signs down, too. Did you notice? No more scaring away the neighbors at gunpoint, I'm afraid." A laugh escaped her, but it died when Jim's frown refused to abate.

"What about Mitchell? Didn't Travis think that removing the gate would make us more vulnerable?"

Meredith tilted her head a bit as she considered Jim's uneasy stance. She'd thought he would be more pleased about the change, seeing as how it would aid his courting plans with Cassie, not to mention being good for his furniture building business. Then again, the locked gate had been a symbol of security to this family for the majority of their lives. It was only natural that such a change would require some adjustment.

"Travis and Crockett discussed it at length this morning. They agreed that if Mitchell's men are bent on causing mischief, a locked gate won't stop them. The night of the fire proved that. All the gate does now is keep neighbors out and Archers in. With the four of you grown and fully capable of handling whatever comes down the path, Travis figured it was time to stop living in isolation."

The grunt Jim gave in reply was hard to read, so Meredith changed the subject.

"How's Cassie?"

Jim's mouth thinned, and a fierceness emerged in his eyes. "She assured me everything was fine. Said her father had given his word not to force her to marry Mitchell. She promised to come to me if he changed his mind." He worked his jaw back and forth. "You don't think they'd lock her in, do you? I watched her house last night and again this morning, and nothing seemed off. Her ma stormed out of the house early in the morning, but I saw Cassie before I left, and she said that except for an ugly argument between her folks, things were normal. She insisted I come home in case Mitchell stirred up trouble for Travis. I told her I'd check on her in a few days."

Meredith nibbled the inside of her cheek. Cassie had always been able to sway Uncle Everett to her way of thinking, but Aunt Noreen was another matter entirely. God had never made a more hardheaded woman. Hearing that she'd gone out early was a bit worrisome. The woman never took idle strolls. But what trouble could she possibly stir up without her husband's support?

"I've never known Uncle Everett to break his word to Cassie," Meredith said, trying to reassure herself as much as Jim. "If he's promised her not to force the marriage, he won't."

Jim made a noncommittal sound.

"Why don't you get cleaned up, and then come in and let me fix you something to eat?"

"Nah." Jim strode away from her and clomped down the steps toward his horse. "I need to talk to Travis."

She thought about stopping him, about mentioning that Travis had expected him to keep an eye on the house once he returned from town, but she held her tongue. Jim's stoic features gave away little; nevertheless, Meredith sensed how the situation with Cassie ate at him. The Archers always handled their problems together. This time shouldn't be any different.

Besides, it wasn't as if she needed a guard, she reminded herself as Jim mounted his horse. She had Sadie. And if the old girl slept under the porch most of the day, what did it matter? Meredith had periodically stayed alone for days at a time at the old homestead. She could certainly manage a few hours at the Archer ranch.

And if Travis didn't like the idea of her being unchaperoned for the duration of the afternoon, he could just come home and watch over her himself.

"You'll be all right here?" Jim turned in his saddle to face her, the tightness around his mouth testifying to his sudden indecision.

"Of course." Meredith's lips curled into a secretive smile. An afternoon alone with her husband? She couldn't get rid of Jim fast enough.

An hour later, Meredith had dusted the parlor, swept the kitchen, and chopped a pot's worth of vegetables for the stew she planned for dinner—a pretty remarkable feat since she spent nearly as much time peering out the window for Travis as she did working.

Surely he would come soon. Unless Jim had trouble locating him. She'd never ridden the north pasture, had no idea how large it was or how wooded. Perhaps finding Travis was more difficult than she'd imagined. And even then, Travis wouldn't leave without at least having a conversation with Jim.

As Meredith poured water over her potatoes, onions, and carrots, another thought struck her. What if Travis felt no urgency to return? What if he had full confidence in her abilities to handle things at the house? Meredith frowned as she set the water pitcher aside. She wanted Travis to trust her, to have confidence in her abilities. But what she wanted even more was for him to jump at the chance to be alone with her.

And wasn't that a muddled mess. Meredith rolled her eyes in exasperation. The man had a ranch to run, for heaven's sake. The last thing he needed was a love-struck wife making demands on his time during prime work hours. They'd have other opportunities—

The sound of a rider approaching banished all practical reasoning, leaving her head swirling and her stomach jumping as she rushed to the bathing room to check her appearance in the shaving mirror.

Travis had come after all.

Anticipation fluttered in her chest as she untied her apron and tossed it onto the table. She pranced down the hall, eager to greet her husband. But when she reached for the door handle, the sound of Sadie's growl stopped her. Caution reasserted itself. Meredith released the knob and instead reached for the shotgun propped nearby.

Whoever was in the yard, it wasn't her husband.

34

Travis guided Bexar through the muddy terrain left from yesterday's storm, methodically working his way back to the ranch. Jim had been none too happy to see the gate down and had given him an earful about how it didn't make sense to reduce security around the house until things with Mitchell were settled. And though Travis still believed that taking down the gate was what God had called him to do, hearing his own doubts voiced aloud left him uneasy.

I'm trying to trust you, Lord. But I feel like I'm fighting against nature. Common sense tells me to lock down, not open up. To protect those I love with every tool at my disposal.

What if he had misunderstood God's intention? What if his actions today were putting his family in danger?

"Is it too late to lay out a fleece?" Travis quipped, tilting an eye toward heaven. "A little confirmation would sure be appreciated."

The more he thought about that fleece, though, the more he remembered what the Lord had demanded of the man who'd laid it out. He'd demanded trust beyond what common sense dictated. God whittled Gideon's army from three thousand men to three hundred, then sent him into battle against an enemy whose troops were too vast to be counted. Gideon purposely made himself vulnerable, ignored his instincts, and put the welfare of his people into the hands of another. And the Lord rewarded him by granting him victory.

Travis squinted into the distance, sighting in on the trail of woodsmoke that marked the location of the ranch house. Was God calling him to do the same?

Bexar ambled into a clearing as Travis pondered. Then from out of the quiet, two muted cracks—gunfire—set both man and horse on alert.

Meri!

Travis kicked Bexar into a run. The animal leapt to his command, his hooves eating up the damp earth as they raced forward. The frantic pace made them reckless, but Travis drove on, his mind focused on only one thing—getting to his wife.

I trusted her to you! his soul cried as trees blurred past.

Shoring up his faith, he held on to the knowledge that she had to be relatively safe in order to fire the signal shots. But even that did little to calm the anxiety raging within. He needed to see her, touch her. Only then would he be able to breathe.

The barn came into view. Travis slowed Bexar with a touch of the reins and yanked his rifle free of the scabbard. His gaze scoured the trees, searching for the threat. Meredith didn't spook easily. She wouldn't have fired those shots without reason.

When he found nothing suspicious behind the barn, he used his knees to steer Bexar into the main yard. That's when he spotted her. Sitting on the porch rocker, the shotgun near but not gripped across her lap, Sadie lying at her feet. She looked safe. Beautiful.

Something wound tight inside him uncoiled a bit.

He could tell the moment she noticed him. She pushed slowly to her feet, as if needing to verify his identity before taking any deliberate action. Once she did, she scrambled down the steps, picked up her skirts, and ran toward him, her limp exacerbated by her hurry.

Travis couldn't yet see her face clearly, but there was a desperation to her movement that twisted his gut. She wasn't just relieved to see him. Something was wrong. Urging Bexar forward, he crossed half the yard in the time it took her to get to the corral. Once he was close enough, he slid from the horse's back and rushed to meet her.

His hands gripped her arms when he reached her, and his gaze roved over her, searching for proof that she was indeed unharmed. "What happened, Meri? Are you all right?"

"It's not me, Travis." Meredith bent her arms and grabbed hold of his elbows, her fingers pressing through the thickness of his coat. "It's Cassie."

He looked over at the house. "Your cousin's here? Jim said he left her in town."

"She's not here. She's at the old homestead. About to marry Roy Mitchell."

His attention snapped back to her face. "What?" Jim was going to be livid. "I thought your uncle gave his word not to force the union."

"Aunt Noreen must've interfered somehow. She hates to be thwarted, and in her mind, Cassie's marriage to Roy is the best way to preserve their livelihood." Meredith was rambling so fast, Travis struggled to keep pace. "She must've warned Roy of Uncle Everett's change of heart, not realizing what measures he would take to ensure he didn't lose the land he'd been promised."

Meri's vivid eyes locked with his. "I think he kidnapped her, Travis. It's the only thing that makes any sense. Mr. Wheeler tried to make it sound like everything was amicable. But I know Cassie, and she'd never—"

"Wait a minute." Travis's eyes narrowed. "Wheeler was here?" That was the man who'd tried to convince him to sell out, and no doubt one of the riders responsible for setting fire to his barn. He'd been here? Talking to Meri?

She nodded. "Roy sent him to deliver the invitation."

"Did he touch you?" Travis shoved the words past clenched teeth. If that snake had so much as laid a finger on her . . .

"He didn't even get off his horse." A gleam shone in Meredith's eyes. "Between Sadie's growls and my shotgun, we managed to welcome him in true Archer style."

Travis grinned. Here he'd torn down gates and disposed of warning signs—things his wife had encouraged him to do—and now she was the one welcoming strangers at gunpoint.

Sadie barked, and for the first time, Travis noticed the dog standing a pace behind Meri. He reached down and stroked her behind her ears. "Sounds like my girls had things well in hand." The old bird dog barked again in appreciation of his approval.

When he straightened, Meredith's eyes were scanning the woods beyond the barn. "Do you think the others heard the shots? Jim will want to know about Cassie. We'll need to strategize, and we don't have much time."

"Don't worry. They'll come barrelin' out of those trees any minute." Especially Jim. The man was already edgier than a new razor. "But for now, I think you better start at the beginning and tell me exactly what Wheeler said."

"There isn't that much to tell." Meredith shivered slightly and rubbed her arms. Her shawl must have slipped off when she left the porch. Funny how she hadn't noticed the cold until that moment.

Travis shrugged out of his work coat and settled the heavy garment on her shoulders. Tenderness softened his face for a moment as he fidgeted with the collar. But when he finished, the hard lines returned. "What did he say?"

"He said that Roy and Cassie were on their way to my father's old property along with my aunt and uncle and a handful of guests. Knowing how close Cassie and I are, Roy asked Wheeler to ride ahead and extend a personal invitation to us. For Cassandra's sake, he asked that we set aside any hard feelings over previous misunderstandings and attend the wedding. It's supposed to be in the cabin at five o'clock tonight."

Travis's eyes widened. "Tonight? That can't be more than a couple hours from now."

"I found that pretty suspicious, too." Meredith pushed her arms through the sleeves of her husband's coat and crossed them over her belly. "I told Mr. Wheeler that when I saw Cassie yesterday morning, she'd had no intention of wedding Mr. Mitchell. He just smiled and said she'd changed her mind."

Meredith searched Travis's face for some clue as to what he was thinking, but his stoic mask gave nothing away. She'd expected outrage or a promise to mount a rescue effort or something. Yet all he did was scowl and stare into the empty space between her and the corral.

"We *are* going to help her, right?" Meredith tried to claim Travis's gaze by searching out his eyes. "I know Cass. She'd never willingly marry that man. Roy must be threatening or manipulating her somehow."

"Of course he's manipulating," Travis growled. "And not only your cousin. He's attempting to manipulate me, as well. Which is why we can't rush off without thinking things through."

Travis twisted his neck back toward the woods. Only then did Meredith hear the sound of riders coming in.

"Mitchell needs both our properties to solidify things with his investors," Travis said, turning back to her. "If we play into his hand, we risk giving him exactly what he wants. We need time to figure out what game he's playing before we can hope to beat him at it."

"But—"

"We'll talk about it more when the boys get here."

Travis strode away from her to signal his brothers, and Meredith couldn't help but feel a little abandoned. Her mind insisted that anticipating Roy's machinations was the wise course, but her heart wanted a take-charge hero ready to ride to the rescue.

Forty-five minutes later, all the Archers stood in the center of the barn, still arguing over the best plan of action.

"What if you're wrong, Travis? I won't take that risk." Jim refused to back down, and Meredith, for one, was glad.

"We don't even know for sure that Mitchell has her," Travis insisted. "More likely it's a ploy to lure us away and leave the ranch open to attack. Only this time, they'll raze everything, not just the barn. It's the only hope he has of driving us off the land. Either that or he has an army of men waiting to ambush us at the cabin. Dead men can't protest an illegal sale, after all."

Crockett pushed away from the post he'd been slouching against. "You did say Cassie was fine when you left her this morning. Right, Jim? Wheeler arrived barely an hour after you did. Mitchell would've had to abduct Cassie and her family, find a minister willing to perform a forced ceremony, and set out for Meredith's cabin in that same time frame. I find it hard to believe that he could pull that off in under an hour with no advance warning."

"He could if he had help." All eyes turned to Meredith. "You forget that Jim saw my aunt leaving the house before he left. She wants this union. She believes it's her family's financial salvation. In her eyes, Roy Mitchell is a saint. I imagine she went directly to his office this morning and probably even aided the man in kidnapping her daughter."

Jim stalked up to Travis and growled in his ear. "If Mitchell had Meredith, you'd go after her. You know you would."

She could tell by the way the two eyed each other in challenge, that Jim's statement hadn't been intended for her ears, but she couldn't stop herself from hoping it would be persuasive. Cassie was in peril. It was time to send in the cavalry.

Jim finally stepped away and let Travis mull over all that'd been said. The quiet ate away at Meredith, but she held her tongue, praying that the Lord would give her husband the wisdom necessary to make the right decision.

"Before Pa died, he made me swear to protect our family and our land. I won't leave the ranch unguarded or let the three of you walk into an ambush without proof that Cassie is truly in danger."

Jim made to protest, but Travis stopped him with a look. And in that moment, something shriveled inside Meredith. The land always came first with Travis. The land and his brothers.

"However," Travis continued, "I agree that we cannot risk Cassie's life, either."

Meredith inhaled a shaky breath. *Please, Travis. Please let us help her.*

"Therefore, I think the best course of action is to let Jim scout out the cabin. The rest of us will stay here in case Mitchell attacks. One man will be harder to spot, but you'll also have no one to watch your back."

Jim nodded, obviously eager to take on the task despite the risk.

"Once Jim determines if Cassandra is in fact at the cabin, he'll return and alert us to the situation—how many men Mitchell has, where they're holding her, and so forth. If she's there, we'll go after her. If not, we'll stay here and elude Mitchell's trap."

It wasn't exactly the cavalry charge she'd been hoping for, but at least it left the door open for a later one.

"I can go with Jim," Meredith volunteered. "I know the property. I can show him the best way to get close to the cabin without being seen."

Jim seemed to be considering her offer until Travis glared the consideration right out of him.

"Not a chance." He turned his glare on her. "If Mitchell got his hands on you, there's no telling what he would do. At the very least he'd use you to get to me. We can't afford that."

"Because it would put your precious land in jeopardy, wouldn't it?" Hot tears threatened to fall, but she forced them back. Any affection he felt for her ran a distant second to his loyalty to the ranch. She'd been a fool to think there could ever be more. "The land always comes first. Doesn't it, Travis?"

Unable to hold the tears at bay any longer, she sprinted past him, her only thought to escape. She headed for the house, but before she reached the porch, strong arms latched onto her from behind and spun her around.

Meredith tried to pull away, but when she saw the pained look in his eyes, she ceased. Even with his callous, overly rational behavior, she loved him too much to hurt him.

"Meri, honey. I know you're worried about Cassie. I am, too." Travis's face hovered above hers, his dark eyes sincere. "But I'm also worried about Jim and Crockett and Neill. We have to take precautions."

She said nothing.

He sighed and loosened his hold on her arms in order to cup her face. His thumbs stroked her cheeks, rubbing away the moisture there with such tenderness it almost set her to weeping again.

"I can't let you go with Jim. It's too dangerous. If something happened to you, I . . ." He glanced up to the sky. His fingers trembled slightly against her face.

Meredith trembled, too. Waiting. *I couldn't bear it*, she imagined him saying. Or . . . *I would be devastated*. How she longed to hear words that would prove her wrong, to prove that his heart was truly engaged.

Travis's eyes lowered to meet hers. She held her breath.

"If something happened to you, Meri, I'd never forgive myself."

Meredith exhaled, and her hopes leaked out with the used air. He still saw her as a responsibility, a duty. Perhaps a pleasant one, but a duty nonetheless.

"I need to know you're safe," he continued, passion firing his words. "I'd give my life to keep you safe."

"I know you would," she said, a sad smile turning her lips upward. Her warrior. So protective. So honorable. He'd no doubt feel the same ardor for anyone under his care.

Placing her hands on his shoulders, she lifted up and touched her lips to his. Just for a moment. A sweet, achingly wistful moment.

Then she stepped away. "I'll be in the house."

"Thank you," he whispered.

As Meredith climbed the porch steps, she knew what she had to do. Travis wasn't the only warrior in the family. No, she had her own protective agenda. Cassie was more a sister to her than a cousin, and though she couldn't explain how she knew, Meredith was certain that Roy had not been bluffing about the wedding.

Cassie needed her. And right now that need outweighed everything else.

35

Meredith watched at the kitchen window until Travis disappeared into the depths of the barn to continue plotting with his brothers. When she could no longer see him, she snuck out the back door and crept down to the corral. Clicking her tongue, she called to Ginger and eased the corral gate open just enough to squeeze the horse through. Darting glances back toward the barn entrance every few seconds, Meredith led her paint around the house and into the woods.

A saddle was out of the question. Too many Archer men around the tack room. She used to love to ride bareback around the homestead as a kid. Surely she could still manage the feat. Meredith found a stump and used it as a mounting block, then urged Ginger toward the road at a fast clip, keeping to the trees.

She didn't have much time. She had to get back to the house before Travis did. If he discovered her missing, the men would divert their attention from defending the ranch to finding her—which could mean Jim would be delayed in going after Cassie. No, it was essential that she be back at the house when Travis came in from the barn. Then, once he and the boys took up positions around the property, she could duck out the back, wind her way down to the creek, and follow it up to the road. She'd have to climb through the barbed-wire fence, but an extra blanket tossed over the barbs to keep her skirts from snagging should help her squeeze between the wires.

It was a sketchy plan, but it was the best she had at the moment.

Meredith steered Ginger out of the trees in order to pass through the newly ungated ranch entrance, then cantered a few strides down the road before dismounting. She led the mare back into the trees and tied her lead to one of the fence posts marking the property line. An observant rider would be able to spot Ginger's white patches through the sparse cover, but she imagined Jim would be too focused on his destination to look back toward the ranch.

Grateful that the house was only a quarter mile from the road, Meredith picked up her skirts and retraced her steps at a jog. A stitch in her side slowed her down about fifty yards from the house. Pressing a hand to her waist to battle the ache radiating there, she walked the remaining distance, stretching her stride as wide as possible.

If Travis was his usual, incredibly thorough self, she might be fortunate enough to return to the house before the men emerged from the barn. She doubted he would release them until they'd considered every eventuality and gone over their respective duties at least twice. However, Jim would be hard to corral for long, so she couldn't count on more than fifteen minutes. And she was pretty sure she'd already used at least ten.

The house finally came into view—along with the men. They all stood gathered around a mounted Jim. Their hats were off and their heads were bowed. Her conscience twinged at the sight of the Archer brothers taking the time to pray over their brother's safety and the situation at large, but she ignored it for the moment and took advantage of their inward focus and closed eyes to dash around the rear of the house unseen.

Once inside, she breathed a sigh of relief, or would have if her corset-laced lungs hadn't already been panting from her brief trot through the woods. Meredith strode through the bathing room and immediately grabbed the half loaf of bread left from lunch and began slicing it into thick pieces. The easiest way to disguise her intentions was to have Travis find her where he expected—in the kitchen. The vegetable soup she'd originally thought to prepare for supper would have to wait for another day, but she could throw together some scrambled egg sandwiches for the men to take with them on guard duty.

She had just cracked the seventh egg into the skillet when the front door opened. Heavy footfalls echoed in the hall. Meredith whisked the eggs frantically with her fork, then moved the skillet directly over the firebox to speed the cooking, hoping that Travis would attribute the perspiration on her forehead to the stove's heat and not comment upon it.

"Jim's on his way, Meri." Travis's quiet voice carried over the sizzle of the frying pan.

Meredith kept her back to him as she stirred the eggs, afraid Travis might somehow discern her subterfuge in the lines of her face. "I'll have these done in just a minute. You and the boys can take sandwiches with you."

He made no comment, but she could sense him nearing.

"I'm sorry I didn't have these ready before Jim left. He's going to be hungry."

Strong hands cupped her shoulders. "He'll be fine."

His touch felt good. Too good. Meredith stepped out of his loose hold and started heaping eggs onto the bread slices she'd set out. Head down, she built the sandwiches, trying to ignore her husband's presence. Which, of course, was impossible. She'd never been more attuned to another human being in her life.

"Meri, stop."

Her hands stilled as she wrapped a napkin around the third and final sandwich.

"Look at me, sweetheart."

Slowly she turned. His light brown eyes shone with a depth of emotion that made her heart pound.

"I swear to you, Meri—the minute Jim confirms that Cassie is at the homestead, we'll all ride out like the devil himself is on our heels. We won't leave her to face Mitchell alone."

He meant every word. She could see it in his face, hear it in his voice. But another voice echoed in her mind, as well—one asking what would happen to Cassie if Jim failed to return. How long would Travis wait before leading the charge?

Tears burned at the back of her eyes. She didn't want to defy her husband. Truly she didn't. It could destroy the trust between them, destroy the chance of love ever taking root in his heart. But she had no choice. She couldn't sit uselessly in the house under Travis's protection when her knowledge of the homestead could mean the difference between success and failure for both Jim and Cassie.

And with Jim's head start, the longer Travis stayed in the kitchen, the less time she'd have to make that difference.

In a desperate grab at the happiness that seemed to be slipping from her grasp, Meredith seized her husband's face between both her hands and kissed him with all the love she'd stored up for him since she was ten years old. It only took a moment for Travis to recover from his shock and respond with equal fervor. Yet when she felt his arms wrap around her back and start to draw her close, she forced herself to tear away.

"Here," she said, shoving the sandwiches at him as much to hurry him along as to keep herself from walking back into his arms. "Make sure your brothers eat."

Then, before he could say anything else, she dodged around him and dashed down the hall to her room. Thumping the door closed behind her, she sagged against the wall and brushed a stray tear from her cheek while she waited for the telltale sound of Travis's boots against the floorboards.

They came down the hall and paused. Meredith squeezed her eyes closed. *Just go, Travis. Please.*

After a long moment, the sound began again, this time fading as Travis crossed to the front door and finally exited onto the porch. His deep voice carried through the walls as he called to Crockett and Neill.

Regret ate at Meredith, and second thoughts flashed through her mind. Then a picture of Jim crystallized behind her closed lids—a picture of him falling to the ground, as still as death. Her eyes jerked open, and her throat closed on a gasp. He was in as much danger as Cassie, heading alone into what was sure to be a den of vipers. She might not be able to bring the cavalry, but she could at least supply him with enough inside information to help even the odds a bit.

And she could watch his back.

Meredith grabbed her cape from the wardrobe and moved to the window. *Lord, keep him safe until I can catch up. Direct my steps and give me the courage to do what must be done. Guard Cassie and . . .* She paused and shifted the curtain just enough to peer out into the yard, where her husband and his brothers were dispersing to their assigned positions. *Help Travis forgive me.*

She released the curtain and turned to leave the room, but when she passed the bureau, she remembered the small tablet of paper Travis kept in the top drawer along with his watch and other odds and ends. After digging out a stubby pencil, she scribbled the few words her raw heart demanded she say, then grabbed an old blanket from the chest and hurried through the house to the back door.

Once outside, she made for the creek without a single backward glance. Regrets were a luxury she could no longer afford.

36

The old game trail was still where she remembered it being. Meredith urged Ginger off the road a couple hundred yards short of the main entrance. The path was almost imperceptible, completely overgrown with brush, but Ginger obediently followed her mistress's silent instruction and plowed through the oak saplings.

Meredith followed the landmarks she recognized more than the path itself, and when she reached the pine she'd long ago dubbed *The Survivor*, she drew Ginger to a halt. Not long after her accident with the trap, lightning had struck the tall, elegant tree. Half of the tree turned brown and brittle, too damaged to support life, but the other half remained green and healthy, flourishing with a will to overcome the adversity thrust upon it. Meredith stared up into the glorious green boughs on the east side and absorbed the hope they had always offered.

As a young girl, the tree had encouraged her to persevere and not let her own injured limb hold her back. Today, though, it inspired strength and fortitude. Meredith breathed deeply, inhaling the scent of the pine and allowing it to solidify her purpose. Time to find Jim.

If Jim had followed the usual Archer strategy of shadowing the road, he should be somewhere in the pines to her right. She'd made up some time by taking the game trail, but there was still no way to guess his precise location. If only there were a way to signal . . . The birdcalls! Neill had been teaching her the distinctive Archer call before the last storm hit. She'd not yet perfected the warble, but she could match the swooping pitch fairly well.

Meredith licked her lips, then cupped her hands around her mouth and threw her cooing voice as deep into the surrounding woods as she could.

She waited a moment and repeated the signal, aiming her call more directly toward the cabin.

The silence stretched out for long minutes. Either Jim hadn't heard her call or he'd been unable to answer. Had he been captured? She prayed not. As she tried to determine her next strategy, a rustling to the south of her hailed a man's approach. Only then did she realize that she might have given her position away to one of Roy's men instead of Jim. The crunch of dead leaves grew louder, and Meredith's pulse throbbed harder.

Gripping Ginger's reins tightly between her fingers, she prepared to flee. The muscles in her thighs grew taut. Her heels twitched. Every instinct screamed at her to race away. But just as she began turning Ginger's head toward home, an answering call floated to her ear, one with a beautiful, well-practiced warble.

"Thank heaven," she whispered, releasing her hold on the reins as Jim emerged on foot between a pair of scrubby post oaks.

Her brother-in-law didn't appear nearly as relieved to see her as she was to see him. The hardheaded man was actually scowling at her.

"What are you doing here?" he hissed.

Meredith dismounted and squared her shoulders. Jim wasn't one to dance around a subject, so she got straight to the point. "I can help you get to the cabin unseen."

He narrowed his eyes at her. "Travis know what you're doing?"

"I left a note." She glared back at him in challenge.

The man let out a breath and rubbed the back of his neck, but in the end, his desire to help Cassie trumped his reluctance to defy his brother.

"I've scouted the perimeter. No obvious guards are posted at the cabin, but I saw evidence of at least four men at the edge of the woods near the house. I think they're patrolling, so it'd be hard to know their exact position at any one time. I imagine Mitchell's got even more inside."

Meredith grimaced. It was a good thing the game trail lay deeper into the woods than Roy's men had penetrated. "So Travis was right. It *is* an ambush."

Jim shrugged. "A trap at least. Hard to know if they plan to pick us off or just ensure our cooperation."

Which would mean either loss of life or loss of land—both options equally heinous to an Archer.

"Have you seen Cassie?"

"No. Haven't been able to get close enough." Jim's gaze shifted, targeting the rooftop of the old homestead barely visible through the trees. "Heard the shrill voice of that mother of hers, though." He twisted his head to face her again, his dark eyes tortured. "She's here, Meri. I'm sure of it."

Meredith touched his arm, a similar dread flowing through her own heart. "Travis needs proof before he'll come, and you can't take on all of Roy's men by yourself." She squeezed his forearm and lifted her chin. "I'll get you to the house."

He didn't ask how or pester her for details. He simply nodded and pointed down the trail. "Show me."

Thankful, for once, for Jim's taciturn ways, Meredith looped Ginger's reins over a low branch and trudged ahead. Lifting her skirts and folding them close to her body to eliminate excess rustling, she kept her eyes to the ground and avoided as many twigs and pinecones as possible.

The trail wound closer to the cabin before forking. The main path led to a watering hole deeper in the woods, but a narrow shoot darted toward the left rear corner of the homestead—the corner that housed her childhood bedroom.

Meredith halted and peered into the thinning cover that separated them from the house. She looked to the right, then to the left. No one. At least, none that she could see.

"Have you spotted any of Roy's men?" she whispered to the man behind her. "I can take you closer, but I don't want to draw the attention of one of the guards." She stared at the foot of her weak leg and winced. "I cannot walk as quietly as you."

"Just tell me what I need to know." Jim came abreast of her, his rifle at the ready.

"If you stay to the left, the pines will give way to a stand of broad oaks. They shade the house in the summer, and since no one's trimmed their branches the last few years, a few limbs stretch all the way to the roof." She watched as understanding dawned in his eyes. His jaw hardened, and he strode forward, but Meredith stopped him with a hand to his arm.

"There is not as much cover near the house, so you'll have to be careful. You might be able to peer through one of the back windows from within the branches of the tree, but if you need to see into the main room, you'll have to crawl over the roof to the front of the house. It's risky, but hopefully none of the men will expect trouble from above."

Jim slid his arm from her grasp and took her hand in his. "Thank you."

She nodded. "Be careful." The earlier vision of his lying upon the ground came back to her, raking a shiver over her skin.

"Stay out of sight," her brother-in-law ordered. "Travis will kill me if anything happens to you." He released her hand and soundlessly moved past.

Meredith prayed over every step Jim took, her throat seeming to constrict at each sound that echoed in the trees. When he rounded the first oak and disappeared from her view, her breathing nearly ceased altogether. This wasn't right. She was supposed to be watching his back. She couldn't do that from this distance.

Taking extra care with her uneven gait, she crept forward, staying in the shadows of the trees until she stood behind the largest oak. Meredith spied Jim between the branches of the tree nearest the cabin and finally breathed easier. His rifle slung over his shoulder, he climbed higher, his footholds secure. The only trouble was the way the brittle winter leaves rattled with his movements.

Jim stretched himself across one of the thicker limbs that reached toward the roof, and began scooting along its length on his belly. Then all at once, he froze.

A twig snapped. But it wasn't from Jim's tree. It echoed lower. Closer.

Meredith silently gathered her cloak more tightly around her and drew the hood over her hair as she tucked her face against the coarse bark of the oak at her side. If she could have climbed beneath the bark itself, she would have.

A rough-looking logger emerged between the trees that she and Jim occupied. His heavy brows scrunched against his eyes as he scanned the area, his ear cocked in Jim's direction. Instead of a gun, the burly fellow carried an ax.

A gust of wind blew across the tree limbs. Meredith's gaze darted to Jim. The branch swayed. Jim's face contorted as he struggled to keep his back perfectly flat so his rifle wouldn't shift and knock into the leaves surrounding him.

The logger jerked his face toward the cabin, as if he sensed the intruder. He slapped the wooden handle of his ax against his left palm and stalked closer to the tree. All he had to do was glance up. . . .

Meredith scoured the ground near her for something she could use as a weapon, but all she found were decayed branches and pinecones. Nothing that would even slow the man down. But maybe she could draw the man away somehow. If she were to dart back toward the Survivor tree, he'd hear and follow, giving Jim time to lay eyes on Cassie and leave. All she had to do was outrun a bear-sized man for the short distance to Ginger. Shouldn't be too hard, right? She'd have a head start and was more familiar with the land.

She inhaled a deep breath and grabbed a handful of skirt. Then, just as she prepared to take flight, a saner idea took shape. Meredith released the fabric of her cape and scooped up a large pinecone. Taking careful aim, she hurled it behind the oaks, back into the forest. It cracked against the trunk of a small pine, and the sound brought Mr. Bushy Brow's head around. The man set off with a determined stride, and Meredith sagged against the trunk of her oak.

Thank the Lord for timely inspiration.

Once the logger disappeared into the woods, Meredith waved Jim toward the roof. The ungrateful man glared at her and jabbed his finger as if ordering her to retreat, but there was no time for a pantomime skirmish. If Jim didn't go now, he might not get another chance. Fortunately, the Archers were an intelligent lot. After a final jab in her direction, Jim resumed his belly crawl and soon lowered himself silently onto the cabin roof.

Shrinking into a crouch, he crossed to the peak. There, he laid flat and peered over the edge. Meredith fisted her hands in the fabric of her cape as he slid out of her view to the front side of the cabin. He seemed to be gone for an eternity. The roof's slope wasn't too steep, but even then, Jim would have to hang upside down from the eaves to see in the front window. What if someone saw him? What if he fell? He would have never been on that roof if she hadn't suggested such an idiotic scheme.

What have I done? Her soul cried out to the only one who could rescue them. *Protect him from my folly, Lord. I should have trusted my husband. I should have trusted you.*

All her big talk to Travis about trusting God to protect his family, about not letting fear dictate his actions, and here she was doing exactly that which she had so adamantly preached against. She should have sought the Lord's will from the very beginning. Instead she'd proceeded with her own plans and only once she was in the midst of them did she think to ask for God's blessing. And even then her mind was set on her own course of action. What if the Lord had inspired that vision of Jim as a warning to her that she not go, but because of her own willfulness, she chose to use it as justification for her actions?

Meredith bowed her head. *I surrender.* A tear trickled down her cheek. *I surrender. Only you can make this right. Show me what to do. Whatever sacrifice is required, I'll make it. Just, please . . . spare Jim and Cassie.*

When she lifted her head, there was Jim, slinking back over the peak of the roof and scrambling toward the tree. Her heart surged in gratitude. *Thank you!*

He had made it as far as the main trunk when the logger charged out of the shallow woods. The bushy-browed henchman ran full out as if he planned to leap into the tree like a cougar after its prey. Jim was too high to drop to the ground without breaking a leg. He struggled to find a defensible position among the branches. He needed his rifle, but his hands were too busy keeping him in the tree to reach for the weapon.

Meredith sprinted toward the logger, her eyes locked on the arm that wielded the ax.

Roy's man latched onto a branch, the soles of his shoes bracing his weight against the trunk. With a roar, he swung the ax in an upward arc, the blade aimed at Jim's flesh.

Meredith vaulted off her good leg midstride and caught the logger's beefy arm as it circled behind him. The logger tried to shove her aside, but she held fast to his right arm and threw what little weight she had to sway him. She had to give Jim time to escape.

She twisted and writhed, kicked out with her legs, anything she could think of to slow him down. The shouts of other men echoed behind her. Reinforcements were coming.

A rifle cocked nearby, and for a split second, both Meredith and the logger froze. Meredith spotted Jim from the corner of her eye. He was on the ground with his rifle aimed at the logger!

He jerked his head to the side, urging her to move away so he would have a clean shot, but a beefy arm locked around her waist, holding her in place.

"Run, Jim!" she shouted between grunts as the logger renewed his efforts to wrench his right arm free of her grasp, no doubt hoping to hurl his ax at his foe. "Get Travis!"

For once Jim didn't scowl at her. His eyes had a desperate look to them, as if he were the one trapped. She knew he didn't want to leave her, that his protective nature demanded he stay and fight. But when the others arrived, he'd be finished.

"For Cassie, Jim," she pleaded. "Go for Cassie."

A yell from the other side of the cabin made his decision for him. He spun and ran.

The instant Jim's rifle was no longer pointed at him, the logger shifted to free his arm. But she hung on—all of her energy focused on keeping him from using his weapon.

"Blasted female!" The logger raised his ax. "Let"—he slammed his arm and hers into the tree—"go!"

Pain ricocheted past her elbows from the force of the collision, and her hands opened against her will.

The logger shouted orders to his compatriots and pointed in the direction Jim had run. The other guards rushed past them, pistols and rifles in hand. Meredith tried to slide away from her captor, but the logger had no intention of relinquishing his prize. He snatched up a handful of fabric at her neck and hauled her upward.

Her hands instinctively circled about his meaty fist, but she had no strength left to pry free of his hold. His dark eyes promised retribution. He gave her a shake as if she were an oversized rag doll and ordered her to cease her fighting. Since he no longer posed a threat to Jim, she obeyed and stumbled along beside him as he made his way to the front of the cabin. He kicked the door in with his foot and dragged her across the threshold.

"I brung you another guest for the wedding, boss."

A movement to her right drew Meredith's attention. Roy stood near the hearth, a shotgun looped casually through his bent arm, the barrel pointed at Uncle Everett, who sat on the floor against the wall with his wrists bound.

She'd heard of shotgun weddings, but never one in which the groom held the gun on the father of the bride.

"Meredith, my dear." Roy smiled, and her stomach recoiled. "So glad you could make it."

37

Travis tucked the butt of his rifle into his shoulder and sighted down the barrel from his position among the pines nearest the old gate. The quiet rumble he'd noted a moment ago had grown louder, more distinct. Hoofbeats. A rider approached. And fast.

Inhaling a cleansing breath, he forced his pulse to calm. He needed a steady hand and a clear head to deal with whatever came down the path. His mind turned heavenward for an instant—not long enough to form a complete thought, but long enough to connect.

Finger hovering over the trigger, Travis peered into the shadows. Before man or horse came into view, a shrill whistle pierced the air. *Jim.* Travis blew out his tension and lowered his rifle. Expecting the hoofbeats to slow, he was unprepared for the second whistle or for the sight of his brother's mount racing past him.

New urgency speared through Travis, and he took off at a dead run for the house. Jim knew their positions. He would have stopped or at least slowed to call out his findings unless a threat existed that was too imminent to spare the time.

Cassandra must truly be in danger. Travis pumped his legs faster, his lungs burning with the sudden heavy intake of cold air. He leapt over a small gully and pushed forward, his energy solely focused on getting to Jim. The others were positioned closer to the house, so they'd be waiting on him. Thankfully, their horses stood saddled and ready in the corral. They could be on their way in minutes.

By the time he sprinted through the clearing, Jim was giving orders from the saddle. Travis overheard him sending Crockett into the den to collect extra pistols. Neill was hustling to the corral to gather the mounts. Travis pulled up so as not to startle his brother's horse. Between heaving breaths, he asked Jim for a report.

"Cassie and her folks are being held at the cabin," Jim said, his face grim. "Mitchell has Mr. Hayes tied up and at gunpoint. The women are under guard, as well, but not restrained. He's got at least four men patrolling. Two more inside. They're armed and don't seem too hesitant about attacking."

"Then we ride." Travis caught his breath and straightened his shoulders. "I'll tell Meredith and be back in a trice." She'd be beside herself with worry, but he couldn't keep it from her. Cassie was like a sister to her.

He had just cleared the porch steps when Jim's voice stopped him.

"She's not there, Travis."

He turned to face his brother, not comprehending his meaning. But when he saw the discomfiture etched into Jim's features, the regret in his eyes, his gut turned to lead.

"I tried to send her back, but she refused to go." Jim stiffened in the saddle then, as if ready to do battle. "I wouldn't have gotten a look in the cabin without her help, Trav. She saved my life. Twice. I'm not sorry she came. Just sorry I couldn't get her out before Mitchell's men swarmed us."

Meredith at the homestead? How could that be? She was in his room. Waiting for him. Safe. Wasn't she?

Holding down the bile that threatened to erupt, Travis spun back to the house and threw open the door. It crashed against the wall as he shouted his wife's name.

"Meredith!"

He ran down the hall, his boots slapping the floorboards. It was a mistake. She was there. Safe in his room.

Travis burst through the door. The emptiness hit him like a sledgehammer to the chest. He scanned every corner as if she might be hiding somewhere. He even wrenched open the wardrobe in desperation.

"Meri." The anguished whisper fell from his lips. This couldn't be happening. She told him she'd be in the house. How could she leave the ranch when he'd expressly forbidden it? How could she leave *him*?

In a daze, he pivoted back toward the door. He took a step, but something about the room whispered to his subconscious mind, something out of place. His attention shifted back to the bed, then the dresser. He blinked, sharpening his focus. There. The tablet. Travis pounced on the paper. His eyes devoured the words.

Travis,

I love you with all of my being, but I love Cassie, too. And right now she needs me more than you do.

Forgive me.
Meri

She loved him. The wonder of the statement seeped into him, but the joy that should have accompanied the knowledge faded beneath his growing frustration and fear. How could she possibly think that anyone needed her more than he did? She was his heart, his very life. If anything happened to her . . .

Travis tore the top page from the tablet and hardened his jaw. He'd just have to make sure nothing did happen. After all, if a wife was going to tell her husband she loved him, she ought to do it in person. And he aimed to see that she did precisely that. Right after he kissed the living fire out of her and showed her exactly how much he truly needed her.

Stuffing the note into the shirt pocket beneath his coat, Travis dropped the tablet on the bed and stormed out of the house. Crockett met him on the porch and handed him a second revolver. Since he only had one holster, and it was already full, he stuffed the gun into his waistband at the small of his back. He collected Bexar's reins from where they hung over the railing and mounted in a single motion.

Travis shared a look with Crockett and Jim and turned to Neill. "I want you to ride into Palestine and fetch the sheriff. All you have to do is head south once you hit the road. If you push your mount, you can be there before sundown. We can't afford to let Mitchell get away this time. We need the law on our side." And *he* needed Neill out of harm's way. The kid could handle himself well enough, but if things went badly, he didn't have the experience necessary to improvise. And if things went really badly, Travis wanted to ensure that at least one Archer lived to see another day.

"Archers stand together, Trav," Neill spat impatiently. "Isn't that what you always say?" He looked from one brother to the next. The errand was a pretense, and he knew it. "Y'all are already outnumbered. Why give Mitchell a bigger advantage? You have a better chance with me riding with you."

"Maybe, but someone's got to get the law involved, and you're the logical choice."

Neill opened his mouth to argue further, but Travis cut him off. "We're wasting time. You have your orders, Neill. Carry them out, like the Archer you are." Travis nudged Bexar past Neill's mount, effectively ending the conversation.

"Boys, I believe we've been invited to a wedding," Travis said, steel lacing his tone. "Let's not be late."

Meredith clasped her cousin's hand as the two girls sat huddled together on the settee. The dreadful Mr. Wheeler loomed over them, legs braced apart, gun in hand. But it was the way he looked at her that frightened Meredith most. That wolfish gleam in his eyes, and the way his gaze kept traveling down her body as if he could see right through her clothing. He'd smile after perusing her in such abominable fashion, and the leering promise on his face turned her stomach.

"Should we start the ceremony now, sir?" A man standing in the back corner of the room posed the question. His black suit and white preacher's collar should have offered reassurance, but his bored expression as he scanned the room full of armed men and hostage women only served to confirm his complicity. There would be no help from that quarter.

"Not yet," Roy said. "Although I'm anxious to wed my lovely bride, I believe we're due to have a few more visitors soon, and I'd hate for anything unpleasant to interrupt our nuptials."

"Very well, but I'm charging you for the extra time." The preacher, if the mercenary little man could be called by such a title, leaned against the wall and slid a silver flask from inside his coat. He unscrewed the lid and imbibed a large swig.

Cassie's grip tightened on Meredith's hand. "I hope he chokes."

"It would be a rather poetic form of justice," Meredith agreed softly. And such a lovely wrench to throw into Roy's plan. But then she remembered the logger going after Jim with that ax and decided it might be better for all concerned to keep Roy happy. At least for the time being.

Aunt Noreen paced across the carpet and glowered at Roy. "I don't approve of liquor, Mr. Mitchell. It's bad enough that my daughter's wedding is not taking place in a church, but I refuse to have a drunkard officiate her ceremony."

Roy's lips thinned as he peered down at the woman before him. "Let me remind you, madam, that I was only too happy to sponsor a church wedding, but Miss Cassandra would not consent. Hence our current predicament. If you feel the need to complain, kindly take it up with your daughter."

"But *you* were in charge of finding the minister. This one is unsatisfactory." She folded her arms and frowned at Roy as if he were one of the ladies on her civic beautification committee who had failed to follow her instructions.

"Noreen . . ." Uncle Everett murmured her name in warning from his position on the floor across from her.

"Hush up, Everett. None of this would have happened if you hadn't given in to Cassandra's whining. The girl can't see past her nose. She's just young enough to think that some flutter in her heart is worth more than financial security. You should have taken her in hand. But, no. Like everything else, you bowed out and forced me to deal with it. You've got no backbone. That's the real reason the mill is failing. I probably should have taken that over, too."

"Mama!" Cassie gasped. But the woman paid her no heed. She'd built up too much steam.

"And as for you . . ." Aunt Noreen pivoted back to face Roy and jabbed his shoulder with her finger, apparently too full of her own agenda to notice the anger brewing in his eyes. "If you want to be my son-in-law, you had best find a minister who isn't incapacitated with drink! I won't allow—"

Roy backhanded her across the mouth with enough force to send her crashing to the floor. "You're not in a position to disallow anything, madam. You might flay your husband with that sharp tongue of yours, but turn it on me, and I will bite you back."

Aunt Noreen glared up at Roy, not all of her fire extinguished. "How dare you raise your hand to me!"

In a flash, Roy had the shotgun cocked and aimed directly at her head. "You know, it just occurred to me that married life would be much easier without a harpy for a mother-in-law."

"No!" Cassie lunged to her feet. Wheeler immediately grasped her arm.

"Please," she cried out to Roy, struggling against Wheeler's hold. "I'll marry you right now. Willingly. Just leave my mother alone."

Roy pulled the gun back. "Such an ardent declaration, my sweet. How could I refuse?" He stepped toward the settee and clasped Cassie's hand, his gentlemanly veneer back in place. Wheeler released her arm, and Cassie lifted her chin.

As Roy led her toward the hearth, Meredith pushed to her feet. There was no way she was letting Cassie face this horror alone.

"Where do you think *you're* going, darlin'?" Wheeler's gravelly voice grated against her nerves. Then his arm snaked around her waist and pulled her roughly against his side.

"I intend to stand up with my cousin, sir," she ground out between clenched teeth. "Release me."

Roy glanced over his shoulder and smirked at her. "Let her come, Wheeler. But keep a firm grip on her. She has a bad habit of starting trouble."

"I'll keep her under control," the man said as his arm tightened around her, nearly cutting off her air.

She stumbled past Aunt Noreen, who seemed to be in a state of shock, numbly letting Uncle Everett loop his bound arms around her and scoot her back against the wall.

The parson gulped down another swig from his flask, then pulled a Bible from his coat pocket and made a great show of flipping pages as he stepped out of the corner to join Roy and Cassie at the hearth.

"Dearly beloved," the man droned in a ponderous, self-important tone. "We are gathered here—"

The front door crashed open.

Meredith's head swiveled.

"What is the meaning of this?" the parson sputtered.

"Found these two riding up the path."

Her ax-wielding "friend" waved to his cohorts, and they shoved two dust-covered men, the obvious recipients of some very rough handling, into the room. One fell to his knee, his arms tied behind his back. The other, though also bound, managed to catch himself and halt his forward momentum before tumbling to the floor.

Meredith's heart recognized them the instant they came through the doorway. And when the man in front lifted his head and met her gaze beneath the brim of his hat, she instinctively stepped toward him.

"Travis."

Wheeler jerked her back against him, a wicked chuckle echoing in her ear. Travis's face hardened in an instant. He surged forward only to be brought up short by a shotgun barrel in the chest.

"Nice of you to finally show up, Archer." Roy tugged Cassandra behind him and nodded to the logger, who muscled Jim back down to his knees before he could fully regain his feet. "For a while there, I thought you decided to decline my invitation."

38

The metal gun barrel dug into his chest, but Travis barely felt it. All his energy was focused on Mitchell.

"I've come for my wife." The words rumbled out of him like thunder gathering in the distance, low and ominous.

The guards had confiscated his rife and gun belt, but the hidden revolver itched against his back, begging him to take it in hand. Never before had he actually wanted to shoot a man. But now it was all he could do not to reach for his weapon.

Mitchell's lips turned down in a mock pout. "I'm devastated. And here I thought you'd come to offer your felicitations."

Travis glared his disgust at the man.

"I assure you, Mr. Wheeler is taking very good care of our dear Miss Meredith. Aren't you, Louis?"

"Indeed I am, Mr. Mitchell. Indeed I am." The man tightened his hold on Meri, his arm deliberately pressing against the underside of her breasts. Meredith clawed at his sleeve until he lifted his right hand and stroked the side of her face with his pistol. "Easy now, kitten." Meri stilled. "You might not want to jostle me too much. It'd be a shame if someone got hurt."

Rage steamed through Travis. Wheeler had just etched his name on one of the bullets in Travis's gun.

Gritting his teeth, he forced his focus away from Wheeler and settled it again on the man behind the shotgun. "I know you designed this meeting, Mitchell. Why don't we skip all the small talk and get down to business. What do I have to do to ensure Meri leaves this cabin unharmed?"

"Not much." Mitchell smiled that ingratiating smile of his that made Travis want to slam his fist into his face. "All I need is your signature on a little document I had my attorney draw up." He gestured to the table that stood on the opposite side of the room near the cookstove. "Should only take a minute. Then you and your bride will be free to go. Unless, of course, you'd like to stay for the wedding."

"Fine," Travis growled. "Bring me a pen. And get one of your men to untie my hands."

"No, Travis," Meredith gasped. "You can't."

But he could. He'd give up anything for her. Without a moment's regret. What he couldn't do was look at those big blue eyes of hers without getting distracted. So he set his jaw and marched toward the table, tipping his head so his hat blocked his view of her.

As he moved, he tallied Mitchell's men. Mitchell and Wheeler made two. The thug with the ax wrestling with Jim was three. And the two fellows who had trussed him and Jim up were loitering outside the door; he could see their shadows through the front window. According to Jim's earlier count, that left only one for Crockett to track down and disable before returning to the cabin. Their plan to draw the men out of the woods had worked. Now they just had to figure out a way to get Jim's hands untied and take out five armed men without endangering the women. He was still working on that part.

Meredith watched with swelling dread as Travis made his way to the table. He couldn't sign away his land. He just couldn't. That land was everything to him. If he sacrificed it for her, it would kill whatever hope they had of making a love-filled marriage together. Oh, he'd never voice his regrets. He was too noble. But he would grow to resent her. How could he not? Because of her, he was breaking his deathbed promise to his father and forfeiting the one thing he treasured above all else—his land.

She bit her lip. He'd never even looked at her. Not since Roy named his price. And that more than anything ate away at her hope.

"You mind untying my hands, Mitchell?" Travis twisted sideways, aiming his bound arms at Roy. "I can't exactly sign your papers with my hands behind my back."

Roy hesitated a moment, then nodded to the only man on his payroll without a gun in his hand. "Parson? Some assistance, please."

"All right," the man huffed. "But it will—"

"Cost me extra. I know." Roy glared at the minister. "Just do it."

The man pulled a blade from his boot and sawed through the rope at Travis's wrists. When her husband was finally free, he rubbed his chafed skin and immediately took up the pen that lay beside the document on the table. He only spared a moment to glance over the words before inking the nib and scratching his name across the bottom of the page.

A silent sob caught in Meredith's throat. It was done.

"A pleasure doing business with you, Mr. Archer." Roy nodded his head toward Travis in a mockery of a bow. "You and your wife may leave if you wish."

Travis strode toward her, but his narrowed eyes focused at a point above her head. Wheeler pressed the side of his pistol against her chin and forced her head around. Then before she knew what he was about, his mouth crashed down on hers. A sound of protest reverberated in her throat as she struggled to free herself from the violation.

From somewhere behind her, Travis shouted, and Cassie cried out for Wheeler to stop. Meredith could hear her husband's pounding footfalls, but right before he reached her, Wheeler yanked his horrible mouth from hers and threw her into Travis, nearly knocking them both to the ground. His wicked chuckle echoed through the cabin as Travis's arms closed around her.

Meredith scrubbed the vile man's taste from her lips with the back of her hand, wishing she could crawl into Travis and hide.

"Go outside and get on Bexar," Travis whispered close to her ear. "Ride for home."

Meredith stiffened. "I can't leave Cassie."

"Jim and I will take care of Cassie." There was no soothing in his tone. Only command. "I need you to go."

How were he and Jim, who was still bound as far as she could tell, going to take care of Cassie? It made no sense.

Travis's grip tightened on her arm ever so slightly. "Trust me, Meri."

The words cut through her. She'd not let him down a second time.

Meredith nodded and slowly stepped away from him. He released her arms, then staggered forward as if her moving had thrown him off-balance. She turned back and grabbed for him, but he'd already recovered. He found her hand within the folds of her skirt and slid a small cylindrical object into her palm. Her eyes widened, and in an instant he glanced toward Jim, let her go, and gave her a little nudge toward the door.

Not only was he asking her to trust him, he was trusting her in return.

Not knowing exactly how to fulfill her mission, Meredith exacerbated her limp so she had an excuse to slow her pace. Stomach fluttering, she made her way to where the logger was kneeling with a knee against Jim's hunched back near the doorway.

"Would you mind letting him up," she asked the man, struggling to minimize the nervous quiver in her voice. "I'm afraid I'll trip over his legs if I try to step over him."

The logger muttered something about "worthless cripples" but did as she requested, hauling Jim to his feet.

When the man was holding Jim only by the elbow, Meredith seized her chance and slid up against Jim's side, reaching for his hands as if to assist him in gaining his feet.

"Get away from there." The logger scowled at her and jerked Jim away from her grasp. But the transfer had been made.

"Sorry," she mumbled, praying he hadn't noticed anything. "I was just trying to help."

She turned back to the door, intending to leave as she'd promised, when one of the outside guards burst into the cabin, sending her skittering back toward Jim.

"We got comp'ny."

39

Roy cursed. "What is it *now*?"

Meredith flinched at his harshness.

"There's about a dozen townsfolk coming down the path, screechin' and carrying on with drums and washboards and such. They look like a bunch of crazies. What do you want me to do?"

"What I want you to do, Mr. Elliott," Roy answered through gritted teeth, "is to go out there and dissuade them."

"Dis . . . what?"

Roy slammed his fist onto the table, rattling the ink bottle Travis had used mere moments ago. "Scare them off, you idiot!"

Mr. Elliott recoiled from the shout and backed away. "Y-yes, sir." He spun around and lumbered past Meredith, leaving the cabin with all possible haste.

Meredith darted a glance toward Travis. Her husband seemed as surprised as anyone by the guard's announcement. The distraction was buying Jim some much needed time, though.

He'd gotten the penknife open and was working on the ropes at his wrists. Meredith maneuvered her way closer, using her body to shield Jim's hands.

The logger moved to the window and reported, "They're mostly darkies. Women and men. Only one feller looks like he'd be worth much in a fight, but even from here I can see a big stupid grin on his face. They're more nuisance than threat."

Could Moses be the man he referred to? A little thrill shot through Meredith. Perhaps the Lord had sent them assistance. The sound of drums, shakers, and other crude noisemakers grew louder as the group advanced on the cabin.

Then she heard the man called Elliott yell out a warning. "You're not welcome here. Turn around and go on home." His rifle boomed, but the oncoming noise never lessened.

"We heard Miss Cassie done got herself hitched," a strident female voice called out. *Myra*. "We come to give her a shivaree, and we ain't leavin' until we give it."

Roy shoved the paper Travis had signed into the pocket of his coat and stomped to the middle of the room, where he grabbed hold of Cassie. "Of all the ill-conceived, dim-witted— We're not even married yet!"

The logger turned a questioning glance to his boss. "What do you want to do?"

"Bar the door," Roy ordered. Then he turned back to the minister. "Get the deed done, Parson."

The door slammed shut. If Moses and Myra were out there, it was possible Crockett and Neill were, too. She had to find a way to let them in.

The preacher began the rushed service, mumbling the words more to himself than the bride and groom as his finger ran down the page of his prayer book in search of the vows. ". . . signifying the mystical union betwixt Christ and his Church . . . not to be entered into unadvisedly . . . If any man can show just cause why they may not be lawfully joined together, speak—"

"I've got plenty of cause." Jim's deep voice brought the clergyman's head up.

"Shut up, you!" The logger brought the handle of his ax across Jim's jaw, knocking his head against the wall beside him.

The penknife clattered to the floor. Meredith leapt forward to cover it with her boot and dragged it under the hem of her skirt. But before she could figure out how to retrieve it and get it back to Jim, her brother-in-law let out a mighty roar and snapped free of the weakened ropes. He lunged at the logger and tackled him.

Travis rushed Wheeler in the same manner.

Roy shouted.

A gun fired.

Cassie screamed.

Meredith's heart froze.

All she could see of her husband was a tangle of arms and legs. She wanted to run to him. See if he'd been shot. Help fight off his foe. But she forced the desperate urge aside. The help he truly needed stood on the other side of the door.

Kicking the penknife into the corner, she moved to the door and threw the latch. The swarm had overtaken the guards—Crockett and Moses at the center, throwing punches and wresting away rifles. Myra's iron skillet got in on the action—and was that Seth Winston clobbering Mr. Elliott with a washboard?

Josiah and Neill brought up the rear.

The cacophony of the shivaree drowned out the noise of the fight but also made it impossible to call out to her friends and neighbors, so Meredith waved her arms above her head until Neill caught sight of her and began steering the mob toward the house.

Meredith stayed at the door to ensure the portal remained open until Seth Winston hustled forward to relieve her of the duty. "Get on over by the horses, girlie." His raised voice barely carried over the din. "We'll cut the heifers out of the herd and let the steers fight it out." He frowned at her when she hesitated. "Go on, now. It's what your man would want."

Travis.

The old man was right.

With a prayer on her heart and a fingertip hold on her faith, Meredith walked away.

Fire burned across Travis's side from where Wheeler's bullet had creased him, but he spared it little thought as he grabbed for the man's gun hand and pounded it into the plank floor. Wheeler's knee surged into Travis's gut, stealing his wind, but he held on. He crushed the man's hand down again, this time aiming for the clawed foot of one of the settee's legs.

Wheeler let out a cry. The pistol fell from his grasp. Travis reached for it, but something hard slammed into his shoulder blade. His arms collapsed, and he fell fully atop Wheeler. The man wasted no time in kicking him aside. Travis thumped onto his back with a groan.

"It's over, Archer," Mitchell said as he switched the grip on his shotgun. The stock that had felled Travis twirled back toward Mitchell's shoulder. "You've been a thorn in my side long enough."

Mitchell took aim, pointing the double barrels at Travis's chest. Travis tightened his jaw and stared at his nemesis, refusing to cower. His only regret was that he'd never told Meri he loved her.

Then, as he inhaled the breath he fully expected to be his last, men and women, neighbors and friends poured into the cabin, carrying on with their blessedly ridiculous shivaree. Old Seth Winston guarded the door as the rest of the company wound through the room like a snake, whoopin' and hollerin'. Travis caught Moses's eye and then spotted Crockett, who moved to casually assist Jim with the ax-wielding logger as the rest of the parade wandered deeper into the house.

How had they known to come? What miracle had brought them at just the right time? Travis struggled to his feet, cradling his aching side, and spied the answer to his question. Neill. He ought to strangle that boy for disobeying his instructions, but he grinned at his kid brother instead. Apparently Neill wasn't too young to improvise after all.

Ever aware of his reputation, Mitchell tried to shoo the crowd away without violence, but when one of the women took Cassie's hand and started maneuvering her toward the door, he snapped. He fired his shotgun into the rafters, and the resultant *boom* and debris shower succeeded in silencing the revelers.

"Unhand my bride, madam. Now!" Mitchell lowered his weapon, the dark-skinned woman his new target.

She obeyed, slowly lifting her hands into the air. Then she darted a glance at Moses. Her chin twitched to the side.

As if he'd been waiting for the signal, Moses launched himself at Mitchell and knocked him to the ground. "Get outta here, Myra!" he ordered as he fought to separate Mitchell from his shotgun.

Pandemonium broke out. Women scurried for the door. Men brought out weapons.

"Wheeler!" Mitchell screamed as he fought to defend himself against the larger Moses. "Get the girl!"

"There's a window in the back room," Everett Hayes called out to his daughter. "Remember, Cass?"

"Come on, Mama," Cassie urged her mother to follow them, but the woman never moved, her blank expression unnatural.

Wheeler lunged toward Cassie.

"Go!" Travis yelled, as he grabbed Wheeler's arm.

"Now, Cassandra," Everett demanded. "I'll stay with your mother."

Finally, Cassie turned and veered toward the small room visible off the kitchen. Myra followed. At the same time, Wheeler tore his arm free and smashed his elbow into Travis's side.

Travis cried out. Pain stabbed through him like a sword's blade as Wheeler moved toward the back room. He'd catch the women before they could get the window open.

Travis reached behind his back, hissing at the pain. His fingers dug beneath his coat and fastened around the handle of his revolver. He pulled it from his waistband, brought his arm around, and squeezed the trigger.

Wheeler fell.

Neill and Josiah charged past Travis and seized Wheeler's arms. He moaned at their treatment, and relief washed over Travis at the knowledge that he hadn't killed the man. He craned his neck to survey the rest of the room, his blood still pumping with the turmoil of the fight. A member of Moses's band crossed his line of vision, pulled a hunting knife from its sheath, and set about freeing Mr. Hayes. Crockett had a knee in the logger's back where he lay sprawled on the floor, and Seth Winston was tying the fella's wrists. Roy Mitchell hung unconscious over Moses's shoulder, and the preacher was beating a hasty exit out the door.

Travis's eyes slid closed, and he sagged against the floor. It was over.

After a moment, the sound of steady footsteps brought his eyes open. Jim stood over him, his hand extended. Travis took it and let his brother haul him to his feet.

"I thought you might want this," Jim said, holding out his other hand.

Travis stared at the paper, his signature glaring up at him from the bottom of the sheet. His chest clenched. Something wet pooled in his eye. He blinked it away and cleared the clog out of his throat.

"Burn that for me, will you?"

Jim grinned and strode toward the hearth. He reached to the mantel, took a match from the iron holder, and scraped the head against the striker. Fire flared at the tip, and Travis watched as Jim hunkered down before the hearth and lit the bottom corner of the paper. While his signature shriveled and turned to black ash, something deep in Travis's soul shouted in triumph.

Then a longing, equally deep, rose within him—a longing to share this moment, this triumph, with the one person who meant more to him than any other.

Meri.

40

When Meredith spied Cassie and Myra coming around the side of the house, she bolted from her spot by the horses, desperate for word of what was happening.

"Did you see Travis?" she demanded of her cousin without preamble. "I heard gunshots. Is he all right?"

"I think so, but I can't be sure. I was too busy climbing out your bedroom window when the second shot went off." Cassie clasped Meredith's arm, her eyes sympathetic. "I'm sure he's fine, though."

Meredith nodded, yet her heart wasn't as sure as her mind. She turned back to the cabin door. Things were quieter. Was that good?

Her stomach roiled. The waiting was killing her.

Finally, someone exited the cabin. Jim crossed the threshold, scanning the yard. "Cassandra?"

Cassie dropped Meredith's arm and hurried toward him. "I'm here!"

Jim pounded across the yard and embraced her with such ferocity her feet left the ground. It was joyous to watch, yet it left Meredith hungry for her own reunion and, at the same time, scared that even if Travis were well, he wouldn't be as happy to see her.

Myra came up behind her and laid a hand on her shoulder. "Our men'll be next. Don't you worry."

"I pray you're right."

When Moses did emerge, the sight of the oh-so-proper Roy Mitchell draped insensible over his shoulder brought a startled smile to Meredith's face.

"Didn't I tell you?" Myra patted Meredith's shoulder and stepped toward her husband. "I better send Josiah to fetch the wagon. Looks like we'll be needing it to haul all the sorry hides we collected."

Meredith actually giggled at that, and the release felt wonderful. Surely Moses would have given top priority to any of their men who had fallen during the melee. If he was carting Roy around, that must mean none of the injuries were too severe on the Archers' side.

She took a step toward the cabin, needing to see her husband, to gain that final reassurance that all was well.

A second step. Then a third. She walked as if in a dream.

Crockett marched through the door, dragging the logger behind him. Seth Winston followed with the man's ax. Her uncle hobbled out next, Aunt Noreen tucked under his arm. Meredith's pulse throbbed. *Where is Travis?*

So intent was she on looking for her husband that she didn't notice that Uncle Everett had paused in front of her until he spoke.

"Forgive me, Meri." His head hung low, his gaze meeting hers only for a moment before dipping back toward the ground. "I want you to know I'll be heading to the bank first thing in the morning to deed the property over to you and Travis, like I should've done right after your marriage."

Meredith nodded, unsure what to say. However, when he shuffled past, a burst of compassion rose up within her. She called his name softly and waited for him to glance back.

"If you allow Cassie to select her own husband," she said, thinking of Jim, "I'll give her the homestead as a wedding gift. Perhaps you and the man she chooses will be able to work together to revive your mill."

Uncle Everett's eyes misted, and for a moment he didn't move. Then he gave his own silent nod before ducking his chin and urging Aunt Noreen forward.

Pivoting toward the cabin once again, Meredith picked up her pace. Another shadow loomed in the doorway. Her feet slowed. Three men moved into the light, none of them Travis. Meredith swallowed her disappointment. Josiah and Neill carried a bloodied Mr. Wheeler down the steps between them.

The last of the men filed out as she reached the edge of the porch. The ones she knew from the freedmen's school smiled at her as they passed. Meredith thanked them for their aid, knowing she should say more, but her mind seemed unable to manage more than a simple thank-you with her heart so focused on locating her husband.

Taking a deep breath, she climbed the steps and entered the dim interior of the cabin. Travis stood near the hearth, his gaze focused somewhere inside the stone opening. He looked so solitary standing there, one hand braced against the mantel. Her heart longed for him with such acute need her chest ached. Yet she held herself back, not sure if he would welcome her intrusion. Not sure if he would welcome *her*.

So she drank him in from afar. His long legs, wide shoulders, the sandy hair at his neck that needed a trim. As she continued her inventory, a frown drew her brows together. His right arm lay curved against his side as if protecting it.

"You're hurt," she said, her reticence dissolving as concern for his health eclipsed all else.

His head came around. "I thought you'd left for the ranch."

She dropped her gaze to the floor as she walked, ostensibly to avoid the hazards of wrinkled rugs and overturned furniture, but in truth she was afraid to meet his eyes—afraid of the disappointment she would read there.

"I stayed with Bexar, intending to ride out if the trouble moved outside, but then Cassie and Myra showed up and people started exiting the cabin. I . . . well . . . I figured the danger had passed."

Travis's hands closed around her shoulders. "I'm glad you're here." Something gruff rumbled in his voice. Something emotional and sincere.

Meredith raised her chin, but she had no time to judge what was in his eyes, for his lips descended upon hers and immediately demanded her full attention. His palms stroked upward to cup her face, and the tenderness in his touch banished her insecurities and planted new hope in the soil of her heart.

Her hands wandered over his ribs, pushing beneath his open coat, circling toward his back. But when her left hand rubbed against his side, Travis flinched. It was only for an instant, and his lips never broke from hers, but it was enough to bring Meredith back to the reality of the moment. She pulled away from his kiss.

She lifted the flap of his coat and grimaced at the sight of torn fabric bloodied from a wound. "I should get Crockett. You need to have that tended." She pivoted and tried to move away, but Travis grasped her arm and refused to let her go.

"It's not serious," he said, stepping close to nuzzle her neck. "You can tend it for me later."

Shivers danced across her skin as his warm breath caressed the lobe of her ear. "I don't understand," she murmured, trying to make sense of what was happening. "I thought you'd be angry with me." His teeth nibbled on her ear, nearly scattering her thoughts. In desperation, she twisted away from him. "Stop that."

Travis straightened and peered into her face, confusion etched across his brow.

Her voice grew scratchy. "How can you kiss me? You didn't even want a wife, Travis. You only married me because your bad luck stuck you with the short straw. And now because of my foolish actions, you've forfeited your land." She closed her mouth against the sob that rose in her throat, but a tear escaped her lashes before she could blink it away.

"Is that what you think?" He loosened his hold on her arm, but only enough to allow his hand to slide down and capture hers. "You think I married you because I lost when we drew straws?" He chuckled softly. "Oh, Meri. Sweetheart. I *won* the straw draw. I didn't lose it."

She stared at him, not comprehending the difference. "What are you saying?"

Travis grinned. "When we sat around the table that night, we didn't decide to draw straws because *none* of us wanted to marry you. We drew straws because *all* of us wanted to marry you."

Meredith blinked up at her husband. Could it be true? Had she been a prize, not a chore?

"And I'll tell you something else." He dipped his head and lowered his voice, his grin turning downright mischievous. "But you gotta swear not to tell the others."

She nodded.

"I rigged the contest."

"What?"

"I made sure that I was the one who ended up with the short straw."

Meredith's pulse quickened. "Why?"

Travis shrugged a bit, and if she didn't know better, she could have sworn his skin pinkened a bit under his tan.

"At the time I told myself that you were my responsibility. That because of our previous encounter, I should be the one to marry you."

A responsibility. Of course. Meredith forced her chin to stay raised and her back straight despite her yearning to curl up into a protective ball.

"But I was fooling myself." Travis's gaze met hers, and she caught her breath. The way he looked at her, it was . . . was . . . "Even then I was falling in love with you."

It was love.

"I couldn't stand the idea of one of my brothers marrying you. You belonged with me. I knew it. I couldn't explain it, but I knew it. And over the last several weeks, I've only grown more sure. I love you, Meredith. I thank God every day for bringing you back into my life."

Her heart felt as if it would burst, so full was her joy. But there was one issue she couldn't ignore. "What about your land?"

Travis squeezed her hand and tugged her into his side, then laid a kiss on her forehead. "You're worth more to me than any pile of dirt. I'd give up the ranch again, in a heartbeat, if it meant keeping you safe."

"Wait . . . again?"

He smiled at her and pointed to the blackened remains scattered across the floor of the hearth. "Mitchell was in no condition to protest when Jim reclaimed the deed paper work."

"Oh, Travis! I'm so pleased."

He returned her smile, but then his face grew serious, his voice unsure. "Meri? Did you mean what you wrote in your note? Have you truly come to care for me?"

Meredith bit her lip, her emotions swirling. "More than anything," she vowed. She reached a hand to his cheek and stroked his strong jaw. "I've been in love with you since that day you rescued me from that steel trap. Only now, I love you with the fullness of a woman's love—deep, abiding, forever."

Travis clasped her to him, his lips once again covering hers. But before Meredith could lose herself in the passion he inspired, a throat cleared. The sound echoed loudly in the nearly empty room. She jumped away from Travis with a start, a blush heating her cheeks.

"Sorry to . . . ah . . . interrupt," Crockett intoned from the doorway. "Wanted to see if we could borrow Meredith's horse. Noreen refuses to ride in the same wagon as Mitchell and his *criminal army*, even if the men are all tied up in the back. And she's declared their mounts equally repulsive. Jim fetched Ginger in hopes of appeasing her, but when she saw there was no saddle, she nearly had a fit of apoplexy. He's giving her his own saddle now, and she stopped screeching, so we thought we'd better head out while the gettin' was good."

Meredith shook her head in sympathy. "I don't envy you the long ride to town with her. But if having Ginger makes it easier, I am more than happy to lend her out."

"Do you have lanterns for after night falls?" Travis strode forward, keeping hold of Meredith's hand as he went. "You'll only have a half moon to light your way."

"Yep. Moses thought to bring a few along. He'll be riding with us to deliver Mitchell and the others to the sheriff while Jim sees Cassie and her folks home. Neill and Josiah wanted to ride along, too, if that's all right with you."

"I don't see why not," Travis said. "After all, it was the boy's job to fetch the sheriff in the first place. Might as well let him finish the job."

Meredith stilled as she did the math. That meant . . . she and Travis would be alone at the house. All night.

Travis turned to look at her and heat flared in his eyes as if he had read her thoughts. "I'll . . ." He cleared his throat and turned back to his brother. "I'll see you off."

Meredith trailed behind, a warm, sunny feeling blooming as she watched her reclusive husband reach out in gratitude to all the men and women who had offered their help. Relationships had been formed today, bonds that would last well into the future. No longer would the Archers be isolated from their community. They now stood among them as neighbors, as friends.

"Moses," Travis said, holding his hand out to the big man. "I can't thank you enough. This day would have ended very differently without you."

Moses clasped his hand. "I's just doing unto others like the Good Book says. Helpin' out is what neighbors do. Bearing each other's burdens, and all that."

"When it comes to burdens, Travis is good at the bearing part," Crockett said, slapping his brother on the back. "It's the letting-others-help-with-the-ones-*he's*-carrying part that needs some work."

Meredith opened her mouth to defend her husband, but Travis responded before she could do more than inhale a preparatory breath.

"You're right," he admitted, his humility so dignified it instantly unruffled her feathers and filled her with quiet pride. "But I think that's going to change after today."

"I believe it will, brother," Crockett said, all teasing gone from his tone. "I believe it will."

As the parties prepared to set off, Meredith hugged Cassie and Myra, then returned to her husband's side to wave her farewells. Once everyone had departed, she found herself wrapped in Travis's arms as the two of them rode double atop Bexar back to the ranch.

The short distance didn't allow for much conversation, but words weren't needed. Meredith simply leaned into her husband and let the sway of the horse's gait soothe away the strain of the last few hours.

Travis loved her. Nothing else mattered.

When Bexar halted, Meredith lifted her head. Travis cupped the side of her face and placed a soft kiss on her lips. It was tender and brief and, oh, so sweet, yet when he pulled away, the tilt of his smile and the heat in his gaze promised more to come.

"I need to see to the horse," he said as he circled her waist with his arm and lowered her to the ground. "But I'll be in soon."

"I'll help you."

He raised an eyebrow at her but made no complaint as he dismounted and led Bexar into the barn. Meredith followed. She needed to be close to him. This was their first night to be completely alone together, and she didn't want to waste a single moment.

Travis removed Bexar's saddle and blankets while Meredith hung up the bridle. She checked the feedbox and water and found them both adequate for the night. Travis came up behind her, his hat brim bumping her head as he nuzzled her neck.

She giggled and danced away, feeling playful yet oddly shy at the same time. Travis gave chase, his husky laughter blending with hers as the two of them darted out of the barn. When they neared the porch, he grabbed her about the waist and lifted her off her feet. Meredith squealed.

"You can't escape me," Travis murmured in her ear as he gently settled her back on the ground.

Meredith turned in his arms to face the man she loved. "I've no desire to."

His eyes darkened, and for a moment she thought he would kiss her. But then he scooped her into his arms and carried her up the porch steps. The front door proved more of a challenge to conquer. Travis had to juggle his hold on her a bit before he could get the latch open. Meredith laughed in delight, endeared by his awkward efforts. Once the door was cracked, he kicked it wide with his boot and carried her over the threshold.

"Welcome home, Mrs. Archer."

Welcome home. As if their marriage had just taken place and he had brought her home for the first time. Meredith's smile trembled as she met her husband's gaze. He was offering her a new start, offering a marriage based on love.

He carried her through the hall until they reached the kitchen. There he set her down and slowly undid the fastenings on her cloak. A shiver tingled against her skin wherever his fingers touched. His eyes held hers as he slid the garment from her shoulders, breaking contact only when he turned to hang the cloak on a hook.

While his back was to her, Meredith discovered a boldness she didn't know she had, and reached for the shoulders of his coat. She eased it down the length of his arms, admiring the play of his muscles beneath the flannel of his shirt. Placing his coat on the hook next to hers, her shyness returned.

Travis nudged her chin up with the edge of his hand. "Will you be my wife tonight, Meri?"

She bit her lip, her heart fluttering so fast she felt light-headed. But she knew what her answer would be. "Yes, Travis. Tonight and always."

No longer was she a short-straw bride, Meredith thought as she took her husband's hand and allowed him to draw her down the hall to their room. With the gift of Travis's heart, she'd been transformed into a well-loved wife. She couldn't imagine a greater blessing.

Stealing the Preacher

To all the ministers who proclaim God's truth
with boldness and care for his flock with loving-kindness.
Thank you for answering his call,
even when the path he directs you to
is not the one you expected.

A man's heart deviseth his way:
but the Lord directeth his steps.

Proverbs 16:9

Burleson County, Texas—1885

Crockett Archer stretched his legs into the aisle as the train pulled away from the Caldwell station. Only a brief stop in Somerville remained before his arrival in Brenham—the place where his life's work would begin. A wide grin spread across his face as he contemplated his future.

Was this how Abraham felt as he'd journeyed to Canaan? Anticipation thrumming through his veins. Certainty of purpose pumping with every heartbeat. That rare sense of satisfaction that came only when one responded to the direct call of the Lord.

"Mama, that man is laughing at your hat." A young boy peered over the seat in front of Crockett, pointing an accusing finger at him.

His mother huffed and reached up to pat the back of her hat—as if it might have had its feelings hurt. "Some people have no manners," she muttered, shooting a scathing glance over her shoulder as she grasped her son's arm and tried to get him to turn around.

"I meant no disrespect to your hat, ma'am." Crockett leaned forward to offer an apology, but in truth, as he focused on the millinery atrocity in question, the desire to laugh threatened to choke him. Blue feathers poked out at all angles, as if a family of jays had used it as a perch while molting. Forcing down his amusement, he schooled his features into a serious mien. "My thoughts were elsewhere entirely, I assure you."

"Then why was you smilin' so big?" Suspicion laced the boy's tone.

And no wonder. If the sample before him was any indication of the woman's usual taste in headwear, the poor lad probably battled for his mother's millinery honor constantly.

"I was simply thinking of all the exciting things that await me at the end of this trip, and it made me happy." Crockett winked at the kid. "Are you looking forward to the end of your trip?"

The boy shrugged. "Not really. We're goin' to see my great-aunt Ida." He gave Crockett a beleaguered look. "She smells funny."

"Andrew Michael Bailey! How could you say such a thing? And to a stranger, no less." Andrew's mother yanked him around, and Crockett beat a hasty retreat, leaning back in his seat while the woman lectured her son in strident whispers.

At least she seemed to have forgotten about the hat incident. Crockett decided to count that as a blessing. If dear old Aunt Ida lived in Brenham, it would be best if her niece was more concerned with her son's slip of the tongue than the new preacher's opinions on her hat.

The new preacher. His heart swelled in his chest.

After three years of apprenticing with the minister in Palestine, Texas, near the ranch where he'd grown up, and guest-speaking at any church in the area that would let him into the pulpit, he finally was being offered the opportunity to preach full time.

Oh, there was another fellow competing for the position, but Crockett knew in his gut that his time had come.

The Lord had been leading him to this day since the summer he'd turned fifteen and his older brother, Travis, suggested he take over the spiritual instruction of the family. At first it had simply been a chore like any other, but it soon developed into a ministry. With their parents deceased and their lives isolated and uncertain, the four Archer brothers had needed a faith that ran deeper than the occasional blessing over supper. They'd needed a faith that penetrated every aspect of their lives. Crockett assumed the responsibility of nurturing his family's souls, but as he and his brothers reached manhood, an ever-increasing pressure to reach beyond his household drove him to stretch his boundaries.

Apparently, he'd be stretching them all the way to Brenham.

Crockett rested his elbow on the satchel that sat on the seat beside him and mentally ran through the key points of the sermon he'd written and rehearsed for tomorrow's service. His concentration shifted inward, and the scenery chugging past his window blurred. He silently mouthed a verse from 1 Peter, but before he could complete the quotation, the passenger car gave a violent lurch.

His hand caught the seat back in front of him at the last second, narrowly preventing a spill into the aisle when his weight was thrown forward.

The locomotive's wheels screeched against the rails. Passengers flew about the car. Women gasped. Children whimpered. The train slowed slightly as the screeching continued.

"What's happening, Mama?" Andrew wailed as his mother curled her body protectively around her son.

"There's probably something on the tracks." Crockett raised his voice above the chaos. "Once the train stops, the crew will clear it away and we'll resume our trip. No need to be afraid, little man."

Yet even as he spoke the words, a tingle of unease crept between Crockett's shoulder blades. A woman a few rows up let out a shrill scream and pointed at something beyond her window. The man at her side pushed forward for a better look, then shouted the one word guaranteed to strike fear in any traveler's heart.

"Bandits!"

Crockett instinctively reached for his hip only to come up empty. He'd left his guns at the ranch. For more than a decade he'd worked the Archer spread with a rifle within constant reach or a pistol strapped to his thigh. Usually both. Now he was stuck facing a band of train robbers with nothing more than his wits because his mentor assured him that circuit riders were the only preachers who traveled armed.

He should have listened to Travis when his brother advised him to pack a weapon in his bag. Maybe then he wouldn't be sitting here defenseless. But he'd been too intent on making a good impression.

Not one to sit idle, however, Crockett lurched to his feet and fought the forward momentum of the slowing train. Lunging across the aisle, he locked his hands onto a pair of seat backs and hunched over a salesman's sample case to peer out the sooty window.

He counted four men. Guns drawn. Faces covered. Their horses quickly closing the gap between them and the train.

"God help us," Crockett prayed under his breath.

As the train slowed to a near stop, the outlaws drew abreast of the passenger car. One rider fell back, disappearing from Crockett's line of sight. The other three surged ahead.

A thump echoed from the rear of the car. The first man was aboard.

Crockett reclaimed his seat.

Just as the rear door crashed open, two other bandits burst into the coach from the front.

"Ever'body put your hands where I can see 'em!" The lead man pulled a second pistol from his left holster. With a weapon in each hand, he took aim at both sides of the railcar, eyeing the male passengers who seemed most likely to interfere.

As he did so, the train came to a full stop, jerking the passengers a final time. The leader's stance never wavered. He stood as steady as an old sea dog on a ship's deck.

Panicked murmurs slithered through the coach, gradually rising in pitch until one lady shot to her feet.

"I have to get out. Let me out!"

The leader's left gun immediately shifted aim to her chest. "Better control your woman, mister." His steely eyes narrowed above the black bandana he wore over his mouth and nose. "I ain't planning to shoot nobody, but plans can change real fast."

The woman's companion snatched her from behind and hauled her back down into the seat. She whined but turned her face into the shelter of the man's arm and made no further comment.

Satisfied, the outlaw turned his attention to the crowd at large. "There's no reason to get all worked up, folks. As soon as we get what we came for, we'll be on our way."

He took a step down the aisle. Then another. The bandit who'd entered with him hung back by the coal stove at the front of the car.

Crockett stole a glance at the man in the rear. He blocked the exit, his gun hand steady. Crockett shifted his attention back to the leader.

Something was off about these outlaws. From accounts he'd read and stories he'd heard, robberies usually featured hotheaded, cocky kids eager to prove they were fast with their guns. This group seemed too steady. Too self-controlled. Too . . . *old*.

Crockett examined them more closely. The one by the stove turned to glance out the window, and Crockett spotted graying hair at his collar beneath his hat. The middle one had leathery skin—what little was visible above the bandana. Deep creases around his eyes testified to a life lived outdoors, squinting against the sun. And though his glare was intent, the slightly crooked posture of the man at the back reminded Crockett of his sixty-year-old mentor when the man's joints were paining him after too much work in the garden.

Crockett was still chewing on his observations when a man in a business suit held out a fancy gold watch, the chain dangling from his fist.

"Here. Take it and leave."

The leader scowled down at the watch as if it offended him. "Put your valuables away," he groused. "That's not what we came for."

Why would they take over the passenger car if they didn't intend to rob the passengers? Were they simply keeping the crowd in check while the fourth man rummaged through the baggage car?

Crockett leaned forward, just enough to see out the opposite window. The fourth man had gathered the horses on the west side of the tracks and was pointing a rifle in the direction of the engine.

"Then what *did* you come for?" the man with the watch demanded. "Tell us so we can hand it over and be done with you and your gang."

The creases around the outlaw's eyes deepened as he scanned the coach for what he sought. When his gaze touched on Crockett, it hovered a moment before moving on. Crockett's mouth went dry.

The man's brows formed a V of displeasure as he concluded his search. A growl rumbled in his throat seconds before his intention exploded across the coach.

"I came for the preacher!"

2

Crockett stiffened.

He came for the . . . what? Surely his mind was playing tricks on him. The man couldn't have said what he thought he'd heard.

The outlaw glared at the passengers and waved his guns from side to side. "Which one of you is the parson? Don't think you can trick me by not wearin' one of them white collars. I know he's on this train, and I ain't leaving 'til I find him."

Crockett's hand nearly lifted to the string tie at his neck, but he halted the movement before giving himself away. He'd never worn a clerical collar. Brother Ralston insisted that a man's character, not his clothing, should identify his calling. Following in his mentor's footsteps might have saved his life.

"You!" the outlaw barked at the salesman across the aisle. "You look like a preacher with your fancy duds and soft hands."

"N-n-no, sir." The man who had raised his hands in surrender the minute the bandits boarded the train now turned his palms inward, worry creasing his brow as he inspected his smooth palms. "I'm j-j-just a drummer. See?" Slowly he opened his traveling case. "Patent medicines."

"Bah!" The outlaw turned away in disgust and swung around to face Crockett.

Pale, steel-blue eyes took his measure. Accustomed to staring down unwanted strangers after years of protecting his ranch from interlopers, Crockett held the man's gaze, although the task had been much easier when he'd been the one holding the gun. The outlaw's eyes narrowed to slits, then turned their attention to Crockett's suit. One brow lifted to the brim of the man's dark hat as he took in the formal attire, but after a glance at Crockett's work-roughened hands, the bandit grunted and strode past.

Never had Crockett been more thankful for calluses and scars.

As the outlaw continued his progress through the car, Crockett made his own assessment of the passengers. Which one was the preacher the bandits were looking for? The man at the front who had offered his watch? The one two rows up dressed like a farmer but whose head was bowed like a man in prayer?

The coincidence of the robbers invading this particular train in search of a preacher didn't sit easily on Crockett's shoulders. Yet he was sure they couldn't be searching for him. He'd never been in this area before. Shoot. Until a couple years ago, he'd never been *anywhere*. No one knew he was on this train except his family, Brother Ralston, and the elders at Brenham.

"I'm losin' patience, folks." The leader growled his warning as he stomped back up the aisle. "If the preacher man don't fess up, I'm liable to get a might upset. And my trigger finger tends to get twitchy when I'm upset."

"Mama, is that man gonna shoot us?" Andrew's tiny voice cut through Crockett's heart.

"Hush, Andy," his mother hissed as she tucked him more firmly under her arm.

Crockett set his jaw. *This isn't right*. Tormenting women and children. Something had to be done. "How do you know that the man you seek is even on this train?" Crockett slowly pushed to his feet, careful to keep his hands raised.

Steel Eyes met his challenge without flinching. "Read him the handbill." He barked the order over his shoulder with a jerk of his chin.

The man by the stove reached into his jacket and pulled out a folded sheet of paper. Holding it by one edge, he shook it open. "'Meet the . . .'" He paused, cleared his throat once, and then stretched the handbill farther away from his face and squinted. "'Meet the preachers. Welcome our two cand-i-dates at Brenham Station on Saturday afternoon. They will arrive on the noon train from Houston and the two fifteen from Milano. Cookies and lemonade will be served.'"

A heaviness pressed against Crockett's chest as the bandit's stilted words drove into him like nails into a coffin.

How . . . ? How could he be the preacher they sought? Denial raged through him, but he smothered it and straightened his shoulders. The *why* didn't matter. What mattered was getting these bandits off the train.

"I'm your man."

"You ain't no parson." The leader waved his gun at him. "Sit down."

Crockett stood his ground. "Check my bag. You'll find my Bible, and inside the front cover is a folded page of sermon notes."

Steel Eyes cocked the pistol in his right hand and pointed the barrel an inch from Crockett's chest. "Step aside, son."

Crockett obeyed, moving into the aisle.

Keeping his stare locked on Crockett, the outlaw holstered his left gun and reached for the satchel. Crockett gave serious thought to knocking the pistol out of his hand the minute he glanced down to open the bag, but the man never gave him the chance. Once he had a grip on the satchel, he tossed it to his partner at the rear of the coach, all without taking his eyes from Crockett's face.

"It's here, boss," the third bandit called in confirmation. "The Bible. The notes. He's even got some journals underneath—all with religious-type names."

"Well, folks," Steel Eyes announced. "It looks like we found what we came for." He latched onto Crockett's arm with an iron grip. "Now, Mr. Preacher Man, let's get you off this train so these good people can enjoy the rest of their trip."

Crockett submitted to the forced escort, the pistol barrel jammed into his back keeping him in check. The outlaws might have the upper hand now, but he'd bide his time. Once away from the women and children, Crockett wouldn't have to worry about an innocent getting caught in the crossfire. He'd make his move when the time was right.

He had an appointment to keep and a job to win. No gang of long-in-the-tooth train robbers was going to derail his plans.

An hour of hard riding later, the leader finally called a halt near a stream bed. Crockett had managed to stay in the saddle during the grueling ride despite the fact that his hands were tied behind his back. His shoulders burned from the awkward position, and his thighs ached from working so hard to keep him atop his mount. The pain had kept him alert, however, and his mind sharp.

The man who had stayed with the horses during the abduction was the first to dismount. "We still got it, eh, Silas?" He eyed the gang's leader. "Don't get that kind of excitement herding cattle, do ya?" He tugged his bandana down to his neck and took a long drink from his canteen, apparently unconcerned that Crockett could see his face.

"I'm too old for that kind of excitement." The man to Crockett's right released a mighty groan as he stood in the stirrups. "You didn't have to jump the train, Carl. I swear I ain't gonna be able to walk right for a month after slammin' my hip into that railcar." He rubbed the offending spot and made a great show of hobbling as he led his horse over to the stream.

"Quit your whining, Frank." Silas kept a firm grip on the reins to

Crockett's horse as he swung down out of the saddle. He'd had them in hand the entire way, not trusting his captive to follow meekly.

Smart fellow.

Crockett had already concluded that they needed him for a particular purpose, and whatever that purpose was, it would probably keep them from lodging a bullet in his back should he make a run for it. But it was unlikely he could keep his seat at a full-out gallop with his hands bound behind him, even if Silas relinquished the reins. So, instead, he'd spent his time plotting what he would do when they stopped.

Now that they had, it was time for action. All he needed was for Steel Eyes to come a little closer.

Silas moved, but only as far as the head of Crockett's horse. He paused to stroke the animal's muzzle. Crockett bit back his disappointment.

"Jasper, bring the preacher man your canteen. He looks a little parched."

The third bandit did as ordered, but as he approached, Crockett caught a glimpse of the censorious look he turned on his leader. "This is crazy, boss." His low voice barely carried, but with little noise around them, Crockett was just able to hear his quiet words. "You promised Miss Martha to give up your thievin' ways. I've never known you to go back on your word. Especially to your wife. We've been livin' honest for too long to risk it all on some fool stunt like this."

"I haven't broken my word," Silas growled, his face reddening as he clearly fought to control his fury. "Martha was the best thing that ever happened to me, and I'd not dishonor her memory by soiling a vow I made to her. I didn't steal a single trinket today, and you know it."

"You stole the parson." Jasper tilted his head in Crockett's direction, though neither of them looked his way. Good thing—since they might have noticed him slipping his boots out of the stirrups or loosening his bonds as he stretched them on the cantle.

"I didn't steal him," Silas insisted. "I just borrowed him. We'll let him go when Joe's through with him."

Jasper sighed and shook his head, his long gray mustache doing nothing to hide his frown. "I know you love that kid of yours, Si. We all do. But this ain't right."

"I'll decide what's right for my family." Silas snatched the canteen away from Jasper and stalked over to Crockett's left side.

Carl and Frank were watering their horses several yards away. Jasper had his back turned. There wouldn't be a better opportunity.

Crockett flung up his knee, planted his left boot against the man's chest, and shoved with all his might. The canteen clattered to the ground. Silas stumbled back, his bellow sounding an alarm. Crockett leapt from the horse's back and managed to wrench his right arm free of his bindings. He smashed his fist into Silas's jaw before the man could regain his balance. The outlaw tumbled backward, the horse's reins still tangled in his fingers.

The horse whinnied at the rough treatment and thrashed about, trying to gain his freedom. Crockett used the diversion to make a run for the trees. A building of some kind lay to the north. A building meant people. People meant help. He just prayed he'd been right about the bandits not wanting to lodge a bullet in him.

A shot rang out, followed by angry shouts demanding he stop. But no lead slammed into him, so Crockett kept running.

He ducked beneath post oak branches and zigzagged from one tree to another, taking advantage of any cover the terrain afforded.

The building was getting closer. A barn, maybe? He just had to keep his legs under him.

Hooves pounded into the earth behind him. Crockett's heart rate tripled. They were running him down. And he was running out of trees.

Open grassland lay between him and a fenced pasture. Keeping to the trees would only allow him to delay capture, not elude it. His only chance was to scale that fence and hope that Silas and his gang wouldn't risk discovery by pursuing him onto private property.

Lungs on fire, Crockett burst out of the woods and sprinted for the fence. The hoofbeats behind him escalated.

A soft whirring caught his ear a second before a lariat dropped over his head and shoulders. Crockett made a desperate grab for the rope, but before he could get his thumbs hooked, the noose tightened around his chest and yanked him backward. In a flash he was flat on his back, staring at the sky.

He'd just been lassoed like a new calf at branding time. Lying still, head throbbing from where it had collided with the earth, Crockett prayed there'd be no hot iron involved when Silas presented him to his son. Then again, whoever this Joe person was, he was bound to be as off his rocker as everyone else involved in this farce. Who knew what the kid would do? After all, he was the one who'd talked his outlaw father into stealing a preacher in the first place.

Silas Robbins didn't know what to make of the man at the end of Jasper's rope. All the sermonizers he'd ever come across were soft, bookish men partial to the sound of their own voices. Silas rubbed his bruised jaw with one hand as he shifted in his saddle and glared at the preacher struggling to gain his feet.

This parson was anything but soft.

"I thought you fellers believed in turnin' the other cheek." Silas's saddle creaked as he leaned forward. The preacher man's fine black suit was covered in dust, his hat lay upended a few feet away, and his arms were pinned to his side by a snare that wouldn't give an inch. Yet the man met his stare without a hint of fear.

"King David was a mighty warrior," the parson answered, "and the Bible calls him a man after God's own heart. If he can slay his enemies and stand before the Lord with a clean conscience, I think I can defend myself and do the same."

Silas straightened, a grudging respect poking him like a mosquito prick. In other circumstances, he could imagine himself liking this fellow. But a preacher? He'd run barefoot across a bed of cactus before he'd give his hand in friendship to one of them holy hypocrites.

"Whatever lets you sleep at night, Parson. Heaven knows the only man better than a lawyer at twisting truth to serve his own purpose is a preacher." Silas crossed his wrists over his saddle horn and waited for the man's reaction.

Would he sputter denials? Call down curses? Staunchly defend his profession?

Nope.

All the fellow did was arch an eyebrow and make a quiet observation. "Seems odd that you would go to so much trouble to collect a clergyman when you hold the occupation in such low esteem."

Odd? It was downright unnatural. But what a man chose to do for his kin was none of this sermonizer's concern.

"To the house, boys." Silas gave the signal to head out. He trotted his gray gelding to where the preacher's hat lay on the ground. Without slowing, he pulled his rifle from the scabbard, leaned deeply to the right, and plucked the thing off the ground by jabbing the gun's muzzle into the head hole. Guiding his horse with his knees, he unhooked the black felt slouch hat from his rifle barrel and slapped it onto the parson's head.

Gotta have the man looking respectable for Jo.

It gave him a sense of satisfaction to have the upper hand again. The preacher might be a couple decades younger and fleeter of foot, but Silas Robbins still had a few tricks up his sleeve. King David, here, wouldn't be getting the drop on him again.

"You want me to put him up on his horse, boss?" Jasper wrapped the end of the rope around the saddle horn and prepared to dismount, but Silas stopped him with a shake of his head.

"He seemed so all-fired anxious to run across our pasture, I figure we might as well grant him his wish."

The parson's attention snapped to meet Silas's before shifting to the barn and back again. The disbelief lining his face was priceless. The poor fellow thought he'd been running for freedom when all along he'd been heading directly into the den of the thieves he'd meant to escape. If there hadn't been the little problem of him ruining Jo's surprise, Silas might have let him go just to see his expression when they rode into the yard and met him at the barn door. Might've made catching the parson's fist with his jaw worthwhile.

Silas set a leisurely pace as they circled the pasture's perimeter. The man leashed to Jasper's horse masked his fatigue well, but he had to be tuckered out after that mad dash through the trees.

Besides, everyone knew preachers were only good for one thing—talking. It stood to reason that if Jo wanted a preacher, she'd want to talk to the fellow. What kind of gift would the hypocrite make if he was so out of breath when he met her that he couldn't get a word out? If Silas was going to all the trouble of surprising her with this gift, it'd be foolish to break it before she could use it.

But would she like it?

Last-minute doubts nibbled the corners of his confidence. Martha had always been the one who'd selected Jo's birthday gifts in the past. Last year, their grief had been too raw over Martha's passing to celebrate anything.

But this year Jo was turning twenty-one. She deserved something large, something meaningful, something she never dreamed she'd actually receive.

Ah, Martha. As they gained the road that led to his ranch, Silas turned his eyes heavenward. *I miss you something fierce, love. You should be the one arranging things for our Jo. Not me.*

Jasper was right. Martha never would have approved of his methods, but somehow he thought she'd approve of the gift. She always was partial to preachin' and church-goin'. And Jo followed in her mama's footsteps.

When he'd asked her last week what she wanted for her birthday and she'd told him she wanted a preacher, Silas had seen the truth of her words in her eyes—eyes so like her mother's. She'd laughed afterward and tried to play like she'd just been foolin', but he'd known better. His Jo was hurtin', and for some reason she thought a preacher man would make it better. Silas had no patience for religion, but if Jo wanted a preacher, by George, he'd get her a preacher.

It was only as they pulled up in the yard and the door to the ranch house cracked open that it occurred to Silas that he maybe should have tried to fashion a bow out of some of the rope around the parson's middle to make him look more like a present and less like a prisoner.

Joanna Robbins stepped from the house, her gaze, as always, drawn to her father. The dappled gray he rode stood out among the brown quarter horses, just as he stood out from his men. Mama used to say he was a man born to lead, and Joanna had to agree. He exuded authority, but it was his unwavering dedication to those closest to him that won their loyalty. His men would follow wherever he led. As would she. Yet in the one thing that mattered above all else, she needed him to follow *her*, and that he would not do.

But he was her daddy, and she loved him. So when a smile crinkled his eyes as he swung down from his horse, and his arms stretched wide in invitation, Joanna banished her worries and ran to him.

His strong arms surrounded her with the love and acceptance he'd shown her all her life. She reveled in it as she circled his waist and squeezed her own love back into him, nestling her head against his chest.

"Three days is a long time, Daddy. I missed you."

"I missed you, too, darlin'." His grip loosened, and he leaned back. "But I brought you something real special."

"For my birthday?" Giddy anticipation bubbled up inside her, as if she were a girl turning twelve, not twenty-one. But the men were looking on, so Joanna harnessed her excitement.

Saddle leather groaned, drawing Joanna's attention to Jasper Mullins, her father's foreman. He swung a leg over his mount's back and unwound a rope from the saddle horn. He dragged his hat from his head, exposing a circular crease in his white-gray hair, then leaned forward and bussed her cheek. The tickle of his droopy mustache made her smile, but the rope he placed in her hand brought a furrow to her brow.

"Happy birthday, Miss Jo."

"Thank you, Jasper."

Frank Pickens and Carl Hurst called out similar well-wishes before making themselves scarce by following Jasper to the barn. It was only when they'd all led their horses away that she got a clear view of what stood tethered to the end of her rope.

"You brought me a . . . rustler?"

The tall man was dressed better than any rustler she'd ever seen—not that she'd ever really seen any. But she imagined they'd wear something more practical for their thieving. Denim trousers, perhaps. And a cotton work shirt. Not a fancy suit and tie. Although the coat *was* rather rumpled, and the trousers were coated with a thick layer of dust.

"He's not a rustler, Jo." Her father's deep voice penetrated her thoughts.

She questioned him with her eyes.

He struggled to meet her gaze and failed. Blowing out a heavy breath, he plucked the hat from his head and beat it against his thigh. "Dad-burn it, girl. You said you wanted a preacher, so that's what I brung ya."

A preacher?

Joanna's knees nearly buckled. She dropped the rope as if it had become a snake and pressed her empty hand to her belly. A preacher. How fervently she had prayed for a man of God to cross her path, one who would aid her in fulfilling her calling. This should be a time of great rejoicing and thanksgiving. Instead she felt ill.

"You stole him?" She bit back a moan. "Daddy, how could you?"

"I didn't steal him," he shouted at her back as she rushed to the preacher's side and began loosening the knot. "I just encouraged him to pay you a visit for your birthday. That's all."

Joanna didn't respond. Nor did she meet the parson's eye. She just focused on the knot above his waist.

"I was real careful not to hurt him none—which is more than I can say for him. That preacher man nearly broke my jaw!"

That brought her head up. "You did?" she whispered.

The man shrugged. "Seemed prudent at the time. I was trying to escape a band of ruthless kidnappers."

Lord have mercy, but the man was handsome. His eyes were the exact shade of the Caledonian brown pigment in her paint set, though infused with a light that would be nearly impossible to duplicate on canvas. His jaw was strong and slightly squared. His nose perfectly proportioned to the rest of his face.

The artist in her had begun cataloging the position of his ears and the line of his throat when he wiggled against his bindings and reminded her of more pressing matters.

"I'm so sorry," she said, fumbling once again with the knot. Finally it loosened enough for her to expand the loop and free his hands. He immediately flung the lasso over his head and rolled his shoulders.

She instinctively stepped back, not sure what he would do. The sound of a gun being cocked directly behind her made it clear her father was taking no chances, either.

The parson seemed unruffled by the show of force, however. He simply continued rubbing his arms and wiggling his fingers in an effort to repair his circulation.

Curious. Most men of her acquaintance had difficulty standing up to her father when he was in a stern mood, even without a gun pointed in their direction. But this preacher, if he truly was a man of the cloth—she was beginning to have her doubts—acted as if standing in a yard at gunpoint was an everyday occurrence.

"Who are you?" She hadn't realized she'd spoken the thought aloud until he turned to her.

He swept his hat from his head, revealing russet hair neatly trimmed. "Crockett Archer, miss." He dipped his chin politely.

She stepped closer. "I'm Joanna Robbins."

"Well, Miss Robbins. As much as I've enjoyed this little side trip, and as delighted as I am to have the honor of wishing you felicitations on your birthday, I really must take my leave. I'm afraid I have a prior engagement that is of the utmost importance. A congregation awaits my arrival in Brenham."

His gaze held no malice, and his smile seemed genuine enough, but she sensed a layer of iron beneath his words.

"You ain't going nowhere, preacher man." Her father moved to her side, his gun less than a foot from Mr. Archer's chest. "Not until my Jo gets what she wants from you."

Joanna's eyes slid closed in mortification. What *his Jo* wanted right now was for the earth to open up and swallow her whole.

4

It appears I am at your disposal, Miss Robbins." Crockett made little effort to hide his irritation, and only felt the tiniest twinge of guilt when his abductor's daughter winced.

What in heaven's name did the girl want with a preacher, anyhow? Did she have some potential husband tied up inside the house waiting to be hitched? Poor wretch had probably been kidnapped, too. Gagged and chained to the stove, no doubt.

Not that this woman would need chains to capture a man's attention under normal circumstances. Her milky skin, soft eyes, and that mad riot of reddish-gold corkscrew curls that gave her a pixie-like appearance would see to that task. But with a train robber for a father and his gang having free rein on her ranch, circumstances were anything but normal.

Part of him wished she was indeed the *Joe* he'd imagined. At least then he could fight his way free. Her being a woman complicated matters. And this ridiculous situation was complicated enough already.

Joanna Robbins raised her head, her gaze meeting his for only an instant before skittering away to somewhere near his chin. "If Mr. Archer agrees to accompany me on a short stroll, I'd be happy to loan him a mount so he can ride into Deanville later this evening. From there he can arrange transportation to Caldwell and be on about his business."

The gun pointed at Crockett's chest lowered a few inches as Silas turned to study his daughter. "That's all you're wanting, Jo? A stroll?"

Crockett found it hard to believe, as well. Yet her voice rang with a quiet earnestness he couldn't discount.

Slowly she raised her chin. Her blue-gray eyes pleaded with him. "It's not all I want, but it's all I'm asking."

How was a man supposed to fight against that? Crockett sighed inwardly. To deny her request would be well within his rights. Yet even considering the notion left him feeling small and petty. No. He'd been called to a higher road, a narrower road.

Besides, if taking a stroll with the gal satisfied her father and thereby gained him his freedom, it'd be worth the concession. He needed to get to a town as soon as possible and wire the elders in Brenham. They would have heard what had happened by now and were surely concerned. And while he wanted to allay their fears, what he really wanted was to allay his own by rescheduling his audition. The elders had communicated their wish to have a decision made and a permanent minister installed as soon as possible. Today's delay, no matter how outrageous the circumstances, would not do him any favors.

"I'd be pleased to escort you wherever you wish to go." Crockett sketched a brief bow, then fit his hat to his head and offered her his arm.

Joanna's lashes dipped over her eyes and pink stained her cheeks, but she only hesitated a moment before sliding her fingers into the crook of his arm. A tiny smile wavered upon her lips. "Thank you."

She swiveled to face her father next. "We'll just walk down to the churchyard and back, Daddy. We won't be long."

"You won't be alone, either," Silas groused. "I plan to keep my eye on you." He spoke to his daughter, but Crockett had no doubt where the implied threat was aimed.

"No." The solidity of the single word brought Crockett's head around to the woman he'd thought docile. "I need privacy for my conversation with the parson. The churchyard is visible from the dormer windows in the attic. You can watch us from there if you feel you must. You can even use your spyglass. But we walk alone."

Silas took hold of Joanna's free arm and tugged her away from Crockett. "I don't like it, Jo. He's a stranger."

"You're the one who brought him here, Daddy."

Crockett hid a grin. Joanna might not wield a Colt .45 like her father did, but her marksmanship was flawless nonetheless. The old man looked as if he'd swallowed a prickly pear.

"He's a preacher," she reminded her father as she gently yet firmly extricated herself from his hold. "I'll be fine."

Joanna moved to Crockett's side and reclaimed his arm. "Shall we?" Her smile was all for show. He could tell by the tremble of her fingers against his coat sleeve and the way her gaze flitted between his eyes and his left ear.

He deliberately waited to respond until her eyes flickered back to his. Then he winked, feeling more himself than he had in hours.

Her brows arched and her eyes widened. Then the edge of her mouth twitched with the beginnings of a genuine grin.

The stress he'd carried since being forced off the train fell from Crockett's shoulders, and he found himself answering her grin with one of his own. "Lead the way, Miss Robbins."

"You got yer knife?" Silas barked out from behind them.

Joanna sighed but twisted her neck to answer. "Yes, sir."

Crockett glanced over his shoulder, as well, and was immediately gutted by a glare that promised dire consequences should any harm befall the lady at his side.

"She knows how to use a blade, Parson." Silas retrieved his own knife from the sheath attached to his gun belt and ran his thumb along the sharpened edge. "Taught her myself. You might wanna keep that in mind during your stroll."

"A comforting notion, indeed," Crockett quipped, "seeing as how I'm without a weapon. I'll be sure to let her take charge of our defense should we come across any bandits."

Silas glowered at his barb, but Crockett ignored it. Joanna Robbins could probably handle a variety of weapons with a skill that would put most men to shame, but Crockett's gut told him she wasn't the type to use them unless forced.

And the more he watched Silas interact with his daughter, the more certain Crockett became that the man was more bluster than bite. In fact, he reminded him a lot of his brother Travis. Oh, if push came to shove, he would strike and strike hard. Until then, however, he'd just growl out the meanest warnings he could think of.

"I'll be watching, preacher man." With a flick of his wrist, Silas flung his knife. The tip of the blade stabbed the earth a mere inch from Crockett's boot.

Crockett's pulse ricocheted in his neck, but he resisted the urge to jump back. Raising his gaze from the hilt of the knife to Silas's face, Crockett watched victory flare in his adversary's eyes. Perhaps the old dog had teeth after all.

"And Joanna," Silas said with a point of his finger, "if you're not back in an hour, I'm comin' to fetch you, private matter or not. Understand me?"

"Yes, Daddy."

Apparently the pixie had challenged the dragon enough for one day.

Feeling as if she were trapped in an hourglass with sand threatening to bury her if she didn't get all her words out in time, Joanna blurted out her desires the moment they reached the road and were safely out of her father's hearing.

"I prayed for a preacher to come."

Mr. Archer's stride stuttered a bit, but he recovered quickly. "Why do you need one?"

She tugged her hand from his arm and focused on the ground in front of her as they walked. Touching him was a distraction she could ill afford at that moment. And though his voice sounded kind and politely curious, she suddenly felt very young and foolish. Why was it that thoughts and plans always made more sense when confined to one's mind than when they exited one's mouth?

"To save my father's soul."

The crunch of the parson's footfalls ceased. Joanna plodded on, however, sure he would snap out of his stupor momentarily. Besides, it was easier to keep moving than to look at whatever shocked expression surely lined his face.

"He's a good-hearted man." She rushed to add, "Truly," before he could dispute the point. "My father might not open himself up to many, but when he does, he gives his all. You should have seen the way he loved my mother. She softened him, he said. Made him laugh. Made him a better man. I tend to think he was always a good man; he just needed someone to believe in him. Losing her nearly broke him."

They passed beneath the shadow of a large oak, and Joanna fought down the sadness that stirred at the thought of her mother. "He made a point to stay strong for me. For his men. For our ranch. He's not one to let down the people who depend on him."

"Yet he holds up trains." Brother Archer's long legs caught him up to her quickly.

She snuck a peek at him. His furrowed brow spoke more of a man wrestling to make sense of a contradiction than of one handing down tacit disapproval. Thanking the Lord for small miracles, she continued her explanation.

"He's been an honest rancher for sixteen years." Joanna kicked at a pebble in the road in front of her, her hackles rising in her father's defense. "In his younger days he might have robbed a few stagecoaches and a handful of trains, but he's reformed."

"Begging your pardon, miss," the parson interrupted her. The laughter she heard in his voice rankled. "But the man I met today held a carload of rail passengers at gunpoint and abducted one of them. He doesn't seem all that reformed to me."

Joanna spun to face him, words coiling inside her like a nest of baby rattlers. "Can't you see that he only did what he did out of love?" Her hand slashed the air. "I don't condone his methods, but his motives were pure. He had no idea what I wanted with a preacher. If he did, he likely never would have fetched you. All he knew was that I missed my mama. Since she and I always attended services together, he must've hoped that having a preacher at hand would ease my grief a little. That's what drove him. Not some twisted need to terrorize people."

Mr. Archer said nothing. He simply stared at her as if she were an oddity in a curiosity shop. Maybe that's what she was. Heaven knew that's how she felt most days. Odd Joanna Robbins. The girl who'd rather hide away in her father's loft with her paints than attend a barn dance. The one who never knew what to say or how to fit in. Whose skin was too pale, freckles too plentiful, and eyes too colorless to ever catch a beau. Hair that resembled copper wire fresh from the spool, its coils springing every which way no matter how many pins she scraped against her scalp.

Some of the starch went out of her. What did she expect? That this stranger whom her father had held at gunpoint and dragged all over creation would be moved by her impassioned plea? The man was only walking with her as a means to an end. He wanted his freedom, and she was the price he was being forced to pay. Man of God he might be, but he was still a man—one who had every right to resent her and her family.

Joanna turned from him and set off through the trees. Thankfully, he followed. She could hear his boots crunching the dry grass and dead twigs behind her. The usual route between her house and the church took about twenty minutes, and while she lived closer to the building than any of her neighbors, today the distance stretched too far. Cutting across the open field would save them about five minutes. With her father no doubt counting down each tick of the clock until he could storm out to fetch her, five minutes might prove crucial.

Soon the back of the old church came into view. A door at the rear led to the previous parson's personal quarters, which he'd built onto the building so as not to be a burden to the area families who felt obligated to take him into their already overcrowded homes.

Hackberry trees lined the sides of the weathered clapboard structure, their small, dark purple fruit littering the ground. Joanna tromped past them and rounded the corner to the steepled front entrance.

Whether Mr. Crockett Archer was a direct answer to her prayers or just some unfortunate fellow her father happened to kidnap, he was here, and she wasn't about to pass up the opportunity she'd been given.

She waited until her companion emerged from around the corner, then gestured to the decaying building. "Do you see this church, Mr. Archer?"

The long-legged stranger propped a boot on one of the front steps and pressed his forearm into his thigh. He made a great show of examining the old structure, tilting his head back to take in the very tip of the spire. "Yes, ma'am. I do."

Joanna inhaled a fortifying breath, braced her hand against the balustrade, and set her chin. "I want to bring it back to life."

5

Bring it back to life?" Crockett echoed, pretty sure his strolling partner was talking about more than slapping on a new coat of paint but wanting to hear the details from her. He'd stopped making assumptions when it came to the Robbins clan.

"Yes." Joanna stared him down as if expecting him to laugh, but Crockett felt no such compulsion. What he felt was a burgeoning curiosity.

Unless he'd missed his guess, Miss Joanna Robbins possessed the soul of a missionary. How that had come to be when she'd been raised by an outlaw and his gang, Crockett couldn't fathom. Yet he sensed her passion. Respected it. He'd not belittle her dream.

Crockett straightened his stance and angled his head toward her. "I'm listening."

The defiance in her eyes softened, as did her posture. She loosened her grip on the balustrade and used it as a pivot to swing herself toward the chapel steps. After climbing three, she smoothed her navy blue skirt beneath her and took a seat on one of the slightly warped boards that had once been a proper stair.

Joanna nibbled the edge of her bottom lip and turned her attention to the sky, as if searching for a place to start. While he waited for her to find the words she sought, Crockett claimed the bottom step, braced his back against the rails, and stretched his legs across the width of the stairs.

"My mother was a godly woman who believed her life's foremost duty lay in leading the members of her family to Christ." His companion's quiet voice drew Crockett's head around. Joanna's gaze no longer peered into the heavens but rested firmly upon her lap, where her palms lay open like a book that held a story only her eyes could see.

"When she died last year, that responsibility fell to me." A quiver vibrated her breath as she paused to inhale. "I'm afraid I'm not up to the task."

An urge to debate that point shot through Crockett, startling him with its vehemence. Why he should feel the need to defend her against her own self-criticism, he couldn't imagine. He'd just met the girl, knew next to nothing about her. However, the burden she carried was palpable, to the point of nearly being visible upon her slender shoulders. Her capabilities or lack thereof were not the issue at the moment. Her weary spirit was begging for someone to lighten her load—if only for a few minutes. God had placed him here to be that someone. Crockett held his tongue and waited for Joanna to continue. He'd take on as much as he could for as long as he could, and when he left, if God was merciful, he'd take it with him.

"She begged me not to give up on Daddy. To keep sowing seeds and praying that the Lord would lead them to fertile ground so they could take root." Joanna gave a tiny sniff and jerked her chin skyward again, blinking against the afternoon sunlight. Or an unwanted tear. "I've tried. Lord knows how I've tried. But I don't have Mama's patience. And without her to lean on, the discouragement grows too heavy."

Finally her eyes met his. "I need help, Mr. Archer. I need a preacher to bring this old church back to life. One who can inspire a community to revive its dormant faith and reach past the barricades erected around a stubborn ex-outlaw's heart to save the bruised soul within."

Pieces of the sermon he'd prepared for the church in Brenham rose unbidden in Crockett's mind. His fiery call to evangelism. His encouragement to seek out lost souls from among those close to home. To testify with actions as well as words. How no soul is beyond the reach of grace. Crockett raised a hand and rubbed away the prickle at the base of his neck.

"I understand you have another commitment, so I will not ask you to take on this mission," Joanna said. "But surely you know other ministers—men who might be interested in such a position. All I ask is that you pass on word of our need. And if you see fit, make a recommendation."

"A recommendation?" Crockett sputtered before he could stop himself.

Joanna stiffened, her shoulders squaring off as she thrust out her chin. "And why not? Our pasture may be small, but our sheep are just as worthy of a shepherd as any other. Or are you the type to condemn an entire community for the mistake of one man?"

"Mistake? It's not like what happened to me was an accident, Miss Robbins. Your father plotted his actions in advance, and as far as I can tell, feels not one speck of remorse."

"Because his motives were pure!"

Crockett held his hands up in conciliation. "Fine. I'll concede that his actions were driven by his desire to please his daughter, but that doesn't make them acceptable. How can I honestly recommend a position here to a colleague? The only men I've met out here are train robbers and kidnappers."

"'They that are whole have no need of the physician, but they that are sick,'" Joanna recited.

The words of Christ pierced Crockett's heart and deflated his defenses. "'I came not to call the righteous, but sinners to repentance.'" The remainder of the quote fell from his lips and lashed his conscience like a whip. "Forgive me, Miss Robbins. You're right, of course. I *can* recommend. With caution, certainly, but with sincerity, too."

And if the Lord was leading him in the direction Crockett believed, there just might be a young minister who would be grateful for an alternative position once the elders in Brenham made their decision. He'd be sure to mention the possibility to him.

"Thank you, Brother Archer. I'll be praying that God will lead the right man to us. *Without* my father's help this time."

Her smile asserted itself once again, and Crockett found himself returning it.

He laughed a deep chuckle that unknotted his belly and expelled the last of his resentment. Joanna's soft chimes added to the music, and for the first time, Crockett was actually glad to be exactly where he was.

"So, how did this old place come to be abandoned?" he asked, his gaze lifting to trace the outline of the neglected building.

"A few years back, the folks over at Deanville offered our preacher a church in town. They already had a cotton gin and grist mill and plans for a school. New families were moving in. It was a good opportunity for him, and I don't blame him for taking it."

"But it left you without a minister."

She nodded, looking back at her hands. "Some of the folks who live farther north make the trip into town on Sundays for services. Most in the area, though, find the journey too long. It's a good ten miles into Deanville from our place, and many live farther away." Joanna grasped the rail nearest her hip and stroked it as if it were the arm of a dear friend. "This old building sits right in the center of the largest cluster of farms and ranches. No one in the area has to travel more than five miles to reach its doors. We still gather here for socials on occasion, but we haven't come together for worship in over two years. I miss it."

The longing in her voice struck a familiar chord. Hadn't he hungered for the same thing? For a community of believers to worship with outside his immediate family? His brothers had been his church for longer than he could remember, and while he loved them and found their encouragement and support invaluable, something within him had cried out for a broader community. For different opinions and perspectives. For friendship. For mentorship. For prayer. When Amos Ralston took Crockett under his wing and introduced him to the congregation in Palestine, he'd felt as if he'd been invited to a feast. What an emptiness it would leave to have that taken away.

Crockett leaned forward and touched Joanna's hand. "I will help you find a new preacher. I promise."

She stared at him a long moment, then nodded. "I believe you."

Joanna quickly ducked her chin and tugged her hand from his. She pushed to her feet, and minding his manners, Crockett stood, as well. His attention lagged behind, however, remembering the passion in her eyes, the determination etching her brow.

In the last three years, he'd met many women. Young. Old. Pretty. Plain. Devout. Flirtatious. After living only among men for years, he found he enjoyed the company of women. Their gracious manners. Their gentle ways. Their lovely figures. But never had he felt anything deeper than a surface admiration. Perhaps because he'd been so focused on his training. Yet after only a handful of minutes, Joanna Robbins had touched something deep inside him, as only a kindred spirit could do.

She'd experienced the Lord's call on her life as surely as he had. And while he'd been called to minister to many, she'd been called for one. Who was he to say her calling was any less significant than his own? In fact, her dedication to the one in her care humbled him, gave him a perspective he'd been lacking. In other circumstances, he could easily imagine the two of them becoming friends. Maybe after he settled in Brenham, he could write to her, encourage her.

One thing was for certain. He'd keep his promise. An Archer never went back on his word. Joanna Robbins would get her preacher. It just wouldn't be him.

"So I guess this means I owe you the use of a horse." She smiled up at him as she dusted her hands together. "You held up your end of the bargain, after all."

Crockett tipped his hat. "As much as I've enjoyed our walk, I really do need to be on my way. I'm sure the congregation in Brenham is concerned for my safety."

She led him to a path that meandered back toward the road. "Is that where you preach?"

"I've spoken there on two occasions," Crockett answered. "Tomorrow was to be my third. I'm hoping to be selected for a permanent position there."

"And my father's ill-timed interruption has put that position in jeopardy, hasn't it." She halted, her expression pained. "I'm truly sorry."

Crockett drew even with her and gestured for her to continue on. "Don't fret, Miss Robbins. My future is in God's hands. All will be well."

"I wish I had your faith," she said, not yet moving.

"I wish I had your horse." He shot her a wink to let her know he was teasing. Mostly.

Joanna grinned, then dutifully resumed her march toward home. Crockett stayed close to her side, enjoying her company now that the tension hovering over them had lifted.

She was telling him something about the creek that ran behind the old church when his senses suddenly sharpened.

Someone was watching them.

Crockett swiveled his head, searching the empty road behind him and then scanning the trees like he used to do at the ranch when standing guard. A movement caught his eye. Furtive. Menacing. Near the blackjack oak they'd just passed to the left of the road. His muscles grew taut, and for the second time that day, he reached for a holster that wasn't there.

A figure jumped from behind the tree. The glimpse of a rifle barrel was all Crockett needed. He grabbed Joanna, ignoring her startled cry as well as her resistance. He pressed her to his chest and curved his larger body around hers, shielding her from the attack.

"Get your hands off my woman, mister, or I'm gonna put a new crease in them fancy duds of yours."

Joanna wiggled against the parson's protective hold. She recognized that bothersome voice. And as soon as she found her freedom, she was gonna strangle the scrawny throat it came from.

She shoved against Brother Archer's chest, a rather firm and well-muscled chest that never would have given way to her puny efforts, she was sure, had she not muttered some disparaging comment about the man's intelligence that finally seemed to clue him in to their lack of true danger.

Once free, Joanna darted around the preacher, dodged the rapidly lowering rifle, and smacked Jackson Spivey upside the head.

"Owww, Jo," the twelve-year-old whined as he jerked away. "What'd ya go and do that for? He's the one that grabbed ya."

"He never laid a hand on me until you jumped out at us like some crazed coyote. What were you thinking, waving a gun around like that? You could've hurt somebody!" Joanna's chest heaved as she dug her fingernails into her palm in a bid for control. "You got no business spying on me, Jackson, or making ridiculous claims on me."

The sandy-haired boy set his mouth in a mutinous line and stretched himself to his full height, which put the top of his head at least an inch above hers. How was she supposed to give him a good dressing down when she had to look up to do it?

"It ain't ridiculous, Jo." His rebellious eyes dared her to contradict him. "Soon as I get old enough to offer for you all proper like, I'm gonna. I done told ya that. And I won't hold with no fancy-pants rooster moving in on my territory in the meantime."

Jackson's eyes narrowed and shifted to Joanna's right, where Brother Archer had come to stand.

Could mortification kill a person? Because at that moment, she was feeling precariously close to expiring.

"You do much hunting, Jackson?" The parson's deep voice rumbled beside her, but it was his question that took her off guard. So nonchalant and . . . well . . . man-to-manish.

Jackson glowered at him. "Now and then."

"Winchester's a good gun. That the '73 Carbine?" The parson stepped forward, his attention on the rifle.

"Yep."

"I prefer the sporting rifle, myself. Longer barrel, more cartridges. But the carbine is lighter weight. Better for when a man's on foot. You clean it after every hunt?"

"Yes, sir."

Joanna's jaw nearly came unhinged. With a few simple questions, Brother Archer had drained all the posturing right out of the boy. Jackson was even holding the rifle up to the preacher for his inspection.

"That's good." The parson smiled and clasped the boy's shoulder in praise. Something that almost looked like pride flashed across Jackson's face. "Make sure you keep it oiled even when you're not hunting. A man's weapon can save his life. You can't get lazy with its upkeep."

"No, sir. I always clean it real good. Pa's, too, when he's . . . ah . . . sick." Jackson's gaze dropped to the ground and stayed there while he kicked at a dirt clod.

Joanna ached for Jackson's embarrassment. He might be a pest and the cause of more headaches than she cared to count, but he only acted that way because he was starved for attention. His pa was a no-account drunk who spent more time at the saloon in Deanville than at home. Jackson had basically been rearing himself for the five years since his ma up and ran off. Which was why Joanna usually didn't put up much of a fuss when he came around and pestered her. But today he'd gone too far.

Brother Archer didn't seem offended, though. Instead he smiled at the boy as if Jackson hadn't just aimed the very weapon they were discussing at his back and threatened bodily harm. As far as she could tell, the parson had no intention of taking the boy to task for his actions. Yet the next man Jackson took aim at might not be so forgiving. *Someone* had to set the boy straight, and apparently that duty fell to her.

"Your pa get sick often?" Brother Archer asked before Joanna could regain her footing in the conversation.

Jackson shrugged, still staring at the dirt. "Often enough."

"Ever had to use your gun to ward off trouble when he was feelin' poorly?"

He ventured a glance up, his eyes wary. "Some."

"Two-legged trouble?" The parson's passive face revealed nothing of his thoughts. His voice remained calm, giving no sign that he felt any of the alarm rising within her own breast. She knew Jackson had it hard, but she never imagined him fighting off trouble harsh enough to require weaponry.

"Once or twice." The boy's matter-of-fact tone left Joanna certain that he'd understated the frequency.

"Why didn't you tell me, Jackson?" Joanna reached out a hand to him, but he shied away, shooting her a glare that made it clear he'd not welcome her pity. "You should have asked for help. My father could have—"

"I handle my own problems."

"With what? A gun?"

He bristled at her, but she didn't care. The kid was twelve years old, for pity's sake. He shouldn't be wielding anything more deadly than a slingshot.

Brother Archer's hand came to rest at the small of her back. The touch was so brief she barely registered the warmth of his fingers before it disappeared, but the surprise of it scattered her thoughts.

"Sometimes it takes a gun."

Shock stole Joanna's breath. How could he stand there and say such a thing? He was a man of God. A man of peace. "He's just a boy!" She flung the accusation at him, but it bounced off his stoic shoulders without an ounce of impact.

"Some boys grow into men slowly," Brother Archer said, his attention trained on Jackson, as if his answer were more for him than Joanna. "Others have manhood thrust upon them whether they're ready for it or not.

"I was eleven when my father died, leaving my brother, Travis, and me to run the ranch, care for our two younger brothers, and defend our home from those who thought they could take it from us. We grew up fast because we had to. Used our guns for the same reason. But all those years, the fear that I might one day have to kill a man haunted me. Nothing scars a man's soul like taking a life, whether justified or not."

A shiver crept down Joanna's back. What kind of parson was this? Weren't preachers supposed to be gentle, compassionate creatures, preferring words to weapons? Crockett Archer sounded more like her outlaw father than a preacher. Perhaps it was a good thing he had other ministerial commitments keeping him from starting up her church.

"Did ya ever hafta do it?" Jackson's low tone rumbled with trepidation. "Kill a man?"

Joanna held her breath, waiting for the answer.

"No, thank the Lord." Brother Archer lifted his face heavenward and closed his eyes for a moment before turning back to Jackson. "Every time you point a gun at someone, though, you run that risk." He paused to glance meaningfully at the carbine in the boy's hand. "A wise man draws his weapon only in the direst of circumstances."

Jackson swallowed hard, his Adam's apple bobbing in his throat. But he nodded—nodded with the maturity of a young man, not a boy. And suddenly Joanna didn't care if Crockett Archer was like other preachers. He had a gift for reaching people. A gift that could make him more valuable to her than the most rousing speaker or genteel scholar.

"Name's Crockett, by the way," the parson said, his face breaking into a smile that banished the solemnity hovering over the trio. "Crockett Archer." He offered his hand, and Jackson shifted the hold on his rifle in order to shake it.

"Crockett? As in Davy Crockett?"

"Yep." The twinkle Joanna had noted earlier returned to the parson's eyes. "My ma named all us boys after men who fought at the Alamo."

Jackson scrunched up his nose. "Why didn't she just call ya Davy?"

Brother Archer laughed, and the rich sound spread through Joanna's chest like molasses on hot oatmeal. "Crockett's not so bad. My younger brother got saddled with Bowie."

"Yer pullin' my leg."

"Nope. That's his name. Although Pa eventually took pity on him and dubbed him Jim. We only use Bowie now when we're wantin' to needle him."

He spoke of his brothers with such affection, Joanna found herself wanting to delve deeper into the Archer clan's history. Until she remembered he was leaving.

"Jackson," she said, feeling a bit like an interloper when two sets of male eyes fastened on her as if they'd just been reminded of her presence. "Mr. Archer needs to get back to the ranch. He has to ride into Deanville before nightfall."

"What's the rush? Ain't he gonna stay for your birthday supper?"

For a boy who'd tried to run the man off a few minutes ago, he sure seemed eager for him to stay.

"He has a previous engagement."

Jackson's brow furrowed. "If it's so important, why'd he come here in the first place?"

"Ha!" The preacher grinned and elbowed Jackson in the ribs. "Her father kid—"

"—*interrupted* his travel plans and persuaded Mr. Archer to come for a short visit in honor of my birthday tomorrow." Joanna shot Crockett a glance that begged him to keep the details to himself. "Unfortunately, because of a pressing appointment, he won't be staying for this evening's supper. But I fully expect to see you there, Jackson. Six o'clock, sharp. You hear?"

"You still gonna have cake?"

"Made a chocolate one this morning."

His grin nearly engulfed his face. "I'll be there."

Joanna hid her pleasure as the boy set off across the field. She'd guessed right. She'd questioned him the other day under the guise of having him help her decide what dessert to use to celebrate her birthday but hoping to discern *his* favorite. Her mama had always made apple pie, knowing Joanna preferred the fruity pastry over cake. But making a pie without Mama didn't seem right, so she'd opted to celebrate with something new. Watching Jackson devour her cake would be a gift in itself.

"Why'd you cut me off back there?" The parson's question brought Joanna back to the present. "I had a great yarn ready to go."

She much preferred his current good humor to the barely leashed indignation he'd displayed when her father had first presented him to her, but she couldn't let him endanger her family, even with a seemingly harmless tale.

"Jackson doesn't know about my father's past. No one outside the ranch does."

"But . . ." His voice trailed off.

Joanna bit back the retort that sprang to her lips. There was no reason for Brother Archer to act so surprised. It wasn't as if reformed outlaws went around telling tales of their exploits at parties to entertain the neighbors.

"I already told you that he's been making an honest living as a rancher for the last sixteen years. Folks around here know him as the owner of the Lazy R. That's all they need to know. That's who he is." She crossed her arms over her middle, determined to drive her point home, when all at once it occurred to her there was another risk she'd managed to overlook.

Crockett Archer.

He knew the truth about her father, had experienced it firsthand. When he got to Deanville, the town marshal was sure to hound him with questions.

Her arms went limp and unfolded of their own accord. "Will you turn him in?" She stepped closer to him, wanting to grab the lapels of his coat but fisting her hands in her skirt instead. "Please. He meant no harm. You were inconvenienced"—a vision of him trussed up like a calf at roundup time flashed through her mind, stirring her conscience—"and mistreated to a certain extent, I suppose, but surely not to the point where you wouldn't be able to extend forgiveness to a man who was simply trying to give his daughter a gift."

The parson's brown eyes hardened, but when his palm closed around her shoulder, the gentleness of his touch instilled hope.

"I won't lie to cover up anything, Miss Robbins," he said, "but neither will I seek retribution. You have my word."

"And if the marshal presses you for details?"

"I'll do my best to be vague, but I will not dishonor my calling with lying. Sin carries consequences. And while a man might escape earthly repercussions, his soul cannot escape the eternal ones. Not without a Savior."

"I know," Joanna murmured, her heart squeezing painfully in her chest. "That's why my father needs more time. Please give him that."

Brother Archer tightened his grip on her shoulder for an instant, then stepped away. "I'll do what I can."

But would it be enough?

7

Crockett couldn't seem to extricate Joanna Robbins from his mind during his ride to Deanville. Every time he started to mentally compose a telegram message for the Brenham elders or review his sermon points, memories of a certain redhead intruded.

The woman was a series of contradictions. His first impression had marked her as a shy, timid creature, yet she defended her father with fiery passion. And when given the chance to solicit help for her mission, she finagled time alone to plead with a stranger. Her wild hair and elfin features were more girlish than womanly when it came to feminine charms; but when her eyes sparked with humor or enthusiasm, her face lit up in a way that made his breath catch. And though she fussed at Jackson Spivey as if he were the bane of her existence, she went out of her way to include him in her birthday supper.

Yep. Joanna Robbins was the kind of woman a man could take his whole life trying to figure out. Not that he was in the market for that kind of puzzle. He had enough to worry about with solidifying his position in Brenham.

Perhaps he could check in on her after he was settled, though. They'd forged an odd sort of friendship, after all, during their brief encounter. Then again, that might prove awkward for whomever she found to fill the pulpit of that old church of hers. Better to focus on the here and now and let tomorrow take care of itself.

Deanville was a tiny place compared to Palestine and Brenham, but it boasted all the necessities of an up-and-coming town—general store, schoolhouse, cotton gin, grist mill, saloon, and two churches. He wondered which of the two was shepherded by the preacher who'd left Joanna's church.

Crockett dropped his horse off at the livery and paid for its board, instructing the stable hand that the animal would be collected by someone from the Lazy R in a day or two. Then, after untying his travel bag, which Joanna's father had returned to him with a belligerent glare, he solicited directions to the telegraph office.

Crossing to the opposite side of the road, Crockett sidestepped a farmer hefting a pair of feed sacks into a wagon bed and tipped his hat to a middle-aged woman carrying a market basket who'd halted to stare at him outside a shop window that read *Dean's Store*.

"Ma'am." He offered one of his most charming smiles. The woman nodded in return, yet he felt her disapproving stare follow him down the street. He was several steps past the store when the rattle of the door and the soft jangle of a bell announced the end of her perusal and the resumption of her shopping.

He probably looked a sight in his rumpled suit coat and dirt-stained trousers. The Lord only knew what the woman must've thought of him. A hot bath and change of clothes would work wonders, but they would have to wait. He had to contact the Brenham church.

The telegraph office stood a few yards north of the general store, a tiny shack of a building with wires strung from wooden poles stationed behind it. Crockett entered and strode to the counter. A short man wearing black sleeve protectors sat hunched over a desk, scribbling furiously as the machine beside him clicked out a pattern of long and short signals. When the clicks ceased, the operator tapped back a brief response, then pushed to his feet.

"What can I do for you, mister?" The fellow's mustache twitched as he talked.

Crockett grinned. "I need to send a wire to Brenham."

The operator shoved a tablet across the counter to him and reached above his ear to extricate a pencil. "Nickel a word."

"Thanks." Crockett wrote out his message, then struck through as many words as possible. He handed the paper back to the operator and tossed a fifty-cent piece onto the counter.

ABDUCTED FROM TRAIN.
RELEASED.
IN DEANVILLE.
WILL ARRIVE LATE TOMORROW.

As the operator scanned the message, his eyebrows arched high onto his forehead. "I done heard about that holdup this morning. The wire's been buzzin' with it for hours. You telling me *you're* the fellow those bandits took from the train?"

Crockett hardened his gaze. If he answered one question it would only open the floodgate for myriad more. "Just send the telegram, please. To Mr. Lukas Hoffmann."

"How'd you escape?" The little man leaned his elbows on the counter and stared up at him, nearly salivating in anticipation of a tale Crockett had no intention of telling. Telegram contents were supposed to remain confidential, but something told him this particular operator relished juicy tidbits too much to keep them to himself.

Crockett braced his palms atop the counter near the operator's elbows and bent his head close enough to growl his response in the man's ear. "Send the telegram."

The man jerked backward. "No need to get your dander up, mister. I's just curious." He carried the paper back to his desk. "Wanna wait for a reply?"

"I'll stop back in after I clean up a bit. That is, if you can direct me to a place where a fella can buy a bath."

"Harold's Barber Shop, across the street. And the boardinghouse is around the corner if you need a place to hang your hat for the night."

"Thanks." Crockett nodded to the operator and turned for the door, his gut telling him that news of his arrival would be all over town before his bathwater cooled.

Maybe he was wrong. Maybe the little operator with the big mustache really did keep things to himself. Maybe he just wanted to assuage his own curiosity. But as Crockett approached the barber shop, a reflection flashed in the window of a man with dark sleeve protectors scurrying down the street. Crockett sighed. Maybe he better make his bath a quick one.

Fifteen minutes later, dressed in his spare trousers and a clean blue chambray shirt, Crockett tucked his soiled suit under his arm and opened the small bathing chamber's door. A man with a tin star on the lapel of his dark gray coat stood waiting on the other side.

"Evening, stranger."

"Evening." Crockett adjusted his grip on his satchel and summoned a smile for the lawman as he stepped past him.

"Thought you might like to share a cup of coffee with me over at the office, so's we can get better acquainted." The man didn't lay a hand on him, but the authority in his voice gave his suggestion the weight of a command.

Crockett slowed his step. "That's mighty neighborly of you, Marshal, but I've had a rather trying day. Perhaps we can visit tomorrow?"

"Won't take long, son." The barrel-chested lawman strode forward, firmly took charge of Crockett's bag, and extricated his clothes from beneath his arm. "Harold will secure a room for you at Bessie's place and see that your belongings are delivered." He handed the bag and clothes to the barber, a thin man with heavily pomaded hair. Then he dug out a coin from his vest pocket and pressed it into the barber's hand.

"Harold, have Miss Bessie clean and press our guest's suit. On me."

"Yes, sir, Marshal Coleson. I'll see to it." Harold spun around and headed to the front of his shop while the marshal gestured toward a side door.

"After you, mister."

Out of options, Crockett nodded and moved toward the exit. "Of course."

Once outside, the lawman steered him back in the direction of the livery, to a stone building boasting an uninviting small barred window high up the south wall. The glass-paned window at the front promised a warmer reception, but Crockett's chest only tightened as his promise to Joanna ran circles in his mind.

The inside of the marshal's office was dim but tidy, the man's desk empty except for an inkstand and a half-finished plate of food. Crockett frowned. The man had left his supper to chase him down. Such a man wouldn't be easily put off.

"What's your name, son?" the marshal asked as he dragged a chair from against the wall to a spot nearer his desk.

"Crockett Archer, sir."

"Brett Coleson." He offered his hand and shook Crockett's with an iron grip. "Have a seat, Archer."

The man's age and manner reminded Crockett of Silas Robbins, and an odd sort of recognition filled him as he took his seat. Marshal Coleson moved past him to the stove behind his desk, where a coffeepot sat waiting.

"Thanks for taking care of my laundry," Crockett interjected into the growing silence. "You didn't have to do that."

The lawman filled a chipped crockery mug, set it on the desk in front of Crockett, and then grabbed his own half-full one and splashed in a couple inches of fresh brew to reheat the dregs. "Glad to do it, son. You've had a trying day, after all." The marshal peered meaningfully at him over the top of the pot as he echoed Crockett's earlier words. "One I'd like to hear more about."

Crockett grasped the mug's handle and held it between the desk and his lips. "What would you like to know?"

"Is it true that you're the man those bandits took from the Gulf, Colorado, and Santa Fe this morning?"

"Yes."

Coleson lowered himself into his chair and took a swig from his mug as if he had all night to get the answers he sought. "What'd they want with you?"

A rueful grin slid into place on Crockett's face. "You wouldn't believe me if I told you."

"Try me."

Crockett shook his head, then met the lawman's eye without flinching. "I was supposed to be a birthday present."

Coleson held his gaze, assessing. Silence stretched, but Crockett didn't turn away. He left himself as open as possible, hoping to disarm the marshal with his honesty so that the vague answers he'd be forced to give later might cause less suspicion.

Finally Coleson blinked. "You know those fellers?"

"Nope. I was as surprised as anyone when they forced me from the train. I thank the Lord they decided they didn't need me after all and let me go. I'm supposed to be in Brenham tomorrow."

"That's right," Coleson said, lifting his cup. "The witness accounts said the men were looking for a preacher. Seems like a strange request for a gang of outlaws."

"Doesn't it, though? They didn't even steal anyone's belongings, even when the passengers offered them up. I tell you, this adventure will make a great tale to add to a sermon. Jesus warned that he will return like a thief in the night. I experienced a thief in the daylight, but it was certainly no less unexpected. Goes to show one must always be ready to meet one's Maker."

"I reckon so." Coleson thumbed his hat back on his forehead. "You hear any names or see any faces you could identify?"

"They wore bandanas over their faces." Which was true—at least for the first part of the encounter. Crockett worked to change the direction of the conversation before Coleson demanded more details. "I appreciate your thoroughness, Marshal, but I won't be pressing charges." Crockett set his mug down, scraped the chair backward, and stood. "The men let me go, and except for a little inconvenience, no harm was done. Besides, what kind of parson would I be if I preached forgiveness from the pulpit but failed to extend it to those who do me wrong?"

"No charges, huh?" Coleson gained his feet, as well, his eyes narrowing slightly, as if he saw right through the conversational maneuver. "Well, I guess that's your right. The railroad might take a different stand, though, so your testimony is still needed."

"Of course." Crockett edged toward the door. "I'll be sure to leave my home address with the boardinghouse proprietress, in case you hear from the railroad." Praying that would prove sufficient, Crockett lifted a hand in parting. "Thanks for the coffee."

"You know, Archer," Coleson called out before Crockett could reach the door, "justice is a biblical concept, too. A man is to be held accountable for his crimes. To make restitution. Or don't you think the book of Exodus applies today?"

Crockett held his face carefully blank, despite the fact that every nerve ending in his body seemed to be sending alarms to his brain.

Marshal Coleson stepped around the desk. "It sticks in my craw when a criminal eludes justice. Reminds me of a gang I chased around Texas the first couple years I served as a Ranger. They were the only outlaws I chased that never gave in to greed. Smart, really, seeing as greed is what leads most thieves to their ruin. They never went after army pay wagons, government shipments, or banks. I'm guessing because they were too well guarded. They seemed content to rob stage passengers and an occasional railcar. And because no one was ever injured in the robberies, most lawmen saw them more as a nuisance than a serious threat."

He moved closer, his eyes locked on Crockett's. "They up and disappeared fifteen or so years back. Strange how your kidnapping is suddenly bringing them back to mind." He raised a brow. "Always bothered me that them yahoos didn't pay for their misdeeds. Thievin's wrong, no matter how little is taken."

"Indeed it is, Marshal," Crockett hurried to agree. "But remember, though all will be held accountable for their actions on the Day of Judgment, justice is not always achieved through men's efforts."

"Mmm," the lawman murmured noncommittally. "The witnesses had a sense the outlaws you encountered were older men." Coleson obviously wasn't ready to let the matter drop just yet. "Gray hair, stiff gaits. What did you obser—"

The door swung open, cutting off Coleson's question. "Howdy, Marshal." The telegraph operator rushed through the opening, oblivious to the tension filling the room. Crockett felt like kissing the little weasel—or at least bear-hugging him.

"A reply came from Brenham for you, Mr. Archer. Thought you'd want to see it right away."

8

Crockett reached for the slip of paper in the operator's hand and managed to sidle around the fellow, putting the little man squarely between him and the marshal. "You're a godsend, my friend." He tossed the operator a coin for his most timely interruption and turned back to Coleson.

"I'm afraid this is rather urgent, Marshal. Would you excuse me?" He reached behind him for the door frame, eager to make his escape.

Coleson crossed his arms over his chest, his expression none too pleased. "You really ought to press charges, Parson. If not for yourself, then for the poor fella they choose to kidnap next time. Do you want his fate on your hands?"

Recalling the way Joanna had taken her father to task over the day's shenanigans, Crockett felt certain Silas Robbins wouldn't be attempting any future clerical abductions. The train-riding preachers of the area should be safe.

"Your concern is well-meaning, Marshal, but unnecessary." Crockett backed fully into the doorway, pleased when the lawman made no move to stop him. "Today's events were instigated by a misunderstanding that has since been cleared up. These men pose no further threat. Therefore, I insist on extending forgiveness. I'll not be filing charges. Good day."

Crockett hesitated a moment longer, but the instant the marshal grunted and waved him off, he dashed through the door and made for the boardinghouse. He stuffed the telegram in his pocket as he went, afraid that if he paused to read it now, Coleson might corner him again. Better to save it for the privacy of his room.

Orange and red streaked the sky to the west, hailing evening's rapid approach. Crockett lengthened his stride as he rounded the corner where the now-darkened barber shop stood and searched for some kind of a placard to identify the boardinghouse.

The side street only boasted three homes, none of them very large. But the second one on the left had a porch lantern lit. Like a ship seeking safe harbor, Crockett aimed for the welcoming light, hoping his knock wouldn't disrupt a family's meal.

A woman tall enough to look him in the eye answered the door. "Yes?"

He doffed his hat. "Evenin', ma'am. I'm looking for Miss Bessie's boardinghouse."

"Ya found it." She turned and started off down the hall, leaving the door gaping behind her. "Scrape your boots afore ya come in. I don't abide no boarders trailing mud on my rugs." Her voice filtered back to him and smacked him into action like a wooden spoon across the knuckles.

Crockett darted to the edge of the porch. He'd polished his boots yesterday before boarding the train, and except for some dust, they'd survived his adventures relatively unscathed. But he didn't want to risk offending his hostess, so he gave them an obligatory scrape against the end of a floorboard and then hastened after Miss Bessie, taking care to close the door behind him.

"You'll be in the west room. Here." The woman pointed to a doorway on the left of the hall but moved past without stopping. "Harold put your belongings in the room. Parlor's to the right."

Crockett barely spared the rooms a glance in his effort to keep up.

"I'm dishin' up supper now," she said as they entered the kitchen. "Breakfast's at six thirty. Food hits the slop bucket at seven, so don't be late."

"Yes, ma'am."

The woman marched up to the stove and ladled some kind of soup from the bottom of a small pot. As she poured it into a bowl, he thought he smelled chicken. But when she slapped the bowl onto the roughhewn table, all he could identify were a few orange chunks that he guessed might be carrots and a green bean or two. Nothing resembling meat floated in the pale broth.

"I don't eat with the boarders, so don't lollygag." She opened the door to the warming oven and brought out a pan of yeast rolls that smelled heavenly. Man might not live on bread alone, but Crockett suspected the rolls would do more to sustain him through the night than the watered-down soup.

That was unkind. Crockett harnessed the uncharitable thought and forced his mind onto a godlier path.

Miss Bessie hadn't been expecting company. She'd probably diluted her own small portion in order to share with the guest thrust upon her. He should be thankful for her generosity.

The woman covered the rolls with a dish towel and set them on the table along with a crock of butter. Then spoon and knife clattered beside the bowl. When she finally glanced his direction, it was to singe him with the heat of a perturbed glare.

"Don't just stand there sucking up the air. Get to eatin'."

"Yes, ma'am." Crockett took hold of the chair nearest him and pulled it out. Before he dropped into his seat, however, he favored his hostess with a bright smile. "Thank you for the fine meal, Miss Bessie."

The woman grunted and turned her back on him. "Just make sure you leave the night's payment on the table—it'll be two dollars." Then without another word, she disappeared into what he could only assume was a back bedroom and shut the door with a decisive thump—a thump followed by a click that sounded suspiciously like a key turning in a lock.

Did she think he would do her harm? Or was she simply protective of her privacy? He supposed the precaution wasn't wholly without merit. An unscrupulous man might attempt to take advantage. Although Crockett imagined Miss Bessie could hold her own with most. She'd probably have any disrespectful fellow hog-tied and booted out the back door before he could sneeze.

The woman was as no-nonsense as they came and seemed an expert at keeping folks at a distance. She'd never even asked his name. Nevertheless, she provided a roof over his head, food for his stomach, and a place to lay his head. If he'd wanted conversation, he could have stayed with the marshal.

Crockett laid his hat on the corner of the table and took his seat. After saying grace for the meal, asking the Lord's blessings on Miss Bessie, and thanking God for watching over him during the craziness with Silas Robbins, he took a few extra minutes to petition the Almighty on Joanna's behalf.

Provide the right man for her mission, Lord. Work through him to reestablish a flock of believers and assist Joanna in her efforts to win over her father. Soften Silas's heart to your message. Penetrate it with your truth.

As he mentally closed out the prayer, it occurred to him that he'd not mentioned the Brenham congregation. Adding a quick postscript, he asked that the elders be granted wisdom in their decision and that the members be blessed as a result.

His memory jogged, Crockett dug out the telegram from his trouser pocket and set the crumpled paper beside his spoon. Too hungry to resist the call of the rolls any longer, he slathered one with butter, ate it in two bites, then buttered another before unfolding the message.

STAY IN DEANVILLE.
ELDERS WILL MEET AND SEND INSTRUCTIONS.

Crockett's jaw halted midchew. His eyes moved over the words a second time.

Stay in Deanville? Really? He'd expected them to encourage him to make all possible haste.

Well, if he were to be completely honest, he'd expected them to arrange a late afternoon service to accommodate his tardy arrival. Pretty vain expectation, now that he thought about it. People had farms to see to, families to tend. It would be unrealistic to ask them to stay in town all day or to make a long return trip. And in truth, that wouldn't be in his best interests, either. Surely only a handful of members would turn out for an evening service. Did he really want a decision to be made when the majority of the members had only heard the first candidate?

Crockett resumed his chewing, though he barely tasted the buttery bread any longer. His mind was fully consumed with generating convincing arguments as to why he shouldn't feel threatened or disheartened by the telegram.

While he slurped his soup, he lectured himself about how God was in control, how he knew what was best. During the consumption of his third and fourth rolls, he imagined scenarios where waiting for a later date to speak would actually prove beneficial. Perhaps a member of considerable influence in the congregation was currently out of town. Maybe an afternoon service would require preaching over wailing babies who'd missed naps. Or maybe the Lord knew that a tree was fixing to fall on the church roof at precisely 3:42 tomorrow afternoon, and keeping him away meant saving his life and the lives of dozens of church members.

All right, so that last one was a bit farfetched. But stranger things had happened. Like a preacher being stolen from a train instead of watches and jewelry. Who would've believed that would happen?

Crockett stood and carried his dishes to the washtub. As his bowl and utensils slid beneath the murky water, he cast a glance at the bolted door to his right. Washing the dishes himself might not do much to improve Miss Bessie's hospitality, but perhaps the small kindness would ease her burden a little. Crockett added some warm water from the kettle on the back of the stove, rolled up his sleeves, and got to work—not only on his dishes but on the few others he found in the bottom of the tub.

When he'd washed, dried, and stacked them on the counter, he hung up the damp towel and rolled down his sleeves. Then he covered the rolls he'd left on the table and collected his telegram. Scanning the kitchen to make sure he was leaving it as tidy as he'd found it, he placed two silver dollars beside the bread pan, where his hostess would be sure to find them, grabbed his hat, and headed for his room.

His travel satchel sat waiting for him on the end of a too-short bed atop a brown patchwork quilt that needed mending. He ran his finger along a frayed square that had come unstitched on one side. Miss Bessie would have his hide for sure if he snagged a satchel buckle on that and tore it further.

He hung his hat on the bedpost and moved the satchel from the bed to the small desk beneath the room's single window. A plain lamp with a slightly sooty chimney jiggled when the bag hit the desk, and its low flame flickered. Crockett adjusted the wick to allow more light to fill the dim room, then unbuckled the satchel and extracted his Bible. A page of sermon notes fell from inside the front cover and fluttered to the floor. Crockett bent to retrieve it.

That's when the idea struck.

An idea that would bless a particular young lady on her birthday while, at the same time, improving his chances at landing the Brenham job. An idea so perfect, it had to be inspired.

Blowing out a deep breath in an attempt to calm his suddenly racing pulse, Crockett ordered his notes, took his Bible in hand, and began preaching in hushed tones to the lacy throw pillows on Miss Bessie's bed.

9

Joanna huffed out a breath and watched her disobedient hair flutter in the mirror. Why did she even bother? The coils never stayed where she put them. Why couldn't she have lovely blond wisps like Holly Brewster? *Her* hair never pushed out of its pins or frizzed into an orange halo. Joanna had even overheard Holly complain to Becky Sue one time that it took her an hour to brush it out every night since it had grown past her hips. Joanna could barely keep hers long enough to reach the bottom of her shoulder blades. Any longer and the weight of it when piled atop her head induced headaches.

Maybe she should give up trying to look like a lady and simply wear it in a thick plait behind her neck. Heaven knew it would be easier to manage. But somehow the thought of giving up on arranging her hair felt like giving up on her chances of finding a husband. She was only turning twenty-one today. Surely that didn't qualify her for old-maid status yet.

Stiffening her spine, Joanna shoved another pin into the fluffy knot at her nape. Then, almost as if her mother were in the room, Joanna heard the echo of a tender voice soothing long-ago tears.

"A woman's hair is her glory, Joanna. And yours is truly glorious."

Joanna closed her eyes and recalled the feel of her mother drawing a brush through her thick tresses as the two of them sat on her bed.

"It's vibrant like a sunrise. Untamed like the most beautiful landscape. It reminds me of your father—wild, yet full of love. Your hair is a gift from God, Joanna. Don't despise it because it is different. See the beauty in his gift."

She opened her eyes and stared hard into the mirror. Her mother had taught her to examine the world through an artist's eye, to find splendor in a landscape where others saw only dirt and rocks. Under her mother's skilled tutelage, Joanna had learned to turn a dry creek bed into a beacon of hope through the stroke of her brush, portraying what could be instead of what was. Yet when she looked upon her reflection, her training proved ineffectual.

"'Tis a gift, Joanna." She scowled at the woman in the mirror. "To scorn it would be to dishonor the Giver."

So she looked again. Past the recalcitrant curls. Past the inadequate length. Past even the unnamable color that existed somewhere between ginger and cinnamon. She allowed her vision to blur slightly so that no details distracted. A minute passed. Then another. Until she realized her perspective had shifted. She saw not her own bright tresses, but the darker, russet tones of her father's hair. And not his alone, for her mind also recalled the light brown curls of her mother. The hair her father had always loved to touch, to twist around his finger when the two of them snuggled together on the settee during quiet evenings. Mama would lean her head against his shoulder, while Daddy wrapped his arm around her.

Joanna blinked, her gaze reluctant to focus on the present. *I see the gift now, God. Thank you.*

Wiping the sentimentality from the corner of her eyes, Joanna gave a little sniff and turned away from her mirror. She smoothed the wrinkles from her Sunday-best dress—a periwinkle polished muslin with indigo trim—and collected her Bible from the small table beside her bed.

She might not yet have a preacher, but she had a Lord who deserved her worship, and though her father and his men had made themselves scarce the minute breakfast ended, she intended to start her twenty-first year with a positive outlook. There'd be no quiet Bible reading in the parlor for her this Sunday. No, it was time to wake up the old chapel with hymns and brush the dust from the pews.

Joanna arranged her favorite straw bonnet upon her head, the one decorated with clusters of periwinkle blooms that made her eyes look more blue than gray, then tied the ribbons beneath her chin and tugged her mother's gloves over her hands.

Today she was going to church.

By the time Joanna neared the chapel, the sunny sky and quiet morning had restored her good humor. She hadn't encountered a single soul on the walk over, even with taking the road instead of the shortcut through the field. But she didn't mind the solitude. In fact, she welcomed it. She'd never been good at making idle chitchat. She much preferred to be alone with her thoughts. No one around to try to impress. No one to interrupt her musings. No one to hear should a song suddenly rise to her lips.

Grinning to herself, Joanna put voice to the hymn that had been running through her head since she left the house. "'For the beauty of the earth, for the glory of the skies.'" Timid at first, her breathy tones slipped softly into the morning air. She twisted her head to peer behind her, making sure no one was within earshot.

"'For the love which from our birth, over and around us lies.'" Joanna's voice grew stronger as she entered the churchyard. The words brought her mother to mind as well as her God, and her heart swelled as she moved into the chorus. "'Lord of all, to Thee we raise, this our hymn of grateful praise.'"

Her gaze caressed the trees by the church walls as she sang the second verse, the lyrics proclaiming God's glory in his creation. Joanna's voice grew bolder as she climbed the steps. Swept up in the moment, she turned around and truly raised her song to the heavens.

"'For the joy of human love; brother, sister, parent, child. Friends on—'"

"'Earth and friends above,'" a rich, masculine voice sang from behind. "'For all gentle thoughts and mild.'"

Joanna gasped and spun around.

Crockett Archer, eyes twinkling, stood in the chapel entrance.

Heat flooded her cheeks. Would she forever be embarrassing herself in front of this man? And how had he even come to be here? A dozen questions raced through her mind, but they all dissolved on her tongue as the handsome parson ignored her distress and continued singing, his deep baritone resonating through her.

"'Lord of all, to Thee we raise, this our hymn of grateful praise.'"

She expected him to stop after the refrain, but he continued unabashedly on to the final verse and turned to her, silently urging her to join him.

Unable to resist, and not really wanting to, Joanna shyly added her melody to his, while returning her attention to the sky, away from Brother Archer's all-too-penetrating stare.

"'For thy church that evermore lifteth holy hands above.'" Gradually, she increased her volume until she matched his, finding an amazing freedom in singing without reservation. "'Off'ring up on every shore her pure sacrifice of love.'"

When they came to the final refrain, she switched from the melody to a line of harmony and closed her eyes as the blend of notes reached into her very spirit. "'Lord of all, to Thee we raise, this our hymn of grateful praise.'"

The final chord hung in the air between them, the memory of its sound filling the silence. Neither of them spoke for a long moment, then Brother Archer murmured a quiet, reverent "Amen."

The Lord had blessed her with another gift, Joanna decided. A perfect moment to treasure in her heart.

Brother Archer turned to her then, a rascal's grin curving his lips. "Surprise."

That was stating it mildly.

Joanna darted a smile up at him, amazed at how comfortable she'd grown beside him as they sang. Usually her encounters with men left her acutely aware of her shortcomings, despite their efforts at politeness. But Brother Archer was different. Instead of kindly overlooking her flaws, he acted as if he were completely unaware of their existence.

"What are you doing here?" Joanna blurted, needing to change the directions of her thoughts before she could examine them too closely.

The parson winked at her. "Granting a birthday wish."

Joanna's breath caught. *Does he mean . . . ? Is he . . . staying?* Her heart hammered wildly in her breast until logic asserted itself. The man had a job waiting for him. Whatever his reasons for returning, she'd be foolish to read too much into them.

Brother Archer took her arm and led her into the small entryway. "After I wired the elders in Brenham, they responded by asking me to hold up in Deanville until they could meet and decide on a new plan. So, since I won't be delivering my sermon there this morning, I thought it might be nice to deliver it somewhere else. To someone who might appreciate it more than the pillows in my room at the boardinghouse."

He grinned at her with such sincerity and good humor that Joanna felt guilty over the pang of disappointment that shot through her at his words. He'd gone out of his way to give her a precious gift. The least she could do was show some appreciation.

Manufacturing a smile, she did her best to beam it up at him. "But how did you know I would be here?" she asked. "I usually conduct my Sunday devotions in my parlor at home."

Brother Archer glanced sheepishly at the floor, where a piece of rope lay huddled in the corner. "I'd intended to ring the bell as a call to worship, but the pull cord appears to have rotted." He brushed his hands together as if ridding them of leftover fibers. "I was fixin' to saddle up and ride to your place when your singing drew me to the front of the church. I'm sure Sunflower appreciates the reprieve."

Hearing her mare's name emerge from such masculine lips struck Joanna as quite ridiculous, and she found herself fighting down a giggle. Crockett Archer seemed the type to ride a steed named Hercules or Samson, not an animal named after the yellow blossoms that cover Texas fields in autumn. But since *she'd* been the one to offer him a horse, she hadn't felt right about assigning him one of her father's mounts. Therefore, she'd lent him her palomino. The mare was sturdy and strong and had enough fire in her to keep even a man like Crockett Archer on his toes.

"I didn't see her when I arrived." If she had, she never would have burst into song. Although, she had to admit, she'd rather enjoyed it when the parson had joined his voice to hers. It almost made her embarrassment worth it. Almost.

"I tied her up around back. Here . . ." He took her arm and led her down the center aisle. "I cleaned off the first few rows at the front. I wasn't sure where you usually sat."

"Third row on the left," she said as she surveyed the chapel. The man had been busy. A broom stood propped against the edge of a windowsill on the far wall next to a pile of leaves, dirt, and something that looked like a nest. She prayed it was from a bird and not one of God's furrier little creatures.

Suddenly the quiet of the building registered. Her footsteps echoed loudly in her ears as she made her way down the aisle. The utter emptiness of the place soaked into her bones and left them cold. Abandoned. Like the pew she used to share with her mother.

Brother Archer handed her into the pew, and Joanna sidled along the edge of the bench and took her seat, bracing herself for the loneliness that would strike the moment he left her to take his place at the podium.

But the parson didn't leave. Instead he folded his tall frame into the pew beside her. Her coldness vanished.

"When my brothers and I worshiped together at home," he said, reaching over the back of the pew in front of them to collect a slender book, "Neill led the songs. As the youngest, his voice was the last to change."

Joanna smiled, imaging a younger version of Crockett Archer, his adolescent voice cracking while his big brothers looked on.

"When it did finally lower, it didn't deepen as far as the rest of ours did. As the only Archer who could sing a decent tenor, he got stuck with the job."

"Does he mind?"

"Neill? Nah. He's always had a hankerin' for music. Took to playing Pa's fiddle when he was about half grown. Made such a screeching racket, Travis banished him to the barn. But now folks actually pay him to play for their shindigs." Brother Archer shook his head as if such a thing was hard to believe, but an unmistakable gleam of pride shone in his dark eyes. "It gives him a reason to get off the ranch every now and again, which is probably a good thing."

The parson settled back into the pew, his shoulder brushing hers so slightly she doubted he was even aware of the contact, despite the fact that she found it hard to be aware of anything else.

"I found a couple of these behind the pulpit." He rubbed the cover of the hymnal he'd retrieved against his trouser leg, gave it a quick inspection, and handed it to her. "I'm no troubadour, but I'd gladly join you in a hymn or two before the sermon. If you'd like."

Taking the book, she thumbed through the pages, seizing the excuse to look anywhere other than his face. Because, really, how could she be expected to converse with any semblance of rationality when the warm kindness in his brown eyes was turning her insides to mush?

"This one," she managed to squeak as she smoothed the pages open.

He nodded, inhaled, and led her in the familiar strains of Charles Wesley's "Love Divine, All Loves Excelling."

She added her alto to his baritone, one song after another. Joanna would have been edified aplenty just staying in that pew with him and singing all morning. But all too soon he set the hymnal aside and strode to the front of the sanctuary.

"Brothers and sisters," he began, his gaze sweeping the invisible congregation before landing on her with a wink, "how blessed we are to come together on this Lord's Day, sanctified by the blood of Christ. But there are others outside these walls whose souls are perishing. Men and women, neighbors, friends, even members of our own families who are in desperate need of the living water that only Christ can provide. Their souls are parched and withering away, yet they don't admit their thirst."

The parson's eyes glowed with compassion as they met hers; however, the ache that usually came when she contemplated the state of her father's soul did not come. For there was passion in Crockett Archer's eyes, too—fiery passion that filled her with hope, with purpose.

He didn't speak with religious rhetoric designed to impress and elevate his standing as a holy emissary of God. Nor did he shout out condemnation and dire warnings in order to frighten his listeners into obedience. No, Crockett Archer spoke in the same charismatic manner that had endeared him to her yesterday when he'd disarmed Jackson Spivey with friendly banter and genuine concern. His voice carried authority, but more than that, it carried authenticity. And it was the latter that held her enthralled.

She followed where he led, opening her Bible to 1 Peter and reading along as he quoted verses that brought evangelism into a new, more personal light. In chapter two he emphasized how all of God's people are a royal priesthood, not just the ministers in the pulpit or the missionaries in foreign fields. And as such, they are called to live holy lives so that others might see and be influenced. Like the wives in chapter three who won over their husbands, not with words but with chaste and reverent behavior. Yet verse fifteen also spoke of the need to always be ready to give an answer as to the reason for the hope evident in one's life.

The parson's words penetrated her heart on a level so personal, so deep, it was as if God himself were speaking truth into her soul. Crockett Archer might have written this sermon for a church dozens of miles away, but in that moment Joanna knew that the Lord had intended its message for her.

10

Silas Robbins reined in his gray, dismounted, and walked the beast to the barn. He and Jasper had gotten caught wrangling one of his heifers out of a mud pit in the far west pasture. Thanks to the stubborn gal's refusal to cooperate, it'd taken longer than expected to haul her sorry hide out of the mire, leaving him late for lunch and wearing more dirt than a wallowing hog.

Some prize of a father he was turning out to be. First his birthday present ran off to Deanville without granting his little girl's wish, then he'd run off himself this morning to avoid the daughter he loved more than life.

Silas's jaw clenched as he hefted the saddle from Marauder's back and slapped it onto the half wall that marked the edge of the first stall. After dragging the blankets off as well, he grabbed a strip of toweling and rubbed down his horse.

Why couldn't he have just sat in the parlor with her for once and let her read him a handful of those infernal verses she put such stock in? It wasn't as if they were gonna flay his skin or set fire to his heathen ears. He wouldn't even have had to listen, really. Just sit there and pretend for a few minutes. It was her birthday, for pity's sake. He coulda done it just this once.

He ran the towel in small, firm circles across Marauder's side, cleaning away the animal's sweat and wishing he could clean away his guilt as easily.

Jo asked so little of him. So little, yet so very much. More than she could comprehend. Martha hadn't understood, either. Probably 'cause he'd never had the heart to explain. She'd seen such goodness in everyone, especially her church folk. It woulda broken her heart to learn the truth. That those holy fellers sittin' beside her on the pew every Sunday were just as vile beneath their shiny veneer as any drunkard or thief. Worse, even.

No, he'd not had the heart to destroy his wife's illusions. And the same held true for his daughter. He'd thought he could set his memories aside for Jo's sake. Just for today. But across the breakfast table, he'd read the invitation in her eyes before she gave it voice. And in that moment, nausea had rolled so viciously through his innards that he'd nearly spewed the contents of his stomach all over the platter of toast Frank had just passed him.

He'd ridden out five minutes later.

Silas finished up with his horse and turned him loose in the corral. Then, straightening his shoulders, he gritted his teeth and marched up to the house.

Pulling the back door open, Silas stepped into the washroom and quickly divested himself of his mud-splattered shirt and pried his caked boots from his feet. His trousers would have to wait for the privacy of his bedroom. He washed his hands, face, and chest, and ran his fingers through his rusty hair before entering the kitchen. His stockinged feet made no noise as he shuffled across the floor to lift the lid and peek into the stew pot Jo had left simmering on the stove.

As he inhaled a tantalizing whiff of beef, onions, and potatoes, the sound of voices carried to him from down the hall. So sure he'd find his quiet little Jo waiting for him somewhat sullen and forlorn thanks to his hasty departure, he was shocked to hear her voice echo so animatedly through the house. Her subdued laugh even reached his ears, bringing a smile to his face.

That smile disappeared the instant a masculine chuckle hit the air. Silas reached for the gun at his hip.

Jasper and the others were still out wrestling cows. Which meant a stranger was in his parlor. Alone with Jo.

Silas cocked his weapon and charged down the short hallway, a growl rumbling in his chest. He burst through the open doorway, not taking time to do more than register the tall man's position by the mantelpiece.

"Touch my daughter and I'll be digging your grave before the day's out, stranger."

"Daddy!" Jo gasped and lurched protectively into the line of fire at the same moment the man turned from his perusal of one of Martha's landscapes. Recognition slammed into Silas like a well-aimed fist.

"Mr. Robbins," the preacher man said with a nod of calm acknowledgment as he stepped out from behind Jo's intended shield. "It appears I'm a little overdressed for Sunday dinner." Archer ran his hands along the lapels of his coat, leaving Silas all too aware of his lack of shirt.

"What're you doing in my parlor, preacher man?" Silas demanded. He held his gun arm steady, determined to regain the control that seemed to be sifting through his fingers. He'd not let this young pup put him on the defensive.

Before the man could answer, however, Joanna shoved herself into her father's face, forcing him to lower his weapon.

"Brother Archer rode in from Deanville this morning to deliver a birthday sermon for me." She threw the words at him. "A gift *you* arranged, I'll thank you to recall. I invited him to join us for dinner, as any hospitable person would. Now quit your barking and put some clothes on. The food will be on the table in fifteen minutes."

With that, she stormed out.

Silas glared at the parson, sure he was somehow responsible for his daughter's switch in loyalty. Archer met his scowl with an annoying degree of nonchalance. Silas holstered his revolver with a grunt. Honest living had apparently robbed him of his ability to intimidate properly.

"Thought you was in a hurry to leave, preacher man. Why'd ya come back?" Silas crossed his arms over his chest and braced his legs apart. He might be forty-six, but there wasn't a speck of flab on his frame. He didn't need a firearm to enforce his will. Archer would be wise to take note.

The parson's grip tightened on his lapels, but the man's eyes never wavered. Silas got the impression that Crockett Archer was fightin' hard against the urge to remove his coat and square off with him.

Curious. Preachers, in his experience, went out of their way to avoid confrontation and faced it only when trapped. This Archer fellow seemed exactly the opposite. He was itchin' for the chance to take him down a peg or two. Silas shifted his jaw, remembering the blow the parson had dealt him yesterday. But the man had been trapped then. What was driving him now?

"Due to my interrupted travels yesterday," the parson explained, "I missed my appointment in Brenham."

Ah, so the feller held a grudge. *Ha!* He might preach forgiveness, but he was as much a hypocrite as the rest of his kind.

"Since I had to wait for a new one to be scheduled, I thought I would spend my time in a worthy pursuit. And I could think of nothing more worthy than delivering a sermon as a birthday gift to your daughter."

Archer released his lapels and held out a hand to Silas. "I really ought to thank you, sir. You caused me no small amount of trouble yesterday, it's true, but you also brought a blessing into my life. Your daughter has a pure heart and a sense of spiritual purpose that humbles me. I am better for having known her. Thank you for giving me that opportunity."

Silas frowned down at the preacher's outstretched hand. What game was he playing? He lifted his focus to search Archer's eyes, hunting for any hint of sarcasm or sanctimony. He found none. Maybe the sermonizer was just better at hiding his motives than most. One thing was for sure, though, he'd not give Archer the satisfaction of thinking himself the bigger man. Silas unfolded his arms and grasped the preacher's hand.

The pressure built as both men tightened their grips. Their gazes met, challenge rife between them. Archer finally released Silas's hand, but Silas didn't kid himself by thinking it was due to any lack of stamina. The man's grip was like a vise. He'd let go as a matter of choice. What bothered Silas was not knowing what drove that choice.

"I think I'll see if I can lend a hand in the kitchen." The parson smiled and stepped around him.

Silas stared at the spot on the parlor rug that Archer had just vacated. Something about that man ate at his craw. He dressed like a preacher and spoke like one most of the time, but beneath that window dressing stood a man who acted more like a hardened cowman.

As Silas trudged to his bedroom to change his muddy trousers, he continued chewing over the Crockett Archer puzzle. He didn't fit Silas's expectations. He wasn't soft or overly scholarly. Although the man did carry more books and journals than clothes in that satchel of his, his hands boasted calluses, and his skin was tanned from the sun. Plus he spoke like a normal person, not with a bunch of highfalutin words that didn't mean nothin' to nobody but himself. The man was strong and willing to stand up for himself yet was not prideful or sanctimonious. He'd fled yesterday to fulfill some private mission but came back this morning to give Jo a gift.

Silas gritted his teeth as he pulled a new work shirt over his head. The man didn't fit any of his tried-and-true notions for preachers. He was a riddle. Silas didn't like riddles. They were messy, unpredictable. And they forced a man to reconsider things that were better left alone.

Silas wanted him gone.

11

After enduring the weight of Silas's disapproval all through the tasty meal of beef stew, corn bread, and leftover chocolate cake, Crockett decided he'd worn his welcome thin enough and took his leave. Joanna insisted he keep Sunflower for his journey, so he and the little mare returned to Deanville, making good time.

Worshiping with Joanna Robbins had been a singular experience. Awkward at first, yet incredibly intimate as time went on. He'd never been one to believe the size of one's audience was an indicator of success. Shoot, for years his audience had consisted solely of his three brothers. God could impact hearers' hearts no matter the size of the congregation. And Joanna's heart thirsted like none other he had encountered.

As he'd stood in the long-abandoned pulpit, he'd made an effort not to stare directly at her for more than a few seconds at a time, not wanting to cause her discomfort. Yet he'd been continually drawn to her—her lovely face tipped up to meet his, her gaze intent and unwavering. He'd preached enough to know when a congregant was thinking more about Sunday dinner than the sermon and could easily recognize the glaze of sleepiness that numbed folks' attention after a too-long Saturday night.

Joanna's avid interest had inspired him, bringing words to his mouth that he hadn't rehearsed and fostering an energy that continued to hum through him even now. There had been times in the past where he'd felt the Spirit moving within him, granting him words beyond what he had prepared, but never before had he felt more like a vessel in the Lord's hand than he had as he stood in front of Joanna Robbins. It was quite humbling, yet exhilarating at the same time.

His mind busy mulling over the morning's events as he strolled from the livery to Miss Bessie's, Crockett nearly missed the frenetic waving of the telegraph operator scurrying across the street toward him.

"Mr. Archer! Mr. Archer!" The little man dodged two buggies and a mule cart before finally reaching Crockett's side.

"Yes?"

Slightly out of breath, the man leaned against the hitching post as he reached into his vest pocket. "I've been waiting for you for an age," he huffed. "This telegram arrived for you an hour ago. It's from that church in Brenham you been correspondin' with. It seemed real urgent, and I worried when I couldn't find you. Miss Bessie said you left early this morning but that your belongings were still in your room. I hoped that meant you was comin' back."

Crockett frowned and held out his hand to accept the paper. "I appreciate you tracking me down."

"It says you're to meet that fellow in Caldwell tonight."

"Yes. I can see that." Crockett looked up from the message to glare at the nosy operator. Mr. Hoffmann was taking the afternoon train from Brenham to Caldwell and asked Crockett to meet him at the hotel restaurant for supper at six so they could discuss the elders' decision.

An unwelcome heaviness settled in the pit of Crockett's stomach. Why were they sending someone to talk to him? Why not just have him come to Brenham?

"How far is the ride to Caldwell?" Crockett stuffed the telegram inside his coat and slipped a coin into the operator's waiting hand.

"About eight and a half miles if you take the northeast road. You got plenty of time to make it, as long as that horse of yours ain't too winded."

"I'll rent a fresh one from the livery." He wouldn't take Joanna's horse out of Deanville. She'd been kind to loan Sunflower to him, and he'd not abuse her generosity. Besides, he couldn't be sure he'd be returning. Despite the knots tightening in his gut, there was a chance he'd be taking the train to Brenham with Mr. Hoffmann after their meeting.

He needed to pack his things and get on the road.

"Thanks for your help, Mr. . . ." Crockett held out his hand as he searched his mind for a name to fit the little man with the big mustache.

"Stallings. Ed Stallings." The operator shook his hand and stepped back. "You better be on your way, Mr. Archer."

"Can't argue with that." Crockett smiled, feeling slightly more charitable toward the interfering fellow. He waved farewell to Mr. Stallings and made for the boardinghouse with long, purposeful strides.

Miss Bessie must have seen him coming, for her bedroom door was firmly shut with her behind it by the time he arrived in the kitchen.

Shaking his head, Crockett crossed the kitchen and raised his voice so that it might pass through the wooden barrier. "I'm checking out, Miss Bessie. Thank you for the room."

He turned to go, but the creak of a hinge stopped him.

"Will ya be comin' back?" His cloistered hostess emerged through the small opening, an unreadable expression on her face.

"I suspect not, but one never knows for sure." The way he figured it, from Caldwell he'd be catching a train headed in one of two directions—either on to Brenham or home to Palestine.

"Well." Miss Bessie fiddled with her apron, not quite meeting his gaze. "Should ya ever wander back this way, you'll have a room waiting for ya." A touch of color stained her cheeks, and she immediately surged out of the doorway to start bustling about the kitchen. She collected pots and pans from where they'd been drying on the counter and piled them into her arms like homemade armor. "Unless I'm full-up, o' course."

"Of course." Crockett grinned and wondered what Miss Bessie would do if he plunked a thank-you kiss smack-dab in the middle of her cheek. The poor woman would probably suffer a heart seizure. He opted to tip his hat to her instead. "Thank you for the invite, ma'am. I'll be sure to stop by if I find myself in Deanville again."

She nodded, then turned her back, signaling she'd said her piece and didn't aim to expand upon it.

Oddly reluctant to say good-bye, Crockett held his tongue as he exited the kitchen. It took only a couple minutes to gather his things from his room and buckle the straps on his satchel. He glanced back into the kitchen on his way out but didn't see any sign of his hostess. Once outside on the road, however, he glanced over his shoulder at the small house and caught the motion of a curtain in the parlor window falling back into place.

"Bye, Miss Bessie," Crockett whispered, a smile tugging his lips upward.

He certainly wouldn't have chosen to be pulled from a train by a gang of retired outlaws, but at least he'd touched a life or two during his little side trip. It just went to show how the Lord could bring good out of any situation. And a reminder that his God was more than capable of working things out with the Brenham elders, as well.

Crockett sent a prayer heavenward as he stepped into the hotel dining room and spotted Brother Hoffmann at a table near the window.

See me through, Lord. See me through.

The Brenham elder caught his eye and stood to greet him as Crockett approached. "Brother Archer. Good to see you again."

Crockett nodded and accepted the man's hand. "Mr. Hoffmann. It was good of you to travel all this way to speak with me, though I would have been happy to meet you in Brenham."

"I know you would've, but I was headed this way on business, anyway, so it was no trouble." The older man waved him toward a chair, and the two seated themselves at the table.

After a waiter took Crockett's order, Lukas Hoffmann kept up a steady stream of friendly banter. He asked about the abduction and oohed and aahed in all the right places as Crockett recounted the adventure—minus a few key details. Crockett asked after the man's family and listened to several delightful anecdotes about Hoffmann's grandson and the scrapes the young lad seemed determined to get into.

Crockett liked Lukas Hoffmann—had since they first met a month ago. He was a jolly sort, always ready with a smile, a laugh, and a thump on the back when a man was feeling low. But as the waiter cleared away their empty plates and poured fresh coffee in their cups, Crockett knew the time for pleasantries had passed.

Hoffmann stirred a heaping spoonful of sugar into his coffee and stared at the swirling liquid, his face losing its cheerful mien. Crockett waited, his unease growing the longer the silence stretched between them. Finally, Hoffmann let out a heavy sigh and looked up from his coffee.

"We've decided to hire Stephen Middleton."

The suddenness of the statement hit Crockett like a fist to the gut.

"I see." The two words were all he could manage past the tightness in his throat.

This wasn't right. He deserved a chance to prove himself. Hiring his competitor simply because the man managed to survive his train travel without incident was grossly unfair! He'd fostered such hopes on this appointment, such dreams. God had been leading him to Brenham; he was sure of it. So how could they just cut him loose without a proper trial?

"You've got to understand, son. None of us took this decision lightly."

Yet you made it in a matter of hours without the benefit of hearing me preach.

"For weeks we have been asking for the Lord to make our path clear. To make our choice evident. When you failed to arrive yesterday, many of us saw it as a sign. A clearing of the path, you might say, leaving us one candidate for the position.

"When we learned of the abduction, however, we questioned our conclusion, considered that perhaps a force other than God was at work." Hoffmann paused to sip his coffee, but the fervor in his eyes didn't dim. "Then you wired that you were safe, and it brought to mind all the times the Lord worked his will even through the evil deeds of others. Joseph's brothers selling him into slavery. Pharaoh's oppression of the Israelites.

The trickery that sent Daniel to the den of lions. Who were we to say that the Lord wasn't at work in a similar way with you?"

Hoffmann took another sip, his gaze challenging Crockett to ask himself the same question. "When Brother Middleton's sermon was well received by the congregation this morning, our conviction solidified. The Lord had made our choice."

If the Lord had made their choice, where did that leave him?

Unable to hold Hoffmann's scrutiny any longer, Crockett's attention fell to the coffee before him. He lifted the white china cup to his mouth and drank in the bitter beverage, its heat lightly scalding the back of his throat as it went down. Much like the painful truth he was mentally trying to swallow.

God had chosen another man to pastor the church in Brenham.

"I'm sorry it didn't work out the way you'd hoped, son." The genuine compassion in Lukas Hoffmann's tone soothed away a bit of the sting, though Crockett's heart still railed against the injustice of being removed from the running by an event so totally beyond his control.

"Me too." Crockett set his cup down, suddenly eager for some time alone.

"God has plans for you, Crockett Archer. Don't let this little setback sour your outlook." Hoffmann pulled a couple bills from his wallet and tucked them under the edge of his saucer, enough to cover the cost of both their meals. Then he pushed his chair back, tossed his napkin on the table, and rose to his feet. "His timing might not be our timing, but it is always perfect."

With that, he left.

Crockett lingered long enough to finish his coffee, then wandered to the hotel desk and rented a room for the night. There wouldn't be another train to Palestine until tomorrow.

The decision on his destination had been made.

Yet as he stood in his room discarding his suit coat and removing his boots, a vague disquiet nagged at him like the itch of a mosquito bite. And the more he tried to define it, the itchier it became.

Had his confidence been misplaced? He'd been so certain God was leading him to Brenham. How could he have mistaken the Lord's purpose so completely? Or had this detour been God's plan all along? And if so, what did that mean for his future?

"What am I supposed to do, Lord?" Crockett whispered the question against the glass of the window that overlooked the dim side street below. He unfastened the buttons of his vest, undid the tie at his throat, and rolled up the sleeves of his shirt. None of the adjustments to his clothing made him comfortable, though. He reached for his watch, intending to set it on the small desk behind him, but when his fingers closed around the brass casing, Hoffmann's words echoed again in his mind.

"God's timing is not our timing."

Pieces of a verse flashed through his consciousness, a verse he'd read recently, during his study of Peter's epistles.

Crockett strode to the bed and unlatched his satchel. Taking up his Bible, he sank onto the mattress and flipped to the end of the second epistle. Pages crinkled as he searched for the passage. Then it was there.

"But, beloved, be not ignorant of this one thing, that one day is with the Lord as a thousand years, and a thousand years as one day. The Lord is not slack concerning his promise, as some men count slackness; but is longsuffering toward us, not willing that any should perish, but that all should come to repentance."

"'Not willing that any should perish . . .'" The whispered words fell from his tongue almost of their own accord. Crockett barely noticed, for at that moment other words bombarded his senses.

"I prayed for a preacher to come. To save my father's soul."

"I need help, Mr. Archer. I need a preacher to bring this old church back to life."

"I will help you find a new preacher. I promise."

Crockett rose from his seat on the bed, his finger sandwiched between the closed pages of the Bible he still grasped, and returned to his position at the window. Staring over the top of the building across the street, he found the steeple of a church a couple blocks away. A tiny smile touched his lips as the persistent nagging that had plagued him the last half hour suddenly dissipated.

"I'm not going home to Palestine, am I, Lord?"

12

Joanna whacked at the weeds daring to encroach her butternut squash plants as the late morning sun warmed her back through the fabric of her brown calico work dress. Once she finished her garden chores and ate a bite for lunch, she'd be able to escape to the barn loft for a few hours to paint. And, oh, how she needed that time away. After all the excitement of the last couple days, she craved the quiet serenity of her studio. Not even her father would bother her there. That sanctuary was hers alone.

The gentle thud of hoofbeats echoed in the distance. An ordinary sound on a ranch, but as Joanna tilted her head to listen better, she realized they were coming not from the pasture or barn but from the road. She straightened, resting her weight against the handle of the hoe. The floppy hat she wore blocked much of the sun, but it still took her a minute to recognize the approaching horse.

"Sunflower?"

Jasper had promised to retrieve her mare when he went to town tomorrow for supplies. Who would be riding . . .

Brother Archer?

Joanna recognized the black hat the preacher had worn the past two days, yet his clothes had changed. Gone was the black Sunday-go-to-meeting suit. Instead, the man riding her horse wore a pair of new denims and a tan work shirt. If it wasn't for the way he sat in the saddle, and the fact that she'd memorized that particular combination of man and horse yesterday as she watched him ride off, she probably would have mistaken him for a wandering cowhand looking for work.

As he dismounted near the barn, he must have caught sight of her, for he lifted a hand in greeting and strode toward the garden.

Her heart skipped a delighted beat, barely able to believe what she was seeing. Then her delight turned to horror as she realized the state of her attire.

Joanna bit her lip and spun around. *Good heavens!* She was covered in dirt. Probably had smudges on her face. And her nails? Joanna moaned as she examined the dark stains around her cuticles. Could his timing be any worse? Not only had he caught her in her ugliest dress with one of her father's old hats plopped on her head, but she probably smelled of the cabbage she had harvested before she checked on her squash. *Wonderful.* Just what a man wanted to smell when visiting a lady.

"Miss Robbins?"

Joanna pivoted and bit back a groan of despair. Crockett Archer was even more handsome than she'd remembered. Somehow his rancher's clothing made him seem more approachable, more . . . within her reach. And if that wasn't the most ridiculous notion, she didn't know what was. A man with his looks and kind heart could have any woman he chose. He'd never settle for a shy, freckly redhead with an ex-outlaw for a father. She was everything the ideal preacher's wife was *not*.

"Brother Archer. What a surprise." Joanna forced her lips to curve in welcome, praying there wasn't a big blotch of dirt on the end of her nose where she'd rubbed an itch a moment ago. "I didn't expect to see you again."

"I hadn't anticipated a reunion this soon, either, but it seems the Lord had other ideas."

His smile was so warm, it took a moment for his words to penetrate. "The Lord?" Joanna scrunched her eyebrows as she tried to puzzle out his meaning. "What ideas?"

The parson removed his hat and held it before him, worrying the brim as if he were actually nervous. "If you're still looking to fill the local pulpit, ma'am, I'd like to apply for the job."

"You'd like to . . . apply . . . ?" Joanna couldn't even form all the words. In fact, she barely managed to hold herself upright. No, truth be told, even that meager feat was beyond her, for she was listing dangerously to the right.

In an instant, Crockett Archer was by her side, steadying her elbow with a solid grip. He angled himself slightly behind her, as if he were a stake propping up a drooping bean plant. "Miss Robbins? Are you all right?"

When she continued teetering, he slapped his hat back on his head and wrapped his right arm around the back of her waist. Her knees quivered from the close contact and from the way his decadent brown eyes searched her face in concern.

His arms felt heavenly about her, and his attentive regard left her breathless, but she needed to clarify his words. Bracing her legs more firmly beneath her, she steadied herself and stepped away from his support. "Are you saying you'd like to . . . to preach here on a regular basis?"

His furrowed brow eased a bit as he nodded. "Yes'm. Every Sunday, if I can find work to support me until the church can pay my salary."

"But what about Brenham?"

From the moment he disarmed Jackson Spivey with nothing but a calm demeanor and a display of respect, Joanna had known in the depths of her soul that Crockett Archer was the minister she needed to reach her father. But she'd watched him leave—twice. Had God truly brought him back to stay?

"They apparently filled their vacancy yesterday."

"I'm sorry." And she was. For him. He'd been so excited, so full of plans when they spoke on Saturday. He must have been devastated.

And it was her fault.

If her father hadn't abducted him, he would have auditioned on schedule, and she knew firsthand how marvelously he could deliver a sermon. A day later, her heart still swelled when she recalled his passionate oration. The man had a gift. A gift she'd stolen from the people of Brenham.

Joanna pushed her father's floppy hat off her head, letting it dangle down her back from the string around her neck. She needed to see Brother Archer's face, his eyes. "How could you want to preach here when it is because of me that you lost your position?"

"Ah, Joanna." Her given name fell from his lips as his gaze melted into hers. "It was never my position to lose. If it had truly been God's will that I preach in Brenham, no abduction could have prevented my appointment. You are not to blame. And I know your rascal of a father's not, either—despite my carrying on the other day. God is the one in charge, and it is he who led me back here. Will you have me?"

Although she knew he only meant in an official preaching capacity, her heart fluttered with a little thrill at his words as she let herself imagine for the briefest of moments what it would be like to have Crockett Archer ask her the same question with a much more personal implication.

Foolish girl. She stood on the verge of having her dearest wish granted. Why did she have to go and start hungering for more?

Joanna resolutely turned her mind back to the gift Brother Archer was offering her, and a genuine smile burst across her face. "Of course I'll have you!"

As soon as the words left her mouth, heat sprinted to her cheeks. Heavens, that wasn't how she'd intended to answer. She cleared her throat, and dropped her gaze. "Having you here would do our community a world of good, Brother Archer. We'd be honored to have you serve as our minister."

There. That sounded better. More formal. Perhaps that would cover her earlier blunder. However, when she looked up, the parson's eyes twinkled with far too much merriment for her peace of mind.

"Wonderful!" he declared, and his enthusiasm eased some of her embarrassment. "Now, all I have to do is find sufficient employment to keep me in food and supplies until we can get this church of ours established."

This church of ours. It was amazing what that simple phrase did to her insides. Ours. This was *their* project. Both of them. Together. She wasn't alone in her mission anymore. And she'd make sure he wasn't alone in his.

"I can ask around. Introduce you to a few . . . " An idea struck her so hard while she was speaking, she almost felt the blow. "Wait! I know the perfect person to ask." Excitement buzzed over her nerve endings faster than a message on a telegraph wire. She'd taken three steps toward the barn before she remembered she was leaving a thoroughly bewildered preacher standing in the middle of her squash rows. She couldn't stop, though. Not now. Not when her mission was so clear.

"Go take stock of the parsonage," she called over her shoulder as she picked up speed. "See what you'll need to make it habitable. I'll meet you there in an hour."

Crockett watched Joanna dart through her garden like a rabbit fleeing a shotgun blast. Only it wasn't fear that drove her. It was purpose. She was definitely up to something.

Once she disappeared into the barn, Crockett broke out of his bemused stupor. He grinned over his own foolishness. What was it about Joanna Robbins that took his attention hostage whenever she was near? The expressive features that displayed her every thought? The delightful way she blushed when he teased her? Or perhaps it was the way she threw herself wholeheartedly into those things that were important to her. Whatever it was, it was certainly compelling.

Rubbing the back of his neck, Crockett glanced around. Apparently he wasn't the only thing Joanna had abandoned in the garden. Her hoe lay fallen atop the winter squash plants she'd been tending so carefully moments ago. And near the garden gate, a small burlap sack with a head or two of cabbage peeking out from between the folds sat forgotten.

Since Joanna was off to do him a kindness, it was only fair that he return the favor. Crockett retrieved the hoe and collected the cabbage on his way through the gate. He was halfway to the house, thinking to set the cabbage inside the kitchen door, when a brown blur thundered past him.

Joanna Robbins tore out of the barn astride a magnificent chestnut quarter horse. She leaned forward in the saddle, hat flopping against her back, hair streaming out behind her in a wild, curly mass as she urged her mount to a full-out gallop. Unable to do anything but stare, Crockett stood dumbstruck as she raced past.

She was the most amazing horsewoman he'd ever seen.

Joanna Robbins. The shy creature who claimed painting and reading were her favorite pastimes had just bolted across the yard like a seasoned jockey atop a Thoroughbred. She might have inherited her mother's grace and manner, but the woman rode like her outlaw father. Maybe better.

13

Sweat dripped down Silas's neck as he set his hatchet aside and signaled to Jasper. "Ease 'er back slow."

"You got it, boss." Jasper nudged his mount forward, and the rope that tethered the gelding to the fallen tree stretched taut.

Carl had discovered the deadfall on his rounds that morning. One of the post oaks had collapsed into the fence. Probably fell victim to the high winds they'd had last week. They'd been hacking at the branches the past half hour, trying to free it from the barbed wire so they could drag it away without taking half the fence line with it.

"Whoa!" Frank called out from the opposite side. "She's catchin' on my end." He groaned heavily as he forced his way past the outer branches to reach the spot where it had snared. "Confounded limbs, stabbin' a man like he was some female's pincushion," he grumbled as he strained forward. "I oughta just set ya on fire and let you burn your way free. Then I'd take my shovel and poke ya 'til there was nothin' left but ashes. Wouldn't be stabbin' me then, would ya?"

Silas rolled his eyes and reached for his bandana. After being partnered with the man for over twenty-five years, he knew better than to interrupt Frank during one of his rants. Not if he wanted to get the job done before sunset. So he held his tongue and swiped the bandana along the back of his neck, rubbing away his perspiration. He twisted his neck to the side to work out a kink, and caught sight of his daughter riding toward them as if a hangin' posse were in pursuit.

"Jo!" His gun clearing leather in an instant, Silas sprinted away from the tangled branches, planted his gloved palm against the rounded trunk, and vaulted over the tree that stood between him and his daughter. As he ran to meet her, his eyes scoured the landscape in search of whatever threatened her, but he saw nothing.

He held up his arms to slow the racing horse, but Joanna had the beast well under control. In a flash, she reined in the horse and bounded off its back.

"Daddy! I have the most wonderful news!" She jogged up to him and flung herself into his arms like she used to do when she was just a little bit of a thing. He caught her against his chest, and the laughter that bubbled out from her calmed his thundering pulse.

He embraced her tightly, a father's tenderness momentarily overriding his common sense. Then he shoved his weapon back into his holster and took her by her upper arms, setting her away from him as he schooled his face into a stern line.

"You scared a year off my life, ridin' in here like that. I thought fer sure a pack of coyotes must be on your heels."

"Sorry, Daddy." Her smile dimmed slightly, but not enough to count. The little scamp wasn't the slightest bit sorry. "I promise not to go over a trot on the way home. And I'll give Gamble a thorough rubdown when we get there. I swear. I was just too excited to hold him back, and you know how he loves to run."

Of course he did. He'd handpicked the animal for just that reason. He just didn't expect his genteel daughter to be the one tearing across the countryside on his back.

Although he couldn't fully suppress his pride in seeing her do so. No doubt about it—his girl could ride.

"Everything all right, boss?" Silas turned to find Frank, hatchet in hand, a few steps behind him. Jasper and Carl stared in his direction, as well.

Silas waved him off. "Yeah." He lifted his voice to carry to the others. "Nothin' to worry about. Go on and see to that tree. We need it hauled off and the fence repaired before the end of the day."

Jasper saluted and started calling out instructions to Carl, while Frank let out a beleaguered sigh and muttered under his breath before plodding away.

Once the men returned to their duties, Silas steered his daughter back toward Gamble, using the horse's body to shield them from the curious looks he knew would be darting his way the moment he turned his back.

"All right, girlie. Spill it. What's got you in a dither?"

Jo bounced on her toes, fixin' to explode with her news. "Brother Archer wants to pastor our church! Can you believe it? I know I fussed at you for bringing him here against his will, but it's turned out to be the best birthday present ever. It's exactly what I wanted! Oh, Daddy. I'm so happy!"

That preacher man was worse than a bad penny. He just kept turnin' up. "What's he doin' back here? I thought he had some all-fired important engagement to get to."

"God changed his plans." She reached out and clasped his hand, and he swore he could feel excitement dancing through her veins. "He's back to stay. All he needs is a place to work until the church gets established. That's where you come in." She gave his hand a squeeze, and Silas's throat closed up.

"He's not working here," he choked out. Just the thought of it gave him hives. "I ain't no charity house for out-of-work sermonizers. And you know how I feel about strangers. We've never had an outsider workin' on the Lazy R, and I ain't about to start now."

"But what about Frank's rheumatism and Jasper's bad knee? Just think of how much help Mr. Archer could be."

"The gal's got a point, Si," Frank said from a few paces away. The fool dropped a handful of twigs from the dead tree into a pile that had no business being so close to where he and Jo were talking. "My rheumatism *has* been flarin' up lately."

"Bah!" Silas snatched a fist-sized stone off the ground and chunked it at the man's head. "Your rheumatism flares whenever it suits your fancy, you sorry dog."

Frank ducked, narrowly avoiding the stone. "Watch it!" He glared at Silas, but there was no real heat behind the look. He knew he'd stuck his nose where it didn't belong. "I'm just sayin' that it wouldn't be so bad to have a young buck around to do the heavy lifting for a change."

Having said his piece, Frank held out a conciliatory hand and headed back to the fence line.

"He's right," Jo said, laying her hand on Silas's arm. "Crockett Archer grew up on a ranch, so it's not like he's some greenhorn who doesn't know a heifer from a steer. He'd be a help to you. I swear. Please, Daddy? Please? It would mean the world to me."

Consarn it! Why did it have to be a preacher that made her happy? It was one thing to have the feller at the church, but on his land? He'd rather house a cougar.

The denial of her request sprang to his tongue, but he just couldn't push it past his lips. Not when the sadness that had lingered in her eyes for more than a year had finally vanished.

"If he fails to do a proper day's work, I'll fire him on the spot." Silas scowled and jabbed a finger in Jo's face.

Unperturbed by his posturing, Joanna squealed in glee and threw her arms around his neck. "Thank you, Daddy! You won't regret it. I promise."

He already regretted it. But after she smacked half a dozen kisses on his cheek and nearly squeezed the breath out of him with her huggin', the dread that had built inside him lessened to a tolerable level.

Looked like he and the preacher man were fixin' to get better acquainted.

Crockett opened the firebox on the stove in his new accommodations and winced as a pungent smell hit him in the face. Instinctively squinting and jerking his face to the side, he hastily identified the source of the stench. Some kind of rodent. Squirrel or mouse, most likely. Whatever it was, it was dead. His stomach churned, but he steeled himself against the compulsion to gag. Casting a desperate glance around for the stove shovel, he finally clapped eyes on the end of its handle protruding from behind the cobweb-strewn kindling bucket. He seized it and quickly scraped it along the base of the firebox, scooping up the indistinguishable furry mass and removing it from its tomb. Trying not to breathe, Crockett made for the door with all possible haste.

He'd be lighting a fire to sanitize that box just as soon as he ensured the stovepipe was clear of debris. No way would he be cooking on that thing tonight, though.

Once outside, Crockett moved toward the edge of the field that bordered the church and hurled the foul-smelling remains as far from him as he could.

"You treat all your visitors that way, Parson?"

Crockett did a brisk about-face. He'd been so intent on ridding himself of one varmint that he'd completely missed the arrival of another.

"Silas." Crockett tossed the stove shovel back toward the church and pulled out a handkerchief to wipe his hands. Heaven knew there wasn't a clean spot left anywhere on his clothes after an hour of sifting through the rubble of his new living quarters.

Joanna's father glared down at him from atop his big Appaloosa. "I hear you're thinking about stickin' around these parts." He made no move to dismount, just crossed his wrists over the pommel, enjoying his position of power.

"That's right." Crockett tucked his thumbs into his suspenders and adopted a bored air, refusing to be intimidated.

All at once, Silas swung down from his horse and stalked up to Crockett, his eyes carrying deadly promise. Crockett freed his hands and formed them into fists, his muscles tense and ready.

"My little girl has her heart set on starting this here church up again. I ain't gonna try and stop her, but understand this, preacher man—I *will* see that nothing hurts her along the way. You already done left twice. If you're planning on leaving again, you best do it now. 'Cause if you leave after you get Jo's hopes up, I'll track you down and feed your liver to the buzzards. Got it?"

Crockett stiffened. "Keep your threats to yourself, Silas." He matched the man scowl for scowl. "You'll not be chasing me off. God brought me to this place, and I'll stay until the job he has for me is finished." And judging by the belligerent attitude of the hardheaded man in front of him, that job was going to take a while.

"What're you planning to do for food and supplies?" Silas challenged. "Don't look like the old parson left you much."

"The Lord will provide." Crockett crossed his arms.

"Ha! That's where you're wrong." Silas smiled, but the expression looked too much like a wolf eyeing his prey to be comforting. "The Lord ain't gonna do the providin'. I am."

"*You* are?" Crockett jerked, his arms unfolding.

"Yep. Startin' tomorrow morning, you'll be working for the Lazy R." He stated it as if everything had already been decided. "Two meals and a dollar a day. Breakfast's at six. Come late, and you don't eat. Fail to handle the work I give you, and you're out on your ear."

Having delivered his dictates, Silas turned to leave. He made it all the way to his horse and had one foot in the stirrup when he stopped and shot a final hard look at Crockett.

"And no sermonizing. I'm hiring you to work cattle and tend to ranch chores, not spout nonsense at me all day. Understand?"

Oh, he understood. Better than Silas himself did. "Tomorrow at six," Crockett agreed, relaxing his stance. "I'll be there."

Silas muttered something under his breath, then mounted and rode off without another word.

Crockett watched him go, an odd satisfaction swelling in his chest. Silas had no idea what was in store for him. The Lord had indeed provided—provided not only a vocation for Crockett but also an opportunity for him to spend time with Joanna's father day in and day out. No wonder Joanna had lit out of the garden as if her skirts were on fire. She'd received divine inspiration. And it was brilliant.

He might be preaching on Sundays, but the rest of the week he'd be living out the message on a more practical level.

Help me make an impact, Lord. His heart is as hard as his head, but I know you are stronger. Work through me, and bring about your glory.

Crockett headed back to the mess that awaited him inside, a grin creasing his face. Silas might think he was coming to the ranch to work cattle, but in truth, he planned on fishing. Fishing for men.

Joanna adjusted her position on the high stool she had dragged to the loft window and studied her subject for several uninterrupted minutes before glancing away to add more details to her sketch. The way his hair brushed his collar at the back of his neck. The angle of his hat. The set of his chin. The way his rolled sleeves exposed muscled forearms.

His likeness was difficult to re-create exactly while he moved about the yard, but she hadn't been able to resist the lure of trying to capture him on paper when he'd driven the wagon in from the upper pasture and began stacking the split logs he'd transported into the woodshed.

Crockett Archer made an arresting artistic specimen.

When her father had ordered her to take Gamble home yesterday after her riotous ride and insisted on following up with the parson himself, she'd worried that he'd try to scare Brother Archer off. But the parson had knocked on her back door before six this morning and even helped her set out the platters of flapjacks and bacon.

She should have known better than to worry. Crockett Archer had never yet allowed her father to cow him. It'd been foolish to think he'd start now.

Joanna stroked her pencil firmly against the tablet as she delineated Crockett's profile, bringing definition to the soft outlines of her preliminary sketch. She idly nibbled her tongue as she shaded in the black of his hat and the long, dark lines of his trousers. The more she worked, the more the drawing came to life beneath her fingers. When she finished and held it out for a final inspection, her heart fluttered at the image before her.

Careful, Jo. God brought him here for your father—not for you.

"Afternoon, Miss Robbins." Brother Archer's deep voice echoed directly below the loft window.

With a guilty start, Joanna slammed the cover of her sketch pad closed. "A-afternoon."

"What are you doing up there?" His hat shaded his eyes, saving her from the teasing twinkle sure to be in evidence otherwise.

Taking a moment to regulate her pulse, Joanna slid from her stool and moved to the window ledge, picturing an invisible book on her head just as her mother had taught her. However, she probably needed an entire imaginary library to ground the hopes that kept trying to take flight within her.

"This is where I paint," she said, proud that her voice sounded normal. Then, not wanting him to question her further about her activities, she hurried to redirect the conversation. "How's your first day at the Lazy R going?"

"It's been anything but lazy—that's for sure." He chuckled a bit, and the sound drew a smile from her. "I'm accustomed to working my family's spread and having a say in what my day looks like, so taking orders from your father will require some getting used to, but we're managing. He hasn't drawn his gun on me today. I count that a success." He tipped his brim back and winked.

"And how is the parsonage working out? I had intended to help you clean it yesterday, until my father placed me on horse duty."

"It'll do." His lack of explanation, more than anything, told her how bad it truly was. "I wrote to my brother and asked Jasper to post the letter for me the next time he goes to town. Travis can box up my things and ship them here. That will make it feel more like home."

"Well, don't worry about the sanctuary. I'll round up some of the ladies in the area, and we'll give it a good scrubbing."

"With all the work I'll be doing here during the day, having one less thing to do to get ready for Sunday would be a tremendous blessing. Thank you." All hint of teasing left his voice, and what remained seeped into her pores like warm bathwater. She wanted to close her eyes and sink into it, but good sense prevailed.

"I'm glad to help, Brother Archer. We're partners in this endeavor, after all."

His gaze held hers, shrinking the distance between them as well as her resolve to be sensible. "Call me Crockett. At least when we're not in church. We are partners, after all." He grinned as he echoed her words.

"Yes, we are." Her pulse started up those crazy flutters again. "And as such, I think we need to—"

A furtive movement near the chicken coop stole her attention.

"What is it?" Crockett asked.

"I'm not sure." The shadow vanished. She peered at the corner of the coop, searching for a clue to help her decipher what she had seen. Nothing.

Except . . . There! A thin rod poked out from beneath the roof. A rod that looked suspiciously like . . .

Joanna spun away from her perch and clambered down the loft ladder as fast as her skirts would allow, ignoring Crockett's concerned calls. When she dashed into the yard, the parson dogged her heels.

"I know you're behind that coop, Jackson Spivey." Joanna eyed the rod as it twitched once, then disappeared behind the wall. "Show yourself."

She halted just short of the coop, wanting to give Jackson the chance to emerge on his own. He might be a boy, but he had his pride. And that pride was much in evidence when he marched around the corner, chin jutted, arms crossed.

"I ain't done nuthin' wrong, Jo. You don't have to lay into me like I'm some sort a criminal or somethin'."

"Didn't my father warn you about sneaking around the Lazy R? He told you not to do any more hunting on our land without permission."

Jackson blasted a puff of air out of the side of his mouth, as if her concerns needed shooing like some kind of pesky insect. "He just didn't want my rifle shots spookin' his cattle. Besides, I wasn't huntin'. I was fishin'. He ain't never said I couldn't do that." His glance shifted from Joanna to the man behind her, and his eyes widened as his belligerence drained away. "I made sure to stay clear of the pastures," he said, turning his attention back to her. "The best fishing holes and game trails are in the woods to the east, anyhow.

"I almost snared me a rabbit." This comment he directed to Crockett, a touch of excitement creeping into his voice. "He slipped the noose, though."

It irked a bit to know that a virtual stranger could inspire such a change in Jackson without saying a single word, while all her efforts to help the boy stay out of trouble seemed only to provide fodder for arguments. It must be a man thing—some kind of code. Her father could do the same thing with his men. She often left the dinner table feeling like an entire secondary conversation had taken place with nothing more than glances and grunts.

"You use fishing line for the snare?" Crockett asked as if there weren't more important issues to pursue.

"Yep. But I didn't have much time to set it up and got the knot tangled. It didn't close right."

"I can show you a quick knot my brother Jim showed me when we were kids. He was in charge of our meals, so he had the most practice—"

"Can we discuss this later, please?" Joanna glared a warning at Crockett. The rogue had the grace to look slightly abashed, but the way Jackson cocked a grin left her feeling as if the two had somehow allied against her.

"Jackson." She lightly gripped his shoulder to get his attention. "It's not just about scaring the cattle. My father has strict rules about knowing where each of the hands are, and he makes sure to always let me know where I can find him should there be a need. What if you were injured? No one would know where to find you."

"I could get injured in the wild lands behind my house and no one would find me there, either." The boy straightened his shoulders and stepped away from her mothering touch. "I'm man enough to know how to take care of myself, Jo. You don't have to worry about me."

The kid was all bravado, but she didn't have the heart to call him on it. "Would you please just ask permission first? I'm sure my father wouldn't mind letting you fish or snare small game in our woods now and again."

Jackson made no response, but the way his gaze darted toward the trees and back, she got the feeling he made more than the occasional foray through the Lazy R woods. Joanna swallowed a sigh. He probably had a hard time finding much game on that barren patch of land his father owned. And there was no telling how often Mr. Spivey actually remembered to bring home supplies after his drinking binges in Deanville. Taking access to the woods away from Jackson might mean taking away his food supply.

Before she could come up with a decent solution that would soothe Jackson's pride without riling her father's temper, Crockett voiced a suggestion.

"If you've got time to go fishing in the afternoons, I would guess you'd have time to put those muscles of yours to more profitable use."

Interest immediately lit Jackson's face. "You talkin' cash money, profitable?"

"Yep." Gone was the twinkle from Crockett's eye. The parson approached Jackson with all the seriousness and respect of one man doing business with another. "With me working at the ranch now, I'll need someone to run errands for me and help with repairs around the church. And since I don't know the area yet, I'll need someone to show me around and introduce me to folks. You interested?"

"How much you payin'?" Jackson crossed his arms, but not before Joanna noticed the trembling in his fingers.

Most people ignored Jackson, their lack of respect for his wastrel of a father leading them to keep their distance from him, as well. His penchant for trouble didn't help much, either. Yet as he stood there trying so hard to act as if he didn't care about Brother Archer's offer, Joanna could almost feel his hunger to prove himself worthy of the respect that had been denied him.

"Fifty cents a week."

Jackson's eyes doubled in size. She doubted the boy had ever had more than a couple pennies of his own to rub together.

"You got yourself a deal, Preacher." He held out a slightly shaky hand, and Crockett grasped it.

"Excellent. Can you meet me at the parsonage tonight around seven? We can discuss more of the details then." He slapped the boy on the shoulder, but then a small frown crept across his brow. "Unless you're needed at home, of course," he said. "I don't want you to neglect your other responsibilities."

"I ain't got none when Pa's away. And when he's home he's always shooing me out so he can do his leatherwork in peace. His head pains him a lot," Jackson added by way of explanation, "and noise makes it worse. As long as I leave him something to eat before I head out in the morning and show up long enough to fix him supper in the evening, he don't care what I do the rest of the time."

Joanna caught Crockett's quick glance and knew he felt the same sympathy she did for the boy. Thankfully, he did a good job of hiding it.

"Well, I'll plan to see you tonight, then, Jackson."

"I'll be there, sir." He spun away to collect his fishing gear and a string of three small catfish and a carp. "Tell your pa thanks for the fish, Jo." He winked and dodged out of her reach when she pretended to give chase, then set off for the road.

"Having a job will be good for him," Joanna said, stepping closer to Crockett. "Keep him out of trouble."

"Maybe it will keep him out of your hair for a while." The skin around the parson's brown eyes crinkled slightly when he smiled. She'd have to add that detail to her sketch later.

Joanna returned his smile, then dragged her thoughts back where they belonged—on Jackson. "I really don't mind having him around. In truth, some days I want to tie him to a chair and feed him 'til he fattens up. Other times I want to hug him until that chip on his shoulder falls off. That boy needs some serious mothering. Unfortunately, I don't think I'm the right one to do it."

"Because he's sweet on you." She could feel Crockett's eyes on her when he spoke, but she didn't turn. What she *did* do was wonder what he saw when he looked at her.

Perhaps she'd be better off not knowing.

"I just don't want to give him the wrong idea and end up being one more adult who lets him down." She kicked at the dirt with her foot. "He has an abundance of those already."

"So you harp at him like a big sister instead."

That brought her head up, along with an affronted gasp. Until she saw the teasing gleam in his eyes.

"You show all the classic signs," he said. "You order him about, take him to task when he misbehaves, and bake him chocolate cake on your birthday because you know it's *his* favorite. All because you care and want to protect him." He shook his head in mock despair. "Yep. You've got a bad case.

I've seen it before. My brother Travis still exhibits the symptoms, despite the fact that all the siblings who were in his care are now grown men."

Joanna pondered his observation, the revelation clicking things into place in a way that made sense. "I guess I do rather think of him as a younger brother." Somehow, knowing how to categorize her relationship with Jackson made it easier to define their boundaries.

Now she just needed Jackson to see it the same way. Maybe his spending time with Crockett would help with that.

"I suspect I need to be getting back to work." The parson ambled toward the emptied wagon. "Silas will be looking for me."

Joanna nodded, disappointed that he had to leave so soon but not wanting anything to cause friction between him and her father.

Crockett led the horses around, then climbed onto the driver's bench, took up the reins, and released the brake. She lifted a hand to wave.

"You've a good heart, Joanna Robbins," he said from his perch on the wagon seat. "It's easy to see why Jackson admires you."

He touched the brim of his hat in farewell and slapped the reins to get the team moving. As the wagon rolled out, his words lingered, tempting her to ponder other ideas. Like . . . if he could see why Jackson might admire her, did that mean *he* could come to admire her, as well? Or was he just playing big brother, unaware of the growing attraction she felt?

Perhaps she and Jackson had more in common than she'd thought.

15

It'd been three days since that conversation by the barn. Three days since she'd seen Crockett outside of mealtimes. Three days of staring at that silly sketch and wishing for things that would surely lead only to heartache.

Joanna exhaled a long breath and sat up enough to rub the perspiration from her forehead with her rolled sleeve. Her knees throbbed from being pressed into the wood floor for so long, but the dais supporting the pulpit glistened as if it were new.

Earlier in the week, she had arranged for several ladies to meet her at the church this afternoon for a cleaning spree. Together they'd been sweeping floors, washing windows, oiling pews, and even ridding the rafters of cobwebs, thanks to a large crate, a long-handled broom, and Mrs. Grimley's unfashionable height.

"Mother, is it time to go yet? We've been here for *hours*." Holly Brewster's woeful moan cut through the sounds of industriousness to grate on Joanna's nerves.

Grant me patience, Lord. Her mind sent the prayer heavenward while her eyes rolled the same direction. At least Holly had shown up to help. That's what she kept telling herself. But really, all she'd done was flick a dust rag haphazardly over a handful of windowsills—windowsills her mother had made a point to surreptitiously clean a second time when she came through with a bucket of vinegar water for the glass. The girl's apron was still as white and pressed as when she'd arrived and her hair flowed in beautiful blond waves down her back—unlike the rest of the women, who had clothes covered in grime and heads covered with kerchiefs.

"I think we're nearly finished, dear," Mrs. Brewster soothed. "Why don't you see if Joanna has anything that needs doing?"

Holly trudged over to the front of the church and twirled a hair ribbon around her index finger as she smiled prettily down at Joanna. "You don't need me to do anything—do you, Joanna? The angels themselves couldn't make this place any cleaner."

Joanna set aside her scrub brush and pressed her hand into the small of her back as she sat back on her heels. "Actually, if you could dump this lye water out in the field for me, I would really appreciate it. That way, I can start mopping up the excess moisture from the wood right away."

Holly eyed the dark brown water with obvious distaste. "Why, I don't think I could carry that heavy thing without sloshing its filthiness all over this beautiful clean floor. I would just feel dreadful if I caused a mess after everyone's diligent work."

And she'd probably feel even worse about sloshing the dirty liquid on her clean hem, but Joanna kept that opinion to herself. "I'm sure you can manage, Holly. Just walk slowly."

"I don't think you understand." Holly's smile never dimmed, but her eyes hardened. "I'm *sure* to spill. And I know you don't want that."

The not-so-veiled threat hung between them just long enough for Joanna to fantasize about turning the bucket over Holly Brewster's lovely head. In the end, Joanna simply shrugged and asked Holly to hand her the toweling piled in the front pew. She didn't have the energy to deal with a confrontation.

Holly tossed the rags to her with a triumphant grin and meandered over to one of the windows. Joanna had just started mopping up the first small puddle on the dais when Holly's quiet gasp brought her head up. The young woman's face was plastered to the window, her arms braced against the sill to give her a higher vantage point as she peered out toward the field.

"Joanna," she hissed, tossing a quick glance over her shoulder before pressing her nose back to the glass. "Is *that* the new parson? The man walking with Jackson Spivey?"

A curl of unease wound through Joanna's chest at Holly's obvious interest. "I reckon so," she admitted, despite her irrational desire to hoard the information. "Jackson does odd jobs for Brother Archer, so I wouldn't be surprised to see them together."

Holly spun from the window, tidied her already pristine apron, pinched some color into her cheeks, and then did the one thing Joanna never thought to see her do. She picked up the bucket of grungy lye water and started hauling it toward the door. *Without* spilling a drop on her pretty, ruffled hem, Joanna couldn't help but notice.

The girl had impeccable timing, too. She managed to reach the door at the exact moment Crockett did.

"Oh!" she exclaimed, as if coming upon him in the doorway had surprised her. "Pardon me. I hope I didn't get any of this dirty water on you."

Was it possible to hear eyelashes bat? Because Joanna could have sworn she heard heavy fluttering as Holly gazed adoringly up at Crockett.

"No harm done, miss."

Did he have to smile at her with the same twinkling grin she'd come to think of as hers? *Come now, Joanna, you can't really see his eyes from here.* Maybe not, but she could hear the charm oozing in his voice. All right, so maybe it wasn't oozing, but he certainly gave no indication that he saw through Holly's ruse. She'd thought him smarter than that. Really. Could the man not see that there was not a single smudge of dirt anywhere on her person? Nor was there even a hint of perspiration on her brow. Yet as Joanna watched, Holly raised a hand to her forehead as if to blot that nonexistent sheen.

"I'm so glad I didn't get any on you," she said, using that same hand to touch Crockett's arm. "After all the work I've done this afternoon, I'm quite fatigued, and I feared my grip might not be as steady as it should be."

"Why don't you let me dispose of that water for you?" Crockett shifted to take the pail, forcing the hand Holly had laid on his arm to fall back to her side. Joanna's lips curved slightly in satisfaction. Until his fingers encircled Holly's around the handle.

"Oh, thank you, Parson." Holly made no move to extract her hand. "That's ever so kind of you."

"It's the least I can do after all the work you ladies have done." He raised his eyes to glance about the sanctuary, directing his appreciation to everyone present. "The place looks marvelous. I can't thank you all enough." His gaze rested briefly on Joanna, and her breath caught. Had his smile deepened just then? But before she could decide the answer, Crockett turned his attention back to Holly.

"I'll be right back." He gently pulled the pail away, but Holly held on as long as possible.

"I'll come with you," she said. "I could do with some fresh air. My name's Holly, by the way. Holly Brewster."

And with that, the two of them disappeared through the doorway.

Joanna fought the urge to dash to the window and press her own face to the glass. The only thing restraining her was the fear that the other women would notice and comment upon her strange behavior. That, and the fact that her knees had been bent so long, her feet were numb.

"I think Holly's taken a fancy to the new preacher, Sarah." Etta Ward elbowed Mrs. Brewster and favored her with a matchmaker's smile.

"Heaven help us all," Mrs. Grimley muttered, turning her back on the scene.

Joanna amened the sentiment wholeheartedly.

"I'd steer clear of that Brewster gal if I were you." Jackson gave Crockett a man-to-man look as he handed the parson another nail.

Crockett hammered it into the new step he held in place while fighting to keep a smile from his face. "Oh? Why's that?"

Ever since the women left that afternoon, Jackson had been filling him in on all the pertinent details of the families that had been represented. Which ones came from farms versus ranches. How many young'uns they had. The names of their husbands. He'd efficiently rattled off the facts as the two of them repaired the church steps, but this latest comment seemed more personal.

"She acts real sweet and all, as long as things are going her way. But the minute you cross her, she turns meaner than a swarm of fire ants."

Crockett wondered what experience had led the boy to that conclusion, but he knew better than to ask. "I appreciate the warning," he said, reaching for another nail. "However, we need to be careful not to say anything unkind about her when she's not here to defend herself. All right?"

Jackson frowned and looked as if he wanted to argue, but eventually he nodded, and they resumed their work.

Yet thoughts of Holly, now resurrected, stubbornly refused to die. The young lady was certainly pretty. And even though he could tell she'd been exaggerating the tale of her cleaning exploits, the fact that she'd done it to impress him was rather gratifying. What man wouldn't enjoy the overt attentions of a beautiful woman? And while he could easily imagine her turning her lips out in a pout or storming off in a huff if she didn't get her wish, he could hardly picture her turning venomous. Maybe it would seem so to a boy, but it wouldn't be more than an irritant to a man.

Crockett drove in the last nail and straightened, visions of another young woman entering his mind, one who'd conversed with him on these very steps. Joanna's quietly intent nature contrasted sharply with Holly's vibrancy. While Miss Brewster's flirtation stroked his ego, the spiritual maturity Miss Robbins exhibited commanded his admiration and respect. Of course, to be fair, the ten minutes he'd spent in Miss Brewster's company this afternoon offered scant opportunity to form more than a surface opinion. A masculine smile tugged at Crockett's lips. He had to admit, though, his opinion of her surface was quite favorable.

"You want me to start sandin' the steps?" Jackson's question broke Crockett free from the dueling female images wreaking havoc on his concentration.

He cleared his throat. "Yes. They'll need a coat of paint, too, but it will be a while before I can make a trip to Deanville to pick some up."

"You gonna get enough to do the whole buildin'?" Jackson asked, assessing the peeling white clapboard with a critical eye.

"It sure needs it, doesn't it?" Crockett tipped his hat back, braced his right foot on the edge of one of the steps, and leaned his forearm across his thigh as he examined the neglect.

Jackson mirrored his stance from the opposite side. "Yep. But I ain't never painted a building afore. And if we gotta wait for you to get done at the Lazy R every day, it'd take us a right long time."

"I've got an idea about that."

Jackson stared at him expectantly, but Crockett said no more—partly to pique the kid's curiosity, and partly because he wasn't sure he could pull it off.

But if he could, he just might succeed at taking the first major step toward bringing the community together, and—even better—the first major step in bringing Silas Robbins into the fold.

16

Sunday arrived, and with it came an abundance of nervous energy that Joanna could not dispel. Unable to sleep, she'd risen before dawn and dispatched all her chores in record time. She'd even fussed over her appearance longer than usual, wrestling her unruly hair into a soft chignon and trying on both of her Sunday-worthy dresses so many times it was a wonder the shine hadn't worn off the brass buttons. Despite her lengthy attire deliberations, though, when she checked the mantel clock in the parlor, the hands hadn't progressed nearly as far as she had hoped. Services weren't scheduled to start for another hour.

A tiny moan escaped her lips. She couldn't stay here and wait. She'd go crazy.

Joanna entered the kitchen, thinking to check on the roast she'd put in the oven. But what was there to check? She'd already done everything that could be done ahead of time. The roast, onions, carrots, and potatoes were baking. The spinach greens were washed and ready for boiling. Bread baked yesterday waited in the pie safe, and the hard-boiled eggs to top the spinach were already peeled and sitting in a covered bowl on the counter. So what was she to do?

Her gloves and Bible beckoned to her from where they lay on the table. It had been about this time last Sunday when she'd decided to walk down to the church. Of course, that was before services were officially being held. Yet even then, Crockett had been there. He was probably there now, strolling up and down the center aisle, making sure everything was ready for his inaugural service, perhaps going over his sermon a final time. Was he nervous?

He always seemed so calm and in control, but he had no way of knowing if his presence would be readily accepted. *She* had no way of knowing.

Starting the church back up had been *her* dream. What if the community failed to embrace the idea of a new minister? What if no one came?

Joanna's eyes rolled at her melodramatic thoughts. Of course they'd come—out of curiosity, if nothing else. After all, the ladies had shown up to help with the cleaning. They wouldn't expend such an effort if they didn't plan to attend. Still, it wouldn't hurt to offer Crockett some moral support, a friendly face to soothe away any anxiety he might be feeling.

She wouldn't mind the chance to be alone with him again, either.

And wasn't *that* an improper thought to be having on a Sunday morning.

Blowing out a breath, Joanna shoved her hands into her best pair of gloves, grabbed up her Bible, and resolved to purify her motives before she reached the church.

Never one to enjoy stringent lectures, even mental ones instigated by herself, Joanna delighted in discovering a familiar figure a few paces ahead of her when she joined the main road. She quickened her step to catch him.

"Jackson Spivey. Don't you look dapper, all cleaned up," she said by way of greeting as she pulled abreast of the young man. He slowed his step and kicked at a tuft of grass at the side of the road.

"Yeah, well, I ain't been to church since my ma left," he said, a dull red rising up his neck, "but I remember she always made me wash behind my ears afore we came. So I figured I ought to scrub real good today."

A soft smile tugged at Joanna's mouth. It seemed Crockett's presence was already working miracles. The boy's damp hair had been combed into submission and he sported a clean shirt, though the sleeves hung past his wrists. He'd probably borrowed it from his father. Tenderness welled inside her for the young man so eager to please his new mentor.

"I think you look quite fine."

Jackson's face jerked toward hers. "You do?"

The vulnerability he usually tried to hide flashed to the surface for a moment, and Joanna couldn't help but offer the reassurance he so obviously craved. "Yes, I do."

"Fine enough for me to escort you to services?" Just that fast, all hint of self-doubt fled from his expression, leaving only adolescent male swagger in its wake.

Even so, Joanna couldn't ignore the plea for acceptance that lurked behind the cocksure words. "I'd be happy to accept your escort," she said, "as a friend." She gave special emphasis to the word *friend* and breathed easier when Jackson nodded in understanding.

He offered her his arm, and Joanna slipped her fingers into the crook of his elbow.

"If you're gonna walk with me, Jo, you gotta pick up the pace." Once he had hold of her, Jackson lengthened his stride, nearly dragging her in his hurry. "Crock promised I could ring the bell if I got there early enough. We can't be late."

Joanna stifled a chuckle and quickened her steps. It seemed escorting her to services wasn't quite as big a coup as ringing the church bell.

"God loves us all individually," Crockett pronounced as he strode across the dais, making eye contact with imaginary church members seated in the pews, "and he has blessed each of us with talents and spiritual gifts as unique as the shape of a face or the sound of a voice. Yet it is not God's will that we exist solely as individuals. He desires us to be in community with him and with each other. For it is only when individual members unite as a single body under Christ that the fullness of his love can be demonstrated to the world. It was for this unity that Jesus himself prayed in John's gospel, chapter seventeen."

Crockett paced back to the pulpit and his notes, uncertainty stealing his voice as he moved into the next section of the sermon, the part that had kept him up until midnight last night writing and rewriting. Praying over and worrying over. He wanted to call the community together, to bind them, to challenge them. But what if he alienated them or offended them? Would his ministry be over before it began?

He shifted his papers and cleared his throat. He couldn't remember ever being this unsure over a lesson. Ever. Since the time he was a boy, confidence in his calling had always been the foundation that gave him the courage to speak with boldness, more concerned with the message God wanted him to impart than pleasing itching ears. So why was that foundation shaking?

Grant me wisdom to speak what you want spoken, Lord, and nothing more.

Glancing over his notes a final time, Crockett inhaled a cleansing breath, released it, and continued where he had left off.

"For too long, this community has consisted of individuals. Individuals drawn together by geography, or perhaps friendship, or even family. But it has not been united as fully as God desires. It has not been one body under Christ. Today we can change that. Today God has brought us together in a way that pleases him, as the text we read a moment ago from 1 Corinthians 12 attests.

"We don't simply meet together in this building because it is a convenient place to worship. We meet in order to rejoice together and mourn together. To uplift and encourage one another. To gain strength from the strong and humility from the weak. To experience the artistry of the Master Weaver who brings all of our individual gifts together to create a tapestry more beautiful than any one person can achieve alone. A tapestry that proclaims

God's glory to every eye that beholds it. A tapestry that is incomplete without you . . ."

His gaze crossed from a pew halfway back on the left to the second one from the front on the right. "Or you . . . or . . ." His gaze slid toward the back of the sanctuary and collided with Joanna, standing silently in the doorway. "You. . . ." Crockett's voice tapered off.

For a moment, all he could do was stare. Her rapt attention, the tiny smile that brought into relief the freckles dusting her cheekbones, the way the light passed through the doorway behind her to set her hair ablaze beneath the prim straw bonnet she wore. Yet it was her inner light that captured him most. The serenity of her features. The glow in her blue eyes. This was a woman of authentic spirituality. No wonder the Master Weaver had chosen her to be the central thread to anchor his new tapestry.

Crockett had no idea how long he stood there gawking. It would have been longer, he was sure, had Jackson not bounded past her and down the aisle, severing the connection that had held him enthralled.

"I'm ready to ring the bell, Crock. Is it time?"

Joanna dipped her head, further releasing him.

"Not yet. Ah . . ." He coughed a bit and dug in his vest pocket for his timepiece as he stepped off the dais and strode down the aisle. "Here," he said, handing the watch to Jackson. "At a quarter 'til the hour, you can ring the call to worship."

The boy cupped the watch in his hand as if it were a piece of fine china. "I'll be careful with it. I swear."

"I know you will." Crockett thumped him on the shoulder. "Go on, now. Take up your position and prepare the rope like I showed you."

The boy traipsed to the back of the sanctuary, leaving Crockett all too conscious of the woman who had moved down the aisle to join him.

"If you win over the rest of the folks the way you have Jackson," she said in a quiet voice that suggested she had no doubt he would, "you'll soon be in need of a larger building."

Crockett darted a glance at her, then directed his attention to the floorboards, an unseen band tightening across his chest. "He's a good kid." A lonely kid who needed a friend. Easy enough to handle. Crockett understood loneliness. Seclusion. He'd lived it. It was no hardship having Jackson around. He kind of reminded Crockett of his kid brother, Neill.

But meeting the spiritual needs of grown men and women was different. More complicated.

Crockett stared at the notes still in his hand. How inadequate they seemed. What did he know about shepherding a flock? *I'm not ready. I—*

"Everyone is looking forward to the services today." Joanna's innocent comment only fueled his doubts. "I told the women when we were cleaning about the sermon you preached last Sunday—how powerful it was, how it moved me."

"You shouldn't have done that," he muttered, his clothes starting to itch against his skin. He paced behind a pair of pews to the window that overlooked the road and scratched a spot on the back of his neck near his collar. "They'll expect too much of me." *You'll expect too much of me.* "I'd practiced that sermon for weeks. This one . . ." He held up the notes and waved them dismissively in the air. "This one I didn't even finish until late last night."

"But I heard you when I came in," she argued, her footsteps echoing on the floor behind him. "Your words touched me the same way as before. Such wisdom and confidence. I know the others will hear it, too."

Confidence? Ha! What confidence? It had deserted him along with his clarity and focus.

She had no business building up people's expectations. He was just an ordinary preacher, self-taught for the most part. Who was he to bring a community together? Who was he to break through to her father when neither she nor her mother had been able to? It was too much to ask. *I should have never agreed to—*

A gentle hand suddenly covered his fisted one where it ground into the windowsill. Crockett closed his eyes as her calm soaked into his spirit.

"Moses doubted he could lead God's people," she said, her voice as gentle as her touch. "Jeremiah thought himself too young and inexperienced to speak for the Lord. It was only when they realized that success was not up to them but up to God that they were able to accomplish what the Lord asked of them."

Slowly, her fingers worked their way into his until his fist loosened and his hand lay relaxed, cradled within hers. "I, more than anyone, know how heavy the burden can become when we feel incapable of coping with the calling set before us. But as my mother used to remind me, I now remind you. Our only job is to be obedient to the call, to scatter the seed. It is God's job to give the increase. Don't try to carry that load. No human can."

Finally he turned. His eyes met hers, and the confidence that had abandoned him in such haste began trickling back.

"Speak the words God has given you, Crockett. Let him worry about the rest."

At that moment, he wanted nothing more than to pull Joanna into his arms and hold her against his chest, to absorb her strength and refuel his depleted stores. But such an act would be neither proper nor prudent, so he settled for squeezing her hand and smiling into her sweet face—a face that hid the heart of a warrior.

"Thank you." Crockett prayed she could read the depth of his gratitude through those paltry words. "God must have known I'd need you to bolster my confidence this morning."

"So it's *your* fault that ornery rooster sounded off an hour early." She startled a laugh out of him with that sassy retort, and all at once, it seemed as if the earth shifted back onto its normal axis.

Crockett straightened away from the window and reluctantly released Joanna's hand. "Seems only fitting that a rooster would help me get my swagger back." He winked, and she cuffed him lightly on the arm, her own eyes dancing.

"Seems to me, you have swagger to spare." Her voice was playfully prim, but the quick glance she shot at him over her shoulder as she moved away left him fighting the urge to engage in some very rooster-like strutting.

The chiming of the church bell saved him from any barnyard theatrics—that and the fact that his little chick had flown the coop to check on Jackson. Crockett tipped his head back and grinned up at the rafters.

"Impeccable timing—as usual, Lord."

His optimism and good humor restored, Crockett sauntered down the aisle and vaulted back up onto the dais to return his notes to the pulpit before taking up his place at the door to greet his congregation.

Let them come, he thought as the first wagon appeared around the curve in the road. *I'm ready.*

17

Joanna's heart swelled with satisfaction as the service neared its close. Crockett's sermon had been delivered flawlessly, as she'd known it would be, full of the same passion and sincerity that stirred her soul the first time she'd heard him speak. And if the few amens that had echoed in the rafters earlier were any indication, she wasn't the only one who'd been moved.

In truth, the only thing that would have made her happier was if her father were sitting in the pew beside her and Jackson. But she wouldn't get ahead of herself. One step at a time.

"One day is with the Lord as a thousand years, and a thousand years as one day." The familiar verse ran through her mind as Crockett invited the congregation to stand for the final hymn, "Trust and Obey"—a fitting selection, as well as a fitting reminder. Joanna joined her voice with the others as her heart prayed for greater patience and trust in the Lord's timing.

Once the song concluded, Crockett asked the members to retake their seats. "I have a few announcements to make before we dismiss," he said, his smile apologetic. "I promise not to take long."

He waited for the shuffle of bodies settling to quiet before he continued. "I wanted to give special thanks to the ladies who worked so diligently on Friday afternoon scrubbing, sweeping, and shining things up in here." His focus rested briefly on each of the women who'd helped with the cleaning, including Holly Brewster, who was leaning so far forward in her pew to preen that for a moment Joanna thought the girl would rise and take a bow.

When Crockett's eyes finally met Joanna's, the twinkle she loved was in full force, as if he could read her thoughts and was sharing a private laugh with her. Wishful thinking, most likely, but pleasant warmth spread through her nonetheless.

"Now that we have the inside refurbished, I'd like to enlist your aid in fixing up the outside."

One man grumbled something under his breath from a row or so behind Joanna, then another from across the aisle. She had to fight the urge to glare some courtesy into them. This building belonged to all of them. It was only right for everyone to contribute to its upkeep. Especially since Crockett had yet to draw a salary.

"I know everyone is busy," Crockett conceded, moving out from behind the pulpit, "so I thought we would turn our workday into a celebration with games and activities for the whole family. Horse races and shooting contests for the men, pie-baking contests for the women, and maybe a greased pig for the kids."

An excited buzz now hummed through the chapel.

"Instead of a barn-raising shindig, we'll have a church-painting one. I'll need some help in organizing the activities, so if there is anyone who would like to volunteer to chair a planning committee, please speak with me after we dismiss. We'll take the funds collected from the offering today and next Sunday to purchase paint and supplies. Then, two weeks from Saturday we'll gather for the event. Everyone in the community will be welcome to participate, whether they attend services here or not." Crockett looked directly at her as he imparted this last bit, and her pulse leapt at the implications.

Her father. He couldn't resist a chance to show off his marksmanship. And she doubted he could keep from entering Gamble in the races, either. He'd been itching for a chance to pit his new horse's speed against mounts offering more competition than the Lazy R cow ponies. This event would be the perfect enticement.

"Did you know about this?" she whispered to Jackson when Crockett turned his attention to the rest of the crowd.

The boy bent his head close to hers. "Nah. I knew he wanted to paint, but I never guessed he'd throw a party. You think it'll work?"

"We'll just have to make sure it does. Deal?" She extended her gloved hand to shake on it.

Jackson fit his hand to hers, his jaw set. "Deal."

Her mind suddenly swirling with ideas, Joanna reached for the small tablet she carried with her for taking notes during the sermon and flipped to a clean page. She'd never planned any kind of community event before, but she'd attended them. Surely she could figure out what needed to be done. Crockett would help.

Joanna bit her lip as her pencil hovered above the paper. The thought of having an excuse to spend more time with the parson set her stomach to dancing. So distracted was she by the image of the two of them huddled together on the settee in the parlor, that she failed to hear Crockett's dismissal. When Mrs. Grimley stopped by her pew, it startled Joanna to realize that everyone was up and milling around and probably had been for several minutes.

Clutching her Bible and tablet to her chest, she lurched to her feet. "Oh, Mrs. Grimley! I didn't see you there."

"Well, now that you do, what do you think of the preacher's plan?" The stern-faced woman raised a brow at her, but Joanna had known her too long to be fooled into thinking the dour expression actually indicated what was in her heart.

"I think it's a wonderful idea. In fact, I was thinking of volunteering to help with the planning committee."

Mrs. Grimley tilted her head toward the pulpit. "Better get a move on, then. That Brewster gal's already got a jump on you."

Sure enough, Holly had Crockett blocked in at the front of the church. She and Becky Sue stood side by side, barricading the center aisle while Holly gushed all over the parson.

Crockett smiled and nodded politely, but there was a tension about his eyes that Joanna hadn't seen since the day her father brought him to the ranch with a lariat around his middle. Clearly, the man was crying out for rescue.

"Excuse me, Mrs. Grimley," Joanna said as she started backing toward the outer aisle. "I believe I'm needed at the front."

She had already turned and had nearly reached the end of the pew when Mrs. Grimley's quiet chuckle met her ear. "Yes, dearie. I believe you are."

Strengthened by the thought of having at least one ally in her corner, Joanna skirted a pair of farmers discussing the worth of a particular mule another man had for sale, and made her way along the wall to the dais. There wasn't much room to maneuver, what with Holly's mother and Etta Ward working hard to eavesdrop from their position in front of the first pew, where they pretended to converse. Joanna supposed she could walk over the dais to get to Crockett, but somehow it seemed wrong for her to step up there, despite the fact that she'd crawled across it on her hands and knees not two days ago. So instead, she twisted sideways and inched along the edge of the stage until she stood a few feet behind Crockett.

"I have so many wonderful ideas," Holly was saying, "and I know simply *everyone* around here, so you won't have to worry about a thing with me in charge." Holly laid her hand on Crockett's arm, and Joanna had to fight the sudden urge to slap it away.

"I'm grateful for your assistance, Miss Brewster. I have no doubt that you are the perfect person to head up the planning committee."

The perfect person? The words cut a surprisingly deep gash in Joanna's hide. Of course he'd think she was perfect. Perfect hair, perfect figure, perfect smile, perfect connections. Perfect veneer for that perfectly horrid temperament she hid so well from the male population.

"Becky Sue and I can arrange decorations for the tables, and I'm sure Mother would be happy to oversee the food arrangements. Wouldn't you, Mama." Holly finally tore her gaze away from Crockett to draw her mother into the conversation, but when she saw Joanna, she immediately turned back to the parson.

"Mama's the best cook in the county. And she knows what every woman's specialty is. She'll organize a feast like you've never tasted. And I'm sure her dear friend Mrs. Ward would volunteer to plan the pie-baking contest. Her husband would be the perfect judge. Nelson Ward's sweet tooth is legendary in these parts."

"That sounds splendid. I'm sure they'll do a fine job. Now, if—"

"Oh, but what about the games?" Holly interrupted, determined to monopolize his time. Didn't she care that she was keeping him from speaking to the other members? It was essential for a new minister to get to know the people of his congregation. All he needed was for one or two crotchety souls to get their dander up because he didn't speak to them before they left.

Joanna frowned. Her own hurt feelings no longer seemed so important. The important thing was ensuring Holly didn't sabotage Crockett's chance to make the best possible first impression.

"I'll need your input on the arrangements for the men's sporting events," Holly insisted.

Crockett backed away, and began looking past her to the rear of the building, where people were slipping through the door. "I'll be happy to assist you, Miss Brewster, but now is not the time."

"Of course." Holly must have sensed that she'd pushed him too far, for she immediately changed tactics. "How silly of me. I just got so excited. We can discuss it over dinner. Mother insisted that I invite you to join us after services."

Joanna's heart fell. She'd been hoping Crockett would dine at the Lazy R. Did Holly have to beat her at this, too? Apparently so, judging by the triumphant smile the blond beauty shot her when Crockett wasn't looking.

"That'll be fine," he said, his attention more focused on the door than on the woman before him. But even that was small comfort in light of the knowledge that Holly Brewster would have him all to herself this afternoon. "Now, if you'll excuse me?"

Holly beamed at him, successfully drawing his notice once again. Then, like the Red Sea of old, she and Becky Sue parted to let Crockett pass through on dry land.

He hadn't even realized she'd been standing behind him.

"It's too bad Brother Archer had to dash off before you had a chance to speak with him, Joanna." Holly sashayed back toward the pulpit, waving the edges of her royal blue skirt like a jay showing off its wings. No, not a jay. With that predatory gleam in her eyes, she was definitely a hawk. A hawk marking her territory and fluttering her wings to keep another female from chasing after her mate of choice.

Well, she could flutter and glare all she wanted. Joanna wasn't about to scurry away like a frightened mouse. "That's all right," she said. "I can speak with him at breakfast tomorrow."

For a fleeting moment, Holly's mouth twisted into a grimace. It didn't last long before being smoothed away, but Joanna experienced a little thrill of satisfaction, nonetheless. It felt good to score a point.

"If it has anything to do with the church picnic, you can ask me. Brother Archer put me in charge of the event." Her brows lifted slightly, as if checking off a point in her own score column.

"I see." Joanna hated to ask the girl for any favors, but helping Crockett was worth more than her pride. And so was her father. "I *had* intended to volunteer my services for the painting day. Perhaps I could assist with some of the games or sporting contests?"

"Definitely not the sporting contests," Holly barked, then immediately softened her tone. "Your father is sure to enter those. He always does. How would it look if Silas Robbins's daughter was in charge of laying out the racecourse or placing the targets? If he were to win, some disgruntled contestant might cry foul. I'm sure you would never do anything to grant your father an unfair advantage, but we don't want there to be even a hint of impropriety. Why, it could reflect poorly on Brother Archer, and I know you wouldn't want that."

"Of course not, but—"

"And I've already decided on committee members for the food and baking events."

"What about the greased pig for the kids?" Joanna couldn't imagine the always pristine Holly wanting anything at all to do with that event. "I could—"

"No." Holly shook her head. "I've already decided that Jackson should be in charge of that. You know how the parson dotes on him. I'm sure he'd want the boy to be involved."

Jackson *would* be a good choice, Joanna thought sourly, and naming him to the committee was just the kind of action that could endear Holly to Crockett. Which no doubt was the girl's motivation for suggesting it. But that left Joanna without a way to participate.

"How about the paint?" Becky Sue spoke up for the first time, darting a quick glance at Holly before continuing. "You know, since she and her mother were always painting those pictures, she'd probably know what kind of paint to buy."

"Any ninny would know what kind of paint to buy," Holly huffed.

"But if she were in charge of the paint, she'd have to travel to Deanville to pick it up and would probably be gone most of the day . . ."

"And that would free Brother Archer up to help me with any last-minute details. Excellent idea, Becky Sue."

The brunette grinned like a puppy that had just been rewarded with a scrap of jerky.

"I'd be happy to take charge of the paint." Joanna hurried to claim the responsibility before Holly changed her mind. Any opportunity to help was better than none.

Besides, it'd been ages since her father had let her travel to Deanville. Maybe if she made the trip soon enough, she could pick out some fabric for a new dress and actually have time to make it up before the picnic. Something pretty. Something to catch a certain gentleman's eye before the blond hawk of doom swooped down and sunk her talons into him.

18

Rain pounded Silas's shoulders as he pulled Marauder to a halt under a large oak. The branches above him did blessed little to ease the downpour, but it was more cover than the man in the flats below him had. Out in the open, his new hand's only protection was a borrowed yellow pommel slicker and a hat that had been pulverized too long to adequately hold its shape.

The others had had the good sense to come in an hour ago and were drying out by the stove in the bunkhouse. Silas had hunkered down with them for a while, too—until Frank's bellyaching wore on his nerves—but the house was no better, what with Jo's fretful glances and pestering questions about Crockett Archer's whereabouts. Silas's only chance for peace was to head back out into the storm and find him.

He'd expected to find the preacher man holed up in one of the line shacks or limping back after being thrown from his horse. He hadn't expected to find the man knee-deep in mud trying to wrestle a cow out of a washed-out gulley.

A frown tugged on Silas's mouth as he nudged Marauder down the hill to lend a hand. What made the man work so hard for one cow? A cow that wasn't even his?

Over the last three weeks, Silas had worked Archer hard—gave him the worst jobs, demanded he stay late, knowing full well the fella needed every spare minute he could wrangle to plan his silly church-painting shindig. He'd seen the dark circles under the parson's eyes, noted the drag in his step, but still he'd pushed—practically dared the sermonizer to quit.

Not only did the preacher man not quit, he worked harder than any of the other hands.

Frank and Carl were lazy cusses who only did what was required of them, but they'd run with Silas in the early days, so turning them out would be like turning out family. Jasper was capable enough to run things on the ranch, should the need ever arise, but he shied from the responsibility of the place. His loyalty was to Silas, not the ranch.

Archer, on the other hand, worked the ranch as if he were personally vested in the outcome. He worked it like an owner. Like Silas himself. No job was beneath him, because all had to be done. He never complained. Always completed his tasks. And if he saw something that needed doing, he did it, whether it was his assignment or not. Which probably explained why he was out in this downpour instead of inside, where anyone with half a brain would be.

Silas reached the gulley and quickly unstrapped the lariat from his pommel. With ease of practice, he lengthened the noose, twirled it a couple times to get a feel for how it would fly in the rain, and let it sail over the cow's head. Archer's hand flew to his sidearm as his face came around. Silas raised a hand in greeting, knowing any words would get lost in the deluge. Archer released his weapon and returned the wave. Silas wrapped the end of the rope around the saddle horn, patted Marauder's neck, and then dismounted and strode to the edge of the wash.

Archer slogged over to meet him, the mud sucking at his boots. "Her forelegs are stuck," he yelled to be heard above the storm. "I was afraid she'd strangle if I roped her neck. I've been trying to dig her out, but the mud is so soft, it slides right back in."

"I'll work the head, you work the legs," Silas shouted. "Maybe we can get her out together."

Archer nodded.

After twenty minutes of pushing and pulling, digging and squirming, and three armloads of twigs, branches, and leaves to add stability to the mud, the bawling cow finally managed to crawl out.

Silas removed the rope from her neck, mounted Marauder, and herded the heifer back to the group of strays that were huddled front-to-end beneath a stand of pines a short distance away. Once he was sure the ornery thing didn't intend to wander toward the gulley again, he turned his horse and headed back to meet up with Archer. Only the man wasn't on his horse. He was sitting on the edge of the wash, hunched over with his head against his knees.

A pang ricocheted off Silas's conscience. The man had given all he had on that final push, practically lifting the stupid beast onto his shoulder as he strained to free her legs. Silas hated to admit it, but without the parson, he probably would've lost that beeve. He never thought the day would come when he'd feel beholden to a preacher man or, worse, actually respect one.

With a grunt, he swung down out of the saddle and carved his way through the rain and mud until his feet stood boot tip to boot tip with his new man. He waited for Archer's head to tip up and then held out his hand. The parson's gaze moved from his hand to his face, and something in Archer's eyes gave Silas the impression that he recognized he was being offered more than just a hand up.

Archer's stare held his without wavering, and when his hand clasped Silas's, the grip was strong and sure. And as he hauled the parson to his feet, a burning need flared to life in Silas's gut—a need to understand what drove this man. What compelled a rancher who co-owned a family spread to work for another man just so he could preach in a small country church in the middle of nowhere?

Joanna paced back to the kitchen window for what must have been the hundredth time in the last twenty minutes. Crockett should have come home with the rest of the hands hours ago, but he hadn't. Was he hurt? Had his horse broken a leg in a mud hole? No one could work in this rain. She couldn't even see past the edge of the porch.

Her daddy had rolled his eyes at her worrying, but he'd eventually gone out to look for Crockett. As always, Silas Robbins knew exactly where each of his men would be working, and he'd promised to drag the parson back within the hour. Only that hour had become two. Now she had two men to fret over.

Joanna's nails dug into her palms as she strained to see through the downpour. It was barely three in the afternoon, but it was dark as night out there. The cascading rain drowned out all other sounds, so she couldn't depend upon hearing the horses when they returned. All she could do was stare into the torrent and hope to spy the shadowy outlines of Crockett and her father.

Bring them home safely, Lord. Please. Bring both of them home.

She'd already made coffee and laid out towels and blankets—had even fetched two sets of dry clothes from her father's room, knowing all of Crockett's spares were back at the parsonage. She turned away from the window long enough to retrieve a pair of earthenware mugs from the cabinet, then resumed her vigil.

The sheets of rain were so thick she could barely make out the barn, but she probed the darkness anyway, desperate for a sign of . . . There! Movement. Definitely movement. Joanna pressed her palm to the glass and angled her face so she could see farther to the east. Lightning flashed overhead, followed immediately by a loud clap of thunder. But the noise didn't matter, for in those brief seconds of light, the mustard yellow of the men's slickers signaled her like a beacon.

Needing to get closer to them, she bolted out to the porch to watch their progress. Jasper must have been keeping an eye out, as well, for the bunkhouse door slammed open and his stiff-legged, poncho-covered form darted out into the yard and met them at the barn entrance. The men dismounted and handed their reins to Jasper. When they turned, Joanna waved to them in large sweeping motions, hoping they'd see her through the rain. She moved as close to the edge of the covered porch as she dared and cupped her hands around her mouth.

"Come to the house!" she shouted when Crockett started trudging toward the building Jasper had just vacated.

The parson lifted his head and stopped but made no move to change direction.

"Don't make me come out there to get you!"

Crockett would probably accuse her of taking on the bossy big-sister role again, but there was nothing sisterly about the concern she felt for him. And if he turned away from her again, he would see just how bossy she could be. She had no qualms about going after him. Her father's men wouldn't take care of him the way she would, and she aimed to see that he suffered no ill effects from this day's work. The poor man had to be drenched to the skin. He'd easily catch his death if not properly tended.

Thankfully, her father saved her from having to chase the man down. He came alongside Crockett and said something while jerking his head toward the house. After that, Crockett followed him, and soon the two men joined her on the porch.

Her father hung his hat and slicker on a peg and bent to kiss Joanna's cheek. His whiskery face was cold against hers. Crockett had been out twice as long. He must be nearly frozen.

"You got coffee going, Jo?" Her father asked as he made use of the bootjack.

"Yes, and there's plenty of hot water for washing." She wanted to hug his neck but knew he wouldn't want to get her wet, so instead she took charge of his boots once he had them off and stood them up against the wall.

"Thanks, darlin'." He grinned at her, then turned to Crockett. "Don't dawdle, Archer. You won't be any use to me if you start ailin'."

The kitchen door closed behind her father, and still Crockett made no move. "I shouldn't come in," he finally said. "I'm covered in grime and will drip mud all over your floors."

"I'd rather worry about the floors than about you. Come on, now. You're trembling from the cold, Crockett. Come in and get warm."

He was pale, too, and sluggish in his movements. After watching him struggle with the fasteners on his slicker for a long, agonizing minute, Joanna stepped close and took over the task herself.

Even with his weakened condition, standing close to him tickled her insides. Her heart thumped wildly in her chest, but she kept her head down, hiding his effect on her with a mask of efficiency. Once the metal buttons had been worked free, she stepped back to allow him space to pull the slicker off. His trembling became more violent as he hung up the coat and reached for his hat.

Her father's shirt had been damp, and his trousers had been soaked from the knees down, but Crockett looked as if he'd just pulled himself out of the river fully clothed. He was sodden, dripping.

Joanna clasped his arm to steady him when he tried to use the bootjack, then quickly arranged his footwear next to her father's before half pushing, half pulling him into the kitchen and steering him toward the stove. One of the mugs was missing from the table, so she knew her father had grabbed some coffee before heading to his room to change.

Crockett just stood where she'd placed him, as if he couldn't figure out what to do next. Gone was his playful, teasing manner. Gone was the twinkle from those deep brown eyes. Truly, he was starting to scare her. She reached for the coffeepot, thinking that getting something hot and bracing inside him would help. But then she heard his teeth chatter, and she immediately changed tactics. She grabbed one of the blankets she'd set out earlier and threw it around his shoulders, like her mother used to do for her after her baths when she'd been little. Then she began rubbing his arms, trying to warm him with the friction. Frowning at his continued shivering, she stepped closer and wrapped her arms more fully around him, rubbing his shoulders and his back. Only he was so broad she couldn't reach all the way around.

His chin bumped the top of her head as she slanted in for a better vantage. She glanced up and froze. His eyes were anything but lifeless now. Intensity glowed from within their depths, the type of intensity that made it impossible to look away. Or breathe.

The type of intensity that whispered possibilities. If she hadn't trapped his arms with the blanket, would he circle them around her and draw her into a real embrace? Would his face bend to hers and sear her lips with a kiss?

Would her father catch them and tear the parson limb from limb?

This last thought brought sanity. Joanna dropped her gaze and stepped back. Eyeing the table, she grabbed the towel sitting so prim and tidy on the corner and shoved it at him.

"For your hair," she mumbled.

He stretched a hand out from under the blanket and took it from her. Unable to resist the temptation of seeing if that intensity still burned in his eyes, she chanced a quick glance at his face. His features had indeed changed, but the heart-stopping half smile he sported, and the resurgence of the twinkle that had earlier been dormant, left her equally giddy.

As she aimed her attention at the coffee once again and turned her back to the soggy parson with the dancing eyes, a secret smile curved her lips.

"Ain't you poured the man his coffee yet, Jo? He's gotta be half froze." Her father's booming voice nearly startled her out of her skin.

"I wanted to dry off first," Crockett quickly interjected, scrubbing the towel against his hair. "At this rate, I'm going to leave a lake-sized puddle in your kitchen." His teeth still chattered slightly as he spoke, but he was starting to sound more like himself—a fact that soothed Joanna considerably.

"Well, since Jo went to the trouble of laying out a second set of clothes, and seeing as how I don't plan to wear both, I suggest you step into the back room and put those on." Her father jabbed a finger toward the shirt, pants, and socks folded tidily on the tabletop.

Crockett stilled. "Thank you, sir. I will."

But he didn't seem to know how to collect the clothes while holding both the blanket and towel. He couldn't exactly tuck them under his arm. They'd be soaked in seconds.

"Here." Joanna grabbed the dry clothes and reached for the coffee she'd just poured him. "I'll show you the way."

She led him to a small guest room at the back of the house and set his coffee on the edge of the bureau near the door. "Just wrap your wet things up in the blanket when you're through and bring them out to the kitchen. I'll string a clothesline near the stove."

Crockett squeezed through the doorway beside her. Slowly. So slowly that when his eyes met hers and held, she felt as if time had halted altogether. Neither of them spoke, but something was definitely being communicated. Joanna just wished she understood what it was. Her untutored, rapidly pounding heart wanted very much to believe it was two souls recognizing they belonged together, yet her head warned it was probably nothing more than friendship and gratitude.

So when Crockett murmured a quiet "Thank you" and moved into the room, proving her mind wiser than her heart, Joanna hid her disappointment with a gracious smile and a hasty retreat.

She slid into a chair at the table next to her father, drawing in the comfort of his solid, dependable presence. It was too bad she couldn't climb up into his lap like she used to as a child. She eyed his shoulder longingly, took in his pensive demeanor as he stared into his half-empty coffee mug, and finally decided to ignore her head and listen to the urging of her heart. Without saying a word, she scooted her chair closer to his and laid her head on his shoulder.

He didn't turn his head or say a word. The break in the pattern of his breathing was the only indication he was aware of her actions. But then a measure of tension drained from his muscles, and his head tipped toward hers in an armless embrace.

"He's a hard worker, this preacher of yours," her father said after a long minute. He straightened his head and rearranged his fingers around his cup. "If he's not careful, I might actually start to like him."

"Oh no." Joanna sat up, her heart lightening. "Don't do that, Daddy. Just think of your reputation."

"Scamp." Her father chuckled and playfully bumped his shoulder against hers. "It does make me wonder what he's up to, though." His voice turned serious, contemplative. "Why would a man work so hard, going beyond what is asked, when this job is clearly nothing more than a stepping-stone for him."

"Because everything I do reflects upon my Lord."

Joanna and her father swiveled as one toward the sound of Crockett's voice.

He dropped his soggy bundle into the washtub where her father's clothes lay heaped and took a seat at the table across from them. "Scripture instructs God's people to give our best to whatever task we turn our hands to, to conduct ourselves as if we work for the Lord himself, not for man." His focus never wavered from her father.

"I've known plenty of *god-fearing* men who were lazy no-accounts—men who'd rather beat a child than spare him a loaf of bread." Her father spat the accusation at Crockett, but Joanna was the one who flinched. She'd never heard such anger from him, such pain. When had he witnessed such cruelty? Her stomach clinched suddenly. Had *he* been the child?

"And that poisons your view of God, doesn't it." Crockett's words were softly spoken, but the weight behind them was staggering.

Her father gave no response beyond tightening his jaw.

"God desires his people to be abounding in love and good works. To be people of integrity and honor. People who reflect his character. But we are human—sinful people capable of evil deeds."

A snort of disgust erupted from her father, but he quickly pressed his lips together, as if shutting a gate to keep anything else from escaping.

"Sometimes those mistakes have far-reaching effects," Crockett quietly intoned, "ones that can be used by the enemy to drive others away from the God who loves them."

Joanna's pulse stuttered. Would her father actually open himself to what Crockett was saying? Was he softening?

But as she watched, a shutter fell over his face, and he pushed away from the table. "I thought we agreed to no sermonizing, Archer." He turned his back to the table and strode over to the window, staring out at the rain that had finally started to lessen.

"That we did, Silas. That we did. Forgive me." Crockett immediately lightened his tone and leaned back in his chair. "I'm not immune to making mistakes myself, I'm afraid. Just ask my brothers. They'd gladly regale you with tale after tale, I'm sure."

Crockett shot her a wink from across the table, and Joanna found herself smiling despite the forfeiture of the previous topic of conversation. *Give it time*, he seemed to be saying with that wink. *A new seed has been planted. Don't churn up the soil before it can take root.*

For several minutes, no one spoke. The rain spattered against the roof. The parlor clock struck the quarter hour. The stovepipe creaked.

Then her father broke the silence. "You still want to go to town tomorrow if the weather clears, Jo?" He addressed his question to the window glass instead of to her.

"Yes, I would." She shared a look with Crockett before turning to regard the back of her father's head. "Brother Archer gave me the money from the offering to buy the paint for the church, and I'd like to get everything purchased as soon as possible." Including that dress fabric.

She'd hoped to get to town before now, but there had been too much work on the ranch for a hand to make a trip solely for workday and picnic supplies.

"I don't think I can spare Jasper," her father said, and Joanna's hopes withered. "But after his hard work today, I'd thought to give Archer some time off. If you can convince him to make the trip, I'd not be opposed to letting him drive you."

Joanna's gaze flew to Crockett's, her breath catching in her throat.

"I'd be honored to escort you, Miss Robbins." He dipped his head in a gentlemanly gesture, but it was the twinkle in his eye that set her heart aquiver.

Had her father really planned to reward Crockett with a day off, or was this simply a ploy to keep the parson and his arguments away for a time?

Did she really care, since it meant she'd be spending an entire day in Crockett's company? The bubbles of delight effervescing in Joanna's middle provided her answer.

19

Crockett arrived at the Lazy R bright and early the following morning, despite his supposed day off. He'd much rather eat Joanna's cooking than his own, and truth be told, he was half afraid Holly Brewster might somehow discern that he'd been granted time off and show up on his doorstep with more ideas and plans for him to consider. The woman's constant need for attention and affirmation drained energy out of him faster than water ran through a sieve.

Unlike Joanna, whose very presence seemed to pour strength into him.

Watching her bustle about the kitchen, making sure the men had plenty to eat and coffee mugs that never ran dry, memories of yesterday flooded his mind. The way she'd fussed over him when his fingers were too numb to unfasten his own slicker. The way she'd warmed him with her hands through the blanket. The way her hair smelled and the softness of it as it brushed his chin. He'd wanted to pillow his head against it. More than that, he'd wanted to throw the blanket aside, take her in his arms, and taste her lips. Not the most parson-like instinct.

He'd never experienced such strong desire before. He enjoyed the company of women, had even flirted a little, but never had he been stirred to any deeper emotion. After fourteen years of being secluded with only brothers for company, he'd found women a delightful experience—their smiles, their softness, their lilting voices. Each encounter had been like a bee flitting to a new blossom—every bloom beautiful and sweet in its own way. But the more time he spent with Joanna, the more addicted he became to her particular nectar. It was as if the rest of the flowers had begun to fade, losing their attraction.

"Honey, Mr. Archer?"

Coffee nearly exploded from Crockett's mouth. Had the woman somehow divined his thoughts?

Joanna arched her brows, a line of puzzlement crinkling her forehead. "For your biscuit." She lifted the small crock in front of her, nothing but innocent inquiry in her eyes.

He managed to choke down his coffee, only too aware of the strange looks he was garnering from the other men around the table. He dipped his chin in a desperate bid to compose himself and found a lone biscuit sitting uneaten on his plate.

"No . . . uh . . . thank you. Butter will suffice." He immediately picked up his knife and set about the task of buttering said biscuit, throwing in a mental lecture on the dangers of undisciplined rumination for good measure.

Thankfully, breakfast soon concluded. Silas and the others scattered to their chores, and Joanna cleared the table. Crockett offered to help her with the dishes, but she shooed him to the parlor, claiming it was his day off and insisting she wasn't going to let him lift a finger until it came time to drive the wagon to Deanville.

Determined not to give his mind a chance to wander into perilous territory again, Crockett picked up one of the three books stacked on a small table between a pair of armchairs. Taking a seat, he opened the book to a random page, only to come face-to-face with the skeletal anatomy of a horse. He twisted the volume to examine its spine. *The Diseases of Livestock and Their Most Efficient Remedies* by a Dr. Lloyd V. Tellor. Well, it could have been worse, he supposed. It could have been a treatise on beekeeping.

Chuckling to himself, Crockett turned to a section that explained how to properly diagnose the source of a horse's lameness.

He'd always enjoyed studying medicine. As youngsters, his brothers came to him with aches and pains as well as their more serious injuries—probably due to the fact that his bedside manner was sunnier than that of Travis, who preferred barking orders. Whatever the reasons, Crockett had embraced his role as family healer and studied every medical text and home-remedy manual he could get his hands on. Admittedly, there hadn't been many, but he made good use of the ones he'd found. Much like he was doing today, although veterinary science didn't hold the same allure for him as the treatment of human ailments. Yet a rancher couldn't expect to be successful without at least a rudimentary knowledge of how to doctor his stock. So with a determined tilt to his head, Crockett turned back to Dr. Tellor's symptomatology.

Unfortunately, he was only a few pages in when a light melody drifted into the parlor, effectively stealing his attention from the discussion of splinting shins and diseased knee joints.

Joanna was singing.

He thought of the first time he'd heard her sing, the morning he'd surprised her with a birthday sermon. At the time, he'd contemplated hiding his presence in order to listen longer to the sweetness of her voice, to the emotion she projected behind the words. In the end, however, he'd been unable to resist joining her. Even now, the lure was strong. Setting aside his book, Crockett leaned back in his chair and softly hummed a companion harmony.

His gaze idled about the room, taking in the little feminine touches that warmed the place. The lacy handkerchief beneath the lamp. The bow in the curtain sash. The embroidered sampler perched on the table near his elbow. Were they evidence of the late Mrs. Robbins, or had Joanna contributed to the styling?

He examined the framed sampler more closely. Noah's ark floated atop a wavy blue line of floodwater, beneath which had been stitched the following verse: "*Now faith is the substance of things hoped for, the evidence of things not seen.*" An olive branch and a dove served as a divider between the verse and the next line of text. "*1874—Joanna Robbins—age 10.*"

Crockett grinned, imagining a little red-headed girl bent over her needlework, her tongue caught between her teeth as she concentrated on getting the stitches just right. What pride she must have felt at having her efforts deemed worthy of such a prominent display. Not as prominent as the large oil painting above the mantel, however.

Crockett pushed to his feet and walked to the hearth to get a closer look at the magnificent rendering of a picturesque river vaguely reminiscent of the one that ran behind the chapel. The work was extraordinary, really, the way light glowed throughout. It was as if the sun had purposely broken through the clouds to beam upon the land in honor of the artist's visit.

"One of my mother's finest," Joanna said beside him, and Crockett turned to face her.

"Your *mother* painted this? It's masterful." His eyes veered back to the landscape searching out the signature in the bottom corner. *M. E. Robbins.* "I did wonder how Silas came by such a piece."

Hearing how that sounded, Crockett pivoted, an apology on his lips. "I didn't mean to imply—"

"What? That my father had stolen it?" Joanna's mouth quirked, and her eyes danced with delightful mischief. "Yes, because stage passengers are so apt to cart around bulky framed art when they travel."

Crockett smiled, gracefully accepting her teasing censure.

"No," she said, a wistful expression softening her features. "He didn't steal the painting, just the artist. Or at least her heart." Joanna stroked the edge of the frame with a reverence that came from deep affection. "Of course, she stole his right back."

Silas seemed like such a hard man; Crockett had difficulty picturing him as a lovesick swain.

As if she had guessed his thoughts, Joanna stepped closer and whispered like a conspirator in his ear. "You should see his bedroom."

Crockett arched a brow, which only served to deepen Joanna's smile.

"You won't find one inch of open space on those walls. Other than a few hanging about the house, every canvas Martha Eleanor Robbins ever painted is in his room." A little sigh escaped her. "They used to only hang four at a time. Mama would rotate new ones in every few months and keep the rest in storage. But after she died, Daddy hung every last one of them up. I think it helps him feel closer to her, to be surrounded so completely by her work."

Silas Robbins had more depth to him than he liked to let on. Crockett clutched his hands behind his back and rocked onto the balls of his feet as new thoughts took shape in his mind. A man who loved his wife and daughter with such fervor would love the Lord with similar ferocity. If he ever gave his heart in that direction.

An hour later, Crockett steered the wagon around a particularly ominous-looking mud puddle as he and Joanna slowly made their way to Deanville. The sun had broken through the clouds to warm the air, but the road remained decidedly soggy in places. He'd looked forward to this outing too much to risk being mired to a halt.

He glanced over to the woman at his side, all buttoned up in her Sunday gloves and bonnet. *Entrancing* was the word that came to mind. If it was possible for a face to sparkle, hers did as she drank in the scenery. He imagined her cataloguing the rise and fall of the land, the position of the trees, the way the yellowed grass bent with the breeze. Is this what she painted in the barn loft?

Silas had left strict instructions naming the makeshift studio off limits. Even he never ventured into his daughter's sanctuary. That was where she could express herself through her art without fear of censure, where she could truly be free. And where, Crockett assumed, she felt closest to her mother.

"Do you paint landscapes, as well?" he asked, hoping she'd open the door just a bit and let him peek inside those secret places.

She turned toward him and smiled. "A few, though I find myself more drawn to human subjects." Her eyes traced the lines of his face for a moment, and Crockett found himself wondering what she saw. Did she simply perceive angles and shadows, or did she truly see *him*?

"My mother tutored me in the style of the Hudson River School," she said, aiming her attention back toward the road, "the style she fell in love with after viewing a Thomas Cole exhibit as a young girl. The paintings idealized nature in such a way that it built a craving within her to someday explore the untamed wilderness in the West."

"Is that how she met your father?"

Joanna peeked at him from beneath the brim of her bonnet. The look would have been coquettish had it not been for the fact that her features were alight with little-girl eagerness. He sensed he was about to be regaled with a well-loved Robbins family tale.

"She was considered quite a spinster back in New York," Joanna began. "Not handsome enough to catch a society beau but too educated to attract the average working man. So she dedicated herself to teaching. Art mostly, though she also gave instruction in music. Each year she rewarded her top students with a trip to Frederic Edwin Church's latest exhibit. He was her favorite contemporary artist, you see."

She mentioned the man's name almost reverently, so Crockett quickly nodded in response, as if he comprehended the significance. He hadn't a clue who the fellow was, of course, but Joanna didn't need to know that.

"Church would travel to far-off exotic places and then return to New York in the winter to paint. Mama longed to follow in his footsteps. She knew, as a woman, she'd never cultivate the type of investors who would allow her to travel to South America as he had, but she'd gained a small inheritance from her father's estate and saved every spare penny of her earnings, hoping that one day she'd be able to take her own wilderness excursion."

"What made her finally leave home?"

"A painting, naturally." Joanna winked at him. Crockett was so charmed to be on the receiving end of the gesture for once that he nearly laughed aloud.

"*Twilight in the Wilderness*," Joanna said, as if that explained everything. "Church had captured a rugged landscape of tree-covered mountains embracing a quiet river, all beneath a darkening sky swept with clouds still colored with the lingering pink of a sunset that had just passed. Once she saw that painting, Mama knew she had to go west—had to capture her own piece of the wilderness before civilization swallowed her for the rest of her days.

"So she finished out her school term, packed her sketchbook and supplies, and set out to find her wilderness."

"And found your father instead." Although a young outlaw like Silas Robbins was bound to be wilderness enough for anyone.

"Yep." Another sideways peek from under her bonnet. "He held up her stage."

Crockett did laugh then. It was too perfect.

"She'd been traveling for several months and had made it as far west as Texas when her funds ran out. The stage was to take her to Galveston, where she planned to board a ship for home. When Daddy and the boys held it up, she handed over her few valuables without a quibble. But when one of the men—Frank, I think—took the satchel that held her sketchbook, she fought like a wildcat to get it back.

"Jasper tried to restrain her while Frank dumped the contents of the bag. They all thought she had a hidden stash of jewels or something. Daddy was the one who first took hold of the sketchbook. He opened it and gazed upon her work. He told me later, that was the moment he fell in love with her—said any woman who could see such beauty in an unforgiving land had to have a pure soul. And Mama said that when the outlaw leader returned her sketchbook to her, his blue eyes glowed above his mask with an admiration she'd never seen in any man back east. It was as if he'd seen her heart when he looked at her sketches, and that glimpse made her beautiful in his eyes."

Joanna turned to look at him then, a wistful smile curving her lips. Crockett's gut clenched. He didn't have to see her sketchbook. She was already beautiful in his eyes.

Clearing his throat, Crockett adjusted his grip on the reins and adjusted his thoughts in a less dangerous direction. "So did he abduct her?"

Joanna laughed, a light, airy sound that wrapped itself around his heart. "Of course not. He did follow her, though. And that evening, he risked his life by coming to town to court her. Mama recognized him immediately but was too enamored to turn him away. They took a table in a dark corner of the café and talked for hours. When he learned she was set to leave in the morning, Daddy proposed that night."

"And she agreed?" Crockett couldn't quite keep the incredulity out of his voice.

"Not at first. She was worried about the difference in their ages. She was four years older than him, you see, and she worried that such a young, spirited man would grow weary of her as she aged. But Daddy convinced her that once his loyalty was given, nothing could sway him. So she agreed. But she gave a condition—he had to stop his thievery."

Crockett did some quick figuring. "But you told me he's been a rancher for the last sixteen years, so he must not have stopped robbing stages until after you were born."

"That's correct. Unfortunately. It was the only spot of contention between them in the early years. Daddy had promised to go straight as soon as he had enough money to buy a ranch and provide a home for her. He and his gang had always played it safe by stealing only enough to provide for their immediate needs, so he hadn't stored up much of a cache. They never pulled heists large enough to draw significant attention from the authorities. And they *never* harmed anyone." Joanna gave special emphasis to this last point.

"My mother continued to plead with him to stop, insisting she didn't need a large house or fancy things. He could hire on at a ranch somewhere or take a job at a mill or a mine. But Daddy refused to work for anyone other than himself, so he continued with his gang until he'd saved up the money to buy a ranch of his own."

Her description of her father's exploits sounded eerily familiar. Crockett frowned as he looked ahead to the outskirts of Deanville. Hadn't Marshal Coleson said much the same thing when he'd questioned him about his abduction?

"Oh, you don't need to frown, Crockett." Joanna gave his shoulder a playful nudge, clearly misinterpreting his concern. "Mama and I got him on the straight and narrow soon enough."

"What role did you play?" he asked, not wanting her to guess his thoughts about the marshal.

A light blush pinkened her cheeks. "Well, according to Mama, I captured Daddy's heart the moment I was born. Whenever he was home, he'd tote me around with him—teaching me how to ride, showing me animal tracks, and carving me wooden toys. I adored him, having no inkling of the secret life he lived. All I knew was that he was my father and he loved me.

"Then one day, he and his gang held up a coach heading for Bremond. When he opened the door to demand the passengers' valuables, he found a woman traveling with her daughter. The little girl was about my age, with red hair and freckles. When she saw him, she screamed in terror and nearly tore her mother's skirts in a desperate bid to get away from him. Daddy slammed the door closed and rode away without taking a single penny from anyone that day, or any day after. He told me later that all he could see that day was my face on that little girl. My terror. Of him. And he couldn't bear it."

Crockett absorbed her words. "Your father might be a stubborn man," he said after a moment, "but he loves fiercely and has proven capable of radical change. Your story gives me hope for our other endeavor."

"Do you think so?" Her eager face shone up at him as if he had just given her a handful of gold.

Crockett nodded, and her answering smile was glorious.

As he steered the team toward the general store, Crockett couldn't help but wonder what stories Joanna would someday tell her own children about how she met their father. Would it be a rousing adventure tale to rival her parents' story, or would it be an ordinary account of a gentle romance that developed over time? Somehow the latter just didn't seem to fit.

Crockett set the brake, climbed down, and turned to assist Joanna. His hands clasped her waist, and an unbidden image of Silas dandling a grandchild on each knee filled his mind—children who were begging to hear the tale of how Grandpa stole their daddy from a train as a birthday present for their mama.

He jerked his hands away from Joanna's waist as if she'd burned him. *Slow down, Crock*, he warned himself. Admitting his attraction to Joanna was one thing. Imagining their future children was quite another.

"Let's . . . uh . . . let's go find that paint." Crockett took Joanna's arm and quickly steered her toward the boardwalk before the quizzical look on her face had time to become an actual question.

20

Selecting the paint didn't take long, and when Crockett offered to cart the canisters out to the wagon, Joanna urged him to get out and explore the town afterward, thereby granting her some time for personal shopping.

"It's so rare that I get the chance to wander through the store myself," she explained when he offered to wait. "I usually just give Jasper a list and have him pick up the necessary items when he comes into town, but since I'm here, I'd love the chance to linger over the pretty ribbons and sweet-smelling soaps."

Surely *that* would scare him off. What man wanted to be caught up in a cloud of perfumed soaps and toilet water?

"I'll just stroll down to the livery for a bit," Crockett said, his easy agreement rankling a bit, despite the fact that he was doing exactly what she wanted.

Botheration. Why did her feelings always have to be in such a jumble whenever he was around?

"When you're finished," he continued, "we can have lunch."

Joanna forced her mind back to the task at hand. *Fabric*. "That would be lovely." She smiled and shooed him toward the door. "I'll come find you when I'm finished here."

"I'll keep an eye out for you." He winked and dipped his head to her before taking the last of the paint outside.

She hovered by the window, waiting until he'd situated the paint cans in the wagon bed and started making his way down the street toward the livery. Then she made a beeline for the fabric display along the back wall.

Dean's Store didn't boast a very wide selection, and most of it was simple calico, but Joanna eagerly fingered every bolt of cloth, imagining what each might look like done up into a dress. The golden brown material dotted with tiny maroon roses might work well with her coloring, but it was too subdued, too safe. For once, she wanted to stand out instead of blending into the background. A hard enough task when Holly Brewster was prancing around. It'd be even worse now that the woman had actually set her cap for Crockett. Joanna sighed as she considered the choices before her. All the tans and dark greens weren't going to help much.

Taking the gold calico in hand, she reached for a bolt of deep russet, thinking it might be close enough in color to the rose pattern to make a pairing, but when she tugged it loose, she discovered a length of blushing pink polished muslin hiding underneath. Joanna sucked in a breath, the russet bolt falling from her hand to thud against the table.

She carefully extracted the pink fabric from the bottom of the pile. The sheen of it caught the light, drawing a sigh from her as she stroked her hand along its length. It had probably been left over from last spring; the color was far too pastel to be fashionable this time of year, but Joanna didn't care. In fact, the lighter color suited her purposes precisely. Even better, it would pair well with the chocolate brown underskirt her mother used to wear with her lemon polonaise. The pale yellow hue had always turned Joanna's complexion rather sallow, so she'd never remade the gown, but the underskirt was a different story. It would add an elegant touch to the cheery pink muslin. Not to mention saving her a great deal of time in the sewing.

Joanna gathered the bolt into her arms and turned to walk to the counter, only to find a woman blocking her path. The lady's hair was pulled back into a rather severe knot, her charcoal dress clean but nondescript. Yet it was her assessing stare that stirred Joanna's unease.

"I seen you with him." The accusation lacked heat and was almost conversational in nature, but Joanna still did a quick scan of the store to make sure she had a clear path to the exit should a mad dash become necessary.

"Who?" she asked, drawing the fabric bolt closer to her chest.

"The parson. Archer."

"Yes. He works for my father and was kind enough to drive me to town." Joanna pasted on a grin and retreated a step, thinking to make her escape down another aisle.

"He's a good man." The woman blushed slightly and fidgeted with the cuff of her sleeve as her gaze slid to the floor. "If ya ain't in too big a hurry, I'd be pleased to have the two of ya lunch with me at the boardinghouse. Archer knows where. Just tell 'im Bessie said come."

Joanna halted her retreat, touched by the awkward invitation. This woman was no threat. She was simply uncomfortable around strangers, a trait Joanna understood all too well. What must it have cost her to initiate the conversation? It was obvious she held Crockett in high esteem—which proved her a woman of good sense.

"How kind of you, Bessie. We'd be delighted to join you for lunch. I'm Joanna." She extended her hand.

Bessie nodded but barely touched her fingers to Joanna's. As if she'd suffered through all the socializing she could manage, Bessie spun around without further word and left Joanna alone with her new dress fabric.

"Care for some more greens, Parson?" Bessie held the bowl out to him, and Crockett accepted it, still in a daze over actually having the woman seated at the table with him. The presence of another female apparently made socializing a less threatening endeavor.

"Thank you, ma'am." He placed a small spoonful on his plate and passed the bowl on to Joanna. "I'll take another one of your yeast rolls, too, if you don't mind."

The woman couldn't have blushed more prettily if he had named her the fairest maiden in the land.

"I remembered how much you liked 'em," she said as she reached for the towel-covered basket.

"They are truly a piece of heaven, Miss Bessie." As he reached under the towel to claim a roll, Crockett winked playfully at her. But he regretted his unthinking gesture when his hostess nearly toppled out of her chair from the shock of it.

Thankfully, Joanna quickly attempted to smooth things over. "You must meet a lot of interesting people, running a boardinghouse. Do you enjoy it?"

"Not particularly."

Crockett ducked his chin and fixed his attention firmly upon his plate, intending to shrink from the conversation so that Miss Bessie could regain her footing.

"It must be hard work," Joanna said, impressing him with how quickly and sensitively she adjusted to Bessie's blunt response.

"It ain't the work. I been tendin' house since I was old enough to wrangle a broom." She shifted in her chair, and her thumb tapped restlessly against the tabletop. "It's havin' strangers showin' up uninvited and expecting me to wait on 'em hand and foot that puts me in a foul mood."

Crockett stuffed the roll in his mouth before she could catch him grinning. He could certainly attest to the truth of that statement.

"If it were up to me, I wouldn't take on boarders at all." Bessie leaned back in her chair and crossed her arms with a huff.

"Why do you do it, then?" Joanna's voice held no censure, only curiosity. It didn't surprise him at all when Miss Bessie's arms relaxed. Joanna's calm manner invited openness. Though not the social whirlwind that Holly Brewster was, she had a way of reaching out to those society missed, those most in need of compassion and a listening ear.

"It was my brother Albert's idea. All because of that wife of his. She wanted him to sell this place, our parents' house, so that she and Bertie could move into a nicer one themselves up in Caldwell. He assured me I'd be given a room of my own—a room off the kitchen, I'm sure, so I can do all the cookin' and cleanin'. Heaven knows that's what I end up doin' every time I go for a visit. At least here I can keep my independence and don't have to put up with Francine's hostility."

Crockett gave up all pretense of eating and sat back to watch the two women, who seemed to have forgotten his presence.

"So how'd you convince your brother to let you keep the house?" Joanna asked.

"I think he knew what a disaster it would be to have me and Francine under the same roof, so he offered to let me keep the house if I would agree to take in boarders so that he could lower my monthly stipend. It was his way of tryin' to make both of us happy, I guess."

"Do you attract enough business to make up the difference?"

"Some months are better than others, but I got extra put aside, so—"

A loud knock cut off the rest of her explanation.

"Miss Bessie?" A gruff masculine voice echoed through the hall as the front door eased open. "I hear ya got comp'ny."

A start of recognition hit Crockett, followed by a jolt of apprehension.

"Yep," Bessie hollered, making no move to greet the visitor in person. "We're in the kitchen, Marshal. You're just in time for a piece of pie."

Crockett looked to Joanna, his pulse growing a bit erratic. Had Marshal Coleson come to question him again? Or had he somehow figured out Joanna's connection to a particular ex-outlaw? Was she in danger?

His eyes raked her face. She surely wasn't acting like she considered herself to be in danger. After Bessie got up to retrieve another plate and cut the pie, Joanna simply wrapped her hands around the delicate china cup in front of her and lifted it to her lips for a sip, the picture of serenity. What she didn't do, however, was meet his gaze, so he had no way of judging whether her composure was legitimate or strictly an act.

He had the oddest urge to grab her and dash out the back door.

Then common sense prevailed. He was pretty sure Silas couldn't be arrested for crimes committed sixteen years ago, especially without witnesses or evidence. But when Brett Coleson strode into the kitchen, pulled his hat from his head, and sat in the vacant chair next to him, it dawned on Crockett that there *was* a crime for which Silas Robbins could be prosecuted—kidnapping.

Joanna eyed the marshal over the rim of her cup. She had too much of her father in her to be comfortable around lawmen, but too much of her mother in her to let it show. Slowly, she lowered her cup to the table and smiled a welcome to the newcomer.

He nodded politely and took his seat. "Brett Coleson, ma'am," he said by way of introduction.

She dipped her chin in return. "Joanna Robbins." Thankfully, the marshal seemed more interested in Crockett than her. After he mumbled something perfunctory, he turned his full attention to the man beside him.

"I didn't expect to see you 'round these parts again, Parson. You decide to take my advice and press charges against those yahoos that abducted you from the train?"

Her pulse bucked like an unbroken horse. Joanna darted a glance at Crockett, knowing even as she did so that the gesture would be telling if the marshal happened to notice. Crockett apparently had better self-control, for he kept his attention on the lawman. She told herself she was glad even while she ached for his reassurance.

"No, sir," Crockett replied, and the denial soothed Joanna's ragged nerves. "That misunderstanding was worked out weeks ago. I'm here because I took a job in the area. Came into town for supplies. That's all."

"Mmm." The sound carried a decidedly unconvinced tone.

Thankfully, Bessie arrived with dessert before the marshal could say much else. "Stop interrogatin' my guests, Brett, and eat your pie."

She plopped an extra-large piece in front of the marshal and slid a slightly smaller one toward Crockett.

"Yes, ma'am, Miss Bessie," the marshal replied, all smiles as he picked up the fork she'd laid out on the plate. "A man'd be foolish to waste his mouth on talkin' when he could be chewin' on your de-lectable blackberry pie."

The woman grunted, unimpressed by the compliment. She retreated to the counter to collect the remaining plates, served Joanna, and returned to her place at the table.

A blessed few minutes of silence fell upon the room as everyone ate their dessert. Joanna loved blackberry pie, but she didn't taste a single bite. How could she when the marshal kept looking at her? She felt as if the truths of her heritage and her father's past sins were rising to the surface under the lawman's perceptive study. If she didn't leave soon, she feared they'd emerge through her skin like a tattoo inked upon her forehead.

"I don't think I can eat another bite," Joanna declared, pushing her half-finished pie away from her. "Bessie, thank you for a wonderful meal. I truly enjoyed getting to know you, but I'm afraid I have several tasks needing my attention back at the ranch. We really must be on our way." She stood.

Crockett took his cue. He pushed to his feet and collected his hat. "Miss Bessie, it was a pleasure to see you again. I'll be sure to stop by and say hello the next time I'm in town."

"You do that." She grabbed the roll basket from the table, tied off the towel around the bread inside, and handed the soft bundle to him. "Take these with you. You might get hungry later."

"Thanks." He accepted the gift, then ushered Joanna toward the front door.

"Hey, Parson?" The deep drawl brought them to a halt.

Crockett pulled slightly away from her in order to pivot and regard the marshal.

"I got a sermon idea for you," the lawman said, his dark eyes narrowed slightly. "Proverbs 21:3. 'To do justice and judgment is more acceptable to the Lord than sacrifice.' Might want to spend some time ponderin' that one."

"I've been leaning more toward Proverbs 16:6," Crockett answered without so much as a blink. "'By mercy and truth iniquity is purged: and by the fear of the Lord men depart from evil.'" Before the lawman could respond, Crockett took Joanna's arm and led her out of the house.

As he steered her to where their wagon waited, Joanna hid her concern over the odd conversation. She doubted either man had actually been talking about sermons. They'd definitely been tugging on opposite ends of a doctrinal rope, though, and she could only deduce that her father was somehow at the center of it.

21

Sitting in the kitchen where the light was best, Joanna bent over the pile of shiny pink fabric in her lap and pushed her needle in and out of the seemingly never-ending yardage that made up the hem of her new polonaise. She'd taken her mother's yellow brocade apart and used it as a pattern for cutting the pink muslin after she and Crockett returned from Deanville on Wednesday. Then yesterday, she'd kept the treadle machine whirring for hours, only stopping when she had to cook meals for the men. Fortunately, none of them complained about the simple fare of vegetable soup at midday or the only slightly more substantial beef hash at supper.

Now, if she could just finish the handwork in the hems and trim today, she might actually have her dress ready for the picnic tomorrow. Little frissons of excitement skittered along her nerve endings, energizing tired fingers and blurry eyes. The men wouldn't be back for another couple hours. Surely that would be enough time to complete the hem on her overskirt and add the lace she'd taken from her mother's gown to the sleeves and neckline. Joanna straightened her posture for a moment in order to stretch the kinks from her back, then exhaled a determined breath and set back to work.

When her thread grew too short to easily work with, she knotted it and snipped off the end. As she unwound another length for her needle, the sound of a wagon approaching the house brought her head up.

Had one of the men returned early? What if it was Crockett? She didn't want him to see her working on the dress. It would spoil the surprise. Joanna grabbed up the folds of pink fabric, lace pieces, and thread spools and scurried to her room. She tossed her armload onto the bed, closed the door, and hustled back to the kitchen. Stabbing her needle into the pincushion, she looked for a place to hide her sewing basket. Not finding anything overly promising, she shoved her scissors, pins, and needle case inside the basket and covered the top with a bread cloth. She hurriedly brushed the tabletop with her hand to clear it of cut threads and fabric scraps, gave it a couple blows to send the residual fuzz flying, and spun toward the door. As she stepped onto the back porch, she gave a quick pat to her hair to make sure her mad rush hadn't loosened her pins. She might not want Crockett seeing her dress just yet, but neither did she want him seeing her looking like a frazzled ragamuffin.

That thought set her to dusting off her apron, so it took a moment to realize the wagon had pulled to a stop. She didn't recognize the team, or the man climbing down from the bench seat—although there was something about his long-legged stride that seemed oddly familiar. When he drew a little closer and smiled a greeting, recognition toyed with her, itching the back of her brain like a mosquito bite she couldn't quite reach.

"Afternoon, ma'am." He touched his hat brim. "This the Lazy R?"

"It is." Joanna sensed no threat from the man, who couldn't have been much older than she, judging by his unlined face and slender build. But her father didn't like her welcoming strangers when he and the hands were away, so she kept her place on the porch and addressed him with caution. "Do you have business here?"

She didn't see how he could. Daddy never invited anyone to the ranch without telling her, and Jasper always took care of town business himself, never arranging for deliveries. Joanna eyed the two trunks in the wagon bed with suspicion.

"Yes, ma'am. I do."

Her eyebrows lifted.

The young cowboy shifted his weight and snatched the hat from his head, as if his hands needed something to fiddle with. "My brother wrote that he hired on here. Crockett Archer? I brought his things."

She could have smacked herself in the forehead for not recognizing the resemblance earlier. Of course he was an Archer. The strong chin. The rich sepia hair. The smile that made his eyes light. He was much too young to be Travis, though, the brother Crockett spoke of most often. She searched her memory for the correct name and mentally pounced as she recalled a discussion about a youthful song leader whose voice was the last to change in the Archer household.

"You must be Neill." She poured all the warmth and welcome she'd been holding back into her burgeoning smile as she stepped off the porch. "I'm Joanna Robbins. Crockett works for my father."

Relief flashed across the young man's features. He swiped his palm down his trouser leg, then held his hand out to her, his grin as wide as the sky.

"Pleased to meet you, Miss Robbins. Crock mentioned you were the one who arranged his new preaching position. That sure was kind of you."

Joanna clasped his hand briefly and then stepped back. "He's doing *me* the favor, I assure you. Our little church has been in need of a preacher for far too long, and your brother fills the pulpit better than I dared hope. He's done more to bring this community together in three short weeks than most could accomplish in a year. Why, he's even organized a church picnic to reach out to those who don't regularly attend services. You should stay. See your brother in action."

Neill peered at her oddly, tilting his head just a bit, as if to look behind her words for some deeper meaning. Only then did she realize how she'd been gushing about Crockett's accomplishments.

"But then you've seen him in action all your life, haven't you." She gave a little laugh to cover her embarrassment. "Why don't you come inside? I'll fix you a glass of spring water and treat you to some leftover fried pies."

"I don't want to put you to any trouble, miss." Yet his eyes had gone quite wide when she'd mentioned pies.

"They're apple . . ." she teased.

"Well, if you're sure it wouldn't be no hardship." A huge grin stretched across his face, and for a moment his eyes danced just like Crockett's.

Joanna found herself caught up in his enthusiasm as she led him into the kitchen. The sewing basket on the table brought her up short, though. Ruthlessly, she swept away the reminder of her unfinished dreams, whisking the basket from the table and dropping it on the floor against the wall.

There'd still be time to work by lantern light after supper. And if not, well, there'd be other picnics, or so she told herself as she set about fetching the water pitcher.

She had just reached into the pie safe to retrieve the leftover pastries when someone knocked on the back door. Before she could take a step in that direction, though, the door cracked open and a golden-brown head popped into view.

Joanna grinned. "Come on in, Jackson. There's plenty for you, too." How the boy knew she'd been about to serve pies, she couldn't fathom, but then Jackson had always had a sixth sense about food. He had a talent for showing up whenever it was being handed out.

"Saw this stranger roll up your drive and thought I better check it out." Jackson straightened to his full height and eyed Neill. "He ain't botherin' ya, is he, Jo?"

She shook her head and moved the platter of pies to the table. "No. He's a guest, Jackson. Neill Archer. Crockett's brother."

The boy snagged one of the small pies as his attention veered sharply back to Neill. "No foolin'? The one who plays the fiddle? Crock told me all about how you used to scare away the barn cats with your screechin' before you got the hang of it."

"Jackson!" If she'd had a spoon in her hand, she would have smacked his knuckles. As it was, she gave serious consideration to yanking the half-eaten pie from his mouth and banishing him from her kitchen. But that would only compound the already poor impression they were making.

Neill, however, didn't seem to take offense at Jackson's insulting comment. He chuckled good-naturedly as he rubbed the back of his neck. "Yeah, Travis wouldn't let me play in the house, so the barn critters made up my audience. Fortunately, our mule and milk cow couldn't escape as readily as the cats."

Jackson laughed and reached for a second pastry, leaving three on the plate for Neill. "Crock says you're pretty good now, though. Played at a barn raising last year, right?"

"Yep. The cats even stuck around." Neill turned to smile up at Joanna when she reached past him to set his water glass on the table. "Thanks."

She dipped her chin in acknowledgment and moved back to the stove.

"Hey," Jackson said, speaking around cheeks bulging with apple filling. Joanna groaned inwardly and tried to pretend she hadn't noticed. "If I can scrounge up a fiddle, would you play at our shindig tomorrow?"

"You wouldn't have to scrounge one up." Neill winked at him. "I brought my own. Never have liked the quiet around a campfire at night. But we best not get ahead of ourselves. I'm supposed to meet up with a friend of mine later, and I haven't even talked to Crockett yet."

Jackson's eyes lit with purpose, and she knew the boy would do everything in his power to see that Neill stayed for the picnic. "I'll go fetch Crockett." He pushed back from the table so fast the chair nearly toppled. "Where's he workin', Jo?"

She bit back a grin. "In the north pasture. Why don't you take Sunflower?" she said, knowing how rarely he got to ride. "You can meet up with the men in the large clearing. They're cutting out the calves for weaning and driving them into the lower pasture."

"You mean it, Jo? You'll let me ride Sunflower?"

"Sure."

Jackson was sprinting for the door the moment the word left her lips.

"Just make sure you saddle her properly," she called after him. "I don't want to have to cart a pile of busted bones back to your pa's house. Understand?"

"Yeah, yeah." He waved her off and disappeared through the door. His excited footsteps clomped across the porch floorboards in a rapid staccato, then quieted into softer thuds as they hit the packed dirt of the yard.

Joanna shook her head and smiled. It took so little to make the boy happy. She poured a second glass of water from the pitcher and joined Neill at the table.

"I could have sworn the two of you were brother and sister," he said, his eyes alight with humor. "My brothers used to scold me the same way. Still do from time to time."

"You aren't the first Archer to accuse me of taking on the bossy big-sister role with Jackson." Joanna chuckled. "I guess that's what happens when a gal doesn't have real siblings to practice on. She badgers poor, unsuspecting neighbor boys."

Neill grinned. "He doesn't seem to mind."

Joanna ducked her chin, his tone bringing a touch of heat to her cheeks. Eager to turn the conversation in a different direction, she questioned him about growing up as the youngest of the Archer pack. He regaled her with stories that made her laugh and some that made her ache for the four boys who'd been forced to raise themselves in the harsh Texas landscape.

"And then there was the time I thought it'd be a hoot to trick my brothers into eating fish bait. I threw a handful of worms into Jim's squirrel stew when he wasn't looking. But somehow Crock must've figured out what I done because when it was suppertime, he insisted I eat my bowl first. They all just sat there watching me until I finished every last bite. Then they gave their portions to the dog and took out some cold ham and stale biscuits instead. Watching them eat, I was sure I could feel those worms wigglin' around in my stomach. It was enough to send me runnin' for the outhouse. I tell you, I never pulled a prank involving food again."

Joanna grinned at the tale, easily imagining him as a boy running wild and getting into one scrape after another. Before she could ask if he ever discovered how Crockett had outsmarted him, the sound of pounding hooves announced his brother's arrival.

Neill's eyes brightened with an excitement that could only be inspired by deep affection. He launched to his feet and was halfway to the door when he recalled his manners. "Excuse me, miss."

But she was every bit as excited as he, and dashed past him when he paused, beating him to the door. "Come along, Neill," she said with a smile. "Your brother's here."

She opened the door and hurried out, but she halted at the edge of the porch and allowed Neill to race down the steps alone. Wrapping her arm around the support post, Joanna watched the brothers embrace. And when Crockett lifted his gaze to include her in his pleasure, a longing struck her with such force she had to tighten her grip on the post to keep herself from trotting down to join the reunion.

Neill said something that set Crockett to laughing and drew his full attention. When his gaze left hers, Joanna turned and slipped back into the house. Back to the dress that would hopefully help Crockett see her not only as a partner but as a woman.

22

Crockett thumped Neill on the back as he embraced his brother a second time. It was just so good to see him, to reconnect with family. As eager as he'd been to leave the ranch and start his ministry, he'd never imagined how hard the separation would be. Forged through trials and survival, trust and mutual respect, the Archer bond went deeper than blood. Having Neill here was like regaining a piece of himself that had been missing.

He glanced up to the house, intending to invite Joanna to join them. Yet when he scanned the porch, all he saw was the back of her skirt disappearing through the kitchen door.

"It must be rough working for such a pretty lady." Neill lifted his chin toward the house.

His brother's knowing stare penetrated a place Crockett wasn't ready to expose. Doing his best to cover his reaction with his usual wink and grin, he draped his arm over Neill's shoulders and steered him toward the wagon. "You haven't met her father yet."

"I still can't believe you took a job with the man who kidnapped you." Neill shrugged out from under his brother's arm when an approaching rider broke through the trees on the far side of the house. "Of course, now that I've seen his daughter, it makes a little more sense."

Avoiding his brother's scrutiny, Crockett turned to greet Jackson as the boy barreled into the yard on Sunflower. Crockett strode back to his own mount and gathered the reins he'd left draped over the saddle horn.

"Do you mind seeing to my horse as well as Sunflower?" He drew his bay's head up from where he'd been nibbling on a tuft of grass near the corral fence and paced over to where Jackson had dismounted. "Silas gave me the rest of the afternoon off, and I'd like to show Neill my place at the church."

"Sure." Jackson collected the reins from him and patted Sunflower's neck. "I'll rub 'em down and turn them out in the corral for a bit." He started to lead the animals to the barn, one on either side of him, but stopped to glance back. "You want me to come by when I'm done? We still gotta set up the shootin' targets and lay out the racecourse tonight, 'cause the gals expect us to help with the decoratin' in the morning. Although why they think they gotta hang ribbons and bows on everything is beyond me."

Crockett shared a grin with Neill over the boy's youthful disdain. The Archer brothers couldn't claim much understanding of females, either, but they had enough sense to know when to go along with one.

"Well, we want the ladies to enjoy the picnic, too," Crockett said in conciliation. "And if dressing the old churchyard up adds to their pleasure, I suppose we can handle decoration duty."

"I guess." Jackson sighed heavily and plodded on into the barn.

"He reminds me a lot of you," Crockett said, returning to Neill's side at the back of the wagon. "He runs wild with little or no supervision, but he's got a heart that's eager to please and a work ethic that, when properly motivated, can be quite impressive."

"Are you calling me impressive?" Mischief danced in Neill's eyes.

Crockett shoved his brother's shoulder, pushing Neill around to the left side of the wagon as he strode to the right. "Only when properly motivated."

Stifling a chuckle, Crockett jammed a booted foot onto a wheel spoke and hefted himself onto the wagon seat. Neill flashed a grin, joined him on the seat, and took up the reins.

On the way to the parsonage, Crockett answered questions about the church, the upcoming picnic, and the work at the Lazy R. But once there, he turned the conversation toward home.

"I'm surprised Travis let you come all this way alone." Crockett hopped over the seat into the wagon bed and scooted the two trunks toward the open end.

"He didn't." Neill hauled one of the trunks up onto his shoulder. "Josiah's waiting for me in Deanville. The lady running the boardinghouse hired him to fix her roof when she heard he had carpentry experience. Said her attic was gettin' musty and insisted he find the leak causing it."

"Ah. Miss Bessie." Crockett jumped to the ground and took up the second trunk. "If he finds that leak, she'll treat him like a king." He led the way to his living quarters, wincing slightly at the weight of his trunk. Travis must've packed his books in this one. No wonder Neill had claimed the larger one.

As they entered, Neill cleared his throat. "Frankly, I was surprised she asked Josiah to stick around. She hardly said two words to him and never sat at the table with us during meals. Made me kinda mad, to tell the truth."

Crockett lowered his trunk to the floor at the foot of his bed and motioned for Neill to place his against the wall. "I'm certain it has nothing to do with the color of Josiah's skin. Miss Bessie's just a little afraid of strangers, men especially. When I stayed with her, she locked herself in her room instead of eating with me. Yet the other day, when I took Joanna to town, the woman insisted we come for lunch and actually stayed in the room. I'm pretty sure having another woman as a buffer precipitated the change."

Neill planted himself in the one chair the room boasted while Crockett opened the first trunk. His gun belt and revolvers lay on top next to his rifle wrapped in flannel. He reached for the rifle, pulling away the protective cloth.

"I've missed having my own guns," he said as he stroked the familiar barrel and tucked the stock into his shoulder, the oiled walnut sliding into place as if it had never left. "Silas lent me a sidearm for working on the ranch, but it's just not the same as having a weapon that's more companion than tool."

Neill nodded. "Yeah. Travis packed the guns. Meredith packed the books."

A fond smile curved Crockett's lips at his sister-in-law's name. He set the rifle on the cot and reached for his copy of D. L. Moody's *The Gospel Awakening*, the volume she'd given him for Christmas last year. "How is Meredith?"

"I've never seen her happier. Or fatter."

Crockett cuffed his brother on the side of his head. "She's pregnant, you dolt, not fat."

"Ow." Neill rubbed the spot where Crockett had smacked him, but his eyes glowed with humor. "Travis is the one you should be worried about, not Meri. After losin' Ma the way we did, he ain't too keen on letting Meredith go through childbirth."

"As if he has any say in the matter at this point."

Neill smirked. "You know Travis."

Yes, he did. His brother had always been one for controlling things. Meredith had helped him mellow over the last few years, but Crockett could imagine those old habits creeping back now that he had a baby on the way.

"Travis asked Josiah's ma to move out to the ranch for the last weeks of Meri's lying-in."

"Weeks?" Crockett sputtered. "I can't picture Myra agreeing to that. Not with the school to run and her own brood to see to."

"No, but she did promise to make regular visits." Neill stretched his long legs into the middle of the room. "That combined with me swearing to fetch her at Meri's first twinge seems to have satisfied him for now."

"And Jim?" Crockett set aside all pretense of unpacking. He craved news from home more than anything stowed in his trunks. Leaning his shoulder blades against the wall, he gave Neill his full attention.

"He's fine. Finally got around to trimming back those oaks around the old homestead last week. I think he and Cassie are planning another trip down to Palestine to visit her folks soon."

Crockett winced in sympathy. "Poor Jim." The man's mother-in-law was a harridan of the first order, but Jim put up with her in the same stoic manner he handled everything else in life, and somehow they made it work. Cassie's happiness obviously meant more to him than his own.

That's what love did to people. It prompted sacrifice. Crockett suppressed a sympathetic chuckle. And helped you endure disagreeable in-laws.

Like stubborn-minded ex-outlaw kidnappers?

"Yoo-hoo," a sing-song voice called from outside. "Are you in there, Brother Archer?"

Still a bit rattled from the picture of his future being tied to Silas Robbins—he could almost feel the lasso tightening around his middle as it had when the man had stolen him from the train—it took Crockett a minute to gather his wits and respond.

When he did, he pushed away from the wall and lurched for the door. About the same time, Holly Brewster's delicate little fist rapped against the wood and sent the unlatched door swinging gently in on its hinges.

"Oh, there you are," Holly said, an almost too perfect smile shaping her lips. "I saw the wagon outside and hoped that meant you were here. I was just delivering the last of the decorations for tomorrow. They're all in the back of the chapel, as you suggested." Her lashes lowered at a languid pace before lifting to reveal a heated stare that sent a shiver of warning down his spine. She took a step closer, and he could have sworn her eyes pleaded with him to invite her in. But that couldn't be right. Surely she knew how improper it would be for her to enter his private quarters.

Taking no chances, Crockett took her arm and steered her out to the yard. The heat in her eyes turned a bit more snappish until she caught sight of Neill coming up behind them.

Her eyes widened, and she latched onto his arm. "Who's your friend, Crockett?"

His name slipped off her tongue as if she'd used it a hundred times. Familiar. Possessive. Far too presumptive.

"My youngest brother, Neill," Crockett ground out, using the introduction as an excuse to extricate himself from Holly's hold. "Neill, may I present Miss Holly Brewster."

"Miss Brewster." Neill touched his hat brim and bent his head. "What's a pretty lady like you doin' hangin' around with this ornery old cuss?" He jerked his chin toward Crockett.

Holly's tinkling laugh filled the air. "He's not *that* old."

"Positively ancient." Neill rolled his eyes in exaggeration. "And don't let those smooth sermons fool you. He can be as ornery as a coyote when he's riled."

Crockett tightened his jaw, restraining the wolfish urge to smack the teasing grin right off his brother's face. He was only twenty-eight, for crying out loud, not exactly in his dotage. And he was the sweetest tempered of all the Archers. Everyone said so.

Yet as he listened to Holly giggle and flirt with his brother, the gulf between their ages seemed to widen. He hadn't felt this old with Joanna. Of course, Joanna had left him and Neill to reunite on their own. Even so, there was a depth to Joanna that lent her a mature air, despite the seven years difference in their ages. Until this moment, in fact, he'd never even thought to calculate it.

"Miss Brewster is the picnic committee chair," Crockett interjected, dispelling the lingering laughter with his impassive tone. "She's been a great help in planning the events and organizing the food and decorations."

Holly preened under the praise, like a cat being stroked in its favorite spot.

"Impressive," Neill said. "It's too bad I won't be able to see the results of such fine handiwork."

"You're not staying?" She pouted prettily. "Crockett, you must insist he stay. With all the young ladies sure to be in attendance, we need all the handsome young men we can get."

Crockett didn't care a hill of beans about the ratio of men to women at the picnic, but he *had* hoped to visit with Neill longer. "Are you sure you can't delay your departure for a day? It would give us more chance to talk."

Neill regarded his brother with serious eyes. "I told Josiah our visit might last overnight, if you had a place for me. I could swing another day, if you don't mind the imposition."

"Of course he won't mind," Holly enthused. "Will you, Crockett?"

"Not one bit." Although he did mind Miss Brewster speaking for him when he was perfectly capable of forming his own sentences. But she was probably just excited about the picnic and got a little carried away.

"I'll have to leave around midday, though." Neill favored Holly with an apologetic look before turning back to Crockett. "You know how Travis worries. And with Meredith expecting, it's even worse. I best not leave him alone too long. Josiah and I need to get on the road to Caldwell before dark. That way we can catch the early train back to Palestine."

"Well . . ." A cracking adolescent voice echoed behind them. "As long as you're here, you might as well help us set up the shooting targets."

The three turned to find Jackson manhandling a set of large wooden discs with white Xs painted in the middle. Crockett reached out to grab one as it slid from the boy's grasp.

Then, unable to resist the boyish urge, he flung the oversized disc directly at his brother's gut. Neill reacted in time to catch it but not before an *oomph* of air forced its way from his lungs.

Satisfied that his place in the Archer ranks was once again secure, Crockett grinned and slapped Neill on the back. "Looks like we're putting you to work, little brother."

"Well, let's get going, then . . . old man." Without batting an eye, Neill slapped the flat side of the disc against Crockett's rump and raced past.

Jackson guffawed.

Holly gasped.

Crockett grinned and gave chase.

23

Come on, Jo." Silas rapped his knuckles twice against his daughter's door. "You're the one who wanted me to go to this shindig. At this rate, it's gonna be half over afore we get there."

Dressed in overalls and an old flannel work shirt for painting duty, Silas stalked down the hall to the kitchen and snatched up the knapsack that held the clean trousers and fancy shirt Jo had pressed for him that morning. He swung the strap over his shoulder just as a door creaked open down the hall.

"It's about ti—"

The vision walking toward him stole his speech as well as every thought in his head save one—his little girl had grown into a full-blown woman right under his nose.

Ah, Martha. Can you see her, darlin'? You'd be so proud.

The fancy pink dress Jo wore swished when she walked. A matching blush stained her cheeks, and she refused to lift her gaze from the floor as she entered the kitchen.

Silas swallowed the lump that had swollen in his throat. "Jo." His quiet rasp of her name rumbled almost too low to be heard. Nevertheless, she lifted her face, her teeth catching the edge of her bottom lip. "You're the spittin' image of your mama in that dress. She looked just like you do on the day I met her. All frilly and lacy and more beautiful than a woman had a right to look." He stepped closer and ran a light finger down the edge of her sleeve. "It's a good thing I'm takin' my rifle for the sport shooting later. I'll need it to run off all the young men."

"Don't be silly, Daddy. You know Jackson's the only young man to ever pay me any attention, and he's too young. Save your bullets for your targets." Jo tapped the bib on his overalls and moved past him to drape a piece of cheesecloth over the large bowl of potato salad sitting on the table.

Silas frowned. It was true that no young man had ever paid court to her. 'Course she'd never hinted at harboring feelings for any of them, neither. So who was the dress for? Because one thing was for certain—she hadn't gotten this gussied up just for a picnic. They had picnics every Fourth of July, and never once had she donned such a fancy getup. Was she trying to attract a beau? His fingers curled into a fist around the strap of his knapsack.

He had known the day would come when some fella would strike her fancy. He just hadn't expected it to be *now.* Watching her graceful movements as she packed plates and flatware into a crate, a sense of inevitability prompted a bittersweet ache in his chest. He wanted her to be happy, to find a love like he had found with her mother. But there was no way he was gonna stand by and let some sweet-talkin' cowhand make off with his Jo before the fella proved his worth to Silas's satisfaction.

So who was he?

The only new man around these parts was . . .

The parson? Absolutely not!

If Jasper and the boys hadn't already ridden down to the churchyard with Gamble in tow, Silas would have leapt on the beast's back and raced in the opposite direction.

How could his daughter . . . *his* daughter . . . fancy a preacher man? He never should have brought Crockett Archer to his ranch. He shoulda left him on that train where he belonged. He should fire him tomorrow. Send him packing.

"Everything's ready, Daddy." Jo turned that sweet smile of hers on him, and Silas bit back a groan. "Would you carry this crate out to the wagon? I'll get the potato salad."

Not daring to open his mouth for fear of what might come out, Silas gave a brisk nod and snatched up the crate of dishes. His jerky motion rattled the crockery, and he had to remind himself to be gentle—with more than just the dishes.

Once outside, he inhaled a calming breath, settled the crate in the wagon bed alongside the two small kegs of cider he'd loaded earlier, and tossed his knapsack on top of the pile. Jo met him near the front of the wagon, hope shining in her eyes. A hope that made him want to snarl like a trapped cougar.

Careful not to let her see his inner turmoil, he took the salad from her, tucked it into the crook of one arm, and gave her a hand up with the other. After she gained her seat and arranged her skirts, he returned the bowl and scrambled up beside her.

They didn't speak much during the short drive, but when they pulled up to the churchyard and that scoundrel of a parson moved to greet them, the pleasure on Jo's face spoke loud enough to ring his ears.

"Miss Robbins." Crockett Archer couldn't take his eyes off her. The bounder. He practically ran up to the wagon, so eager was he to get his hands on Jo and assist her to the ground. His grip on her waist didn't linger long enough to be improper, but his fingers took their sweet time disengaging. "You look lovely, Joanna," the man said so low Silas doubted anyone but he and Jo heard it.

Silas stared a hole in the parson's head until the fella finally remembered someone besides Jo existed. Tempted to upend Jo's potato salad on the man's head when he finally looked back to the wagon, Silas restrained the impulse and contented himself with a glare that would melt iron.

Archer blinked, then smiled up at him as if he hadn't just been scorched. "Silas! So glad you could come. I understand you're the man to beat when it comes to target shooting."

"You needin' some lessons, Preacher?" He was more than willing to do some teaching. Especially if Archer was the target.

"No, sir." The parson's smile widened, but determination glittered in his eyes. "I'm needing some competition."

"Ha!" Silas surprised himself with the shout of laughter. "If you think you can beat me, preacher man, you best save some room after lunch for the humble pie you'll be eating."

"You're probably right, but it will be interesting to see, won't it?" Challenge radiated from Archer as he reached up to the wagon seat and took hold of the potato salad.

Silas tried to glare him down, but the man didn't even flinch. He simply turned and offered Jo his arm before leading her over to the food tables.

Dratted sermonizer.

The crazy thing was, if Archer were just a cowhand, Silas would probably favor a match between him and Jo. The man worked hard, lived up to his word, and refused to be intimidated, even by Silas. He was the kind of man who would be a good provider, a good protector, and if he truly loved his girl, a good husband.

But how could he trust his daughter's future happiness to a preacher? To the type of man who knew how to trick the world into believing his holy façade while wielding a cruel rod of tyranny behind closed doors? His gut told him Archer was different, that he would never strike down a woman or a child, but the vision of little Andy Murdoch, broken and battered, flashed an unforgettable warning in his mind.

His gut had been wrong before.

It seemed the entire community had turned out for the church painting and picnic. Joanna was amazed at how quickly the men had the exterior white-washed. Jackson and some of the older boys even scrambled up the hackberry trees and onto the roof in order to paint the steeple.

She had brought an apron and planned to carry water around to the workers, but Holly commandeered the bucket and ladle from her before she could move past the food tables, insisting that she and Becky Sue had been assigned that task. Holly even went so far as to suggest that Joanna should round up the younger children for a game of hide-and-seek or other entertainment.

"Their mothers so rarely get a chance to sit and visit without having to worry about the little ones getting into mischief," Holly had said. "Just think what a boon it would be to have you tend them for an hour or so."

Then she and Becky Sue had sauntered over to the men. Holly inserted herself between Crockett and his brother Neill, sidling close as Crockett gratefully accepted the refreshment she offered. She turned to Neill next, and the man must have made some teasing comment, for she threw her head back and tittered a laugh that grated worse than fingernails on a schoolroom blackboard.

Holly loitered and lingered while Becky Sue dashed from one thirsty man to the next, and when she finally moved on, she made a point to arch a superior brow in Joanna's direction before approaching the next gentleman.

The vile woman. She'd done everything in her power to keep Joanna away from Crockett while insinuating herself into the very position Joanna coveted. And all Crockett did was smile at her. Stupid man.

Yet despite her raging jealousy, Joanna had recognized the truth in Holly's earlier statement. The young mothers really could be blessed by having someone else tend their children for a while. Deciding it would be better to focus her energies in a positive direction instead of sitting around brooding over missed opportunities, Joanna spent an hour organizing footraces, a pinecone toss, and a game of leapfrog for the boys and hopscotch for the girls.

When the church bell finally rang, the signal for everyone to gather in the yard for lunch, the children whooped and scampered back to their mothers. Joanna lagged behind, savoring the quiet of the uninhabited field, and steeling herself for more of Holly's machinations.

She arrived in time to hear Crockett's prayer of thanksgiving for the food and for all the neighbors who had worked so hard that morning. She halted on the fringe of the crowd to bow her head, but not before catching a glimpse of her father across the way, head uncovered, eyes respectfully closed. Her heart swelled in her chest.

I have so much to be thankful for, Lord. Forgive me for forgetting that there are more important things at work here than my own desires.

The men had all washed up and changed into their picnic attire behind the church's shuttered windows. The painting done, now their only concern lay in piling their plates as high as possible with the feast Mrs. Brewster had organized.

Crockett stood in the center of it all, smiling and chatting. Bowing to the ladies. Clasping men on the arm. Ruffling a boy's hair as he dodged between the adult legs to get closer to the food. His face gradually turned in her direction, and she lifted a hand to wave, her lips curving upward in anticipation. But Mrs. Grimley snagged his attention by pushing a plate into his hands and steering him over to the food.

The woman could be a force of nature when set to a task, so Joanna knew Crockett had no choice but to follow. Yet that knowledge did little to keep the disappointment at bay.

Focus on what's important, Joanna.

Squaring her shoulders, she sought out her father and his men. They'd spread out the blankets she'd packed under one of the hackberry trees near the back of the chapel. Thinking to make sure they had everything they needed before claiming a plate for herself, she skirted the edge of the crowd, pressing as close to the building as she dared without brushing up against the wet paint.

She had just come even with one of the shuttered windows, when Becky Sue's distinctive nasal voice echoed from within the church.

"The parson *kissed* you? However did you manage that?"

Shock stopped Joanna midstep.

"I just created the opportunity for him to do exactly what he's been wanting to do for the last several days."

Holly Brewster? Crockett kissed Holly Brewster? No. It had to be some kind of mistake. He wouldn't. Would he? Joanna's palms pressed against her stomach as she fought to find a breath.

"We've grown quite close, Crockett and I."

The sound of his given name on Holly's lips bruised Joanna's sore heart.

"We spent long hours talking in the evenings on my mama's porch, and not always about picnic business—if you know what I mean."

"But how did you get him to kiss you?" Becky Sue pressed. "Here. At the picnic."

Holly's voice grew quiet and conspiratorial. Joanna had to strain to hear. "While the men changed out of their work clothes, I snuck around to the back of the church and waited for him to show up. I figured he would drop his painting clothes off in his living quarters before rejoining the group over by the food. He's the tidy sort, you know." She imparted this last bit as if she were a relative or sweetheart, someone intimately acquainted with the nuances of his preferences and personality. It made Joanna want to scream. Or sob. Or yank Holly's shiny blond hair out by the fistful.

"Well, just as I suspected," Holly continued, "he came around the corner and disappeared into his room. I ran up to the door and met him as he came out. Finding me there, he wrapped his arms around me, and his lips caressed my forehead. He couldn't risk anything more since someone could have come by, but it was enough to assure me that his feelings are indeed engaged."

"His feelings are indeed engaged." The words echoed in Joanna's mind like a death knoll.

Biting back a wounded cry, Joanna spun around and sprinted back the way she had come. She couldn't let her father see the tears streaking her cheeks. She couldn't let anyone see. Plunging back into the field where she'd romped so cheerfully with the children, she headed for the one place she could hide.

The river.

24

Mrs. Grimley bulldogged her way through the crowd, dragging Crockett in her wake. The woman could have given Moses instructions on sea parting. She refused to rest until she had him firmly planted at the head of the line. Not used to being mothered, Crockett shrugged apologetically at the men whose places were being usurped, but none of them seemed to mind. They just grinned and slapped his back as he passed.

Once the lady had shoved a plate at him and ordered him to heap it full, she apparently considered her duty accomplished, for she left his side in order to shoo away a pair of boys who were trying to stuff extra cookies into their trouser pockets down at the dessert table. Crockett recognized the scamps from the group that had been playing with Joanna earlier.

She'd been so good with the kids. Laughter and squeals had carried to the work crew from the field, bringing smiles to many of the fathers' faces. He'd smiled, too, though not because of the children. Because of Joanna.

His eyes had followed her all morning. He'd been aware of her when she assisted at the food tables, and again when she helped unload an elderly couple's wagon and set up their rockers beneath the shade of a large oak. He'd noticed, too, when she lingered to visit with them so they wouldn't feel excluded from the activities. More than once, his arm had gone slack, leaving paint to drip unused from his brush before he roused himself and got back to work. He couldn't seem to stop himself from searching her out. Even when he'd opened his eyes after offering the blessing, a flash of pink in his periphery told him she was near.

Crockett glanced back to the place where he'd last seen her, hoping to meet her eye or share a smile. This was *their* day, their success. Something inside him stretched toward her, needing to connect, to share the moment in whatever way possible.

But she wasn't there.

He craned his neck to see over the heads of the people milling about the yard. There. Was that her by the chapel? Where was she . . . ?

A red-haired pixie in a fancy pink dress bolted down the side of the church and disappeared around the corner, swiping a hand across her cheek as she ran—the way a woman would swipe at a tear.

If someone had hurt her . . .

Crockett's gut hardened to stone.

He turned to the man behind him in line and forced his lips to curve enough to pass for a smile. "Go ahead of me, brother. I just realized there's something I need to attend to." He set the plate Mrs. Grimley had given him well out of the way of the lunch traffic, and squeezed between the men huddled around him and the food.

"Can't it wait, preacher?" one of the men he was pushing past asked. "You're gonna miss the best pickin's."

"I won't be long," Crockett said. "Besides, the way the women around here cook, they're all good pickin's."

"You ain't tried my Maybelle's corn pone, then. Stuff's drier than a dust storm in August."

That set the men to cackling, and Crockett used the distraction to make his escape. He stretched his stride as long as the crowded yard would allow, but the minute he reached the far side of the chapel, he broke into a loping run.

He crossed the field in the direction he'd assumed she'd gone but had to halt when he couldn't find her. He scanned east, then west, his heart thudding against the wall of his chest. Where was she?

Fighting the urge to cup his hands around his mouth and shout her name, Crockett bit the edge of his tongue and scoured the landscape again. As his head turned south, a red cardinal shot into the air above the water oaks that lined the river and chirped an alarm.

Joanna.

Crockett made for the trees.

He found her beneath the branches of a pecan, her back to him. Her left arm was braced against its trunk, her head hanging low, her shoulders heaving with quiet sobs. The sight broke his heart.

He stepped forward, every instinct screaming at him to take her into his arms and soothe away the hurt, but she must have heard his approach, for she gave a little squeal of distress and dodged behind the tree.

"Jo, wait. It's me." He hurried after her, reaching out to capture her hand and draw her to him, but she recoiled. She scooted farther around the tree, forcing more distance between them and keeping her face averted.

"Go away, Crockett." Her voice hitched as she struggled to subdue her tears. "You should be at the picnic. You'll be missed."

He dug a handkerchief from his pocket and handed it over her shoulder, careful not to crowd her. "You're more important to me than the picnic."

She clasped the white cotton but offered no thanks. "I know we've been friends," she said between sniffs and a delicate blow, "but you shouldn't say things like that to me. Not when you're courting someone else."

"Courting?" The idea jarred him so thoroughly that his response shot from his mouth like a bullet from a gun, throwing him back a step. "What are you talking about? I'm not courting anyone."

At least not yet. And certainly not someone other than the woman standing before him.

"Maybe not officially," Joanna allowed, "but from what I heard, the young lady in question seems to believe that a certain understanding has been established."

"What young lady? I swear to you, Joanna, any *understanding* this person believes she has is a *mis*understanding. I've made no promises. I've not even hinted at promises."

She spun around to face him then, her eyes the dark blue-gray of a stormy sky, her chin jutting, her reddened nose sniffing in disdain instead of distress. "A kiss is more than a hinted promise, Crockett Archer. At least for an honorable man. But maybe you're not as honorable as I thought."

"Now, hold on a minute." Crockett raised a hand to ward off her accusations, his clenched jaw clipping the ends off his words. "Before you go impugning my honor, let me make it perfectly clear that I have kissed no one."

"So you deny being with Holly outside your personal quarters less than an hour ago?"

Crockett's brow furrowed. What did that have to do with anything? "No . . ."

"I heard her describe the encounter to Becky Sue in vivid detail." Joanna advanced on him, hands fisted at her sides. "The way you wrapped your arms around her and pressed your lips to her forehead."

"Heaven help me!" Crockett's arms sliced upward through the air like twin sabers, then slapped down against his thighs. "If she considered that a kiss, the woman is deranged."

"Deranged? Just because you're too ill-mannered to consider such a gesture a kiss doesn't make her deranged. How dare you toy with a woman's affections in that manner? You . . . you . . . toad!" She flung his soggy, crushed handkerchief directly into his face along with her ridiculously innocuous insult.

Suddenly Crockett wanted to laugh. Either that or show the little firebrand exactly how he defined a kiss. But he dared not let his mouth so much as twitch for fear she'd assume he was belittling her pain. For he saw now that that was exactly what it was. Her pain. Not Holly's. Hers.

And though he hated himself for finding joy in her distress, that pain gave him hope. Hope that her feelings might run deeper than friendship.

Stepping over the handkerchief that had bounced off his nose and fallen to the ground, Crockett gently clasped her upper arms. He'd not let her back away from him this time.

She trembled at his touch, and a tiny gasp echoed in the air between them.

"Joanna," he said as he stroked the bottom of her shoulder with his thumb. "The contact I made with Holly was nothing personal. I ran into her—almost sent her tumbling to the ground, in fact. That's why I put my arms around her. To keep her upright. Nothing more."

The skin between her brows scrunched, and her eyes searched his. "But—"

"Shh. Let me finish, sweetheart." Her damp lashes blinked in surprise at the endearment, bringing a smile to his face. "When we collided, my chin banged against Holly's forehead. That's it. I separated myself from her as quickly as I could, made my apologies, and hurried back to the gathering. There was no rendezvous. No embrace. And definitely no kiss."

"So Holly was wrong about your feelings being engaged?" She tilted her head farther back to examine his reaction to her question. Of course, that only strengthened his reaction to *her*. Joanna's face was at the perfect angle for a kiss. Her lips parted ever so slightly as she awaited his answer.

Oh! His answer.

"I have no feelings for Miss Brewster beyond gratitude for her help with the picnic." That and a bit of suspicion of her motives. Holly had a way of twisting the truth to suit her purposes, and he was leery of what exactly those purposes might be since they seemed to involve him. He needed to keep her at a distance from now on.

"You don't intend to court her, then?" Joanna's soft mouth curved ever so slightly, and his stomach clenched in response. Heaven help him, but he wanted to kiss her.

"No." The hoarse reply came out so low, he added a slight shake of his head for clarification.

"I'm glad," she whispered. At least he thought she whispered. It might just have been the increased thudding of his heart against his rib cage that kept him from hearing.

"If I were going to instigate a courtship with a kiss," he murmured, "it wouldn't be a quick peck on the forehead." He tightened his grip on her shoulders as he spoke.

"It wouldn't?" She swayed toward him slightly.

Crockett shook his head, his eyes never leaving her upturned face.

"What would it be?" Her breathy question dissolved the last of his reserve.

"This." Crockett drew her toward him and lowered his head. He stopped a fraction of an inch from her mouth. Gave her a final chance to change her mind and pull away. When she made no move beyond shifting her focus from his eyes to his lips, he closed the last of the distance.

His mouth covered hers. Instinctively, he tugged her closer. She came to him—her hands on his waist, the feathery touch speeding his already charging pulse.

Releasing her shoulders, he slid his palms around to her back. She felt so good in his arms, so right. He wanted to hold her there forever, to kiss her until they both forgot everything else.

He deepened the kiss.

She startled at the change, then softened against him. But her momentary shock was enough to bring him back to his senses.

Swallowing a groan of reluctance, Crockett lifted his head. Joanna rose up on her tiptoes as if to follow, but his greater height kept her from her goal.

His hands shook slightly as he released her. Merciful heavens. He'd never experienced anything so intense. So exhilarating. And terrifying. It was as if some element of his very being had been altered.

Had she felt it, too?

Joanna's eyes flickered open, and a pretty pink blush washed over the pale freckles bridging her cheeks. Her eyes, now more blue than gray, gazed at him with a wonderfully bemused expression—one that filled his heart with tenderness.

And protectiveness.

"Joanna."

She blinked, her eyes slow to focus. "Mmm?"

"You need to get back to the picnic, sweetheart. Before someone notices that both of us are missing."

"Oh . . . yes . . ." She stepped back and darted a glance behind her. "But you better stay here for a while. Daddy is probably looking for me by now, and we wouldn't want him to get the wrong idea."

Crockett imagined Silas would get precisely the *right* idea, but it wouldn't do to have the man jumping to unsavory conclusions before Crockett had a chance to declare himself. And to do that, he and Joanna needed time to explore this new direction their relationship had taken. Not to mention the time still needed to break through Silas's distrust of preachers. As long as her father held on to his prejudice, Joanna would be caught in the middle. Having to choose would tear her heart out, and Crockett refused to put her through that. No, he'd have to win Silas's favor first. Only then could he ask Joanna to be his wife.

25

Somehow Joanna navigated the busy churchyard and ended up at her blanket with actual food on her plate. Her father brushed the crumbs from his lap and stood to assist her, taking her plate and then her hand as she lowered herself to the ground.

He started to hand the plate down to her but stopped halfway, his brow furrowing. "Playin' with them kids sure stirred up an odd appetite in you, girl."

Joanna accepted the plate from him, puzzling over his comment. Until she got a fresh look at what sat upon her dish—three carrot sticks, a spoonful of pickled beets, a slice of chocolate cake, and two helpings of Maybelle Parker's atrocious corn pone. She had to press her lips together with extreme force to keep a burst of laughter from exploding into the air. She had no recollection whatsoever of serving herself such a strange assortment. Beets? Really? She hated beets.

"Things were rather picked over by the time I went through the line." Not that she remembered, but it was bound to be true since nearly everyone had already eaten. Although why she'd taken beets, she couldn't possibly imagine.

Her daddy raised an eyebrow at her, so she stabbed one of the magenta circles with her fork and popped it into her mouth. The briny taste assaulted her tongue as she chewed, puckering her face against her will. She managed to swallow, though, and considered that a great triumph until her father hunkered down beside her and felt her head with the back of his hand.

"You feelin' all right, Jo? You look a little flushed."

Which, of course, only made her flush more. Especially when his mouth curved down in a frown, and his eyes narrowed as if he could see the truth of what had happened to her written across her features.

"I'm fine, Daddy." Except that she wasn't. She was better than fine. *Much* better. So much better, in fact, that even a plate of pickled beets couldn't sour her mood.

Her father let out a noncommittal grunt as he settled back on the blanket beside her, but Joanna ignored the sound along with the scowl that accompanied it and stuck a carrot stick in her mouth to keep from smiling too big.

Crockett had kissed her. Well and truly kissed her. On purpose. Joanna fought down a giggle as she pictured the awkward tangle that must have resulted from Holly's manufactured collision—the one Crockett had scrambled to escape. He hadn't scrambled to escape *her* down by the river. No. He'd taken his time. And what a lovely time it had been.

She could still picture the intent look on his face as he bent his head and waited for her silent permission. His eyes had roamed her face as if he yearned for her, his mouth curving just enough to let her know she pleased him. *She* pleased him. Her—the shy little wallflower with the ungovernable hair and freckled skin; the woman no one ever looked at twice; the daughter of the man who'd kidnapped him. She pleased him.

And heavenly stars, how he pleased her.

Unable to resist the lure, Joanna turned her head to scan the crowd for a glimpse of him. Just a peek, she promised herself. It wouldn't be wise to let her father catch her mooning over the preacher. But when she finally caught sight of him horsing around with Jackson and Neill over by the greased pig enclosure, his smile was so bright, she couldn't help staring. He was so handsome. And kind. And fun-loving. And . . . courting her!

Crockett must have sensed her attention, for he lifted his face. His gaze found hers, and a subtle change crept into his expression. His grin never dimmed, but somehow it deepened, became personal, private, between the two of them. She couldn't have looked away had a herd of longhorns stampeded through the churchyard.

Then he winked and turned back to his brother, freeing her to look elsewhere. But what else could possibly capture her interest after that? Joanna dropped her attention to her lap and held the moment close to her breast, as if it were a kitten begging to be stroked and snuggled for a little longer before squirming away.

"I would've thought a smart gal like you would have better taste."

Joanna jerked her head up at her father's grumbled comment, her stomach clutching. He was staring at her just like he used to when she was a girl and he caught her doing something she oughtn't have.

He'd never been one to throw out verbal accusations. He didn't have to. All he had to do was stare at her until she recognized the error of her ways and confessed everything. Even now she could feel the truth about Crockett's kiss creeping up her throat and knocking on the back of her teeth.

But then her daddy let out a ragged sigh and nodded his chin toward her plate while he pushed up to his feet. "Even I know to avoid Miz Maybelle's corn pone, Jo."

Air whooshed from her lungs, turning unspoken admissions into harmless giggles. "Somebody's got to eat them, Daddy," she said, lifting one to her mouth. "It would be an embarrassment for her to take a full platter back home."

"You got a bigger heart than I do." He grunted and adjusted his suspenders, his attention briefly captured by something behind her and at an angle very much in line with where she'd last seen Crockett. Then he shook his head and gathered up his rifle from where it leaned against the hackberry's trunk. "I'm gonna go check on Gamble, make sure he's ready for the race."

"All right." Joanna smiled up at him, guilt pricking at her conscience for the relief she felt at his departure. "I'll pack up our things."

He waved a hand to let her know he'd heard, then ambled off toward the rope corral that had been strung in the trees behind the church for the horses. He muttered something under his breath as he strode past her, something that sounded an awful lot like *Archer* and *shooting*.

Not a good combination.

Abandoning the beets, carrots, and pone, Joanna went straight for the cake. Somehow a suspicious father armed with a gun seemed less threatening when chocolate was melting on her tongue.

Crockett made a point to keep his distance from Joanna during the afternoon activities. At least in body. In mind, well, that was a different matter. She constantly crept into his thoughts, despite his best efforts to concentrate on the discussions and people around him. Thankfully, once the games started, everyone's attention turned to the children and their bumbling efforts to tackle the greased pig, leaving laughter to outrank conversation.

After little Joey Anderson successfully captured the pig, Neill took out his fiddle and played a set of sprightly songs that had the crowd toe tappin' and hand clappin' in rhythm. Some of the kids even swung partners around in an impromptu dance full of elbows and knees that kept getting tangled together.

One fellow pulled a mouth harp from his pocket and took up a position next to Neill, and another grabbed a pair of spoons and added some percussion to the ensemble. The audience began throwing in whoops for musical emphasis and urged the musicians to a faster tempo by quickening the pace of their clapping.

Neill's bow flew over the strings, his fingers moving to capture all the notes. Then all at once, the crescendo climaxed, and he stabbed his bow into the air with a final flourish. The crowd roared its approval. Neill bowed.

The kid had gotten better since the last time Crockett had heard him play.

Smiling to himself, Crockett hung back, allowing Neill to accept the appreciation that was his due without big brother hovering. Once the back slaps and handshakes concluded, however, and the crowd dispersed to witness the pie-baking contest, he made his way to his brother's side.

"You sure you can't stay longer?" Crockett asked, even though he knew the answer.

Neill placed his fiddle in the carrying case that lay open atop one of the emptied food tables and carefully fastened the lid. "Yep, but I imagine I'll be back before long."

"Oh?" Crockett raised a brow. "Why's that?"

Neill slanted a sly look at his brother. "Well, with as hard as that blonde is working to draw your attention away from your boss's redheaded daughter, I figure one of the two will end up leg-shacklin' you before too long, which means I'll be returnin' for a wedding." He paused to tuck his fiddle case under his arm, then leaned close. "My money's on the redhead, by the way."

Mine too, Crockett thought, yet he hid his opinion behind a scowl of displeasure. "Mind your own business, pup," he growled.

Neill laughed and clapped a hand on Crockett's shoulder. "Now, where's the fun in that?"

Incorrigible kid. Crockett cuffed him on the arm. "Yeah, well, someday some woman will run *you* around in circles, and we'll see who's laughing then."

The two of them walked to the wagon that waited across the churchyard, close to the road. Neill set his fiddle in the back and turned to Crockett. "It was good to see you, Crock."

"You too. Thanks for making the trip out here."

Neill shrugged off his gratitude. "You know me. Always ready to use any excuse to escape the ranch for a few days."

Crockett yanked him into an embrace. "Give everyone my love." He pounded Neill on the back a time or two, then stepped back.

"Will do." Neill climbed up onto the bench, gathered up the reins, and released the brake. "Take care, brother."

Crockett nodded and watched the wagon roll away.

A gunshot cracked through the air. Crockett's pulse skittered. He whipped his head around, instinctively searching out Joanna for the brief seconds it took his mind to recall the reason for the sound. The horse race. Crockett chuckled at himself and hurried to the edge of the designated course. He arrived just in time to see a blur of horses approaching the first turn. He glanced across the way and found Joanna with the Lazy R hands. She was bouncing up and down and shouting encouragement to her father. Her delight ignited his own.

Someone nudged his side as the horses thundered past. He scooted aside to allow whomever it was to pass, but the person pressed closer to him instead and even slipped a hand into the crook of his elbow.

"I'd say our picnic is a rousing success," a warm feminine voice purred.

Crockett fought down the urge to yank his arm from Holly Brewster's grasp. The woman had a tendency for boldness and far too creative a manner of reading meaning into situations where there was none, but she was still a lady and deserved his kindness. Digging deep, he found a polite grin for her.

"You organized a fine event, Miss Brewster."

Was her thumb stroking the inside of his arm?

"After all the hours we put in together during the planning, Crockett, I think you know me well enough to call me Holly." She smiled so sweetly at him it was hard to believe she was purposely being forward, yet the way she leaned into him made him blasted uncomfortable.

He patted her hand and gently disengaged it from his arm, subtly removing her hold on him without drawing any attention from the spectators crowded around them. "We wouldn't want anyone to get the wrong idea, Miss Brewster," he said, emphasizing the more formal name. "That's how rumors get started."

She pouted prettily, then glanced sideways at him. "If you think that's best." Her gaze drifted slowly downward from his face to his chest, dipped nearly to his waist, then gradually lifted again. "I'll be careful to address you as Brother Archer when we're around others."

But not when we're alone. He wasn't so naïve as to miss the message hanging unspoken between them.

And in that instant, he knew the time for polite consideration had passed. Like Joseph in the clutches of Potiphar's wife, it was time to flee.

He muttered a brief "Pardon me" and without further explanation darted through the dispersing crowd, spotted Jackson giving a smaller boy a leg up into the hackberry tree that stood closest to the front of the church, and broke into a jog.

"What's going on over here?" he asked, hoping the flimsy excuse of checking up on the boys would be viewed as reason enough for him to have scurried across the yard like a lizard who'd just had his rock overturned.

The younger boy paid Crockett no mind, immediately scrambling up to a higher branch. He planted his feet, grabbed the trunk for balance, and pushed to his feet. "They're coming up to the halfway marker!" he shouted. "Three of 'em are bunched together at the front. The rest are falling behind."

Excitement buzzed through the crowd as anticipation built to see who the leaders would be.

"I bet Robbins wins again," one nearby man commented. "That new chestnut of his looked to be even faster than his gray."

Another turned to Crockett. "You work out at the Lazy R, don't ya, preacher? Ever seen that horse run?"

The magnificent image of Joanna bursting out of the barn on Gamble's back came immediately to mind. "Yep. He's got the speed for sure, but I'm not sure how he'll hold up under Silas's weight. Some of the other riders are much smaller. It might give them an advantage."

"Not against Silas," the first man said. "He races all out—like a bandit tryin' to outrun the law."

The men chuckled over the comparison. Crockett choked.

"You all right, Crock?" Jackson pounded his back until Crockett held up a hand to assure him he was fine.

"They're comin' round the bend!" came the announcement from the treetop.

Crockett welcomed the distraction. The top three horses pounded toward the churchyard, the largest starting to pull away.

"Yeehaw. Get 'em, Silas!"

Crockett grinned, recognizing Carl's voice. Jasper and Frank were walking toward the finish line with Joanna in tow, her eyes alight. She glanced across the yard, her gaze finding his as if she'd known precisely where he was all the time. A smile of pure joy beamed from her face, leaving Crockett helpless to do anything but smile in return.

At the last minute, she turned back to the race and applauded as her father plunged to victory two lengths ahead of the next horse. A loud cheer rose from the crowd. Silas's arm shot into the air in triumph. Crockett added a hurrah to the chorus, then waited for the rush of congratulations to fade before joining the Lazy R crew gathered around their leader.

"Great race, Silas," Crockett said, taking hold of Gamble's bridle. "I'd be happy to cool him down for you while you celebrate."

"Oh, I ain't celebratin' too much just yet, Parson." Silas swung down from the saddle and handed Crockett the reins but didn't release his own grip. "Not 'til I beat you in the shooting contest." His eyes held something more than friendly challenge, and when Crockett tugged on the reins, Silas held on. A look passed between them—a look that Crockett suspected had little to do with horses or shooting.

The line between respecting Silas as an employer and the father of the woman he wished to court, and proving himself a man equally worthy of respect was growing thinner and more precarious by the minute.

Crockett made no move to tug the reins away, but neither did he release his own grip. "You don't expect me to go easy on you, just because you're my boss, do you?" He injected humor into his voice, though he was only half teasing.

"You do and I'll fire you on the spot," Silas growled. "I ain't no charity case, boy. And I ain't afraid of your best. Shoot to win, and I'll still beat ya."

"We'll see." Crockett winked at a wide-eyed Joanna, who stood beside her father. Jasper and the other hands looked at him as if he'd lost his mind.

Silas's face took on a red hue, but he kept his temper in check. He tossed the reins at Crockett and smacked his shoulder with the force of a small grizzly. "You're a big talker, Parson. But we already knew that, didn't we? Time to see if your actions match up."

26

Nearly everyone at the picnic turned out for the shooting contest. Man after man stepped up to the line and took aim at the first target. The crowd held its collective breath until a shot was fired and then either cheered or groaned, depending on whether or not the bullet hit the scoring disc.

Nelson Ward, still waddling a bit after tasting all the pies during the baking contest, served as referee. Following each shot, he emerged from one of the safety positions, circled the mark where the bullet struck the target with a carpenter's pencil, and wrote the shooter's initials below it. Only shots that hit within six inches of the center of the painted *X* would qualify to move on to the next round, where the distance would be increased.

Crockett eyed Silas as he came up to the line. The man strolled forward with the swagger of a marksman confident in his abilities. Previous contestants had taken the time to check the wind or bend their bodies into the perfect stance before raising their rifles. When Silas reached the line, though, he simply lifted his weapon and fired a shot in one continuous motion. The whole exhibition was over in an instant.

A twinge of unease settled in Crockett's gut. It *was* a rather impressive display. Of course, the first target stood only one hundred yards away, so it didn't require excessive finesse to place a shot near enough the center to continue in the competition. At least not for a skilled shooter. And Silas was definitely skilled.

"You're up, Parson." Silas regarded him with such a superior air that when Crockett stepped up to the line he had to close his eyes for a moment to clear his head of the raging voice that demanded he shoot even faster and straighter in order to wipe the smug grin off his employer's face.

But only a fool would play the game on his competitor's terms instead of his own. Crockett waved to the onlookers who were busy shouting encouragement, most of it none too flattering. It seemed no one expected a preacher to be able to hit the broad side of a barn.

Well, it was time to open the eyes of the blind.

Silas might be a sharpshooting ex-outlaw, but Crockett was no slouch. The Archers had lived by the gun since they were boys. Life on their secluded ranch required it, both for protection and for food. If he could outshoot Travis, which he had done on more than one occasion, he could outshoot anyone, even a stubborn, middle-aged kidnapper turned rancher.

Inhaling a calming breath, Crockett raised his rifle, sighted down the barrel, and squeezed the trigger.

Wood splintered in gratifying fashion as the target vibrated with the force of the strike.

"You hit it, Parson!" The boy who had scampered up the tree to call out the racers' positions earlier looked up at him with a mixture of shock and awe.

"He did more than that, boy," his father said, coming up behind him, his own rifle draped through the crook of his arm. "If I don't miss my guess, he hit it dead center." The man held his hand out to Crockett. "Best shot of the round."

Crockett grinned and accepted the man's hand. It didn't take long for others to follow suit. Men who had respected his position as minister now suddenly seemed to respect him as a man—as one of them.

Jackson ran in from the target range, the scoring disc held out before him like a giant serving platter. "You won the round, Crock!" he shouted. "Here, look." He held out the target for all to see, then pointed to the mark at the center of the white X with the initials CA printed beneath.

"Looks like I'll have plenty of company in round two," Crockett said in answer, noting the number of markings within the designated advancement area. "Must be at least fifteen qualifying shots there."

"Yep." Jackson pulled a piece of crumpled paper from his pocket. "Mr. Ward gave me the list."

As he started calling out the names of the men moving on in the competition, Crockett checked to see where Silas's shot had landed. It was only about an inch away from his own, up and to the right. For a fellow who'd done such little preparation, the result was impressive.

"Don't get cocky, Archer." Silas slid in beside him while everyone else circled around Jackson to hear the reading of the names. "We still got us two rounds to go."

Crockett clapped his boss on the shoulder with the same degree of force Silas had used on him earlier. "Should make for a good contest." With that, he edged away from the center of the crowd so the other competitors could examine the scoring disc.

Joanna caught his eye from where she stood among the spectators. She lifted her hand in front of herself, just enough for a small wave. No one else would notice, but the tiny gesture went straight to his heart. She was rooting for him.

Of course, she was probably rooting for her father, too, but right now her smile and encouragement were solely for his benefit.

The target in the second round had been nailed to a tree approximately two hundred fifty yards from the shooting line. Carl was the only Lazy R hand who'd failed to qualify. While he grumbled under his breath about nature's cruelty in stealing his eyesight, Jasper and Frank both took their turns at the line. When Silas was up, he demonstrated greater care and deliberation in taking aim, but he still fired faster than any previous competitor. And put his shot directly in the center of the X.

Crockett's bullet veered a little to the left, leaving Silas the winner of the round.

Only six names graced round three's list. Half of them belonged to the Lazy R.

"Your last shot went a bit wide back there, preacher man," Silas said as he tucked the stock of his weapon into his shoulder and sighted an imaginary target somewhere among the trees that lined the river. "Too bad. I thought I might finally have some competition."

Crockett grinned, recognizing the intimidation tactic for what it was. "Oh, I won't let you down, Silas. Don't worry. We're fighting for Lazy R pride, after all. If you and Jasper both miss, I'll be there to clinch the victory."

Silas raised a sardonic brow.

"Might even be worth an extra afternoon off, huh?" Crockett gripped the man's collarbone in a friendly squeeze.

"You beat me, boy, I'll give you two afternoons off."

Crockett winked and released his hold. "Deal."

Two afternoons to spend with Joanna. Now he had even more incentive.

"'Course, if I win, you'll be giving me an extra hour after supper each night for a week. We got plenty of harness that needs mendin' and saddles in want of oil."

"Fair enough." He wouldn't mind a little extra work, especially if Joanna found reasons to come visit him out in the barn.

"You want in on the action, too, Jasper?" Silas nodded to the quiet man standing a few steps away.

"No thanks, boss." Jasper shrugged. "I still remember the contest last Fourth of July. You were the only one who even hit the final target. I'd rather keep my evenings free, thank you."

Crockett lifted his head and searched the trees along the river for the third scoring disc. *There*. It was easily five hundred yards out. The X on its face had been painted twice as large as the previous ones, but he still had to squint to make it out. Not quite the same as shooting cans off the woodcutting stump with Travis. Eager to outdo each other over the years, he and Trav had worked their way past the barn all the way to the tree line, which was a fairly comparable distance to today's target. But even as men, they'd missed those cans as often as they'd hit them.

Winning today would be no small feat.

The first man was called to the line. Crockett's belly started aching. Each marksman had his own ritual, and these rituals seemed to grow ever longer as the men set and reset their stances, waiting for the perfect conditions to shoot.

The first two missed the target. The crowd groaned in sympathy and offered polite applause for their good showing. The third man nicked the rim of the scoring disc. The spectators roared their approval.

Jasper stepped up to the line next. The onlookers hushed. He fit his rifle into his shoulder and searched for the best line, making tiny adjustments to his grip. Once satisfied, he stilled. And waited. And waited. The instant the gentle breeze swirling around them died, he pulled the trigger.

The scoring disc jerked as the bullet struck near the top.

"Great shot." Crockett slapped Jasper on the back as whistles and applause rose from the crowd. "Maybe you should have joined in on the wager after all. You might end up with the best mark."

Jasper shook his head, though a smile lit his face. "Nah. Silas will find a way to beat me. The boss man don't know how to lose. Never has."

Crockett could well believe that. The man exuded confidence and skill in everything he did. Whether he was working the ranch or leading a group of bandits on an abduction mission, one thing remained constant—the man fought hard to accomplish his goals. And never failed.

Could it be that the very self-sufficiency that allowed him to be such a successful rancher and leader of men was also his biggest barrier to accepting Christ? A man who needed only his own strength and wits to succeed in life would be blind to his need for a Savior.

Conviction settled in Crockett's gut as he watched Silas stride up to the line. The man's face showed nothing beyond concentration. No perspiration beaded his forehead. No tremors seized his hands. His legs stood solid beneath him; not even a heel dared swivel for better purchase. The *crack* of his shot rent the air, followed quickly by a distant *thunk* as his bullet collided with the target.

As a shout exploded from the crowd, Crockett's attention turned inward. If he could hand Silas a loss, would it put a chink in the man's armor? A chink that could weaken his defenses, giving truth a better chance to find its way inside?

If so, Lord, I ask that you steady my hand. Make my aim true. And grant me victory today, so that you can claim the victory tomorrow.

Silas backed away from the line, and gestured with a sweep of his arm for Crockett to take his place. Crockett hesitated, then slowly moved forward. The knot in his gut tightened with each step. He braced his right foot behind him, digging his boot into the dirt for better balance. He eyed the scoring disc and tried to picture a can on a tree stump. Well-wishers called out encouragement and advice, but their words were nothing more than a faint buzzing in his ears. He lifted his Winchester into position, and the buzz faded into silence.

Crockett inhaled. Sighted the center of the target. Adjusted for the breeze that ruffled his hair. Exhaled just enough air to relax his lungs. Then with a prayer in his heart, he squeezed the trigger.

The rifle butt kicked into his shoulder. A touch of smoke leaked from the muzzle. The shot blast rang in his ears.

But what made his heart sing was the telltale jerk of the scoring disc as his bullet lodged into its wooden surface.

Mr. Ward wandered out to mark the shot and take the necessary measurements. Then Jackson retrieved the target and ran ahead, collecting spectators as he went. By the time he reached the firing line, the entire community swarmed at his back. Everyone pressed forward, eager to hear the results, but Jackson held the large disc flat against his midsection as he struggled to catch his breath after the long jog.

A cool hand slid into Crockett's overheated palm. The light touch only lasted a moment before it pulled away, but a moment was all he needed to recognize its source. *Joanna*. He twisted his neck in the direction of the touch and found her at his side, her shy smile throwing his heartbeat into an erratic rhythm.

"The winner of the shooting contest," Jackson shouted, tearing Crockett's attention away from Joanna's sweet face, "with a mark only two and a half inches from dead center—" he paused, then twirled the scoring disk around for all to see—"is Crockett Archer!"

A loud cheer arose, but it was the pride glistening in Joanna's eyes that reverberated loudest in his heart. She smiled and clapped, but when others moved in to offer their congratulations, she quietly retreated. While he appreciated the handshakes and good-natured back thumping, what he really wanted was to sweep Joanna into his arms and twirl her around until her laughter spilled over them both. Then he'd kiss her and take that laughter inside himself as together they reveled in the joy of the moment.

But when the next hand firmed around his and Crockett found himself staring into Silas's face, he remembered that this moment was not about him at all. It was about what the Lord had done through him.

"Looks like you earned yourself some time off, Archer."

For once, Crockett offered no grin, just a slight nod of acknowledgment. "It was a fine match. One that I can't take credit for."

"What do you mean, you can't take credit for it?" Silas's grip tightened, grinding Crockett's fingers. "You find some way to cheat?"

"No," Crockett said with a little chuckle as he eased his hand out of Silas's vise. "I just meant that my abilities are not my own—they come from God. He provided the training during the hardship of my youth and helped me hone them as an adult. He deserves the credit."

"But he wasn't the one standing here pulling the trigger. You were."

"Oh, he was here," Crockett said, taking encouragement from the confusion that pushed past the defiance in Silas's eyes. "I visited him in prayer before raising my rifle and felt his presence throughout."

"Why would he care about a stupid shooting contest?"

"He doesn't, Silas. He cares about *you*."

27

Two days later, Silas was still puzzling over Crockett Archer's declaration as he rubbed Marauder down after a long ride through the woods. Crazy preachers. Always talkin' in riddles. He drew the currycomb through the gray's coat, wishing he could use the same method to untangle his thoughts.

What in the world did a shooting contest have to do with God? And why would his losing be a message that God cared about him? More likely God was showing favoritism—helping Archer win. Silas wanted no part of a God who cheated. But then, he'd always known the Almighty didn't play fair. For if he were truly interested in justice, Andy Murdoch would still be alive and that Bible-totin', child-bashin', sermon-spewin' stepfather of his woulda had his brains fried by some holy lightning.

Instead, God had turned a blind eye to the preacher's faults and let an innocent suffer.

Silas blew out a harsh breath, stormed out of Marauder's stall, and flung the currycomb onto the shelf. He kicked the wall hard enough to jangle the tack above, then bent over the half wall that sectioned off the milk cow's quarters and pressed his forearms against the wood.

"Daddy?"

Silas bit back an oath at the sight of his daughter climbing down the loft ladder.

"Are you all right?" she asked, wiping her hands on the painting smock that protected her dress. "I heard a crash."

He turned to face her, rubbing the dents out of his forearms. "I'm fine, Jo. Just had some bad memories sneak up on me and stir my temper. Nothing to worry about."

She glided toward him, a penetrating look in her eyes that reminded him so much of her mother he wanted to spin on his heels and run. Martha had always been able to see past his bluster to the doubts and pain beneath. But he didn't want his sweet Jo exposed to that darker side. It was his duty to protect her, to shield her from the ugly part of the world, even to the point of preserving her illusions about a loving God.

Jo halted in front of him and touched his arm. "Can I pray about it for you?"

He flinched.

"If it'll make you feel better," he grumbled. Silas turned away from the compassion in his daughter's eyes. He knew she was only trying to help, but doggone it, prayer was the last thing he wanted. The very idea chafed like a pair of sandpaper drawers.

"I'm not the one who needs to feel better, Daddy. You do. God can heal those old pains if you let him. He loves you."

"Ha!" Silas shoved away from the half wall and glowered at his daughter. Maybe he'd kept her too sheltered. Maybe it was time for a dose of reality. Something to protect her from the wiles of smooth-talkin' preachers.

"If your God was interested in sparin' me pain, he shoulda restrained the evil that caused it in the first place. You and Archer can go around spoutin' off about how God cares, but all I've ever seen from him is cold indifference. So forgive me if I'm not too eager to deepen our acquaintance."

"Did he feel indifferent toward you when the soldiers stripped the clothes from his only Son's body and plied him with whips until flesh was torn from bone?" Jo's quiet voice knocked him back. He wanted to discount her example. God had sent his Son for all mankind, not for him individually. It wasn't personal.

Yet somehow, when Joanna murmured the words, it felt personal.

"Did he feel indifferent when they pierced his Son's hands with nails and spat upon his face? Was it coldness he felt when his Son's tortured cry punctured the heavens, accusing him of forsaking him? It must have been agony for the Father to turn his back. Yet he could not gaze upon the sin clinging to Jesus. *Your* sin. *My* sin. Was it indifference that kept him from intervening? No, it was love. Love for you."

Silas couldn't answer. He couldn't look at her, either. Why wouldn't she just leave? He wished she would quit muddying the water. He was entitled to his opinions, to his anger—justified in them.

So why was he still listening?

She stepped closer. He could feel her, though she didn't touch him again. "Evil exists in this world, Daddy. When people choose that path, there are harsh consequences. Innocents are hurt. Once in a while God chooses to intervene. Many times he doesn't. Why? I don't know. But what I do know is that he promises to work things out for good for those who love him. He finds ways to create blessings even in the wake of disasters."

"I've never seen any such blessings." Silas muttered this observation more to himself than her, but Jo must have heard, for a sad little laugh fell from her lips.

"Oh, Daddy. You blame God for the bad in your life, yet you refuse to acknowledge his hand in the good. How many times have you bragged about the fact that you never get sick and can outwork any man? Who do you think blessed you with such a strong constitution? And Jasper's always talking about how smart you are, how you can lay out plans to perfection."

"Jasper should keep his mouth shut."

"God gave you that intelligence," Jo continued, determined to ride this train all the way to the end of the track. "And what about Mama?"

That brought his head around. "What about her? Your God had nothing to do with Martha. I found her on my own."

"Did you?" She raised a doubtful brow. "So it was nothing more than chance that placed Mama in the very stage you were set to hold up. A woman who would eventually convince you to leave your life of crime, who would bring you joy and comfort. A godly woman who prayed for your salvation every day of her life, and whose last wish was for her daughter to take over her spiritual vigil so that she might one day see her beloved husband again in eternity."

"She asked that of you?" Something rasped the back of his throat. Martha had always been a religious woman, but he never realized his lack of faith was such a burden to her. A burden she passed on to their daughter.

"She did. But she didn't have to ask. I would have done it anyway. I love you too much to give up on you."

Silas leaned his arm against the half wall behind him, suddenly unsteady. "I . . . I don't understand."

"Why do you think I wanted a new preacher so desperately? I didn't have Mama's support any longer. I needed help. And God answered my prayer by sending me a parson who is so much like you that he's probably the only preacher in the country you could come to respect."

Archer was in on this, too? Of course he was. Suddenly his comment at the end of the shooting match made sense. It was all a plot, a plan. They were ganging up on him, herding him places he didn't want to go.

"The best part of all, Daddy, is that God used *you* to bring him here. I never would have found Crockett if it hadn't been for you."

"I'll send him back," Silas threatened, panic setting in. He needed space to breathe, to think. He hated being chased, cornered.

"God's pursuing you," Jo pressed, relentless. "He wants you as his own. All you have to do is stop run . . ."

Her words died away as he sprinted out the barn door.

28

A cool breeze ruffled Crockett's shirt as he rode onto the Lazy R at the conclusion of his afternoon visits. He'd borrowed Joanna's mount to pay calls on the folks who'd not attended services following the picnic and to check in on the few he'd heard were ill. Everyone welcomed him warmly, although most had been more eager to discuss the shooting contest than church attendance. But he wouldn't complain. A foot in the door was a foot in the door, no matter how it came to be there.

The only true disappointment of the day came when he realized how much time those visits had consumed. He'd intended to spend only two or three hours paying calls and instead had spent nearly four. That didn't leave much time for courting.

Crockett grinned as his mare trotted toward the barn. It was a good thing Archers knew how to make the most of limited resources.

Frank was washing up at the pump near the corral trough. Crockett waved, thinking it might be a good idea to freshen up a bit himself before searching Joanna out. He had just tugged the reins to steer Sunflower in that direction when Silas burst out of the barn like a cat with his tail on fire. The mare reared, her shrill neigh a scream in Crockett's ears. He instinctively tightened his knees and leaned forward in the saddle to keep his seat.

"Easy, girl. Whoa now." He patted her neck, and Sunflower finally returned her forelegs to the ground.

Frank hobbled after his boss as fast as his stiff gait would allow. "Silas?" he called.

The fleeing man ignored his shout and soon pulled so far ahead, Frank was forced to give up the chase. He shuffled back to Crockett and ran a hand through his damp, graying hair. "What in tarnation was that all about?"

"I have no idea," he said, staring after his employer's retreating back. "It was like he didn't even see us." Which was odd. The man prided himself on his detailed awareness of all of the ranch's workings.

"Didn't hear us, neither." Frank grunted and crossed his arms over his chest, obviously put out by Silas's callous dismissal. "Something musta got him riled."

Crockett dismounted, continuing to stroke Sunflower's neck as she snorted and tossed her head. Her chest heaved, and a large breath expelled from her lungs. "That-a-girl," Crockett crooned. He kept a snug grip on the reins, still leery of the mare trying to bolt.

Bolt. Crockett turned to where Silas was disappearing into the trees out past the corral. "He's not mad," he murmured. "He's scared."

"Scared?" Frank scoffed. "You're out of your gourd if you think that. I've known Silas Robbins for more than twenty-five years, and I can promise you that man ain't afeared of nothin'."

Nothing but preachers and religious discussions, Crockett thought with a smile. Then all at once, a picture of what must have happened crystallized in his brain, and his gut lurched.

"Joanna!" Her name echoed across the yard ahead of him. He spared only a moment to toss Sunflower's reins to Frank before breaking into a run.

He found her huddled against the tack wall, arms wrapped around her middle, shoulders trembling. Her eyes lifted to meet his, her teeth digging into her bottom lip as she fought to contain the tears that swam in her eyes.

"I've ruined ev-everything." The hitch in her voice broke his heart. "I pressed him too hard. Said too much." A fat tear crested the dam and rolled slowly down her cheek. "He ran from me, Crockett." She swallowed a sob. "He ran from *me*."

He opened his arms and caught her as she staggered toward him. Folding her into his chest, he laid his cheek against her hair and stroked her back. "Shh, sweetheart. He didn't run from you. He ran from the truth."

"I never should have said anything." She tipped her head back, gently dislodging him. Her eyes shimmered, but she held the remaining tears at bay. "I thought it was the right time. He actually seemed to be listening. But then I went too far. I told him about my promise to Mama and the real reason you came here. I even pointed out how he'd unwittingly played a role himself by abducting you from that train."

Joanna braced her palms against his shirtfront, her touch ricocheting through him as she leaned backward against his hold. "He threatened to send you away, Crockett. And heaven knows if he'll ever let me speak of this again. You warned me to be subtle, to be patient, but I just blundered forward and made a mess of everything."

Crockett released his hold on her waist with one hand and moved to cup her chin with his other. "There's a time for subtlety, and a time to be bold. If the Spirit was moving you to speak, it would have been a sin not to."

"But what if it wasn't the Spirit? What if it was just me?"

Crockett sighed and snuggled her head back into his chest. "I battle the same question every time I write a sermon."

"How do you know?" She mumbled the question against his shirt, leaving her head where it rested in the hollow between his shoulder and neck. The place that seemed to be made for her.

Crockett rubbed her arm and dropped a gentle kiss on the top of her head before answering. "I don't always know. Not for certain. The best we can do is ensure our hearts are right, our motives pure, and then listen for God's guidance, praying that he will correct our path if we veer off course."

"Do you think I veered off course?" The quiet question tugged at his heart.

"No." The memory of Silas's agitated dash convicted him. "I know you, Jo. For years, you've prayed for your father, wanting only what is in his best interest. If you believed the time was right for you to speak, it was right."

"Then why did he run?" She didn't pull away, but she did tilt her head to meet his gaze.

For a moment her upturned lips distracted him. Steeling himself against the ill-timed surge of desire, he dragged his focus back up to her eyes.

"He needs time to think," Crockett said, "to examine his beliefs. You can't make the choice for him. He has to choose it on his own. We'll give him some time, see where the Lord leads next."

"But what if he makes you leave?" Her fingers wrinkled the cotton of his shirt as if she meant to hold him captive.

If she only knew how captivated he already was.

Crockett smiled down at her, his heart full of promises as he covered her hand with his own. "He might fire me, darlin', but he can't make me leave the area. I've got a church to run, you know. Besides"—he winked—"I get the feeling the woman who hired me might fancy me a little. I think I can convince her to let me stay on."

At last the clouds cleared from her eyes, and her mouth curved flirtatiously. "Oh, you do, do you?"

Crockett waggled his eyebrows. "I'm not above using my masculine wiles for a good cause." He shifted his grip on her hand and raised it toward his lips. "Do you think she'd let me stay in exchange for a kiss?" He lowered his head and lightly caressed the skin just below the bend of her knuckles, in the valley where her first two fingers met.

Her breath caught, and a tremor passed through her, a delicate version of the one pounding through him.

"You know, Archer," a gruff voice rasped behind them, making Joanna jump, "I don't reckon the boss's mood would improve much if he were to come home and find you dallyin' with his daughter."

Crockett squeezed Joanna's hand before slowly pivoting to face Frank.

The older man dropped Sunflower's reins, his right hand moving to hover above his holster. "Can't say I like it much, either, seein' as how Jo's practically my niece." His steely stare moved to Joanna and examined her from head to toe, assuring himself she was unharmed.

"I'd never take sinful advantage of a woman, Frank," Crockett ground out, his jaw clenching as he strove to keep a lid on his temper. He took a step closer to his accuser. "Especially not one whom I respect and care for as much as Joanna."

Frank's bow-legged stride closed the remaining distance between them. His eyes latched onto Crockett's, his palm resting on the butt of his pistol. "You telling me you got honorable intentions toward our gal?"

Crockett gave a clipped nod. "Yes, sir, I am—I do."

Instantly the man's face cleared, and the old grump actually smiled. "Hot diggity!" He cackled and slapped his thigh with his empty gun hand. "I knew it! Wait'll I tell the boys. Jasper's gonna owe me twenty bucks."

"Frank?" Joanna slid around Crockett's side, her fingers trailing down his arm until her slender hand nestled into his palm. "I don't understand." She tipped her face up to Crockett, puzzlement evident in the lines upon her brow.

He shrugged slightly, then closed his hand around hers and stroked his thumb over her knuckles.

"I ain't so old I can't remember what it's like to be young. I ain't blind, neither. I seen the way you look at her across the supper table when you think no one's watching." Frank jabbed his bony elbow into Crockett's ribs. "Why do ya think I waited so long to follow ya in here? Didja think Sunflower and I were out in the yard shootin' the breeze? Ha!"

Truth be told, after finding Joanna, he hadn't thought of anything but how best to comfort and reassure her. Now his little pixie was blushing up a storm and doing her best to hide her face behind his shoulder. It was all he could do not to grin.

"You mind keeping this information under your hat for a bit, Frank?" If the old buzzard went squawkin' to Silas about his and Joanna's courtship, her father would have him hog-tied and thrown off the Lazy R before he could blink. It wouldn't keep him away from Joanna, of course. Crockett had meant what he'd said about hanging around no matter what. However, Silas was at a crossroads. The fewer distractions he had to deal with, the better. "We'd like Silas to hear about it from us. When the time is right."

"All right," Frank grumbled, his usual grim demeanor reasserting itself. "But don't take your sweet time about it. I ain't met the man yet who can pull the wool over Si's eyes for long. In fact, it wouldn't surprise me if he already suspects something's afoot. Ever since the picnic, he's had a peculiar look about him when he watches you work—like he can't decide if he should keep you around or send ya packin'." Frank socked him in the arm. "Might be a good idea to stay upwind of him when we go huntin' tomorrow."

The man cackled at his own witticism, then finally moved on, leading Sunflower to her stall near the back wall.

"You're going hunting tomorrow?" Joanna's soft question pulled him away from the complications mushrooming in his mind.

"Your father grumbled something about putting my rifle skills to use for the Lazy R before I take another afternoon for myself." Crockett winked. "If you ask me, though, I think he just wants to see if I can hit a moving target."

A teasing smile lit up Joanna's face. "Can you?"

"I've been known to take down a squirrel midleap between trees." The Archer ranch had crawled with the little rodents. As kids, he and Travis used to have contests to see who could bag the most—until Jim threatened to quit cooking if they didn't start giving him some variety. Of course, Jim wouldn't be the one cooking this time. Crockett grinned at Joanna. "I think I can manage to bring something home to your table."

It was her turn to wink as she slipped from his hold and headed back toward the loft ladder. "I'll look forward to it."

29

Silas veered west through a stand of post oaks, separating himself from the rest of the hunting party. He knew these game trails as well as the Tonkawa Indians who roamed the area a hundred years ago had, and frankly, he wasn't in the mood for company. The conversation he'd had with Jo yesterday had replayed over and over in his mind during the course of the night, robbing him of sleep and leaving his temper dangerously ragged. Worst of all, it'd made things awkward between him and Jo.

He hadn't been able to look his girl in the eye this morning, not after running out on her like some kind of coward yesterday. He hated himself for that. She was his baby girl. His Jo. And he couldn't look at her.

Not without seeing her mother and recalling the promise Martha had extracted from her.

All those years they were together, she'd never harped at him about God. She had invited him to services once in a while and insisted on praying before meals, but she'd never nagged him about it. Probably 'cause she knew it wouldn't do any good.

Had she really prayed for him every day? Fought some kind of unseen battle for his soul that he'd never even been aware of? Apparently she'd passed the duty on to Jo, leaving their girl to take up the fight. A fight that drained her so much, she'd felt she had to call in reinforcements.

Archer.

Silas spat at the ground as he trudged deeper into the woods. What kind of man let his womenfolk fight his battles? So what if he'd known nothing about it. He did now. And that meant he had to make some changes. What exactly those changes were supposed to entail he hadn't quite figured out. Tightening his grip on his rifle, Silas squinted up at the sky.

"Why do you care about an old reprobate like me?" The harsh whisper rasped in his throat. "Did you tangle me up with a God-fearin' woman just to lure me in? 'Cause I ain't biting. It don't make no sense for you to go to such lengths to lasso my soul when you wouldn't lift a finger to stop one of your own sermonizers from caning Andy to death. So you can just quit chasin' me."

I love you too much to give up on you.

The words had been Joanna's yesterday. Yet the voice ringing in his head now sounded nothing like his little girl and everything like the roar of rushing waters.

Silas gritted his teeth and halted in the shade of a hickory tree—away from the early morning sun forcing its warmth onto the earth. Silas didn't want to be warm. He wanted the numbness the cold offered. A numbness that would keep him from thinking, keep him from feeling.

A rustle to his right brought his senses to alert.

Finally. A distraction.

Moving deliberately, so as not to make a noise that would give away his position, Silas shifted his rifle into a ready position and stole a careful glance around the hickory's trunk. About two hundred yards downhill and to the south, a white-tailed deer stepped out from the trees to nose the grass of a tiny clearing. Sunlight glinted off the buck's rack. The beast was strong. Mature. And easy pickin's.

A smile of triumph curved Silas's lips. The others were safely to the north—too far away to poach his find. He'd be the one with the first kill of the day. And judging by the size of the specimen in front of him, he'd be bringing in the best of the day, as well.

Silas eased into a secure stance and took aim. Drawing a line up from the buck's front leg, he sighted the center of the chest. A lung shot. He'd take no chances on the head or spine. Anything less than an instant kill would send the deer bounding into the trees, never to be found. No, this was his chance to prove his marksmanship. To prove his self-sufficiency. To regain the control Jo had shattered in him yesterday.

A tiny sound echoed somewhere downhill from him, between his position and the buck. Some varmint with bad timing, blast it all. The buck lifted his head and blinked, poised to leap away, but Silas wouldn't allow it. Without a second thought, he squeezed the trigger.

But it wasn't the buck that fell.

A slender figure had emerged from the brush fifty yards downwind at the same moment Silas's rifle cracked its shot. The buck bounded away. The figure crumpled.

No! Silas's mind screamed the word his constricted throat couldn't voice. How . . . ? Where had he . . . ? It wasn't possible. All of the men were farther north.

But it wasn't a man.

Acid churned in his stomach as the truth dawned in horrifying clarity. "No. Please, God. No!" Leaping forward, Silas sprinted down the hill, stumbling over tree roots, slipping on sandy soil. Thick shrub branches tore at his face and hands. He shoved them aside.

He forced his way through the last bramble and fell to his knees beside Jackson Spivey's writhing form. The boy was belly down, moaning, trying to reach behind his shoulder to the place where blood oozed from a bullet-sized hole. A bullet Silas had put there.

"Easy, Jackson." Silas snatched the bandana from his neck, wadded it, and pressed it hard against the boy's wound.

Jackson cried out, the sound lacerating Silas's soul.

"Don't worry, son. I'm gonna get you out of here. You're gonna be fine." He *had* to be fine. Silas couldn't be responsible for another boy's death.

Holding the dressing in place, Silas rolled him over. A whimper echoed in the air between them, but Silas wasn't sure if it emanated from Jackson or himself.

Muddy streaks marred the kid's face, where tears had coursed over his cheeks. His breaths came in shallow little pants as he struggled to keep a brave front. "It hurts, Mr. Robbins."

"I know, boy. But you're tough. You'll pull through." Maybe if he said it enough times, one of them would start to believe it.

Silas searched Jackson's chest for an exit wound. He found none. Biting back an oath, he scanned the hillside for any sign of his men. *Where are they?* They should have headed his way after hearing his gunshot—if for no other reason than to see what type of game he'd bagged.

His grip tightened on Jackson, remorse hitting him so hard, his head spun. He squeezed his eyes shut and gathered his wits. Regret wasn't going to get the boy home. A strong back was. Silas slid his hunting knife from the sheath at his waist and yanked the tail of his shirt free from his trousers. Slicing the flannel with the blade, he tugged and tore until he had a strip long enough to wrap around Jackson's chest. Trying not to jostle the boy too much, he wrestled the bandage until it securely bound the dressing to the wound.

When he finished, Jackson's eyes had closed. The fight seemed to be draining from him along with his blood. Silas swallowed the growing lump in his throat. He couldn't let another minute pass without saying what needed to be said.

"I'm sorry, Jackson." He hugged the boy gently to his chest and squinted away the moisture pooling near his lashes. "So sorry."

"It ain't your fault." Jackson's eyes cracked open a slit. "Jo fussed at me 'bout not hunting without permission. I was . . . too stubborn to listen.

Guess . . . she was right, huh?" He tried to chuckle, but the weak sound turned into a cough.

Silas winced.

He'd been too stubborn to listen, too. What if she was right again? What if God really did care?

Jackson's head lolled to the side as the boy lost consciousness. His face ashen, his body limp, he was knockin' on death's door.

Silas lifted his face to heaven. "I know you and I ain't seen eye to eye for quite some time, and I know I'm to blame for this predicament. But if you could see your way to intervening on the boy's behalf, I'd take it as a personal favor."

The sky didn't open. No angelic chorus started singing. No beam of heavenly light fell across Jackson's face. The kid just lay there as broken as before.

Fine. He'd handle it by himself. It'd been crazy to think God would listen to him anyway. Maybe he listened to people like Jo and Martha, but to bitter old outlaws with blood on their hands? Not likely.

"All right, kid," he grunted as he shifted to take Jackson's weight. "Let's get you out of here." He collected the fallen rifles and hoisted the boy over his right shoulder like a gangly sack of potatoes. Using the rifles as if they were a cane, Silas levered himself up to a standing position and quickly braced his legs. Once he had Jackson's weight distributed evenly, he set off for the trail using the arm with the rifles to shield the boy from the worst of the brush as he pushed them through.

A pair of shots echoed some distance to the north, drawing a scowl from Silas. If the men were off chasing their own game, there'd be no one to help him with Jackson. The kid would never make it.

"Why won't you do something?" Silas groaned beneath his labored breath. He would have shouted his frustration to the sky, but he had no energy to spare. The vegetation thinned as he neared the edge of the gulley. He struggled to put one foot in front of the other, the ground beneath him growing increasingly steep.

His boot slipped. He tightened his one-arm hold on Jackson and leaned into the hill, digging his toes into the sandy soil. Silas rammed the rifle butts into the ground to help him stabilize. His gaze lifted to where the hill leveled out above him. Still twenty yards to go.

Sweat beaded his forehead despite the cool morning breeze. Silas set his jaw and took another step. He'd get the boy home or die trying.

Ten yards. Five. Something caught the toe of his boot. A root, maybe? He staggered to the right, Jackson's weight nearly toppling him sideways. Not now. He was so close. Just a few more steps.

He thrust the rifle butts into the earth as he corrected his balance. Once steady he started onward, but the sandy slope shifted beneath his boots. As his feet struggled to find purchase again and again, his defenses weakened. Determination alone wasn't going to save Jackson. Nor would stubbornness or strength of will.

The next slip took Silas to his knees. As his legs absorbed the impact of his collision, his soul absorbed the realization that relying on himself was hopeless. A forty-year-old grudge against God had no place on this hillside nor in his heart. Not when a boy's life hung in the balance.

Arms shaking, he clung to Jackson while his pride and bitterness crumbled to dust. "I need your help." Though God knew he didn't deserve it. "Please. No favors. No bargains. I'm just a sinner on his knees beggin' for mercy. Beggin' you to spare the life of this boy. Please. I ain't demandin' a miracle or a flock of angels to swoop down and flutter their wings around him. I ain't got no right to ask for such things. All I ask is that you give us a fighting chance."

His breath shuddered as he inhaled. "I'm done running. If you want me . . . I'm yours."

Silas made no effort to get up. He *did* make an effort to trust—to trust in a God he didn't understand. Leaning on the faith of his daughter and his wife . . . he waited.

Barely a moment passed before the sound of his name being called met his ears.

"Here!" Silas yelled in response. "Hurry!"

Footsteps pounded faster, louder.

Silas struggled to stand, bracing himself against the slope and clasping Jackson's legs tight to his chest.

"Give me your hand," a voice called from above.

Silas lifted his head as he swung the rifles up over the ridge. "Archer. Thank God." Never had he meant two words more.

The parson's solid grasp encircled his wrist, and with his strength counterbalancing the downward slope of the hill, it only took two long strides for Silas to regain the trail.

"Is that Jackson?" Archer paled, taking in the kid's limp form.

Silas swallowed hard, guilt tearing at his throat. "He jumped in front of my bullet when I tried to take down a buck. I never knew he was there." Moisture pooled in his eyes, but for once he didn't care. His pride no longer mattered. All that mattered was Jackson.

He braced himself for Archer's disdain. It was what he deserved. But the man met his gaze head on, nothing more than concern etched on his face. "Come on," he said, slinging his rifle strap over his shoulder and gathering up the other two. "I'll help you get him to the house."

Each man took one of Jackson's arms and wound it about his neck.

Their greater height kept all but the toes of the boy's boots from scraping the ground as they stretched their stride in the rush to get home.

"How'd you know to come?" Silas huffed out between steps. "I heard the others hunting farther on."

"It's hard to explain," Archer replied, his own breath heaving between the words. "As soon as I heard your shot, my gut reacted. The guys assured me you were fine, but I couldn't shake the feeling that I was supposed to check on you."

God brought him back. Archer didn't make the claim, but Silas knew it was true. God had intervened. Even before Silas had been aware of the need.

Silence fell between them again as they concentrated on putting one foot in front of the other as quickly as possible. Finally, the barn came into view. And with it another slew of problems. They might have gotten the boy home, but the doctor was miles away. Fetching one from Deanville would take at least a couple hours—if they could even find the man.

Silas regarded the preacher from the corner of his eye. "You prayin', Archer?" Heaven knew the boy needed someone with more pull than he had with the big man upstairs if the kid was gonna have a shot at surviving this mess.

"With every step, Si," he grunted out, twisting his neck to meet his gaze. "With every step."

Silas nodded, the vise around his heart loosening just a touch. "Me too."

30

Joanna plucked another weed free from around the new carrot tops that had recently pushed through the soil, her mind far from her task. Crockett had invited her to go riding with him when he returned from hunting. Just the two of them. A flutter of anticipation danced in her belly. She planned to show him some of her mother's favorite painting spots, and if she could muster the nerve, she might even ask permission to sketch his likeness. Not that she hadn't sketched him already. She'd completed at least a dozen drawings, but they'd all captured Crockett from a distance.

What would it be like to study him up close? To take her time with each feature of his face in order to replicate it on paper? The strong line of his jaw. The sparkle in his eyes when he teased her. The curve of his mouth when he smiled.

The way his lips softened right before they met hers.

Joanna's hands stilled. Would Crockett kiss her again? Mercy, but she hoped so. Her breath caught in her throat as her eyes slid closed to savor the memory of the kiss they'd shared down by the river. Would their second kiss be as heavenly as the first?

She blinked against the sunlight, and a smile bloomed across her face—until she noticed three men limping toward her from the edge of the woods.

Instantly alert, she shot to her feet and lifted a hand to block the sun's glare.

Someone was hurt. She couldn't tell who from this distance, but she knew what her father expected of her in such a situation.

Dashing through the open gate, Joanna abandoned the garden and ran for the house. She bounded up the back porch steps and grabbed the metal rod that hung from the large metal triangle she used for calling the men to supper. She circled the inside of it again and again, striking metal against metal with a strength borne of fear. The clamor nearly deafened her, but she kept it up until the ache in her arm forced her to stop. She prayed the others were within earshot. If so, the alarm would have them running for the house.

The entire time she rang the dinner bell, her focus remained locked on the trio of men approaching from the north. The one on the right had the build of her father, but he was so hunched over from the weight of the injured man, she couldn't be sure. The one on the left was slightly taller, and her heart wanted so badly to believe it was Crockett—that both he and her father were unharmed.

She longed to sprint out to meet them and see for herself who'd been hurt and how bad the injuries were, but practicality drove her into the house instead. Rushing out to them would only assuage her curiosity, but it wouldn't actually help anyone. She'd be of better service gathering medical supplies and preparing a sickroom.

Working the pump at the sink, Joanna quickly scrubbed away the garden dirt from her hands and under her nails, then ransacked the linen closet for the rolls of bandages and wads of cotton wool she always kept on hand. By the time she'd gathered the medicine box and the shears from her sewing basket, and stripped the quilt from her bed, heavy footfalls from the porch announced the arrival of the men.

She'd purposely left the back door ajar, and as she rounded the corner into the kitchen, a male boot kicked it wide.

"Bring him around to my room," Joanna instructed before she'd even gotten a look at the men. "I've got things set up for him in there."

She held the door open as the threesome finagled their way through. A breath she hadn't known she'd been holding whooshed from her lungs when she recognized her father and Crockett.

Thank you, Lord, for keeping them safe.

Crockett dropped the rifles he'd been toting to the floor. The injured man didn't even flinch at the racket. That's when she noticed the sandy hair and the slender build.

"Jackson?" The name escaped her in a strangled cry.

How had this happened? He was just a boy. A boy who should be pestering her with inappropriate marriage proposals, not drooping lifelessly across her daddy's shoulders. She moaned, pressing her hand over her mouth to mute the sound. Was he dead already?

"Is he . . ." She couldn't quite voice the question as the men shuffled past her into the hall.

"He's still breathing, but there's a bullet in him," Crockett answered, his grim expression offering her little comfort.

She followed the men into her room, and when she realized they meant to lay Jackson facedown, she darted to the head of the bed to remove the pillow. Better not take any chances. If he survived the bullet, she didn't want a pillow suffocating him.

The men grunted as they slowly lowered Jackson to the bed, taking care not to jostle him too much.

"Hand me those shears," Crockett said from the far side of the bed and immediately set to work extricating Jackson's shirttails from his trousers.

Joanna grabbed the scissors from the bedside table and held them out handle first.

"Thanks." He barely spared her a glance, so focused was he on Jackson. He snipped through the makeshift bandage that held the blood-soaked dressing in place and then started in on the shirt, cutting it from tail to neck.

She retrieved the discarded bandage from where he'd tossed it on the sheet. Only then did she recognize the fabric as being from her father's shirt.

"Daddy . . . ?" Joanna turned, intending to ask what had happened, but the haunted look etched into his features dissolved her words.

He stared at Jackson as if he didn't really see him, as if his mind recalled another horror. She held her hand out to him, but he backed away until his bootheels hit the wall on the opposite side of the room. Then he slowly lowered himself to the floor. His hat knocked against the wall and tumbled to the rug. He never even blinked. He just covered his face with his hands and bowed his head over his knees.

She'd never seen him like this—defeated. It frightened her.

"I'm going to need water, Jo," Crockett said, bringing her attention back to the boy on the bed. "Warm if you have it. And sponges or rags to clean the injured area."

She met Crockett's gaze over the top of Jackson's prone form. Compassion glowed there, along with a rigid determination that helped her own spine stiffen. They would fight this. Together.

"You can start with the water in the pitcher." She hurried to the washstand and filled the porcelain basin with water, then carried it to Crockett's side of the bed, setting it on the edge of the dresser at his elbow. "The stove reservoir should have warm water, and I'll put on a couple of kettles, too."

He caught her hand before she could dash off to the kitchen. "Heat some of the reservoir water nearly to a boil and bring me the strongest lye soap you've got. Oh, and a knife. A thin, sharp one. And tweezers if you have 'em." He spoke softly, as if he didn't want the unconscious boy to overhear and start fretting.

His gentleness nearly brought the tears she'd been battling to the surface, but she blinked them back and nodded her understanding before slipping out to the kitchen.

She had just set the second kettle on to boil when the rest of the hands burst into the house.

Frank and Carl bent double as soon as they saw she was unharmed and started wheezing as they gulped air into their lungs.

"What happened?" Jasper demanded, apparently the only one who had enough breath to talk.

"Jackson's been shot. We'll need to fetch a doctor." She glanced back at the hall, expecting to see her father emerge. There was no way he couldn't have heard the thundering herd arrive. He'd snap back to his usual self, start barking orders, and set everything to right. But he never came.

"The boss?" Jasper asked, obviously at as much of a loss as Joanna.

"He and Crockett are in with Jackson." They didn't need to know what state he was in at the moment. It would only rattle them, and right now Jackson needed them at their sharpest.

"What do ya want us to do?" Frank wheezed.

Joanna straightened her shoulders and spoke with authority. "Jasper, you and Frank ride to Deanville. One of you fetch the doctor. The other better track down Sam Spivey." After years of watching her father lead his men, she easily mimicked his manner and tone. "Search the saloons first. Sober him up before you bring him back here, though. The last thing we need is someone yelling and knocking things around when we're trying to save his boy's life."

Jasper and Frank nodded, then spun and headed out the door without another word.

"What about me, Jo?" Carl stepped forward. He dragged his hat from his head and scrunched it up in his fist. His eyes barely met hers. "I ain't much good around sick folk." His Adam's apple bobbed as he leaned close. "The sight of blood makes me woozy."

The poor fellow's face burned deep red at the admission, and his feet shuffled as if he couldn't wait to leave.

"That's just as well," Joanna said. She twisted to check the steam on the kettle, hoping to relieve his embarrassment by acting as if she hadn't noticed. "With my father and Crockett tending to Jackson, and Frank and Jasper gone to Deanville, the care of the ranch falls to you. I need you to see to the stock and handle all the regular chores while we're short-handed."

"Yes'm. I can do that." He slapped his hat over his thinning hair and dashed for the back door before she could change her mind.

Judging the water in the first kettle to be close enough to boiling, she palmed a folded dish towel and removed it from the fire.

After pouring the hot water into a small dishpan, she balanced the tray containing the lye soap, her two sharpest knives, and clean towels atop it and carried the materials to the sickroom.

Disheartened to see her father still huddled on the floor, Joanna tried not to look at him as she circled the bed to set the dishpan on the dresser top. She could only imagine one thing that could have brought her father this low.

"It's his bullet in Jackson, isn't it?" she whispered when Crockett turned toward her and started rolling up his sleeves.

His eyes met hers. "An accident."

She nodded. It could be nothing else. Her father would never intentionally harm Jackson. But, oh, how her heart ached for both of them, and she worried that neither would recover.

Bring healing, Father. Please. For both of them.

Crockett's breath hissed out of him as he dunked his arms elbow deep into the near-scalding water.

"Do you want me to cool it down a little?" Joanna moved to collect the pitcher from the washstand.

"No. I can handle it." He latched onto the cake of soap and started scrubbing. "How long until the doctor arrives?"

"I don't know. A couple hours, at least. Jasper and Frank are fetching him from Deanville." She returned to his side and held a towel out for him.

His head jerked toward her. "Deanville? There's not one closer?"

"No."

He hung his head for a moment, eyes closed, shoulders hunched forward. She thought she heard him murmur, "Not again, Lord." Then his back straightened and he spoke more distinctly. "Grant me strength and skill."

Opening his eyes, he accepted the towel from her. "I need you to go to my room at the church, Jo, and fetch my medical books. They're in the trunk that Neill brought me. Do you remember it?"

She frowned. "Yes, but why . . . ?"

"I might have need of them, and I'll feel better having them on hand." His jaw hardened and his brown eyes darkened with resolution. "We can't wait for the doctor. I'm going to have to get the bullet out and patch Jackson up myself."

"You . . . you can't do that, can you?" What could he possibly know about surgery? He would just make things worse. No, they should wait for the doctor.

She started shaking her head, but his answer stopped her.

"I've done it before."

A short bark of laughter erupted from her father. "Of course he has."

The comment puckered her brow, but Joanna was too stunned by Crockett's claim to respond. "I-I don't understand."

"Pulled a bullet out of my brother Jim's shoulder when we were kids. He was about Jackson's age. I wasn't much older. But there was no one else to do it." He sighed, then bent his mouth in a crooked half grin. "He's got a nasty scar, but he lived through it."

She steadied herself with a hand on the dresser top. Heavenly stars. He had dug a bullet out of his own brother when he was just a child. How was that even possible?

"After that day," Crockett continued, "I was in charge of all the doctoring on the Archer ranch. I read every medical book I could get my hands on and memorized most of them. I can do this, Jo. I have to."

She couldn't seem to move. Or speak. She just stood there staring at him.

Then her father's voice broke her stupor. "Have faith in your man, Jo, and go fetch his books. The Lord brought him here. Remember?" The words were slightly mocking as he flung her earlier comments back at her, but there was an edge to them she'd not heard before. Resignation? Or maybe bewilderment, as if someone had just solved an impossible puzzle in front of him, leaving him no longer able to discern between what could and couldn't be done. "Might as well let the two of them get to work."

So consumed was she in trying to decipher the change in her father, she was halfway to the barn to collect Sunflower before the full impact of what he said hit her. He'd called Crockett *her* man. And heaven be praised, he'd actually acknowledged not only God's presence but his involvement in their lives.

Tears of thanksgiving clouded her vision, and new energy surged as she raced the rest of the way to the barn.

31

Crockett blew out a prayerful breath as he gently removed the dressing from Jackson's back and started cleaning around the wound. His fingers shook. He paused, clenched them into a fist a couple times, and then continued.

Could he do this? His hands were so much larger now than when he'd dug that bullet out of Jim. What if he caused more damage than good?

Don't let me hurt him, God. Help me save him. I can't do it alone.

Crockett swished the dishrag he was using in the hot water to rinse away the blood and dirt, then set back to work on the wound.

The sound of Silas adjusting his position against the far wall drew Crockett's attention. He wished he could somehow ease the man's burden. Guilt and worry seemed to have cut the man's legs out from under him.

Silas raised his head slightly, the glazed look in his eyes giving Crockett serious cause for concern. "It's Andy all over again," he muttered.

"Who's Andy?" Crockett spoke softly, giving Silas the opening to answer or not, whichever he chose. Jackson wasn't the only one in the room with wounds that needed tending.

"A kid I knew back in Missouri before I lit out for Texas." Silas stared straight ahead, as if he were peering through a window into the past. "He died."

The stark words hit Crockett like a blow. He turned back to Jackson. It wasn't right for children to die. Jackson should be scampering all over the countryside—poaching fish, climbing trees, snaring rabbits—not lying here with a hole beneath his shoulder blade.

"An accident?" Crockett washed some fabric fibers from the entry wound.

"Nope," Silas answered, his voice flat. "His preacher stepfather beat him to death with a cane."

"What?" Crockett's near shout destroyed the calm he'd worked so hard to maintain in the room. Jackson's body flinched, and he let out a muffled moan. Crockett whispered an apology and steadied the boy by clasping his uninjured side until he stilled.

How could a man of God thrash a child to death? It was unthinkable. No wonder Silas held such a deep-seated revulsion of preachers. Crockett felt soiled by association.

"It was my fault." Silas rambled on, unfazed by Crockett's outburst. "I was always getting Andy into trouble. I was a year older and had a talent for mischief. I didn't have no folks to steer me straight. All Mr. and Mrs. Washburn cared about was how much work they could wring outta me on their farm. And when Mr. Washburn got a hankering for the corn whiskey down at his still, I'd sneak away to town.

"Andy was a sickly kid. Scrawny. An easy mark for the bigger boys to pick on. Three of them ganged up on him one day out behind the schoolhouse, and when I came across 'em, something inside me snapped. I launched myself at the biggest one and blackened his eye before he even knew what hit him. Knocked out another kid's tooth, and bloodied the third one's nose. I made it clear that anyone who messed with Andy in the future would get more of the same."

Crockett listened intently as he finished cleansing Jackson's wound. Only a tiny amount of blood seeped from the hole now, but Crockett worried more was leaking inside. At least the boy's breathing seemed normal, if a bit shallow. Surely if the bullet had punctured a lung he'd be in a lot more distress. Maybe things weren't as bad as they'd feared.

Or maybe the damage was hidden. Like the damage inside Silas. Perhaps he could cleanse that wound a little more, too.

"I imagine you earned Andy's loyalty that day."

Silas snorted. "Kid followed me around like a puppy after that. I acted all put out, like having him around was a hassle, but in truth, he'd become the little brother I'd always wanted.

"So when we sneaked down to the creek for a swim one afternoon and I saw the bruises on his back, I was livid. I demanded he tell me who had hit him so I could pound some decency into him. He made up some excuse about tripping on the church steps, but I didn't buy it. Finally he admitted his stepfather had punished him for lying about Mrs. Carson's bloomers."

Bloomers? A smile edged its way onto Crockett's face as he placed a clean dressing over the torn flesh of Jackson's back. He took the whiskey bottle from Joanna's medicine box and poured a portion over the blades of the knives she had brought him, thinking he'd need to pour some in the wound, too, eventually. His smile dissolved.

"I was the one who'd stolen the bloomers, of course, and tied them to the weathervane atop her house," Silas rattled on. "Andy was just the lookout. But the old man didn't care. All that mattered was making someone pay for the crime. He insisted that Andy stay away from me, but Andy refused. He snuck out every chance he got. And every chance *I* got, I plotted how to get even with the old man for hurting my friend."

Crockett bent over Jackson, peering intently into the wound. Now that the bleeding had slowed, he could judge the bullet's path more readily. The angle seemed to head outward, toward a spot under the boy's arm. Thank God. He hoped that meant no major organs had been hit. There were some bone chips that would need to be cleared out from where the bullet appeared to have grazed the ribs, but as long as the bullet wasn't lodged behind bone, he shouldn't have too much trouble extracting it.

Silas had grown quiet again. Crockett decided he'd done all that he could for Jackson until Joanna returned. He'd need her help swabbing the blood when he went in, or he'd never be able to see what he was doing. Her father was in no shape to assist.

As a precaution against infection, Crockett poured a generous splash of whiskey in and around Jackson's wound, holding the boy down when he screamed and tried to raise up off the bed. Once the initial shock passed, Jackson collapsed against the mattress, and Crockett managed to apply a fresh dressing without further reaction.

Crockett's gut told him Silas wouldn't continue his story if Joanna was around, and expecting she'd be back in minutes, Crockett said a quick prayer over Jackson, then strode across the room to seat himself next to Silas on the floor.

"So what'd you end up doing?" He directed his question to the air in front of him, though he watched Silas from the corner of his eye.

A sad crooked smile turned the corners of Silas's mouth. "I dropped a snake on his head from the rafters of the church during one of his sermons."

Crockett bit back a grin.

"The fella squealed and flailed as if the brimstone he'd been calling down had set his hair afire. I dropped from the rafters to a spot in the aisle right in front of him—wanted to make sure the lout knew it was me that done it so his anger would have the proper target. Then I lit out of there and raced for the farm.

"I was only gone a couple hours. Just long enough for church to finish and Sunday dinner to be eaten. But by the time I got to Andy's house ready to take my punishment, the parson had already spent his rage. I could hear

Andy's mom wailing and begging her husband to let her fetch the doctor. Then a loud crash echoed through the front room, and the wailing stopped.

"I shimmied up the tree that shaded Andy's window and forced my way inside." Tears rolled down Silas's cheek as he spoke, but he made no move to brush them away. Crockett wasn't sure he was even aware they were there.

"He looked so tiny in that bed. Tiny and battered beyond recognition. I was afraid to touch him. Afraid I'd hurt him more. He made horrible rasping sounds when he breathed, and his chest barely moved. But when I came closer, the less swollen of his eyes cracked open a slit, as if he knew I was there.

"'It doesn't hurt, Silas,' he told me. 'It doesn't hurt to go to heaven.' After that, he didn't rasp anymore."

Silas's legs fell flat upon the floor and his arms circled closed in front of his chest as if he were clutching Andy's broken body to his breast.

"All this time I blamed God for not protecting him, for siding with one of his own and abandoning Andy to the brutality of a madman. But I was the one to blame. I was the one who prodded the bull and left Andy to face the horns alone."

Silas's voice grew husky. Eyes still straight ahead, he cleared his throat. Crockett wanted to lay a supporting hand upon his shoulder, to console him with assurances that it wasn't his fault, either, that the blame rested solely with the fiend who vented his rage on a child. But Crockett sensed his touch would jar Silas from his vulnerable state and possibly bring his walls back up. He didn't need pity. He needed to finish his story.

"God didn't abandon Andy. I see that now." Silas swallowed long and slow. "I remember the peace that settled over his face as he took his last breath. The smile that touched his lips as the angels welcomed him home. It was the same look Martha had when she . . ."

Crockett couldn't stop himself this time. He put his hand on Silas's shoulder and squeezed. The man finally turned to look at him.

"I been running from God for forty years, Archer. Today I stopped."

Moisture collected in the corner of Crockett's eye as his soul shouted praise for the lost sheep that had finally been dragged home.

"Something happened out there while I was trying to get Jackson home. I still don't understand it, but I guess God don't need me to understand everything. He just needs me to trust."

The simple statement of faith seared Crockett's heart. His hand tightened reflexively on Silas's shoulder as the man's gaze burned into his with a conviction Crockett had never witnessed in him before.

"God brought you here, Archer. Brought you here for this moment." Silas reached out his hand and clasped Crockett's shoulder. "A preacher with doctorin' skills." He grinned and shook his head as if he still couldn't quite believe it. "I might've pulled you off that train, but God was the one who put you there. Put you there for Jo. For me. And for Jackson."

Silas shoved up to his feet, then held out a hand and yanked Crockett up, as well. "The boy's going to be fine, Parson. I trust you. But more importantly, I trust the God who brought you here."

He slapped Crockett on the back, his vigor returning in force, causing Crockett to stagger forward a step.

"Now, show me what I can do to help."

32

Joanna tossed Sunflower's reins to Carl and slid from the horse's back, all while cradling the two medical books she'd found in Crockett's room. It had taken her longer than she'd expected to find the volumes, since they were mixed among two dozen or so other books in a small trunk under his bed. She prayed the delay would not prove too costly.

After sprinting across the yard, she burst through the back door, dashed down the hall to the sickroom, and careened to a halt.

Her father and Crockett, sleeves rolled to their elbows, fingers covered in blood, stood over Jackson, their heads only inches apart. Discarded wads of cotton wool stained bright red littered the floor around her father's feet. A strong metallic tang filled her nostrils, and she fought against the urge to gag.

Too much blood. Too much . . .

Crockett glanced up. "Good. You're back. I need tweezers and a needle and thread."

A wave of dizziness hit her, but she pushed through it to concentrate on his words. Needle and thread. Her sewing basket. The kitchen.

Slowly, she bent at the waist and lowered the books to the floor. Then she backed into the hall and hurried to escape . . . er . . . fetch the items. Grabbing up the entire basket, she thrust it over her arm and turned to face the hall.

You can do this, Joanna. Crockett needs you. You can be strong for him. Strong for Jackson.

Setting her shoulders, she marched on to the sickroom. Keeping her gaze averted from Jackson, she rounded the bed and placed the sewing basket on the dresser top.

"I have the needle and thread," she said, tugging a needle free from the pincushion. She always kept two or three of them threaded and ready to go for mending projects. She'd plucked out the one with black thread. Somehow it just seemed a sturdier color than white or blue.

"Soak it in the whiskey in the tray over there." Crockett didn't even look up. He didn't have to. His tone said everything for him—complete assurance that she would accomplish whatever he asked of her. "Then wash up yourself. You need to be clean before you handle any of the instruments."

She hadn't planned on staying long enough to handle any instruments. Surely her father could see to that task. He seemed recovered and back to his usual capable self. Joanna opened her mouth to say just that, then closed it. If Crockett had need of her, she'd stay.

The smell of the whiskey wrinkled her nose as she dropped the needle and thread into the shallow puddle on the tray. She couldn't decide if that smell was better or worse than the blood. Maybe if she kept her back turned, her stomach would stay where it belonged and not jump into her throat again.

Breathing more through her mouth than her nose, Joanna unbuttoned her cuffs and rolled her sleeves. She had just finished scrubbing to her elbows with the lye soap when Crockett's voice cut through the quiet.

"Hand me the tweezers. I can see the bullet, but I can't quite reach it." Crockett held his bloody hand out in expectation.

Joanna stared helplessly at the tweezer-less tray. "I . . . um . . . don't have any tweezers."

Crockett finally glanced her way, a frown scrunching his brow. His eyes raked the tray as if hoping she'd overlooked them. Not finding them, his scowl deepened. His gaze traveled over the entire dresser top, then narrowed in on her. All at once the lines cleared from his forehead.

"Towel off and bring me your hands. Your fingers should be slender enough."

"Slender enough for *what*?" But she knew the answer. She shook her head even as she reached for the towel. She stared at Jackson, at the hole in his flesh, at the blood. "I-I can't."

"Joanna." The firmness in Crockett's voice brooked no argument. She forced her eyes to meet his. "Come here." He spoke in the same authoritative tone he used from the pulpit, and before she consciously chose to obey, her feet carried her to his side.

"The more I cut, the more chance there is of damaging something that can't be repaired. The top of the bullet is exposed. All you have to do is pull it out." He circled his left arm around her, careful not to touch her clothing with his hand, and gently nudged her into position directly in front of him. He pressed close, his heat warming her back. Then his cheek came alongside hers, and he spoke directly into her ear. "You can do this, Joanna. I wouldn't ask it of you if I didn't believe you could do it."

She glanced across the bed to her father. He winked at her and nodded. "Easy as cleaning the innards from a chicken before throwing it in the pot."

The comparison was absurd, but somehow it grounded her. If she could reach into a chicken to pull out its gizzard, surely she could pull out a bullet.

Only Jackson didn't look a thing like a chicken, and that tiny circle of lead Crockett was pointing out to her was no gizzard.

"As soon as we blot away the excess blood, reach for it." Giving her no time to formulate an adequate reason to delay, Crockett signaled her father with a nod of his head. "Silas."

The two of them patted the area with clean cotton, then held the wound open for her. Biting her tongue, Joanna reached for the bullet. The warm squish around her finger and thumb set her legs to trembling so fiercely, it was only by God's grace she stayed upright.

As if sensing her weakness, Crockett braced her with his own frame, surrounding her, steadying her.

Her fingertip brushed against something solid. Metal. So close. She just needed to get a grip on it. All thought of where her hand was faded away as she concentrated solely on retrieving the bullet. She burrowed deeper, twisting her wrist to get her thumb nearer the target.

She could feel it. Almost there. Just as her thumb and forefinger closed around it, it slipped away. A frustrated grunt echoed in her throat. If only she could push it toward her from the other side.

Well . . . why not? Joanna pulled her fingers out and reached around to press on Jackson's side, estimating where the exit wound would have been if his rib cage hadn't slowed the bullet's progress. Easing the fingers of her left hand into the wound, she searched again for the bullet. Once she could feel it, she experimented with different angles and pressures with her right hand until she found one that lifted the bullet ever so slightly. She reached with her fingers, praying the metal ball wouldn't slip away again.

Her thumb was too short, but she managed to trap the bullet between her first two fingers. Holding her breath, she clasped the hunk of lead between her fingertips and slowly tugged it toward her. Movement! Ever so slight, but it definitely moved. She tugged again. Gently. Afraid the slightest jostle would steal it from her grasp. Again, it moved with her.

"I think I've got it," she whispered.

Crockett's arms seemed to firm around her, though in truth he barely touched her. He drew in breath as she did, their chests rising together.

Joanna maneuvered her thumb into the small opening and secured her grip on the piece of lead. She pulled her arm back, and the bullet finally slid free of Jackson's flesh.

Staring at the mangled lead between her fingers, not quite believing she'd really removed it, she dropped it into her palm and pivoted to face Crockett.

"It's out." A tremulous smile lifted the corners of her mouth.

Crockett's answering grin was tender yet beaming with satisfaction. "That it is." He lifted the bullet from her palm and bent his forehead close to hers. "I never doubted you." His lips brushed against her hair as he spoke, and his cheek rested against the top of her head for a single precious moment before he stepped aside.

"Why don't you get cleaned up while I finish things here." Crockett nodded toward her hands as he reached for the needle soaking on the tray.

Joanna glanced down at her bloodstained fingers and staggered a bit as light-headedness assailed her. Now that the bullet had been retrieved, her queasy stomach was back in full force. "I think I'll . . . um . . . wash up in the kitchen."

Holding her hands awkwardly in front of her, she circled the bed and headed for the door. Before she reached it, her father's voice stopped her.

"You did good, Jo." His eyes glowed, and Joanna stood a little taller. Her stomach settled a bit, and her head no longer felt as if it were going to roll off her shoulders.

All her life she'd strived to please him, whether it was with her riding skills, her painting, or even just the way she cooked his beefsteak. Never a great dispenser of flattery, her father rarely spoke his approval aloud. Yet when he did, she treasured the words as if they'd been crafted from the finest silver.

Not trusting her voice, Joanna simply nodded in response and exited.

It didn't take long to wash up, yet even after cleaning away Jackson's blood, her hands continued to shake, causing her fingers to fumble with the button at her cuff.

Maybe tea would help. Joanna refilled the empty kettle, set it over the hottest part of the stove, and dug in the cabinet for her tea tin. She grabbed the coffee, too, thinking of the men. As she worked the handle on the grinder, her mind returned to Jackson. So pale. So still. So young. Too young.

"Please, Lord," she whispered under her breath. "Please bring him through this."

Once her tea had steeped, she poured a cupful and stirred in a teaspoon of honey, hoping the sweetness would serve as an extra balm to her ragged emotions. She sat at the table, circled her fingers around the heated cup, and blew gently across the brew's surface. Inhaling the flavorful steam, she closed her eyes and let her head loll forward. The tension she'd carried in her neck for the last hour finally loosened.

"Is that coffee I smell?"

Joanna jerked her head up to find Crockett approaching the table.

"Yes," she answered, scrambling to her feet. "Sit down. I'll pour you a cup." Joanna grabbed a towel to protect her hand, then lifted the coffeepot from the back of the stove and filled a mug. She turned to place it on the table in front of his usual place, but he wasn't sitting at the table. He was standing two feet from her, his eyes drinking her in as if he needed her more than any hot beverage.

Crockett Archer was the strongest, most capable man she'd ever met. Never once had he projected anything less than confidence as he dealt with Jackson's injury—with her father, as well. She was no fool. Something had happened between the two men while she'd been gone. Something that had restored her father's wilted spirit.

Yet as Crockett stood before her, she saw the toll it all had taken. The weariness etched into his forehead, the vulnerability in his eyes.

Without a word, she set the ceramic mug on the table, then stepped up to Crockett and wrapped her arms around him. She held him fast, laying her head upon his chest and squeezing him close, her only thought to give him the comfort he so readily gave others.

He stiffened at first, then with a strangled sound that could have been a swallowed sob, he clutched her to himself and buried his face in her hair.

Tremors coursed through him. Joanna gathered him closer, as if she could protect him from the storm running its course. After a long moment, the tremors subsided and his hold on her changed. His grip loosened slightly, allowing his hands to roam her back. One traced the line of her spine up to her nape, the light touch of his fingers bringing on another case of light-headedness.

The softness of his lips pressed into her scalp, and his warm breath fanned across the edge of her brow. "I love you, Joanna Robbins."

Everything inside her froze for a single moment, only to be followed by a deluge of reactions that nearly buckled her knees. Her heart pounded. Her stomach danced. And her mind swirled so fast, she could barely keep a grip on the words she thought she'd heard.

Tilting her face up, she searched Crockett's face for the truth she so desperately wanted to believe. She found no teasing smile, no laughing eyes. Only an intensity that stole her breath.

"I love you, Jo."

Then his lips were bending to hers, and all thought scattered. She stretched up to meet him, thrilling at the way his arms tightened around her. His mouth was soft, insistent. A little bit desperate yet achingly gentle. Joanna melted into him, tasting the promise in his kiss. The hope.

She wanted to linger, to savor, to stretch the kiss into forever. But they weren't alone. Her father could come in at any moment. And Jackson . . . Well, Jackson should be their focus now.

Slowly she pulled away. The hand Crockett held at her nape slipped around to cup her cheek, and for a moment she didn't think he would let her go. But then he seemed to remember their circumstances, as well, and lifted his head.

Her breathing ragged, she looked up into the deep brown eyes she loved so well. With a hand that was none too steady, she reached up and combed a bit of his unruly hair off his forehead. Then, as if her fingers were one of her paintbrushes, she stroked the lines of his face, tracing his eyebrows, his cheek, his jaw.

Suddenly shy, she dropped her gaze. Her hand followed, coming to rest against his chest, the beat of his heart thudding against her palm.

"You're a dream for me, Crockett," she whispered. "A dream I never imagined would come true. I love you so much my heart aches with it."

His arms encircled her again, drawing her firmly against him. She laid her head in the hollow beneath his shoulder, her arms wrapping around his waist.

Neither spoke. They simply absorbed strength and comfort from one another, silently rejoicing in the precious gift they'd found.

But they couldn't stay as they were forever, not with all that was going on around them. So after lingering as long as her conscience would allow, Joanna eased away from Crockett's hold.

"How's Jackson?" she asked in a soft voice, reluctant to completely break the spell that had been woven over the two of them. "Do you think he'll recover?"

Crockett cleared his throat as he stepped away. He bent to pick up the forgotten mug of coffee, then took a sip before answering.

"I'll feel better after the doctor examines him," he said, finally meeting her eye. "But yes, I think he'll recover. The bullet didn't strike any vital organs as far as I could tell." He paused for another sip. "There's always a danger of infection, though."

"Maybe when his father comes to collect him, I should try to convince him to leave Jackson here so I can tend him. Sam Spivey's not the most dependable sort."

Crockett dipped his chin in agreement. "If he does take the boy home, it might be a good idea for one or both of us to make periodic visits."

"I'm sure Mr. Spivey would welcome a meal or two if I was to come by. I could make some broth for Jackson and leave his father a heartier soup."

"That's a good plan." He winked at her, and her heart turned a flip. It was such a little thing, yet his approval warmed her inside and out.

Silence crept back into the kitchen, but it was a comfortable one. One that allowed Joanna's thoughts to flow from one to the next unheeded.

"Is Daddy sitting with Jackson?" She traced the edge of the table with her finger as she moved toward the stove. "I should probably take him some coffee." She reached for another mug and filled it with fragrant brew.

Hesitating at the edge of the table, she turned back to Crockett. "How's he doing? He looked more like his old self when I came back from your place, but I know he still feels responsible."

"If you ask me," Crockett said, a slight smile touching his lips, "he looks more like his new self than his old one."

Joanna's brow furrowed. "His new self? I don't understand."

"He's praying, Jo." Crockett reached out and clasped her hand. "Truly praying. I think for the first time in forty years, he's letting go of the past and opening himself to the Lord."

Her knees did buckle then. She thunked the coffee mug she held onto the table—not caring about the liquid that sloshed over the brim—and all but fell into the nearest chair. Her vision blurred as tears pooled in her eyes and rolled down her cheeks.

Crockett moved behind her, his hands massaging her shoulders. "Those seeds you and your mother planted are coming to fruition, Jo. He's finally stopped running."

Joanna leaned her head back against Crockett, her mind too overwhelmed to pray anything more than *Thank you*.

33

Crockett clasped Jackson's good arm above the elbow and levered him to a sitting position. It'd only been four days since the accident, but the boy was already itching to return to his free-spirited ways.

"Easy does it," Crockett cautioned as Jackson tried to stand on his own. "Let me help you." He adjusted his hold, moving his hand to grip the boy's upper arm.

"Aww, come on, Crock. Quit treating me like an old woman." He tugged his arm free and staggered a bit at the sudden loss of support. "The doc came by yesterday and said I was mendin' just fine. I ain't got a fever no more, and so long as I wear this stupid sling, I can go about my business."

"Within reason." Crockett raised a brow until Jackson squirmed sufficiently to let him know he'd caught the message. "If you try to do too much too soon, it could set you back."

"Yes, *Ma*." Jackson rolled his eyes.

Crockett chuckled and gently ruffled his hair. "You're a mess, kid." But he was improving, praise God. This was the second day he'd been out of bed, and he seemed stronger.

Jackson made his way gingerly across the one-room Spivey cabin and lowered himself into a chair at the rickety table in the corner by the stove. He reached for the towel-covered plate Crockett had brought.

"What'd she make this time?" He peeked beneath the cloth. "Mmm. Oatmeal cookies." He grabbed one and shoved it into his mouth. "I should get shot more often," he said around a mouthful of cookie, "if it means Jo will keep sending me treats."

"It might be less painful if you just stopped by the house every once in a while." Crockett winked, and Jackson, cheeks bulging, grinned.

Helping himself to a cookie as he joined Jackson at the table, Crockett took a bite, then surreptitiously surveyed the cabin. Cooking wasn't all Jo had done. The cabin glowed with a cleanliness that must have taken her hours to accomplish, even with the room's small size. The walls looked as if they might crumple like a pile of sticks if the wind blew too hard, and the furniture was a broken, mismatched mess, but there wasn't a speck of dirt to be found.

He frowned as he surveyed the cot Sam Spivey used. Apparently dirt wasn't the only thing scarce around here.

"Your father's saddlebags are gone." Crockett strove to keep his voice free of condemnation. "He light out again?"

"Yeah, well . . ." Jackson shrugged, the reddish tinge creeping up his cheeks belying his air of nonchalance. "Three days is about his limit, you know. And with the doc's good report, he figured I'd be all right. Said he had a job lined up with one of the ranchers closer to Deanville and was worried the man would give it to someone else if he didn't show up soon." He jutted his chin forward as he grabbed another cookie from the plate. "All his hoverin' was driving me batty, anyway. We're both better alone."

Crockett met Jackson's skittery gaze and waited for the boy's attention to settle. "You're not alone."

Jackson swallowed the bite he'd been chewing. "I know."

A confirming silence passed between them before Crockett pushed to his feet. "Why don't you let me take you back to the Lazy R? If nothing else it would save Joanna from having to drag food over here twice a day."

"Nah. Tell Jo I got enough to tide me over for a while. Pa laid in supplies before he left. She don't have to keep coming."

"She will anyway. You know how she is."

"Yeah. But a man don't want his lady to see him weak. If I were to stay there, she'd probably coddle me like some kind of baby or something." His face screwed into a comically disgusted expression.

At his words, though, memories assailed Crockett of the way Joanna had held him after he'd emerged from Jackson's sickroom. She seen him at his weakest, yet instead of diminishing him, the sharing of the burden made him stronger. Her love made him stronger.

Jackson's heavy sigh from across the table pulled Crockett from his thoughts. "You're gonna marry her, aren't ya?"

A pinprick of guilt poked Crockett's conscience for depriving the boy of his infatuation. Nevertheless, he straightened in his seat and nodded once. "Yes."

"Figures." Jackson leaned back in his chair. "Well, if I had to lose her to somebody, I'm glad it's you."

"No hard feelings?"

The boy looked more resigned than pained, but Jackson was good at putting up fronts, so it was hard to tell.

Jackson sat a little straighter, his demeanor changing from boy to man as he eyed Crockett with surprising maturity. "If I didn't think you'd be good for her, I'd fight you for her. But I trust you, Crock. I been around you enough to know that you don't just spout nice words from the pulpit—you live 'em. She'll be in good hands."

For once, Crockett had no words at the ready. Humbled by the boy's faith, all he could manage was a gravelly "Thanks."

"'Course, you still gotta get through Silas." The smile that twisted Jackson's face made it clear he wouldn't mind witnessing his friend endure a little fatherly torture.

And Crockett fully expected to suffer some. Silas might have opened up to him in a moment of weakness after Jackson's injury, and he might have even worked through some of his issues with preachers, but the man was still an ornery cuss who wouldn't give away his precious daughter without demanding his pound of flesh. Crockett hid a grin behind his hand. He actually looked forward to the challenge.

"Well, anything worth having is worth working for, right?" He winked at Jackson.

"Yep." Jackson grabbed the towel that had guarded the cookies and wadded it in his good hand. "Don't worry." He launched the towel at Crockett's head. "I'll put in a good word for you. Silas promised to bring his checkerboard over tomorrow to entertain me while you and Jo are off at church."

Crockett hid his disappointment. He'd hoped Silas would attend services. According to Joanna, he'd been reading her mother's Bible the last few evenings and even asked a question or two. But Silas was a man used to making his own way—a leader, not a follower. Nagging him about attending church would only create friction. The man needed to come to his own conclusions and decide for himself whom he would serve. Like Joshua, all Crockett could do was offer the invitation and proclaim his own allegiance through his words and deeds. It was up to Silas to do the rest.

"You think you can manage to ring the bell without me?" Jackson interjected into the silence.

Crockett shook off his ponderings and smiled. He snagged the towel from where it had fallen across his shoulder and tossed it back at Jackson's face. "Maybe. But just this once." He crossed his arms over his chest and spoke with his best mock-lecture tone. "You don't need two arms to pull the bell rope, you know. I fully expect you to be back at work next Sunday. No more lazing about, you hear?"

Jackson chuckled. "You got it."

As it turned out, Crockett missed Jackson for more than his bell ringing skills the next day. With the boy at home, Crockett had no one to run interference for him when it came to dodging Holly Brewster. The gal seemed to be constantly circling like some kind of hungry buzzard, swooping in every chance she got to pick at his flesh. She arrived early and offered to ring the bell in Jackson's place. Yet when he unhooked the rope for her, all she did was bat her eyelashes and plead with him to help her.

What if the rope slipped through her fingers? What if she did it wrong? Wouldn't it be better for him to hold the rope, too? Preferably by holding her in the process.

She hadn't said that last part aloud, but it projected through the sultry glances she kept aiming in his direction. He'd finally instructed her to yank on the rope however she liked, then left her to her own devices and strode away to the podium to review the sermon notes he'd finished reviewing not five minutes before.

Thankfully, Joanna arrived soon after, saving him from Holly's more blatant machinations. But all through the service, Miss Brewster continued her subtle attack. She sang a touch too loudly from the pew behind his, ensuring he heard her voice above any other. He strained to hear Joanna's gentle lilting from across the aisle, but Holly's brassy tones drowned her out.

During the sermon, Holly stared at him with a far-too-enraptured expression. As much as he would've liked to believe that his message could hold her so in thrall, not even his pride could swallow that much rot. Then she started toying with the buttons on the bodice of her dress, and that's when he gave up all pretense of acting as if he didn't notice her. He locked his focus on the left side of the congregation from that moment on and never veered to the right again.

Her brazenness had gone too far. It was no longer just a matter of his being uncomfortable with her forward manner; it had progressed to the point where he worried about moral implications. He couldn't simply strive to avoid her. He needed to confront her. Not only as a man who wished to discourage her interest but also as a minister who needed to caution her about the slippery path she was walking.

But he hated confrontation. Growing up, he'd been the keeper of the peace in the Archer household. If Travis got too uptight, Crockett would tease him into a better frame of mind. If Jim wanted to pound Neill into a pulp for ruining his stew, Crockett intervened with a funny anecdote to diffuse the tension. He was an expert at charming people back onto the honorable path. Unfortunately, charm wouldn't work with Holly. It would only inflame the problem.

So he had no choice. He had to confront her directly. Which meant he'd have to hurt her, because the truth was not what she wanted to hear.

Is there any other way, Lord? Couldn't you just change her heart? I have little experience in talking to women. I'm bound to muck this up.

No peace came with the prayer. Only a recollection of a verse from James. *"He which converteth the sinner from the error of his way shall save a soul from death, and shall hide a multitude of sins."*

Apparently, he couldn't charm God, either.

As Crockett stood at the rear of the church, shaking the hands of departing members, he forced himself to smile and make polite conversation despite the sick mound of dread swelling in his stomach. A confrontation with Holly was sure to be awkward, possibly even volatile. But he'd been called to minister to all the members of his flock, not just the easy ones.

So when Holly and her mother made their way toward him, he steeled himself for what needed to be done.

"Another wonderful sermon, Brother Archer," Sarah Brewster gushed. "As always." She tittered like a young girl as she held her hand out to him. "Won't you come for lunch? I'm frying chicken, and Holly baked a wild blackberry cobbler that will melt in your mouth."

"It sounds wonderful, ma'am," Crockett said as he clasped her hand, "but I'm afraid I'm already promised elsewhere today."

"At the Lazy R?" Holly interjected, her lips puffed into a pretty pout. "Pish. You eat there all the time. I'm sure Joanna wouldn't mind sharing you."

Actually, he figured she'd probably mind quite a bit.

The possessive thought cheered him considerably. "I'm sorry, ladies. I've given my word. However . . ." He drew the word out to keep Holly from arguing further, then turned his attention to her mother. "I would like to ask your permission to call on Holly tomorrow evening. Perhaps around seven? There is a matter of some urgency I need to discuss with her."

He'd tried to make it clear that his visit would not be a courting call by his last remark, but judging by the way Holly's pout disappeared beneath the onslaught of a beaming smile, she hadn't caught on.

Pressing the issue with so many parishioners within hearing distance didn't seem wise, and he supposed she'd understand soon enough, so he held his tongue.

Mrs. Brewster squeezed his hand and nearly bounced in her delight. "Of course you can pay a call, Parson. We'll be sure to hold back a serving of cobbler for you."

"Thank you, ma'am."

She finally released his hand and grabbed hold of her daughter. "Come along, Holly. Let the man get to his lunch. You'll see him tomorrow."

Holly captured his hand despite the fact that he hadn't extended it to her. "I'll be looking forward to it."

He wished he could say the same.

The following afternoon, Joanna steered her wagon through the Lazy R gate after a visit with Jackson and spotted Crockett striding out of the barn to meet her. He halted by the edge of the building and rubbed a bandana over the back of his neck before stuffing the blue cloth back into his pocket. He stood so tall; his long legs braced apart, the fabric of his shirt outlining the breadth of his shoulders and arms. Her heart fluttered as she rambled closer.

This man loved her. This strong, handsome, godly man truly loved her. It didn't seem possible.

She bit her lip, yet her mouth stretched into a wide grin anyway when he raised his hand in greeting. Joanna returned the gesture, keeping one hand on the reins as the team plodded toward the barn.

"How's Jackson today?" Crockett's eyes danced as he waited for her to set the brake.

Joanna wrapped the harness straps around the brake lever and bent to retrieve the food basket from the floorboards. "Oh, as ornery as ever," she said as she gathered her skirts to one side. "He was outside trying to chop wood one-handed when I got there."

Crockett's warm hands circled her waist as he lifted her from the wagon, and they lingered even after her feet were solidly aground.

"I chopped a pile for him two days ago." One of his brows arched, nearly disappearing beneath the rim of his hat. "Surely the kid hasn't depleted it already. Especially with you doing all the cooking."

"The woodpile was still stacked high in the shed. I think he was trying to prove something to himself," Joanna said, finding it hard to concentrate on the conversation with Crockett's fingers stroking her sleeves. "I don't mind him testing his capabilities; I just wish he wouldn't use such sharp implements until he's sure of what those capabilities are."

His fingertips had worked their way up to her shoulders and she abandoned all hope of coherent thought and leaned into the caress. His thumb brushed the edge of her jaw, and her eyes slid closed. The feel of his breath on her face was the only warning she received before his lips met hers.

Joanna reached up to stroke his cheek. Crockett tugged her closer and began to deepen the kiss, then suddenly drew back.

"Sorry." His voice shook a little, then turned into a soft chuckle. "I hadn't intended to do that when I came to help you down."

Joanna lowered her lashes, not quite able to meet his gaze after the sweetness of the kiss. "I didn't mind."

He laughed outright. "Heavens, Jo. That's not the thing to say to a man when he's battling to hang onto his self-control and good intentions." His words were lighthearted, but she didn't miss the way he stepped back and released his hold on her.

Did she really tempt his self-control? Red hair, freckles, and all? If she'd ever needed proof that he really loved her, he'd just given it to her.

"You're a good man, Crockett Archer. I trust you."

"That's good, because I need to tell you something you're not going to like."

She frowned at the change that came over his features. Gone was the teasing suitor. Like a storm cloud blowing in to cover the sun, Crockett's eyes darkened with a seriousness that immediately set her on edge.

"The horses will be all right for a minute," he said, relieving her of the basket and taking her arm. "Let's go sit on the porch."

She didn't want to sit on the porch. She wanted him to spit out the bad news. He wasn't leaving, was he? If he was, would he take her with him? And what about her father? They'd been making such progress. And Jackson. He would be devastated.

By the time Crockett led her up the porch steps and into one of the rockers, Joanna felt as brittle as a week-old cookie, ready to crumble at the slightest tap.

"What is it?" She scooted to the edge of the seat and braced her feet against the porch floor to keep the chair from rocking. Her neck craned up to gauge Crockett's expression, and her gaze followed him as he took the seat next to hers. The chair creaked as it accepted his weight, and Joanna feared she might scream right along with it if the man didn't hurry up and end her suspense.

Finally he turned. He ran his palms down his pant legs and took a breath before looking up to meet her eyes. "I'm paying a call on Holly Brewster tonight after supper."

Joanna frowned and blinked several times. Did that mean he wasn't leaving? Relief whooshed the air from her lungs until the rest of the message sank into her brain. "Why are you going to see Holly?"

She fought to control the alarm rising in her breast. Just because he was going to see Holly didn't mean he had feelings for her. He couldn't and still kiss her the way he had down by the wagon, right? "Are the two of you planning another church picnic?"

A picnic. That's probably all it was. Holly always loved to be at the center of any event, and she *had* done a decent job with organizing the last one—even if she did stick Joanna with babysitting duty to keep her away from Crockett.

"No. We're not planning another picnic."

Not a picnic? Then what was he going there for? "Is she . . . uh . . . ill?"

She'd looked fine at church yesterday. Better than fine, actually. The lavender dress she'd worn had shown off every one of her feminine curves to perfection, and her pretty blond hair had practically shimmered beneath her stylish matching bonnet. She'd seemed in disgustingly good health.

"No, she's not ill, either. I'm going to talk to her about a personal matter that I'm worried might soon have some serious spiritual implications." The corners of his mouth pinched, and lines appeared on his forehead. This wasn't a call he was looking forward to making.

Somehow that made everything better.

He ran a hand over his face but didn't quite manage to erase his grimace. "I'm afraid I can't give you any specifics since it's a private matter. However, I didn't want to keep my visit a secret from you. After Holly twisted events at the picnic to make you think something happened that actually didn't, I worried that something similar might happen with this situation." He bridged the space between them, covering her left hand with his right. "I love you, Joanna. I don't want you to doubt that for a moment. No matter what anyone says."

The fact that he knew her well enough to recognize her weaknesses and cared enough to help her fortify them spoke volumes. "Thank you for telling me. Is there anything I can do to help?"

"Pray." Crockett's eyes bored into hers. "Pray for the Spirit to provide me with the right words. And for Miss Brewster's heart to be receptive."

"I will," she vowed, and started that very moment.

Lord, I don't know what has happened or what the ramifications are, but I ask that you guide Crockett tonight. Give him the words you wish him to say and the courage to say them. May they find fertile ground in Holly's heart.

Crockett must have been praying, too, for though his eyes were open they lacked focus. Not wanting to disturb him, Joanna simply held his hand and silently repeated parts of her own prayer until the sound of an approaching horse brought her head around.

A single rider trotted down the drive. From a distance, Joanna recognized neither the mount nor the man, but as the rider neared the porch, an awful tightening wound about her chest. Surely not . . .

Crockett slipped his hand from hers and pushed to his feet, sending his rocker into a gentle creaking motion. "Marshal Coleson. What brings you out to the Lazy R?" He stepped to the edge of the porch and leaned against the support beam. Tipping his hat back, he grinned a welcome that set Joanna's teeth to grinding.

"Came to see Mr. Robbins. He around?"

Joanna's hands fisted in the fabric of her skirt. What did the lawman want with her father? Had he figured out who Silas Robbins used to be? Or had this visit been prompted by something else? She'd been uneasy about the marshal ever since that odd exchange between him and Crockett at Miss Bessie's place, and now he was here. At the Lazy R.

Crockett glanced up at the sky, then back at Coleson. "Silas and Jasper are checking on one of the heifers out in the eastern pasture. She's fixin' to drop a calf."

Saddle leather groaned as the marshal brought his mount to a halt and crossed his wrists over the horn. "Mind fetching him for me?"

"I'll go." Joanna sprang from her chair, her mind racing. She could warn him. Maybe even take him some food if he decided to run. There was cheese in the kitchen. And apples. She could pack the bread she'd baked this morning, too. She could have it together before the marshal even dismounted. All she had to do—

"If it's all the same to you, miss, I'd prefer the parson fetch him."

She swallowed nervously, looking from Coleson to the barn and back again. She couldn't just stand by and let this man take her daddy away. He'd changed. He was a good man. A good father.

"Joanna." Crockett's voice echoed quietly in her ears. He was facing her now, his hands massaging her rigid shoulders. "It will be all right. Do you hear me? God is in control. It will be all right."

She dragged her attention from the lawman and found Crockett's face. He smiled. She latched onto that smile, desperate for a taste of the peace it offered.

"We don't even know why the marshal's here." He brushed a stray curl off her forehead and back over her ear. "Just invite him in and give him some of that great coffee you make. Treat him like any other guest."

But he wasn't any other guest. He was a lawman. A lawman who wanted to talk with her father. She didn't want to pour him coffee, she wanted to send him packing.

Yet a more rational part of her brain had her nodding agreement.

"That's my girl." Crockett started to pull away. Joanna grabbed his hand.

"Promise you won't leave for Holly's until we work whatever this is out. Please?" If he left, she'd shatter.

Crockett, his hand still trapped in her death grip, raised her hand to his lips and kissed her whitened knuckles. "I promise. You're my top priority, Joanna. Everything else but God comes second."

Finally, she let him go, clinging now to his vow instead of his hand. The marshal dipped his chin to Crockett when he strode past, then touched the brim of his hat in a salute to her.

"If you don't mind, miss, I'll water my horse."

She forced a smile to her lips, hoping it didn't look as quivery as it felt. "Of course, Marshal. Help yourself."

"I'll see to your team, as well." He dismounted and took hold of his horse's bridle. "It's only right since I'm the reason Archer won't be around to do it." He turned and led his horse toward the corral trough.

"Thank you." The words fell automatically from her lips as she watched him go. Then she remembered Crockett's instructions and called after him. "Come up to the house and get some coffee when you're finished. I'll make a fresh pot."

"I'll do that, miss. Thanks."

As Joanna walked into the kitchen and set about tossing out the old coffee and making up new, she couldn't shake the feeling that she'd just invited Disaster to dinner.

35

Silas reined in Marauder and stared down at the roof of the ranch house. He'd always enjoyed the view from this small rise. Many a time he'd ridden in from a long day on the range only to pause at this spot and absorb the vision of home. Martha had always seemed to know when he was there. Maybe she watched for him; maybe she just sensed his nearness. Either way, she'd usually come out into the yard and wave.

Man, how he missed those waves.

I got the law waitin' on me, Martha. Waiting in our home. At our table. There ain't no runnin' this time.

He closed his eyes and tried to visualize his wife, but her face didn't appear. His gut clenched. Martha had always been his rock. His support. His conscience. Even after her death. She couldn't abandon him now. Not when he needed her most.

"'Fear thou not; for I am with thee.'"

Silas swiveled and stared at the man behind him. Archer sat peacefully atop his mount, not even looking in Silas's direction, just spoutin' verses into the wind.

"'Be not dismayed; for I am thy God: I will strengthen thee; yea, I will help thee; yea, I will uphold thee with the right hand of my righteousness.'" Finally Archer turned to look at him, and his gaze seemed to penetrate to the very marrow of his bones. "Whatever happens, Si, God is with you. Lean on his strength, and you'll get through."

Then the parson nudged his horse and headed down the rise.

Silas watched him go, a prickle in his chest. What if *gettin' through* meant enduring a prison term? He'd been reading about that Paul feller, the one Jo told him had written so many of them church letters. Seemed he wrote most of 'em from jail. Not exactly the way Silas wanted to spend his twilight years. But what if that's what God had in mind for him? Heaven knew he deserved it.

"I can't say as I trust where you're leadin'," Silas said, squinting up at the clouds as Marauder pranced beneath him, eager to follow Archer's mount, "but I gave my word to stop running, and that's what I aim to do. If you're . . . uh . . . of a mind to send some of that help the preacher was yammerin' about, I'd not turn my nose up at it. . . . Just so you know."

The clouds offered no reply, so Silas gave Marauder his head and plunged over the rise.

The marshal stood waiting on the porch, hip cocked against the rail, coffee cup in hand.

Silas scowled. The man looked downright comfortable.

"I hear you're lookin' for me," Silas said, swinging his leg over Marauder's back. Archer appeared at the horse's head and led the beast away, giving Silas an unobstructed view of the lawman trespassin' on his porch.

"Need to ask you a few questions, if you don't mind."

Silas got the distinct impression it wouldn't matter if he minded or not. The man's casual pose failed to soften the steel in his eyes.

"I reckon I can spare the time to answer a few." Silas climbed the porch steps and eyed the marshal from head to toe, taking in the gun slung low on his hip, the badge pinned to his vest, and the hard lines of everything in between.

The lawman straightened to his full height and met Silas's stare with one of his own.

Silas deliberately turned his back and stepped to the door. Pulling it wide, he waved the marshal ahead of him into the house. "I hear you're an ex-Ranger. That true?"

The man paused halfway over the threshold. "I hear you're an ex-outlaw. *That* true?"

Years of living by his wits kept Silas's expression bland as milk toast. "Marshal, if that's the kind of question you plan on askin', this is gonna be a real short visit."

"We'll see." The marshal held his gaze for a long moment before continuing into the kitchen.

Yep. He'd been a Ranger all right. Silas could see it in his eyes. Jasper had suspected as much, even warned Silas about him five years ago, when Coleson had taken over as town marshal.

Now that he'd stared the man down, though, an eerie feeling of destiny crawled up Silas's spine. Coleson knew who he was.

"Daddy?" Joanna's blue eyes rounded with concern as she skirted the kitchen table and hurried toward him.

Something caught in his throat when he thought about the possibility of being dragged off in front of his little girl—of never seeing her again. He opened his right arm and pulled her into a half hug.

"Everything's all right, Jo." His voice sounded like gravel under a wagon wheel, but she burrowed closer anyway. He patted her shoulder once and dropped a quick kiss against her forehead, turning slightly so the marshal wouldn't catch the gesture, and stepped away. "Ya got some of that brew for your old man?"

She nodded, blinking the moisture from her eyes. Then she stiffened her spine, lifted her chin, and marched past Coleson as if he were nothing more than a new piece of furniture in the room.

Pride in his Jo would have brought a smile to Silas's face if he hadn't been so determined to keep his features schooled. Couldn't give Coleson even the smallest advantage.

"There a place we can talk, Robbins?" The lawman barely waited long enough for Jo to put the mug in his hand before starting in.

"Here's as good a place as any." Silas deliberately moved to the head of the table and took a seat. "Pull up a chair, Marshal."

Coleson glanced meaningfully at Jo. "You sure you want your daughter hearin' all I got to say?"

Jo scraped chair legs against the floor and plopped into the seat to Silas's right. "I'm staying."

Silas's mouth curved a tad at the corners. Family stood by family.

The marshal shrugged and chose a chair near the stove, probably so he could keep an eye on the door. "Suit yourself."

Coleson set aside his coffee and pushed his hat brim up onto the high part of his forehead with a bent knuckle. His focus never wavered from Silas's face. "I understand there was a shooting here a few days ago."

Somehow Silas managed not to flinch. *That* was what this was about?

"Yep. Hunting accident." He paused to take a sip of coffee. "Scared the beans right outta me when I saw Jackson go down."

Coleson's eyes widened a bit at his ready answer. Silas stifled a grin. Nothing like knocking a lawman off his high horse with a little straight shootin'. They never expected it.

"Sam Spivey claims you're the man who shot his son."

The accusation jabbed him right in the sore spot of his heart. Silas winced and dropped his chin. "It's true." Regret clogged his voice. He coughed a bit to clear it. "I wish it weren't."

Triumph flashed in Coleson's eyes. "So you admit to back-shooting the boy in cold blood."

"Now hold on a cotton-pickin' minute, Marshal. I ain't no back-shooter!" Silas slapped the flat of his hand against the table with a loud crash. If Coleson thought he could twist a horrible accident around into a hangin' offense, this friendly chat was gonna end up with Silas introducing the business end of his boot to the lawman's backside.

"Doc Granger confirmed that the bullet entered the boy from behind." Coleson narrowed his eyes. "You saying the doc's wrong?"

"You're making it sound like my father shot Jackson on purpose!" Jo sprang to her feet, her voice quivering. "It was an accident. Daddy was aiming at a buck and had no idea Jackson was even there until after he pulled the trigger."

Coleson raised an eyebrow at her. "Were you there, miss?"

"No, but Crockett told me—"

"If you didn't witness the shooting yourself," the marshal interrupted, "then I'll thank you to refrain from spoutin' opinions and hearsay. I'm interested only in facts."

"If you're truly interested in facts, Marshal," a deep voice echoed from the doorway, "perhaps you should interview the only other person who was there at the time of the shooting."

Archer.

Silas never thought he'd actually be glad to have the man around, but when the parson crossed the room to stand directly behind Jo and placed his hands on her shoulders in a show of support and protection, an odd sense of relief washed over him. If this sorry excuse for a lawman managed to drag him out of here, Archer would take care of his little girl.

"Jackson's recovering quite nicely thanks to Silas's quick actions in the field as well as his assistance with the surgery." Archer's usually polite tone carried an undercurrent of iron as he addressed the marshal. "I'm sure the boy would be happy to answer your questions with all the facts you need. I could even escort you to the Spivey place myself, if you'd like."

"Thank you, Parson. But I prefer to interview the boy without anyone around who might feel obliged to influence his testimony."

Silas grunted. "You interested in finding the *truth*, Marshal? Or you just lookin' for someone to confirm the assumptions you already made?"

"Usually my assumptions aren't too far off, Robbins. Lucky for you, though, this badge keeps me from acting on them without proof." He slowly unfolded his lean frame from the chair and rose to his full height. "I was planning on payin' Jackson a visit anyway. His pa asked me to look in on the boy—maybe even stay a night or two. So you can count on me takin' my time gettin' to the bottom of this. I intend to be real thorough."

His hard expression lent credibility to his threat, but Silas stared right back, refusing to be intimidated. Finally the marshal turned away. He found a smile somewhere behind that iron wall of his and tipped his hat to Jo. "Thanks for the coffee, miss." He lifted his gaze to Archer next. "Parson," he said, and then ambled to the door.

"I'll see you out, Marshal." Jo followed the man to the porch and accompanied him across the yard, all those manners her mother had drummed into her coming into play.

Keeping his eye on Jo and the marshal through the open door, Silas got down to business, not knowing how much time he'd have.

"I've seen the way you look at my daughter, Archer." The words came out as much of an accusation as any of the statements Coleson had unleashed. "You intend to do right by her?"

"I do." The parson came up alongside him, his focus, too, on the redheaded angel beside the barn. "I aim to make her my wife if you'll give us your blessing."

"Swear to me you'll look after her if this mess goes south."

"You have my word." Archer's voice rang with conviction, and the pressure gripping Silas's chest eased slightly. "She's my heart, Silas. I'd give my life for her."

Silas nodded and extended his hand toward the preacher. Neither of them looked the other in the face, but as Archer's hand moved to clasp his, understanding passed between them.

The pact had been sealed.

36

Supper at the Lazy R that evening was a somber affair. Brett Coleson's earlier presence lingered over the room like a burial shroud. The ranch hands picked at Joanna's baked beans instead of wolfing them down with their usual gusto and even failed to finish off the corn bread she'd browned to perfection. Not that she'd noticed.

Crockett eyed Joanna from across the table. Spoon tipped downward, she listlessly dragged a bean from the edge of her dish to the pile in the center, the same way he would've driven a stray calf back into the herd. The comparison tempted him to smile, but the fact that he couldn't recall any of the little critters on her plate, stray or otherwise, actually making their way to her mouth stole his frivolity.

"Well, aren't we a bunch of sorry hangdogs?" Silas scraped his chair back, yanked his napkin from his shirt collar, and chucked it onto the table. "Enough of this moping. Frank. Carl. You boys have saddles to oil and harnesses to mend. Get to it. Jasper, meet me in the barn. We need to talk about Henderson's bull and start makin' plans.

"Archer?"

Crockett met his employer's gaze while the men around him shuffled to fulfill their assigned tasks.

"Don't be late for your appointment." Silas glanced briefly at Joanna and then back at Crockett before pivoting away and striding for the door.

"Your appointment?" Joanna paused in the middle of collecting the dirty dishes from the table. "Oh, that's right." Crockett hadn't thought it possible for her eyes to dim any further. He'd been wrong. "I had forgotten about Holly."

He wished he could forget about her, too. All he wanted was to hold Jo in his arms and lay tiny kisses on her head until she smiled again.

Crockett moved to her side and took the stack of plates from her hands. "I don't have to go just yet," he said, setting the dishes on the table and tipping her face up with the crook of his finger. "Come sit with me in the parlor for a minute?"

She responded with only a nod. Crockett slid his palm into the slight indention of her back and gently guided her toward the sitting room. He led her to the small sofa and took a seat beside her.

"It's going to be all right, Jo." He cradled her hand in his. "Who knows? This trial might be just what your father needs to solidify his faith."

"But it's so new to him!" Her fingers dug into the flesh of his hand with almost painful force. "What if he sees this as proof that God doesn't care about him? He rejected God for so long. What if this gives him the excuse to revert back?"

"What if God delivers him and thereby reveals his mercy?" Crockett stroked his knuckles along her cheek, needing to touch her, to soothe her. "Or what if Silas needs adversity to grow? He started out as an orphan without a penny to his name, and now he's an established rancher supporting four men and a beautiful daughter. Who's to say his spiritual maturity won't be forged in the same fashion? We can't know what is best for him. Only God knows. What we *can* do is stand by him, support him, and love him through it all."

An unexpected lump suddenly lodged in Crockett's throat. That's what he wanted to do for Joanna. Stand by her. Support her. Love her with every fiber of his being. Forever.

He gazed into his love's sweet face and knew. Now was the time. She was nodding and saying something about needing to trust God more, but in all honesty he could barely hear her over the thudding of his heart and the urgent demand ringing in his mind.

"Jo, I . . . er . . ." He stumbled. He *never* stumbled over his words. Never. Yet his tongue seemed to have swollen to twice its normal size in the time it took him to suck in a single breath.

She glanced quizzically up at him, her mouth slightly parted. Only then did he realize he'd interrupted her. Heat crept up his neck.

She nodded and gave him a brief smile. "Yes?"

Crockett cleared his throat and tried again. "I know this might seem like an inappropriate time, but everything in my heart is telling me it's exactly the *right* time. For you. For me. For the two of us together."

The furrows in her brow deepened, and her head tipped at an odd angle. She stared at him as if he were spouting gibberish.

Which, of course, he was.

A laugh exploded from his chest. He shook his head at his complete ineptitude and tunneled his fingers through his hair, hoping to stimulate some cohesive thoughts. "Just my luck," he muttered, "the one moment a man wants to be his most eloquent, and I fumble around like I haven't a thought in my head."

"Crockett? What's wrong?"

"You." He groaned. "No, not you." He was making a complete muck of this. Desperate to find some way to salvage the situation, he surged to his feet, paced a couple steps, and turned back to face her. Drawing in a deep breath, he dropped to his knees by her feet and reclaimed her hand.

"We can't know what the future holds, but what I *do* know is that I want to share my future with you."

The frown lines on Joanna's brow smoothed, and her eyes grew misty. She caught her lower lip between her teeth, her body going completely still.

Crockett lifted her hand to his mouth and pressed his lips to the soft skin above her knuckles. "Joanna Robbins, you've stolen my heart. I've fallen in love with your quiet smile, your tender soul, your compassionate nature. I love the way you rush to defend those you care about and stand and fight when danger threatens."

He lifted his hand to brush at a stray ringlet that had fallen to frame her face, marveling at how it wrapped itself around his finger as if it belonged there. "I love the way your hair curls with unleashed abandon." He cupped her cheek in his palm, and she leaned into his touch. A surge of desire pulsed through him as her eyes warmed beneath his gaze. "And I adore those tiny freckles dancing across your cheeks."

Joanna dipped her chin and lowered her lashes as a pretty pink blush stole over her skin. But she didn't hide herself for long. Her lashes lifted, revealing eyes rimmed with anticipation and love. The intensity nearly knocked the breath from his chest.

"Marry me, Jo?" The simple words were all he could manage.

She nodded, shakily at first, then with growing vigor. "Yes, Crockett. Oh, yes!"

In a flash he was on his feet, catching her as she sprang up from the sofa and into his arms. His mouth found her sweet lips, and triumph sang in his veins.

She was his.

Crockett's arms tightened about her as he drew her close and buried his fingers into the curls at her nape, luxuriating in their softness as they spiraled around him. He broke away from her lips to feather kisses across her cheeks and the bridge of her nose, not wanting to miss a single freckle.

"I never dreamed I could be so happy," Joanna whispered, her breath warm against his chin.

He was kissing a line past her ear when he felt her stiffen. Lifting his head, he forced his attention from the pale expanse of neck that he longed to explore and instead focused on her face. "What is it?"

"Do you think Daddy will give his blessing?" Her fingers clasped his shirt. "I want to be your wife more than anything, Crockett. Truly I do. But the thought of defying my father to do so . . . it . . . well, I fear it would leave my heart in shreds."

"Shh." He tucked her head beneath his chin and rubbed gentle circles over her back. "I would never make you choose between your father and me, darling. I know how much he means to you, and frankly, he's rather grown on me, as well."

She tilted her head and locked on his gaze. He winked, and the smile that creased her face, though small, made his heart swell.

"Silas and I came to an understanding a short time ago. He approves my suit."

The last of the tension leaked from Joanna's body, and when she raised up on her toes, he met her halfway, sealing their commitment with a kiss so deep and joyful that when he finally brought it to a close, his breathing was ragged and his hands trembled as he struggled to release his hold on the woman who would soon be his wife.

Later, as he hiked up the rutted drive to the Brewster homestead, Crockett replayed that moment in his mind. The way Joanna's face brightened. The way she sought his kiss. The way she felt pressed up against his chest when her arms circled his waist. Such memories put a man in a right cheerful frame of mind, even when embarking on a distasteful task.

Why, he actually found himself whistling as he trudged past the Brewsters' corral and bending to pat the head of the old hound dog that trotted out from under the house to sniff his boots.

"Leave the parson alone, Clancy." A large man rumbled the order as he stepped down from the front porch. He thumbed his drooping suspenders back onto his shoulders in a well-practiced motion as he strode across the yard. "Go on, now. Git!"

He kicked at the dog halfheartedly. Clancy evaded the strike with a quick stutter step and scampered off to investigate the mud by the water trough.

"Parson." Holly's father offered his hand in greeting, though his expression remained rather closed. Crockett smiled anyway and clasped the man's hand.

"Alan. Good to see you, sir."

The two slowly made their way up to the house.

"Your visit's got my womenfolk all in a dither," Alan complained. "Kicked me out of my own kitchen. Sent the boys to the barn as if this were some kind of special occasion. It's not like you haven't been here before with all those plannin' meetings and such." He halted at the porch steps and eyed Crockett with a wary glance. "Unless this call you're payin' tonight is different somehow." His eyes narrowed even further. "Is it, Parson? Different?"

Dread tickled his nape as he faced Holly's father, but he strove to keep his voice steady with no hint of apology. "I'm not here to plan another church event, but I am here in an official capacity."

"What kind of official capacity?" Suspicion darkened the man's features.

Crockett met his stare without a blink. "I'm afraid it's a private matter between Holly and me, but your concern does you credit, sir. In fact, I would welcome your supervision should you care to keep an eye on things."

"Plan on it."

Crockett nodded. Having Alan Brewster chaperone the visit might not be terribly comfortable with the grizzly-bear stare the man was aiming at him, but he'd rather suffer that discomfort than the type Holly dished out.

"Sarah!" Mr. Brewster yelled up to the house. "Parson's here!"

Holly's mother burst out of the door like a plump quail freshly flushed from her nest. "Well, for heaven's sake, Alan. Quit your hollerin' and show the man up here."

"He can find his own way," Alan groused. "I'll be out by the corral. Keepin' an eye on . . . things." He shot a meaningful glance at Crockett.

Crockett stepped aside to let the man pass, feeling the heat of that glance between his shoulder blades as he climbed the steps to the front porch. Removing his hat, he dipped his chin to Sarah. "Ma'am."

"Brother Archer, we're delighted to have you pay a call on us this evening." The woman's hands fluttered about like a pair of birds that couldn't decide where to alight. "Holly could talk of nothing else all day."

"Mother," a second feminine voice chided from just inside the door, "you're going to embarrass him *and* me with talk like that."

Crockett crossed the threshold and found Holly standing just inside the door. A fading sunbeam fell through the westward facing window to dance upon her blond hair, making it glow like a golden halo. She smiled prettily and held out her hands to take his hat, but she waited for him to come to her, as if she knew the sunlight in that particular spot showed her beauty off to its best advantage and was loath to leave it.

"We saved you some cobbler," Holly said, finally abandoning her sunbeam to take his arm and lead him to a chair. "I'll dish some up for you."

"Only if you ladies will join me." Crockett aimed his smile at Sarah, but Holly was the one who answered.

"Oh, Mother has some mending to attend to in the parlor. Don't you, Mama?"

"Ah . . . yes. That's right. Mending. Big pile."

Crockett felt himself being maneuvered into a corner. Time for a quick dodge. "Well, in that case, why don't you and I enjoy our dessert out on the porch, Miss Brewster?" He favored Holly with his most charming grin. Two could play this game. "The swing would make a cozy place for our talk—private yet still proper."

"That's a wonderful idea, Parson," Sarah gushed. "I'll dish up the cobbler while you two get comfortable."

She shooed them out the front door, and Crockett escorted Holly to the wooden swing that turned out to be a bit narrower than he had originally thought. It didn't help matters when Holly seated herself several inches away from the arm on her side, leaving barely enough room for him to sit without having his leg rub up against hers.

Reminding himself of his reason for coming, he aimed an apologetic grin her way. "I'm sorry, Miss Brewster. Would you mind scooting over a bit? I don't have quite enough room."

Her lips tightened in a disgruntled expression before quickly softening into a smile. "Of course." She shifted a negligible amount. "Is that better?"

"A little more please."

Something unpleasant flashed in her eyes, but she complied.

"Thank you."

The cobbler arrived, saving Crockett from having to say anything more, and he welcomed the reprieve. He tucked into the dessert, the sweetness of the sugared blackberries helping to improve his mood. He scraped every last bit of the deep purple syrup from the inside of his bowl before finally setting the dish on the floor to his side. The reprieve was over.

"You're a fine cook, Miss Brewster. That cobbler was delicious."

Her cheeks pinkened at his compliment, her lashes lowering demurely. "Thank you. But please, Crockett"—her lashes lifted as she drew his given name across her tongue as if it were the dessert—"call me Holly."

"No, ma'am. I don't think I will."

She blinked. "What?"

"This is what I wanted to talk to you about, Miss Brewster." Pressing his back against the swing arm, Crockett turned to face her more squarely as he tried desperately to ignore the jittery surging of his pulse. He needed to present a strong, confident front, not prove himself a bag of nerves. Clearing his throat, he forced himself to meet her gaze. "I'm concerned that you are playing a game that could lead you to serious harm."

"Why, I-I have no idea what you mean." She put up a good front, but when her fingers started plucking at her skirt, he knew he'd unsettled her.

"Miss Brewster, I'm not unaware of the special attention you've been paying to me. It is quite flattering, but I fear, not . . . appropriate." Crockett spoke slowly, thinking over each word as he strove to find the proper balance of gentleness and reproof. *"Restore in the spirit of meekness,"* Scripture admonished. "I do not wish to injure your feelings; however, I must make my position clear. I will *not* be pursuing a courtship with you. My heart is already engaged elsewhere."

Deep lines marred the pale perfection of her brow. "But you're here . . . now. Didn't you come to see me?" Slowly the lines eased, replaced by the pout she had perfected.

"I came as your minister, not as a beau." Crockett leaned forward, willing her soul to heed his warning. "You are young and lovely, but some of your behavior of late has been shockingly forward. To tell the truth, it has made me quite uncomfortable. I worry that if you continue in this manner, other men might get the wrong idea and attempt to take advantage of you."

"But I'm not interested in any other men, Crockett. I'm interested in *you*." She reached between them and placed her hand on his knee.

Frowning, he took hold of her wrist and dropped her hand back onto her lap. "You see, Miss Brewster? This is exactly what I mean. I have told you that my heart belongs to another, yet you continue to press yourself upon me, despite my warnings. I really must insist that you stop."

Crockett stood, setting the swing in motion. "I'm sorry to have to be so frank, but you need to understand and accept that the only relationship I am interested in having with you is that of preacher and parishioner."

Holly stopped the swing's motion with the sole of her shoe and launched to her feet. Her blue eyes crackled like a midday sky after the hiss of lightning. "Who is this woman who claims your heart? Someone you knew before?" Gone were the pretty pout and the languid lashes. Fire was all that remained when she jammed her fists onto her hips and stood toe-to-toe with him.

"Her identity doesn't matter. What matters is that you curb your forward behavior. It attracts the wrong kind of attention from the wrong kind of man and has no place in a Christian woman's life. Hold yourself to a higher standard, Miss Brewster, and accept the truth that there will never be anything between us."

"You know what I think?" She poked him in the chest. "I think there *is* no other woman. I think you're just frightened by what I make you feel. I tempt you, don't I? I make you feel things you think a preacher ought not feel."

"Miss Brewster." Crockett growled the warning, barely keeping his ire leashed. But Holly took no heed as she rushed on.

"Passion is not evil, Crockett. It's a gift from God. Haven't you read Solomon's Song? And what about Paul? Didn't he say that marriage is the godly solution for those who burn for one another?"

"Enough!"

She jumped at his bark, but Crockett no longer cared about her comfort. The time for gentleness had passed. He longed to throw Joanna's name into her arguments like a stick of dynamite and blow them all to bits. Holly would hear the news soon enough anyway. However, a shred of caution stayed his tongue. He'd be doing his love no favors if he dragged her into this ugliness.

Instead he forced other words through his teeth, spitting out one at a time. "I am not now, nor will I ever be, interested in a relationship with you, Miss Brewster, and I'll thank you to never speak of this again."

With that, he strode across the porch to the front door, opened it, and leaned inside to collect his hat from the hook on the wall. Slapping it on his head, he marched down the steps into the yard, his only goal to escape this place and the irrational woman who refused to take no for an answer.

He didn't miss the wail that pierced the evening air nor the slam of the door that echoed behind him, but neither did he turn to look. He wouldn't have stopped at all had not a shadowy figure emerged from the barn.

"I don't know what your game is, Parson," Alan Brewster murmured in a lethal voice not two feet away, "but if you hurt my little girl, the only preachin' you'll be doin' is from six feet under. Understand?"

Crockett nodded with a sharp downward thrust of his chin and without a word continued his march home.

37

The following evening found Crockett equally weary as he trudged home. Silas had taken it into his head to show Crockett the ins and outs of the ranch in excruciating detail—everything from riding the borders of the property to going over the account ledgers to discussing his plans for breeding and future expansion of the herd. Silas hadn't stopped once all day, even discussing business through lunch and supper. Crockett feared his head would explode if he tried to squeeze one more piece of information between his ears.

Silas had tried well to hide his desperation, but Crockett had felt it with every instruction he gave, every plan he shared. He was like a condemned man talking over the sound of sand rushing through his hourglass. When Crockett reminded him that Coleson had made no move to pursue an arrest after speaking with Jackson, Silas had just clasped his shoulder and told him that once he and Jo were married, he would be a partner in the Lazy R anyway, so there was nothing to lose in showing him the ropes now.

Crockett grinned as he crossed the field to the churchyard. The man who'd hated preachers for forty years was not only welcoming one into the family but handing over the reins of his ranch. If anyone doubted the existence of God, they'd have only to witness Silas Robbins's turnabout to be convinced. No other explanation would suffice.

Thank you, Father, for your patient wooing, for never giving up on any of us. Keep working on Silas. Guard his newfound faith through whatever trials may arise, and help him to fully accept you as Lord. Give Jo and me wisdom as we walk alongside him and—

A clanking noise from inside his rooms interrupted his prayer as he approached the rear of the church. Had a coon found its way inside? He hoped the little bandit hadn't gotten into his books. Most were safely stored in his trunk, but he'd left a few sitting out on his table last night, including his Bible. He'd had to read all three epistles of John to calm down after his run-in with Holly. He'd gone to bed meditating on 1 John 4:11—"Beloved, if God so loved us, we ought also to love one another"—before he'd finally reclaimed enough peace to sleep. Some people were a trial to love, but with God's help, he'd find a way.

Having reached his door, he yanked it open and scanned the interior for signs of a furry intruder. The intruder he found, though, was neither furry nor likely to scamper away with a stomp of his foot or a wave of his hat.

Crockett stiffened. "What are you doing in my house?"

Holly Brewster smiled sweetly and held out a cup of coffee and a plate bearing some kind of wedge-shaped dessert. Crockett didn't take the time to assess if it was pie or cake. All of his attention, and fury, were focused on the woman making herself at home in his personal sanctuary.

"I came to apologize for that little misunderstanding we had last night and to bring you a peace offering." She lifted the plate toward him again, but Crockett just scowled at her, not about to accept anything she offered. "Come on," she cooed. "It's my vanilla cream cake, guaranteed to bring a smile to even the grumpiest of faces."

"You need to leave. Now." Crockett strode forward and swiped the plate from her hand. He dumped the dish, cake and all, into the ribbon-covered basket sitting on his table.

Finding a shawl that could only be hers draped across his bed, he snatched it up and tossed it at her, not caring if the coffee she held splattered the fine wool.

"Do you have no care for your reputation?" He growled the question, barely restraining the shout clawing its way up his throat. "Or mine? You can't be in my rooms."

She set the coffee cup aside and folded her shawl over her arm as if his reaction didn't perturb her the slightest bit. "You're overreacting, Crockett."

"It's Brother Archer," he ground out between clenched teeth. "I am your minister, not your beau." He clasped her elbow, maintaining enough self-control to keep his grip only firm, not painful, while he *encouraged* her toward the door.

She tried to yank her arm free from his grasp, her eyes finally widening in alarm, but he refused to release her.

"How dare you treat me this way," she sputtered. "You have no right!" She fought his hold yet was no match for his strength.

"I not only have the right," he said, grabbing the basket from the table as they passed, "I have the obligation as a Christian man to protect your virtue." He reached the door that still hung ajar from when he'd entered and pushed it fully open with the toe of his boot. "You're like a child who keeps wandering too close to the stove. You won't heed my warnings, so my only choice is to put you out of the kitchen."

"A child?" Holly screeched. "Why, you condescending, manhandling barbarian! You think you're so noble, but you're nothing more than a bully. A bully!"

With a swing of his arm, Crockett set her forcibly out of his home, thrust the basket at her, and then stepped back and closed the door in her disbelieving face.

Something crashed against the wall. Probably a plate, by the sound of it. Crockett leaned his back against the door, some part of his brain wondering if the cake had still been on it when she threw it.

"You'll pay for this, Crockett Archer! Do you hear me?" Something else thudded against the side of the building. The basket, perhaps? "You'll pay for this!"

Another screech. Then something that sounded like tearing fabric, followed by feet stomping in rapid succession. He'd never witnessed a grown woman throw a temper tantrum, but Holly Brewster seemed to have a definite knack for such things.

Through his window he caught a glimpse of her back as she huffed off. She'd worked herself up to such an extent, half her hair was coming out of its pins. Crockett shook his head, pitying the man she did finally wrangle into marriage. She'd either walk all over him or shred him to pieces with those claws whenever he did something she didn't like.

"'It is better to dwell in the corner of the housetop, than with a brawling woman in a wide house.'" Crockett chuckled to himself as his anger cooled. "Now I know why Solomon saw fit to record that particular proverb twice."

Thanking God for his providence in providing a peace-loving woman like Joanna for him to share a house and life with, Crockett pushed away from the door and headed for the table. Lighting the lamp to chase away the encroaching darkness, he settled in his chair and reread that passage from 1 John before starting in on his evening prayers.

He prayed over a different household from his congregation each night. However, instead of moving on to the Wards as he had originally planned, he decided to return to the Brewsters. Heaven only knew what kind of upheaval they'd be facing once Holly got home. And Holly herself needed prayer, too. Prayers for wisdom, for a forgiving heart, and for comfort. Now that he had his own emotions back under control, he could see that her tantrum was driven by hurt. He'd rejected her quite adamantly. Probably bruised her pride as well as her heart.

Guilt pricked his conscience. Had he been too hard on her? Too forceful?

Had he acted more in anger than admonishment? Crockett bowed his head again and added a plea for his own forgiveness to his list of petitions.

An hour later, Crockett had a completely different petition on his lips when Alan Brewster kicked in his door and started throwing punches.

Crockett barely had enough time to throw a hand up to ward off Alan's meaty fist before the enraged man grabbed him by the shirtfront and slammed him into the wall. Crockett twisted his body at the last second to take the force of the collision on his shoulder instead of his skull, sending shards of pain down his arm.

"You call yourself a man of God? You wretch!" Alan's fist slammed into Crockett's gut as his left hand pinned his shoulder to the wall. "You're a demon who preys on the trust of young women!" Another blow came, but Crockett hardened his muscles to deflect the force while knocking away Alan's hold with an upward thrust of a stiff arm.

He ducked and spun toward the door. "What are you talking about?"

Alan roared and charged like a bull. Crockett braced his legs, but the man's weight and momentum were too great. Alan wrapped his arms about Crockett's middle and drove him through the open doorway, taking him to the ground.

The air rushed from Crockett's lungs as he hit. The back of his head bounced against the hard-packed earth, stunning him.

Arms from behind hoisted him to his feet, dragging him out from under Brewster. Crockett was about to thank whomever had stepped in, when those same arms tightened like manacles around his biceps. Crockett strained against the hold, but the men on either side of him gave no quarter.

"I haven't done anything!" He swiveled his head from side to side to plead with his captors, men who seemed slightly more rational than Holly's father. He recognized them as kin to Alan and Sarah. He'd met them at the picnic but had never seen them at church.

Brewster staggered forward, winded but still packing plenty of rage to fuel another attack. "Are you saying that you never laid hands on my girl?"

Crockett hesitated for a split second, thinking of the way he'd grabbed Holly's arm and ushered her out the door. That second was all it took to reignite Alan's fury. His fist crashed into Crockett's jaw, knocking his head into the chin of one of the men holding him.

"I didn't harm her," Crockett insisted, desperate to insert some reason into this situation before things got any worse. "She was in my house when I arrived home from the ranch, and I escorted her out. I was concerned for her reputation and made her leave. That's all."

"That's all?" Alan bellowed and landed a blow to his ribs. Crockett groaned. "My Holly comes home bawling her eyes out, her dress torn clear off her shoulder, her hair falling down around her ears, leaves and sticks poked every which way, dirt in her nails as if she had to claw to get away from you, and you dare to tell me you were protecting her reputation?" A volley of punches to Crockett's midsection punctuated the accusation.

Crockett's legs sagged, but his captors held him upright to accept the blows. He tasted blood in his mouth. Agony throbbed in his side. His strength was nearly gone.

Thankfully, so was Alan's.

The man took a step back, his chest heaving from his exertion.

Crockett slowly lifted his head and met Alan Brewster's glare with the fierce dignity of one unjustly accused. "With God as my witness, I did not harm your daughter. Holly was upset when she left me but unharmed. Perhaps she fell on her way home. Perhaps someone else attacked her. I don't know what happened. All I know is that it wasn't me."

No one spoke. Crockett's avowal simply hung in the air like a righteous beacon. And he started to hope.

"Did Holly actually *say* the parson attacked her?" one of the men at Crockett's back dared ask.

Please, God, let them see the truth.

"You think I'm gonna ask for all the gritty details?" Alan snapped, his eyes dark as the surrounding night. "The evidence spoke for itself. My baby girl threw herself into my arms and sobbed her heart out. 'Make him go away, Papa,' she said. 'Make Brother Archer go away and never come back.' I aim to do just that. To make sure this man never hurts another young girl like he did my Holly. Do you boys stand with me or not?"

The arms holding Crockett tightened, hefting him nearly off the ground.

"We're with you, Alan."

"Good," Brewster said. "Then, let's string him up."

38

Joanna stood before the canvas she'd been working on for the last several months and gazed into the beloved eyes she missed so keenly.

"Oh, Mama. I'm going to be married. Can you believe it?" A thrill coursed through her at the thought of becoming Crockett's wife.

Her mother's likeness smiled back at her, serene and loving, just the way Joanna remembered her. She hoped she'd captured her the way her father remembered her, as well, for the portrait was to be his birthday present. If he was still at home and not in prison somewhere when his birthday came around next month.

Don't think about that. It was much more pleasant to think about Crockett. Her betrothed. Joanna grinned as she stepped to her worktable to rinse out her paintbrush. She swished the bristles in the small Mason jar of turpentine, the pungent smell familiar and well loved, one that never failed to bring her mother to mind. But at the moment, a handsome man with twinkling eyes and strong arms consumed her thoughts.

Those thoughts drew her to the barn loft window and lifted her gaze over the trees to focus on the church. Would Crockett be in his room composing his next sermon or crawling into bed after a grueling day of ranch work? Her heart leapt at the thought that she wouldn't have to wonder much longer. Soon she would be there with him, perhaps mending quietly in a corner while he worked on his notes, or maybe rubbing the soreness from his shoulders as they readied for bed.

Joanna nibbled on her lip, her stomach fluttering in a way that sent delightful shivers through her core. But then something caught her eye in the direction of the churchyard. Were those lights? She braced a hand against the frame of the window and squinted into the night. It looked like two—no, three—lights. Lanterns.

Crockett hadn't mentioned any appointments. Could there be an emergency of some kind? An illness or injury? Word had gotten around about his skill in tending Jackson's wound. Yet something didn't feel right. An odd urgency prodded her, turning those belly flutters into needle pricks. Reaching behind her back to untie her painting smock, Joanna whirled from the window and dashed to the loft ladder.

Once her feet hit the ground, Joanna ran for the bunkhouse. "Jasper!"

Her father's most trusted man had the door opened and was several steps into the yard, his pistol in hand, by the time she met up with him.

"Saddle Sunflower and Gamble. There's trouble at the church."

He didn't waste time on words, just nodded once and jogged toward the barn.

"Jo?" Her father must have heard her shout for he was crossing the yard with long strides, buckling his gun belt as he went.

She ran to him and grabbed his arm. "Daddy, something's going on at the church. There are lights in the yard. I can't explain it, but I just know something's wrong. Will you ride with me to check on Crockett?"

Silas wrapped his arm around her shoulder and steered her toward the barn. "I don't see the harm in payin' Archer a little visit."

"Thank you, Daddy."

He gave her a firm pat and rushed forward to take over Gamble's preparation, freeing Jasper to see to Sunflower.

The instant the cinch was fastened on her mount, Joanna stuck her foot in the stirrup and hoisted herself astride. Without waiting for her father, she kicked Sunflower into an easy canter. The deepening darkness kept her from the gallop her heart demanded. By the time she crossed onto the main road, her father was at her side, urging Gamble to take the lead.

"Stay mounted until we know what's going on," her father ordered.

She knew better than to argue.

Cutting through the field would be too treacherous for the horses at night, so Joanna and her father kept to the road. As they approached, she could make out a handful of men in lantern light under one of the large, spreading oaks that had shaded the crowd during the picnic. She leaned forward in the saddle, trying to get a better view of what was going on. A pair of horses stood ground-tethered nearby, but there seemed to be one in the middle of the men.

Had it been injured? Is that why they all huddled around it? But their attention didn't seem to be on the horse directly. No, they seemed to be focused on something else. Something writhing against them. They were beating it; she could see that now. Beating it and throwing it on top of the horse.

That's when a snake fell down from among the tree branches. A snake whose tail was looped at the end. Her stomach dropped. Not a snake. A rope.

And the thing on the horse was . . .

"Crockett!" She screamed his name at the top of her voice and urged Sunflower to a gallop. But her father cut in front of her before she could race into the fray.

"Stay behind me." His voice was harsh. Harsher than she'd ever heard it. Then he pulled his rifle from his scabbard without breaking stride and fired a shot in the air. Once fully upon the men, he pulled Gamble to a halt and aimed his weapon at the belligerent fellow in the front of the pack—Alan Brewster.

"What's going on here?" Her father's voice echoed calmly in the night, as if meeting a neighbor at an impromptu hanging was nothing out of the ordinary.

Joanna reined Sunflower in a few paces back as her father had instructed but close enough that she could see Crockett. And the sight wasn't pretty. His beloved face was beaten and bloody, his hair dusty and disheveled, his hands bound behind his back.

Oh, Crockett. She moaned and had to restrain herself from running to him. Fear for his safety rooted her to the earth, however. For while they'd ridden in, one of the men had slipped the noose over Crockett's neck and tightened the knot. If the horse he sat on spooked, or if one of the men gave the beast a slap, Crockett would be left dangling.

"This is none of your concern, Silas." Mr. Brewster planted his hands on his hips—hips that supported a gun belt with a revolver at the ready.

"You're about to string up one of my ranch hands, and my future son-in-law. That makes it my concern."

"Son-in-law?" Mr. Brewster turned his head to spit, then lifted the back of his hand to wipe his mouth. Only then did Joanna notice that he sported several cuts and bruises of his own. "Seems to me I'm doing you and that girl of yours a favor, then. When you hear what this skunk did to my Holly, you'll be beggin' to help instead of asking me to stop."

A sick feeling churned in Joanna's stomach. *Holly.* No doubt that girl had twisted the truth into something ugly and vile. But surely not even Holly could be so cruel as to crave a man's death.

"What is she accusing him of?" Her father shifted slightly in his saddle, laying his rifle across his lap as if he no longer saw a need for it.

Joanna longed to snatch the weapon from him and demand Crockett's release . . . until she noticed her daddy's finger hovering over the trigger. He'd not surrendered. He'd just removed the appearance of the threat to put Brewster's men at ease.

"My girl stumbled home tonight with her dress torn, hair a mess, sobbing about how she hated Brother Archer and wanted me to make him leave and never come back. If your Jo had done the same, what would you have done?"

"Beaten the man responsible to a bloody pulp."

"Exactly." Mr. Brewster nodded in satisfaction, righteous indignation glowing in his eyes.

"But I wouldn't hang him. That's the law's job."

Mr. Brewster's face darkened, his jaw working back and forth as if it were in danger of locking. "There ain't no law around these parts, Silas. A man's gotta see to his own justice."

"But there is law around. Marshal Coleson's up at the Spivey place."

Joanna shot a look at her father. Would he actually bring the law in on this, put himself in the marshal's path to save Crockett?

"Let me go fetch him."

Apparently he would. Moisture clouded Joanna's eyes. Never had she loved her father more.

"You sure bringin' in the law is the best idea, Alan?" the man holding the horse's head asked.

Mr. Brewster hesitated.

"You hang that man, you're doing it out of anger and vengeance, not justice." Joanna's father slowly brought his rifle back around and aimed it at Alan Brewster's chest. "Besides, as sure as you are that Archer's guilty, I'm equally sure he's innocent. I know this man. I've worked with him day after day. You think I'd trust him with my daughter if I wasn't completely convinced of his character?"

"Every man's got secrets, Silas. Even you." The threat hung in the air. Joanna peered at the man, her pulse erratic. Did Mr. Brewster know something about her father's past?

"I'm getting the marshal, Brewster." Her father's voice had hardened to stone. "He'll sort this out. If I'm wrong, Coleson will take care of Archer. But if I'm right and you hang him before I get back, you'll be the one the marshal carts off to prison. For murder."

"Fine," Mr. Brewster shouted, spooking Crockett's horse.

Joanna gasped, her knees tightening around her own mount, causing Sunflower to sidestep. Thankfully, the man tending Crockett's horse held the beast steady.

"Fetch the marshal," Mr. Brewster conceded. "While you do that I'll send Buck after Holly." The man who had been up in the tree securing the rope slithered down and hurried to his horse. "We'll see who Coleson believes."

"That we shall." Joanna's father reined Gamble around and came up alongside her. "Take my rifle, Jo." He pushed the weapon into her shaky hands.

"Shouldn't I be the one to fetch the marshal?" Joanna eyed the angry men around her. She hated the idea of leaving Crockett, but of the two of them, her father would prove the bigger deterrent. Alan Brewster wouldn't consider her much of a threat, even with the rifle.

Her father shook his head. "No, stay here. I know Archer didn't lay a hand on Holly, but somebody else might have. I don't want you riding alone in the dark." He clasped her shoulder and gave her one of those looks that made it clear the discussion was over. "Watch over your man."

Joanna steeled her spine and nodded. "I love you, Daddy."

His lips turned up in a strained smile. "I love you, too, darlin', and I swear to you that I'll make this right."

All she could do was nod in response.

Taking up the reins, her father brought Gamble's head around and touched his heels to the animal's flanks. Gamble leapt forward and the two of them raced up the road that led to Jackson's cabin.

"Hurry," she whispered.

39

Silas's heart pounded as fast and hard as Gamble's hooves while he raced up the path to Jackson's home. When he caught sight of the marshal's horse sheltered under the broken-down lean-to west of the house, a heavy exhale released the pressure that'd been building in his chest.

If Coleson had already returned to Deanville, Archer would have been in a world of hurt. Not that he was all that dandy now.

Silas had spent most of his younger years doing everything possible to keep his neck out of a noose, but when Joanna screamed Archer's name as if her heart were being torn from her body, all he could think was that it should be him wearin' that rope necktie, not the parson.

Reining Gamble in, Silas leapt from the saddle, not surprised in the slightest when the marshal shoved the door open and came out to meet him, pistol in hand.

"Mount up, Coleson." Silas paid the gun no heed, just rounded Gamble's head and faced the lawman straight on. "You're needed down at the church."

"The church?" Coleson scoffed. "That's rich coming from you, Robbins. Don't think I'm fool enough to go haring after you in the dark on some manufactured pretense. I know you want me gone."

"What I want is your butt in the saddle." Silas's hands clenched into fists, but he kept them at his sides as he marched up to where the lawman lounged against the doorframe. "An innocent man's gonna be lynched unless you put a stop to it."

"And who's the poor soul I'm supposed to save?" Coleman straightened a bit at Silas's approach but gave no indication he intended to follow him to the churchyard.

"The parson."

"Archer?" Laughter sputtered out of the lawman. Silas's right hand twitched. He ached to shut the man up with a quick jab to the mouth.

Coleson pushed his hat back on his forehead. "I guess I'm supposed to believe he stepped on the wrong toes in one of his sermons, huh? Come on, Robbins. I expected better of you. At least come up with a tale that's remotely believable."

Silas was debating the merits of forcibly installing the man on his horse when Jackson pushed past Coleson, his face whiter than milk on snow.

"Who's got Crock?"

"Alan Brewster." Silas focused on the boy, letting the marshal fade from his vision entirely. "He's got it in his head that the parson attacked Holly."

Color surged back to Jackson's cheeks. "Crock would never hurt a woman. Never!" The kid stomped over to Silas's side, then hopped from one foot to the next as if he couldn't quite contain his outrage. "Holly Brewster's been chasing after him for weeks, always throwin' herself in his path and makin' eyes at him in church. I kept telling him he needed to set her straight, but you know Crock. He's too nice. Every time he tried to discourage her, she doubled her efforts. She must've cornered him, pushed him so far that he stopped worryin' about her feelings and finally told her flat out to leave him be. That woulda made her madder than spit."

"Well, right now the only thing standing between Archer and a stretched neck is Jo and my promise to fetch a lawman to sort things out." Silas glared at Coleson. "So, you comin'?"

The marshal glared back, holding his answer hostage.

"I am." Jackson shoved his foot into Gamble's stirrup and reached for the saddle horn.

"Watch that arm, boy." Worried Jackson would damage his still-healing wound, Silas hurried over to give him a leg up. "You sure you're ready to ride?"

"Crock's the best friend I got. I'm goin'." Jackson's mulish expression as he settled into the saddle kept Silas from arguing. He nodded instead and swung up behind the boy.

Coleson approached the pair and laid a staying hand on Jackson's leg. "You really believe Archer's in trouble, son?"

"Yes, sir, Marshal." Jackson glanced over his shoulder at Silas, then turned back to Coleson. "I know you think he used to rob them stagecoaches, and maybe he did way back when. But that don't make no never mind to me. I've known Mr. Robbins for near half my life, and I trust him."

"Even after he shot you?"

"On accident—how many times do I have to tell you?" Jackson corrected, his defense a salve on Silas's conscience. "And yes, I still trust him."

Coleson's gaze narrowed as it slid from the kid to Silas. "Maybe I'd trust him, too, if he stopped hiding his past."

"Come with me now, and I'll tell you everything you want to know." The words surprised Silas as much as the lawman, but something inside clicked into place with the saying of them. He'd vowed to let God have his way with him, but that couldn't happen if he was still holding on to the sins of his past, could it? Time to put the old to rest and take up the new.

After they saw to Archer.

"I plan to hold you to that, Robbins," the marshal said as he strode toward his horse.

Silas maintained his stoic mask despite the rapid thump in his chest. He'd face what he had to face when the time came, but for now what mattered was keeping his promise to his little girl.

Touching his heels to Gamble's flanks, he set off for the church, praying he'd find Archer still breathing when he got there.

Joanna's arms ached and had begun to shake, but she refused to lower her rifle, despite the fact that Alan Brewster was no longer paying her any mind. It was the only thing she could do for Crockett, and she had to do something. She couldn't tend his wounds, couldn't hold him, couldn't even get that foul rope off his neck. All she could do was watch, pray, and keep her rifle trained on the man who threatened his life.

She spared a quick glance toward the road. *Where are you, Daddy?* Had the marshal moved on? What would happen if he wasn't there? Would they be able to stop Mr. Brewster without the law to intervene?

A bead of sweat rolled down her spine, slowing over each bump of her backbone. Joanna felt each rise and fall of the droplet as if time had slowed. And when the trail ended at the small of her back, she couldn't escape the morbid sensation that Crockett's time had reached its end, as well.

"This is taking too long," Alan Brewster grumbled. He stopped his agitated pacing and strode over to Crockett. "I shouldn't have sent Buck after Holly. She's been through enough tonight without being forced to see this scum again. I say we just take care of business now and spare her the ugliness."

"No!" Joanna jumped from Sunflower's back and raced toward the men. She raised her rifle like a club, fully prepared to swing it at Mr. Brewster's head, but he turned, and with a mighty sweep of his arm, knocked the weapon out of her hands. She cried out in surprise and despair, staggering slightly from the blow, while the second man dashed over to collect the rifle.

"Jo!" Crockett jerked against his bonds, fighting to get free. But his struggles only served to upset his horse. His body stretched dangerously backward, the rope pulling taut as his mount skittered forward.

"I'm fine, Crockett," Joanna rushed to assure him. She attempted to dodge Holly's father in order to get to the horse, but he grabbed her about the waist and set her aside.

"Not so fast, girlie. You ain't getting near my prisoner."

"Then get your man to control that horse," Joanna demanded.

"Walt?" Mr. Brewster didn't even have the decency to glance at Crockett's predicament, so intent was he on glaring her into submission.

"I got him, Alan." The man reclaimed the reins and backed the horse up a step, then two. Finally, Crockett sat at a normal angle, and Joanna breathed easier.

"Please, Mr. Brewster." Joanna grabbed his sleeve in supplication. "Undo the rope. Marshal Coleson will make sure justice is done when he arrives. There's no reason to risk an accident taking Crockett's life in the meantime."

Holly's father shook off her hold. "You know, a decent woman would have more compassion for the female who'd been hurt instead of pleading for the release of her attacker."

Joanna's spine stiffened. She straightened to her full height and stared the man directly in the eyes. "A decent woman stands by the man she loves no matter what vile lies are used to condemn him."

"Are you calling my Holly a liar?"

Joanna said nothing. She just stared back at him, letting her certainty do the talking for her.

"Why, you . . ." He raised his hand, his intent clear.

Joanna braced herself but never took her eyes from his.

"Lay a hand on that woman, and you'll be the one I cart off to jail tonight, mister. No questions asked."

Marshal Coleson. Joanna spun to face the lawman, not surprised to see two guns trained on Mr. Brewster, the second belonging to her father. What did surprise her was the blond beauty peering over the marshal's shoulder from the back of his horse, and the truly horrified expression marring her usually lovely features.

"Papa! What are you *doing*?"

40

Alan Brewster lowered his hand, and the wildness rising to a fever pitch inside Crockett subsided.

"Holly?" Alan stepped away from Joanna and took a step toward his daughter.

Joanna took advantage of his distraction and ran to Crockett. She grabbed hold of his leg and laid her cheek against the bend of his knee. Crockett's eyes slid closed as he absorbed the feel of her, wishing his hands were free to caress her face and stroke her glorious hair.

"Are you all right?" he managed through a tight throat, the rope keeping him from bending his chin enough to see more than the top of her head. "He didn't hurt you, did he?" Crockett hated the helplessness of his position. He could deal with the bonds and the noose and the stupidly skittish horse when he was the only one in danger, but when Brewster turned on Joanna, he'd nearly gone out of his mind.

She raised her head and leaned back enough to allow him to see her eyes glittering in the lantern light. "I'm fine as long as you are alive and well."

"I love you, Joanna. No matter what happens, know that."

A fierce look swept over her face, much like the expression she'd worn when she confronted Alan Brewster with nothing but her faith in his innocence—a faith that made him want to shout in triumph and kiss her senseless all at the same time. "The only thing that's going to happen, Crockett Archer, is you getting out of that awful rope and off this horse so you can marry me like you promised. You got that?"

A grin pulled against his split lip, but Crockett welcomed the prick of pain. "Yes, ma'am."

"This your daughter, mister?" Coleson called out, drawing Crockett's attention as the marshal gave Holly an arm down from her perch behind him. "We found her walking along the road with some fella named Buck. She seemed surprised to hear what was transpirin' down here at the church. Asked if she could ride with me the rest of the way."

Holly slid to the ground and rushed to her father. She had changed her dress and repaired her hair, and Crockett prayed her improved appearance would play in his favor.

"Papa, this is wrong," she murmured, her voice quiet after the booming tones of Marshal Coleson, but it still managed to carry through the night air. She cast a guilty glance toward Crockett, and then her gaze fell on Joanna and her eyes widened before shooting a look back at Crockett's face. She bit her lip and turned back to her father. "Let him go, Papa."

"But he hurt you, darlin'. I can't let him get away with that." The tender way he spoke did nothing to dim the hostility in his stance. "Either the marshal takes him in or I mete out the justice myself, but I ain't leavin' here tonight without making sure he pays for what he done to you."

"He did hurt me," Holly began, and Joanna stiffened beside Crockett.

"Easy," he whispered. "Give her a chance to do what's right." He'd seen the way Holly looked at Joanna. She knew now—knew that Joanna was the woman he'd spoken about, knew that he'd told the truth about being promised to another.

"He hurt me," Holly said, her gaze dropping to the ground, "but not in the way you think. He only hurt my pride."

"But your dress," Alan sputtered. "Your hair. The dirt and leaves. I know what I saw when you came home, and the damage was to more than your pride, girl. Don't let this lawman intimidate you and keep you from speaking the truth."

Holly's head snapped up. "When have I ever let a man intimidate me?"

Crockett nearly choked on the sudden urge to laugh.

"Are you sayin' you lied to me, girl?" Brewster growled, grabbing onto Holly's arm.

"I never lied," she shot back. "I just let you draw your own conclusions."

Brewster shoved his daughter away and clasped his hands behind his back, as if afraid of what they might do if he didn't rein them in. "Land sakes, girl! I nearly killed a man, and you're tellin' me it was all some kind of game?" He strode toward Crockett, muttering under his breath.

Holly followed on his heels. "I never asked you to hang him, Papa. I just wanted you to make him leave."

"Why?" Brewster spun to face her. "Because he chose to court Joanna Robbins instead of you?"

Holly drew up short, her eyes going wide. "What?"

"Don't think I haven't heard you and your mama scheming. I knew you were anglin' after the parson, but I never believed any child of mine could be so spiteful as to mar a good man's reputation just because she didn't get what she wanted from him. You're a spoiled, deceitful girl, Holly, and I'm ashamed of ya." Brewster turned his back on her, pulled a hunting knife from the leather sheath at his waist, and reached behind Crockett to slice the ropes binding his wrists.

Crockett's arms sprang apart, and hundreds of needle-sharp pricks stabbed into his hands as blood began to flow back into his palms and fingers. Without giving his flesh time to recover, he reached to his neck, grasped the rope chaffing the underside of his jaw, and flung it over his head. In the next instant he was off the saddle—clutching Joanna to his chest and wiping the tears of relief from her cheeks while trying to keep his own from falling.

Her arms wrapped around his middle and drew his bruised body up against her softness. "Thank you, God," she whispered. "Thank you. Thank you. Thank you."

His heart echoed her sentiment while his face buried itself in her hair. Inhaling deeply, he exulted in the clean, sunshiny scent of her. He was going to live. Live to be a husband, a father. To love Joanna for however many days the Lord granted them together.

So lost was he in the woman in his arms, that when another feminine voice clamored, he startled.

"Papa! How can you say such horrible things?" Genuine shock and hurt laced Holly's voice. Crockett lifted his head and winced when Brewster yanked his arm away from his daughter's attempted touch. "I never once uttered anything untrue," she insisted. "It was you who drew the wrong conclusion, your rage that put Brother Archer's head in that noose."

Brewster's shoulders slumped, and his hand trembled as he rubbed it over his face. "It's true that I let my rage spin out of control, and when I think of what almost happened, it turns my stomach. I can only pray that God and the parson will forgive me."

Holly stood straighter, a smile brightening her face. But when her father saw that smile, he stiffened.

"I got a scare today, Holly. A scare that will keep me from making a mistake like this again. What have *you* learned?"

She blinked and tipped her head sideways, as if trying to puzzle out her father's meaning.

"You're not innocent of wrongdoing," Alan said, his voice heavy, tired. "It was you who instigated these events with your manipulations and deceitful ways."

Her brow scrunched, and she opened her mouth as if to protest, but he cut her off. "You don't have to lie with your tongue to be deceitful. Satan himself tried to tempt Christ with the truth of Scripture twisted to his own purposes."

"Are you comparing me to . . . to *Satan*?" Holly reared back as if he'd struck her.

Crockett's heart stirred with compassion, and he thought to intervene, but Joanna squeezed his hand. "Easy," she whispered, echoing his earlier words to her. "Give him a chance. He knows her better than we do."

Crockett smiled down at the beautiful woman looking at him with wise blue-gray eyes and squeezed her hand in return. "You're going to make me a fine wife, Miss Robbins."

She favored him with the wink he would have given her if his left eye hadn't swollen nearly shut. "I vow to do my best, Mr. Archer."

He wanted nothing more than to tug her close again, but Alan Brewster had turned his back on Holly in order to face them.

"I owe you an apology, Parson." Brewster lifted his chin and met Crockett's stare head on.

Crockett nodded quickly and without reservation. Then he held his hand out to the older man. Brewster hesitated a moment, then shook it with a firm grip.

"I promise you that I'll be taking the girl firmly in hand after this. And I'll be havin' a talk with her mother, as well." The man didn't wait for a response, just barked at Holly to get herself on his horse and marched back toward the church where his mount waited.

Walt collected the lanterns without uttering a word, and Holly scampered after her father, keeping her attention glued to the ground in front of her.

Once they rode out, Joanna sagged against Crockett's side. "Praise God that's over," she sighed. Maintaining her grip on his hand, she swung around to regard him more fully. Her eyes scanned his face, and her lips pursed in displeasure at what she saw. "Those cuts are going to need some attention."

"You volunteering for the job?" He did his best to waggle his brows in a rakish manner, and was thoroughly enjoying the bloom of her smile when Jackson came running up from across the churchyard.

"Crock! Crock, come quick." The boy waved his good arm in frantic motions above his head. "The marshal's arrestin' Silas!"

41

What?" Joanna's already frayed emotions shredded like a piece of antique lace being dragged across a thistle patch.

This can't be happening. Not now. It had to be some kind of mistake.

She looked past Jackson to her father. His hands were outstretched, wrist-over-wrist before him while Marshal Coleson secured them with a strip of leather, as if her father were a horse to be hobbled.

"Wait!" She lurched forward, her legs nothing but trembling sticks as she fumbled over the ground separating her from her father. "Stop!"

Crockett was at her side in an instant, his warm hand gripping her elbow, supporting her, strengthening her, as his steady gait propelled her securely across the remaining distance. Jackson fell into step behind them.

"What are you doing?" Joanna wrenched her arm away from Crockett's hold when they reached the men and threw herself at the marshal. She shoved against his shoulder, hard, forcing him to stumble backward a step. "You can't arrest him. Jackson's shooting was an accident."

Marshal Coleson stoically regained his footing and regarded her with a cool gaze. "I'm not arresting him for the shooting."

"Then why are you treating him like a prisoner? He hasn't done anything!"

"On the contrary, ma'am, he's confessed to multiple counts of robbery. Coaches, trains, even admitted to kidnapping the parson, here."

"Which I still have no intention of pressing charges for," Crockett said from behind her. But his generosity didn't matter, not really. Not if her father had admitted to the rest.

"Daddy?" She searched his face for answers, but his oddly composed features revealed nothing.

Why would he confess? Why now, after all these years? Was it greedy of her to want to keep both the men she loved? Must she sacrifice her father now that Crockett was safe?

Her father lifted his bound arms and looped them over her head. She flung her arms about his waist and clung to him with desperate strength, closing her eyes to block out the truth of what was happening. In her mind, she was a little girl again running to her father for comfort. And when his lips brushed her forehead in the same manner they used to press against a scraped elbow or a hen-pecked hand, her tears fell.

His arms tightened about her, and his husky voice echoed softly in the night. "It's time, Jo. Time to stop hiding from the past."

She shook her head adamantly against his chest, squeezing her eyes shut so firmly that her cheeks nearly met her brows.

"Come now, Jo. It's the right thing to do. Deep in your heart you know that. Doesn't the Good Book say we need to confess our sins to receive God's forgiveness?"

"First John 1:9," Crockett murmured softly.

"See," her daddy said, a near laugh in his voice, "the parson knows what I'm talking about." He lifted his arms back over her head and gently eased himself from her hold.

Determined to be strong for him, she didn't fight. She stepped back and dried her cheeks with the back of her hand. When the knuckles of his bound hands chucked her softly under her chin, she bit her lip to keep it from trembling and raised her gaze.

"Don't you see, darlin'? If I'm gonna be joinin' up with the Lord, I can't keep hangin' on to the secrets of my past. I have to own up to what I did and face the consequences. He ain't the kind to be satisfied with me handin' over half the loot. He wants the whole thing."

Shivers coursed over her skin at the same time a floodgate of warmth opened in her heart to surge through every vein. This was the moment—the moment for which she and her mother had prayed year after year.

Tears rose to blur her vision, but she blinked them away. She didn't want him to remember her tears; she wanted him to remember her joy. Joanna beamed a smile at him, a smile that wobbled a bit, but one that matched the feelings of her heart.

"I'm proud of you, Daddy. Prouder than I've ever been in my entire life."

"Yeah . . . well . . ." He coughed and turned away, but not before she noticed how his eyes gleamed suspiciously bright in the moonlight. He coughed again, then focused on a point above her head. "You'll see her home, Archer?"

"I will." Crockett placed his hands on her shoulders, his thumbs making comforting circles on her back. And while his confirmation was what any gentleman would offer, the solemnity of his voice carried a weight that extended well beyond escort duty.

Her father nodded once, then turned and reached for Gamble's saddle horn with his bound hands. "No sense dragging this thing out, Coleson," he said gruffly as he mounted in a less than graceful manner. "Let's get the boy home so we can be on our way at first light."

The marshal gathered Gamble's reins and climbed aboard his own mount. "Come on, Jackson. You can ride with me." Coleson removed his boot from the stirrup and reached a hand down to help the boy mount behind him.

Jackson shot a questioning glance at Crockett, then at his nod, scrambled up behind the marshal.

As the threesome disappeared into the night, Joanna stood frozen, too numb and exhausted to do more than stare after them. Her soul rejoiced at her father's spiritual surrender, but her heart agonized over the price he might pay. Crockett wrapped his arms about her shoulders and pulled her back against his chest. His heat soaked through her chilled skin as he held her close. Then he leaned his face down, pressing his cheek against hers, and whispered words that revived her weary hope.

"It's not over yet, Jo. It's not over."

42

The following afternoon, Joanna marched out of Miss Bessie's boardinghouse, ready to do battle with Marshal Coleson. Crockett had driven her to Deanville first thing that morning, settled her at the boardinghouse, and then rode on to Caldwell in search of a lawyer. Jasper, Frank, and Carl had chipped in from their savings to cover the attorney's fee, but they chose to stay behind and tend the ranch. That and keep themselves out of the marshal's line of fire.

She didn't blame them. In fact, she was glad they were staying away. Her heart was battered enough already. It couldn't take much more.

Thankfully, she had reinforcements marching alongside her. Miss Bessie, looking stern as ever in her tight bun and pursed mouth, matched Joanna's stride. Both women's arms overflowed with items geared to a man's comfort. Blankets, reading material, food. Miss Bessie had even scrounged up a deck of playing cards that had been left behind by one of her boarders. Knowing her father didn't sleep well if he didn't have her mother's paintings around him, Joanna had brought two of his favorites from home, along with her mother's Bible.

No way would she let him rot in a stark jail cell, surrounded by nothing warmer than stone and iron. When she ran into the marshal coming out of the bank that morning, he'd approved her bringing her father a few personal items. Well, her definition of *few* might be a bit liberal, but she aimed to see that Coleson stood by his word, even if she had to bully him to do it.

As she stepped onto the boardwalk that ran in front of the jailhouse, one of the paintings under her arm began to slip. Without a free hand to adjust its position, all she could do was clench her elbow to her side and bend her posture so her thigh could slow its downward progress. Fortunately, the door to the jail stood ajar, and Joanna managed to nudge it open with her foot. Hurrying to reach a raised surface before she completely lost her grip on her mother's *Sunrise on the Brazos*, she surged forward and dropped her load onto the first table she came to. A table that happened to be the marshal's desk.

One thing she could say for the marshal—he had good reflexes. The man jumped to his feet and in the same motion snatched his coffee cup and a stack of wanted posters out of the avalanche's path before the *Brazos* could inflict any damage.

He raised a supercilious brow. "Are you thinking to bribe me, Miss Robbins?" His dry tone reeked with sarcasm. "I'm afraid I'm not much of an art collector."

"Don't be ridiculous, Marshal." Joanna jutted out a hip to keep the *Brazos* from sliding off the edge of his desk and quickly stacked *The Lazy R Pines* on top of it, freeing her hands to settle her special surprise on the floor against the front of the desk. "These things are for my father. I only brought a few," she said with a smile. "Just like you instructed."

Bessie came in behind Joanna, looked directly at Marshal Coleson, and deliberately dropped her market basket atop the handful of telegrams sitting on the one section of his desk that hadn't been overrun by artwork.

"Land sakes, woman! You're in on this, too?" The lawman growled, looked around for a place to set his coffee, settled on the back of the small cast-iron stove behind him, and growled again. "Listen, ladies. This here ain't no pleasure palace. It's a jail. It's not supposed to be cozy. It's supposed to be hard. Cold. So downright disagreeable, in fact, that once folks visit, they decide to change their ways so's they don't have to come back."

Joanna crossed her arms over her chest and raised her chin, not about to give in. "But my father doesn't have to be convinced. He changed his ways sixteen years ago. Therefore no harm will come from a few blankets and knickknacks."

"Knickknacks?" A rather sour chuckle rattled in his throat. "Lady, your knickknacks are about to swallow my desk."

"You don't plan to starve your prisoner—do you, Brett?" Miss Bessie flung back the towel covering her basket to reveal the feast waiting within. "Fresh bread, jam, cheese, apples. Just some snacks to sustain him between those paltry meals Mrs. Elliott brings." The marshal leaned close to inspect the hamper and inhaled deeply.

"Those your strawberry preserves, Bess?"

"Yep. I thought you might enjoy sampling the wares, too." She pushed the basket more directly under his nose. "If you dig deep enough in there, you might even find a thick square of my lemon pound cake."

The man's head jerked up, and Joanna swore she could hear him salivating. "You *are* trying to bribe me." He slashed a frown at Bessie, but his gaze twitched back to the hamper, giving him away.

"It's not a bribe. It's a reward for doin' a good deed." Bessie reached across the desk, and for a moment, Joanna thought she was going to touch the marshal's hand. But then her fingers detoured to the towel and drew it back over the food. "Let her hang her pictures, Brett. It ain't gonna hurt nothing."

"Seems a waste of time to me," Coleson grumbled, but he picked up the first painting and started scrutinizing the frame and the back, as if checking for contraband. "The circuit judge is gonna be here next week. Hearing's set for Tuesday."

Tuesday. A moan rose in Joanna's throat. Six more days of wondering what would happen. Six more days of separation from her father. Joanna's spine started to slump along with her spirits, but she forced them both straight. Six more days to pray for a favorable outcome.

"What's this?" Coleson dug a hammer out of the food basket and waved it under Joanna's nose. "Trying to sneak weapons in to your father?"

Bessie harrumphed in disgust. "Don't be an idiot. That's to hang the pictures. There's a handful of nails down there, too. We just didn't have enough hands to carry it all. Had to put it in the bottom of the hamper to keep it from smashing the bread."

Coleson turned to face Bessie and raised a doubtful brow. "You expect me to just let you waltz into that cell with a weapon that Silas Robbins can use against me?"

"No." Bessie aimed a look at the lawman that seemed to question the man's intelligence. "What I expect is that you will take charge like you always do and go in there and hang the pictures yourself. Really, Brett. It's what a gentleman would do."

"For pity's sake," the man grouched. "Give me them nails. You can hand me the blasted paintings through the bars." He stomped off toward the back of the jailhouse, muttering under his breath about fool women and their crazy schemes.

Bessie smirked at Joanna, then picked up the blankets, playing cards, and Bible, leaving the food hamper on the marshal's desk. She shrugged off Joanna's questioning glance. "I really made it more for him than your father. To soften him up, you know. He loves my cooking."

Joanna hid a grin as she collected the paintings. If she didn't know better, she would swear Miss Bessie had a soft spot for the town marshal beneath that prickly exterior. And judging by the man's reactions, he was probably fond of more than her food.

By the time the women made it back to the trio of cells at the rear of the building, the marshal had already restrained Joanna's father by placing his arms through the last cell's bars and cinching a leather strap around his wrists. Her father leaned submissively against the bars while Coleson fit a key into the door's lock.

Joanna set the paintings against the wall and rushed up to her father, covering his hands with her own. "Are you all right, Daddy?"

He smiled at her and nodded. "I'm fine, darlin'. You don't need to be fretting about me."

"Crockett's on his way to Caldwell to hire a lawyer. We're going to fight this. It's not over."

Her father's gaze met hers through the bars with a level of peace that stunned her. "God's in control, Jo. Whatever happens, he'll take care of me." He raised his bound hands along the bars until his fingers were able to capture a piece of her hair that dangled by her temple. "He'll take care of you, too. If I didn't believe that, I wouldn't be here now."

Her eyes grew moist. "I know," she said, her voice trembling slightly. "I trust him, Daddy. I do." After so many years of hoping and praying for her father to express such faith, it nearly undid her control to hear him do so. But a weepy woman would serve no good purpose. So she blinked away the unwanted liquid from her eyes and cocked her chin enough to shoot him a grin. "I brought you a few things."

Marshal Coleson snorted. "A *few*? The woman's trying to turn my jail into a lady's parlor."

"Oh?" Her father quizzed her with a look.

Joanna shrugged, then turned and clasped a frame in each hand. "I know how you like having Mama's paintings around, so when I left the house this morning, I brought a couple with me."

His eyes lit with surprised delight. "The *Brazos*?"

Joanna smiled as she held up the painting for her father to see. "Of course." She handed it through the bars to the marshal, who had come up alongside them. Her father's gaze followed its trail, caressing the familiar scene with hungry eyes.

"I brought our pines, too." She held out the last painting her mother had completed before her death, the one she'd claimed was her favorite because it was bathed in the love of home.

He stretched a reverent fingertip toward the canvas. "Ah, Martha." The words were whisper-soft. Joanna bowed her head, her heart squeezing.

After a pair of thumps from the hammer, the marshal returned to collect the second painting. The first hung rather crooked on the wall above the cot that served as a bed, but it was up. Joanna nodded her thanks to the grumbling lawman and handed him the next one.

Her stomach lurched as she reached for the final item stashed by the wall to her left. "I brought one of mine, too. A new one." Heat rushed to her cheeks, and she found it hard to look her father in the face. Her hands shook as she lifted the recently framed piece before her.

"One of yours?" Curiosity warmed his voice. "That's wonderful, Jo. I haven't seen a new work from you since . . . well . . . in a long time."

Not since her mother's death.

Joanna bit her lip and slid the portrait free of the pillowcase she'd wrapped it in. Holding her breath, she let the white cotton fall to the ground and turned the painting around to let her father see it. "I had planned to give it to you for your birthday, but . . ." She lifted her head, and the rest of the sentence turned to dust in her mouth as she saw what could only be described as awe wash over her father's face.

He offered no compliments. No flowery praise. Not even a smile. He just stared at the likeness of his wife as if nothing else existed. His hands opened, and Joanna set the bottom edge of the frame across his wide palms. His lips silently formed her mother's name at the same time that a tear rolled down his weathered cheek.

Joanna glanced away, the moment too intimate for even her to invade. It was only then that she noticed the complete stillness surrounding her. Bessie stood by the cell door, eyes wide in disbelief and wonder. Even the marshal looked nonplussed.

"I'll just . . . uh . . . place a nail and let you hang that one when you're ready." Coleson backed away and quickly pounded a nail into place near the head of the cot.

The two sharp taps from the hammer seemed to break Silas from his trance. He blinked and finally lifted his head.

"You brought her back to life, Jo," he rasped. "Thank you."

"She'd be so proud of you, Daddy." Joanna scooted close and wrapped her hands under his as he held the frame.

The cell door rattled closed, shaking the bars. Joanna stepped back, taking the painting with her when the marshal approached. As soon as Coleson unfastened her father's bonds, however, she passed the painting through the bars.

"I put the blanket, cards, and Bible on the cot, Robbins."

Her father hugged the painting to his chest but focused his attention on his daughter. "Martha's Bible?"

Joanna nodded. "You've been reading it so faithfully lately, I thought you'd like to have it. I was hoping you'd find strength and comfort in its pages."

"I'm sure I will." He set the painting down, leaning it against the bars, and held a hand out to her. "Come here, Jo."

She went immediately, stretching her arms through the bars to hold as much of him as she could.

"I love you, darlin'," he said, the words burning a hole directly to the center of her heart.

"I love you, too, Daddy, and I'll be praying for you every day."

He patted her shoulder in that slightly awkward way of his that always made her smile. "You do that, girl, but remember . . . if God don't give you the answer you're wantin', don't be holdin' it against him. He can still be trusted, even when he says no."

Joanna had to work hard to swallow the melon-sized lump in her throat. Her father had truly made his peace with God. She locked her gaze with his and lifted her chin. "I'll remember."

43

All of Deanville turned out for the hearing—the nosy telegraph clerk, the barber, even the minister who used to preach from the pulpit Crockett now occupied. Crockett recognized several faces from his own congregation, as well.

Joanna hadn't wanted to leave her father in the days leading up to the court date, so after Crockett returned to town with the attorney, he'd left her in Miss Bessie's care and returned home, not only to conduct worship services, but also to organize a special prayer meeting Sunday evening. He had been humbled by the number of families that had turned out. And when he put out the word to recruit character witnesses willing to testify on Silas's behalf, several volunteered and were in the courtroom now, waiting.

Jackson had begged to be included on the witness list, but Mr. Gillman, the attorney, had been afraid the marshal would bring up the shooting incident if Jackson took the stand, and that wouldn't do Silas any favors.

The door to the judge's chambers cracked open, and Joanna squeezed Crockett's hand. He stroked the pad of his thumb over her knuckles and shifted closer to her on the wooden gallery pew, his own nerves on edge.

The judge, a surprisingly short, slender man with a balding pate, strode into the courtroom. He seemed to grow in stature, however, as he ascended to the bench, and when he pounded his gavel, all chatter died. With no more than a flick of the wrist, the man had taken command of the room.

Crockett and Joanna rose to their feet along with the rest of the crowd, but the judge quickly waved them all back down. Gillman had assured him that Judge Wicker was a fair man who didn't stand on ceremony, and it appeared that at least the latter half of that assessment was true. Crockett prayed the first half proved accurate, as well.

"Silas Robbins." The judge's voice echoed through the crowded room with an impressive boom. Mr. Gillman stood and urged Silas to do the same. The judge shuffled some papers around on his desk as he continued. "You are charged with an ambiguous number of robberies." He looked up and pierced Coleson with a glare of displeasure. "Apparently the good marshal, here, was unclear as to how many crimes to actually charge you with."

"That's my fault, Your Honor," Silas said, ignoring the lawyer at his side who was muttering furiously at him to be quiet. "When I made my confession, I couldn't recall the exact number of stagecoaches. Probably around twenty or so. I only robbed three trains, though. Four if you count the time I abducted the parson." He jabbed his finger over his shoulder.

Crockett raised his hand and waved at the judge.

"What are you doing?" Joanna hissed.

Crockett bent toward her and whispered out of the side of his mouth. "Trying to show there are no hard feelings over that incident."

The judge raised a brow at Crockett and turned back to Coleson. "I don't see kidnapping listed among the crimes."

"That's because the parson refuses to press charges." The marshal folded his arms across his chest, and Crockett had no doubt the lawman's glare would've scorched him if he had actually glanced in his direction. "'Course, I hear he's marryin' up with the defendant's daughter, so that might have something to do with it."

"The parson's matrimonial prospects are not the concern of this court, Marshal. I'll thank you to keep your suppositions to yourself so that we may progress in an orderly manner. Do I make myself clear?"

Coleson scuffed the sole of his left boot against the oak floorboards. "Yes, sir."

The judge redirected his attention to Silas. "Now, Robbins, since you have been so forthcoming about the events for which you are charged, and since I have a statement from Mr. Coleson indicating that you have confessed to the crimes in question, may I assume that you are entering a guilty plea?"

Silas straightened his posture and lifted his chin in a way that reminded Crockett of Joanna when she was determined to see something through. "Yes, Your Honor."

Joanna whimpered softly, and Crockett wrapped his arm around her, wishing he could do more to protect her heart from this emotional pummeling.

"An honest criminal," Judge Wicker remarked. "That's a rarity in my line of work. Refreshing." He made a note on one of the papers in front of him, then gestured to Mr. Gillman. "Before I pronounce sentence, do you have any witnesses who wish to offer testimony on Mr. Robbins's behalf?"

"Yes, Your Honor," the lawyer replied.

"Very well. Call your first witness."

"I call Silas Robbins."

After giving his oath to tell the truth, Silas took the stand.

Mr. Gillman strode up to Silas, then turned slightly to include the audience as well as the judge in his questioning. "Mr. Robbins. How many years have passed since the last time you stole something? A material possession of any value."

Silas cleared his throat. "Sixteen years."

The lawyer paced before the judge's bench, hands behind his back. "And after sixteen years of lawful living, what prodded you to suddenly confess these past wrongs?"

"Got tired of carryin' the past around with me while dodgin' God and my conscience. Finally stopped dodging and realized it was time to come clean. I couldn't be God's man otherwise."

Mr. Gillman smiled. "I see. So not only have you been a law-abiding citizen for the past sixteen years, but you have also recently become a man of religious conviction. Admirable, indeed. No further questions."

"You may be excused, Mr. Robbins." Judge Wicker directed Silas back to his seat. "Call your next witness."

Gillman turned to face the gallery. "I call Mrs. Idabelle Grimley."

A shuffle echoed behind Crockett as Mrs. Grimley made her way forward, clutching her handbag nervously before her. Her gaze found his as she passed his row, and Crockett nodded encouragement to her.

At Mr. Gillman's prompting, she told the court about the time Silas had shown up on her family's doorstep with two of his men in tow offering to cut hay after her husband had been laid up with a broken leg. Mr. Robbins hadn't accepted a thing in payment beyond the cherry pie she forced him to take home in thanks.

Two other church members took the stand following Mrs. Grimley, each painting a picture of Silas as a hardworking rancher who kept mostly to himself but who could always be counted on to help his neighbor in time of crisis. When the attorney turned toward the crowd to call the fourth witness, however, Judge Wicker interrupted him.

"You've made your point, Gillman. Robbins has been a model citizen and a decent neighbor to these folks." He waved his hand impatiently, as if trying to erase names from an invisible blackboard. "I think we can dispense with the rest of the witnesses if they all have a similar testimony."

"Yes, Your Honor." Gillman took his seat.

Judge Wicker turned to Coleson. "You have any refuting witnesses?"

The marshal slowly gained his feet. "Uh . . . no, Your Honor. But the man's confessed," he hurried to add, "so that should tell you all you need to know."

The judge frowned. "Did you not wire area lawmen to see if there were witnesses willing to testify regarding Mr. Robbins's crimes?"

"I did. But of the two men who came forward, neither could identify him. Robbins always wore a bandana over his face, you see. And with all the years that've passed . . . well . . . the witnesses weren't willing to swear on a Bible that he was the man who'd robbed them."

Judge Wicker glared his displeasure at the marshal until the man finally took his seat. "This is highly irregular," the judge grumbled. "A confession of decades-old crimes from a criminal with no accusers." He set aside his papers and let out a heavy sigh.

Joanna tensed. Crockett rubbed her arm, his own chest growing tight.

"Mr. Robbins," the judge intoned, his scowl locking on Silas as Joanna's father pushed his chair back and rose to accept his sentence. "You present me an unusual dilemma. You have pled guilty to the charge of robbery. Therefore, I must assign a sentence appropriate to the crimes for which you have confessed. Usually a minimum of five years."

"No," Joanna whispered, her quiet anguish a shout in Crockett's ear.

"However," the judge continued, "I find myself asking what, exactly, that five years in prison would be expected to accomplish.

"Incarceration serves a twofold purpose. First, it is a punishment for crimes committed against society and a deterrent against future illicit behavior. But second, and I believe most crucial, incarceration provides an opportunity for reformation of the criminal character. That is why we have libraries and chaplains in our prisons, why we teach our inmates a marketable trade. We want them to reenter society changed and prepared to contribute in a positive manner."

Judge Wicker paused for breath, then pointed a stubby finger directly at Silas.

"You, sir," he declared, a note of accusation ringing in his voice, "have already reformed."

44

Joanna blinked. Had she heard correctly? Had the judge just accused her father of being *too* rehabilitated? She shared a brief glance with Crockett, but he appeared equally perplexed. He rubbed her arm again, though, and the simple touch buoyed her. She didn't know how she would have survived this day without him by her side, always ready with a smile or a gentle reassuring touch.

Her father stood so straight and tall, his shoulders squared as he listened to the judge's pronouncement. He'd stood the same way at her mother's funeral, as if braced for a blow he couldn't defend against.

"Since you have already renounced your criminal ways and have been an exemplary citizen for the past sixteen years, I am reluctant to enforce prison time."

Joanna's heart hiccupped in her chest. She grabbed Crockett's knee. *Please, Lord. Please.*

"However," the judge continued, his expression grave, "there is the element of punishment that must be addressed. In such cases, I would normally insist that you make restitution to those you have wronged. Yet it seems we have no victims on which to confer such compensation. Hence my dilemma. I cannot let a guilty man go free with no consequences for his actions. Nor will my conscience allow me to sentence to prison a man who has already proven himself reformed.

"That leaves me with only one recourse. Therefore, it is the ruling of this court that you, Silas Robbins, will make restitution to the community at large in lieu of individual victims. Instead of time served in prison, your five years will be probated on the condition that during each of those five years, ten percent of all income, whether personal or the product of the

Lazy R ranch, be donated to local charitable or civic organizations approved by the court. The court will appoint a business manager to oversee your finances during this period and to keep an accounting of all earnings and expenditures. Do you agree to abide by these conditions?"

"Yes, sir." Her father gave a shaky nod. "I do."

"Then the ruling stands. This court is adjourned." Judge Wicker pounded his gavel, rose from the bench, and strode to his chambers.

Applause reverberated through the room along with a handful of hearty cheers, but it was nothing more than a buzz in Joanna's ears. All of her attention focused on her father and her need to get to him. Now.

She tried to squeeze past Jackson and Miss Bessie to get to the aisle, but they were too busy celebrating—Jackson with loud hollers and Bessie with timid claps as she backed up to avoid being impaled with a flying elbow or jerking knee. Crockett must have sensed Joanna's growing desperation, for when she turned his direction to look for an escape route, he seized her about the waist and hoisted her over the barrier separating the court from the gallery. With a wink, he shooed her toward her father.

Loving him for knowing her so well, she blew him a kiss, then pivoted and threw herself into her father's arms, not caring that he was occupied with a handshake from Mr. Gillman at the time.

"Oh, Daddy! You're free." Free from the past. Free from prison. Free to be the man God always intended him to be.

His arms tightened around her, and he dropped a kiss on her head. "That I am, darlin'. That I am."

Joanna pulled slightly away, her gaze drinking in his beloved face. He smiled, and the light in his eyes shone brighter than she'd ever seen it. A laugh of pure joy bubbled out of her, and her father's rich chuckle joined it on its journey to the rafters.

"Hey, Parson!" Her father loosened his hold on her in order to include Crockett in their circle. "I need you to do me a favor."

"What's that, Si?"

This time her father was the one to wink. "Find me some water."

Joanna was slow to understand, but when the Deanville preacher stepped up and pounded her daddy on the back, saying he knew just the place to do the deed, comprehension dawned. Joanna's stomach swirled in jittery delight as her former minister led the way down the aisle, his pulpit voice ringing out in song.

"Shall we gather at the river,
Where bright angel feet have trod,
With its crystal tide forever
Flowing by the throne of God?"

The man gestured to the crowd to follow them, and soon an entire throng was singing and laughing on their way down to the town creek. Joanna grinned through the tears pooling in her eyes and added her trembling voice to the mix as she allowed herself to be herded along with the rest.

> "Yes, we'll gather at the river,
> The beautiful, the beautiful river,
> Gather with the saints at the river,
> That flows by the throne of God."

The longer she sang, the stronger her voice became. Crockett grabbed her hand, his deep baritone blending with her alto as they escorted her father to a tree-shaded area out behind the schoolhouse.

The Deanville preacher stepped aside once they arrived at the swimming hole, giving the three of them some privacy as he led the congregants in another hymn.

> "What can wash away my sin?
> Nothing but the blood of Jesus.
> What can make me whole again?
> Nothing but the blood of Jesus . . ."

The singing continued, but Joanna's voice faltered. The reality of the moment pierced too deeply.

"Archer?" Her father shrugged out of his suit coat, and then paused and regarded Crockett with an intense gaze. "Son, would you do the honors?"

"Nothing would make me happier, sir." Crockett clapped him on the shoulder, then quickly divested himself of boots, coat, and tie and waded into the water.

Joanna collected the discarded clothing and held it tight to her breast, as if doing so would enhance her connection to the two men she loved more than life.

Can you see this, Mama? Your prayers are being answered.

The men ventured away from the bank until they were waist-deep in the creek. The crowd hushed. Crockett asked her father for his confession, and when her daddy claimed Jesus as his Lord, Joanna couldn't hold the tears back any longer. Tiny sobs of long-awaited joy shook her shoulders as Crockett buried her daddy in the water and brought him back up a new man in Christ.

And as the crowd shouted their amens and burst into a rousing rendition of "Let Every Heart Rejoice and Sing," Joanna could have sworn she heard her mother's clear soprano joining in the praise.

Epilogue

Crockett stood before his congregation three months after that triumphant day, a pile of ravaged nerves. Knots twisted his stomach and tiny pinpricks needled his neck as he gazed over the heads of the crowd, a condition that hadn't beset him since his first day in the pulpit. But then, he wasn't in the pulpit today. His mentor, Amos Ralston, had that distinction. After all, a man couldn't perform his own wedding ceremony.

Jackson waved at him from the back of the sanctuary, sporting his new duds. Silas had offered the kid an official position at the Lazy R along with a set of clothes and an assigned horse to ride while on duty, and Jackson had been strutting around the ranch ever since, his pride nearly busting the buttons off his store-bought shirt. He still showed up early at the church every Sunday to ring the bell, and that was where he stood now—manning the pull rope in order to set the church bell to ringing the instant Brother Ralston pronounced Crockett and Joanna husband and wife.

Husband and wife. Crockett swallowed hard.

"If you tug on your collar one more time, Crock, the thing's gonna pop clean off."

Crockett glared at his big brother. "You know, Trav," he muttered out of the side of his mouth, "Jackson volunteered to stand up with me. It's not too late to switch you out."

"Yes it is." Travis chuckled softly and nodded toward the back of the church. "Your bride's coming."

Crockett's pulse leapt at the telltale squeak of hinges. The gap in the door widened. Silas, wearing the new suit coat Joanna had bought him for the trial all those months ago, stepped through the entrance and held his arm out to his daughter somewhere behind him.

Straining to see past his soon-to-be father-in-law, Crockett stretched his neck only to have his breath catch in his throat.

Joanna glided through the doorway, resplendent in a dark green gown dripping in ivory lace. Her glorious red curls hung loose past her shoulders with a halo of golden wildflowers and streams of ivory ribbon as adornment. Her chin dipped in demure shyness, she was halfway down the aisle before she raised her lashes and met his gaze.

When she did, Crockett felt the impact clear through his chest. Soon this beautiful woman would be *his*. His helpmeet, his partner, his wife. The love glowing in her blue-gray eyes banished his nerves, and his heart swelled with pride.

His attention never leaving her face, he stepped forward and accepted her hand from Silas. Her gloved fingers curved around his and his pulse thrummed. Her pixie face, delicate within the mass of those burnished curls, blushed at the intensity of his stare. Reeling in his desire, he winked at her to break the tension, then grinned like an idiot when she smiled at him.

As Crockett turned to face the minister, he caught Travis rolling his eyes at his smitten behavior. But then a gurgling noise from the front row transformed his brother's mocking expression into one of indulgent adoration as his six-week-old son, Joseph, flailed his arms in happy, jerky motions from where he lay cradled in Meredith's lap.

Yep, the Archer men were soft as cornmeal mush when it came to their women. Apparently their children, too. Even Jim, the most stoic of the bunch, hinted at a smile when his Cassie snuggled close as the minister began addressing the congregation. Maybe Neill would be different when his turn came around, but as Crockett hugged Joanna's arm into his side, he sure hoped not.

Loving a woman might soften a man's heart, but receiving her love in return made him infinitely stronger than he could ever have been alone.

Two-time RITA finalist and winner of the coveted HOLT Medallion and ACFW Carol Award, CBA bestselling author **Karen Witemeyer** writes historical romance because she believes the world needs more happily-ever-afters. She is an avid cross-stitcher and shower singer, and she bakes a mean apple cobbler. Karen makes her home in Abilene, Texas, with her husband and three children. Learn more about Karen and her books and sign up for her free newsletter at www.karenwitemeyer.com.

More From Karen Witemeyer

To learn more about Karen and her books, visit karenwitemeyer.com.

A teacher on the run. A bounty hunter in pursuit. Can Charlotte and Stone learn to trust each other before they both lose what they hold most dear?

A Worthy Pursuit

Nicole Renard is on a mission to find a *suitable* husband. But when her plans are waylaid by a dashing yet eccentric researcher, can she stop her heart from surging full steam ahead?

Full Steam Ahead

Eden Spencer prefers books over suitors. But when a tarnished Texas hero captures her heart, will she deny her feelings or create her own love story?

To Win Her Heart

You May Also Enjoy...

Brought together by the Madison Bridal School in 1890, three young women form a close bond. In time, they learn more about each other—and themselves—as they help one another grow in faith and, eventually, find love.

Brides of Seattle: *Steadfast Heart, Refining Fire, Love Everlasting*
by Tracie Peterson
traciepeterson.com

When Brook Eden's friend Justin, a future duke, discovers she may be an English heiress, she travels to meet her alleged father. In Yorkshire, she finds herself confused by her emotions and haunted by her mother's mysterious death. Will she learn the truth—before it's too late?

The Lost Heiress by Roseanna M. White
Ladies of the Manor
roseannamwhite.com

Entering her fourth season, Lady Miranda Hawthorne secretly longs to be bold. But she is mortified when her brother's handsome new valet accidentally mails her private thoughts to a duke she's never met—until he responds. As she sorts out her growing feelings for two men, Miranda uncovers secrets that will put more than her heart at risk.

A Noble Masquerade by Kristi Ann Hunter
Hawthorne House
kristiannhunter.com

BethanyHouse